Goddess of the Sea

Goddess of the Sea

LESBIANS, PIRATES, & DRAGONS
BOOK TWO

BRITNEY JACKSON

Contents

1. An Unworthy Child — 1
2. Mount Drakon — 13
3. Ash and Bone — 40
4. Sword and Flame — 71
5. A Dragon Rider — 107
6. A Captain — 131
7. A Surgeon — 144
8. An Interrogation — 172
9. Slowing Down — 194
10. Not Wrong — 218
11. To Belong — 258
12. The Serpent and the Sword — 291
13. A Warning from a Goddess — 307
14. Sharp Swords and Dirty Moves — 329
15. A Message from the Dead — 344
16. The Nature of Fire — 366
17. Learning the Ropes — 394
18. Stay with Me — 413
19. Strays — 434
20. Her Place — 450
21. It Spreads Among You — 479
22. Gods and Seashell Stew — 495
23. Goddess of the Sea — 522
24. Uncharted Waters — 552
25. The Kraken — 577
26. Here Be Sirens — 602
27. The Turquoise Palace — 639
Book 3 — 657
The Aletharian Appendices — 659
Appendix A — 660
Appendix B — 662
Appendix C — 665
Appendix D — 668

Author's Note 671
Also by Britney Jackson 675
About the Author 677

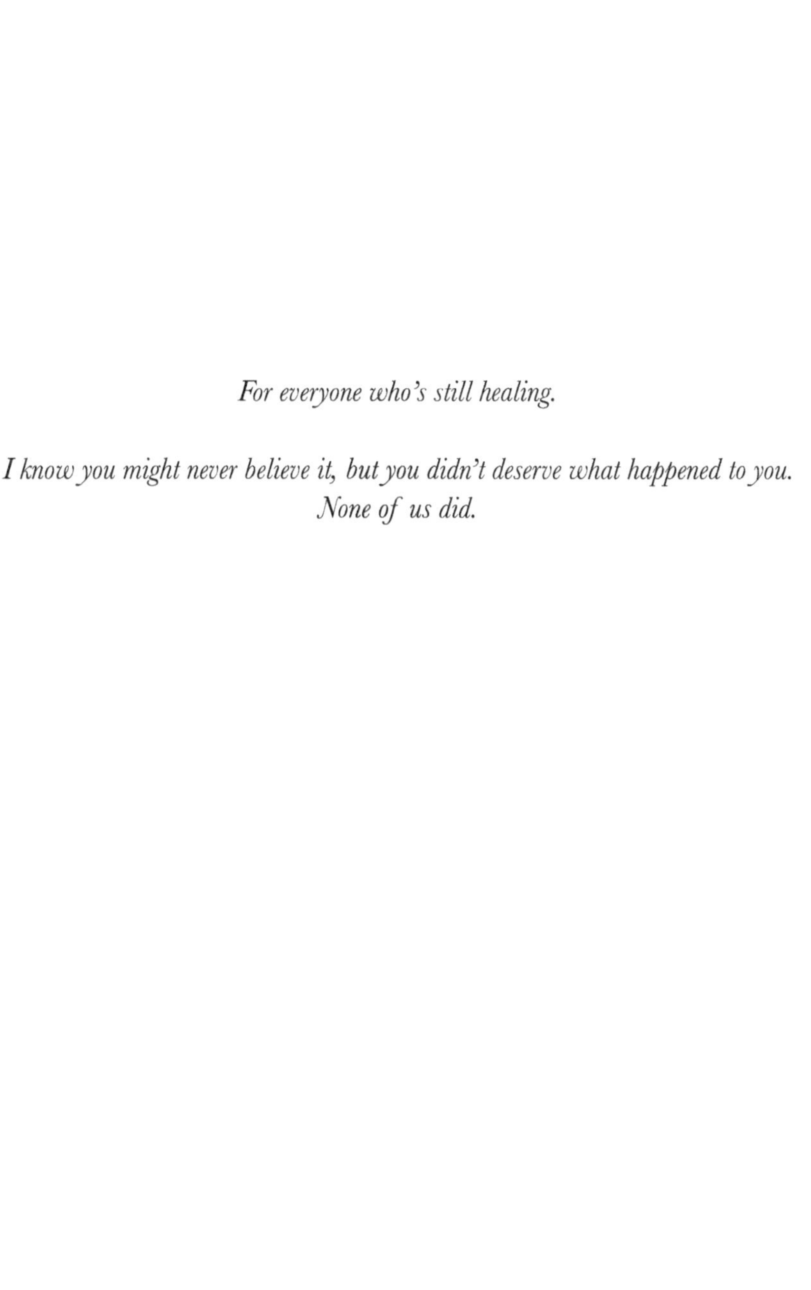

For everyone who's still healing.

I know you might never believe it, but you didn't deserve what happened to you. None of us did.

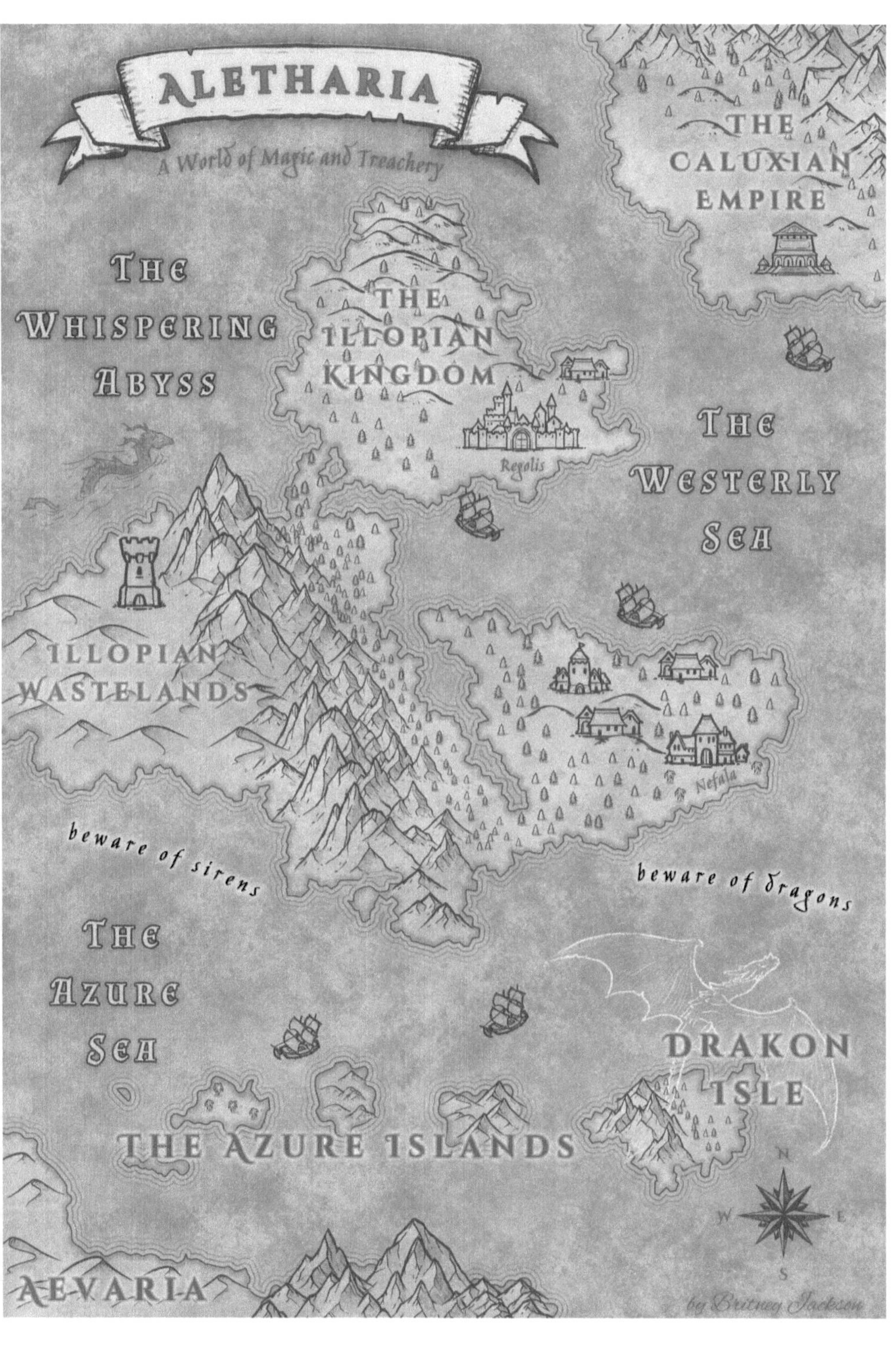
ALETHARIA
A World of Magic and Treachery
THE CALUXIAN EMPIRE
THE WHISPERING ABYSS
THE ILLOPIAN KINGDOM
Regolis
THE WESTERLY SEA
ILLOPIAN WASTELANDS
Nefala
beware of sirens
beware of dragons
THE AZURE SEA
DRAKON ISLE
THE AZURE ISLANDS
AEVARIA
by Britney Jackson
N
S
E
W

CHAPTER 1
An Unworthy Child

Eighteen years earlier…

To an outsider, a young child spending all of her time amongst magical, fire-breathing beasts might've sounded unwise.

Even a little dangerous.

But that was only because the outsider hadn't met Emilia Drakon's mother.

Dragons were gentle, compared to Nydia Drakon.

A young Emilia Drakon pushed herself onto her hands and knees, pain radiating through her body.

Blood dripped from her nose and lips, darkening the dirt beneath her, like drops of black ink.

A dull thrum of magic tickled the edges of Emilia's senses, as the earth drank in her blood.

Magic lives in everything.

The dragons had once told her that.

The flash of a red tunic in Emilia's peripheral warned her that her opponent—an adolescent boy by the name of Mateo—had just stepped toward her.

With a derisive laugh, he said, "Used up already?"

The other children laughed along with him. Their laughter irritated Emilia's senses—discordant and sharp, cruel and repulsive.

Mateo was right, though.

Emilia had used every ounce of magic within her.

She'd lost.

Her mother could see that. Anyone could see that.

Any moment now, a healer would come to help.

A healer should've *already* come.

With no magic left to defend herself, any further attacks could kill Emilia.

Emilia didn't want to die. The dragons had promised to take her to a shipwreck later that week. She didn't want to miss it.

Her mother wouldn't let her die, would she?

A silly, childish thought.

Emilia's mother had already killed her once.

That was the cruelty of a child's mind, though.

No matter what their experiences told them, a child always wanted to trust the adult—to believe *this* time would be different.

It was natural.

It was biological.

So, Emilia waited—tired, bleeding, and hurting—for her mother to send the healer.

If she'd been any other child, her mother would've done it.

If she'd been any other child, her mother wouldn't have thrown her into this match in the first place.

This wasn't training.

It never had been.

It was punishment.

CAMILA, CHIEF HEALER OF THE DRAKON PEOPLE, RUSHED TOWARD the wall of fire that guarded their training grounds—only to have the flames shoot upward, further blocking her path to the wounded child.

With a growl of rage, she whirled on her chieftess. "She's done, Nydia. Withdraw your fire."

Nydia lifted her chin. The light and shadow of the flames played along the angular lines of her cheekbones. "I decide when she's done."

No one wielded destructive magic as easily as Nydia Drakon. Not even other warriors. Had anyone *else* produced a wall of flames as high as this one, they would've looked sickly or weakened afterward, but not Nydia.

Nydia didn't show a hint of weakness.

She never had.

Camila had once found that impressive, just as the rest of the Drakon people had. Lately, though, she'd grown increasingly frustrated with Nydia's icy demeanor.

Mostly because of Emilia.

The little girl was already a dragon-rider, and she'd become a brilliant healer, too—*if* her mother didn't kill her first.

Or…*again.*

Camila wished her vote had been enough to stop the execution last time, but she'd be damned if she'd watch it happen again.

"She's wounded," Camila said—not that she doubted Nydia had seen the blood.

Nydia didn't even look her way. "She'll live."

"She might not," Camila argued, "if you let that boy attack her again."

Nydia lifted her shoulders. "Then, she won't."

Camila could hardly believe her ears. "Why would you put her up against Mateo in the first place? He's a trained warrior, and she's an untrained healer."

"She hasn't taken her rune yet," Nydia said dully—as if watching someone hurt her daughter had bored her. Perhaps she just wished for an excuse to do it herself. "She's nothing until she takes her rune."

"She's a healer," Camila said, "and you know it."

Nydia raised a dark eyebrow. "So, what if she is?"

For Aletha's sake, Nydia knew *what if!*

If Emilia was a healer, then setting her up against a warrior was pure and simple cruelty. Even if she'd been older, *trained*, she still would've lost.

Her magic wasn't meant for fighting.

It was meant for healing.

Nydia taught destructive magic to every child on the island—no matter what kind of sorcerer they might turn out to be—and though the children had always described her methods as cruel and ruthless, Nydia had never intentionally harmed the kids.

Their parents wouldn't have stood for that.

Nydia had always matched them up against children their own age—with similar styles of magic.

What she'd done to her daughter was beyond cruel, and there was no *parent* here to save Emilia.

So, Camila tried.

"This is wrong. End it—before it's too late."

Nydia turned her sharp gaze on Camila. She stepped forward, standing toe-to-toe with Camila, as she'd often done when they were younger. Sparks of fire flashed within Nydia's green eyes, and her sleek, black braids shone in the firelight.

She was beautiful.

Unmovable.

Deadly.

"Wrong?" Nydia sneered. "Was it wrong when *our* leaders set me up against you?" She leaned closer, and her lips curled into a dangerous smile. "When I nearly killed you? Every day? For a month."

Such a fucking bitch.

Camila had once slapped her, actually—only to find out that Nydia enjoyed that. A little too much.

Camila flexed her lightly wrinkled, dark-skinned fingers, as if that might give her strength. "You and I were the same age," she reminded Nydia, "and once they'd trained us in our respective magicks, they stopped setting us against each other."

That didn't mean they'd stopped fighting, though.

Nydia had continued to pick fights with Camila *outside* of training for the next several years. She'd only lost interest after Camila bonded with a dragon.

"Perhaps you've forgotten," Camila added, "but your daughter is *seven* years old."

Nydia wrinkled her nose in distaste. It had become a habit of hers, whenever someone mentioned her biological connection to Emilia—ever since the child had returned to them, barely a year ago.

"She's old enough to train," Nydia said coldly.

"Against a boy twice her age?" Camila challenged.

Nydia rolled her eyes. "You can teach your students however you like." Apparently, whatever enjoyment she'd found in fighting with Camila had waned—because she turned her attention back toward the fighting students. "These are *my* training grounds."

And didn't they all know it?

The most blood-soaked earth on the entire island.

For a woman who constantly kept healers in work, Nydia clearly didn't have any respect for their wisdom.

Camila often wondered, though, if it were more about her being a dragon-rider than her being a healer.

Nydia had been cold and ruthless, even as a child.

Most warrior sorcerers were.

But Nydia had *enjoyed* competing with Camila.

The fights and taunts—Nydia had loved it.

Their relationship hadn't changed until Camila bonded with the blue dragon, Caelu.

The day Camila had ridden her dragon for the first time, the other children had cheered her on, while Nydia had looked on in confusion…

At first.

Then, in anger.

Camila hadn't ridden her dragon in years, though—not since her arthritis set in. Caelu hadn't wanted Camila to feel any more pain than she already did.

Between the flickering flames, Camila caught sight of Emilia's small, blood-streaked face, and she *saw* the moment the child accepted her mother's betrayal—when a bit of innocence faded from her green eyes.

"Get up," Nydia snarled at the wounded girl, "you unworthy, pathetic excuse for a child."

Any other child might've cried or pleaded, hoping to appeal to some long-forgotten motherly instinct, but Emilia Drakon did no such thing.

Emilia Drakon forced herself to her feet and faced the boy who'd soon kill her—who probably didn't even realize how severely he'd *already* wounded her.

Camila glanced from the girl to the wall of flames and back again. She couldn't overpower Nydia's destructive magic on her own, and Nydia knew that.

Nydia wielded every ounce of power she had—magical and political—with the knowledge that no one could stop her.

No one *except*…the dragons.

Perhaps, if Camila called to Caelu…

"Ask Aster to explain her future to you," Nydia said, suddenly, "*all* of it—not just the part he told the others." Her unfeeling, green eyes shifted toward Camila. "*Then*, tell me I'm being too hard on her."

But…Camila already knew. Aster, Nydia's brother, had looked into the future *before* Emilia's birth and informed them she'd be the last dragon sorcerer.

What more could he have seen?

"Whatever it is, she hasn't done it yet," Camila told her. "She's an innocent child who deserves to live."

Nydia rolled her eyes. "This isn't about what *she* will do. It's about what *they* will do," she corrected, "to her."

Camila didn't have time to ask for clarification—because, at that moment, the older boy flung a ball of fire at Emilia.

Emilia lifted her small hands and squeezed her eyes shut, trying desperately to conjure a wall of her own, but even a trained warrior couldn't have done that, while drained of magic.

An untrained healer certainly couldn't.

The fire hit the girl, unhindered, and the pure agony of her screams nearly sent Camila to her knees.

Camila pressed her hands to her head, fingers sinking into dense curls, as she resisted the urge to cover her ears and shut out the heart-wrenching sound.

Yet, somehow, Nydia Drakon's only response was, "How embarrassing."

Camila could've strangled the woman.

Apparently, Camila wasn't alone in that sentiment.

A furious roar erupted near the peak of Mount Drakon, where just *one* of the dragons usually rested.

The other dragons began to roar, too, from separate parts of the island, and something inside of Camila recognized the roar of her own dragon among them.

Everyone around the training grounds fell silent—children and adults alike—and they looked toward the clouds.

A few of the children screamed, and the adults exchanged worried looks.

After all, you didn't live on an island full of dragons without understanding how easily one's wrath could end your life.

Nydia, though—she just sighed, "Every time."

A gust of wind flowed downward through the forest, and a hint of magic whispered in the trees.

When the massive, black dragon emerged from the clouds, most of the children fled—including the young warrior who'd just attacked Emilia Drakon.

Good choice, on his part.

Dragons weren't always rational in their attacks.

As a former dragon-rider, Camila understood that better than most.

The power of the dragon's tremendous wings wreaked havoc on the clearing, scattering dust and leaves into the air—and easily extinguishing Nydia's wall of flame.

Nymeth.

Even the adults gasped at the sight of *her.*

Nymeth was the most ancient and mysterious of their dragons. The most the Drakon people usually saw of Nymeth was when she shed her smooth, black scale—and they collected it for use in riding-armor.

Her spikes were sharper than any blade, her size reminiscent of a small mountain.

A second dragon swooped in beneath Nymeth.

It was Emryn, the small, green dragon, who Camila had once seen chasing Emilia, as if they were *playing*.

He landed in front of the burned child, his green, serpent-like eyes wild and whirling.

Curious—that it was those two who came.

Emryn was the dragon Emilia had been named after, whereas Nydia had been named after Nymeth.

Yet, both were here—not for Nydia, but for Emilia.

Nymeth opened her massive jaws and roared with so much force that Nydia's thick, black braids flew backward, and her red gown whipped around her curvy figure.

And though all the remaining children and adults ran, fearing dragon-fire, Nydia stood her ground.

"She's my child, not yours."

Nymeth opened her mighty jaws and roared again.

The steam of Nymeth's breath left Nydia's red clothing visibly damp. Yet, she didn't yield an inch.

On the now-vacated training grounds, Emilia reached out and curled her small, burned hand around one of the green dragon's enormous claws—as if she were trying to comfort *him*.

Emryn fluttered his wings and exhaled a distraught puff of smoke through his snout. Then, he turned his anxious, dragon-green eyes toward Camila.

"Help her," he pleaded in Camila's mind.

If there was anything the Drakon people believed, it was that their loyalty belonged, first and foremost, to dragons. So, Camila ignored the shriek of fury from her chieftess and rushed to help the child.

Nydia surged forward, but Nymeth dropped onto the scorched earth in front of her, blocking her path.

The ground beneath them quaked, as Nymeth dug her giant, black claws into dirt and stone.

Nymeth opened her jaws yet again—teeth as large as any human and sharper than any blade—and deep within her throat, a glow of fire emerged.

"I'm not afraid of fire!" Nydia screamed at the dragon. "I am a Drakon chieftess. I am a warrior!"

"Don't forget psychopath," Camila said under her breath—as she gathered the child into her arms.

A puff of black smoke escaped Emryn's snout, as he seemed to laugh at her remark.

Camila smiled at the playful, green dragon.

She'd never ridden Emryn.

Like most dragon-riders, Camila had only bonded with one dragon. Emilia was the only Drakon sorcerer ever known to have bonded with all of them.

Caelu was sweet and kind, and Camila loved her for it—but she didn't have Emryn's sense of humor.

Camila held her hands near Emilia's face but hesitated to actually touch her. It was easier to heal through touch, but Camila feared the melted skin would pull away from the bone if she touched it.

Still, she *needed* to heal Emilia's mouth and nose.

All third-degree burns could kill, of course, but the child would die much faster, if she couldn't breathe.

How could Nydia have let this happen?

It was too soon to know how deep those burns had gone. Camila could only hope the boy hadn't been powerful enough to kill someone with one strike.

Emryn lowered his head and pressed his snout beneath Emilia, helping Camila support her weight.

Perhaps he'd lent a bit of his own magic, as well—because Camila noticed Emilia's burns receding faster than before. Her mottled, black-and-red skin grew pinker, then whiter, as the skin mended itself.

That is, until you reached her neck—where it was still mottled grey and bleeding, like the rest of her.

The stench of charred skin still burned Camila's nose, but she was relieved to see Emilia's eyes open.

The sound that escaped the little girl's lips was more rasp than voice, and all she managed to say was, *"Hurts."*

The dragon whined, and Camila's heart broke, too.

"I know. I know, baby." She'd never had her own child, but the soothing tone came naturally to her. "It hurts so much. I know." Camila looked up at the distraught, green dragon. "I have to stabilize her first, but as soon as I'm sure she'll live, I'll go get her something for the pain."

Emryn blinked his massive, green eyes at her. *"Hurry."*

She nodded and moved her hands to Emilia's neck.

"She's weak! I have to strengthen her," Nydia screamed at the black dragon. "Don't you understand what she'll have to endure? For you?!"

"She is a child," Nymeth told the chieftess. *"Even I do not burn my children."*

"She's not your child, though," Nydia growled. "She's mine."

Camila didn't know whether to admire the woman's courage or despise her arrogance.

Nymeth gave a dangerous growl of her own in return, and another spark of fire burned within her throat.

Nydia acknowledged the warning with a lift of her hands, and when the dragon snapped her massive jaws shut, extinguishing the flame, Nydia turned to leave.

Emilia turned her head, the movement slow and weak, and when she caught sight of her mother, she whispered, "Don't."

Camila's eyes widened in disbelief, as Emilia extended a burned hand, as if she meant to grab something. "Oh, no, you don't." Camila tried to hold the child still, but she didn't want to put pressure on any of her burns. "Be still, you stubborn girl! You think because you said *one* word, you're healed?"

Two more puffs of smoke escaped Emryn's snout, and Camila glared at him. "If you're so amused, perhaps *you* should hold the child still!"

Emryn lifted one of his massive front legs and wiggled his dangerously sharp claws at Camila.

Well…yes.

He did have a point.

In that brief moment of distraction, Emilia managed to sink her burned fingers into the soil beneath her.

Camila frowned. "What are you—"

A familiar crackle of magic drew Camila's attention away from the girl, and she looked up, just in time to see Nydia hurl a ball of magical fire at the smallest dragon.

Nymeth roared in fury, but it was Emilia—the injured, barely conscious child—who reacted first.

She pulled something from deep within the earth—something ancient and powerful. The telltale glow of magic enveloped the child, burning within her eyes.

Then, Emilia lifted her dirty, injured hand, and an impossible, green fire burst forth.

Her strange, impossible magic collided with her mother's magic, and Nydia's flames dissipated, like dandelion dust, beneath the child's magic.

How…had she done that?

Emilia was a healer.

Healers wielded restorative magic well, but failed with most destructive magic. Until now, Emilia had fulfilled that expectation— both in her strengths and her weaknesses.

But had that even *been* destructive magic?

Camila had never seen green fire before.

She cast a puzzled look at the green dragon that leaned over them, but his eyes never left Emilia.

Emilia had gone limp in Camila's arms—either succumbing to her injuries or to the loss of energy.

Nydia stood nearby—next to Nymeth's huge front leg—and she

smiled, as if she weren't at all surprised by her injured daughter's defense of the dragon.

As if the entire incident hadn't bewildered Camila enough, *now* she had to process the fact that Nydia Drakon was smiling at the daughter she hated.

She might've assumed the woman was just baring her teeth, like some kind of beast, if her strong cheekbones hadn't lifted, as well.

Oh, Aletha.

What an unsettling sight.

Nydia's green eyes shifted toward Camila, and her smile widened. "I told you she wasn't done."

Nymeth lowered her massive head and growled at the chieftess. Yet, she didn't kill her, even though Camila had no doubt the dragon had considered it.

This time, Nydia took the hint and left.

Emilia was far too injured and drained to regain consciousness now. So, only Camila heard the words the ancient, black dragon spoke to Emilia.

"Good work, Dragon Child."

CHAPTER 2

Mount Drakon

"Em?"

"Em!"

Emilia looked up at her captain, heart pounding in her chest.

Maria held Emilia's shoulder, and she'd tilted her head, as if she were trying to see Emilia through the smoke.

Smoke?

No.

There was no smoke.

Was there?

How long had Maria been calling her name?

How long had Emilia stared at the charred earth that had once been her mother's training grounds?

When Emilia's gaze tried to drift away again, Maria pressed her fingers to Emilia's jaw, drawing her back.

"Not yet, love."

The gentle lilt of Maria's voice enthralled Emilia's disoriented mind.

"Eyes on me," Maria said. When Emilia obeyed that order, she continued, "Now, I need you to *breathe.*"

She enunciated the words carefully, as if she knew, somehow, that Emilia would struggle to hear them over the deafening *whoosh* of blood in her ears.

Worry twisted at Maria's brows, and Emilia wanted to smooth it away.

If only she could remember how.

"Em," Maria said.

Goddess, she was spellbinding—with those wide, brown eyes and that mass of little, brown curls slipping out beneath her headscarf and tricorn.

The thin sheen of sweat that coated her brown skin shimmered like gold in the sunlight, and her tall and muscular form seemed to glow and blur like a…

Wait. Blur?

Air!

Emilia couldn't breathe.

She folded forward, gasping.

With a sigh of relief, Maria said, "There you are."

The first deep inhale hurt, like a steel blade slicing through lungs that were too tight to accommodate it.

The second breath hurt, too—and then the next several after that.

Slowly, though, Emilia's chest loosened, and the sharp pain eased into a dull ache.

She lost count of the number of heartbeats that passed before her pulse stopped rattling her head.

The shame must've been waiting for a gap to slip through—because it filled her as the pain eased.

Emilia had tried to hide it. She'd tried *so* hard.

But this place pulled her under—hiding the present behind a wall of smoke, while she suffocated on the past.

Panic churned in her stomach, and bile rose in her throat.

She fought it back.

It was bad enough that Maria had witnessed yet *another* of her panic attacks.

She needed to regain control of her body.

If anyone else had touched Emilia in that moment, she might've screamed or fought, but even in a whirl of panic, she recognized the steadiness of her captain's touch.

Maria's hand trailed along Emilia's shoulder blade, and her thumb traced slow circles against her skin.

And while Emilia couldn't deny that it soothed her, she also didn't understand *why* Maria was doing it. No one had ever done that to her before.

Emilia had nearly fought back the panic when another cannon blast wracked the island. That was all it took to bring up the contents of her stomach.

Maria reacted not with shock or disgust—but with calculation. The hand on Emilia's back slid down to curl around Emilia's waist, and she steadied Emilia as her muscles violently convulsed.

Maria reached forward with her other hand and swept her fingers along the side of Emilia's thick, black hair.

Since their first sword fight, when Maria had unintentionally chopped off some of Emilia's hair, it hadn't grown long enough to really get in the *way*, per se, but Maria pulled it away from her face, anyway.

Maria didn't say a word. She just…held Emilia steady.

Her demeanor seemed almost cold and practical—except Emilia had known cold and practical people.

None of *them* would've done this.

When Emilia finished, Maria released her and stepped back. She pulled out her leather pocket-flask and held it out, waiting silently for Emilia to take it.

Emilia straightened and wiped her fingers over her mouth. The humiliation burning her skin was even more excruciating than the spasms of her stomach.

What was she supposed to say now?

How could Emilia explain her panic? How could she explain the way her mind and body had slipped out of her control?

She'd have to lie—say she'd come down with an illness or something.

But when she turned to do that, she met the calm, understanding gaze of Captain Maria Welles.

And only one word fell from her lips. "Sorry."

"For what?" Maria said—with enough casual dismissiveness to stun Emilia into silence.

She waved the flask impatiently, and Emilia took it.

"Thank you." Emilia lifted the flask to her lips.

Maria's gaze didn't waver. "Anytime, love."

Emilia spat out the first sip and swallowed the next.

Despite Maria's dismissive response, the shame continued to press against Emilia's chest. She took a few more sips, but the weight only seemed to grow.

"I didn't realize I'd—" Emilia stammered, "that my mind had—"

"I know," Maria interrupted.

Again…dismissive. Yet, her eyes didn't match her tone.

Maria's gaze didn't flick away from Emilia the way her words had. No, those large, brown eyes remained steady and focused on Emilia—soft with concern.

"I'm sorry," Emilia said again.

Maria sighed, "If you apologize one more time…" She didn't finish, which probably meant this was another one of those idle threats she liked to throw around.

Emilia almost apologized *again*, out of pure habit, but she clamped her mouth shut, just in time.

Maria must've noticed—because she lifted a scarred eyebrow.

Emilia didn't understand. If her mother had seen her have a panic attack, she would've ridiculed her.

She would've called Emilia *weak*.

Mocked her.

If Catherine Rochester had seen Emilia in such a vulnerable state, she would've used it against her.

But Captain Maria Welles—a pirate known for her ruthlessness—had rubbed Emilia's back, held her, and offered her rum to rinse her mouth afterward.

Maria had confessed her love for Emilia less than an hour ago, and though Emilia couldn't say she'd actually processed it, she hadn't discounted it either.

No, it wasn't that Emilia *doubted* Maria's love. It was more that… Catherine had said she loved Emilia, too, and clearly, that hadn't meant much.

And, more importantly, there was the simple fact that no amount of love could make Emilia Drakon deserving of kindness.

Didn't Maria know that?

Emilia took another drink. The rum stung her raw throat, but it also washed away the taste of panic.

"We can still go back—take the other path down," Maria offered. "I don't remember seeing any," she winced, before saying, "*destruction* on the way up."

Emilia let out a small laugh—one that felt more like a release of hysteria than humor. "That's because there were no people there," she said, "that day."

Maria jerked her head toward the charred grounds, a new clarity lightening her deep, brown eyes.

Without Nydia Drakon's magic, there was nothing to designate this as anything other than a burned clearing.

Perhaps Emilia should have let Maria think that was all it was.

"Fucking hell," Maria breathed. Her eyes—wide and flashing— shifted back toward Emilia. She grabbed Emilia by the arm so suddenly Emilia nearly spilled the rum. "Come on. We're going back."

"We can't," Emilia said. She planted her feet in place. "It took us all morning and afternoon to climb the mountain. We don't have that kind of time."

Maria couldn't argue with *that*. She turned. "Em," she sighed, "you can't put yourself through this."

"I'll do better," Emilia assured her. "I promise."

Maria released her abruptly, as if Emilia's skin had burned her. "Better?" She fell back on her heels, and pain twisted at the scars on her face. "Em…"

They had to take the quickest path.

The dragons would divert the naval fleet's attention for as long as they could, but they needed a dragon-rider.

And the *Wicked Fate* needed a captain.

Emilia had just opened her mouth to explain this, when Maria reached out and touched Emilia's cheek.

"Em, you're perfect."

Pure shock decimated every argument on Emilia's lips.

Every time Emilia managed to process *one* of the shocking statements Maria had made today, the enigmatic pirate captain spat out another.

Maybe she'd said, *'Em, you're pathetic.'*

It sounded similar.

Sort of.

'Pathetic' was one of Emilia's mother's favorite adjectives, and it made a lot more sense than *'perfect.'*

Maria must've realized she hadn't made her point—because she continued, "This isn't a sword fight. You can't beat it with skill." She dropped her hand, and her brows creased. "All we can do is endure."

We.

Why had Maria included herself in that statement? Had Maria experienced these same…symptoms?

Emilia found that hard to believe—because if she had, then that would mean it *wasn't* weakness.

Because Captain Maria Welles was anything but weak.

Maria nodded toward the flask. "Are you finished with that?"

Still too stunned to speak, Emilia simply held it out.

Maria took the leather pocket-flask and tipped it back, drinking deeply.

Emilia didn't know how to respond to the strangely kind remarks Maria had made. So, she returned her attention to the issue of time, instead. "This path will cut hours off of our return journey."

Maria lowered the flask, and her eyes narrowed. "There's another reason, isn't there?"

Damn her and her uncanny perceptiveness.

"The other reason is…less important," Emilia said.

"Em," Maria said, tone sharp with warning. "Tell me."

Emilia sighed, "The other problem is Catherine."

Maria tensed—but didn't retract the question.

So, Emilia continued, "If she sends people to look for us, she'll send them up the other path."

Maria didn't ask why Emilia thought Catherine was still alive. She didn't argue that it made more sense to think Catherine had drowned—that the naval fleet had tracked them down without her.

Judith had said something like that once.

So had Pelt.

Zain had, too.

But Maria never had. Ever since the day Catherine jumped, there'd been an understanding between the two of them that Catherine was still out there.

Maybe that was the reason Maria had once given her the nickname *'Cat.'*

The woman clearly had plenty of lives to spare.

"You were with Catherine for quite some time." Maria clenched her jaw, as if the thought pained her. "What makes you think she didn't learn this path, as well?"

Emilia didn't meet her gaze. "I was careful," she said, her chest tight. "Catherine never saw this path."

Maria's eyes widened. "You hid it from her."

The accusation made Emilia's stomach churn.

"It wasn't like that," Emilia insisted. "We kept her in a healer's tent, near the coast." She looked down, squeezing her forefinger with her opposite hand. "Why would I show her a path that would take her through the most vulnerable parts of the island?"

One corner of Maria's mouth quirked up. "Why wouldn't you?"

For whatever reason, this revelation seemed to please Maria, but it had the opposite effect on Emilia.

"If I'd known," Emilia said, defensiveness edging into her voice, "I would've warned someone."

Maria's smile softened. "I know that, love."

"I never took her to the cliff-side either, but," Emilia rambled nervously, "that was only because the dragons didn't like her." Her lungs constricted. "I did trust her. I did!"

"Em."

When Emilia didn't respond, Maria closed her fingers around Emilia's elbow and tugged her closer.

Emilia looked up.

Maria's warm touch unraveled some of the tension in Emilia's chest, and her heart rate instantly slowed.

"You thought you trusted her," Maria said slowly, "and to a certain extent, you did."

Her fingers traced the gentle curve of Emilia's arm, and her dark gaze warmed Emilia's skin.

"Sometimes, we survive not because of our choices, but because we're more clever than we give ourselves credit for," Maria told her. She let go of Emilia's arm and straightened. "Take it from the renowned swordsman who almost lost a sword-fight to you. You're clever. *Too* clever."

Emilia's mouth fell open. "Almost? You *did* lose!"

Maria shrugged her strong shoulders. "That isn't how I remember it."

Emilia glared at her. "Oh, you liar!"

Maria laughed loudly. She pocketed her flask and leaned toward Emilia. "Aren't you glad you chose to stay with me?" she teased. "Now, you can almost beat me over and over. For years to come."

Emilia closed the sliver of space that Maria had left between them. "I can *stab* you," she corrected, "over and over. For years to come."

Delight flashed in Maria's large, brown eyes, and her smile widened. She glanced at the sword that hung at Emilia's waist and murmured, "One can only hope."

"Hope?" An incredulous laugh spilled from Emilia's lips. "Why would you hope—"

But Maria stole her words and her breath with a single kiss.

It was quicker than the other kisses they'd shared, but it drew Emilia's muscles tight, all the same. And she *knew* it would linger in her mind for hours to come.

"You're right. Unfortunately," Maria admitted. "About saving time *and* avoiding Catherine."

Emilia lifted her eyebrows. "I'm sorry, Captain," she said slowly, "but did you just say I was right?"

Maria rolled her eyes. "I won't say it again."

Emilia just smiled. "Once was enough for me."

Captain Maria Welles tried not to laugh, as her surgeon attempted to push a whole, fucking boulder.

Emilia Drakon's strength was found in her courage, brilliance, and endurance—*not* in her biceps.

Maria moved to the other side of the stone, and when Em looked up, she said, "You push. I'll pull."

With a nod, Em resumed her efforts.

Maria's own muscles strained at the weight of the stone, but it eventually shifted loose and rolled from its place. She stepped out of the way before the stone could trap her against the side of the mountain.

Maria moved to stand beside Em, and her stomach fell at the sight of the sharp, moss-covered descent.

Em had called this a path. This was *not* a path.

It was a near-vertical *fall*!

"What the fuck, Em?" Maria turned to give her surgeon a look of disbelief. "We moved that for *this*?"

Like any ship captain, Maria preferred *not* to sail through uncharted waters, and for her, descending this mountain—or *any* mountain, for that matter—was what she'd call uncharted waters.

She knew port cities. She knew the seas.

She didn't know mountains.

What little she *did* know about them, she'd learned from Zain, who'd grown up in the high peaks of the Illopian Mountains, but Mount Drakon wasn't like the mountains in the Kingdom of Illopia.

The elevation was lower, and it felt…*older*, somehow.

One side of Mount Drakon eased languorously toward the sea,

while the opposite side fell sharply. They'd climbed up the easy side of the mountain that morning.

Apparently, Em intended to take them down the *other* side.

Em leaned forward with her hands on her knees, her face flushed with exhaustion. "I know how it looks…"

"Do you?" Maria said.

Em continued, "But my people use—*used* this path all the time." She straightened to her full height, which was still a few inches shorter than Maria's. "Pretty much every time Nymeth and my mother fought over me."

Maria's brows furrowed. "Who's Nymeth," she said, "and why was she fighting your mother?"

"The big, black dragon," Em told her. She brushed a hand over the dragon-scale cuirass she'd worn over her black shirt. "The one who gave me my armor."

Maria glanced down at the cuirass. She'd assumed it was just ordinary leather, but looking at it now, she noticed the woven thread between each scale.

"I don't remember seeing a black dragon."

Em offered an uneasy laugh. "You haven't met her yet," she explained. "She's not very sociable."

Gods, how many of those things *were* there?

"She and my mother disagreed a bit about my magical training," Em said. "My mother liked it deadly. Nymeth—not so much." She waved a hand. "You know, typical parental disagreement—with growling and fireballs." She tilted her head and squinted. "And people running and screaming…"

Maria blinked. She never knew whether to laugh or scream with this girl.

A little too enthusiastically, Em added, "We also used it before hurricanes! It's totally safe."

"Before hurricanes?" Maria said.

"We live—*lived* close to shore during the dry months." Em tensed when she corrected herself, but her voice didn't waver. "But during storms, we'd move to a higher elevation."

Maria thought of the storm surges in Nefala and wondered how much worse they were on the islands.

She tried to imagine Adda packing up an entire tavern and moving it to a higher elevation—and then realized…she hadn't seen a building all day.

There should've been ruins, at least. The cannons couldn't have obliterated them completely.

With a curious frown, Maria said, "You must've traveled lightly."

Em shrugged. "We took our tents and most of our possessions," she said, confirming Maria's suspicion. "We just didn't *possess* as much as Illopians do."

"Tents?"

Maria wouldn't have admitted it, at the time, but from her first day aboard, Em's adaptability had impressed her.

Most new sailors—older sailors, too, for that matter—griped and groused at every opportunity, and why shouldn't they? Ship life was hard.

Em, though—she'd accepted it all.

Even when Maria *tried* to elicit a reaction, Em only ever took offense to Maria's power play.

Which had become a button Maria *loved* to push.

A woman had to have hobbies, didn't she?

But now, Maria understood. Adaptability was in Emilia Drakon's blood.

Em squinted thoughtfully. "I think that's the closest Illopian word for it," she muttered. "Stretched hide?"

Em spread out her arms—because in her mind, that apparently represented a fucking tent.

Maria snorted. "Yes. I know what a tent is."

Em dropped her arms and nodded. "I take it you didn't evacuate before storms in Nefala?"

"What? With our stone buildings?" Maria scoffed. "Nah, I suppose some people did," she amended, "if the mountain priests predicted a particularly bad season. Most of us just boarded our shit up, though."

The adolescent memories that came to mind when Maria considered *that* left her grinning shamelessly.

"Well," Maria laughed, "Adda boarded up. I mostly just skirted my chores and went out looking for pretty girls who might want to board up with *me*."

Em's green eyes seemed to wander for a moment—before abruptly shifting back toward Maria.

Em blinked, shook her head, and returned her attention to the mountain. "We had *vastly* different childhoods."

Maria raised both eyebrows. "It was my sex life that told you that?" she said. "Not the dragons?"

Em turned to frown at her. "No, no, no. You have it all wrong." She held up her hand. "The dragons were the most normal *part* of my childhood."

Maria couldn't help but laugh. "You're only proving my point, love."

Em rolled her eyes, but her lips twitched with amusement. "I'd be careful, if I were you," she teased. "You don't want the dragons to dislike you. They threaten to eat people they don't like."

Maria pulled out her leather pocket flask and took another sip of rum, before offering it to Em. "Well, I hope they threatened to eat Catherine, then."

Em straightened and accepted the flask. "Thanks."

Maria suppressed her smile.

No one understood the gravity of that small act of trust the way Maria did, but then, no one else had noticed the way Em's eyes used to flare with panic every time someone offered her food or drink.

Maria had, though.

That panic had faded with each shared moment between them, and now, Em accepted Maria's flask without a second thought.

Em trusted Maria, and *that* had been no small feat.

"Emryn *begged* me to let him eat her," Em assured Maria, after she'd taken a sip of rum, "but, you know, he's always hungry. He has the appetite of an adolescent. Well, he basically *is* one—in dragon years. He's only seven hundred years old."

Maria sputtered in shock, "Seven *hundred?*"

How old were the adult ones?

Em returned the flask. "They all hated Catherine, though, whether they threatened to eat her or not."

"Smart creatures," Maria muttered.

Em beamed like a proud mother. "The smartest."

Gods.

A smile like that could crumble mountains.

It faded too soon, though, and Maria mourned its loss.

"If only I'd trusted their…perception of her," Em said with a pained sigh. "They couldn't tell me *why* they didn't like her. I just knew they didn't." The familiar shadow of guilt passed over Em's face. "Maybe if I'd realized—if I'd thought about it—would I have let my mother kill her, then?"

Sympathy twisted at Maria's chest. "Em—"

Em glanced at Maria. She straightened and lifted her chin. "Right. We should get started."

Maria wanted to pull her back, to urge her to keep talking, but…it wasn't the time. Instead, she followed Em along the lush mountain path. "None of your dragons have offered to eat *me* yet, have they?"

Em turned to face Maria, walking backward. A hint of mischief sparkled in her bright, green eyes. "That, my captain," she teased, "is privileged information."

Maria had always found *this* side of her surgeon particularly enticing, and she let that feeling pull her forward.

"Privileged for whom?" Maria increased the pace of her steps, easily overtaking Em. "I outrank you."

Em's pupils dilated—just a moment before her foot slipped over the moss.

Maria reached out and caught the leather strap of Em's scabbard. She tugged her forward, and Em's soft curves collided with the front of Maria's body.

"W-well…" Em cleared her throat. "Not in the dragons' eyes."

Maria chuckled. She tilted her face and brushed her mouth against Em's.

Em leaned forward, too, her eyes fluttering closed.

Boom.

Maria had only a moment to realize this blast of cannon fire had been louder than the last—before the mountain began to rumble and crackle around them.

Maria snaked her arm around Em's waist and caught the tree limb behind her, just as the ground crumbled beneath their feet.

The tree snatched them backward, and their bodies rocked, before Maria's boots found the ground again.

Em didn't scream, but Maria nearly did.

"Huh." Em watched the loose rocks and dust slide down the side of the mountain with a frown. "That's never happened before."

Maria pressed her face into Em's silky, black hair and inhaled deeply. The gentle, floral scent that lingered there was enough to reassure Maria's racing mind that they'd survived.

Maria had always suspected Em bathed with something other than just seawater—something more than what Illopian sailors used.

The floral scent was faint, but it was always there.

Soft and soothing.

One of Em's hands slid around the slight curve of Maria's waist, and her face pressed against Maria's leather doublet. "Thank you," she said, "Captain."

Maria shook her head in frustration. "You're lucky I had hold of you already. You *said* this way was safe."

"It was. Before," Em said. Her voice wavered. "I'd never traveled it under cannon-fire before. How was I supposed to know?"

Maria merely grunted.

The danger seemed to have passed, but that didn't mean Maria was ready to let go of the tree limb.

Or Em.

Em tilted her head back, peering up at the tree that had saved their lives. "Hey! I can use that!"

"What?" Maria said, but Em was already reaching.

Her fingers curled along the bend of Maria's elbow, as she raised herself onto her toes. When Em realized she *still* couldn't reach it, she turned in Maria's arms.

Maria cast her gaze downward, her brows high.

It was bad enough that Em's touch—casual as it might've been —raised chill bumps over Maria's arm.

But her round ass sliding against Maria's waist was just…too much.

Heat spread through Maria's lower half, and under her breath, she muttered, "Oh, for fuck's sake."

Em snatched some kind of purple flower from one of the tree limbs and waved it like a flag. "Got it!"

Maria forced a smile.

Clearly oblivious to the effects her body had on Maria's, Em turned on the narrow ledge, and the wide curve of her hips brushed against Maria once again.

"It's for a salve," Em told her.

Maria raised both eyebrows.

As Em pocketed the small, purple flower, Maria peered over the edge of the mountain—in hopes that the terrifying fall might quell the arousal now pulsing throughout her entire body.

It did not.

"So, if we stick close to the rock face—and avoid the crumbling edge," Em was saying, "we'll make it around the curve, and the path widens from there."

Couldn't Maria just…take Em by those luscious hips, pin her against the tree, and kiss her senseless?

It wasn't as if the danger bothered *Em*.

Clearly.

Sure, Maria's ship was under fire, at the moment, but Emilia Drakon was…*here*.

Sexy.

Beautiful.

And here.

Stop.

Stop it.

"What do you think?" Em asked.

Maria straightened. "I wasn't thinking anything!"

Em frowned, probably puzzled by the forcefulness of Maria's answer. "Umm," she stammered, "about continuing?"

"Oh," Maria said, blinking. "Yes."

Em squinted suspiciously—before turning to examine the crumbling ledge.

Maria took a moment to adjust her tricorn, which had cocked backward during their near fall.

"I'm obviously the heavier of the two of us, so I'll go first," Em said. "If it holds me, it'll hold you."

Maria instantly forgot her tricorn. "What?"

But it was too late.

Had Em given her the chance to argue, Maria might've used the argument that regardless of their physical weight, Maria wore heavier clothing.

Heavier swords, too. Surely, those added a few pounds!

And if that hadn't worked, Maria would've pulled rank.

But her bizarrely fearless surgeon hadn't given her the chance. She'd just stepped out onto the fucking ledge.

With her back pressed against the rock face, Em called back to her, "It held!"

"Gods, Em!" Maria snapped. "What if it hadn't?"

With slow, careful steps, Em inched to the right. "Then, you'd know not to come this way."

Maria could fucking kill her.

If the mountain didn't beat her to it.

Maria followed Em's example, turning to press her back against the rock face. Her stomach jumped into her throat at the sight of the fall that awaited them.

Em must've noticed a change in her expression—because she called out, "If it makes you dizzy, try turning toward the rock face."

Maria appreciated the thought, but anything less than eliminating the chance of falling was probably *not* going to help.

Unless…

Maria let her gaze follow the steep, green slope of the mountain —to the place where trees gave way to sand. Beyond that sand was the only sight Maria had ever needed.

The sea.

Her pulse slowed.

As long as Maria could see the ocean, she could keep herself calm. "I'm fine," she told Em. "I'm a sailor. I'm not afraid of heights."

Em seemed to accept that. "Okay."

Maria chose not to mention that it'd been over a decade since climbing the rigging had been part of *her* job description.

She didn't think that piece of information would calm either of them.

Maria took her first step. The narrow ledge held beneath her boots. "This doesn't bother you?"

Em followed her gaze downward, before saying, "I've fallen mid-flight before. I was much higher, then."

Maria momentarily forgot to keep her gaze on the rocks beneath her boots and glanced, instead, at her dragon-riding surgeon. "What?"

"About six more steps," Em called.

The adrenaline made Maria want to grasp the hilt of her right sword out of habit, but she resisted—keeping her palms against the rock face behind her.

She took note of each vine and jut of rock—in case she found herself in need of it.

Now, Maria spoke to keep *herself* calm. "How long have you been considering this? Staying with us?"

Em cast a wide-eyed look at her. "You want to talk about that right *now*?"

"Yes," Maria said.

Em cast a wary look at the rocks beneath her. "Step lightly. These feel a bit loose."

Maria had never done anything *lightly*. "Answer the question, surgeon."

Em took another step. "Had I been honest with myself," she said, after a bit of hesitation, "I might've realized I couldn't leave you weeks ago."

The honesty of Em's statement caught her so off-guard that she nearly fell. "You couldn't leave *me*?"

"Captain!" Em yelled. She reached out, grasping for Maria's

hand. She caught hold of it and squeezed. Her voice rose with anger and panic. "I told you I could treat anything except death! *Except!*"

Maria regained her balance, but Em didn't let go. Her fingers were soft but fierce around Maria's.

Maria's chest tightened at the sensation. When was the last time she'd felt anything like this?

Before the imprisonment?

In a tone that was somehow both panicked and scolding, at once, Em said, "I would've missed the crew, too! Just so you know."

"And the cats," Maria said breathlessly.

"And the cats," Em agreed.

They took two more steps, and Maria began to suspect that Em had underestimated how far it was.

As the shock and delight of Em's answer faded, Maria's ego urged her to say, "Just weeks? Not more?"

Despite the danger beneath their feet, Em glared at her. "Captain," she said, "the first time you had sex with me, you said it was fun—but that it was over."

"I didn't think you'd *believe* me," Maria muttered.

"Yes, you did," Em argued.

Maria tilted her head in acknowledgment. "Fine, I'll take weeks."

Em took her final step.

A smirk tilted at one corner of Maria's mouth. "In my defense, though, it *was* fun."

Em cast an incredulous look her way. "Do you *want* me to push you to your death, Captain?"

Maria laughed loudly at the threat. She couldn't help but notice, though, that Em's protective hold on her hand had never wavered.

Maria took her last step, as well. Relief washed over her, as her boots landed on stable ground.

The footpath opened around them, loose rock giving way to high grasses and wide-trunked trees. The mountain must've shielded this side from the cannon-fire.

Maria couldn't help but wonder if *all* of Drakon Isle had once been this beautiful.

Something about the wistfulness of Em's smile told her it had.

"You know," Em said with a sheepish smile, "if you don't count the *slight* setback of the ground crumbling beneath us, we're actually making good time."

Maria scowled.

"I'm not an oracle," Em reminded her. "I couldn't have predicted that." Seizing the opportunity, she added, "Now, if I summon the sea goddess, *she*—"

Maria didn't wait for her to finish. "*Never* do that again."

Em blinked. "Never do…what?" She looked down at their joined hands, and her face reddened. "Oh!"

Maria was so stunned by the sudden flush of Em's cheeks that she didn't realize what Em had assumed—until after her soft fingers had released Maria's.

Maria frowned at her now empty hand. "Not *that*."

A bizarre urge flared up inside of Maria—the urge to reach out and take Em's hand back into her own—but she resisted it.

Instead, she pressed a knuckle to Em's chin, urging Em's enchanting, green eyes away from the ground. When Em made eye-contact with her, Maria said, "Stop risking your life for—"

She hesitated.

For me.

It was hard to say those words—because saying them meant thinking about what they *meant*—and Maria had been doing nothing *but* thinking about what they meant for weeks.

Ever since the day Em had offered her life in exchange for Maria and her crew.

This time, the crew wasn't even involved. She'd done it for Maria alone, and Maria didn't like it.

The transparency of Em's actions didn't stop her from trying to deny it. "It was the rational choice."

"No," Maria said. "You're done risking your life."

Em scrunched up her nose, as if she found something confusing about Maria's demand.

"Do you understand me?" Maria lifted an eyebrow, waiting for her usual, *'Yes, Captain.'*

Instead, Em said, "You've clearly forgotten we're under attack right now."

"No. Risking. Your life," Maria said, enunciating each word. "That's an order."

Em shrugged. "I mean, I could *pretend* to agree, if that's what you want."

Maria dropped her hand.

Em continued to ramble, "Me—I prefer honesty."

"For fuck's sake, Em," Maria grumbled.

"How about a *'Maybe, Captain?'*" Em offered. She smiled and pointed her forefinger. "I can do that."

Maria shook her head in disbelief. Over a decade in this job, and she was powerless against a fucking surgeon.

A fearless surgeon.

With the undying loyalty of both dragons and cats.

And a beautiful smile—that she happened to be directing at Maria right now.

So not fair.

"Oh!" Em said. Delight sparkled in her bright, green eyes. "I have to show you something!"

Maria would've followed Em anywhere to keep *that* smile on her face.

Fortunately, Em only led her about three steps forward and two to the left. She placed her hand on a large tree with a wide, moss-covered trunk.

"This is it!"

Maria quirked her head, brows furrowing.

Clearly, the dragon sorceress had bewitched Maria with her smile and caused her to miss something.

"That," Maria said, "is a tree."

"Yes." Em looked up at the tree and then back at Maria. "Do you remember the day we talked about books?" She bounced on the balls of her feet, as if she could barely contain her excitement. "I was injured, and you were writing in your log."

How could Maria forget?

She stepped forward, and Em took a step back.

"You mean the first day you called me Captain and meant it?" Maria took another step forward, backing Em into the tree. "The day you decided to trust me?"

Em pressed her back against the tree trunk and looked up at Maria, but Maria continued to close every inch of space that opened between them.

Maria leaned in, tilting her face—so that she could whisper the next question against Em's lips, "The day you let me fuck you while you were tied up?"

Em inhaled sharply. Blood rushed to the surface of her fair skin, turning it an enticing shade of pink.

Maria pulled back slightly—so she could peer into Em's dark, dilated eyes. "Is that the day you meant?"

"Mm-hmm."

The faint vibration of Em's mouth against hers sent a shockwave of arousal through Maria's body.

Maria forgot the battle, forgot the danger.

She forgot everything except the nearness of Em's body and the need to feel Em's mouth beneath hers—to curl her fingers around Em's hips and hold her close.

Maria captured Em's lips with her own—and smiled, when the surgeon melted against her.

Maria pressed her tongue into Em's mouth, tasting the rum and coconut that lingered on her tongue. She felt the slow vibration of Em's moan against her own tongue, and then, Em opened further to her.

With one hand, Maria slid her fingers along Em's soft jawline and lifted her face, and with the other, she grasped the soft curve of Em's hip—just beneath her scabbard—and pulled her waist against Maria's.

The thick roots of the old tree had already separated Em's feet, so Maria pressed her thigh into the open space. When Em jerked back in surprise, Maria tightened her grasp, holding Em in place.

"Was *this* what you wanted to show me?" Maria whispered against her lips.

"Uhh," Em said with a gasp, "no."

Maria pulled back, and for a moment, Em looked as if she wanted to chase her. Em's fingers toyed with one of the leather thongs of Maria's doublet, and her gaze traveled from Maria's mouth to her throat.

Maria stroked her thumb along the curve of Em's hipbone, the soft flesh dipping beneath her touch. Em's breath caught. "I'm not sure I believe you."

Em's eyes widened. "What? Why wouldn't—"

Maria kissed her again, and Em apparently forgot her argument.

Then, the distant rumble of cannons brought Maria's mind back to her ship. With a sigh, she leaned back, resting her weight on the heels of her boots. "What's the significance of the tree, Em?"

Em blinked slowly, as if she couldn't remember anything before the kiss, but eventually, her eyes brightened. "Oh! Right!" A bright smile burst across her face. "This is where I did it!"

Maria had only one action on her mind, at the moment. So, she'd need a bit more than that. "Did what?"

"Read," Em said, as if it were obvious. She smiled up at the canopy of leaves above her. "Isn't it perfect? The stolen books we talked about—this is where I read them! It's my favorite tree."

Maria chuckled. She licked her lips, still warm from Em's kiss, and she shook her head. "Why am I not surprised," she said, "that *you* have a favorite tree?"

"Because everyone does," Em said with a shrug. "You can't read *without* a shade tree. You'd get sunburned." She eyed Maria's dark skin. "Oh, that's probably not as much of an issue for you, is it?"

Maria laughed. She brushed her thumb along the soft, pink skin beneath Em's cheekbone and longed to stay like this forever.

"Emryn and Astral would lie there," Em continued, pointing at something behind Maria, "and whine about my reading choices." She looked up at Maria. "They only like stories with dragons."

Maria nodded. "Astral and Emryn are…dragons?"

"Yes," Em said. "You met Emryn earlier. He was the one with the green scales. Astral had violet scales."

"Mm-hmm." Maria offered an indulgent smile. "You read to your dragons?"

"Of course," Em said—as if they *weren't* discussing some of the most terrifying beasts in all of Aletharia—and Maria adored her for it.

"My sweet surgeon," Maria murmured.

She let each word linger on the tip of her tongue—words she'd once said with contempt, but now said with affection.

She should've known it would turn out this way.

Maria had always had a weakness for sweet things—even ones with prickly outer layers.

Especially those, apparently.

A sudden tremor traveled throughout Em's body, and with her lush curves pressed so closely to Maria's form, Maria felt every moment—shooting from her head to her toes like a bolt of lightning.

Maria leaned back, frowning worriedly.

Quick gasps spilled from Em's mouth, and she blinked rapidly, her green eyes wide with terror.

Maria grasped her shoulders. "What's wrong?"

Maria had learned to recognize some of the subtle signs before Em's panic attacks. She'd worsened one once, and even if Em had freely taken the blame for her mistake, Maria didn't want to do it ever again.

A subtle distance would usually shutter over Em.

Sometimes, her eyes would dart, as her senses grew over-stimulated.

Her voice would rise.

Her skin might flush.

Her breath might quicken.

Sometimes, her breath stopped completely.

Given the chance, Em would flee, but if you pushed her, she *would* fight.

Whatever this was, it wasn't *that*.

Perhaps Maria shouldn't have been so confident of that, but this had come on *too* suddenly—as if Em had opened a window for someone *else's* fear.

"Oh, no, no, no," Em whispered. "Igrunn."

"Em? Love?" Maria tried again. "Who's Igrunn?"

Em pressed a hand against her left side, and Maria released her and stepped back so Em could bend forward. "The one who looks like fire in the sunlight."

Maria's brows furrowed at the unhelpful description. "One of the...dragons?"

"Yes," Em gasped. "Orange and yellow scales."

Maria nodded. She didn't understand the magical connection Em shared with her dragons, but she figured, somehow, this was happening because of that. "Is something wrong with him?"

"He's injured." Em straightened, still clutching her side. "He's hurting *here*. I can feel it."

"You can *feel* it?" Maria repeated.

That was absurd.

Who'd decided it should work like that?

"Captain?" Em's eyes sought out Maria's with a desperation Maria had never seen in them before. "They have a weapon that can pierce dragon-scale."

Maria's frown deepened. She'd always heard cannon fire *couldn't* pierce dragon-scale, but perhaps the Royal Navy had found a way to change that.

"Were the dragons flying *above* the sails?" Maria asked. "No one's foolish enough to fire a cannon vertically."

"Of course they were flying above the sails," Em said, in a rush of breath. She held out her hands. "It's—it's...something else. Something with a blade."

Maria couldn't think of anything. The naval sailors carried swords and belt knives, of course, but none of those could've reached above the towering sails of a warship.

"Wait." Em extracted herself from her little nook and began to pace. She pressed her hand to the top of her head and squeezed her eyes shut, as if too many people were talking, at once—though no one was talking at all. "Caelu's going to show it to me."

Show?

How did *that* work?

None of this made sense to Maria.

Em opened her eyes. "It's like a crossbow," she said, "except it's massive—with projectiles that have blades like swords."

"A ballista," Maria said.

Em froze. Her brows creased, and a hint of pain flashed in her green eyes. "You knew they had a weapon that could hurt dragons, and you didn't tell me?"

"No," Maria said. "It was eleven years ago, Em."

Em didn't relax.

Not yet.

Maria sighed, "It was just a rumor. Someone was testing it against leather and steel, but…everyone said dragon-scale was unlike either of them."

Curiously, Maria reached out to touch Em's black, dragon-scale cuirass, and Em, cautiously, let her.

Her fingertips slid over the nearly impenetrable scale. It truly *was* unlike either—more like leather in texture, while still tougher than the strongest steel.

Maria let her hand fall. "It was a siege weapon," she explained, "but if the rumors were true, then…I suppose they've modified it for use against dragons."

Em bit her lip nervously. "You've never used one?"

"Never," Maria said.

"Okay," Em breathed. She stepped past Maria—and then turned back. "With Emryn, sometimes, I'd fly through the trees." She mimicked the motion with her hand. "Twisting and swerving, like a snake."

Maria's eyebrows lifted. "They wouldn't be able to take aim," she realized. She nodded. "I like it."

Em shook her head. "I don't think the others can do it, though," she sighed. "Maybe if I demonstrated—"

Maria no longer liked it. "How would you do that?"

Em stepped forward. "We need to get to shore."

"Yes," Maria agreed, "but why, exactly?" She really needed to hear the rest of Em's plan—so she could most likely order Em *not* to go through with it.

Em closed her eyes and rubbed the side of her head. "But I can't let the dragons continue to fight. Not if it's putting them in danger."

Maria wished Em would use the same caution for herself that she used for her dragons. "How many ships have they armed with the new weapon?"

Em glanced up at her. "Umm, let me ask," she said, before falling silent again. "One! They only see one."

"That's the flagship," Maria said. "It's Catherine's."

Em's eyes widened. "Do you think she's on it?"

"Maybe," Maria said, but really, she knew better. She knew Catherine well enough to know she wouldn't have stayed on the ship.

As soon as she'd realized Maria and Em had gone ashore, she'd have come after them.

Catherine was somewhere on the island. Maria had no doubt about it.

"Tell your dragons to avoid that ship," Maria said. "They'll be cautious with their flagship, which means *you* can be cautious, too."

Em nodded. "Okay," she whispered. "Okay."

Noticing the familiar flare of panic in Em's eyes, Maria stepped closer and curled her fingers around Em's arms. "Before we go, I need you to breathe."

Em nodded again—the movement quick and jerky.

Maria squeezed her arms to get her attention. "Em."

Em looked up, blinking. The glaze of her eyes cleared, and she exhaled slowly. "Yes, Captain."

Maria released Em's arms and adjusted her tricorn. "Let's go, then."

"Oh, umm," Em interrupted. She pointed at Maria's hair and grimaced. "I can just...get it, if you want?"

Maria lifted her eyebrows. "Get what?"

Em reached out toward the brown curls that had escaped Maria's headscarf—but didn't touch them. "May I?"

Maria widened her eyes and nodded.

Em raised herself onto her toes and plucked a shard of white stone from one of Maria's curls. She smiled and held it out in front of her. "Oh! It's only a rock."

Maria frowned. "What did you *think* it was?"

"Bone," Em said—with far too much nonchalance for Maria's taste. "Do you want it? It's a pretty one."

Actually, after this, Maria didn't think she'd ever touch a *rock* again. "You keep it."

"Thank you!" Em pocketed it.

Maria shook her head slowly. "You don't see any more possible *bones* on me, do you?"

Em circled around Maria, clearly taking the question more seriously than Maria meant it. "Nope!" she chimed. "You're good, Captain."

"Lovely," Maria muttered.

CHAPTER 3

Ash and Bone

In hindsight, Maria supposed it had been naïve to think the charred clearing they'd seen earlier was the worst…*scenery* they'd encounter on this path.

There'd been a reason, after all, that Em hadn't taken them this way before.

That being said, Maria doubted anything could've prepared her for the destruction that stretched before them now.

The blackened remains of trees jutted from the ash, like shards of broken glass—along with the few stone tables and tools that had survived the cannon-fire.

Most cultures would've left behind crumbling structures—the skeletal ruins of a city—but Em's people had left nothing but ash and bone.

Maria cast a concerned glance in Em's direction.

Em kept her expression blank. "Stay here."

Maria arched an eyebrow. Clearly, her poor surgeon had forgotten who she was talking to.

When Em stepped forward, Maria followed.

At the sound of Maria's footsteps, Em stopped and turned

toward her. "It'll only take me a moment," she tried again. "There's something I have to get."

"All right," Maria said. "Lead the way."

Em frowned. She gestured toward the rock face beside them. "There are places to hide here." She turned toward the open expanse of ash behind her and added, "There's nowhere to hide out there."

"I'm Captain Maria Welles," Maria said simply. "I don't hide."

Em bounced on the balls of her feet. It was interesting—how similar her mannerisms were when she was worried or excited. Maria might not have known which one this was—if it hadn't been for the crease of her brows and the darting of her eyes.

It was fear.

Not for herself, but for Maria.

"You're not going alone," Maria informed her. "If it's important enough for you to go out there, then it's important enough for me to go with you."

With a pleading look, Em said, "Captain…"

Maria stepped forward. "That's right. *Captain*. You'll take me with you, and that's an order."

Normally, Em would've fought back, but she only sighed and spread out her hands. "Fine."

That, more than anything, worried Maria.

It made her feel helpless, and Maria *hated* feeling helpless. "Fine, what?"

Even now, Em didn't rise to the bait. "Captain."

"Darling," Maria said, before Em took the first step, "is it absolutely necessary?"

"Yes," Em said without looking at her.

Maria breathed out a regretful sigh. "All right."

Em was about to walk into a kind of hell most people wouldn't wish on their worst enemies.

If Maria couldn't stop her, she at least intended to be at her side.

Something beneath the shallow layer of ash crackled beneath Maria's boot, and Maria could only *hope* it was a stick or dead leaf, rather than bone.

She lightened her steps.

As they ventured toward the outer rim of the field of ash, the babble of nearby water grew louder—its peaceful sound at odds with the disturbing sight.

Almost as if she knew what Maria was thinking, Em called back, "Our healers lived near the river."

This *was* where her people had lived, then.

Maria had assumed as much—with the amount of destruction—but the confirmation only deepened the ache in her chest.

She grasped for words to fill the haunted silence.

"You lived with other healers?" Maria asked. "Not with your mother?"

If Maria's mother had been anything like Em's, she wouldn't have wanted to live with her, either, but she still found the living situation strange—compared to the way Illopian families lived.

"Some children lived with their parents until they were older," Em said, "if they wanted." Her shoulders drew together in a sort of uneasy shrug. "My mother never wanted…that."

In that brief moment of hesitation, Maria heard the word Em *hadn't* said, rather than the one she had.

My mother never wanted me.

"Heartless bitch."

Maria hadn't meant to say it out loud. She didn't even realize she had—until Em froze mid-step.

Em turned to face Maria, her brows high.

"Have I said something inaccurate?" Maria asked.

Em winced a little. She cast a quick glance around them and lowered her voice. "You realize it's easier for them to, umm, straddle the line here, right?"

Maria frowned at that. "What line?"

"The line between life and death," Em said.

Maria's eyes widened.

Just as Em had done a moment before, Maria glanced around at the grey ash that surrounded them, and a chill slid down her spine.

She remembered the crackle beneath her boot and hoped—with renewed vigor—that it *hadn't* been a bone.

"They can't touch you," Em assured her. "I'm the only one of us who's…*near* them, in that sense."

What the fuck was that supposed to mean?

"She *can* hear you, though," Em warned.

Maria glanced at Em. A spark of excitement overtook the horror that had been creeping under her skin. "She can?"

Em's eyebrows inched higher. "That was *not* supposed to encourage you."

Maria cast another bewildered glance at the empty field around them, and the chilling realization that Em might've been seeing… *more*, in that moment, settled over Maria. She shuddered at the thought.

Em's lips twitched. "We're almost there."

Maria followed Em, watching her step with a bit more caution than before. "What makes you think it survived the fire?" She eyed the few items that had survived. "Whatever you're looking for, I mean."

"Dragon-scale doesn't burn," Em explained.

Maria looked up, her unsettling suspicions growing. "Why do you need dragon-scale?"

Em didn't answer. "Here we are."

She knelt and brushed away the ash with her bare hands. She unearthed a stone mortar and set it aside—before digging through another pile of ash.

Maria watched with rising levels of concern.

"Ah!" Em said. "I knew it!"

She lifted a piece of black, dragon-scale armor.

Wait, no.

Not a single piece—but two.

Black, dragon-scale tassets for each thigh, held together by a thick, leather belt.

"Em," Maria said warily.

Em's gaze darted toward her. "They need me."

Maria's heart raced at the mere thought of what Em was suggesting. "My crew needs you."

"And your crew will have me," Em assured her, "afterward."

Maria's adrenaline only rose. "Em…"

Em set the tassets aside and returned to searching the piles of ash. "I need the rest of it," she mumbled. "Have you seen any gloves?"

Maria stepped forward to order Em *not* to do this—but her boot slid across something soft. She stepped back and brushed the ash aside with the toe of her boot. Something black and leathery lay beneath.

Maria knelt and picked it up. A black, dragon-scale cuirass, almost identical to Em's, emerged from the ash.

The pain in Em's exhale was so audible it wrenched Maria's chest. "It's Camila's."

Who was Camila?

It didn't matter. She was clearly someone Em had grieved, and Maria had accidentally trudged up the memory.

Maria returned the cuirass to where she'd found it—and, once again, tried to fill the painful silence.

"I always figured you just liked the color black," Maria said playfully. "I didn't realize you all wore it."

A faint smile pulled at Em's lips. "I do like the color black," she admitted, "and we don't *all* wear it."

Maria lifted an eyebrow. "No?"

"Only our dragon-riders wore black," Em told her. "Warriors, like my mother, wore red. Our healers usually wore blue, but Camila and I were dragon-riders, as well as healers. So, we wore Nymeth's scale, instead."

"What? Like a uniform?" Maria said.

Like the naval uniform?

Em bit her lip thoughtfully. "We had more freedom, I think. If we liked trousers, we wore trousers. If someone liked dresses, they wore dresses. There were no requirements. The colors were just… tradition."

"Red, blue, black," Maria listed. "What else?"

A hint of life returned to Em's eyes. "Oracles, like my uncle, wore violet—the color of Astral's scales," she explained. "Agrarian sorcerers, like my possible-father, wore green—the color of Emryn's scales."

Maria held up a hand. "Let's…revisit that for a moment." She suppressed a laugh. "Did you just call someone your *possible*-father?"

Blood rushed to Em's cheeks.

Perhaps she'd thought Maria was criticizing the nickname, rather than just being…puzzled by it.

"If it helps, I never called him that to his face," Em said quickly. "Well, I did that once, but—"

Maria shook her head. "So, you suspected this person was your father, but you never…asked?"

"Of course I asked," Em assured her. "I was told it was an inappropriate question."

Maria nodded slowly, her eyes wide.

"Silas was his name," Em said. "He and my mother were often together at night. They barely spoke a word to each other in the daylight, so…"

"So, you guessed," Maria realized.

Em nodded. "I inherited most of my physical traits from my mother," she explained, "but my skin tone was closer to Silas's."

Maria could just imagine Em, as a child, tallying up all the reasons this *Silas* might've been her father. "Oh," she teased. "So, he was pink, too, then?"

"I'm not *always* pink!" Em laughed.

Maria feigned shock. "You're not?"

Em rolled her eyes, but her cheeks, indeed, took on a slight pink tint, as she did. "He was paler than I am, if you can believe it. His hair was brown, though, and mine's black, like my mother's. His hair was curly, and mine's not—except mine's not as straight as my mother's was, either."

Maria knelt in front of her to listen. "Was he kind?"

Em's brows furrowed. "I don't know, but he wasn't cruel," she said. "He didn't make eye-contact much, and he spent more time around plants than people—with the exception of my mother, that is. Sometimes, I thought…maybe his mind worked like mine."

The deep loneliness behind those words made Maria's heart ache.

Em looked up. "Wishful thinking, I guess."

"Maybe," Maria said gently, "or maybe not."

"Did you know who your father was?" Em asked.

Maria shook her head. "Adda met him once, but she didn't know his name," she said. "When I was a child, she told me he was a merchant sailor, but—" Amusement tugged at the edges of her mouth. "If he sold to Adda, he was probably a pirate."

Em smiled. "So, *that's* where you got it from."

Maria snorted. "Well, I certainly didn't take after my mother. Farming?" She shook her head in horror. "I could *never* stay on land that long."

Em's smile deepened, and for just a moment, the two of them forgot their dreadful surroundings.

Then, like clockwork, a distant blast of cannon-fire reminded them.

While Em returned to her search, Maria stood to keep watch. She admired how well Em was holding herself together through this all, but she also worried about how much pain Em was bottling up for later.

"Not that I am, in *any* way, agreeing to your plan," Maria said carefully, "but what would the dragon-scale protect against, exactly?"

Em climbed to her feet, shaking the ash from a pair of black, leather gloves. "Burns." She held one glove beneath her arm, as she slid her fingers into the other. "Dragon-fire heats the air around you —and the scale beneath you. I've flown recreationally without armor, but during a battle, I need protection."

"What about falling?" Maria said. "Does it protect you, then?"

Em lifted her eyebrows in amusement. "From that height, Captain," she said, "even water is deadly."

Maria narrowed her eyes at that. "Which is exactly why I don't want you to do this."

"The dragons taught me to fly when I was a child," Em told her. "I've survived this long, haven't I?"

Maria crossed her arms, her leather doublet clinging to her shoulders. "Did that sound reassuring in your head? Because it's not!"

Em slid her fingers into the second glove. "The only thing that's ever successfully killed me was my mother." She offered the kind of quirky smile that only Emilia Drakon would offer at such a time. "Dragon-riding is *far* less terrifying than she was."

"You could still die," Maria said.

"Name one time the risk of death has stopped me from doing anything," Em challenged. She looked up at Maria. "I joined your crew, didn't I?"

She…*might* have had a point there.

Maria pursed her lips. "You're my surgeon, Em."

"Yes," Em agreed, "but I'm also a dragon sorceress. I have the chance to burn our enemies to the ground—or, well…sea. I intend to take it."

Maria couldn't help the rush of excitement that coursed through her at the thought.

Em stepped closer, more lovely and dangerous than Maria had ever seen her—in her thick, black armor. "Isn't that what you want? To see them all burn?"

Desire buzzed in Maria's blood, like rum. "Yes."

Em tilted her head, and her lips curved into the most *enticing* smile. "Then, let me give that to you."

Sunlight sparkled in Em's intensely green eyes, and Maria found herself closing the inch of space that remained between them.

"Oh," Maria breathed, "you are…lovely."

Em's eyes widened, as if she hadn't expected that reaction, but she should have.

After all, this had been the side of Em that had enthralled Maria from the start. She'd come to adore the soft and sweet side of Em, too, but that didn't mean the sharp and vengeful side had lost any of its appeal.

Emilia Drakon was a multi-faceted stone, whose every side was just as enchanting as the last.

If Maria kissed Em now, would she taste like fire and vengeance?

Or honey and warmth?

Maria tilted her face closer, and she reached out and touched Em's side—just inches above her waist. Em released a shaky breath at her touch, and Maria brushed her lips against Em's.

She trailed her hand downward—along the pliant dragon-scale that covered Em's soft curves, down to where Em's hips flared wider, where her thin sword hung from its scabbard.

Maria paused when her fingers brushed the soft fabric of Em's black trousers, and Em leaned back.

"Oh," she said breathlessly. "The tassets."

Maria crossed her arms, as Em retrieved the final pieces of her armor. Perhaps she should've moved a bit faster with that kiss.

Em returned with the tassets—which consisted of two large pieces of dragon-scale armor, suspended from a heavy, leather belt. She turned them over in her hands, analyzing each strap and buckle.

"I've never worn it with a scabbard before."

Maria's gaze drifted toward Em's hips, where she carried the sword Maria had given her. "It fastens around your waist?" Maria assumed.

"Part of it does. Around my thighs, too." Em sighed, "Camila used to help me put it on—when she was alive."

Maria's chest tightened. "And, erm, was she...before Catherine?"

Em's brows furrowed. "You mean," she asked, "was she *born* before Catherine?"

Maria scowled. "No." She dropped her arms. "Was Camila your lover before you met Catherine?"

Em lifted her eyebrows in disbelief. "My lover?"

Maria regretted even asking.

"Camila was my mother's age," Em pointed out.

"What does that matter?" Maria asked.

"Well," Em said, draping the armor over her arm, "part of the time we're discussing includes my childhood."

Maria blinked—and then frowned. "Oh! She wasn't a lover, then?"

"No, Captain. She wasn't a lover," Em said with an amused smile. "She was our chief healer—*and* the only dragon-rider of her generation."

Maria nodded. "Are all dragon-riders healers?"

"No," Em said, "but the dragons do seem to favor healers. My mother always found that strange."

"I bet she did," Maria said with a roll of her eyes.

"Camila taught me everything I know," Em added, "except for the surgical methods, of course. I learned those from all the Illopian medical books I found."

"Oh, yes," Maria said with a wink. "Found."

Em rolled her eyes, but a sheepish smile tugged at her lips. "Camila—she… She cared about people."

Maria's gaze softened. "She was like you, then."

Em's eyes widened. "What?" she stammered. "No, no. I could never—" She stared at the thin layer of grey ash beneath her feet. "Camila would've never made the mistakes I made. No one would have."

Maria's stomach sank. "Em…"

Em forced a smile. "Sorry." She lifted the black armor in her hands. "I should put these on."

Maria longed to lift the guilt from Em's shoulders, but she didn't know how. Perhaps the best she could do, at the moment, was allow Em to keep moving.

She stepped forward. "Would you like me to help?"

With a hesitant nod, Em said, "If you don't mind."

No woman had *ever* looked that cute while wearing armor.

It simply wasn't possible.

"I don't," Maria assured her. She held out a hand, and Em gave it to her.

It was heavier than it looked—lighter than steel, of course, but heavier than simple leather.

Maria examined each piece. Despite the difference in material,

Em's armor had enough in common with Maria's doublet and scabbard that she didn't think it'd be hard to figure out.

Em unbuckled her scabbard, and Maria closed the remaining space between them. She slipped her own fingers through the thin, leather belt and loosened it.

She lifted it higher. "Hold it here," she murmured.

Em held the belt and sword against her stomach.

Maria unlaced the tassets and set them aside. She slipped the leather around Em's waist. She tugged lightly, and Em stumbled toward her.

Maria smoothed the leather over the soft, lower curve of Em's stomach. Heat pulsed through Maria.

Em looked up, briefly meeting Maria's gaze, and Maria searched those emerald-green eyes for signs of the same desire that burned inside of Maria now.

Em's eyes darkened, and Maria's lips twitched.

Maria fastened the belt—and then dropped to her knees.

She suppressed a laugh, when Em's eyes widened.

Maria picked up the tasset and smoothed it around Em's left thigh. Beneath her fingers, the dragon-scale felt unlike anything Maria had ever known—moving as effortlessly as leather, while remaining as impenetrable as steel.

Maria held the armor against Em's thigh with her hands, and when her right hand slid up Em's inner thigh, she heard a sharp intake of breath above her.

Maria didn't bother to hide her smile, as she laced up the armor. "Em? Your, uh, dead mother isn't still eavesdropping, is she?"

"No," Em said breathlessly. "Not for some time now." Her brows furrowed. "Why do you ask?"

"No reason," Maria lied.

Em's thighs were a luscious combination of muscle and soft flesh, and with such a perfect opportunity to caress them, Maria simply couldn't help herself.

Em's knees nearly buckled at her touch. "Captain!"

"Do you want them to come loose?" Maria asked.

With a growl of frustration, Em said, "No."

"Well…" Maria slid two fingers upward, smoothing the armor along the inside of Em's thigh.

Up, up, and…

Em gasped the moment Maria's fingers pressed into the center of her trousers. "I *will* stab you."

Maria chuckled. "Total accident."

Em narrowed her eyes at that. "Mm-hmm."

Maria picked up the other piece of armor and slipped it around Em's other thigh. "Would you like me to be less," she paused to grin at Em, "*thorough?*"

Em glanced down at her, eyes wide. Blood gathered in her cheeks, and she released a shuddery breath.

Maria finished lacing the second piece of armor.

"Is that a yes, love," she asked slowly, "or a no?"

Slowly and carefully, Em shook her head.

Maria's lips curved into a deep smile. With her lovely surgeon's consent, Maria succumbed to the temptation—and trailed her fingers up Em's thigh.

When she reached the edge of the dragon-scale, Maria continued upward. She found the slight give of flesh between Em's thighs and traced it with her forefinger.

A breathless moan spilled from Em's lips.

Maria curled her fingers inward, and Em trembled against her. With those thin, black trousers Em wore, Maria felt…*everything*—more than she would've felt through leather, anyway.

Maria wondered…if she made Em wet enough, could it soak through these trousers? Would Maria feel it against her fingers?

Maria rubbed, and Em clasped a hand over her mouth to muffle her moans.

With a chuckle, Maria murmured, "I've found a weak spot in your armor, love."

"It's not *supposed*," Em gasped, "to protect me there."

Maria chuckled. "How about here?"

She nuzzled her face against Em's thigh—and then bit her, just beneath the last lace.

Em nearly collapsed. "You—*achk. Goddess…*"

She must've panicked at the loudness of her own voice—because Em suddenly clasped both hands over her mouth, leaving her sword to fall and nearly clack Maria on the top of the head.

Maria moved in time to avoid a concussion—and instead, rested her face against Em's thigh, as her own body shook with laughter.

Maria peered up at Em, watching her reactions with an amused smile.

"Captain," Em moaned. "This wasn't a good—*ah*."

Maria cut her off with another press of her fingers.

Still, she climbed to her feet and leaned toward her trembling surgeon. "It wasn't a good idea?" Maria assumed. "Why? Because Catherine might find us?"

Em nodded, eyes glazed with desire.

"I suppose you're right," Maria said, but she didn't move her hand—*yet*, "but can you imagine the look on her face? If she found me here? Fucking you?"

Em stiffened, and her eyes widened. "Captain!"

With a smug laugh, Maria removed her hand.

Em stumbled forward, and she made a sound that was delightfully similar to a whimper.

Maria caught her by the arms. "Are you *sure* we don't have time?"

Em swallowed hard.

Maria chuckled. She trailed her fingers—still warm from friction—over Em's soft, pink mouth, and she watched as the black in Em's eyes swallowed up the green.

Maria's hand drifted upward, and she traced the high curve of Em's cheekbone with her thumb. She cradled Em's face, and then, she dipped her head.

Em moaned the moment Maria's mouth met hers, and Maria thought that sound might actually kill her.

Em clung to one of the thongs of Maria's doublet, and Maria responded by tugging at the upper strap of Em's scabbard. Em's lips parted as she laughed, and Maria pushed her tongue inside.

When they parted to catch their breath, Em said, "I never should've trusted you to help with my armor."

Maria snorted. "No," she admitted, "but you'll let me every time, won't you?" She grasped Em's chin and leaned in close. "And you'll always love it."

Em tried to reply, but Maria clasped her hand over Em's mouth —as the distant murmur of a man's voice caught her attention.

Em must've noticed it, too, because her eyes widened.

Maria uncovered Em's mouth and silently mouthed the words: *"Where do we go?"*

Em motioned for Maria to follow. She fixed her scabbard as quietly as possible, as she led Maria back toward the mountain they'd just descended.

The layer of ash thinned, and, slowly but surely, the grey and black beneath their feet turned to green.

The murmur of voices followed them every step of the way, and Maria resisted the urge to move faster.

Rushing was clumsy.

Rushing made noise.

A thick grove of trees separated the mountain and the bubbling riverside, and Em and Maria slipped into the shadows of those trees now.

Em turned to Maria and gestured toward the rock face— patches of brown and grey barely visible through the trees—but before they could even start in that direction, a leaf crunched behind them.

Em swung around, her eyes wide.

Maria turned, too.

Yet, nothing but the stillness of trees lay behind them. It must've been an animal.

The nearby voices grew louder, and Maria knew there was no time to wait for the animal to reveal itself. Her gaze returned to Em.

"Go," she mouthed, but before Em could take off, Maria caught her by the elbow and added, *"Slowly."*

Someone was clearly on their trail.

The last thing they needed was to make that trail *audible*.

～

Maria didn't hate adrenaline.

Sometimes, she even enjoyed it. It was useful during a sword fight.

Useful, while running.

But walking?

Creeping slowly through a silent forest?

Not so useful, then.

With no small amount of effort, Em and Maria reached the end of the grove.

Only a few more trees stood between them and whatever hiding place Em had in mind—when the razor-sharp tip of a sword pressed into Maria's back.

Maria froze. "Em?"

After such a long silence, it came as no surprise that Em jumped at the sound of Maria's voice.

Em turned carefully to face Maria, and though she must've guessed already, her face still paled at the sight of the armed sailor who stood behind Maria.

The sailor extended his opposite hand, pointing a second weapon at Em, and Maria cursed inwardly as the end of his flint-lock pistol entered her line of sight.

"Found them!" he called out.

Em glanced toward Maria's swords—a silent question—but Maria gave a subtle shake of her head.

Not yet.

Two more sailors invaded the grove with their swords already drawn, flanking each side of Em.

When Maria saw the familiar face on Em's left—aged by a decade or so, since she'd last seen it—her eyes narrowed.

"Lieutenant Ingelby," Maria said, and when Em stiffened at the name, Maria's anger flared hotter.

She'd have to add whatever Ingleby had done to *Em* to the reasons she wanted him dead.

"It's Captain Ingelby now, pirate," Edward Ingelby sneered. He jabbed his sword at Em, nearly slicing into her shoulder. "I suppose I have our little witch to thank for that. Her and her dead friends."

Rage rippled through every muscle of Maria's body, and the only thing that kept her from doing something exceedingly foolish was the knowledge that the fucking coward hadn't drawn blood.

Yet.

Ingelby jabbed at Em again, but she didn't respond. She didn't even seem to register the pain. She kept her gaze straight ahead—eyes wide, skin flushed…

Oh, shit.

Signs of panic.

Ingelby stepped closer, and the words spilled from Maria's lips before she could stop them.

"Touch her, and you'll fucking die!"

Edward Ingelby stopped and raised a dark eyebrow at his former captain. With a malicious twist of his lips, he took yet another step toward Em.

Maria's hand strayed toward her sword, and she flexed her fingers in an effort to resist the temptation.

Ingelby pressed his blade against Em's throat, and Em's gaze darted toward him. She lifted her chin.

Good.

She'd noticed him that time.

Maria tried to meet her gaze—to calm Em in any way she could —but Em had *always* kept her gaze low when she was nervous.

Gods, Maria despised Ingelby's nasty, little sneer.

She always had.

"Admiral Rochester *did* mention you might have a weakness for the witch."

The mention of Catherine sent another rush of anger through Maria's veins. She stepped forward, aware of the sword that pressed into her back as she did.

"Oh, I'm sure she mentions plenty to *you*," Maria taunted, "or has she tired of using you in that way?"

Outrage flared in Ingelby's grey eyes, and Maria couldn't help but grin at the sight.

Her attention strayed back toward her surgeon, and she froze. Maria's smile faded, and her stomach dropped—because Em had folded in on herself, cringing away from the scarred sailor on her right.

Maria had missed something.

That scarred sailor crept toward Em, and Em jerked back, nearly falling onto Ingelby's sword.

Maria didn't recognize this sailor, but Em clearly did. "What the fuck are you doing to her?"

That kind of rage from Captain Maria Welles tended to elicit a reaction from most people, but this man barely acknowledged her.

Apparently, he only cared to torment Em. He leaned toward her and whispered in her ear. Em stiffened, her eyes flaring wider.

Ingelby was less selective about who *he* tormented. "Oh, they're old friends, I hear," he told Maria. "According to the stories *I've* heard, your little witch gave him his scars."

Em's chest heaved beneath the black cuirass, and her trembling fingers strayed toward her sword.

What had that asshole whispered to her?

"Nasty business," Ingelby added. "Torture."

And with that, the pieces of the puzzle clicked into place.

Maria glanced at the sailor's scars.

Scattered burns and cuts.

Nothing deliberate.

Nothing done with a blade.

A shattered lantern, perhaps?

Maria remembered a glass lantern on the table in the Regolis dungeons. They'd dragged her to a dimly lit room for interrogation, shackled her to the chair.

It had burned her eyes—after so long in the dark. Maria remembered it because it had burned her eyes.

Perhaps Em had knocked it over—or caused someone *else* to knock it over.

When the sailor reached toward Em, Maria noticed the scars on his wrist, too.

A partial circle.

Bite marks.

The sailor had touched Em, and she'd defended herself in the only way she could. She'd bitten him.

This time, when the scarred sailor whispered something to Em, Maria read his lips.

"Feral, little animal."

Em closed her fingers around the hilt of her sword, and Maria drew both of her own.

The *shing* of steel drew Ingelby's attention toward Maria, and he lunged at her.

Maria stepped forward and to the left, dodging the stab behind her and catching Ingelby's sword with one of her own.

She thrust her other sword at Ingelby, and he stumbled back.

With two more well-timed steps, Maria dodged his next blow and forced a collision between the two naval sailors.

Maria stepped back yet again, forcing the two naval sailors to approach her from the same side.

A sudden scream pierced the air.

The scarred sailor.

Ingelby shot a worried look in the shipman's direction, and Maria couldn't help but worry, too.

How well could Em fight through the panic? How much of Em's obvious trauma would her tormenter use against her?

Still, Maria took advantage of the distraction and slashed her sword at Ingelby.

He spun in time to avoid lethal injury, but her blade still caught his arm.

He yelled out, blood flowing.

The *thump* of a body hitting the ground caught Maria's attention. When she saw the scarred sailor still standing—covered in blood and snarling in rage—she quickly searched the ground for her surgeon.

Grass rustled nearby, as Em crawled toward her fallen sword. A trail of blood followed her, soaking her skin from the bottom of her ear to her shoulder.

Despite being disoriented, Em had injured the scarred sailor, but *he'd* cut her throat.

Maria panicked. She wanted to rush to Em's side, but Ingelby slashed his sword at her before she could.

Maria caught his blade between both of her own and shoved forward, throwing him off-balance.

She could only pray to any goddess who listened that Em had regained enough mental clarity to flee *from* her tormentor and not toward him.

At least Maria had the comfort of knowing one of the goddesses *liked* Em.

Ingelby slashed again, and Maria parried.

Why hadn't the other sailor fired his pistol yet?

Wet powder?

Or perhaps he'd already used his shot.

Maria blocked Ingelby's next attack, while she searched the trees for signs of the third sailor.

Nothing.

He was gone.

Goddamn it!

Blood stained the blue sleeve of Ingelby's waistcoat, and his movements slowed.

Maria parried with one sword and shoved the other into his stomach. When she ripped the sword free, he stumbled and fell back into the high grass.

Maria stalked toward him.

Thump.

Thump.

Thump.

Maria hesitated. She *knew* that sound. She didn't think she'd ever forget it—the sound that had sent her rushing to end the fight between Em and Buchan.

A boot against flesh.

When Em finally cried out, Maria raced toward the sound.

She didn't think Ingelby could run while bleeding out, anyway, but even if he did, he was the last thing on her mind.

Maria found Em behind one of the nearby trees, bleeding into the dirt, as that monster kicked her.

There were easier ways to incapacitate someone.

That's not what this was.

This was cruelty.

This was malice.

Em continued to reach for her sword, throughout the merciless beating. Her fingers closed around it.

Maria ran toward the scarred sailor, sword raised, but…apparently, Em hadn't needed her at all.

The sorceress rolled onto her back, hair and skin slick with blood, and shoved her sword upward.

Before Maria could slash her sword downward, the sailor froze. A choking sound escaped the man's scarred lips, and a spurt of blood shot outward.

Maria stepped back and lowered her sword.

She looked down to find that Em's sword had opened the man's abdomen and pierced his chest.

Blood and entrails spilled into the grass, and when Em let go of her sword, the sailor collapsed with Em's blade still buried in his chest.

Maria sheathed her own swords, and without thinking, she went to retrieve Em's sword.

Still too disoriented to understand what she was seeing, Em gasped and shuffled away from Maria.

Maria dropped the sword immediately and lifted both of her hands—hoping Em could see they were empty. "Em," she hissed. "Em, it's me. It's only me."

Em didn't hear her.

She scrambled backward.

Maria dropped to the ground and crawled on her hands and knees. The limbs and roots scraped her palms, and Maria wondered what *Em's* hands must've looked like by now. "It's me, love. Maria."

Normally, Maria wouldn't have called herself by name—so close to her enemies, like this—but when recognition flickered in Em's eyes, she knew she'd done the right thing. "I won't hurt you, Em. I swear."

Em stopped, her breasts still heaving beneath the black, dragon-scale cuirass. "Captain?" she breathed.

"Yes." Maria crawled closer, and Em let her.

Em's trembling elbows finally gave out, and cloaked in the shadows of the grove, Em collapsed.

When Maria reached the injured dragon sorceress, she leaned over her. She cupped Em's pale face in her hands and breathed, "Oh, my sweet surgeon."

For once, Maria didn't worry about the relief that betrayed itself in her voice. No one would hear her, anyway, and after the fear she'd just felt for Em, she didn't have enough worry left for anything else.

Maria moved her hand downward, intending to check the wound that ran down the side of Em's throat, but Em caught her hand before she could.

Em blinked up at Maria, her eyes somehow greener than the grass around her. She gave Maria's hand an affectionate squeeze. "I'm sorry."

Maria narrowed her eyes at the wounded surgeon. "*You* have nothing to apologize for."

"I drew my sword," Em said. Her face grew paler with each word. "I tried to wait, but he—he was—"

"I know," Maria interrupted. "I'd already drawn my swords, anyway—before you drew yours."

Maria chose *not* to mention that she'd drawn her swords because she'd known Em was losing the battle with her mind.

That wasn't relevant.

"Oh," Em said tiredly.

Maria cast another glance at the shallow wound on Em's throat. It wasn't gushing. So, why was Em losing color so quickly? "What did he do to you?"

"He didn't cut the artery, if that's what you're worried about," Em said. Yet, her voice grew more strained with each passing moment. "I'm fine."

Maria was worried about *far* more than Em's artery, but she had no intention of admitting it.

Em tried to sit up, but when the ground scraped against her bruised back, she gasped and fell back.

"Em?"

How many times had that bastard kicked her?

Em had proven on her first day aboard the *Wicked Fate* that she could survive a beating, but that didn't mean Maria worried about her any less now.

By the time Em spoke again, she'd apparently found a way to mask the strain in her voice.

"I killed him, didn't I?" Em asked. "He's dead?"

Even though Maria had already seen the state of the sailor's corpse, she glanced at it again.

It didn't get much more *dead* than that.

"Very much so."

Em relaxed against the blood-slick grass.

Had there ever been a more beautiful sight than Emilia Drakon, lying in the grass? With her green eyes so much brighter than the grass around her?

Maria would prefer she weren't injured, of course, but that didn't mean she couldn't see Em's beauty now.

"I bit him," Em admitted. "That's why he hated me." She closed her eyes and sighed, "I vaguely remember a fire, but that part wasn't my fault." Her brows furrowed. "I don't think it was, anyway."

Maria didn't need to ask *why* Em had such a vague recollection of the event. She already knew.

They'd drugged her. The little sips of water Em had accepted to keep herself alive had also kept her weak and disoriented.

"I can't imagine why he didn't like being bitten," Maria muttered. "*You* seem to like it well enough."

Em opened her eyes. "Very funny, Captain."

Maria grinned. "You gave him what he deserved," she said, "and it was far worse than a bite or burn."

A hesitant smile tugged at the corners of Em's lips. "What about the other two?"

"Ingelby's wounded," Maria said, noting the way Em's shoulders tensed at his name, "and the one with the flintlock ran—probably for reinforcements." Em didn't tense for that one. "Did you recognize him?"

Em shook her head. "He's the only one who wasn't here, when —" She swallowed. "When it happened."

"I still intend to kill him," Maria informed her.

Em's eyebrows lifted. "I have a dire question, Captain," she said, suddenly, "about Ingelby."

Mirroring her seriousness, Maria nodded.

"What could Zain have *possibly* seen in him?"

Maria gave a surprised snort—and then burst into a fit of laughter that was nearly impossible to stifle.

Well…

Em had conquered her panic, after all.

"I have *no* idea," Maria admitted. She brushed Em's shortened, black hair away from her face, comforted by the familiar smile that curved at Em's lips. "Let me finish off Ingelby. I want you to go to that hiding place of yours and wait for me there."

Em shook her head. "I'm not leaving you."

"Yes, you are," Maria stated. "It won't take long."

"I *won't*," Em insisted, "leave you."

"You need to tend to your wounds, Em," Maria said. "Find the crevice, and heal yourself—if…that's possible." She hoped it was. "I'll find you afterward."

Worry twisted at Em's soft face. "I can't leave you."

Maria rolled her eyes.

Em had to have known she needed time to heal. Yet, she argued, anyway.

Maria leaned closer. "It's an order, surgeon."

Now, it was Em who scowled. "Yes, *Captain*."

Oh, Maria did love that tone.

If nothing else, it told her that Em was still herself—in spite of the people who'd tried to break her.

Maria climbed to her feet, while Em raised herself into a sitting position, hissing in pain with each movement.

Maria offered her hand, and with a reluctant look, Em took it. She twisted and writhed, as she climbed to her feet.

Em was in no shape to fight.

Maria could only hope she realized that—and kept herself safe.

EMILIA CLUTCHED HER SIDE, AS IF THAT MIGHT SLOW THE INTERNAL bleeding, and her steps grew more unsteady.

She didn't like this plan.

Even if it *was* the only one that made sense, Emilia didn't like it.

What if she lost consciousness after healing herself?

What if Catherine found Maria, while Emilia was unconscious?

Emilia found the gap in the mountain and slipped between it. The cold rock pressed against her back, and she closed her eyes. She inhaled through her nose, exhaled through her mouth—pushing the memories of torture from her mind.

Emilia's entire body ached and throbbed from the beating, but she'd endured far more pain than this.

After all, that was what her mother had trained her to do.

Endure.

The cool rock behind Emilia soothed the pain in her back, but the dizziness only worsened.

In the dark shadows of the small cave, Emilia held her hand in front of her and channeled all the energy she had into a healing spell. A subtle glow enveloped her fingers—shimmering and gentle, like starlight.

Already, she felt the strength seeping out of her.

Emilia pressed her fingers to the sword wound that ran from her jaw to her throat—mostly because she knew this particular wound had worried Maria.

Warm, soothing magic seeped into the wound, mending the blood-soaked skin beneath her fingers.

Her eyelids grew heavy.

The magic flickered out, and Emilia sagged against the rock

wall. Pain radiated through her body, pulsing outward from her left side and lower back.

Emilia summoned her magic once more and flattened her hand against her side. Warmth enveloped her insides, sealing the ruptured organ and repairing the damage.

The pain receded, but exhaustion rose to take its place. The cost of healing her own injuries had always felt so much steeper than the cost of healing someone else's.

Emilia slipped down the wall, her legs sliding out in front of her. Her rear collided with the rock floor.

Her head lolled to the side, and her mind drifted.

Emilia might've lost consciousness entirely, if it hadn't been for the sudden *crunch* of a limb beneath someone's boot.

She straightened, peering through the crevice.

The naval sailors wore the same style of leather boot Maria wore, but theirs were uncreased and shined—whereas Maria's boots were old and faded.

Grass rustled near the crevice, but Emilia couldn't get a good look at the boot—or the person who wore it.

"Em?"

At the sound of Maria's familiar lilt, Emilia relaxed against the wall behind her. "In here," she called.

Maria followed the sound of her voice and slipped through the crevice with more ease than Emilia had.

Emilia closed her eyes.

The darkness had nearly dragged her under again—when a drop of something alarmingly *warm* splattered against Emilia's ankle.

Her eyes flew open.

Captain Maria Welles stood between Emilia's legs with a damn *head* dangling from her hand. "You don't look so well."

Neither does Ingelby, Emilia thought.

"Have you healed your injuries?" Maria asked.

Another drop of Ingelby's blood splashed against Emilia's leg, and she pleaded with her exhausted muscles to move. "I don't remember inviting *him*."

Maria followed her gaze to the disembodied head. "Oh," she said, as if she'd forgotten she was holding it. She dropped the head between Emilia's ankles.

Then, Maria crossed her arms and grinned with the smugness of a cat who'd just presented her human with a dead rat.

Emilia wouldn't call Ingelby a rat, though.

That would be insulting to rats.

"Shall we add a bow, and give it to Zain?" Emilia asked.

Maria's smile faded. "Zain will never hear of this."

Emilia lifted her eyebrows in amusement. "You have that much confidence in my ability to lie?"

"I have no confidence in your ability to lie, my love," Maria informed her. "My confidence is in his ability to not *ask*."

Emilia rolled her eyes at that.

Maria bent and retrieved the head. She lifted it by the hair— long, brown hair that was tied off with a gold ribbon. She placed it in the corner of their small cave and then crouched between Emilia's legs.

Emilia eyed the head, hoping they wouldn't stay long enough for it to attract flies.

"You look awful," Maria told her.

Emilia scowled at her. "Thank you, Captain."

Maria didn't bother to apologize. She reached out and traced the line of blood on Emilia's throat, clearly looking for the wound. She found nothing but blood.

"What about the internal injuries?" Maria asked.

"I don't remember admitting to having those," Emilia complained. When Maria narrowed her dark brown eyes, Emilia sighed, "I healed them, too, but considering your history with my armor, I hope you won't ask me to remove it so you can see."

Maria's full, sensuous mouth curved at the corners. "I was being thorough."

Emilia gave her a skeptical look. "And just so you know, I look awful *because* I healed my injuries."

Maria's smile faded. "I don't understand."

"Magic comes at a cost," Emilia said. "I paid it."

Maria frowned, likely remembering the times she'd seen Emilia use magic in the past, but Emilia hadn't healed her own injuries any of those times.

After the fight with Buchan, she had, but even then, she'd had more time—and the help of a tincture.

"Can you still fight?" Maria asked.

Emilia nodded. "I'm not entirely drained. Yet."

The look Maria gave her suggested she hadn't understood that part, either. "And are you all right?"

Emilia's brows furrowed. "I just told you I—"

"Not physically," Maria interrupted. Her dark gaze darted toward Ingelby's head, before returning to Emilia. "The ones who hurt you—*these* ones, at least—are dead. Did it help?"

Emilia's eyes widened, and she, too, glanced toward the head in the corner.

Maria had killed him for *her*?

Ingelby had betrayed Maria during the mutiny. Wasn't *that* why she'd killed him?

"We'll kill the other one, too," Maria said, "when he returns." She tilted her head, and one of her beaded braids brushed against her doublet. "Did it help?"

Emilia nodded, her throat too tight to speak.

"Good," Maria said simply. She climbed to her feet. "Now, tell me. How do we get to shore from here?"

"If we went back the way we came, past the tents—past...where I once lived," Emilia corrected herself, "we could reach the shore that way."

"But there are other ways," Maria assumed.

"A few," Emilia said. She hooked a thumb over her shoulder. "There's a small gap on the left side of the grove. It leads to shore, but if something went wrong, none of the dragons could reach us." She winced. "Not that they could reach us here, either..."

Maria crossed her arms, her black, leather doublet stretching tight. "And the right side of the grove?"

"If we stay close to the mountain, we'll come out by the river,"

Emilia explained, "but if we go the opposite direction, we'll reach the shore—close to where you anchored the *Wicked Fate*."

Maria nodded. "So, that's the way we're going," she realized. "Do you need more time to recover?"

Emilia tested her muscles, bending her legs. She pressed her hands against the rock wall behind her and tried to stand—only to nearly collapse.

Emilia sighed. "A few more minutes might help."

Maria gave another nod. "Take your time, love."

Emilia blinked at her usually impatient captain. "Since when are you willing to wait for *anything*?"

A smirk twitched at one corner of Maria's lips. "I think you underestimate how long I waited for you."

Emilia frowned. "Waited for me to…do what?"

Maria's smile only widened. "You'll figure it out, eventually."

Emilia doubted that.

Maria didn't wait for things. She grumbled and pestered everyone—until they moved at *her* speed.

The grass outside rustled, and Maria's infuriating smile faded. Her gaze flicked toward the crevice.

Emilia made a second attempt at standing. Ready or not, she needed to prepare herself for a fight.

Maria's tattooed fingers closed around the hilt of her sword. "It's him," she hissed, and then, with no further warning, Maria slipped through the crevice.

Emilia rolled her eyes.

So much for patience!

Emilia forced her weakened legs to follow. Her exhausted muscles protested each step, but she refused to let them rest.

Damn pirate!

Arrogant, impatient fool.

A flash of blue between the trees caught Emilia's attention, and she quickened her steps.

I can barely walk!

How am I supposed to rescue you like this?

Apparently, Emilia's anger strengthened her—because her legs wobbled less with each silent insult.

Emilia was beginning to understand why the crew had elected Zain as quartermaster.

He was cautious to a fault—unlike their bloodthirsty captain, who plunged into possible traps for a *chance* of stabbing an enemy!

Emilia reached Maria just in time to see the horror and desperation flash across the blonde sailor's face as Maria plunged her sword into his chest.

At the sound of Emilia's footsteps, Maria ripped her sword free and spun toward Emilia, lifting the blood-soaked blade into the air.

Emilia didn't even flinch.

Maria, on the other hand, stumbled back a step. "What the fuck, Em?" She lowered her sword, her brown eyes wide. "I almost stabbed you!"

"I noticed," Emilia assured her.

Maria spread out her arms, blood dripping from her sword. "Why didn't you stay in the cave? I would've brought the head back to you."

Emilia squinted at that. "I don't care about the head." She worried that might've sounded ungrateful and quickly added, "I mean, Rat-Slayer would be proud, of course, but—"

"Rat-Slayer?" Maria interrupted. "What does the *cat* have to do with it?"

"*But*," Emilia continued, "did you even stop to think this might be a trap?"

"Stop? No," Maria said. "Think? Yes."

Emilia stepped closer. "Well, next time—if we live to *see* a next time—try stopping and looking around you."

Maria stepped forward, too. "I *did* look around."

Barely an inch of grass separated them, their bodies close enough that Emilia could feel blood dripping from Maria's blade onto her left shoe.

"Look again," Emilia said.

Maria's brows furrowed, and a hint of worry flickered in her self-assured, dark brown eyes. She lifted her gaze, scanning the trees behind Emilia.

"Fuck."

Emilia nodded. "Behind you, as well."

Maria turned to look at the six naval sailors who'd emerged from the trees behind her, and Emilia cast a glance over her shoulder at the six behind *her*.

"They must've been hiding," Maria mumbled.

"You think?" Emilia said sarcastically.

Maria spun toward her, eyes dark and dangerous. "This is not the time for your snark."

"Isn't it?" Emilia challenged. She took one last step forward, and heat crackled between them. "I'd prefer you *knew* how angry I was before we both died!"

Maria grasped Emilia's chin between three fingers, and Emilia's racing heart stuttered to a stop.

Maria leaned in, and her warm, unyielding fingers lifted Emilia's face, forcing Emilia to meet her gaze.

Sunlight danced between the canopy of leaves above them, casting skitters of light and shadow over Maria's gorgeous, brown skin.

Her dark eyes scanned Emilia's face. "Hide it."

Emilia blinked at the strange remark. "What?"

"I can see the exhaustion in your face," Maria said quietly. "Don't let *them* see it."

Easier said than done, Captain.

Maria released her hold on Emilia's face and let her hand drift downward. Her thumb stroked the blood-stained skin of Emilia's neck, and Emilia tried not to shudder at her touch. "You should've cleaned this."

With an incredulous look, Emilia said, "With *what*, exactly?"

The corners of Maria's rosy-brown lips quirked upward. "Stay angry, love. It helps."

"Shouldn't be a problem," Emilia said.

Maria laughed. She turned to face the six sailors behind her. "Draw your sword."

Emilia unsheathed her sword and followed Maria's lead, turning to face the opposite direction.

Six shipmen watched her, but none of them moved.

They seemed to be waiting for something.

Or someone.

Maria took a deliberate step backward, pressing her back against Emilia's.

Emilia straightened at the unexpected contact.

"They'll try to separate us," Maria whispered over her shoulder. "*Don't* let them."

With an ease that made no sense in their current predicament, Emilia said, "Yes, Captain."

Leaves crunched somewhere to the right of Emilia, and a familiar, tall form emerged from the trees.

Out of the corner of her eye, Emilia could see her yellow-blonde braid and her long, blue waistcoat.

The naval sailors *had* been waiting for something, of course.

They'd been waiting for her.

CHAPTER 4

Sword and Flame

"So nice of you to *finally* come out of hiding," Catherine said. Each word lilted delicately, her voice, as always, so deceptively light. "We've been searching the island for hours."

Maria stiffened at the sound of Catherine's voice, and with Maria's back against her own, Emilia *felt* the vibration of hatred that ricocheted through Maria's body.

Catherine stopped to consider the corpse Maria had left. "Another hero," she sighed, "slain by pirates."

Emilia cast a look of disbelief in her direction. She didn't know how long the naval sailors had hidden, exactly, but she was fairly certain they'd had time to save that guy.

Maria shifted her sword to her left hand so that she could reach behind her and grasp Emilia's free hand.

Emilia glanced down at their joined hands, her eyes wide.

Maria had *never* held Emilia's hand.

On the mountain, perhaps, after her near-fall—but even then, it'd been Emilia, who'd grabbed *Maria's* hand.

This, paired with the knowledge that Maria had sacrificed one of her dual-sword-wielding hands to do it, told Emilia there must've been a reason.

"Listen to me," Maria said in an urgent whisper. "The Royal Navy is trained to respond to silent commands."

At the reminder of the other sailors, Emilia quickly tore her gaze from Maria's hand and redirected it toward the armed shipmen who surrounded them.

"Whatever she says, whatever she does," Maria continued, "do *not* let her distract you." Her leather-clad shoulder brushed against Emilia's, and her grip tightened. "Keep your attention on *their* blades."

Grass shifted near Emilia's right ankle as Catherine neared them, and it took every ounce of Emilia's self-control to not look at her.

Maria's shoulder brushed against Emilia's again—as Maria glanced back at her. "I need to know you heard me," she hissed, and then, before Emilia could wonder what she meant by that, she said, "Say it."

Anxiously, Emilia whispered, "Yes, Captain."

Maria's muscles slackened behind Emilia, and a quick sigh of relief escaped Maria's lips.

"Emilia?" Catherine began.

Emilia grimaced. It might've been her real name, but she only liked to hear it from Maria these days.

"This madness is typical of her," Catherine said—from an alarmingly close distance, "but you? You're smart. Reasonable. Emilia, I know *you* know better."

It amazed Emilia how much perspective could change things. Once, that might've sounded like a compliment. Now, it sounded like condescension.

Manipulation.

Catherine had come to the girl who'd never heard a kind word in her life and had showered her with them.

Despite her proximity, the steady *thump* of Catherine's boots continued.

Emilia tried not to question Maria's advice, but…didn't she need to know where Catherine's sword was, as well?

Catherine's voice came from somewhere behind Emilia now. In

front of Maria, possibly? "There's two of you, against who-knows-how-many of us."

Emilia eyed the six sailors in front of her with a frown. "There are thirteen of you," she informed Catherine. "Have you forgotten how to count?"

Catherine's footsteps came to an abrupt stop—near Emilia's left ear, this time.

She was circling them.

After a moment of shock, Catherine resumed her steps. She entered Emilia's line of sight, before she stopped a second time.

Catherine stood just outside the reach of Emilia's sword, her own sword drawn and ready to use.

She wore her dazzling, golden hair in a tight braid that slid over the shoulder of her blue waistcoat like a snake. Her small, pink lips thinned into a tight line.

"I was *trying* to imply," Catherine said, "that I might have more men hiding in the tree-cover."

"Well, you should've said that, then," Emilia said.

Catherine's blue eyes narrowed, but the tremble of Maria's shoulders, behind Emilia, suggested that *she*, unlike Catherine, had found Emilia's remark funny.

Catherine hid the flex of her muscles well.

Emilia might not have noticed it at all, if the gold-laced buttons of Catherine's coat sleeve hadn't twitched, refracting a beam of sunlight.

A key difference, Emilia realized, in Admiral Rochester and whatever version of Catherine she'd once thought she loved…was that Admiral Rochester didn't like for people to interrupt her speeches.

Emilia made a mental note to interrupt *more*.

"My point was," Catherine said, tone sharp, "the two of you don't stand a chance, and you know it."

Remembering Maria's warning, Emilia returned her attention to the armed sailors who surrounded them.

"You're letting this pirate infect you with her madness," Catherine said—with such fervor that Emilia almost wondered if she believed it. "How many people have died because they followed her into a war they couldn't win? Don't be the next."

Emilia lifted her eyebrows. "Right, because my prospects look so much better with *you*," she said sarcastically, "who would execute me for existing."

Catherine lowered her voice—likely so that her own naval sailors wouldn't hear. "We can negotiate," she offered. "You've committed some terrible crimes, Emilia. There isn't much hope for you, but perhaps we could spare your dragons—if you cooperated."

"They'd never spare the dragons," Maria called over her shoulder. "She's only here for the dragons."

Catherine shot a murderous look at the back of Maria's head, and Emilia frowned suspiciously.

"I'm here," Catherine corrected, "because *you* fired the pistol, Maria. You wanted my fleet to find you."

Maria ignored Catherine's argument, speaking only to Emilia. "It was always about the dragons," she tried to explain. "She let one of the naval ships sink—so that she could board the *Wicked Fate*."

'I meant for this one to sink,' Catherine had said.

"She put on a show for us, like she always does," Maria said, her voice thick with disgust, "but it was always about finding you— about finding your dragons."

But why would Catherine expect to find Emilia with Maria?

Unless…Jonas had sent word, somehow?

She searched Catherine's face for any confirmation, but Catherine showed no emotion whatsoever—a bit of annoyance, perhaps, but nothing more than that.

If the Royal Navy had been after the dragons all along, then… the *Wicked Fate* had led them right to them.

A fresh wave of betrayal washed over Emilia.

"If you knew this," Emilia said, struggling to keep the pain from her voice, "why didn't you tell me?"

A hint of satisfaction flashed in Catherine's eyes.

Just because I'm less than happy with my captain, at the moment, doesn't mean I'm coming to your side.

Emilia couldn't see Maria's reaction, but she felt the stiffness of Maria's muscles behind her.

"We'll talk about this later," Maria whispered.

Catherine scoffed at that. "Later? Your madness knows no bounds if you think you'll have a *later.*"

Emilia followed Maria's lead in ignoring Catherine. "Captain, I need to know," she whispered. "If you knew my dragons were in danger, why didn't you tell me?"

Maria's shoulders tightened, and she released a shaky sigh. "I knew something didn't add up, but I didn't know what. I didn't put it together until you told me about the ballista."

Catherine had done so well with concealing her emotions until that point, but the mention of her dragon-killing weapon caused her eyes to widen.

She'd never learned how a dragon-bond worked.

She hadn't expected Emilia to know about that.

Maria squeezed Emilia's hand hard enough to get her attention. "Please. We'll talk later. This isn't the time to question me."

Emilia knew Maria was right, but she simply couldn't take risks when it came to her dragons.

"Isn't it, though?" Catherine objected. Despite their whispers, she'd caught every word. "You shouldn't go to your death, following a pirate you can't trust."

"I know exactly who I can't trust," Emilia snarled, "thank you very much."

Catherine blew out a frustrated sigh. "Forgive me for thinking you'd eventually see reason," she said. "It seems you've let her corrupt you entirely."

Emilia tightened her grip on her sword.

Catherine cast a quick glance behind her—at the naval sailors, who'd begun to fidget nervously.

It seemed Emilia wasn't the only one questioning someone today.

Interesting.

Catherine took a step toward Emilia—and then quickly stepped back, as she realized how close she'd come to stepping into Emilia's reach.

What if Emilia somehow signaled Maria to step *with* her?

No, that wouldn't work.

The shipmen could fire a pistol far quicker than Emilia could kill Catherine.

Catherine lowered her voice once more—to prevent her loyal shipmen from hearing. "The Emilia I knew wouldn't have aligned herself with murderous pirates," she said. "The Emilia I knew was kind."

A visceral combination of hatred and guilt vaulted through Emilia, rattling her to the core.

Kind enough to be manipulated.

Kind enough to cause the massacre of her people.

Maria squeezed Emilia's hand hard enough to hurt, and that one, unexpected action anchored Emilia and jerked her mind back to the present.

"The Emilia you knew," Emilia snarled, "is dead."

Catherine recoiled, as if she hadn't expected such a vicious response.

What response *had* she expected?

You know what? You're right. Let's kiss and make up, and you can try to execute me again. Just like old times?

"When your mother wanted to kill me, simply for *being* an Illopian who washed up on your shore," Catherine continued in a quiet tone, "you said no. You said, 'That's murder, Mother. Murder is wrong.'"

Yes, well, Emilia had regretted that choice every day since Catherine's betrayal.

"A human response from a witch!" Catherine said, suddenly raising her voice. "Imagine my surprise!"

Startled by the sudden increase in volume, Emilia jerked back.

Apparently, Catherine wanted the naval sailors to hear that part?

When a wave of laughter rippled through the men who surrounded them, Emilia understood why.

Catherine had *never* seen Emilia as anything other than a witch, had she? Emilia had been foolish to think any human would.

Then again…Maria saw her as more, didn't she?

Judith, too.

"Of course, that didn't last long, did it?" Catherine's smile cut as sharply as her words. "Do you even *know* how many people you killed in Regolis?"

Emilia's throat constricted.

She'd tried so hard not to think about it.

Catherine stepped forward. "Do you know how many screams I listened to," she murmured, "while I lay there, bleeding out around my own sword?"

Emilia's stomach turned with guilt.

Catherine drove the knife deeper with every word. "How many people did you burn," she sneered, "witch?"

Maria had remained stoic and unwavering throughout all of Catherine's manipulative tactics, but for whatever reason, *this* evoked a reaction.

"She became what you made her," Maria snapped. She turned, glaring at Catherine. "Just as I became what you made me."

Catherine tilted her head, braid sliding along the front of her coat.

Her eyebrows lifted. Despite all her words about Maria's 'madness,' she clearly hadn't expected Maria to be the one to crack.

Changing her target in the blink of an eye, Catherine finished the circle. "Oh, I'm to blame now?" She stopped in front of Maria, and her usually delicate voice turned sharp. "I'm to blame for *all* the evil in Aletharia. Piracy. Witchcraft. The one law-abiding person you've ever known is to blame?"

The shift in Catherine's focus allowed Emilia to regain her composure—and find clarity, along with it.

Now, when Maria stiffened behind her, Emilia understood it was *her* turn to anchor Maria.

Emilia cast a quick glance over her shoulder, as Maria's fingers began to unfurl.

Maria stepped toward Catherine and *tried* to let go of Emilia's hand. "*You*—"

Emilia didn't let her. She squeezed her own fingers around Maria's hand and jerked her back. Maria's backside collided with Emilia's, and the blade of her sword clanged against the blade of Emilia's.

Not the safest move—but it worked.

Catherine looked down at their joined hands. "What was that?"

The press of Maria's fingers returned, and her muscles relaxed, as she released a slow breath.

Catherine stepped to the side, but her gaze never left their clasped hands. "What *is* this?" Her voice rose in pitch, and her light blue eyes flashed with something akin to—

Wait…

Was that *jealousy?*

Catherine was jealous? Now, of all times?

"What kind of villainous pirate holds someone's hand?"

The surrounding sailors shifted on their feet, likely unsettled by the, uhh, *intensity* of Catherine's reaction.

"It's a hindrance in a sword fight!" she exclaimed.

With her thumb, Maria stroked the side of Emilia's forefinger, and though Emilia would've liked to have thought it was some rare show of affection, she knew Maria well enough to know that Maria was enjoying Catherine's reaction and wanted to exacerbate it.

It worked, too.

Catherine stepped toward them. "You were about to say something!" She pointed her blade at Maria. "Tell me what it was!"

Maria eyed the sword with a dangerous smile. "Come closer," she said, "and I'll fucking show you."

Catherine took a quick step backward. She dropped her sword to her side—but her grip remained tight, her posture rigid. She glanced at the watching sailors.

Once or twice, Maria had mentioned to Emilia the prejudice women faced in the Royal Navy. How fragile *was* their trust in Catherine?

The next time she spoke, she'd regained control of her voice. "So, that's it, then," Catherine said. "You want to fight—with no chance of survival. At least, if you surrendered, you could try to orchestrate one of those daring escapes you both seem so fond of."

Her mocking tone wasn't lost on either of them.

"You mean, like the escape you made," Maria said, "from my ship?"

Catherine chuckled.

Emilia didn't think that was a good sign.

"Oh, I think that was more of an exit, don't you?" Catherine said. A shrewd smile twisted at her lips. "I never did thank you, by the way—for letting me go."

Once again, Maria's shoulders tightened.

Definitely *not* a good sign.

Emilia's stomach dipped with dread. "Captain," she whispered. "What does she mean by that?"

"Not," Maria hissed, "now."

Two words.

'*She's lying,*' would've also been two words, and Maria had chosen not to use those.

'*She's insane?*' Also, two words.

Catherine watched Emilia's reaction with a self-satisfied smile. "You didn't tell her," she scolded Maria, "that you were the one who taught me?"

Emilia's dread turned to frustration. "Taught her what?" she hissed at Maria. "What is she saying?"

"Not *fucking* now!" Maria snapped.

Emilia rolled her eyes, even though Maria wouldn't see it. She felt ridiculous, still holding Maria's hand, while they argued, but she kept hold of it, anyway.

Like a predator, Catherine pounced at the first sign of weakness. "Wow, Maria," she taunted. "You don't tell your little dragon-whore anything, do you?"

All of the naval sailors laughed at that remark.

Emilia didn't laugh.

She flinched.

Partly because she'd never heard Catherine use that word before. It seemed a bit undignified for her.

Mostly, though?

Because the culmination of dishonesty from her current lover and prejudice from her former lover was starting to eat away at Emilia's self-worth.

Maria surprised her with an instant reaction.

"Em is my surgeon." She growled the words through her teeth. "You can refer to her by name or by her *correct* job title. Insult her, demean her, and I *will* gut you."

As foolish as the threat might've been, it actually lifted some of the weight from Emilia's chest.

Maria might've lied to her, but she cared enough to take offense on Emilia's behalf. She cared enough to make it clear that she didn't agree with their awful ideas.

That meant something.

To Emilia, it…*meant* something.

Catherine laughed at Maria's threat. "You'd die."

"I can't think of a better way *to* die," Maria assured her, "than with your blood on my hands."

Okay, things were getting out of hand now.

"Captain," Emilia said softly, "we're not dying. We're sticking together, remember?"

Maria glanced over her shoulder, surprise lightening her dark brown eyes. "Y-yes." With a pained look, she added, "Your trust isn't — It isn't misplaced."

"Yes, well," Emilia said with a scowl, "you're going to explain to me *why* later."

The soft chuckle Maria offered in response made Emilia's stomach flutter. "Of course."

"No," Catherine said. Her smile vanished, and frustration sparked in her light blue eyes.

Emilia didn't know if Catherine had heard them—or if she was just upset they were still speaking at all.

"You can't trust her," Catherine said.

Emilia lifted her eyebrows. "As opposed to *you?*"

Catherine shook her head, gripping her sword. "She will lead you to your death, Emilia."

"Or we'll lead you to yours," Emilia countered.

Catherine's jaw tightened. She took one step back and flicked her sword. "You can't say I didn't try."

She took a second step backward, and the shipmen charged.

Whatever the silent command had been—Catherine had just given it.

Emilia blocked the first sword that slashed at her, and the reverberation of the naval sailor's sword against her own ricocheted through her bones.

Emilia pulled back, then *down*, then thrust upward.

The weight that tugged at her sword, as she pulled it back, suggested she'd injured the sailor, and the blood glistening on the edge of her blade confirmed it.

Emilia didn't have time to wonder if she'd killed him, though, because the next attack came from her left.

Catherine wasn't wrong about their joined hands hindering them. It limited Emilia's ability to pivot or turn, but *Maria* hadn't been wrong about the naval sailors.

They were determined to separate the two of them.

As Emilia cut down her second attacker, she couldn't help but think, after her time fighting and sparring with Maria, the naval sailors seemed…clumsy.

They lacked Maria's precision and her ability to build momentum, rather than lose it. They were predictable, too—using the same set of moves Catherine had taught Emilia the first day.

Being outnumbered was never a good thing. A sharp blade in the hands of a person who'd never seen one before could still kill someone.

Usually by accident.

But after fighting Maria—and fighting Catherine, before *her*—this felt almost too easy.

When a blade came rushing toward Emilia from the right, she turned to block it—and caught sight of Catherine.

Catherine walked…not toward them, but away.

With her level of skill *and* the numbers on her side, Catherine could've won this fight within moments. So, why was she putting distance between them, instead?

That brief distraction came with a steep cost.

Pain and pressure exploded through Emilia's left arm and knocked her off-balance. Her hand slipped free from Maria's.

Warm blood slid down her forearm, splitting into two streams around her thumb.

The wound throbbed.

The bone ached.

And Emilia had no idea how deep the blade had gone.

She forced herself not to look.

Emilia was right-handed. She could fight without her left arm— as long as she didn't let the pain blind her.

Fortunately, her mother had given her more than enough experience with that.

Emilia noticed a sailor running toward Maria with the intent of attacking her from behind, and Emilia stepped into his path.

His weight and momentum threw Emilia backward.

Tree roots and acorns dug into her back, and the force of the collision shoved the air from her lungs.

Emilia had managed to impale him on the way down, though.

Maria stepped behind the dead shipman and grabbed him by the shoulder. Casting quick glances around them, she muttered, "Hold tight."

She jerked the corpse back roughly—but had to release him in order to block another attack.

The dead weight slammed back into Emilia, and more blood spilled onto her chest and stomach.

Emilia pushed with her injured arm, bottling up the scream that tried to escape, and Maria assisted with a rough kick to the side of the dead sailor's body.

The weight fell away, and Emilia gasped for breath.

Maria tossed her sword and caught it with the right hand, before extending the left hand to Emilia.

Emilia took her hand, ignoring the pain that exploded through her left forearm as she did.

Maria jerked Emilia to her feet, only looking her way when a spurt of blood splashed against Maria's skin, as well. She looked down, her eyes wide. "That's not his, is it?"

"I can still fight," Emilia said. Her voice sounded weak, even to her own ears. "It's only the left arm."

Maria turned Emilia's wrist, and she sucked in a sharp breath the moment she saw the wound—and the flash of exposed bone within. "Fuck."

"I'm fine," Emilia assured her. "I can still fight."

Maria had never shied away from the sight of gore.

If anything, she reveled in it.

But now, her dark skin grew just a shade paler.

The next two shipmen came at them from opposite sides, and Maria had no choice but to release Emilia's injured arm so they could fight.

Emilia chose to counteract her pain with optimism. Counting the corpse at their feet, they'd killed at least four already and injured several others.

That left eight—possibly injured—shipmen.

They could handle four each.

Maybe.

"She's unguarded," Maria said, suddenly.

Emilia cast an alarmed glance over her shoulder—her unease only rising, when she realized Maria was looking at Catherine, *not* their attackers.

"You said to watch them," Emilia reminded Maria, "not her." Her pulse raced. "Don't you remember?"

Maria didn't even seem to hear her, and Emilia was almost positive that if she could see Maria's dark brown eyes right now, she'd find a familiar flash of obsession within them. "I have a clear path to her."

Emilia's voice rose with desperation. "Captain—"

"I'm taking it," Maria said.

"Captain!" Emilia screamed. "*Again?*"

If Maria even heard her, she didn't react. She raced toward Catherine, sword in hand, and left Emilia standing in the middle of eight fucking shipmen.

You, Emilia thought bitterly. *You were the one who said not to let her separate us. You bloodthirsty imbecile!*

The eight shipmen spread out, forming a circle around Emilia, and the four in her line of sight smiled.

Emilia let out a nervous laugh.

Oh, dear.

ELEVEN YEARS.

Maria had waited for this moment—*craved* this moment—for eleven years.

She'd encountered Catherine a few times, in her pursuit of naval vessels. Maria had lost one battle, won another.

Yet, she'd never had a clear path to Catherine, like the one she had now.

Catherine Rochester—as First Mate, Captain, Commodore, and now Admiral—had always used the people around her as a shield.

Even when she'd boarded the *Wicked Fate* alone, she'd used Em as her shield.

But *now?*

Now, she had no one to protect her, and vengeance was so close Maria could *taste* it.

And like any hungry creature, the taste made her rabid.

Catherine watched her approach with a cruel smile.

Out of the two of them, Catherine had always been the more aggressive fighter, but today, it was Maria who lifted her sword mid-stride and slashed it downward.

Catherine threw her sword up, blocking Maria's blow with a loud *clang.*

Catherine tried to tilt her blade, but Maria jerked her own blade back, before she could.

Maria took a step back and unsheathed her second sword, while Catherine adjusted her grip on her own.

Where was her usual aggression? Typically, Catherine would've stepped forward the moment Maria stepped back. Yet, she hadn't.

Maria slashed at her, and Catherine parried.

Maria slashed again and sent a gold tassel from the shoulder of Catherine's perfect, blue waistcoat flying.

Catherine gasped, as if Maria had cut *her*, instead.

Maria thrust her blade at Catherine's opposite side.

Even blinded by her own hatred, Maria didn't fight to kill Catherine. She fought to injure her—to force a surrender.

She'd had plenty of time to plan her vengeance, and Maria had decided, long ago, she didn't want it quick.

She wanted it slow.

She wanted it painful.

She wanted Catherine to suffer pain and indignity, just as Maria had.

Then, Maria wanted Catherine to beg for her death.

Maria feinted with her left sword, following with a slash of her right.

Catherine cried out, when the blade slid across her left bicep. Her blue coat-sleeve split and darkened with blood.

Yet, when Catherine blocked Maria's next thrust, and her gaze met Maria's, above the clash of steel, Maria found no distress in Catherine's blue eyes.

What she found, instead, was delight.

With a growl of rage, Maria tried again, and when Catherine blocked *that* one, she let out a quiet chuckle.

The sound made Maria's blood run cold.

Something wasn't right.

"What the fuck is so funny?" Maria snarled.

Catherine slashed, and Maria parried.

And Catherine's cruel smile never wavered.

"It shouldn't have surprised me," Catherine said with another thrust of her sword, "when I heard the rumors that she'd joined you."

Maria didn't know for *sure* Jonas was to blame, but if she thought there were anything left of him, at this point, Maria might've dragged him up from the bottom of the sea, just to stab him again.

"You're both so similar," Catherine explained, "in the *worst* ways."

Maria ignored the attempted insult. Even when she and Cat had been close, they'd often taunted each other, while sparring.

This was nothing new.

More honest, perhaps, but not new.

Catherine didn't stop there, though. She parried another strike from Maria and added, breathlessly, "I never liked to be present for the torture, you know?"

The mention of torture sent a jolt of shock through Maria's body, and she missed the next strike.

A moment of numb paralysis followed, and Maria heard one of her swords scrape across the ground.

Rather than following up with another blow, Catherine took a step back. "I find it," she paused to wrinkle her nose, "*distasteful.*"

Maria used the brief respite to recover. She adjusted her grip on her remaining sword and shifted her feet in the grass. "Yet, you don't mind assigning it."

Catherine shrugged, and the gold tassels Maria *hadn't* hacked off wiggled with the movement. "It's necessary," she said, "but unpleasant."

Unpleasant.

Un-fucking-pleasant.

For *her*.

Fury rose inside of Maria, and she funneled every ounce of it into her blade.

Catherine blocked, but the force of the blow sent her back a step.

Maria thrust again, and Catherine stumbled.

Maria had no intention of allowing Catherine to toy with her pulse and adrenaline again, but Catherine simply wouldn't shut her fucking mouth.

"I was present," Catherine said, between swings, "more often than I would've liked," she gasped for breath, "for our dear Emilia, though."

The mention of Emilia caught Maria by surprise.

"Often enough," Catherine continued, "to learn an important detail about her."

Maria relied on muscle memory, as she tried to piece together what Catherine was saying.

Strike.

Parry.

"A detail you might find very relevant," Catherine added, "one you might regret not knowing before now."

Strike.

Parry.

"Spit it out!" Maria snarled.

Strike.

Strike.

Strike!

"It's almost impossible to make her scream."

Maria would've liked to have said she'd understood immediately, but her focus had been too divided, her desire to beat Catherine too strong.

When the words *did* sink in, a naïve part of Maria assumed it had been some kind of innuendo. Catherine had so amusingly displayed her jealousy earlier. A bitter innuendo might've made sense.

But after one last attack, the full context of the conversation settled over Maria, like a dark cloud.

Maria stumbled back, and her stomach plunged.

She jerked her head toward where she'd left Em.

Where she'd *forgotten* she left Em.

Three shipmen held the dragon sorceress, and the other five had circled around them.

The tallest man stood behind Em with a sword against her throat, sunlight gleaming off the sharpened steel.

The other two shipmen held Em by the arms, and one of them had something dark on his fingers.

Blood.

A thick layer of blood.

Maria could barely see Em's face from this distance, but she saw it well enough to notice the tight shut of her eyelids and the deep red flush of her face.

With a sudden onslaught of nausea, Maria looked down at Em's wounded arm and realized that the blood she'd seen on the sailor's hand…was Em's.

Oh, no.

No, no, no.

Shame crashed over Maria, leaving nothing of the obsessive rage that had driven her moments before.

And with the world dissolving beneath Maria's feet, it was all too easy for Catherine to step behind her.

Like the sailor had done to Em, Catherine pressed her sword over Maria's chest and against her throat.

"Go ahead and disarm yourself for me, Maria," Catherine said. "You know you want to."

"Tell them to stop."

Though Maria was too overwhelmed and nauseated by her own guilt to feel the proper amount of rage, her voice still vibrated with it.

Catherine gave her an infuriating laugh. "We can cut your throat or hers," she reminded Maria. "I don't think you're in a position to be making demands."

Over the years, Maria had always told herself that she'd choose vengeance over anyone—that *no one* was that important to her—but at the sight of Em's pain, her hand seemed to move of its own accord.

She dropped her sword.

Catherine lowered her sword, too, and stepped back—but Maria hadn't done this for her own safety.

Em had gone slack in the shipmen's arms, suggesting that *maybe* they'd stopped torturing her, but they hadn't released her.

"She really could've saved us all some time by just screaming," Catherine complained. "Don't you think?"

Maria spun toward Catherine. "Tell them to get their fucking hands off of her," she snarled. "Now."

"Oh," Catherine said with a sneer. "Yes, *Captain*."

Catherine lifted her sword into the air, and Maria's brows furrowed. Catherine brought the sword down, and to Maria's horror, the sailor followed the motion.

The steel hilt of the sword slammed into the back of Em's head, and she fell forward.

Fury and panic seared through Maria, at once—white-hot and consuming—blinding her to everything but the *crack* of her surgeon's skull.

Maria didn't even realize she'd thrown herself at Catherine—until Catherine lifted her sword between them. At sword-point, she forced Maria back a step.

Maria's heart raced, and every sense she possessed narrowed to a single, white-hot point.

Em.

"You fired the pistol, Maria," Catherine reminded her. "For *her*! You invited war. For her!" She stepped forward, and the sharp point of her blade pressed into Maria's leather doublet. "You showed me your weakness. Did you think I'd forget it?"

If Catherine had accused Maria of weakness before, Maria would've denied it, but she didn't have enough strength left to deny it now.

A sharp kick to the back of Maria's legs sent her to her knees.

Most of the shipmen had abandoned the unconscious dragon sorceress the moment they'd seen an unarmed pirate fling herself at their admiral.

The single sailor who'd remained with Em stood over her with a pistol aimed at her blood-soaked hair.

As if that were necessary, at this point.

Maria stared at Em's crumpled form. The curtain of blood that flowed over Em's face left Maria's chest hollow.

Maria's ears rang, and her throat ached.

Had she screamed?

When had she screamed?

Someone behind Maria yelled something, but she couldn't hear them over the sound of her own pulse.

Too many emotions warred for control of Maria, and the best she could do for any of them was to conceal them all.

The anger told her to fight.

The panic told her to give them what they wanted.

The guilt told her it didn't matter which action she took. She'd already fallen into Catherine's trap.

She'd *always* fallen into Catherine's traps.

Maria was a pirate now! She'd become as good of a manipulator as Catherine, hadn't she?

She'd tricked Em.

She'd tricked others before Em.

But not Catherine.

Never Catherine.

Catherine used the blade of her sword to force Maria's face upward. "Don't just wait for us to arrest you," she whined. "I want you to say the words."

Maria met her gaze with a calm she didn't feel.

The point of Catherine's blade pressed against the scar on Maria's throat. "Surrender," she demanded.

Maria raised an eyebrow.

"Why does it matter if she says it?" someone asked.

A mix of disbelief and anger flared in Catherine's light blue eyes. "Are you questioning me, sailor?"

"No, I—" he stammered. "I would never, Admiral."

Maria resisted the urge to roll her eyes. Nothing disgusted her more than the obedience of these cowards.

Catherine glanced down at Maria. "I realize you can't see behind you, but there are no less than eight weapons aimed at you now—including my own."

"I assumed," Maria assured her.

Catherine clenched her narrow jaw. "And the pistol we have on your witch? Did you see *it*?"

Maria's blood boiled at the reminder. Her nostrils flared, and she sucked in a sharp breath. Then, slowly but surely, she forced the emotion down.

"My surgeon."

Catherine rolled her eyes. "Yes, fine! Your *surgeon*."

The difference wouldn't have mattered to Em, but it mattered to Catherine.

Catherine hated to acknowledge Em as anything other than a witch—just as she hated to acknowledge Maria as anything other than a pirate.

Perhaps what she really hated was the reminder that she'd *ever* seen either of them as human.

"Don't get *too* comfortable with the knowledge that King Eldric wants you both alive," Catherine warned. "I've already made peace with bringing one of you back dead—if need be."

Personally, Maria preferred death to surrender, but Catherine might've had a point earlier.

Alive, the two of them might escape.

Dead?

Maria didn't even want to *consider* Em being dead.

"As long as I kill the dragons," Catherine said, "I'll receive a hero's welcome, regardless." A smile twisted at her lips. "And we *will* kill them, by the way."

A distant part of Maria—one that hadn't shattered with fear— wanted to know why. Was King Eldric *that* afraid of a prophecy given by fanatical mountain priests, or did he simply want to destroy every power he couldn't conquer or tame?

Maria had only needed to rise to the rank of captain to learn the monstrous secret of Illopia's slave trade.

How many terrible secrets had Admiral Rochester learned—and then ignored, like a fucking coward?

Or worse.

How many had she *enabled*?

"You never had the pleasure of meeting the witch's mother," Catherine said. "Consider yourself lucky."

Oh, Maria did, actually—because if she'd ever met the woman who'd drowned a defenseless infant, Maria would've tried to kill her.

She might've failed, if Em's mother was as dangerous as people thought, but Maria would've tried.

"Nydia Drakon was cruel," Catherine told her, "but she was also cunning—always one step ahead."

Perhaps that was what it took to predict Catherine's schemes. *Cruelty.*

Perhaps that was what Maria had never developed enough of.

Catherine's thin, pink lips twisted into an unflattering sneer. "She sent the dragons away at the first sign of an attack."

Wait.

Em's mother had *died*, rather than let the dragons protect her people?

"Emilia, though—she *called* the dragons," Catherine said. "For *you.*" A sadistic kind of delight shone in Catherine's light blue eyes. "When there are no more dragons left in Aletharia, I hope you remember that."

That single needlepoint of guilt pricked an already gushing wound.

Catherine flicked her sword at two of the shipmen, and they grabbed Maria's arms and wrenched them back.

Maria flinched at the all-too-familiar *clink* of an iron shackle. A sailor closed the shackle around one of her scarred wrists—before pushing both arms forward.

They shackled the other wrist, and the cold iron dug into Maria's scarred skin, weighing down her arms.

Ten years ago, the sensation would've unleashed the same wave of panic in Maria that it did in Em. As a matter of fact, it *had*— when Maria's recklessness had gotten her captured mere months after her escape.

Time had weakened the power her memories had over her, but that didn't mean they no longer affected her. It didn't mean her muscles didn't still tense—or that her stomach didn't still twist with nausea.

Maria could only hope Catherine hadn't noticed.

Maria's gaze wandered back toward Em. They hadn't shackled her yet, but Maria had no doubt they would. Would they keep them together—so that Maria could at least *try* to calm Em when she awoke?

If she awoke.

Fuck, there was so much blood.

No. Don't let them see your fear, Maria told herself.

She focused on her anger, instead.

Let them see that—not fear.

Wait.

Had Em's finger just twitched?

From this distance, Maria couldn't say for sure, but *maybe*. Maybe she'd seen what she hoped she'd seen.

How long had Em been unconscious?

Catherine must've noticed Maria watching. "I'm not *cruel*. I prefer to immobilize her with the drug," she said defensively. "She doesn't suffer when I do it that way, but with those beasts flying around…" Catherine shrugged, and the tip of her sword twitched upward. "I still haven't figured out how she communicates with them."

Maria cast an incredulous look at her former First Mate.

She doesn't suffer with the drug?

Catherine couldn't be serious.

Maria had *watched* that drug at work—when Jonas had used it on Em. She'd watched Em writhe in her sleep—and wake with its miserable side effects.

Em hid her pain better than anyone Maria had ever known, but when she'd been unconscious, Maria had *heard* it. And the thought of it had tormented her for weeks.

Maria cast another glance in Em's direction—and saw it again.

Em stretched her fingers outward, reaching for her sword, which lay in the grass, near her head.

Maria glanced at the shipman, who stood over Em, but he was

too busy watching Catherine—likely waiting for the order to shackle Em.

Sure enough, Catherine told one of the sailors, "We need to get the witch to my ship, where her beasts can't save her—not without risking their lives, anyway."

If Em *had* regained consciousness, she'd need time.

"Do they know?" Maria blurted out.

Catherine's cold, blue gaze shifted toward Maria—and away from Em. "Excuse me?"

Maria hated the bigotry of the Royal Navy more than anyone, but if she *had* to use it against Catherine, she would. "Do they know you fucked her?"

The shipmen fell silent, and Catherine's eyes blazed with rage.

"Lies," she hissed.

"Do they know you *loved* her?" Maria continued.

"Nasty, vicious lies!" Catherine snarled. She jabbed the point of her sword into Maria's leather doublet. "You have no right to make accusations, pirate!"

Maria flashed a devious smile. "Oh, I don't blame you. She's lovely." She glanced at the two shipmen in her line of sight. "Oh, but I guess *they* would. Oops."

"You awful *wretch*!" Catherine screamed, causing several of the shipmen to shift on their feet.

The rumors would spread quickly now.

Maria didn't feel great about what she was doing, but she didn't feel bad either—not for Catherine.

"What?" Maria said. "You didn't tell them you infiltrated the Drakon tribe with intelligence and skill, did you?" She let her gaze drift downward. "When it was really your cunt."

Catherine's milky-white skin reddened with rage, and something seemed to snap in her blue eyes. She lifted her sword and pressed its sharpened tip into the scarred skin beneath Maria's eye.

Maria's smile faded, and her muscles tensed.

"Should I take your eyesight permanently this time?" Catherine said, voice vibrating with hatred. "You were a lot more subdued without it."

Maria's pulse spiked.

The memory of pain flooded her mind, and Maria wondered if Catherine had already cut her.

There had been periods of numbness the last time.

She'd lost time.

The pain felt so real; maybe it was.

Maria blinked slowly, noting the way her eyelashes brushed her scarred cheek.

Memory.

Just a memory.

A sudden cry, followed by the shot of a pistol, caused Catherine to stumble backward and drop her sword.

The sound of the shot startled Maria, too, and fearing the worst, she searched for Em.

What she found, instead, was the gory sight of a shipman dragging his body across blood-soaked grass. His screams echoed throughout the grove, as he dragged a sword-impaled thigh behind him.

The pistol had fallen when he did.

Em scrambled after him, drenched in blood and clumsy on her hands and knees. When she caught up with him, she jerked her sword free and left him to bleed out.

Slowly and unsteadily, Em climbed to her feet.

Blinking out of her shock, Catherine screamed at the remaining shipmen. "Shackle her! Now!"

Terror gripped Maria, as seven shipmen ran toward the injured, barely conscious dragon sorceress.

She would've thought at least one of them would stay to protect their admiral. Maria was shackled, not *dead*.

Em didn't run from them, though. She simply lifted her sword above her head, pointing it toward the sky.

Catherine frowned. "What is she doing?"

As if in answer, an unnatural wind began to flow down the mountain, and a strange sort of energy whispered through the trees.

The first naval sailor to notice the shadow moving above the trees screamed out, "Dragon!"

The other shipmen screamed and ran for cover, but the stride of a human simply couldn't compete with the flap of a dragon's wings.

"No, no, no," Catherine whispered. "Not here."

A green dragon soared through the trees, twisting and swerving in a way that larger dragons probably couldn't. As he closed in on the sailors, he opened his mouth, and a glow of fire emerged from within.

The screams of the sailors chilled Maria to the bone.

The first stream of dragon-fire didn't hit any of the naval sailors, though.

It hit Emilia Drakon's sword.

She didn't even flinch.

The burst of fire narrowed, engulfing Em's blade in flames, as if she'd coated it in something flammable.

Despite her injuries, Em wielded the blade expertly, adjusting her stance for a fight.

The dragon flew past her, and his next stream of fire engulfed no less than five of the seven naval sailors.

Agonized screams filled the air, and the temperature rose high enough to sting Maria's skin—despite her distance from the burning sailors.

The two sailors who got caught on Em's side of the fire attacked her, and as she met the first sword with her own flaming blade, sparks scattered in the air.

While Maria squinted through the smoke, trying to keep an eye on Em, Catherine watched the sky. When the dragon continued toward them, roaring like a rabid beast, Catherine Rochester tried to flee.

Fucking coward.

The sticks snapping beneath Catherine's boots caught Maria's attention, and she let the rage fuel her.

Maria lifted the heavy, iron shackles and climbed to her feet.

She caught Catherine from behind, throwing the shackles around her head and jerking backward.

As the iron chain dug into Catherine's throat, her screams turned to choked rasps.

Catherine kicked her long legs and dug her fingernails into Maria's tattooed forearms, but Maria only pulled harder.

In desperation, Catherine threw herself backward, bashing her head against Maria's mouth.

They hit the ground together, but the weight of the shackles threw Maria's arms above her head.

She tried to shift her body, but Catherine was faster. She straddled Maria's waist and began to strike her in the face.

Over and over.

Maria fought the disorientation and was preparing to lift the shackles—when the ground quaked beneath her.

A rumble of dissatisfaction resounded above them, and both Catherine and Maria looked up to find the small, green dragon *sitting* on his massive, hind legs.

This one might've been small compared to the other dragons, but up close, it might as well have been a mountain.

The dragon opened his mouth, displaying teeth the size of swords, and his hot breath washed over them.

The air thickened, humid with the steam of dragon-breath. It smelled of copper, singed air, and roasted meat.

"Oh, f-f-u—" Catherine breathed.

Would the dragon open fire on Maria, too?

In order to kill the woman responsible for the massacre of the Drakon people?

Maria wouldn't blame him if he did.

Bone-white with shock, Catherine scrambled backward, but she shook like a quivering bowstring, as she did, falling clumsily to one side or the other.

Maria squeezed her eyes shut, bracing herself for whatever painful death awaited her, but all that emerged from the dragon's jaws…was a growl.

A terrifying growl—one so loud and ferocious that it rattled Maria's bones and the ground beneath her—but just…a growl.

Saliva slid between the dragon's huge teeth, hitting the dirt in front of them with a few loud *splats*.

Catherine flinched at the sound.

Perhaps she'd closed her eyes, too.

But as soon as Catherine realized she was still alive, she scrambled to her feet and ran for the narrow gap in the grove. She must've fallen several times—if the sounds of shifting dirt and rock were any indication.

Maria opened her eyes.

Her heart jolted at the sight of the huge, green-scaled dragon that loomed above her.

He closed his mouth, and Maria couldn't help but flinch again at the *chomp* of his powerful jaws.

If it weren't for that visceral sound, Maria might've thought she'd recently gone deaf—because the screams of the burning sailors had stopped. Based on the stench, however, Maria figured it was safe to assume they'd died already.

The dragon narrowed his green eyes in expectation.

Emerald-green eyes—just like Em's.

There was absolutely no way this fire-breathing beast could understand human language, and yet…

"Thank you?" Maria said. The dragon tilted its enormous head, like a curious wolf pup, and Maria felt it necessary to add, "For not reducing me to ash?"

"Ash and bone," came a familiar, slurred voice.

Em.

Maria climbed to her feet as quickly as she could, but the shackles slowed her movement. "What?"

Em staggered forward, the sword in her hand no longer burning. "Dragon-fire can't decimate bone."

Maria rushed to meet her blood-covered surgeon—relief and guilt pouring through her in waves. When she reached Em, she tried to lift her hands and touch Em's face, before remembering the shackles.

"Do I *want* to know how you know that?"

The side of Em's mouth that wasn't covered in blood seemed to curve. "We cremate our dead with dragon-fire." She hesitated. "Well, we did. Before."

Maria's chest tightened. "Oh."

Em tried to step forward—but swayed as she did.

Maria caught her by the elbow.

Em squinted through a layer of blood. "I need to—" Her gaze shifted downward. "I need to get that off of you."

"What?" Maria said, but then, she noticed Em reaching for the shackles. "No! Em. Don't touch it."

"It's all right," Em assured her, and she pressed her trembling hand against the iron.

Em's breath grew shallow, and her lip quivered.

Clink.

Maria watched in disbelief, as the shackles fell from her wrists. Then, she caught Em, as she fell forward.

"Em?" Maria gasped. "Em!"

The dragon growled, and Maria jumped at the sound.

"It was a necessary use of my magic, and you know it," Em slurred at the dragon. She tried to open her eyes, but her eyelashes fluttered. "You want her to take me to Nymeth, don't you? Before I pass out?"

The dragon made a low, rumbling sound in response—as if the two of them were bickering siblings, rather than totally different species.

Em looked up at Maria, her eyes glazed and distant. "Are you all right?"

"Me?" Maria scoffed. "Em, you can barely walk."

How had she cut down three shipmen in this state?

"I've used too much magic today." Em wiped the blood from her eye. "I'm also bleeding."

That was an understatement.

Maria cupped Em's face in her hands, undeterred by the blood that stained her skin. She crumbled all at once, and any semblance of dignity went with her.

"Em, I'm so fucking sorry."

Em squinted up at her, blinked, squinted again, and then blinked again, as more blood dripped into her eye. "I must be concussed," she muttered, "because I thought I heard Captain Maria Welles apologize."

The laugh that escaped Maria's lips sounded far too much like a sob for her own taste. She needed to pull herself together. "Definitely concussed," she agreed.

Em pressed three bloody fingers against Maria's leather doublet—as if she were testing her distance from Maria.

Was her vision impaired, too?

"They were all on you when I came to," Em said.

Maria lifted both eyebrows. "Well, you fixed that." She couldn't help the awed laugh that escaped her lips. "Gods, that was—*you* were incredible."

Em tilted her head and squinted, and Maria didn't know whether to attribute the action to confusion or the continuous flow of blood dripping into her eye.

"Did you just compliment me, Captain?"

"No." Maria tried to wipe the blood from Em's eye with her thumb, but the steady flow made it impossible. "I was complimenting myself, actually—for my brilliant instincts in hiring you."

Maria ripped part of her sleeve and tried to use the fabric to slow the blood flow, but it soaked through before she even found the source.

It was in Em's hair, on her neck…

Maria jerked her hands back. "Em, you keep *bleeding*!"

"Mm." Em closed her eyes and swayed. "It's just a head wound."

"Just?" Maria caught her by the arms. "I'm going to kill you."

Maria didn't realize her mistake until the dragon behind her growled.

She froze, eyes wide.

The ground trembled beneath Maria's boots, as the green dragon stepped toward her.

The dragon's breath was hot enough to singe the hair on the back of Maria's neck, and when a scalding drop of saliva hit the back of her boot, she realized the dragon had not only stepped closer—but had opened its jaws, as well.

Her voice came out higher than usual. "Em?"

Em opened her eyes wearily, as if she'd just awoken from a nap.

That…probably wasn't a good sign.

Em looked up at the dragon. "No, no. She says that a lot," she assured the dragon. "She doesn't mean it."

The heat of the dragon's breath didn't recede, but a sort of croaky rumble resounded from its thick throat.

"Emryn's concerned," Em said tiredly. "You'll have to reassure him yourself."

"Me?" Maria said incredulously. She didn't know how to talk to dragons! She didn't dare turn around, but she called over her shoulder, "If we're being honest, I've only considered killing her three times."

Maria tensed, as the dragon exhaled another humid breath against her neck.

Em lifted both eyebrows—or…Maria thought she had, beneath all of that blood. "I told you to *reassure* him." She glanced up at the dragon. "You know I'll be upset with you, if you give her a heart attack."

The dragon made a sound that sounded almost like a whine.

If…it were a *volcano* doing the whining.

Then, the scalding breath on Maria's neck receded.

Every muscle in Maria's body sagged with relief, but still, she assured Em, "I wasn't afraid of it."

"Him," Em corrected.

With a wince, Maria repeated, "Him."

Em swayed again, and Maria moved her hands, finding a better place to hold her. In the process, Maria paused to look at the wound on Em's forearm.

Her stomach lurched, and another wave of shame poured over her. "Em, your arm," Maria said in a strained voice. "Oh, fuck."

Em somehow kept *her* voice even. "Ah, yes, that's, umm…what happens to muscle and sinew, when someone plunges their hand into the wound. Over and over."

Maria's throat closed. "Fucking hell."

"I can't move it past here, at the moment," Em said. She pointed at her elbow with her uninjured hand—but didn't dare touch it. "But Nymeth will heal it."

Maria barely heard her. All she could do was think about how badly she'd fucked up—and wonder how much pain Em was hiding from her. "I'm sorry."

Em frowned. "Captain…"

"I said your trust was well-placed," Maria said, "but I was wrong. I left you. I didn't even think—"

"Captain," Em interrupted. "Don't worry. I'm not as arrogant as you." Pain bled into her voice. Yet, somehow, she still teased. "I *know* you make mistakes."

Maria laughed—and barely resisted the urge to fall at Em's feet.

That would've been a mistake, too, considering Maria happened to be the one holding Em upright, at the moment.

"I should've known better than to leave you," Maria sighed. "I mean, fuck, I *did* know better. I just—"

Em offered a weak smile. "Captain, you've wanted vengeance far longer than you've known *me*. I never expected you to choose a surgeon over that."

Maria froze.

What the fuck?

She could've handled Em's anger. She would've welcomed it, even.

But grim acceptance? That fucking hurt.

She didn't know why it hurt, but it did.

"You *should* expect that!" Maria gave Em's shoulders a shake— only realizing she shouldn't have done that, when Em's eyes rolled a bit. "I am your captain. Expect more from me. *Please.*"

"I—" Em blinked wearily. "I think I might be too concussed for this conversation."

That earned another laugh from Maria, and the laughter eased the ache in her chest. She rubbed Em's upper arms. "Do you need to rest for a moment?" she asked. "There's a rock over there we could—"

"If I rest, I'll lose consciousness," Em interrupted, "and I'd rather not do that again."

Maria nodded. "What do we do, then?"

Habit urged her to take control of the situation, but head injuries weren't Maria's area of expertise.

"Nymeth is coming to heal me," Em explained. "I only have to make it to shore like this, and she'll handle the rest."

Maria frowned at the name. She couldn't keep track of all the dragons. "Which one was Nymeth again?"

"Black dragon," Em slurred. "Giant. Ancient…"

Maria didn't think Em would make it more than a couple of steps in this state. "Can't she come to you?" She tilted her head toward the green dragon behind them. "The way that one did?"

Em shook her head, eyes fluttering with every movement. "She's too big to make it through the gap. All of them are, except Emryn," she explained. "That's why he was the only one I could call."

Emryn released another terrifying growl, but Em waved it off, as if it were nothing.

"I *did* try to call you sooner," she grumbled. "Have *you* ever tried to concentrate while some blue-coat-wearing asshole mangles your muscle tissue? It's not easy!"

Maria stared. Her surgeon was arguing with a dragon—while concussed.

After eleven years as a ship captain, Maria had thought she'd seen everything. Fortunately for her, this dragon-riding surgeon had come along to free her of that belief.

"Which part of the shoreline?" Maria interrupted.

"Umm, north," Em said carefully, as if she were listening to something. Maria could only assume Em was speaking to her dragons through that bond of hers—however *that* worked. "Near the *Wicked Fate*."

Maria brushed her hand over her scabbard, and her pulse spiked at the emptiness of the sheaths. "Let me retrieve my swords. Then, we'll go."

When Maria returned with the swords, she found Em leaning forward with her uninjured arm draped across her stomach. "Are you all right, love?"

"Go away," Em groaned.

Maria lifted an eyebrow. "Excuse me?"

Em straightened but kept her hand on her stomach. "I've already vomited in front of you once today. I'd rather not do it again."

Maria rolled her eyes. "I'll be all right." She stepped closer. "Is it the pain or the concussion?"

"Could be either." Em's brows furrowed, and she added, "Or a skull fracture."

Maria remembered the awful *crack* of Em's skull and repressed a shudder. "How bad would that be?"

"I'm fine. I'm fine," Em mumbled. "I'm…fine."

The repetition was only making Maria worry more.

"Em?" Maria said.

Em looked up. "It doesn't matter. Nymeth can heal it," she said, and Maria had almost relaxed, when Em added, "As long as I don't die before I get there."

Maria's eyes widened. "What?!"

Em cringed so hard her ear brushed her shoulder. "Hey," she whined. "No yelling."

Maria winced. "Sorry."

"My head's all," Em paused to think about it, "something."

Maria didn't find Em's deteriorating explanations very comforting. She took Em by the arm. "Rest your weight against me," she urged. "Go on, love."

For a moment, Em looked as if she wanted to argue, but the more Maria urged her, the more she wearily leaned into Maria's side.

Maria led her toward the end of the grove.

The quaking steps of the green dragon followed.

"Why is he following us?" Maria whispered to Em.

"He's keeping us safe," Em explained. "He intends to burn Catherine if she comes back."

Maria snorted at that. "She *won't* come back."

Em looked up at her. "You don't think so?"

"She's back on her ship by now," Maria assured her, and with a wicked grin, she added, "changing her trousers."

"Oh," Em said, wrinkling her nose. "You're awful."

Maria laughed loudly. "If I couldn't have her blood on my hands—*this* time," she admitted, "seeing her reaction to that dragon was a nice consolation."

"And I missed it," Em sighed. She quirked her head, as if she were listening to something, and then said, "Emryn agrees with you." She giggled. "But he says *your* expression wasn't too flattering, either."

Maria's smile faded. "I haven't the faintest idea what he's talking about."

Em's smile deepened. "I'm sure."

Though Em's wounds still worried her, Maria couldn't deny the relief she felt at having Em under her arm. Her obsession could've cost her this.

Her obsession could've cost her everything.

When Em began to close her eyes and slump harder against Maria, Maria spoke to keep her conscious.

"I still can't believe you defeated those shipmen," Maria muttered, "while concussed."

Em opened her eyes. "Emryn killed most of them."

"Yes, I saw that part," Maria said, "but the others?"

Em shrugged. "Believe it or not," she said, "I have a lot of experience with fighting while concussed."

Maria's brows furrowed. "Buchan?"

Em blinked. "Oh, I forgot about him, actually."

Maria narrowed her eyes—at the same moment the giant, fire-breathing beast behind them growled.

"As strange as it sounds," Maria snarled, "I have a feeling I'm going to agree with the dragon."

Em tilted her head at that. "You do seem to share a similar opinion of my mother."

"Your mother?" Maria snapped. "Are you telling me your mother gave you a fucking concussion?"

"Too loud!" Em said. "And that's oversimplified."

"Em," Maria growled. "Anything less than a no was not what I wanted to hear."

"Sorry," Em said—as if Maria were angry with *her*, instead of her horrendous mother. "She wanted to make me stronger."

Maria stared down at the person she'd just watched withstand injury and torture.

Either her mother's methods were effective, or Em had never needed that woman in the first place.

The trees grew sparser and sparser, as they neared the coast, and the grass beneath them turned to sand.

Within a thick, grey cloud of cannon-smoke, Maria spotted the *Wicked Fate*, surrounded by naval ships.

At least it hadn't sunk yet.

CHAPTER 5

A Dragon Rider

Maria searched the deserted beach. Catherine had fled in the opposite direction. If that side of the grove opened anywhere near this one, Catherine was long gone now.

"So, where's your—"

Before Maria could even finish the question, another gust of wind burst through the trees, scattering sand into the air. Maria covered her face with her free arm.

A tremendous shadow settled over them, dark and cool, and the slow beat of dragon wings grew louder, even, than the nearby blasts of cannon-fire.

Sand billowed around them, and the largest beast Maria had ever seen landed right in front of her.

Maria clutched Em closer to her side.

After all, Em was concussed, and with the air so tumultuous, at the moment, she might collapse.

It was *Em* who needed the support, okay?

Not Maria.

Em looked up at Maria, lifting her eyebrows, and a tinge of embarrassment warmed Maria's skin.

The dragon shook out its massive wings, before folding the

membranous extensions around its huge, rippling body. Its obsidian scales gleamed in the sunlight, reflecting hues of silver and midnight-blue.

Unlike the smaller, green-scaled dragon, the large, black one didn't possess smooth, shining scales.

This dragon's scales were jagged—broken in some areas, missing in others. Age and battle had left its mark on the creature, and yet, it projected power in a way no younger creature ever could.

Em laughed beside her. "Emryn says you haven't breathed in a solid minute."

Maria scowled at that. "Emryn is a liar."

The green dragon behind them snorted.

Maria didn't know how to read the emotions of a silent dragon, but something told her the large, black dragon was *less* amused.

The black dragon lowered its head, and luminous, emerald-green eyes blinked within its shadowy face.

"She wants me to come to her," Em explained. She flashed a teasing smile. "You'll have to let go of me for a moment. I hope you can stand on your own."

Maria narrowed her eyes at the playful surgeon. "I am your captain, in case you've forgotten," she said. "All of these little jokes of yours *can* be punished."

Em squinted. "I don't remember a law about jokes."

"I'm adding it," Maria assured her.

Em laughed at that, but it must've exhausted her to do so— because her face paled, and she staggered.

Maria held her steady. "Go. Let it—*her*—heal you."

She thought Em had said *'her'* earlier, but gods, it was hard to remember, while looking at the creature.

The dragon looked like…shadow.

Like night incarnate.

Like a *god*.

Not a person or mortal.

How old *were* these dragons?

Em stepped forward and then stumbled.

Worriedly, Maria reached for her, but the dragon moved forward to catch her.

The black dragon curled her neck around Em in what looked like an embrace, and Em draped her uninjured arm over the dragon's jagged, neck scales.

The dragon emitted a sort of dual-toned hum. One part of it was a low rumble like the one she'd heard from Emryn earlier, while the other was a bit higher—a dyadic harmony.

The longer the dragon made the sound, the more she seemed to glow—much like Em's hands had done, when she'd healed Maria in the galley.

A green glow seemed to emanate from within the dragon, stretching to envelop Em's body, as well.

While Maria couldn't see the injuries from here, the relaxation of Em's muscles made it clear that her pain was receding.

Maria glanced curiously at the green dragon, who watched from behind her. Was he capable of this kind of magic, as well?

Em lifted her injured arm to touch the ridges of the black dragon's face, and Maria sighed with relief.

If Em could freely move that arm again, then the muscles and whatever else the naval sailors had mangled must've healed already.

Em rested her head against the dragon's and whispered something, and the affection that softened Em's blood-stained face tugged at Maria's heart.

Em stepped back, and the dragon lifted her head.

The black dragon rumbled, like a volcano, and the green dragon lowered his reptilian head, as if in answer to whatever she'd communicated to him.

Em returned to Maria. She walked steadily now—with a bit of exhaustion, perhaps, but not confusion.

"Better?" Maria assumed.

Em nodded. "Much better."

Maria needed to see it, though. She looked at Em's healed arm first, and her eyes widened at the closed skin she found there. Like Maria's stab wound in the galley, the gruesome wound in Em's arm had sealed.

Maria lifted her hands and combed her fingers through Em's black, blood-soaked hair, searching for the wound that had been near the top of her head.

When Maria found no opening there either, a sigh of relief spilled from her lips. "You're all right."

Em's dazzling, green eyes softened. "Yes, Captain."

The foolish urge to wrap her arms around Em and pull her close swept through Maria, but with a quick glance toward the nearby ships, Maria squeezed the steel handle of her sword until the urge passed.

"You should've just screamed," Maria blurted out—the words she'd been saving for when Em wasn't in danger. "You wouldn't have suffered as long!"

Em's smile faded. "It would've distracted you," she said, "and Catherine would've used it against you."

Well, yes.

That *was* what had happened.

"Distract me, then!" Maria snapped. The dragons shifted around them, and Maria lowered her voice. "I'd rather you distract me than for you to—to endure that."

Em frowned, as if she hadn't expected that. "It was also what they wanted," she said with a helpless shrug. "I couldn't give them the satisfaction."

Maria's frustration instantly seeped out of her.

Catherine was right. She and Em were alike in the worst ways, and Maria couldn't fault Em for that.

None of it would've happened, anyway, if Maria hadn't believed the lie she'd told herself—that vengeance mattered more than anything or anyone.

Catherine had seen through her twice already, and yet, Maria continued to lie.

The black dragon rustled her wings and adjusted her muscular, hind legs, causing a slight shudder in the sand beneath Maria's leather boots.

Maria eyed the white sand warily.

Em glanced back at the dragon. Her brows furrowed, and

though Maria didn't even understand how telepathic communication *worked*, she suspected Em and the dragon were using it now.

When Em's gaze darted toward Maria, she realized they were using it to discuss…Maria, apparently.

Maria crossed her arms and waited.

When Em's attention finally returned to Maria, she proceeded to *not* explain what the dragon had said about Maria.

Maria wasn't sure she liked the black dragon, after all.

At least the green dragon was *reasonably*-sized.

No one needed to grow to the size of a mountain.

That *mountain* better not have told Em to leave her.

The small, green dragon chose that moment to exhale a puff of smoke, and Maria tried not to think about the slight rise in temperature behind her.

Maria gestured toward the green dragon with a tilt of her head. "Why couldn't that one heal you?"

Em glanced at Emryn. "He hasn't mastered healing magic yet. He's too young." When Maria's frown deepened, Em squinted thoughtfully. "Dragons are a little like our warrior sorcerers."

Both dragons growled.

Maria jumped at the sound—barely fighting the urge to run for cover—while Em just rolled her eyes.

"I *know* you're more powerful," Em assured them. "I was just using an example she might understand."

Maria didn't know why Em thought she'd understand an example that still required Maria to know something about magic, but what she *did* know was that she didn't like it when those things growled.

"Can you stop making them angry?" Maria hissed.

Em raised her eyebrows in amusement—but, fortunately, chose not to remark on Maria's reaction. "Anyway," she said with a smile, "our warriors can conjure destructive magic, like fire, far more easily than restorative magic, like healing."

Maria frowned, as she recalled a few things Em had said about her mother. "Are you telling me your mother considered you weaker than her, when she couldn't even perform the same style of magic?"

The green dragon growled again. Maria couldn't explain it, but this time, she thought the growl had been meant for Em's mother, not Maria.

With a wince, Em explained, "It was more that she thought restorative magic was weaker than destructive magic."

"Convenient," Maria said, "if she wasn't as good at it."

Em shifted uncomfortably—the way she always did when Maria expressed her disdain for her mother.

Maria wasn't sure if some part of Em still expected punishment for questioning her mother—or if Em simply wasn't ready to stop letting her mother's opinion of her dictate her opinion of herself.

No one healed in a day, but Em *needed* to realize how awful her mother's treatment of her had been.

"Right, uhh, fire comes easily to them, even when they're young," Em continued, as if Maria hadn't said anything. "Then, there's telepathy, dragon-sight, and other forms of dragon magic."

Maria lifted an eyebrow. "And healing?"

"That one develops slowly," Em explained. "Some of the dragons can heal smaller wounds. Emryn's the youngest, so he struggles the most." She offered an apologetic smile to the green dragon, who simply cocked his head. "Nymeth heals as well as I do."

The black dragon growled, and Em quickly added, "Better! She heals much better than I do!"

At least the witch *occasionally* had a normal reaction to those creatures.

"So, if age is a factor," Maria said, "how old is *she*?" She jabbed a finger in the direction of the black one.

Em laughed. "No one knows."

Maria's brows furrowed. "You can't...ask her?"

The black dragon lowered her head and let out a dangerous growl, her tremendous muscles rippling.

Maria's eyes widened, and she stumbled backward.

"Nymeth thinks you're rude," Em explained.

"She can understand me?" Maria hissed. She'd suspected, of course—but had hoped against it.

With a soft giggle, Em said, "Yes, she's familiar with all languages known to man. She can't read your thoughts like she can mine, though."

"Thank the gods for that," Maria muttered under her breath.

Nymeth settled back on her hind legs and huffed out a puff of black smoke.

Em held up a finger. "Sorry," she corrected herself. "All languages known to man *and* many others."

"What?" Maria said with a frown.

Em lifted her eyebrows. "You didn't think humans were the only creatures who could create their own languages, did you?"

Well, what the fuck else would she think?

Em must've seen the confirmation on Maria's face—because she laughed in that way that was adorable and frustrating, all at once.

The green dragon made another snorting sound, and Em replied, "I agree. She *is* an arrogant human."

Maria suppressed a smile. "Fuck you."

Em laughed again, but as soon as her gaze found Maria's face, she stopped. Her smile faded, and she stepped closer to Maria. "My vision was too blurry earlier," she mumbled to herself. "I couldn't see it."

Maria's brows furrowed. "Couldn't see what?"

Em lifted her hand and touched a bruise on Maria's cheek. Maria expected the tender skin to sting when touched, but the surgeon touched her with such attentive and careful fingers that Maria barely felt it.

"Goddess," Em breathed. Her green eyes narrowed. "What is her obsession with breaking your face?"

Maria laughed bitterly. "You wouldn't believe how many times I've asked myself the same thing."

Em's gaze flicked upward—toward the scar over Maria's eye. "Did you come up with any theories?"

"I did, actually," Maria said. "I think it's jealousy." She leaned toward Em and flashed a wry grin. "What do you think, surgeon? Is it possible your captain was once more attractive than Catherine Rochester?"

"Once?" Em's frown deepened. "You still are."

Maria's smile faded. "You think so?"

Em gave her an incredulous look. "Don't you?"

"Of course I do," Maria said, but her voice sounded weak, even to her own ears.

Catherine was beautiful. Maria had always thought so. She was hideous on the inside, of course, but deceptively appealing on the outside.

"Just to confirm…" An arrogant smile pulled at the edges of Maria's mouth. "You've always found me more attractive, then? Even when you hated me?"

Em's cheeks reddened. "I don't understand why you feel the need to interrogate me on such matters."

Maria snorted at the evasive answer. "You did!"

Her blush only deepened at that. "Of course I did."

Maria had expected the smug satisfaction that filled her, after that confession, but she *hadn't* expected the warmer, deeper feeling that followed.

Maria kept her voice light, despite the emotions whirling inside of her. "Do me a favor," she teased, "and repeat that the next time our lofty admiral graces us with her presence."

Em rolled her eyes. "I'm starting to think she's not the only one with a jealousy problem."

Maria didn't bother to deny it. "We were friends for a reason." Her smile faded, and she sighed, "Cat and I are more alike than either of us cares to admit."

"Yes," Em said, as if she'd noticed that herself. She stepped closer, and sincerity shone in her green eyes. "But you're different in the ways that matter."

Maria blinked in surprise.

Her heart fluttered, and something inside her chest lifted.

Maria had never realized how much she'd needed to hear that.

Em leaned forward onto her toes. She brushed her finger along the curve of Maria's bottom lip, and it came away wet with blood. "She hurt you here, too," she sighed. "If I had more magic left, I'd heal it."

Maria let out an incredulous laugh. After the things Em had just survived, she was worried about this? "It's a busted lip, Em. I'll be fine."

Maria considered kissing Em just to prove her point—but a nearby blast of cannon-fire brought their concerns back to the *Wicked Fate*.

Through the wall of thick smoke, Maria could just make out the outline of her ship—still intact. She knew the *Wicked Fate* would need extensive repairs if they survived the day, but that was a problem for the future.

If they survived to see a future.

Maria hadn't caught whatever Em had just said to Nymeth, but it must've been some sort of goodbye—because the black dragon unfurled her massive, black wings, straightened her wide legs, and took to the air.

The green dragon, however, kept his wings folded.

Em turned toward the Azure Sea. She, too, squinted into the smoke, searching for the *Wicked Fate*. "Even if we had the longboat, you'd never make it back in it," she mumbled. "You'd be a slow-moving target."

Maria's stomach flipped. "Me? What about you?"

Em turned to face Maria. "We've already discussed this," she said with a frown. "I'm riding."

Maria glanced at the green dragon—and realized why he hadn't flown away with the other one. She returned her attention to her surgeon. "You've been injured since then," she argued. "You could've died!"

"Nymeth healed me," Em reminded her. She shook her head in confusion. "Captain, we agreed that I—"

"I didn't agree," Maria insisted. "I accepted you'd need your riding armor, yes, but that was before I—"

Before I almost lost you.

If sand weren't such a nuisance to walk on, Maria might've paced to calm herself. As it was, she could only shove back the terror surging inside of her—and glower.

Em didn't flinch under her gaze. "My dragons need me, and the

Wicked Fate needs you," she told Maria. "As soon as we've won, I'll return to your ship."

"No," Maria said.

Em lifted her eyebrows in disbelief. "No?"

Maria resisted the urge to grab Em's hand, to plead with her.

Em had said she wanted this. She'd told Maria she *wanted* to stay.

What if she'd changed her mind?

After Maria had failed her so thoroughly, *had* Em changed her mind?

Em's brows furrowed. "Captain?"

Maria stepped closer to her surgeon. "You called it my ship," she said, her voice low. "It's *our* ship."

Em's frown deepened. "Okay."

"Say it." Maria leaned in close—close enough to feel the caress of Em's breath against her sore lips, close enough to see the dilation of Em's pupils. "Say *our* ship."

Em didn't step back, and for once, she didn't break eye-contact.

The cannon-fire rumbled in the distance, but Maria barely heard it above the sound of her own thundering pulse.

She waited for Em to refuse her, but she didn't.

Instead, Em reached out and brushed her hand against Maria's leather-clad hips. Em had never been the one to touch first, but she touched Maria now.

Maria closed her eyes and exhaled shakily. That one point of contact might as well have been *every* point.

Maria felt the heat of Em's touch *everywhere*.

"Our ship," Em whispered.

Maria opened her eyes, and when she saw Em's curious, yet gentle, smile, something inside her chest twisted at the sight.

Gods.

Maria closed her hands around Em's blood-streaked face and kissed her. She exhaled her relief against Em's mouth, and Em leaned into her.

Despite the softness of Em's mouth, Maria's lips stung from the pressure, but she didn't dare pull away.

Maria tasted a hint of blood in the kiss and realized it was her own.

Em lifted her hand and wiped the blood from Maria's bottom lip. "I wish I could heal you now."

Maria couldn't help but laugh. "You're covered in blood, love. Do you realize that? *Covered!*"

"Yes." Em wiped her thumb across Maria's lip once more, somehow leaving the nerves tingling, instead of stinging. "What does that have to do with anything?"

Maria snorted. She stroked her own thumb along Em's blood-streaked cheek and said, "Em, I can't protect you up there."

"No," Em said with a smile, "but I can protect *you*."

That was *exactly* what Maria was afraid of.

"It's not your job to protect me," Maria said.

Em laughed. "Well, I'd like to see you stop me."

Maria narrowed her eyes at the challenge. "I'm your captain." She dropped her hand. "I can order you to come with me!"

Em shrugged easily. "And I can ignore you."

Frustration pulled Maria's muscles tight, and she exhaled slowly. "You are the most insubordinate surgeon who's ever worked on a ship."

"Possibly," Em said, "but that's why you hired me."

Maria pulled back. "What?"

"You pretend to want obedience, but you actually despise it." Strands of Em's short, black hair rustled in the breeze, and an affectionate smile softened her face. "You hired me *after* I proved I wasn't afraid of you. If you wanted obedience, Captain, you wouldn't surround yourself with people who so clearly prefer rebellion."

Maria crossed her arms, but she couldn't help the impressed smile that tugged at her lips.

Em wasn't wrong.

Obedience was Catherine.

Obedience was the Royal Navy.

Obedience was what Maria had rejected.

What she'd seen in *Em*…was courage.

"Fine," Maria said, "but at *least* tell that thing not to drop you."

Complete and utter confusion twisted at Em's face. She glanced at her dragon, who gave a snort in response. "Captain…" She returned her attention to Maria. "That is not at *all* how dragon-riding works."

Maria suppressed a laugh. "Let me rephrase, then," she said. "If you die, I'll make you regret it."

Em tilted her head, her dark hair sliding to the side, and for a moment, Maria thought she'd debate the logistics of that one, as well. Then, she said, "Deal."

Maria grinned. "Darling," she murmured. "What have I told you about making deals with pirates?"

The smile Em offered her in return was as warm and soothing as a balm. "Can you swim?"

"Of course I can swim," Maria said distractedly. "I grew up in Nefala, not Rego—" She stopped the moment she saw Em's eyes widen, but it was too late.

She couldn't have figured it out that easily. Maria hadn't even finished the sentence.

But Em's smile faded, and she took a step back. "It was you."

Maria's stomach plummeted. "Fuck."

"Catherine grew up near the Westerly Sea, where the water was too cold to swim," Em said, "but you didn't. You grew up in a port city on the Azure Sea."

Did they have to do this now?

Wasn't one failure a day enough?

Actually, no. If they *were* going to do this, it was better they did it now—away from the *Wicked Fate*.

Maria closed herself off, letting no emotion show.

"That's what she meant," Em realized. Her green eyes burned brighter with each moment that Maria kept silent. "You knew she'd jump. You told her to!"

Not in…so many words.

"The rest of the crew thought she'd drown, but you knew better," Em accused, "because you taught her to swim. You taught Catherine how to escape a ship."

Em really *was* too clever for her own good.

Maria stepped toward Emilia. "Surgeon."

Emilia scoffed at the show of power. "Captain."

"She's the Admiral of the Royal Navy," Maria said. "It's her duty to choose death over interrogation."

"Catherine Rochester would never choose anything over herself, and you know it," Em argued. "You said you'd explain. So, stop lying to me, and *explain*."

Maria squeezed her eyes shut and exhaled a shaky breath. "If you breathe a word of this to anyone…"

Em flinched, and Maria stopped, sure she'd said something wrong, but not sure what.

"I protected your reputation when I thought I hated you!" Em said, pain bleeding into her voice. "You think I'd stop *now*? Now that I—that I love you?"

Maria's stomach flipped at those words. Somehow, having heard them once before hadn't lessened their impact any. "I thought you said you *might* love me."

"Oh," Emilia scoffed. "Let's not get pedantic."

A surprised laugh spilled from Maria's lips, and the rigid set of her muscles loosened. She stepped closer to Em, white sand sinking beneath her leather boot.

In a soft, pleading tone—that she *knew* was totally unfit for a legendary pirate captain—she said, "It would ruin me."

Empathy twisted at Em's face with the same intensity as physical pain. "Your secrets are safe with me, Captain." Sincerity glistened in her impossibly green eyes. "They always have been."

Something cracked inside Maria's chest. "Oh."

Perhaps Judith had known that before Maria did.

Judith had told Em the truth about Maria's crime, after all.

Maria traced the hilt of her sword absently, her gaze fixed on the sand beneath her boots. "If the crew thought I was too weak to kill Catherine—"

"No one in their right mind would think you're weak!" Em said. She crossed her blood-stained arms. "Emotionally compromised, maybe, but not weak."

Maria lifted her gaze to meet Em's. "In the world of pirates, darling," she said bitterly, "that *is* weak."

"Well, I'm sorry," Em said, her voice thick with sarcasm, "but I don't believe something just because someone says it. You're not weak. I'll tell them that."

Maria snorted. "That…won't be necessary."

Em lifted her chin and stiffened her shoulders, like an angry ship cat. "Who are we fighting? Zain?"

Oh, for fuck's sake.

Maria squeezed her eyes shut, barely suppressing laughter. "He…might suspect."

The confession dampened her amusement a bit.

Em's shoulders fell. "He thinks you let her live?"

"I didn't," Maria insisted. She pursed her lips, and the pressure she inflicted on her bottom lip stung. "She was mine when I taught her—*my* First Mate! Of course, I wanted her to survive. I thought we'd be fleeing a mutiny or battle together, not…" She rolled her eyes. "Not *her* leading the mutiny against *me*."

Em nodded. "Why did you let her jump?"

It didn't matter how gentle Em's voice had been—and it *had* been achingly gentle.

The word *'let'* was still enough to evoke Maria's anger—and the plethora of emotions that hid beneath it.

"She had you, Em!" Maria snarled. "If I'd shot her, she would've used you like a shield. *You* haven't seen her do it. I have!" Near-forgotten memories flashed through Maria's mind, and every muscle in Maria's body tightened in response. "Nothing matters to her! No matter what you'd meant to her, no matter what King Eldric had asked of her, she would've made me—" Her voice cracked. "She would've used you."

Em stared at Maria, as if she couldn't make sense of what she was seeing. "It wouldn't have been your fault."

Maria let out a shrill laugh. "You have to be fucking kidding me."

Em frowned and glanced at Emryn, as if the *dragon* could

explain it to her. Her eyes widened, then, and her attention returned to Maria. "It was fear?"

"No," Maria lied.

"You were afraid," Em said slowly, "for me?"

Why was it so difficult for Em to comprehend that someone might choose her over everything else?

Just that once.

Or…twice.

Hadn't Em already done the same for Maria?

Maria looked away, and her words came out softer, this time. "Legends don't die without an audience. We'd live on—in their fears, their thoughts, their stories…" She sighed, "That's why, regardless of the king's orders regarding the dragons, he'll also have ordered her to bring you back alive—to bring us both back alive."

"Captain Maria Welles is a legend," Em argued. "I'm not."

Maria arched an eyebrow. "The Dragon Child?"

Em grimaced at the phrase. "That doesn't count."

"It counts," Maria said. With another sigh, she added, "Regardless of her orders, though, I think Catherine has proven to *both* of us that she'll choose herself over everything."

Em nodded slowly. "On the day of my execution, she sent the guards away, rather than let them overhear us," she admitted, "and I *knew* she would."

"I wonder what her king thought of that," Maria muttered. She shook her head. "I couldn't kill her, Em. Not when I knew it'd put you in danger."

"You knew she'd flee, if you fired the pistol," Em realized, "but just in case she didn't, you told her to."

Maria nodded.

And Catherine had proven it again.

She wouldn't kill either of them, unless she had to.

In such a quiet, simple tone that Maria couldn't be sure she'd heard her correctly, Em said, "I'm not worth that."

Maria might've asked her to repeat herself, if the next blast of cannon-fire hadn't startled them both.

Maria looked up to find an even thicker cloud of grey smoke—and the faint outlines of two ships sailing toward the *Wicked Fate.*

"We're running out of time," Em said. Without even waiting for a goodbye, she hurried toward the green dragon. "Swim. I'll keep their attention off of you."

"Em, no!" Maria called after her. "Don't do that."

Em barely acknowledged Maria's protest. "Swim!"

The dragon lowered himself to the ground, letting the white sand scrape against the shining, green scales of his neck and torso. Em mounted him with the ease of a practiced rider.

Emryn straightened his large, reptilian legs and unfolded his great, green wings, and Em adjusted her armor-clad thighs, centering her balance—before pulling two black, leather gloves from her pocket.

Em slipped them onto her hands, as both dragon and rider rose above Maria's head. "Stay safe," Em called down to her.

Maria crossed her arms, resisting the urge to reach for Em, to beg her to climb back down. "You, too," she said, "love."

Emryn rustled his wings once more, and Em rested her gloved hands against the dragon's green ridges.

Then, the dragon and his rider took wing.

EMILIA SCREAMED.

Not in fear or pain.

But in pure, uncontainable exhilaration.

The surge of excitement faded into a calmer sort of joy, and Emilia's screams tapered into giddy laughter.

The dragons laughed, too, their voices only audible in Emilia's mind.

"Welcome back, rider," Emryn said.

A flash of violet swooped over them, and Astral's voice filled Emilia's mind, as well. *"We've missed you."*

Warmth swelled in Emilia's chest, and she felt as if she could sob. *"Oh, I missed you, too! Every day."*

It was the only thing that had kept Emilia going in the Regolis dungeons—the thought of her dragons.

And her duty to protect them.

Shadows swirled in the clouds above her, as Astral and Caelu circled overhead.

How many times in those dungeons had Emilia wondered if she'd ever see her dragons again? How many times in the Kingdom of Illopia had she wondered if she'd ever experience *this* again?

The cool rush of wind tugged at Emilia's hair and armor, as the green dragon soared higher and higher.

The air burned Emilia's eyes, causing them to water, and she blinked rapidly to clear her vision.

Far beneath them, cannon-fire rumbled, but Emilia barely heard it over the thunderous beat of dragon wings and the deafening *whoosh* of air that followed.

Each flap of Emryn's tremendous wings propelled them higher into the air, and the thick, white fog of clouds rushed toward them at an unnerving speed.

The scent of water and metal filled Emilia's senses, and the dew dampened her hair, leaving the short, black strands stuck to Emilia's forehead and cheeks.

Emryn gave Emilia no warning *whatsoever*, before twisting midair and swooping downward—nearly throwing Emilia into a free fall.

With a squeak of surprise, Emilia pressed her thighs closer and tensed her stomach. She slid forward and backward astride the dragon's back, but she held her balance.

It wasn't the first time the young dragon had nearly killed Emilia mid-flight, but it *had* been a while.

Emryn's laughter filled her mind. *"Out of practice?"*

Asshole.

It'd been almost a year.

Of course she was out of practice!

"I lost muscle mass—among other things—while starving in those dungeons," Emilia informed him. *"You could have a little bit of mercy on me."*

"You didn't regain your muscle mass while serving on your human's ship?" Emryn said.

Emilia had regained most of it, sure—but not all.

"Perhaps you should ask your shiny human to focus more on the lower parts of your body, then."

Emilia blanched.

The problem with dragon bonds was that as soon as the sorcerer was close enough to speak to the dragons, the dragons were close enough to know *everything*.

Including how Emilia felt about Maria.

The dragons had been supportive about it, of course—enthusiastic, even—but Emilia suspected *Emryn's* approval of Maria hinged more on her continuing to wear that shiny, gold chain around her neck and the shiny, gold loops in her ears.

"You're too young to be making jokes about the lower parts of my body!" Emilia scolded.

Emryn snorted. *"I'm seven hundred years older than you."*

"Dragons don't mate until they're over a thousand," Emilia said. *"Nymeth told me that."*

Caelu dropped down to fly beside them, her light blue scale shimmering in the sunlight. *"Nymeth didn't want to explain dragon sex to a thirteen-year-old witch."*

Emilia's brows furrowed. *"She lied to me?"*

The dragons' laughter filled Emilia's mind, but infuriatingly, none of them answered the question.

"Is Igrunn all right?" Emilia asked them.

Emilia would've seen him by now if he were flying with them. He was impossible to miss—his orange and yellow scales giving him the appearance of fire.

"Igrunn's fine," Emryn told her. *"He'll join us soon."*

"We took Igrunn to Nymeth," Caelu said. *"She healed his wound."*

Emilia's chest tightened. *"Good. That was quite the scare."*

Nymeth, the ancient, black dragon, had perched herself somewhere near the top of Mount Drakon—so she could watch the battle from afar.

After all, for hundreds of years, she'd barely shown herself to the Drakon people. She certainly didn't intend to show herself to the humans below.

Violet scales drew Emilia's attention to her right—where Astral swooped lower to join them. Her voice filled Emilia's mind. *"Nymeth agreed with your order to avoid the dragon-killing ship."* Her powerful, purplish wings beat mercilessly at the air beneath them. *"We haven't flown near it since Igrunn's injury."*

Hearing the dragons refer to Emilia's suggestion as an *order* unleashed a flutter of insecurity in her chest, but this didn't feel like the right time to correct them.

"Good," Emilia thought. *"The last thing I want is for any of you to get hurt."*

"Then, how will we save your shiny human?" Emryn asked.

Fair question.

Emilia risked a glance downward, and her stomach lurched. From this height, she saw only the blue of the sea, the curve of Drakon Isle, a thick, grey cloud of cannon-smoke, and the shadows of ships within.

Fortunately, dragon senses were *made* for these heights.

"Can you show me what you see?" Emilia asked the dragons. *"How many ships are near the one with the ballista?"*

An image flashed in Emilia's mind, unfolding with the same ease as the dragons' voices.

Two ships?

No.

Four.

One on each side.

They'd surrounded the flagship, shielding it.

Shielding Catherine.

"What about my ship?" Emilia asked the dragons. *"The one flying the black flag. How many are near it?"*

"As of now, none," Astral said, voice rising with pride. *"We've burned every ship that's tried to attack your humans. We just destroyed two more a few minutes ago."*

"Perfect. Is there a sufficient distance between the blue-flagship and the one flying black?" Emilia asked.

"Yes," Caelu assured her. *"The dragon-killing ship seems reluctant to close the distance."*

Of course they were reluctant.

Catherine was reluctant.

'*They'll be cautious with their flagship,*' Maria had said, '*which means you can be cautious, too.*'

Astral's sigh filled Emilia's mind. *"Two more ships are closing in on your humans now."* She couldn't have sounded more annoyed. *"They never learn, do they?"*

An amused smile tugged at the corners of Emilia's lips. She'd already explained the meaning of the word 'crew' to her dragons. Yet, they continued to refer to the crew as Emilia's 'humans.'

Not her crew-mates.

Her humans.

"Humans are extraordinarily ignorant creatures," Caelu told Astral. Then, to Emilia, she added, *"No offense to your shiny ones, of course."*

Emilia lifted her eyebrows at the blue dragon.

Caelu was the kindest dragon Emilia had ever known, and Emilia had never heard her insult anyone—unless you counted Emilia's mother.

"Okay," Emilia said. '*Astral, you'll burn any ships that approach the Wicked Fate."*

"Happily," Astral said in that smug tone of hers.

"Caelu," Emilia continued, *"you and Igrunn will take care of the ships in the middle of the formation—if Igrunn's ready for flight, of course."*

From the mountain peak in the distance, a dragon took flight, his bright scales shining like fire.

"I'm ready!"

Emilia smiled, relieved to hear his voice again—especially after the scare he'd given her earlier. *"Emryn and I will take out the four around the flagship."*

"No!" Caelu cried. *"Their weapon can kill you, too!"*

"I know," Emilia said. *"We'll avoid the flagship itself—and only take out the ships around it."* Her chest tightened. *"I won't risk Emryn's life."*

"And I won't risk yours," Emryn informed her.

With a gloved hand, Emilia stroked his green neck scales. *"Emryn and I can swerve in and out quickly enough to take them out,"* she told the other dragons. *"We've practiced this before."*

Not with ships, but…with trees.

That counted, right?

"Trees don't have cannons," Nymeth interjected—from wherever she watched.

"It'll work, though," Emilia thought, *"don't you think?"*

"Perhaps," Nymeth said, *"but be careful, little one."*

Emilia hadn't been little in quite some time, but to Nymeth, *everyone* was little. Even giants were ants to her.

"I will." Emilia returned her attention to the other dragons. *"Remember: fly high, and never stop moving. Don't give them the chance to take aim."*

The wind whipped a few strands of black hair into Emilia's face.

"Anything else, rider?" Astral asked.

"Yes," Emilia said easily. *"Burn them all."*

The dragons roared at that, and one by one, they flew toward their targets—with Astral veering west, while Caelu and Igrunn plunged downward.

The steady beat of Emryn's wings slowed. *"Do we get to have our fun now, rider?"*

Emilia laughed at his enthusiasm. *"I told Nymeth we'd be careful."*

Emryn gave a low rumble of dissatisfaction. *"Now, why would you do that?"*

Nymeth's powerful voice invaded both of their minds, at once. *"Why wouldn't she?"*

Emryn's iridescent, green scales shuddered beneath Emilia's gloved hands, and his voice quietened. *"I hate it when she does that."*

With a soft giggle, Emilia said, *"Ready?"*

She might as well have given Emryn permission to kill her. He rolled mid-flight, before plunging downward, and this time, Emilia's scream *did* carry a bit of alarm.

They plummeted toward bright, azure-blue waters that, at this speed, might as well have been solid ground, and Emilia clung tightly to the dragon's green scales.

"*Don't fall,*" Emryn said unhelpfully. "*Your shiny human might glare at me.*"

Using her thighs to maneuver herself, Emilia regained her balance astride the rough, dragon scale. Only once there was no immediate danger of death, did she reply, "*She's a great swordsman, too.*"

"*I'm terrified,*" Emryn said.

Emilia laughed at his sarcasm.

The glassy surface of the water rose to meet them at an unhindered pace, and Emilia's eyes widened.

He was going to slow down, wasn't he?

"Emryn?!"

Emryn unfurled his green wings and flapped them once, before slamming his spiked tail against the surface of the water.

The dragon glided across the sea, cool water spraying around them and drenching Emilia's armor and skin.

The sensation was *magical.*

Emilia threw her head back, cold, wet hair brushing the back of her neck, and a burst of giddy laughter spilled from her mouth. She loosened her grip, and the familiar urge to spread her arms rose within her.

Long ago, when Emilia had first learned to ride, Nymeth had blamed that urge on Emilia's '*dragon blood.*'

A metaphor, of course.

Despite what Illopians believed about the Drakon people, that was not how they'd *ever* procreated.

'*You long to spread your wings,*' Nymeth had said—so long ago.

Emilia had giggled, picturing herself with massive dragon wings atop her small, human body.

Very little, in Emilia's twenty-five years of life, had come close to the delight that filled her now.

But…sword-fighting with her captain had.

Kissing her captain had.

Her captain had.

Emilia spotted the first naval ship, directly ahead.

The ship's cannons shifted in their direction, and Emilia screamed out, "Now!"

Fire erupted from Emryn's mouth.

He slammed his tail against the water once more and flapped his massive wings. They soared upward—just in time to avoid the burning, naval ship.

Sparks flicked over Emilia's skin, and her hands slid. She bit back a cry, when a jagged piece of wet scale sliced into her glove.

But Emilia held her balance throughout it all.

The screams of naval sailors followed them.

"You're hurt," Emryn said.

"I'm fine." The burns along the back of Emilia's arms stung, but it was nothing compared to the other wounds she'd sustained that day. *"Next ship."*

"I'll be more careful," Emryn promised. Reckless as he was, Emryn usually learned from his mistakes.

And they'd made a lot of them. Together.

Emilia had started to tell him not to worry about it, but when a massive bolt flew past her head, Emilia realized they *both* needed to be more careful.

"Swerve!" Emilia yelled. "Wind, like a serpent!"

Emryn obeyed, twisting and weaving mid-air—just as he'd done when he was avoiding trees.

Two more ballista bolts shot toward them, but both of them missed.

Only when they were far outside the flagship's reach, did Emilia breathe a sigh of relief.

Ships burned around them, and the agonized screams of sailors blended into one, terrible sound. Guilt twisted at Emilia's chest.

Think like your mother, Emilia told herself. *Think like your captain.*

They killed your people.

None of them are innocent.

Still…Emilia's chest ached.

"There's room in your heart for strength and compassion," Emryn said, clearly listening to her thoughts. *"Don't begrudge yourself for having a heart large enough for both."*

Emilia wished she could believe the dragon, but her mother had already told her the truth.

Emilia was weak.

She was unworthy.

She was an embarrassment.

The dragon dove toward the next naval ship, twisting and winding through the air.

"You're drifting, rider," Emryn warned her.

Emilia blinked out of her thoughts. *"Sorry."*

As Emryn swerved around the towering sails of the naval ship, Emilia screamed, "Now!"

Emryn opened his massive jaws and spewed fire on the ship below.

He then twisted sharply, safely avoiding the flames.

Emilia and Emryn took out the next two ships with more ease than the first two, and though each attack brought more dragon-killing bolts their way, Emryn swerved skillfully enough to avoid every one.

In the aftermath, they escaped to a safe distance from the flag-ship and waited to see what it would do.

Nymeth's rumbling voice invaded Emilia's mind. *"Dragon Child?"*

Emilia glanced toward Mount Drakon, where the massive, black dragon waited. *"Yes, Nymeth?"*

"Allow me to fly you to your ship," Nymeth said. *"There's something you and I must do before you go."*

Emilia's heart ached at the thought. She liked her life aboard the *Wicked Fate* and couldn't bear the thought of leaving Maria, but that didn't mean the inevitability of leaving the dragons hurt any less.

"Don't fret yet, little one," Nymeth told her. *"Wait until you hear what I have in mind, before you lose hope."*

The pain in Emilia's chest eased, and a flutter of hope rose to take its place. *"We're coming to you now, Nymeth."*

A Captain

Water sloshed against the wooden hull of the *Wicked Fate*, as Maria swam up alongside it.

She tried waving her leather tricorn above her head, but in the towering shadow of the ship, Maria might as well have been at the bottom of the sea.

She shouted up to anyone who might've been near the rail, but with the chaos ensuing above her, it didn't surprise her when no one answered.

Maria might've *kept* trying, if she hadn't noticed the movement of the cannons above her.

What the fuck were they doing?

Maria scanned the side of her ship. Without a rope ladder, she'd have to use the slick keel as a foothold.

Maria *much* preferred rope.

Yet, when she overheard the command Helen was repeating to the gunners, pure rage propelled her up onto the keel.

Her wet, leather boots squeaked against the slick wood, and she reached for a loose plank. Taking hold, Maria hauled herself up against the hull of the ship and searched for her next foothold.

"Zain Fucking Amari, I'm going to kill you," Maria grumbled.

She wedged her fingers between two loose planks and lifted her waterlogged boot. Something tugged at her ankle. "I leave my ship in your hands once, and what do you do? You fucking—*agh!*"

Maria's boot slipped in the middle of her expletive-laced rant, and the front of her body slammed against the side of the ship.

Wooden splinters dug into Maria's hands, and she kicked her legs, searching for another foothold.

She must've made a lot of noise when she slipped—because one of the sailors *finally* peered over the side of the ship.

He promptly pointed his pistol at her. "I'd suggest you slide on back down."

Maria's boot found the keel again, and she hauled herself back up. She lifted her head and glared at the familiar face. "Want to rethink that tone, boatswain?"

Pelt leapt onto the rail so quickly he nearly threw himself over the side of the ship *with* her. "Captain?!"

Maria raised both eyebrows. "Well, I'm not wearing fucking blue, am I?"

Pelt swung back over the rail to yell at someone. "Rope!" he called out. "Get me some rope! Now!"

A few more sailors climbed over the hull to help, and Pelt returned with a *glorious* rope ladder. He threw it over the side, and Maria took hold of it.

Never in her life had Maria been so pleased to see rope.

Well…maybe *one* other time.

Maria climbed the rope, and the sailors took each side and pulled it upward. Maria decided, in that moment, that if she survived to go on *more* safe excursions with Em, she'd take grappling hooks.

And reinforcements.

When Maria reached the top of the ladder, Pelt leaned forward and grasped her arm, helping her over the wooden rail.

His hazel eyes widened at the sight of her—even though *his* clothes were wet with blood, as well. "What happened to you?"

"Catherine," Maria muttered.

Pelt looked down, eyeing her drenched, leather trousers. "She did the seaweed, too?"

Maria spun toward her boatswain. "Take me to your acting captain," she growled, "so I can *kill* him."

Pelt looked up, eyes even wider than before. "Aye, Captain."

Pelt carefully navigated his way through the chaos, and Maria followed, seawater dripping from her clothes with every step. She drew one of her swords.

With a quick glance in her direction, Pelt mumbled, "Sorry about the, er…" He waved his pistol warily.

"We're in battle," Maria reminded him. "It's fine."

Pelt continued to cast wide-eyed looks at Maria as they walked, and she caught him, more than once, frowning at the tangles of dark seaweed around her ankles.

They found Zain on the quarterdeck, standing next to Henry, and Maria ascended the steps two at a time.

Zain grimaced the moment he saw her. "What happened to *you*?"

Maria raised her sword swiftly, extending her arm to press the blade against Zain's throat.

His hands immediately went up. "Never mind!" he said, his eyes wide. "Seaweed looks great on you!"

Maria stepped closer, letting her sword press into his throat, and as if by instinct, Zain straightened—coming to attention, much like he'd done when they'd served in the navy together. "Belay the order!"

Zain's dark eyebrows drew inward. "What order?"

Maria didn't have time for this shit.

"Belay it," she said, through clenched teeth, "or I'll slice you into more pieces than you can count."

Zain let out a laugh of disbelief. "What crime have I committed?"

"Do you think that matters to me?" Maria growled. "Does it *look* like I intend to wait for a trial?"

Just in case he had any doubt, she pressed her sword forward, forcing him back a step.

Zain stumbled, and his smile faded. "I have captained the ship well in your absence, and this is the thanks I get?"

"If all of your commands have been as foolish as this one," Maria said, "I wouldn't call it *well*.'"

Zain scoffed at that. "What command?"

"The one you *just* gave to Helen," Maria said.

Pelt stepped toward them. "About the dragons?"

Zain glanced at Pelt and then back at Maria, recognition flashing in his dark eyes. "Captain, they've burned every ship around us!" he said. "We have to defend ourselves—*try*, at least—before they turn their fire on us."

"Every ship *around* you!" Maria repeated. She forced him back one more step—at the point of her sword. "Did it never occur to you, you fucking imbecile," she shouted, "that the dragons were *helping* you?"

Zain gave a baffled shake of his hands. "They're *dragons*!"

Pelt winced a little. "The timing of each enemy going up in flames *did* seem a bit…convenient."

Maria narrowed her eyes at both of them.

"Dragons are beasts," Zain argued. "They're not capable of that kind of intelligence."

"Oh, I don't know," Pelt muttered. "Rat-Slayer's a beast, and he scratched *you*." He flashed a mouthful of gold teeth. "That was intelligent."

Zain rolled his eyes at the boatswain. "Are we all calling the feral feline by that ridiculous name now?"

"Well, *I* don't enjoy being scratched," Pelt said.

Maria sighed, quickly losing patience. "I'll put it this way," she snarled. "If Em gets hurt because of *your* mistake, I will tear you apart, limb by limb."

Zain's dark gaze shifted toward her, and his bronze skin paled a shade. "Why would Em—"

Possibly because he *wasn't* being threatened by an enraged pirate captain, at the moment, Pelt actually understood. He straightened. "Em's up there?"

Zain frowned at Pelt. "Up where?" He cast a puzzled glance

toward the raging fires around them—just as a violet-scaled dragon flew past. His eyes widened. "Our surgeon is in the sky?"

Unlike Zain, Pelt didn't wait for clarification. He immediately turned and ran for the gun deck.

"Hey! I didn't even retract the order yet!" Zain called after Pelt. "I'm still acting captain, you know?"

"No, you're not," Maria assured him. She lowered her sword. "You're relieved of duty, quartermaster."

"Fine." Zain dusted off his green waistcoat, as if Maria's sword had soiled it somehow—more so than the blood-stains that were already on it. "Captain."

Henry—Maria's grey-haired helmsman, who'd barely acknowledged the near-murder taking place next to him—tipped his head. "Good day, Captain."

Maria's eyebrows rose. "If you say so, Henry."

Maria sheathed her sword and turned to survey the damage done to her ship.

Wood splintered outward from the hull, and puddles of blood seeped into the deck. Near the rail, sailors hoisted up one blood-soaked corpse after another and tossed them into the sea.

All dressed in blue waistcoats.

So far.

"How many times were we boarded?" Maria asked.

Zain followed her gaze to the pile of dead bodies. "Three."

Maria turned to face him. "Are any still aboard?"

"Not that we know of," he said.

"How many dead?" Maria asked.

Zain sighed, "Thirty or so of theirs. Four of ours."

Maria didn't enjoy hearing *any* of her sailors were dead, but those were good numbers—in the grand scheme of things. "Did you execute the prisoners?"

"Yes, Captain," Zain said. "No quarter given."

Maria nodded. "How many of ours are injured?"

"The last I heard from Fulke," Zain said, "twenty-seven." He glanced up at a dragon as it flew overhead. "They're in the hold, and many of them will die—if our surgeon doesn't come back to do her *real* job."

Maria leaned toward him. She held her thumb and forefinger close together, her nautical tattoos nearly touching. "You're *this* close to having my fist in your face."

Zain spread out his hands. "What did I do *this* time?"

The pounding of boots drew Maria's attention toward the main deck, and she dropped her hand to her side, as Pelt jogged toward them.

When the boatswain reached the quarterdeck, he folded forward, bracing his hands on his knees, as he panted for breath. "Helen called off the gunners, and she swears," he gasped, "they haven't blown up Em."

Maria stared blankly at him.

"She also wanted me to tell you," Pelt said, "that having a surgeon who can destroy an entire fleet on dragon-back is—and I quote—*'fucking badass.'*"

It was, wasn't it?

Maria's chest swelled with pride, unraveling a bit of the tension there. No one was questioning her decision to spare Em's life *now*, were they?

The thunderous beat of a dragon's wings grew louder, and the ship groaned, as the gust of wind unleashed by those wings hit the sails of the ship.

The *Wicked Fate* rocked, and Maria placed her hand on the top of her tricorn to hold it in place.

A dragon with intense, violet scales—the color of the night sky, during a hurricane—unleashed a stream of fire on the ship that sailed toward them.

Zain jumped back, as fire engulfed the sails.

Pelt straightened. "Holy hell."

Maria thrust a hand toward the destruction. "That doesn't look like helping to you?"

"It *looks* terrifying," Zain muttered.

As if to confirm his feelings, the flames funneled downward, and naval sailors began to scream. The scent of burning flesh drifted across the water.

The three of them watched the devastation in stunned silence.

"Captain?" Pelt said—without looking at her. "Do we even *need* cannons anymore?"

"Of course we need them," Zain scoffed. "We're not trusting that *witch* and her beasts with the safety of our ship."

Maria had heard one too many people refer to Em as a 'witch' today—in *that* tone. She spun toward him and grasped the lapels of his forest-green waistcoat.

She snatched him forward so forcefully that one of the brass buttons of his coat popped off.

Zain gasped.

"That *witch* and her beasts saved your life," Maria reminded him. "Show her some fucking respect."

"I'm quartermaster, and she's a surgeon," Zain said with a scoff. "I don't have to respect her."

Pelt tilted his head and averted his gaze—as if he knew Zain had chosen the wrong response.

Too bad Zain didn't know it.

"That's not how it works on my ship, and you know it," Maria growled. She leaned in closer. "You'll respect everyone in my service, or I'll make you."

Zain held his breath. "Yes, Captain."

Maria released him, and he staggered backward. She turned away and gripped the sword at her hip—until the raging fire within her quelled.

Zain straightened his waistcoat, and behind her back, he whispered to Pelt, "She's in a *mood* today."

Pelt chuckled. "I mean," he said, drawing out the word, "Catherine does have that effect on people."

Wasn't that the truth?

Maria released her sword and exhaled slowly.

"So, is she aware of the seaweed or not?" Zain hissed.

Out of the corner of her eye, she saw Pelt shrug.

Maria turned to face her whispering quartermaster and boatswain, and both of them straightened. "The *Wicked Fate* can't take any more fire," she admitted, "and Em has provided us the space we need to flee."

"Then, what are we waiting for?" Zain asked.

"Em," Pelt assumed. He turned to Maria. "She decided to stay with us, didn't she?"

Maria nodded.

Pelt grinned. "I knew it."

"Well, that's...good," Zain said, as if it pained him to admit it. "Our wounded will need her."

Maria lifted her eyebrows. What would it take for him to admit he didn't actually hate Em?

"But we can't wait for the remaining ships to close the distance," Zain pointed out. "We have to go *now*."

Maria hated it, but he was right.

She turned to gaze out at the fiery sea, searching for the green dragon Em had mounted on the island. Through the flickering flames, she caught glimpses of light blue scales and vivid, orange scales, but...no green.

Em was, no doubt, on the *other* side of the fire.

Catherine's side.

Jolts of panic coursed through Maria's veins, and her heart raced.

Why couldn't Em have ridden a different dragon?

Maria understood that the small dragon was the only one who could evade the ballista's bolts, but Em could've ridden a different one! She could've sent the small one into danger without her. She could've kept herself safe!

Safer, anyway.

But...Maria knew why she hadn't. It was why Maria had fallen in love with her.

Em was brave.

Brave, clever, and kind—even if she despised her own kindness.

"If those beasts really do obey her," Zain told Maria, "she can fly out and join us after the battle."

No.

Maria couldn't leave Em.

Even if her crew needed her to do it, even if Em had known she would, Maria couldn't. She just couldn't.

"Captain," Zain said, once again, "we have to go."

Pelt leaned against the taffrail and crossed his arms. "I suppose the question you have to ask yourself is," he said, "do you have faith in her?"

Maria glanced at him, and her decision was made.

"Prepare to wear ship!" she screamed out. "Hard to starboard!"

Zain repeated the orders, and across the ship, one pirate after another yelled out the instructions.

"Prepare to wear ship!"

"Man the braces!"

"Move!"

Sailors rushed to their places, climbing the rigging and loosening the lines, and Henry turned the wheel.

Maria cast one more glance at her boatswain—who'd watched it all with an amused, gold-toothed smirk.

"Thought so."

MARIA SQUEEZED THE WOODEN SPOKES OF THE WHEEL UNTIL ALL sensation left her fingers. Her heart pounded against her chest, and for the twelfth time in the last hour, Maria considered turning the *Wicked Fate* around and sailing directly into the naval flagship.

Em should've caught up with them by now.

Why the fuck hadn't she?

Had Em changed her mind?

Or…

No, Maria wouldn't consider the other possibility.

Em *had* survived the battle. Maria refused to believe otherwise.

"The lookout spotted something," Zain said.

Maria glanced at her quartermaster—and tried her best to conceal the hope that burst through her at the news. "Is it a dragon?"

Zain merely shrugged. "Or another ship," he muttered. "It's not like I can hear him from here."

Maria despised the nonchalance in his tone—even as she reminded herself that *she* should show the same nonchalance.

Maria reached for her spyglass, but the sight of Judith's short, brown hair stopped her.

Judith rushed up the wooden steps—with Pelt following not far behind. "It's Em!" she said with a bright smile. "Captain, they've spotted a dragon!"

Maria's tight grip on the wheel might've been the *only* thing that kept her from sinking to her knees.

Em had survived.

Em had survived, and she *hadn't* changed her mind.

Judith and Pelt stepped onto the quarterdeck.

A rush of relieved laughter spilled from Maria's lips. "Fuck."

So much for nonchalance.

But Judith's smile softened. "I know."

Of course she did. Judith always knew.

Zain looked up, squinting at a dark shape in the blue sky, and Maria followed his gaze, realizing she could see Em's dragon, now, too—though, at this distance, it could've been a bird as easily as a dragon.

A large bird.

A mountain-sized bird.

"She's not going to fly into our sails, is she?" Zain asked.

"The girl's smarter than all of us combined, Zain," Judith scoffed. "I think she knows not to fly into the sails."

"Illopian surgeons are smart," Zain said. "*She's* not Illopian."

Judith's smile sharpened, and she turned toward Maria. "Permission to kick him in the shin, Captain?"

"You've never asked permission for that before," Maria said, "nor have you needed it."

Zain threw out his arms. "Why is everyone so *violent* today?"

Pelt didn't point out the absurdity of that question in so many *words*, but the way he eyed the blood-stains on his own clothes said it all.

"Forgive me," Zain grumbled, "for being a little concerned about our already-damaged ship."

"He does bring up a good point—if you ignore most of it," Pelt said. Zain scowled at him, but he ignored that, too. "As fast as Em and that dragon are moving, they'll be here before we know it. How do you want us to retrieve her?"

Maria hadn't thought about that. The dragon obviously couldn't land on the ship, but she'd never asked Em if dragons could land in the ocean.

"Can she swim?" Judith asked.

That question evoked memories of Maria's last conversation with Em on Drakon Isle—when Em had guessed the secret Maria had kept from them. Another wave of guilt rolled through her.

Em had accepted the truth so easily—even though she'd had every reason not to—but Maria knew if anyone *else* on the ship found out, they'd mutiny.

Captain Maria Welles was merciless.

Cold, unrelenting, and merciless.

Anything less than that, and she wasn't fit for this line of work.

"She's an islander," Pelt said. "Can't all islanders swim?"

Zain pointed a finger at them. "Also, witches float!"

All three of them turned to stare at him, then.

"What?" he said. "Everyone knows that!"

Pelt leaned toward Judith and muttered, "I think he has more superstitious beliefs than he does coats."

Judith scrunched up her nose. "No. Not possible."

"How would *you* know?" Zain asked.

"Oh, it's a game we play," Pelt informed him. "Every time you buy a new one, I have to drink more of Judith's rum."

Maria grimaced at that. "Are you trying to die?"

Zain picked at the forest-green threads of his waistcoat. "I spend my gold wisely, and this is what I get for it?"

"Zain," Judith said with a sigh, "when are you going to realize the things we've heard about Em's kind weren't true?"

Zain looked up at her. "I have realized that. I can see Em's not evil, but she *is* strange." He leaned forward, as if to share a secret with them. "I've seen her talking to the ship cats! As if they're people!"

Even Maria laughed at that.

"We've *all* seen that, Zain," Judith said.

"I think she can swim," Maria told Pelt, "but just in case she can't, let's have some sailors nearby who can."

"That's four of us, Captain." Judith crossed her arms, and her torn, white shirt stretched tight over her chest. "There are four of us who can swim."

Oh.

"Take Fulke, then," Maria told them. "If nothing else, he can pick her up and *toss* her on the ship."

Pelt turned to leave. "Rope-ladder?"

"Yes," Maria said, "and tell them to be careful. I don't want her injured." Worry hammered against Maria's ribs. "Any worse than she might already be."

Pelt nodded once. "Aye, Captain."

The steps creaked as he descended them, and Maria glanced again at the dark shape in the sky. In the brief time they'd spent talking, the dragon's wings had consumed the distance between them.

Maria now saw the dragon's full shape—its spiked tail and massive wings—*and* the color of its scales.

Maria turned to Judith. "Did the lookout happen to mention what *color* the dragon was?"

"Black," Judith said. "Is that *not* Em's dragon?"

Maria gripped the wheel and tilted her head to the side, her own, wet curls tickling her neck. "No, she has a black one, too. It's just," she hesitated, "the black one can be a bit…intimidating."

Amusement sparkled in Judith's bright, blue eyes. "There are dragons you *don't* find intimidating?"

"I don't find any of them intimidating," Maria insisted. "I'm simply concerned that our *crew* might find this one," she paused again, her eyes widening at the memory of the massive creature, "terrifying."

Judith chuckled. "Of course, Captain."

Maria glared at the ship cook. "Go do your job. I haven't eaten all day!" Okay, so, maybe she'd eaten a few coconuts with Em that morning, but those didn't count. "I'm wasting away out here."

"Oh, yes," Judith teased, "you look it."

"Go!"

Maria squeezed the wooden spokes of the wheel, flexing the muscles in her forearms. The wind beat against their sails, rocking the ship, and Maria knew, now, it was no ordinary wind.

Some sailors moved away from the rail, while others rushed toward it. They pointed at the dragon, and murmurs of excitement spread from one side of the ship to the other.

The dragon opened its massive jaws and roared.

The sound sent some sailors running for their lives, while others only cheered louder.

The dragon swooped low, extending its giant, black wings over the water, and Em *finally* came into view.

She rode astride the mountain-sized dragon, as if it were no bigger than a horse, her shortened, black hair whipping across her face.

The crew whooped and cheered, and a thousand emotions flooded Maria with such intensity that she could barely breathe.

Em was safe.

Em was back.

Em was...*so* fucking hot.

Zain cleared his throat, and Maria reluctantly tore her gaze from her dragon-riding surgeon.

"Thought you might want to know," Zain said, "if you're done swooning, that is—" He nodded toward the wheel in front of Maria. "You let go of the wheel."

Maria's eyes widened, and she swiftly wrapped her fingers around the wooden spokes, catching the wheel that spun freely in front of her.

Maybe some of that rocking *hadn't* been the dragon, after all.

With a sullen glare, she said, "Captain Maria Welles does not fucking swoon."

Zain lifted a dark eyebrow. "I would hope not."

CHAPTER 7

A Surgeon

The ambush Emilia expected upon returning to the *Wicked Fate* wasn't the one she received.

She'd expected an impatient pirate captain, demanding to know what had taken Emilia so long.

Perhaps a bit of fear and hostility from the crew, even.

What Emilia received, instead, was…*squeezing*.

The bright orange braid that brushed Emilia's arm suggested that the perpetrator of the squeezing was Helen—though even *that* sight blurred after a few moments of oxygen deprivation.

"I knew you'd come back!" Helen squealed in her ear.

Emilia might've responded, if her lungs weren't collapsing beneath Helen's bone-shattering embrace. Emilia's feet left the deck, and she had no choice but to accept that this was how she'd die.

Crushed to death by the ridiculously huge biceps of their master gunner.

The crew pressed in around them, and a familiar voice interrupted Emilia's impending death.

"Would you hurry up, Helen?" Judith complained. "You're not the only one who wants a hug."

Ah, yes.

A hug.

That was what they called this painful experience.

"Oh, sorry." Helen set Emilia on the deck, and blood rushed back into her extremities. Intensity never fading, Helen clapped two gunpowdery hands around Emilia's face. "What you did with those dragons back there was…*awesome!*" she exclaimed. "Almost as awesome as when you punched Buchan!"

"Oh," Emilia said breathlessly. "Thank you, Helen."

Helen pressed an aggressive kiss to Emilia's forehead before releasing her, and then, a smaller, calmer woman shoved Helen out of the way.

Emilia smiled at the sight of the short-haired ship cook, who'd quickly become her closest friend. It hadn't even been a full day since Emilia had seen her last, but the sight still flooded her with affection.

Judith smiled and shook her head. "How dare you try to leave us?" She threw her tanned arms around Emilia's neck and pulled her close. Her cheek pressed against Emilia's jaw. "I knew you wouldn't be able to."

"You *and* Helen, apparently," Emilia said with a laugh. "Maybe someone could tell *me* next time?"

Hesitantly, Emilia lifted her gloved hand and rested it against Judith's slender shoulder blade. A strange warmth unfurled inside her chest, and Emilia decided she kind of liked hugs.

The ones that didn't kill her, anyway.

"You wouldn't have listened," Judith told her. "You're too stubborn. Both of you are."

Both.

As if summoned by Judith's mention of her, Maria pushed her way through the crowd, complaining all the while.

"Get out of the way."

"Where is she?"

"Don't you all have work to do?"

"What kind of fucking pirates are you?"

At the sound of Maria's voice, Judith pulled back, but she took hold of Emilia's shoulders, gripping them firmly. "Whatever the captain says to you," Judith whispered, "please, keep in mind that she's been a wreck for the last hour."

Emilia frowned.

A wreck?

Maria?

That seemed unlikely.

Judith stepped aside, and Maria strode toward Emilia, her leather boots thudding against the deck. Anger darkened Maria's large, brown eyes, and a slight flush burned beneath her brown skin.

Maria walked as if the deck itself had wronged her, each step heavy and deliberate—forceful enough to jostle the swords against her leather-clad thighs.

Every other crew member shrank away from her, but Emilia didn't budge—not even when Maria cornered her against the rail.

"What the fuck took you so long?"

Emilia suppressed a smile. She'd known those would be Maria's first words to her—after a battle that could've killed them both.

'Thank the gods we both survived' would've been too civil for Maria.

"I came as quickly as I could," Emilia assured her.

Maria narrowed her eyes at that. "You rode a dragon with a wingspan the size of a small continent, and *this* was the quickest you could come?"

Emilia lifted her eyebrows in amusement. "Nymeth is nowhere near as large as you seem to think she is."

Maria didn't smile. "Em."

"I came as quickly as I could," Emilia repeated.

It wasn't a lie.

She and Nymeth *had* left as soon as they could.

Emilia simply couldn't explain what had delayed them on Drakon Isle.

Not to Maria.

Maria stepped closer.

Her gaze slid over Emilia's curves with an aching slowness that Emilia could practically *feel*—on her skin, beneath the armor.

Maria tilted her head, damp, brown curls sliding out from

beneath her headscarf, and she exhaled slowly. "You," she murmured, "are killing me."

It didn't *sound* like an insult—even though she'd surely meant it as one.

Emilia offered a helpless shrug. "I'm…sorry?"

Maria reached out and grasped Emilia's wrist. She extended Emilia's arm—before Emilia could stop her—and examined the scattering of burns that stretched from the end of the leather glove to the bend of her elbow.

Her eyes darkened. "You said the armor would protect you from this."

"It did," Emilia assured her, "in all the places it covered."

Emilia pulled her arm back toward herself and swiftly pushed down her sleeve, covering her bandaged elbow—before Maria noticed *it*, too.

"Perhaps we should have a leather shirt made for you," Maria suggested, "to wear beneath the armor." Her gaze flicked downward. "Trousers, too."

Emilia looked up, blinking. "You'd do that?"

"I'd *pay* someone to do that," Maria corrected—as if the distinction were important. She waved a hand toward the glistening, red burns on Emilia's forearm. "And if it'll keep you from coming back to me with those all over you, then yes, of course I'd do it."

No one had ever worried about a few minor burns on Emilia's arms before.

It baffled Emilia that anyone would.

The sudden twitch of a smile at the corners of Maria's beautiful, full lips stunned Emilia so thoroughly that she forgot everything besides it.

"Em," Maria said slowly. "Why do you have gunpowder on your forehead?"

"Hmm?" Emilia forced her brain back into motion. "Oh," she said with a giggle. "Helen."

Maria lifted her hand and brushed a tattooed thumb against Emilia's cheek. "It's here, too."

Emilia's skin tingled beneath the gentle slide of Maria's thumb, and she longed to lean into Maria's touch, longed for more. "Of course it is."

Maria blinked and glanced around the crowded deck, as if she'd just remembered where they were. She dropped her hand.

The pirate captain glared at the first sailor who made eye-contact with her. "You can stand around later," she snapped. "We're being chased!"

The sailor fled from her presence as fast as his feet would take him.

Emilia's eyebrows lifted.

No wonder Judith had warned Emilia about Maria's temper. *Still…*

A wreck?

Surely, that part had been an exaggeration.

Maria's sharp gaze returned to Emilia. "Follow me."

Without waiting for Emilia's response, Maria spun on the heels of her boots and strode away from her.

Emilia rushed to catch up.

She might've thought Maria was taking her to the captain's quarters—where they could have a moment alone—had she been walking toward the stern of the ship, instead of the bow.

Any remaining pirates in Maria's path scattered, and when one man dared to stop and stare, Maria snarled at him just as viciously as the last.

Emilia's eyes grew ever wider, and when they passed a puddle of blood, she turned to look. "You didn't murder anyone while I was gone, did you?"

Maria threw an amused smirk over her shoulder. "What would you do if I had?"

Emilia shrugged. "I'd be…concerned?"

Maria snorted. "I considered murdering Zain quite a few times, but you'll be pleased to hear I resisted."

Emilia pressed a hand to her chest. "For an entire hour?" she gasped. "What an accomplishment!"

Maria chuckled. "Smart-ass." Her steps slowed, and some of the rage that had radiated from her slipped away. "The navy boarded the *Wicked Fate* three times. While we were on the island fighting, they were fighting here, too."

Emilia's smile faded. "Did—" Anxiety closed around her throat. "Did anyone die?"

"Only four of ours." Maria didn't look at her. "So far."

Emilia froze, horror bounding through her. "Only?"

How could she say it like that?

Maria stopped and turned toward her. "We're lucky to have survived at all, Em," she said cooly. "Without you and your dragons, we wouldn't have."

"I—I know," Emilia stammered. There had been a point when even *she'd* thought they wouldn't make it. "But captain, I can't heal someone who's already dead."

"No one asked you to," Maria said.

Emilia stared at her in disbelief.

Couldn't Maria act human for one moment?

Maria crossed her arms, the leather stretching over her strong shoulders. "I told you the day I hired you," she said. "Piracy is a dangerous profession."

"I know that," Emilia said defensively, "but you have a surgeon now." Pain and guilt whirled within her, and Emilia could no longer tell which had come from the present and which had come from the past. "Shouldn't that change things?"

"It has." Maria's tone was as unwavering as her stare. "Without you, people would've died during Catherine's *first* stunt. Without you, Henry would've died from whatever happened to him. Without you, minor cuts and splinters during our voyage might've become serious infections. Without you, surgeon," Maria said, "all two hundred people on this ship would've died in today's battle."

Emilia stared up at Maria, her eyes wide.

It was as if Maria had been keeping count of every single person Emilia had…

Oh.

She had.

Maria's gaze dropped to Emilia's left arm. Not the one she'd burned during dragon-flight, but the one she'd injured during battle

—the one they'd used to torture her. "You and I were the only ones meant for public execution. They would've executed the rest of them today—while I watched."

Emilia's stomach twisted at the suggestion. She couldn't understand the reasoning behind something so pointlessly cruel—until she followed Maria's gaze and…remembered.

They'd tortured Emilia to force a reaction from Maria.

Why *wouldn't* they have done the same to the crew?

"Four died. Two hundred lived," Maria said. "Did the second number even cross your mind?"

Emilia shook her head.

"I didn't think so." Maria's eyes flashed. "You don't get to count the dead, while refusing to count the living."

Unbearable weight pressed against Emilia's chest.

Maria didn't understand. There'd been no living to count!

They'd all died, and Emilia hadn't saved anyone!

Wait…no.

They weren't talking about the Drakon people.

Were they?

Emilia's mind whirled, and though she tried to sort her thoughts into the right order, they spun out, anyway.

An emotion flickered in Maria's eyes, then—the first one Emilia had seen the entire conversation—and Maria released a pained sigh. "You'll get there, love," she whispered. "It just takes time."

Emilia's stomach fluttered.

Perhaps Maria had understood, after all.

Maria's arms loosened, before falling to her sides, and distress twisted at her previously stoic face. She reached for Emilia, only to drop her hand again.

Since when was Captain Maria Welles indecisive?

"A few more steps, Em," Maria breathed. "Please."

Emilia's frown deepened.

Perhaps it was the tumultuous state of her own mind, at the moment, but Emilia just couldn't make sense of Maria's behavior—or her request, for that matter.

They were nowhere near the captain's quarters.

Nowhere near the surgeon's cabin.

They weren't even close to the hatch.

What difference could a few steps make?

"I said *'please,'* Em." Maria shifted her weight from one boot to the other, clenching and unclenching her fists. "I won't say it again."

She had, hadn't she?

Captain Maria Welles had said *'please.'*

On the main deck.

Where anyone could've heard her.

Whatever this was—it was important.

Emilia nodded. "Of course, Captain." She glanced in the direction they'd been walking before they'd stopped. "Just show me where you want me."

Maria's eyes widened. Like ice, the tension in Maria's muscles melted away, and for the first time since Emilia's return, she actually laughed. "That," she teased, "would be everywhere, Em."

Emilia returned her gaze to her captain. "What?"

Maria blinked innocently. "Nothing." A smirk twisted at one side of her bruised mouth. "Come on."

Maria led Emilia toward several rows of recently stacked barrels —and then behind them, toward the bulwark.

The long shadow of those barrels fell over them.

Maria squinted at the sunlit sails that towered above the barrels, as if searching for something, and Emilia let her gaze wander toward the sea.

She couldn't see Catherine's ship among the azure-blue waves, but she knew it was still out there. They'd barely avoided it in their flight here.

Emilia turned toward the captain. "How many wounded do we have?"

Maria never answered.

In two, quick steps, she closed the space between them and pushed Emilia against the bulwark. Maria closed one hand around the wooden rail behind Emilia and curled the other against Emilia's face.

Maria stifled Emilia's gasp of surprise with the hard press of her mouth. Every muscle in Emilia's body clenched in response to that kiss.

With Maria's lips pressed so hard against her own, Emilia felt every aspect of Maria's warm mouth—including the split in her lower lip and the swelling around it. Maria kissed as if it didn't hurt at all.

Maria kissed like a drowning sailor, desperate for the air from Emilia's mouth, desperate for the touch of her hand.

Her hand slid from Emilia's cheek to her neck, and her fingers curled behind Emilia's neck, drawing her closer.

Maria released the ship's rail, and with that hand, she grasped Emilia's hip and pulled her forward.

The increased pressure of Maria's waist against her own sent a rush of arousal through Emilia's body.

Goddess, what if someone walked up on them?

What was Maria *doing*?

Maria's mouth moved hungrily over Emilia's skin, kissing her jaw, then her neck. Heat washed over Emilia in waves, and when she moaned, Maria pressed her hips harder against Emilia's. "Fuck, Em. I can't—" she gasped. "I can't trust myself to touch you, when they might see." Her fingers slid upward, sinking into Emilia's hair, entangling with the soft, black strands. "I can't trust myself to stop."

Probably for the best, Emilia thought, *because I can't trust myself not to moan when you do touch me.*

Still, Emilia found it hard to believe that Maria would worry about losing control with *anyone*—much less Emilia.

Maria had never relinquished control of anything.

Certainly not herself.

Yet, at that very moment, Maria's fingers trembled against Emilia's skin, and her breath quickened.

The unusual sensation made Emilia pull back, worry stabbing at her chest. She looked up into Maria's widened, brown eyes. "Captain?"

A strange sort of agony twisted at Maria's scars.

Emilia pressed her hand to Maria's face, and to her surprise,

Maria closed her eyes and leaned into Emilia's touch. "Are you all right?"

Maria's jaw clenched beneath Emilia's fingers, and she gave a slow, subtle shake of her head.

Sympathy wrenched at Emilia's chest, leaving it raw and aching. *'She's been a wreck,'* Judith had said.

Maria opened her eyes, pain flashing within their dark depths, and she gripped a handful of Emilia's hair. "You've scared me," she said, "one too many times today."

Emilia noticed the slight tremor in Maria's lips, and a wave of guilt rolled inside her stomach.

Oh, Maria.

Maria leaned closer to her. "No more."

Emilia's heart pounded against her ribs.

Desperation made Maria's voice crack. "No more scares," she said. "Just…" Her teeth flashed. "Not today. Promise me."

Maria had arranged the words like a demand. Yet, it sounded like a plea.

"Captain," Emilia whispered.

Maria's earlier behavior came into sharp focus, then.

Emilia had seen it before—on the day of her trial, when Maria had snapped at everyone who'd come near Emilia. Except for Rat-Slayer, of course, who'd been her accomplice, essentially.

But Emilia hadn't understood what she was seeing, then.

Now, she did.

It was helplessness.

Some people ran and hid, like rabbits, when they were scared.

Maria became a viper, striking at anyone who came close, lest they see what lurked underneath.

Maria pressed her forehead against Emilia's, and her knees buckled. "Promise me, Em. Just for today."

Her weight pressed into Emilia, and Emilia held her steady.

Maria had only asked for a few more steps, Emilia realized, because *she* couldn't make it any further.

Maria couldn't have made it back to her quarters.

She couldn't have made it below deck.

Maria had needed to break, and she'd needed Emilia to catch the pieces.

"No more," Emilia promised.

A sigh of relief wrenched itself from Maria's lungs, and Maria crumbled against Emilia.

The rough wood of the bulwark and rail pressed into Emilia's back, but she only noticed Maria in that moment—the weight, warmth, and feel of her.

Emilia caressed Maria's face in a way that had always soothed her dragons. Slow and careful. She traced every scar, felt Maria's soft skin dip beneath her fingers, traced the swelling of her lips, felt the warm exhale of breath Maria released against her.

Slowly but surely, Maria relaxed against her. "Just for today. I just need to not feel," she gasped for breath, "*this* for a few hours."

Emilia didn't bother to point out that the promise Maria had asked her to make would change nothing, if the naval flagship caught up with them.

Maria likely already knew that, and…

And this was Captain Maria Welles.

The most powerful pirate in all of Aletharia.

The legendary villainess feared by all.

The strongest person Emilia had ever known.

Emilia had never seen her shatter before. Perhaps no one had.

And in that moment, Emilia wanted to do whatever it took to protect Maria from feeling this ever again.

Maria's dark eyelashes fluttered at Emilia's touch. Her breathing slowed against Emilia's wrist, and her fingers slid lazily through strands of Emilia's hair.

The sun eased lower in the sky, casting a fiery glow over Maria's radiant, brown skin, reflecting warmth in her large, brown eyes.

"We saw *her* ship—but not you," Maria whispered. "Do you understand what I—why I…"

She didn't finish, but Emilia understood.

Guilt twisted at her chest. She'd never meant to worry Maria. She hadn't even realized Maria *would* worry.

"Tell her."

Emilia nearly jumped when Nymeth's voice invaded her mind—with no warning whatsoever.

"I don't want you feeling guilty," Nymeth told her. *"I feel what she means to you. We all do. You can tell her the truth, if you want."*

As if to emphasize Nymeth's words, the pain in Emilia's arm increased threefold, the deep burn throbbing against its bandage.

"She wouldn't understand," Emilia thought.

"Then, explain it to her," Nymeth said, *"and if she still refuses to accept it, then perhaps she's not as wonderful as you believe her to be."*

Okay, Emilia had never called Maria wonderful.

Had she?

The dragons just interpreted Emilia's thoughts however they wanted.

Maria pulled back, searching Emilia's face. "Em?"

Emilia straightened—and just had to hope the *'I'm-talking-to-a-dragon-right-now'* didn't show on her face. "I'm sorry. I never meant to worry you."

Maria's brows creased. "Didn't you hear me earlier? You saved my crew, Em. Don't apologize for that." She withdrew her fingers from Emilia's hair and sighed, "I don't make sense to myself right now, either."

Emilia curled her fingers around Maria's wrist to stop her from withdrawing any further. "You make sense to me, Captain."

Maria's soft lips parted. For a moment, she said nothing. She only stared. Then, the moment passed, and she leaned closer to Emilia. "You better not say that too loudly. They'll start saying you're mad, too."

Emilia offered her a baffled smile. "Really? And why would they say that?"

"Oh, I don't know," Maria muttered. "I think I've heard the phrase 'tempestuous madwoman' whispered sixty times in the last hour."

With a stunned laugh, Emilia said, "What have you been *doing* to these people?"

"Nothing," Maria said, though Emilia doubted the truth of *that*. A smile twitched at one side of Maria's mouth. "Do you disagree with their assessment of me?"

"A little," Emilia admitted. "You're tempestuous, yes, but a madwoman?" She shook her head. "No."

The pleasant curve of Maria's lips deepened, and she leaned in to press those lips against Emilia's.

Maria curled one hand against Emilia's face, while the other drifted lower. She traced the dragon-scale armor that melded to Emilia's wide curves.

A rush of heat poured through Emilia in response, following every caress of Maria's warm hand.

"Gods," Maria growled against Emilia's mouth, "I love the way you look in this armor."

Emilia opened her eyes. "You—you do?"

Maria chuckled, the vibration low and lazy against Emilia's lips. That scarred eyebrow of hers inched upward, and a smirk twisted at her mouth. "If you really want to know, you can touch me and find out."

Emilia leaned back, her eyes wide.

She didn't mean—

Emilia's gaze dropped involuntarily to Maria's black, leather trousers, and a burst of laughter spilled from Maria's lips.

Emilia blushed.

Why did Maria enjoy doing this to her?

"This is the main deck," Emilia hissed, "in case you've forgotten." With the way Maria had kissed her, she very well *might* have.

"I haven't," Maria assured her. "No one can see us. I was *very* careful."

Emilia didn't doubt that, but she still wasn't going to slip her hand down Maria's trousers in broad daylight.

Even if part of her *did* want to know if Maria could actually be...wet—with such little provocation.

Even if that same part of her would love to taste the wetness on her fingers afterward.

Oh, goddess.

A terrible part of her.

Ridiculous part of her!

A part of her that should *never* be indulged.

Almost as if she could see the battle taking place in Emilia's mind, Maria let out another peal of laughter.

"Stop that," Emilia grumbled. "I don't know why you keep laughing. Nothing funny has happened."

Maria *didn't* stop, but she did lean forward and capture Emilia's lips in another, deep kiss.

Emilia melted against her.

"Captain?"

Emilia jerked back in alarm, accidentally slamming her lower back against the bulwark in the process.

Maria's hands tightened around Emilia's hips. "Careful, love."

"Captain!" Zain said again, his voice drifting closer. He yelled at someone nearby, "Have you seen her?"

Maria groaned and gave Emilia a pleading look. "I can't take it anymore! You have to let me kill him!"

"I have to *let* you?" Emilia said with a laugh. "Since when do I have power over Captain Maria Welles?"

"Always," Maria said—without a trace of humor. "Why do you think I tried so hard to hide it?"

Emilia's mouth fell open. A multitude of questions whirled in her mind, but Emilia no longer remembered how to form words.

Or *breathe*, for that matter.

Zain continued to yell, "Captain!"

Maria released Emilia's waist and stepped back. Her gaze darted toward Emilia's burns one last time—before she turned and strode out of the shadows.

"There you are!"

"Yes," Maria said. "Now, what the fuck do you want?"

Emilia straightened her dragon-scale cuirass and scabbard. She combed her fingers through her thick hair, hoping Zain would attribute any tangles to flying, instead of Maria.

Then, she, too, emerged from the stacks of barrels.

Zain's gaze darted toward her. "Surgeon," he said in a sort of curt greeting—before returning his attention to Maria. "You're needed at the helm."

Maria glanced Emilia's way, too, but her large, brown eyes held significantly more warmth than Zain's had. "I left you for one moment, Zain. You can't hold the wheel for one fucking moment?"

"I could," Zain informed her, "if I thought holding the wheel was all we needed to do."

"It *is* all we need to do." Maria crossed her arms, muscles flexing beneath her shirt. "I told you to stay on course. How much simpler can I make it?"

"We're on a course to evade a naval ship that is no longer chasing us," Zain countered. He tilted his chin, his long, black hair brushing the collar of his green waistcoat. "How much simpler can *I* make it?"

Maria's brows furrowed. "What?"

"She turned," Zain said.

Maria's arms dropped to her sides, and she stared at nothing in particular. "Why would she do that?"

"Why don't you tell me?" Zain snarled. He stepped closer and lowered his voice. "Since you always seem to know more about Catherine than you let on."

Maria's gaze cut toward him.

Oh, shit. Maria was right. Zain *did* suspect something.

Emilia shifted forward, preparing to defend her captain if the need arose, but Maria barely reacted.

She lifted her chin, and her voice cooled several degrees. "I don't care enough about what you think of me, *quartermaster*," Maria sneered, "to ask questions I already know the answer to."

Zain narrowed his eyes at that. "As I said, Captain," he repeated, "you're needed at the helm."

Maria brushed past him. She took a few steps toward the quarterdeck and then stopped, as if she'd just remembered something.

Maria turned back toward Emilia. "Twenty-seven."

Emilia frowned at the seemingly random number.

"You asked how many wounded we had," Maria said, reminding Emilia of the question she'd already forgotten. "It's twenty-seven."

"Oh," Emilia said, blinking.

Maria pointed a tattooed finger at Emilia. "And…no more."

"No more," Emilia assured her, "Captain."

Maria didn't let a shred of the emotion reach her face, but the muscles in her shoulders relaxed. Zain moved past her, and Maria waited until he could no longer see her to mouth two words to Emilia.

"Thank you."

Emilia offered her a gentle smile, and Maria's dark gaze softened at the sight of it.

Maria turned and followed Zain.

With her opposite hand, Emilia touched her bandaged elbow—both grateful that Maria hadn't noticed it and regretful at having hidden it from her.

Maria would see it eventually, and she'd react just as strongly as she had when she'd seen the first one.

It was only a matter of time.

With that many wounded, Emilia assumed they would've taken them to the hold. The hold wasn't the most sanitary place to perform surgeries, but it was the only one large enough for that many people.

Emilia had performed her surgeries there during the last battle.

She approached the hatch, where she'd venture below deck, but she slowed when she noticed a familiar, slender form perched on the coaming around the hatch.

Judith sat, hunched forward on the raised wood, with her hands clasped between her knees. She'd rolled up the sleeves of her once-white shirt, hiding a few—but not all—of the blood-stains, and glistening beads of sweat slid down her slender neck and arms.

Judith was small, compared to Helen, and harmless, compared

to Maria. Yet, she'd clearly done a bit of fighting herself today—if the blood-stains on her clothes were any indication.

During the last battle with a naval ship, Judith had remained below deck, caring for the wounded alongside Emilia, but no one had boarded the *Wicked Fate* during *that* battle.

Unless you counted Catherine—and her brief appearance.

Her *show*, as Maria had called it.

Emilia wondered if anyone had stayed with the wounded this time—or if they'd left them alone to scream and despair.

The thought made Emilia's chest ache.

"You were waiting for me?" Emilia guessed.

Judith spread out her hands. "Who else?"

Emilia stopped near the hatch. "How did it go today," she asked, "without my assistance?"

With a wave of her hand, Judith said, "Ah, well…"

Two pirates passed behind Judith, discussing some buttons one of them had sliced from the uniform of a dead naval sailor, and Judith peered over her shoulder at them.

The tallest pirate turned a gold button over in his calloused palm. "Do you think it's real gold?"

"Don't know," the other pirate said, rising on his toes to look at it, "but if you'd just let me see it—"

"Hey!" The taller one raised his arm, just in time to avoid the swipe of the other's hand. "Get your own!"

Judith returned her attention to Emilia, arching her eyebrows, as if to say, *'That's a fight waiting to happen.'*

Emilia couldn't help but laugh.

Judith jumped to her feet and continued, as if she'd never stopped, "Well, you know, we skipped the afternoon meal because we were too busy trying not to piss ourselves—or die." She tacked on dying, as if it were an inconsequential afterthought. "I assume you and the captain did the same?"

Emilia couldn't even remember which fight they were fighting at that time. Was that Ingelby?

Regardless, Emilia knew they hadn't stopped to eat. "Something like that."

Judith nodded. "I figured. Captain's been begging for apples even more than usual." She rolled her eyes at that. "But if you get to feeling a bit woozy, we can grab you some hardtack on the way."

Emilia appreciated Judith's thoughtfulness, of course, but she was far too anxious to eat. "I'd rather check on the wounded first."

"Suit yourself," Judith said. She adjusted the pistol at her hip. "The evening meal should be ready soon." She leaned in close to Emilia, as if this next part were a secret. "I chose the simplest recipe I knew—one even the *dullest* sailor could follow. Then, I told Pelt to send me some deckhands he didn't need." She grinned. "You know, I kind of *like* telling people what to do?"

Emilia widened her eyes. "I've never noticed."

Judith snorted at her sarcasm. "Oh, you love helping me, and you know it!"

A sincere smile pulled at Emilia's lips. "I really do."

On the days Emilia had too much of her own work to do to assist Judith with hers, she always missed Judith's presence—along with Judith's ability to fill every silence with words.

With a deep smile of her own, Judith said, "I'll have to slip out now and then to check on the food, but I'm yours for the next few hours, at least."

"Thank you," Emilia said.

The ship rocked over the waves, and a thin spray of water washed over the deck.

Despite Judith's many years of experience, even *she* nearly lost her balance. With a sigh, she swung open the hatch. "Always nice to descend a few ladders when we're moving at *this* speed."

Emilia followed. "So…twenty-seven wounded?"

A knowing smile tilted at the corners of Judith's lips. "Oh! So, she *did* manage to answer your question, then? Even with her tongue down your throat?"

Emilia's face paled. "W-what?"

Judith braced one foot on the corner of the hatch and tilted her head, as she waited for Emilia to process the fact that she'd—*oh, goddess*—she'd seen!

Between the coolness of shock and the heat of humiliation,

Emilia's body couldn't decide whether it wanted to burn or freeze. "The captain said—" she stammered. "She said no one could see!"

Judith shook her head, as if Emilia had fallen for the oldest trick in the book. "The captain's overconfident, mate. If you ever think there's a moment when she's not being overconfident, you're wrong. She is." Her smile faltered, as she noticed something in Emilia's expression. "Hey! It's just a bit of teasing. Gods, Em, I've seen you with your trousers unfastened after she had you tied up."

Really?

Did Judith really have to bring that up now?

Of all times?

"I didn't think you'd be upset over some *kissing*," Judith laughed. "No one else saw you! I promise."

Emilia looked up.

Kissing

Judith had only seen them kissing.

She hadn't seen Maria break down.

Or if she had, she was pretending she hadn't—likely for Maria's sake.

"I only saw because I was looking for you," Judith assured her. "Besides, it's not like anyone on this ship would've been shocked by the sight of our captain making out with a pretty girl." She rolled her eyes. "She was sneaking off to do that before I even knew *how*."

Emilia didn't think she counted as a '*pretty girl*,' but she was too concerned about Maria's privacy, at the moment, to argue.

Maria trusted Judith, obviously—more than she'd ever trusted anyone—but that didn't mean Emilia felt any less protective over the moment they'd shared.

Judith stepped down onto the ladder. "I was so bad at *my* first kiss that the girl never spoke to me again."

Emilia blinked—and then frowned at Judith.

"The captain laughed for nearly an hour when I told her," Judith continued, "before telling me what I'd *probably* done wrong." She shrugged her slender shoulders. "I suppose she was right because the next girl stayed with me for a whole two months."

Emilia tried not to laugh—tried and *failed*. "But you've had longer relationships since then, haven't you?"

"Not really, no," Judith called back.

Ah, poor Judith.

"Unless you count Helen," Judith added, "which I don't."

Then again, Emilia supposed having *no* long-term lovers was better than having one who'd only used you to slaughter your people.

As Emilia followed Judith down, the sunlight streaming through the porthole below deck fell upon Emilia's burned wrist.

Judith hesitated on the ladder, peering up at her burns. "Don't you need to, er, swish that away first?"

Emilia glanced down at the ship cook. "Judith, when have I ever *swished*, while using magic?"

"I don't know how it works," Judith said defensively. "For all I know, you strip naked and dance in the moonlight."

Emilia's brows furrowed. "I do not."

Judith continued down the ladder. "Are you sure?" she said skeptically. "Because I've heard rumors."

"Not about me," Emilia assured her. "*If* any witches have *ever* performed such a ritual," she added, "they were your Illopian village witches, and it was only to get more gold from their patrons."

Judith cocked her head at that. "Would've worked on me," she admitted, "if they were pretty. Are they pretty?"

Emilia's frown deepened. "I've...never met one."

"Neither have I." Judith hopped from the ladder with a soft *thump*. "But wouldn't they look a bit like you?"

Emilia climbed down the last few steps. "Why would they?"

"Well, the village witches are related to you, aren't they?" Judith said. "That's what the captain said."

Either Maria had misunderstood Emilia, or Judith had misunderstood Maria.

Emilia's shoes hit the floorboards, and she turned to face Judith. "They inherited a bit of dragon magic from *a* Drakon sorcerer. Not necessarily one that looked like me."

"Oh," Judith said. "You don't all look the same?"

Emilia rolled her eyes. "Oh, for Aletha's sake."

A sailor snored loudly in one of the nearby hammocks. Usually, the sailors on night watch would be sound asleep, still, but today, only a few of them occupied the hammocks on the lower deck.

The few with the remarkable ability to fall asleep after a battle, apparently.

Judith leaned against one of the support beams. "Other islanders share physical traits, don't they?"

"Well, yes," Emilia admitted, "but they still don't look the *same*." When one sailor grunted, as if he were waking up, Emilia lowered her voice. "The Drakon people, though, aren't—*weren't*—like that. Contrary to your Illopian stories, we weren't all born from the same woman who had sex with a dragon."

"See, I always thought that story sounded strange," Judith said, waving a finger, "because how would she even *do* it?" She widened her eyes at the thought.

"She wouldn't," Emilia said. "They tell you that story so you'll think we're barbaric and inhuman."

"I never thought you were barbaric or inhuman," Judith assured her.

Emilia offered her an affectionate smile. "I know."

Judith motioned toward the next ladder with a tilt of her head, and the two of them resumed their walk.

"The original families of the Drakon tribe were born of magic, not body," Emilia explained. "Even to this day, we all look different —different hair colors, different skin tones, different body shape. The only thing we all have in common is the eye color."

Judith spun toward her. She pointed two fingers at Emilia's eyes. "You all have those weird green eyes?"

"Had," Emilia corrected, "but yes. They're a sign of dragon magic."

Excitement sparked in Judith's bright blue eyes for a moment— before the reminder of what happened to Emilia's people dimmed them. "Oh, gods, this is an insensitive topic, isn't it?" She touched Emilia's arm. "Shit, Em! I didn't even think about it!"

"It's all right," Emilia said. "I'd rather you ask than keep believing their lies."

Judith reluctantly released Emilia's shoulder. She stepped down onto the next ladder, and Emilia followed.

They were a few steps down, when Judith called up, "Is that why some Illopians used to kill babies with green eyes?"

Emilia's shoe missed the next wooden rung, and she nearly fell. "*What?*"

With another soft *thump*, Judith hopped down onto the next level. "Oh, don't worry!" she said. "I haven't heard of babies being born with green eyes in years."

"Judith, that's—that's not a good thing." Emilia descended the last few rungs. "You don't realize what that means?"

Judith held the ladder, while Emilia climbed off of it. "Of course! The witch babies realized they were in danger and changed their eye color."

"Try again," Emilia said.

Judith leaned against the ladder, next to Emilia. "Oh, you doubt it," she said with a playful grin, "but I've seen it." At Emilia's skeptical look, Judith said, "My aunt had this baby with blonde hair, right? And my aunt and uncle were both dark-haired. So, my uncle gets suspicious and threatens to throw out the baby—you know, because he thinks it's a bastard..."

Emilia's eyes widened—again. "He did what?"

"Well, the baby must've heard him," Judith continued, "because over the next ten years, his blonde hair turned brown."

Emilia shook her head—and then brushed back the black strands of hair that fell around her face when she did. "A child's hair gradually darkened over a span of *ten* years, and you think it's magic?"

Judith leaned toward her. "You don't think so?"

"No!" Emilia said with a laugh. "Judith, your kingdom fears magic so much they try to eradicate it. Yet, you all still see it in everything—*because* you fear it. That's paranoia!"

Something rustled behind a nearby barrel, and Emilia rose on her toes to peer over it.

Judith pushed away from the ladder, before following Emilia's gaze. "Probably a rat."

A slow smile spread across Emilia's face. "Oh, I don't think so." She stepped forward and sank to her knees on the floorboards. "Come here, little Winter."

A tiny, white ball of fur sprinted out from behind the barrels and leapt up into Emilia's burned arms.

Judith shook her head in wonder. "How did you know which one it was?"

Emilia scooped up the little, white cat and climbed to her feet. "She's the smallest."

Winter's claws sent jolts of pain lashing through Emilia's injured arms, but she couldn't bring herself to care. After all, for a few moments today, Emilia had feared she'd never see the ship cats again.

Judith watched Emilia stroke the cat's ears with an amused smile. "Paranoia, huh?" she said. "Like when Zain runs from the cats?"

Emilia laughed at the comparison. "Sure."

"All right," Judith said with a nod. "I'll work on it."

Emilia cast a surprised glance at the ship cook, before a fond smile curved deeply at her lips.

Judith reached out a hesitant hand toward the cat. "Do you think she'll let me?"

Emilia turned the kitten in her arms, ensuring at least one fluffy, white ear was available for petting. "It doesn't hurt to try."

Judith scoffed, "Says the only person she's never *clawed*."

Emilia laughed at that.

Winter hissed at Judith, but she relaxed when Emilia leaned in and whispered, "She's our friend."

Judith's bright blue eyes widened the moment she managed to touch the cat's ear *without* losing a finger. "One day, you'll tell me how you control these things."

"I don't control them!" Emilia said.

Judith squinted suspiciously at Emilia, clearly not taking her word for it. She continued to stroke the cat's ear. "She's sort of soft when she's not scratching people."

"Pretty sure she's soft either way," Emilia muttered.

Judith's hand fell from the cat, her thin fingers brushing Emilia's burned arm. She stepped closer to examine the deep red burns. "Surely you'd be in less pain, if you'd healed those *before* you picked her up?"

"I'm fine." Emilia ran her fingers along the cat's neck, and Winter purred happily. "I'll apply a bit of aloe before I perform any surgeries."

Judith narrowed her eyes at that. "Em," she said slowly, "what are you not telling me?"

"Nothing," Emilia lied.

Judith's fierce glare turned into a frown, as Winter pressed her tiny head against Judith's hand, urging her to resume the petting. "During the last battle, you said focus was an important aspect of your magic," she pointed out. "Personally, *I've* never been able to focus well, while in pain…"

Emilia didn't meet her gaze. "Believe it or not, I have a lot of experience with focusing while in pain."

A hint of sympathy flashed across Judith's face, and her resolve faltered. "Because of the imprisonment?"

"Because of a lot more than that," Emilia mumbled.

Concern twisted at Judith's brows, and though Emilia could see Judith wanted to ask more, she was grateful when Judith chose not to.

"You treated a lot of wounded sailors during our last battle…" Judith began.

A lot of wounded for a *show*—if Maria's assumptions were correct.

At least none of theirs had *died*. Catherine had let an entire ship of her own sailors die—for a manipulative tactic.

What information was worth that?

Maria killed with no discretion sometimes. Emilia killed with… perhaps too *much* discretion.

But how did someone reach a level of apathy where *that* sounded like a fair trade?

By slaughtering an entire people after living amongst them for months, Emilia supposed.

Oblivious to Emilia's distraction, Judith continued, "But some of these wounds are gruesome, Em."

"Oh, I prefer the gruesome wounds in some ways," Emilia said. "It's harder to miss things with them."

Judith scowled at her. "It's at times like these, Em, that it becomes abundantly clear why the captain likes you," she said, as if it were an insult. "Some of us prefer to *not* see blood, you know?"

Good thing she hadn't seen Ingelby, then.

Or some of the ones Emilia had killed.

"Point is," Judith said with a roll of her eyes, "you'll need to focus. Tell me why you won't heal yourself."

Emilia's chest tightened. "If I could heal myself, I would."

"Well, why can't you?" Judith asked. "You've done it before, haven't you? After the fight with Buchan?"

Yes, but Emilia had an almost untouched reserve of magic, then —and time for the tincture to set. "I only need focus if I intend to use magic, and I don't."

That wasn't totally true. Surgery required concentration, too, of course, but…not quite as much.

"Why not?" Judith said impatiently.

Worry twisted at Emilia's chest. Admitting her limits—even if all sorcerers had the same ones—felt like admitting weakness, and the prospect unsettled her.

Maria knew, but did Emilia have to tell Judith, too?

Of course she did. If there was a chance Emilia wouldn't be able to save everyone, Judith needed to know.

With a sigh, Emilia explained, "People who don't understand magic tend to assume it's an unlimited resource, but it isn't. Only the gods create from nothing. The rest of us have to *take* from somewhere." She winced a little when Winter kneaded her burned arm. "Sorcerers wield magic. We don't create it."

Judith nodded. "That's why you relied more on surgical methods when there were so many wounded."

Winter must've noticed Emilia's pain because she moved, before kneading again. The small, white cat climbed up Emilia's body and nestled herself into Emilia's breasts, as if they were an armor-clad bed.

Emilia sighed with relief. "Yes."

"I assumed it was only because you were hiding your magic," Judith told her.

"Well, there was that, too," Emilia admitted.

"What are your limits, then," Judith asked, "and how do you know when you've reached them?"

"I can feel it," Emilia breathed. "I feel like I become *less*—like I've severed my connection to things." Her chest ached, as the memories of those months on the run resurfaced. "After a long time of that feeling, I start to forget I was ever anything else—anything more."

Judith's brows furrowed. "A long time?"

Emilia blinked, as she remembered who she was talking to—and *what* she was talking about. "My magic doesn't just exist for a specific amount of time and then vanish. It depletes over time, based on what I do with it and how much I need it. A healer can use more healing magic than they can anything else, but the magic is still finite. It replenishes under certain conditions, but it's not something I can control."

"It's like food, then!" Judith realized. "I can cook, if I have ingredients. If I don't, I can't—until we make port, of course, and replenish our foodstuffs."

Emilia's eyebrows lifted at the simple explanation. "Well, yes."

Judith nodded—with more enthusiasm, now. "So, you used magic on the island to save either the captain or yourself—or both —and you ran out of ingredients."

Emilia laughed at the analogy. "Essentially."

Judith narrowed her eyes, suddenly, and flicked her fingers against Emilia's shoulder. "And this is what has you looking all ashamed, as if you've failed us, somehow?"

Emilia cradled the cat close and stepped back, wary of Judith's apparent anger. "Umm, maybe?"

Judith rolled her eyes. "Em, you treated half the injuries last time without magic! Magic might've made you a sorcerer, but it didn't make you a great surgeon. You did that!"

A cool wave of shock washed over Emilia. "What?"

"Oh, you silly girl!" Judith scolded. "Did you not know that?"

Emilia would've said *no*, if she hadn't thought Judith might throw something at her for it. Then, Winter would likely scratch Judith, and Emilia would have a whole mess on her hands.

So, she opted for staring in shock, instead. "But what if surgery isn't enough to stabilize them? What if they die before I can replenish my magic?"

Judith merely shrugged. "Then, they would've died with a human surgeon, too."

"But I'm not human!" Emilia tried to explain. "I'm supposed to be able to do *more*."

"According to whom?" Judith challenged. "Yourself?"

Emilia sputtered, "Uhh, w-well…"

"Gods, Em," Judith said with a shake of her head. "Who told you there was something wrong with having limits? Who told you it wasn't okay to need time to recover?"

Her mother.

Emilia's mother had told her that.

"It just means you're normal, Em," Judith told her. "You're a normal person." She cocked her head and scrunched up her nose in that adorable way of hers. "I mean…you're also a dragon-riding witch who can win entire battles by herself, but that's all right!"

Emilia frowned.

Judith spread out her arms and shrugged. "I'm…someone who wants all pretty girls to like me. Even the ones I can't possibly please." She winced. "*Especially* the ones I can't possibly please!" In a long exhale, she added, "Because she's so fucking pretty! And hell, maybe next time will be different!"

Emilia squinted suspiciously at the ship cook. "Are we talking about Sarah again?"

"The point is," Judith said, "we all have quirks!"

Oh. *That* was the point.

"And my quirk is dragons," Emilia guessed, "*not* my inability to use magic, at the moment."

"Now, you're getting it!" Judith praised.

Emilia laughed at her excitement. "We should get down to the hold," she reminded Judith. "Winter says Rat-Slayer's waiting for me."

"I take it back," Judith muttered. "You have way more than one quirk."

CHAPTER 8

An Interrogation

Emilia circled the damp, open space—with a large, silver-and-white tabby prowling behind her and a small, white kitten perched on her shoulder.

She'd tried to tell the ship cats she wasn't going anywhere, but after her brief departure, they were, understandably, unwilling to let her out of their sight.

They'd relax, eventually.

Until then, Emilia appreciated their company.

She stopped next to each hammock, preparing some of the pirates for surgery and determining which ones needed treatment first.

A few of the conscious sailors eyed the ship cats warily. Emilia didn't understand why—until one of them finally spoke up.

Emilia had just narrowly avoided tripping over a small, grey cat, who'd scurried out in front of her mid-step, when the sailor in the hammock next to her said, "Those vicious, little things have been down here all day." He shuddered in horror. "They clawed everyone who tried to remove them."

Emilia suppressed a laugh. She'd never get over how terrified these violent pirates were of a few precious, little cats.

Who kept their ship free of *rats*, mind you!

Okay. Not so little, in Rat-Slayer's case.

"They're assisting me," Emilia assured him. "They're not here to eat you."

"So you say," he said with a scowl.

Judith had elected to wait—with her bottle of rum—by the table they'd brought down for surgery.

But when Emilia returned to that table, now, she found two people waiting, instead of one.

A slender, lean-muscled sailor—who didn't *appear* to be injured—sat on the table, and Judith stood in front of him. She leaned toward the sailor, frantically whispering something to him, and when he grinned in response, the flash of gold Emilia saw, even from a distance, told Emilia who he was.

"Hi, Pelt."

At the sound of Emilia's voice, the whispering ceased, and two pairs of eyes slid Emilia's way.

If there was one thing Emilia had learned as the outcast of her own island, it was that when people reacted like *that* to the sound of her voice, it was never a good sign.

Perhaps Emilia had been foolish to assume Judith was above this kind of thing. No one else had ever been.

"Em!" Pelt said with a convincing amount of enthusiasm. He leaned forward on the table, gripping its wooden edge. "Good to have you back, surgeon."

Emilia didn't know whether to believe him or not. People who reacted like that to Emilia's approach often said things they didn't mean afterward.

Emilia might not have understood the reasoning behind it, but that didn't mean she hadn't learned to recognize it. "I'm happy to still have a place here."

Emilia meant that. She might've stumbled into some kind of deceptive social practice, but that didn't mean *Emilia* had to deceive anyone, did it?

Goddess, she hoped not.

Emilia was no good at that.

Pelt snorted, "You're a surgeon, Em. You'll always have a place here."

Emilia turned to Judith, only for Judith to immediately shift her gaze upward—toward the leaking boards above her head.

Despite her evasiveness, the distress still showed in Judith's face —in the twist of her mouth and brows.

Judith was the most laid-back person Emilia had ever met. If something worried her, it worried Emilia, too.

Rat-Slayer circled around Emilia, placing himself between her and the boatswain, before plopping his heavy butt on Emilia's shoes.

Winter dug her claws deeper into Emilia's shoulder.

Pelt cast a puzzled look at the protective, silver-and-white tabby at Emilia's feet and then up at the small, white cat on her shoulder. "Do you always perform surgeries with the cats...*on* you?"

"Not always," Emilia said. "They're a little clingy today, but I see no reason *not* to indulge them."

Rat-Slayer tipped his head back and meowed at her.

"It was an observation," Emilia assured the cat, "not a complaint. I know. You have your reasons."

Pelt glanced from the irate cat to Emilia—and then to Judith, who just shrugged and sipped her rum.

Emilia reached up to rub the furry, white ear of the cat on her shoulder. "Are you injured, Pelt?"

His seemingly warm, hazel eyes shifted toward her. Pelt rocked back on the table, and the flickering candlelight fell over the vicious scar on his cheek. "If I'm not," he said, "are you going to ask me to leave?"

"No," Emilia assured him. "I just think you should tell me before I cut you open."

His eyes flared wide. Then, Pelt snorted and burst into laughter. He held up both hands. "Not injured."

"Good," Emilia said. She turned her gaze toward Judith. "So, what is this about, then?"

"Can't I just stop by to say hi?" Pelt complained. "You let the ship cats do it!"

Emilia kept her attention on Judith. Surely, Judith, of all people, would tell her the truth—if Emilia asked directly.

Judith winced. "I tried to convince him to wait and do this another day," she said, "when there weren't injured sailors who needed you."

Emilia would also prefer to focus on the injured—over whatever *this* was.

Pelt dropped his arms—and all pretense with them. "I don't mind leaving it for another day," he told Judith, "but Zain won't be as amendable." He lifted a thin eyebrow. "Would you rather her be blindsided by him or me?"

Emilia preferred not to be blindsided by anyone, but apparently, her opinion didn't factor into this.

"Fine," Judith told him, "but be quick about it."

Anxiety fluttered in Emilia's stomach.

What had Judith just given him permission to do?

Pelt's attention swung back toward Emilia, and he leaned forward. "What happened out there today?"

No.

He couldn't be serious.

There were people suffering right now, and Pelt wanted her to participate in idle conversation?

"The same thing that happened here, I assume," Emilia said. "We fought—multiple times—and won."

Emilia didn't mention that Maria had fallen into Catherine's trap—and they'd nearly been recaptured.

Those secrets belonged to Maria and herself.

"Who did you fight?" Pelt asked.

"The Royal Navy, obviously." Emilia narrowed her eyes at the boatswain—whom she'd never known to act so absurdly before. "If you're just going to ask questions you already know the answers to, I'd prefer to get started on my surgeries."

Pelt ignored the complaint. "Was she surprised?"

Emilia froze. "What?"

Pelt leaned forward, gold teeth flashing within his mouth. "The captain," he clarified. "Was the captain surprised when she saw Catherine *alive*?"

Oh.

Oh, no.

Emilia forced a small shrug—one that made Winter meow in protest. "I…don't know."

The smug snort Pelt gave in response made Emilia's stomach churn. He turned to Judith. "Do you see now," he asked, "why I wanted to talk to her first?"

Judith gave a single nod.

What was happening right now?

Pelt hopped off the table, advancing toward Emilia so suddenly that Rat-Slayer stood and hissed.

Pelt stopped. "Let's try this again, shall we?"

Shit.

Lie, lie, lie.

But Emilia couldn't lie.

Not well, anyway.

"On the island, when Catherine showed herself," Pelt repeated, "did the captain look surprised?"

'Look.'

Not 'sound.' Not 'seem.'

'Look.'

Emilia didn't need to lie.

"I don't know," she repeated. "We were facing away from each other, at the time. I couldn't see her."

Pelt squinted suspiciously at that. "Why would you face away from each other?"

"We were surrounded," Emilia explained. "We had to watch each other's back."

"The captain trusts you at her back?" Pelt said.

Emilia's brows furrowed. "Why wouldn't she?"

As opposed to a bunch of naval sailors, Emilia supposed Maria would've trusted *anyone* at her back.

Pelt cast a questioning look in Judith's direction.

Judith shrugged. "Why would she lie about that?"

He quirked his head slightly, before returning his attention to Emilia. "Were *you* surprised?"

Emilia didn't bother to lie. "No."

Pelt's eyes narrowed. "Because you knew," he said with a nod, "how she escaped?"

"No," Emilia said honestly, "because she always survives." Pure hatred cooled her tone. "I won't believe Catherine's dead until I've seen her bones."

Pelt actually flinched at that. "Oh."

An injured sailor in a nearby hammock groaned in pain, and Emilia cast a concerned glance in his direction. "If that's all, I should really get back to—"

"It's not all," Pelt interrupted. "*Do* you know how she escaped, surgeon?"

Emilia offered an impatient shrug. "One can only assume she swam."

Judith drank deeply from her bottle of rum.

"Quite a distance, don't you think?" Pelt said.

Emilia fixed her gaze on the bulkhead behind Pelt, resisting the urge to lower her gaze to the floor. "How could I know that," she sighed, "without also knowing where—or how—she'd hidden her fleet?"

Pelt blinked, as if he hadn't fully considered that until this moment. His expression cleared, and he hopped back onto the table.

Rat-Slayer apparently decided the immediate danger had passed and dropped his hindquarters back onto Emilia's shoes.

"You might not know this," Pelt told Emilia, "but I was there that day." He tilted his head, his braided, brown hair shifting over his neck. "The day of the mutiny?"

Emilia's heart sputtered in her chest. She glanced at Judith, who watched with a concerned frown.

Did Pelt know how much Judith had told Emilia?

Pelt must've noticed the anxiety creeping into Emilia's expression—because he suddenly said, "Don't worry!" He flashed a wide, gold-toothed grin that did *not* put her at ease.

"I sided with the captain! Wouldn't be here, if I hadn't, would I?"

"I would hope not," Emilia said.

Pelt gave her that quick laugh of surprise—the same one he'd given her the first day, when she'd insulted the Illopian king in front of everyone. "The thing is, Em," he said slowly, "those of us who sided with the captain—we escaped in longboats. Do you know why that is?"

Emilia didn't answer. She'd grown tired of playing this game she didn't understand—especially when there were so many injured people who needed her.

"Because none of us could fucking swim," Pelt said.

Don't react, Emilia told herself.

Don't.

React.

"That's not true," Judith interrupted. She held out her rum-carrying arm. "I knew how to swim."

"Yes," Pelt amended. "Judith knew." His brows lifted. "Probably because the captain taught her."

Don't react.

Judith frowned. "We learned together, actually."

A hint of amusement twisted at Pelt's mouth, like a hiss of air escaping from a closed container, but he gave no other indication he'd even heard her.

He placed a deeply tanned hand over his stained, white shirt. "Even as far south as the little farm town I'm from, we didn't swim," he assured her. "Whether it was because the water was too cold or because we were scared of sea monsters, it just…wasn't done."

Most sea monsters resided in the Whispering Abyss—the home of sea monsters—and the ones who didn't preferred the warm waters of the Azure Sea.

If any sea monsters even lurked in the Westerly Sea, which surrounded much of Illopia, there couldn't have been more than one or two.

But Emilia supposed even a few sea monsters could evoke fear in a people who feared all forms of magic.

"Now, me? I'm a peasant," Pelt said. "People like me don't vacation in cities like Regolis…"

You do, if they put you in shackles first, Emilia thought bleakly.

"But Zain's been there once or twice," Pelt continued, "and earlier today, he seemed quite sure that people from Regolis aren't taught to swim."

Earlier today.

Then, what Zain had said to Maria above deck—that *was* what he'd meant.

Emilia cast a wary glance at the hammocks that surrounded them. Many of the sailors had lost consciousness already, but some of them hadn't.

"Relax," Pelt said. "They won't hear us, and if they do, we'll just have their testimonies thrown out." A smirk twitched at one side of his mouth. "After all, they're injured, right? Delirious. Unreliable…"

Emilia eyed the boatswain suspiciously, wondering, yet again, which side he was on. "Look, I appreciate the lesson on Illopian customs and all," she sighed, "but I've answered every question you've asked. And there are people who need me. Can I just do my job?"

If Pelt cared for any sailor in Emilia's care, he didn't show it. "Did the captain teach Catherine how to swim?"

"I don't know," Emilia said.

One lie.

One lie, she could do.

Hopefully.

"Come on, mate. You were there for their reunion," Pelt chided. "Surely, you saw something."

"I didn't." Emilia meant to leave it at that, but in a moment of impulsivity, she voiced the question that had been on her mind all day. "It was over a decade ago. If she *did* teach Catherine something, why not just tell us? It's not like we—I mean, *you*—didn't know about her friendship with Catherine."

Oops.

Too much honesty.

Honesty was bad.

Sometimes.

Apparently.

"Because she's ashamed." Judith spoke to Emilia and no one else, as if Pelt weren't even there. "And for good reason—after what Catherine did to us." Pain flashed in her bright, blue eyes. "*All of us.*"

Throughout the conversation, Emilia had thought Judith was in on it—*helping* her keep the secret—but that slight strain of betrayal in her voice suggested that...she'd figured it out when everyone else had.

Maria hadn't even told her closest friend—the one person she'd ever trusted.

"Also because," Pelt interjected, "some of us remember how easily the captain and Catherine used to communicate—wordlessly or sometimes with just...*one* word."

'*Run.*'

He knew. Pelt knew exactly what had happened.

Emilia tried to keep her voice steady, even as her heart pounded against her chest. "I have surgeries to perform. I'm going to need that table vacated."

Pelt smiled and lifted his hands in surrender. He slid off of the surgery table, and Rat-Slayer growled.

"One more question." The boatswain stepped toward Emilia, even as Rat-Slayer raised his hackles. He lowered his voice. "If you knew an incriminating truth about our captain, would you tell me?"

"No," Emilia said.

A flicker of amusement flashed in Pelt's hazel eyes. "Not the answer I expected, but all right," he said with a laugh. He turned to Judith and spread out his arms. "She passed—as far as I can tell. Let's just hope she handles the real thing just as well."

The real thing?!

The real—

Oh, fuck this.

Pelt must not have seen the glint of murder in Emilia's eyes—because he kept talking. "If you need some help moving sailors," he told Emilia, "let me know." He flashed that golden grin of his. "So I can tell Fulke."

Emilia pointed toward the wooden ladder in the corner—where the Aevarian giant stood with his massive arms crossed over his massive chest. "Fulke's already here."

Pelt glanced at him. "Oh."

"Didn't you walk past him," Emilia said, brows high, "on your way down here?"

"Couldn't see him," Pelt said. "He's too quiet."

Emilia ignored the missing-tongue joke. "But *huge*."

Pelt just laughed. "I'll send Helen, then."

In other words, someone with larger muscles than him.

"I appreciate the offer, Pelt," Emilia said. "Now, leave before Rat-Slayer loses his temper."

Pelt's eyes widened. He glanced down at the cat, who continued to eye him as if he were a giant rat in need of slaying.

With no further delay, the boatswain fled the hold.

Emilia whispered, "Good kitty," to Rat-Slayer, before turning to face Judith. Her smile faded.

Judith leaned against the table, drinking the last few drops of her rum. Lines of sadness and anger pulled at every part of her narrow face.

Warily, Emilia asked, "What was that?"

"Practice," Judith said.

Emilia stepped closer to her. "For what, exactly?"

"Zain figured it out hours ago," Judith said bluntly. "Why do you think things are so tense between him and the captain?" She shook the empty rum bottle, as if she still weren't convinced it was empty. "It's only a matter of time before he says something."

Emilia's heart raced. "Figured…what out?"

Judith's nostrils flared, and rage flashed within her bright blue eyes. "No," she snarled. "Not you, too. Not with me." She waved the bottle at Emilia. "*She* keeps enough secrets from me for the both of you!"

Emilia swallowed. Her gaze fell to the floor. "I—I didn't know," she whispered. "For the record."

"Neither did I," Judith said. "She's a real asshole sometimes."

Emilia looked up at her. "Judith—"

"I need more rum," Judith interrupted. She pushed away from the table. "I'll come back later." She gave the empty bottle another shake. "Probably after I've smashed this against her head a few times."

Emilia's chest tightened. "Judith, you don't understand," she tried to tell her. "Catherine is—"

Judith turned, pinning Emilia with a glare she'd only seen once before. "No," she snapped. "No, you don't get to tell *me* about the captain and Catherine." Her eyes flashed with resentment. "I was there."

Emilia had only wanted to tell Judith about Catherine, actually. *Just* Catherine.

Manipulative Catherine—with her many faces.

But the pain and anger in Judith's tone had lashed against Emilia's chest, and now, guilt expanded in her throat, leaving her unable to speak.

Judith didn't wait for Emilia to find her voice. She just spun on her heel and walked away.

Rat-Slayer circled Emilia's ankles, rubbing his silver ears against her black trousers—until she sighed.

"I'm worried about her, Rat-Slayer."

JUDITH FORGAVE EASILY, EMILIA CONCLUDED.

She'd have to—to have been Maria's closest friend all these years.

As much as Emilia loved her captain—a fact that became easier and easier to admit with each passing moment—Emilia had been on the wrong side of enough of Maria's antics to know that.

Judith had returned to the hold midway through Emilia's second surgery, equipped with a fresh bottle of rum and a totally different demeanor.

When Emilia had asked her about it, Judith had said the preparation for the evening meal was going well and that she and the captain had talked.

Emilia wished Judith had told her more. Emilia wanted to know if the captain was all right. Had Pelt confronted her?

Had Zain?

Emilia couldn't stand the thought of Maria being in danger with her so far away—especially when Maria had only done what she'd done out of concern for Emilia.

If asked, Emilia would've told her not to do it, of course, but… what was done was done.

Emilia wouldn't watch Maria suffer for it.

She cared for the crew of the *Wicked Fate*—a *lot*—but Emilia would fight them all for her captain.

And maybe Zain, Judith, and Pelt begrudged Maria for teaching Catherine so many things in the first place—things she'd one day use against them—but Emilia understood what it was like to be deceived.

She might've blamed *herself* for falling for Catherine's lies, but she didn't blame Maria.

As Emilia finished suturing the puncture wound in the sailor's stomach, the noise around her increased. A cacophony of voices filled the large hold, drowning out the usual symphony of creaks and groans from the ship.

Emilia cast a baffled glance toward the ladder in the corner, only to find a crowd of sailors gathered there.

Non-injured sailors, at that.

What the hell?

Perhaps Emilia had concentrated a little *too* hard on her work.

Sure, she'd noticed a few sailors slipping down to talk to Fulke or Judith throughout the day, but what could've brought *this* many people down to the hold?

The hold was probably the least pleasant place to gather on the entire ship—even when it *didn't* smell like literal guts.

Helen's boisterous voice rose above the others, and Emilia thought she caught several mentions of the word 'dragon.'

While she watched, Pelt slipped out from the crowd and

ambled toward her with a half-empty bottle of rum. Emilia had seen a lot of those today—far more than what the usual rum rations allowed.

"Surgeon," Pelt said.

It was funny how different that greeting could sound from person to person.

Pelt said it with enthusiasm.

Zain said it with disdain.

"Boatswain," Emilia said.

Apparently too drunk to notice the blood-soaked sailor in front of Emilia, Pelt hopped up onto the surgery table—next to that unconscious sailor's legs.

Emilia's eyes widened when the table rocked.

"It smells like shit in here," Pelt complained.

"Well, I can assure you," Emilia told him, "your intestines wouldn't smell great either, if I were to slice them open."

Pelt shifted away from her. "Ar-are you…threatening me?"

Emilia merely smiled. "You'll know when I'm threatening you."

Pelt snorted in amusement. "Well, I hope you're getting a bit of fresh air now and then," he said. "I haven't seen you leave the hold in hours."

Emilia found it hard to believe that anyone would notice when she did or didn't leave the hold, but…he wasn't wrong. "I haven't had a chance. Some of these surgeries were urgent."

"Oh," Pelt said.

She resisted the urge to add, *'And you'd delayed them enough already with your ridiculous questions.'*

Emilia tried to remind herself that in Pelt's line of work, those questions might've been important, but in Emilia's line of work, critical injuries came first.

They *kind of* had to.

Pelt held out the bottle of rum. "Need something to drink?"

Emilia lifted her blood-soaked hands for him to see.

His eyes widened at the sight. "Oh."

Emilia laughed at his reaction—before returning her attention to the wounded sailor. "At the risk of sounding as if I don't want you here—again," she said slowly, "what *are* all of you doing down here?"

Pelt snorted. "Helen," he said. "We're all following her, as she gives her rendition of the day's events—as though we didn't all live through it ourselves." He leaned forward to whisper, "We're also a bit drunk."

"I suspected," Emilia assured him. She glanced at the noisy crowd. "And is her rendition…accurate?"

Pelt arched his eyebrows. "If Helen were a fisherman—she's not; she doesn't have the attention span—but *if* she were, she'd tell you every fish she caught was as big as the *Wicked Fate* herself." He stretched his arms wide for emphasis.

Emilia laughed at that. "Of course she would."

"Again," Pelt added, "we're all too drunk to care."

"But if Helen brought the crowd," Emilia asked, as she set aside a needle, "who brought Helen?"

"Who do you think?" Pelt sipped his rum. "Judith."

The mention of Judith caused Emilia to look up. She glanced toward the empty corner of the table, where she'd *left* Judith. "Umm, where is Judith?"

"Where do you think?" Pelt practically parroted. He pointed a calloused finger toward the crowd.

"But," Emilia sputtered, "she was helping me."

Pelt braced a bony elbow against Emilia's shoulder. "Why do you think the captain tries to keep them apart?" he said in a drunken whisper. "They're both useless when the other's around."

Emilia couldn't help but smile at that. "It's cute."

"Sure," Pelt muttered, "until they blow a hole in the side of the ship."

Emilia laughed. "Have they always been like this?"

"Nah." Pelt removed his elbow, and Emilia's sore shoulder cried out in relief. He straightened. "Judith likes to tell everyone that Helen isn't her type—even though she keeps fucking her."

"Because her type is Sarah?" Emilia assumed.

Pelt widened his eyes and lifted the bottle to his mouth. "You don't know the half of Sarah."

Emilia laughed. She *had* gotten that impression. She couldn't even count the number of details Judith had mentioned about Sarah, during their work together, and yet, she still felt as if she knew nothing. "What about Helen? Does she deny Judith is *her* type?"

"Helen doesn't have a type," Pelt assured her. "You might as well be asking her about potatoes, sweet rolls, or hardtack. If she can stomach it, she'll fuck it."

Emilia wrinkled her nose at *that* analogy. "I'm sure she's a little more selective than that."

Pelt just grunted and took another drink of rum.

The hulking shadow that was Fulke stepped up behind Pelt and picked him up by the shoulder, as if he were nothing more than a kitten. He lifted him off of the surgery table and set him on the floorboards.

When Pelt spun around, choking and sputtering in shock, Fulke calmly signed an explanation.

"*'No sitting on the table during surgery?'*" Pelt translated. "Why not? Oh. *'It's rude.'*" He nodded and took another sip of rum, as if the substance hadn't nearly killed him two seconds ago. "Sorry, big guy."

Emilia smiled at the master of arms. "Thank you, Fulke."

"*You're welcome,*" he signed.

Emilia understood that hand gesture without a translation. She was still working on learning the others.

"*Are you ready for me to move him?*" Fulke signed. He pointed a large finger at the sailor on the table.

Emilia had learned that phrase, as well.

Today.

She didn't know if Fulke had chosen to come down to the hold on his own or if Maria had sent him. All Emilia knew was that she couldn't have moved the wounded sailors without him.

For the rest of the day, at least, Fulke was her hero.

"I think so," Emilia said. "He's all sewed up. I just need to—" She swept her gaze over the table, searching anywhere Judith might've left the—

Her eyes widened.

"Pelt?"

The boatswain turned toward her. "Hmm?" He dragged his hand across his mouth, wiping away the rum that had leaked out during his choking fit.

"When you saw Judith earlier," Emilia said, "did she happen to be holding a…punctured organ?"

Pelt's eyebrows knitted together. "Organ?"

"A bloody, fleshy thing?" Emilia offered. She lifted her own eyebrows. "Kind of hard to miss."

Pelt shrugged. "Well, I'm a bit drunk, so…"

Emilia sighed. She turned to face the gentle, dark-skinned giant beside her. "Could you, maybe, keep an eye on the wounded sailor —you know, just make sure he doesn't fall off the table—while I retrieve a spleen?"

An amused smile twitched at one side of Fulke's mouth. *"Of course,"* he signed.

If Emilia weren't covered in blood, at the moment, she might've hugged him.

Not that she was very confident in her hugging skills yet.

"You're the absolute best," Emilia informed him.

A chuckle rumbled low in the giant's belly, and warmth glowed in his dark brown eyes. He looked at her like that a lot.

Like she was a kitten.

Cute, small, and strange.

Emilia rounded the table and stepped over the sleeping cat on the other side of it. She cut between hammocks on her way to the wooden ladder.

As she drew near to the crowd, Emilia realized it looked a bit smaller up close. She reached them just in time to hear the end of Helen's remark.

"…you mean the part where she swooped in on dragon-back to save the day?"

Emilia pushed her way through the small circle of sailors— who all fell silent at the sight of her. "Right," she said, spreading out her blood-soaked hands. "Sorry to interrupt what I assume was a conversation about me, considering all the dragon talk, but uhh…"

Judith lifted her eyebrows curiously, when Emilia turned toward her.

"You walked off with someone's spleen," Emilia pointed out.

Judith frowned—and looked down at her hand. "Ugh!" she said, tossing the organ into Emilia's waiting hand. "Why would you *hand* that to me?"

"You said you wanted to help," Emilia muttered.

The small crowd didn't resume their conversation until *after* Emilia slipped back through—with Judith now trailing behind her.

"Couldn't you have mentioned that you'd given me a piece of someone's *body*?" Judith complained.

"Seriously, Judith?" Emilia said with a smile. "It was in your hand. What did you think it was?"

Judith tried—pointlessly—to shake the blood from her hand. "Oh, I don't know," she grumbled.

When Helen's voice rose above the clamor again and Judith's gaze drifted back toward her, Emilia's smile turned mischievous. "Right."

Judith's blue eyes shifted back toward Emilia. "Oh, no," she scolded, "you don't get to use that tone with me." She quickened her steps to catch up with Emilia. "Not when I had to watch you and the captain stare at each other for weeks."

"I don't stare," Emilia said defensively, but then, her eyes widened at the other part of that. "Wait. The captain stares at me?"

Judith arched her eyebrows, as if Emilia had just proven her point. "Constantly. It's amazing you don't notice."

Emilia's cheeks warmed.

She'd noticed Maria watching her a few times, of course, but she'd always thought Maria only watched her like that because she didn't trust her.

And that *was* the reason.

Wasn't it?

When they reached the table, Pelt stepped toward Judith and

gestured at Fulke with a not-so-subtle tilt of his head. "Don't sit on the table," he whispered. "Big guy doesn't like it."

Judith wrinkled her nose at him. "Why would anyone sit on the table, Pelt? There's a dead guy on it."

Pelt glanced over his shoulder. "Since when?"

"He's not dead!" Emilia told them—before adding, worriedly, "Yet." She dropped the damaged spleen into her bucket of not-so-pleasant things—to be thrown out, at some point—and turned to face them.

Judith took a clean cloth from a bucket of water and scrubbed frantically at her blood-soaked hand. "He can survive without that gross thing?"

"Usually," Emilia said. Honestly, she worried more about the blood loss than anything. Tomorrow, she'd use her healing magic, but the wounded would have to survive the night first. "I can't guarantee he'll live. I can't guarantee any of them will," she admitted, "but I'm doing everything I can."

Judith must've recognized the despair in Emilia's words—because she looked up, and her blue eyes softened. "You're doing great, Em."

Even if Emilia didn't believe herself capable of '*great*,' her heart still fluttered at the kind words.

Clearly not worried about his injured crew-mate, Pelt leaned toward Judith. "Tell me Helen at least *noticed* you ogling her."

With a glare, Judith shoved him—nearly hard enough to knock him flat on his already-scarred face.

As Emilia scrubbed her own hands, Fulke gathered the unconscious sailor into his massive arms and carried him to a nearby hammock.

Pelt tried to take advantage of the now-empty table, but he changed his mind as soon as Fulke turned to look at him.

Fulke's dark eyebrows inched toward the grey headscarf he wore around his nearly bald head, and Pelt took *another* step away from the surgery table.

"Gods forbid anyone rest their feet around here," Pelt muttered under his breath.

Emilia just sighed.

"You should've offered to help him," Judith scolded Pelt. "I haven't seen *you* do any real work in hours."

Pelt sipped his rum. "I'd just be in the way."

Judith stole the bottle from him and drank from it.

Emilia looked up at the boatswain. "Why *aren't* you working, actually?" She glanced at the small crowd near the ladder. "Why are none of you…working?"

"We've reduced sail," Pelt said. "We don't need as many people working now."

"But…why?"

Experienced sailors like Pelt often used terms Emilia didn't fully understand, but Judith usually explained them to her. This one, Emilia thought, meant they'd deliberately slowed down.

Which seemed like a bad idea—considering Catherine's ship was still out there.

Pelt stepped closer to Emilia, and Judith eyed him suspiciously. "Oh, you know," he said with a grin, "because of the mutiny."

Judith nearly choked on her rum.

Emilia narrowed her eyes. "You're joking."

He better be joking.

Pelt braced a hand against the table. "You think I'd joke about something so serious?"

"Yes," Judith muttered—behind the bottle of rum.

Emilia crossed her arms. "I'd know, if there were a mutiny."

"How?" Pelt said. "You've been all the way down here." Gold teeth flashed in his mouth. "For hours."

"Someone would've come for me," Emilia stated.

Pelt squinted at her. "No, they wouldn't have," he assured her. "Everyone knows which side her *lover* would take. They would've kept you in the dark." He leaned forward and lowered his voice. "Can't have you calling those dragons of yours, can we?"

Emilia flushed at the accusation. "You don't *know* the captain is my lover."

Just because Maria and Emilia had been more…*free* in their

affection, recently—in front of everyone—didn't mean everyone *knew*.

Even Judith snorted at that.

"Em," Pelt said with a rueful shake of his head. "We know." When Emilia didn't confirm or deny it, he added, "Besides, why else would you choose to stay with the pirate captain who kidnapped you?"

Emilia's brows furrowed. "The captain never kidnapped me."

"Sure, she didn't," Pelt said with a wink.

"She didn't!" Emilia insisted. She stared at him in disbelief. "You were there when I signed the Code!"

Pelt offered her a careless shrug. "I did warn you," he reminded her, "that Zain wouldn't handle it well."

Emilia liked this joke less and less with every word that came out of his mouth.

"Judith would've known," Emilia pointed out.

"Eh, actually, I've been down here with you," Judith said with a wince. "They might've been keeping me in the dark, too."

"Her lover and her closest friend?" Pelt said. "Of course we kept you both in the dark."

It was a joke.

It had to be.

Judith wouldn't be this calm, if there were any chance the captain was actually in danger.

Still, Emilia's hand drifted toward her sword. "Quit calling the captain my lover."

"There is no one on this ship who doesn't know, Em," Pelt assured her. "No one."

Fulke returned, and at the sound of his heavy steps, Emilia spun toward him.

"You'd tell me if the captain was in danger, wouldn't you?" Even to Emilia's own ears, the question sounded more like a threat.

Fulke nodded.

"Don't believe *him*," Pelt scoffed. "He's here to guard the hatch! What? You think the captain sent the only giant aboard to assist a *surgeon*?"

Fulke laughed, and Emilia glared at him, too.

They were all messing with her.

Every single one of them!

When Emilia turned to Judith, expecting better of her, the cook drank her rum even faster than before.

Emilia was going to kill them all.

Helen's obnoxious laughter echoed throughout the large space, reminding Emilia of *one* group of people who disproved Pelt's entire lie.

"Them!" Emilia jabbed a finger toward the crowd. "Why are they down here, laughing, if there's a mutiny?"

Pelt's smirk didn't waver. "They're celebrating."

"Celebrating what?" Emilia said.

Don't say it.

"Oh, didn't I mention? The mutiny's over," Pelt said. "Zain's probably captain by now."

Don't you dare.

"I mean, he would've had to kill the captain to earn the crew's respect," Pelt said, nudging Emilia's shoulder with his own, "but good riddance, right?"

Emilia snatched a small, surgical blade from the table and jerked her hand forward, pressing the flat blade against the boatswain's throat. "Do not joke about the captain's life with me."

Pelt immediately raised both hands. "Fucking hell."

Fulke didn't even bother to help the boatswain. He simply turned around, eliminating himself as a witness.

"Fuck you, Fulke," Pelt complained.

"Em?" Judith lowered her bottle, eyes wide. "Why don't you put the weapon away, mate?"

"It's not a weapon. It's a surgical tool," Emilia informed her, "that can slice open a carotid artery, if someone doesn't *tell* me my captain is all right."

"Oh, fuck," Pelt whimpered. "She's fine! I swear!"

Emilia instantly removed the blade. "Thank you."

Judith snorted—and then burst into a fit of laughter, which Fulke enthusiastically joined.

Pelt ran his fingers over his throat and examined them—to ensure there was no blood. "Not her lover, my ass," he grumbled.

Emilia ignored that.

Pelt glared at Judith and Fulke. "The concern shown by my *friends* is so touching!"

"Hey," Judith said with a shrug. "We weren't the ones who made the joke."

"It was a good joke!" Pelt insisted.

Judith laughed, "Well, now, it's an even better one."

A snort of amusement broke through Pelt's brief indignation, and then, *he* was laughing, too.

"Oh," Judith exclaimed, suddenly. "Do you know who'd really love this? Helen!" She spun on her heels and stepped toward the crowd. "I'll go tell her now!"

Grasping her slender shoulder, Fulke picked Judith up mid-step and flipped her around to face the table.

Judith blinked. "I'll…tell her later, I guess?"

Fulke nodded.

Aside from a slight smile, Emilia paid them no mind.

Her captain was fine.

She could focus on her next surgery now.

CHAPTER 9

Slowing Down

What in the name of the goddess…

Emilia jumped out of the way just in time to avoid being flattened by a couple of dancing sailors.

"Sorry!" one of the men yelled, as they danced past.

With tattooed arms outstretched, the men kept their calloused hands clasped together. Their leather boots hit the deck with a rhythmic *thuh-thump* that reminded Emilia more of horses galloping than people dancing.

Their clumsy yet gleeful dancing brought a baffled smile to Emilia's lips—even as she wondered what in the absolute *hell* was going on.

It had been a few hours since Helen's drunken crowd had left the hold. So, she'd expected to see a *few* of them above deck, but this wasn't a few.

*This…*was everyone.

Had Emilia missed something while she was in surgery?

Was there not a whole other ship still out there?

Emilia needed to find Maria.

Before someone broke an ankle, preferably.

Dark, moonlit waves crashed against the sides of the ship, and lanterns—with their flickering candles inside—scattered the main deck.

Anxiety churned in Emilia's stomach, as she passed one huddle of drunken sailors after another.

"Em!"

Emilia barely had time to register her name, before a hand dragged her into a circle of singing sailors.

She suddenly found herself beneath the sweaty, thick-muscled arm of Helen, who rocked lurchingly to the tune of an unfamiliar sea shanty.

"Sea! Oh, sea!" Helen bellowed in Emilia's ear.

While Emilia was too fond of the master gunner to voice her own discomfort, Pelt plugged his ears and groaned at Helen's off-key rendition of the song.

Judith—held hostage by Helen's other arm—was apparently *also* drunk enough to have lost all sense of pitch.

"She who will never leave me!" the two of them sang in a wobbly sort of unison.

On the other side of Pelt, a pirate complained, "Those aren't even the right *words*."

"Where's the captain?" Emilia yelled to Pelt—between refrains.

Whether he'd actually heard her or had just read her lips, she didn't know, but the boatswain extracted her from Helen's arm and gave her a helpful shove in the direction of the quarterdeck.

"Thank you!" Emilia called back—even though she doubted the boatswain would hear her.

Emilia found Maria not actually *on* the quarterdeck, but sitting on the steps that led up to it. Rather than drinking from her usual leather flask, she held an entire bottle between her leather-clad thighs.

Maria leaned an elbow against the wooden step behind her, watching as Fulke and a sailor half his size arm-wrestled on top of a wooden barrel.

Goddess, if they kept this up, Emilia would end up back in surgery before she could even speak to Maria.

By the time Emilia returned her attention to her captain, she found Maria's dark eyes fixed on her, instead.

'*Constantly,*' Judith had said. *'It's amazing you don't notice.'*

Well, she'd definitely notice now.

Emilia looked down, breaking the accidental eye-contact, and Maria lifted the bottle of rum to her lips.

Emilia took a few more steps in Maria's direction, before calling out, "What's going on?"

Maria's heated stare didn't waver, but she lifted a tattooed finger and tapped her earlobe. The little gold loop she wore in her ear wiggled in response.

Maria couldn't hear her.

Of course she couldn't.

Emilia glanced around at the raucous crowd of pirates, wondering how *any* of them were communicating with each other.

Maybe they were all just guessing at what the other was saying.

"May I stab you in the gut?"

"Yes, I do like pineapples, actually."

Maria beckoned her closer.

Emilia forced herself to stop shifting on her feet and crossed the remaining space between them. As she moved away from the crowd and toward her solitary captain, the noise softened.

Just a little.

Instead of the question she'd meant to ask, Emilia heard herself say, "Why are you sitting by yourself?"

Maria's mouth—still blood-red and bruised from her fight with Catherine—quirked up at the corners. "I'm watching."

Emilia assumed she meant the arm-wrestling, but when Maria deliberately trailed her gaze down Emilia's body, Emilia wondered if she'd misunderstood something.

Easy to do in this chaos.

"It's a little unfair, isn't it?" Emilia said with a nervous smile. "For a giant to wrestle a human?"

"You expect Fulke to turn down free gold?" Maria said.

Emilia laughed, "I guess not."

He was a pirate, after all.

Maria reclined further against the step behind her. "I thought you'd come up with the others."

Emilia spread out her clean hands. "I was covered in blood and…*other* things." Not everyone wanted to hear the details of her work. "I needed to bathe."

Maria's gaze lingered on the burns on Emilia's arms, rather than the clean hands Emilia had been trying to show her. "You must be exhausted," she murmured. "I know I am."

Emilia's eyes widened. It was rare to hear Maria admit any kind of weakness or vulnerability—even a temporary one.

Except…in that moment, Emilia realized Maria had done it before—before Emilia had even *known* how rare it was.

'My arms are a bit tired,' she'd said that first night.

"Who wouldn't be," Emilia said, "after today?"

Maria tilted her head, and her thick curls brushed her left shoulder. "Then, why the fuck are you still standing?"

Emilia laughed at the question. After the day she'd had, she wasn't sure she remembered *how* to sit down. "I've been working."

Also, Catherine's still out there.

Have you forgotten that, Captain?

Maria shifted her lean hips toward the left rail and tilted her head toward the vacated space on her right. "Come here."

Emilia blushed.

Maria really underestimated the width of Emilia's hips sometimes. Either that, or she just *liked* being pressed up against Emilia.

Maria took another sip of rum, and the shameless smirk she hid behind the bottle told Emilia that it was most definitely the latter.

Emilia eyed the steps warily. She'd been running on pure adrenaline for hours now. Emilia worried the adrenaline would abandon her the moment she sat down, and if it did, what would be left of her without it?

Maria lowered her voice to a whisper—forcing Emilia to read her lips. "Sit," she said, "please."

Emilia forced herself to obey, folding herself onto the wooden step, next to Maria's sprawled form.

Emilia rested her feet in front of her, but the release of pressure only gave way to pain, radiating from her heels to her toes.

She glanced at Maria, only to find the pirate captain watching her with a concerned frown.

Had the pain shown on her face?

Fortunately, the crew's drunken rendition of a sea shanty filled any awkward silence that might've followed.

Maria wrinkled her nose, her concern turning to disgust. "They really *are* just awful." She lifted the bottle to her lips. "I need to hire a musician."

Emilia tried not to wince at one of the higher notes. "They're," she said in a strained tone, "not that bad."

Maria watched Emilia from the corner of her eye as she drank. She swallowed and lowered the bottle. "Have I mentioned that you're a terrible liar?" She tilted her face closer. "*Em?*"

Emilia scowled at her teasing. "I offered to come up with a different alias."

Maria leaned back. A hint of affection softened her dark brown eyes, and she smiled. "You're Em," she said with a shrug. "You could never be anyone else."

Why had that sounded like a compliment?

The sailors belted out a particularly out-of-tune note—earning yet another grimace from Maria.

"In their defense," Emilia said dryly, "how better to sing a song about drinking than drunk and off-key?"

Maria had just raised her bottle again—but lowered it, suddenly. "Em?" she said with a curious smile. "What makes you think this one is about drinking?"

Weren't *all* sea shanties about drinking?

"They mentioned liquor," Emilia said. She hadn't understood all of the lines, but she'd understood that one.

When Maria squinted at her, Emilia held up a finger. She waited for the crew to repeat the line, and sure enough, they did.

Emilia turned to Maria and…frowned, as she found the pirate captain doubled over in laughter.

"Oh. I see," Maria gasped. "I see."

"You see *what?* Why are you laughing?" Heat rose in Emilia's cheeks, and irritation prickled along her skin. "Are you laughing at *me?*"

Maria rested her head against the wooden railing on the other side of the steps, as she tried—and failed—to catch her breath.

Emilia rolled her eyes. "Captain, if you don't tell me why you're laughing, I'm going to stab you."

"Em," Maria said with an amused grin, "oh, my sweet surgeon." She shifted her body toward Emilia's and lowered her voice. "Lick," she said slowly, "her."

Emilia's eyes widened.

Maria held up two tattooed fingers. "Two words."

"Oh." Emilia couldn't have blushed harder if she'd tried.

Maria's smile widened. "The next refrain isn't describing the delightful qualities of a donkey, either, my love."

Annoyance overtook Emilia's embarrassment. "Oh, shut up." When Maria snorted, Emilia added, "It's not my fault they don't know how to enunciate!"

Maria fell back against the step behind her. "Then, you agree!" she said victoriously. "We need a musician." She lifted the bottle of rum to her bruised lips. Drinking deeply, she nudged Emilia's knee with her own. "Want to help me convince Zain?"

Emilia glanced down at Maria's leather-clad knee. The casual touch had unleashed a strange warmth inside her chest—one that eased her rising anxiety.

Now that she thought about it…Emilia had barely even considered the concerns that had *brought* her to Maria, since sitting down next to her.

Her mere presence had eased Emilia's anxiety.

Maria lifted a scarred eyebrow. "Is that a no?"

"Hmm?" Emilia said, looking up. "Oh, umm, no."

A curious smile twitched at the corners of Maria's mouth, but she didn't ask for an explanation. She just took another sip of rum. "We had a musician once."

"Really?" Emilia said with a surprised laugh. "You hired a musician but not a surgeon?"

Maria tilted her head back and groaned, as if she'd heard this question before—from Adda, most likely. "Such an unfair question," she complained. "Do you *know* how hard it is to lure a surgeon into villainy?" Maria pressed her weight into her right elbow, and with deliberate slowness, she trailed her gaze along each of Emilia's curves. "They're not all teeming with murderous anger like you were."

Emilia's skin warmed beneath Maria's heated gaze. "What makes you think I'm not *still* teeming with murderous anger?"

Maria's smile widened. "Oh, I do hope you are."

"Musicians, on the other hand," Emilia said sarcastically, "are notoriously unhappy people."

Maria snorted at that. "Maybe not, but they *are* usually lurking in the taverns already," she said, "just waiting for me to snatch them up."

She was doing it again—describing herself like some dangerous predator that delighted in devouring its prey.

Emilia didn't know if Maria actually saw herself that way—or just wanted others to see her that way.

"Well, what happened to your musician?"

Maria took another sip of rum. "My sword."

"Ah," Emilia said with a shake of her head. "Why am I not surprised?"

"I had a reason," Maria said defensively. She squinted at nothing in particular. "I don't remember what it was, but I did have one."

"Of course you did," Emilia muttered.

Maria leaned forward, resting the bottle of rum between her thighs. "Oh, come on! He was insufferable!" She quirked her head to the side, and her brows furrowed. "I think he stole from someone."

Emilia didn't think those counted as the same crime—especially considering one of them was *not* a crime.

"Maybe you should practice *not* killing your crew members," Emilia said, "before you hire another."

Maria wrinkled her nose. "Why would I do that?"

Why, indeed?

When Maria leaned back again, she rested her arm behind Emilia, and the warmth of her curled around Emilia like a blanket. "While we're on the subject," she practically *cooed* in Emilia's ear, "did I hear that you did…*not* draw a weapon against Pelt today?"

Goddess!

News traveled fast on this ship.

Emilia kept her gaze straight ahead—for fear of accidentally turning and kissing Maria. Heat slid over her skin like a caress, and Emilia wondered how the pirate captain expected her to answer questions in these…conditions.

"I would never," Emilia said—even though they both knew she'd broken that law before. "That would be against the Code."

"Mm-hmm," Maria murmured.

The heat dipped lower.

Emilia closed her eyes and exhaled slowly.

They were discussing a possible crime.

Emilia needed to focus on that, *not* on how close the captain was—*not* on how easy it would be to tilt her head back and press her mouth against Maria's.

Damn it.

"I was teaching him about surgical blades," Emilia said.

That scarred eyebrow of Maria's inched upward. "Directly after he insinuated I was dead?"

Oh, couldn't they have left that part out?

"That," Emilia lied, "had nothing to do with it."

Maria chuckled lowly, and the sound poured into Emilia's ear and into her veins, like warm honey.

Emilia would've preferred interrogation at sword-point to *this*. At least her body had never tried to melt into a puddle of goo at sword-point.

Oh, right.

It had.

Maria relaxed her muscles and muttered under her breath, "Thank the gods you're mine."

That remark jolted Emilia back into action. She turned toward

Maria, but her irritation faltered the moment she saw those sparks of liquid fire in Maria's eyes.

Her warm voice might as well have been ice, compared to her eyes.

"Just because we said…what we said," Emilia managed to force out, "doesn't mean I'm yours."

I love you.

I actually…love you.

Why did Emilia want to say it again? Even now, when someone might hear them?

Pelt *said* everyone knew, but they didn't *know*. They thought, and what they thought didn't even scratch the surface of what Emilia actually felt for Maria.

The crew had always assumed things were more sexual between them than they actually were.

Not that things weren't…sexual.

Clearly.

Behind Emilia, Maria moved her arm. When her warm fingertips skimmed along Emilia's back, a flood of arousal pooled between Emilia's thighs.

Maria's lips brushed Emilia's ear as she murmured, "Keep telling yourself that, darling."

Emilia shuddered, and Maria's dark gaze devoured the movement. Her fingers curled against Emilia's back, pressing hard enough that it might've left marks, if she'd kept longer fingernails.

Emilia gasped and leaned into Maria's arm—either to stop her or plead for more, Emilia wasn't sure which.

The look Maria gave her in response sent jolts of desire spiraling through Emilia.

"You have to stop," Emilia breathed.

Before I kiss you.

Before I do a lot…more than kiss you.

Maria's breath—sweet with rum—fell against Emilia's face. "Stop what?"

Oh, like she didn't know!

"Looking at me like that," Emilia hissed against her lips. "Do you want them all to see?"

Maria's eyes darkened so much that they looked more black than brown, and she let her gaze drop lower, along the curve of Emilia's neck, over the swell of her breasts, down between her spread thighs…

Emilia involuntarily clenched them together, and the slight increase in pressure nearly made her moan.

"Even if they saw," Maria whispered, "they wouldn't know what I was thinking. Picturing."

Emilia blinked at that last part. "Picturing?"

Maria laughed. She removed her arm from behind Emilia's back and straightened, and nearly every sign of what had just happened vanished from her face.

The only remaining tells were the way her fingers curled too tightly around the rum bottle, and the way her leather-clad thighs closed ever-so-slightly around it.

Emilia begged the ache between her own thighs to fade. "Why do you enjoy tormenting me so much?"

Maria snorted. "I could ask you the same."

What?

Emilia had done no tormenting!

She'd done nothing at all, actually. She was innocent of all crimes.

Except the real ones.

"Em?" Maria said, without looking at her. "Ask me the question you came to ask."

Emilia glanced at the pirate captain. "What?"

"When you were standing there—" Maria pointed a finger toward the place where Emilia had caught her…*possibly* staring earlier. "—you were stressing about something. I assume you had a question?"

Stressing?

There was no way Maria could've known that.

Just by looking at her.

Maria watched Emilia's now fidgeting hands, and her tone softened with concern. "Was it just the noise?" she asked. "I know loud crowds bother you."

What was she talking about now?

The noise *did* bother Emilia—but only because it, along with all of the lanterns burning tonight, would lead the navy to them like a damn beacon.

"You think noisy crowds bother me?" Emilia asked.

Maria gave a single nod. "I noticed it in the tavern."

The tavern?

Well, that wasn't fair.

Emilia had been anxious for a *multitude* of reasons the day she'd joined Maria in the tavern.

Her possible capture and death, for one.

Maria, for another.

"That was you," Emilia said with a baffled shake of her head. "You said the tavern made you restless."

Maria's eyes widened. Had she not expected Emilia to remember that? With a subtle nod, she admitted, "It's the walls that do it to me."

She waved her bottle toward the open sky, and Emilia followed the gesture with her gaze. The sight of the peaceful, star-speckled sky drew a sigh from Emilia's lips.

Then, the thought of Catherine shattered her peace, and her pulse returned to its former pace.

What were they even *doing*? Had everyone but Emilia forgotten the danger?

"Even in my quarters, I can still *see* the ocean. I can still feel it," Maria explained, "but when I go home…" She pursed her lips and shook her head.

Emilia glanced at Maria. For a moment, it had seemed impossible, and yet, the captain's honesty had pierced through Emilia's haze of anxiety once again. Her chest warmed with gratitude. "Oh."

The smile Maria gave her in response was achingly gentle. She held out the bottle of rum. "Try it," she urged. "It dulls the senses a little—makes it easier."

Emilia immediately held up her hand. "No. Someone on this ship needs to stay sober."

Maria leaned in close—close enough that her leather doublet brushed Emilia's arm. "I suppose I'll just have to take you to my quarters, then," she said with a taunting smirk. "Calm you down there."

Yet another wave of heat coursed through Emilia's body. "W-what?"

As if she'd said nothing at all, the infuriating pirate captain leaned back and took another drink of rum.

Who just *said* things like that?

Captain Maria Welles, clearly.

With a sigh, Emilia said, "I don't understand what we're doing." Her heart raced. "Why is everyone drunk? Why are they singing and dancing, as if—"

"As if we've won?" Maria said. "We did, Em."

Her cold yet casual tone only worsened Emilia's anxiety.

Why was Maria acting as if she didn't know the same disconcerting information Emilia knew?

"Catherine's still out there."

Maria didn't even look Emilia's way. "She's always still out there."

"Yes, well," Emilia argued, "not this close."

"What do you want to do? Chase her?" Maria said with a scoff. "We're not ready for another battle, Em."

"I know that," Emilia assured her, "which is why I don't think we should light the ship up like a beacon and sing loud enough for all of Aletharia to hear."

Maria breathed out a long sigh and pressed the half-empty bottle of rum into Emilia's hands. "Drink," she demanded, and when Emilia tried to give it back, she added, "One sip. That's all."

With a puzzled frown, Emilia raised the bottle to her mouth. She sipped it slowly, concentrating on the sweet flavor of the liquid and the slight burn that traveled from her tongue to her stomach.

Afterward, she exhaled and tried to return the bottle to Maria.

Maria didn't take it. "Another."

Emilia scowled at that. "You said one sip."

"One more," Maria said. "One sip. One breath."

"That's not—" Emilia didn't have the energy left to argue with Maria's strange, pointless lies. So, rather than finish her sentence, she lifted the bottle to her lips and took a second sip of rum.

Maria waited until she'd exhaled to say—yet again, "Another."

With a peeved glare, Emilia took a third drink.

Maria's lips twitched with amusement, but her voice didn't waver as she repeated, "Another."

Emilia drank.

Sweet.

Burn.

Exhale.

"Another."

Maria's calm repetition of the word reminded Emilia of the chants their agrarian sorcerers used. Silas—Emilia's possible father —had taught several of them to her and the other children during training.

Plant magic was more passive than other styles of magic. You didn't wield it so much as let it wield you. Agrarian sorcerers often used chants to connect with the earth—in order to channel its magic.

"Another."

The rum hadn't had time to reach her bloodstream, and yet, Emilia's hands had already stopped shaking.

"Another."

It *wasn't* the rum that had calmed Emilia.

It was Maria's voice.

Emilia turned to look at her wonderful, infuriating captain— who looked far too pleased with herself. "I'm still worried," she muttered, "just so you know."

Maria chuckled. "I know."

Emilia held it out. "Do you want it back now?"

Maria shook her head. "Keep it. No one should have to deal with my quartermaster without rum."

Quartermaster?

Emilia hadn't seen Zain since earlier.

But Maria climbed to her feet and held out a hand. "Come with me," she demanded, "surgeon."

Emilia stared at the pink scar in the center of Maria's palm—where the blade of a sword had once sliced deeply into the meat—before looking up. "Where are you taking me?"

Maria flashed a taunting smile. "It's an order."

With a sigh, Emilia placed her hand in Maria's.

She didn't think much of the action—until Maria's fingers closed around hers, and her skin tingled.

Until her chest fluttered, and her breath caught.

Maria didn't release Emilia's hand as quickly as she expected, and when Emilia looked up curiously, she found Maria's eyes as dark and deep as the sea itself.

Had Maria felt it, too?

How could she? They were physiological reactions, not…magic.

'Magic is in everything.'

Maria let go of Emilia's hand and then ran her fingers along the top of her blue headscarf, as if she intended to adjust the tricorn that she…wasn't wearing. She dropped her hand. "Come."

Maria climbed the steps, and Emilia followed.

On the quarterdeck, Henry manned the helm, while Zain leaned against the rail, wearing his usual scowl.

When they reached the final step, Maria turned toward her. "Do me a favor, and try not to question me in front of Zain." She swayed toward Emilia, as gracefully as a dancer. "I know you'll fail, but *try*."

Emilia rolled her eyes and tipped back the rum.

Maria pressed a hand against Emilia's lower back—apparently unaware of what her touch *did* to Emilia—and guided her toward Zain. "Quartermaster, I'd like you to meet the only other sober person on this ship."

Emilia glanced pointedly at the bottle of rum in her hand.

Zain scowled at Maria. "Funny, Captain," he said, his teeth flashing with each enunciated syllable.

Emilia remembered Pelt's warnings and wished Maria would take a break from antagonizing him, for once.

"Yes, well," Maria said dismissively, "Em had a few questions for you."

Emilia looked up at Maria. "I did?"

Maria gave the back of Emilia's scabbard a playful tug, before dropping her hand to her side. "You did."

Apparently, Maria was goading everyone tonight.

Emilia narrowed her eyes at her mischievous captain. "Can you tell us what they were, Captain?"

Zain glanced back and forth between them.

"Of course, surgeon." Maria turned her attention to Zain. "When did we last see the naval flagship?"

Zain relaxed his shoulders. Clearly, answering questions didn't bother him as much as dealing with Maria's sense of humor. "If I had to guess," he said with a tilt of his head, "six hours ago."

"Which direction did she sail?" Maria said.

He didn't hesitate. "She went east. We went west."

Maria crossed her arms over her chest. "If she'd turned back, would we have seen her?"

"In the open seas? With good visibility?" Zain said. "Yes." His dark gaze shifted toward Emilia. "Why?"

Maria leaned toward Emilia, and the cool, steel hilt of her sword brushed Emilia's waist. "Oh, Em's just being *thorough*," she teased, "isn't she?"

Emilia couldn't help but blush at that word—at the memory of Maria using it to describe the way she'd helped Emilia with her armor.

Goddess, it barely felt like the same *day*.

Unaware of the private joke passing between them, Zain asked, "Why would our surgeon need to know things that don't concern her?"

Emilia bristled at that, but Maria spoke first.

"How does it not concern her?"

Zain flinched at the abrupt change in tone. He glanced down at the swords Maria carried at her waist, perhaps to ensure she hadn't unsheathed them. "Her only job on this ship is to treat the wounded."

"Well, thank the gods she knows how to do *more* than her job," Maria said. All the previous mirth had vanished from her tone, leaving pure ice in its place. "Remind me." She stepped toward Zain. "Were you asleep when Em saved our fucking lives earlier?"

Emilia looked up at Maria, her eyes wide.

"No, I was here," Zain said slowly, "captaining the *Wicked Fate* in your absence."

Maria took another step toward him, forcing him to look up at her. "Oh, right," she said quietly, "when you were giving the most foolish orders I've ever heard."

"According to you," Zain sneered, "Captain."

Maria tilted her head, and every muscle in her body tensed. "Oh?"

Emilia had never heard a single syllable sound so…*dangerous*.

She knew why Zain was being more difficult than usual—if what Judith said was true, anyway—but what was going on with Maria?

It couldn't have been about the way he'd talked to Emilia. He'd always talked down to her.

Zain straightened. "I didn't ask for an entire *fleet* to attack us." He stepped toward Maria, now. "Do you want to talk about who did?"

Maria's hand strayed to her sword.

"Whoa!"

Emilia stepped between them.

Maria glanced at Emilia—and then let her hand fall away from the sword. In response to Emilia's wide-eyed expression, she just muttered, "Long day."

Emilia swallowed.

Perhaps Maria's joke about needing rum to deal with Zain hadn't been a joke, after all. Emilia offered her the bottle, and Maria took it.

Emilia waited until Maria had tipped back the rum bottle, before she whirled on the quartermaster.

Apparently expecting a less hostile reaction from Emilia, Zain took a startled step backward.

"Thank you for putting my mind at ease—with the captain's help," Emilia said, tone as sharp as a sword, "and I'm *so* sorry for caring about our crew."

Maria snorted midway through her drink.

Zain frowned at the strange apology. "You're…welcome?"

Emilia crossed her arms and waited.

His frown deepened. His gaze darted toward Maria, and Emilia lifted her eyebrows expectantly.

With a sigh, Zain turned to Maria. "Sorry, Captain."

Maria lowered the bottle and blinked at them both. She shrugged and muttered, "Nice…coat."

Emilia's brows furrowed.

Well, so much for apologies.

Zain looked down at his bright, red waistcoat.

"It is," Emilia said, squinting at the color, "flashier than the one you were wearing a few hours ago."

Zain scowled. "Yes, well, I couldn't keep wearing the one with blood on it, now could I?" He pointed an accusatory finger at Maria. "Not to mention, damaged!"

Emilia turned toward Maria. "You damaged his coat," she asked bewilderedly, "by…bleeding on it?"

Maria lifted her eyebrows. "It was a button."

Emilia's frown deepened. "You bled on a button?"

Maria's lips twitched up at the corners. "No."

"Just because you don't mind walking around smelling like seaweed," Zain sneered at Maria, "doesn't mean *I* have to keep wearing the same clothes."

Maria squinted at that. "It wasn't the foul-smelling kind," she mumbled, "was it?" She stepped closer to Emilia and whispered, "Do I smell like seaweed?"

Emilia leaned forward and sniffed Maria's black, leather doublet.

The possibility that Maria's question might've been less literal than she'd taken it didn't occur to Emilia—until Maria's low, amused laughter filled her ear.

Emilia blushed. She slowly eased back on her heels.

But of course, Maria would never let her off that easily. "Well?"

Emilia shrugged. "You smell like you always do."

A curious smile tugged at Maria's lips. "Which is?"

Not like seaweed. Isn't that enough?

Heat gathered in Emilia's cheeks, as she quietly admitted, "Like hibiscus and oranges."

A hint of surprise flickered in Maria's eyes, and her smile softened. She slipped her hand into her pocket and retrieved a glass bottle. She held it out, the cork resting between her first and middle fingers.

"I used some earlier, actually," Maria admitted. "I was a bit sore after it all."

Emilia couldn't stop the delighted smile that burst across her face. "That's," she said shyly, "what I made it for."

Affection warmed Maria's large, brown eyes, and she tilted her face closer to Emilia's. "I know."

"Okay, what is this?" Zain interrupted. "What's happening right now?"

Both of them looked up, startled.

Zain leaned away from them, his lip curling with disgust. "Whatever it is," he said with a flick of his hands, "I want no part of it." He shooed them. "Go."

Emilia blinked.

You'd think they were covered in fish slime!

Maria rolled her eyes and took Emilia by the arm. She led Emilia toward the steps—but not before loudly complaining, "He's so exhausting when I've been drinking."

Emilia admired Maria's ability to never even *consider* the possibility that she might be at fault.

Only when they reached the main deck did Emilia dare to ask, "What happened back there?"

Maria froze, and it was clear in the rigid set of her shoulders that the rum hadn't helped as much as she'd pretended it had.

With her fingers still wrapped around Emilia's arm, Maria jerked Emilia toward her. Her eyes darkened, and Emilia couldn't help but sink into their deep, dangerous depths.

"I've watched too many people hurt you today," Maria growled. "He's lucky I didn't kill him."

As Maria neared the door to her quarters, she cast a quick glance over her shoulder, expecting to find Em—and *only* Em—following her.

The extra set of eyes made her stop.

A jolt of shock traveled from Maria's chest to her extremities, and the extra pair of eyes blinked slowly.

It was only *after* the shock left her body that Maria managed to process the body those small, reflective eyes were attached to.

"What the fuck, Em?" Maria forced herself to let go of her sword. "Where did you even *get* that thing?"

Em barely spared a glance for the sword Maria had almost drawn—before returning her attention to the large tabby cat in her arms. She stroked his silver-and-white fur and scoffed, "He lives here, Captain."

Maria sighed. "That's not what I—" She shook her head. "How did I not hear you pick up a fucking cat?"

Despite the several steps of distance they'd put between themselves and the main deck, the refrain of the next vulgar sea shanty still reached Maria's ears.

With a pointed look, Em said, "How much noise do you think cats make?"

Not as much as pirates when they're singing about sex.

Apparently.

Still, Maria eyed the purring beast in Em's arms skeptically. "Don't you think he's a little too…*well-fed* for stealth?"

Rat-Slayer stopped purring and opened his eyes.

"Oh, look!" Em said. "Now, you've offended him."

As if to confirm her point, Rat-Slayer meowed and leapt from Em's arms, but the heavy *thump* of his paws against the deck only proved Maria's point.

Maria arched her eyebrows.

Em abruptly sank to her knees and covered Rat-Slayer's ears with her hands. "He's only *'well-fed'* because he's good at his job!"

Maria couldn't decide which part she needed to wrap her mind around first—the fact that her lovely surgeon had just sunk to her knees in front of Maria.

Again.

Or the fact that she'd only done it to cover a cat's ears.

The cat in question took advantage of his situation, rubbing his fluffy, silver ear against Em's fingers.

Em obliged him, of course.

When had she ever not?

"It's not his rat-slaying skills that concern me," Maria informed her. "It's *your* skill of summoning cats out of nowhere."

Soft laughter spilled from Em's lips. As she looked up at Maria, the thin, silver beams of moonlight that streamed in from the upper deck reflected in her eyes.

No longer only alike emeralds in color, Emilia Drakon's eyes now sparkled like them, as well.

"He's been following me all day," Em explained. "I just asked him to wait while I went to find you." She leaned forward, as if sharing a secret. "I didn't want him to get squashed by all the dancing sailors."

Maria snorted at that. "Good thinking."

Em's smile deepened. Her fingers continued to move over the cat's fur, but her enchanting gaze never left Maria. "Honestly…" she trailed off, blushing.

Maria waited for her to finish.

Impatience had always been one of Maria's weaknesses—though she preferred to blame it on the slowness of those around her—but every now and then, with Em, Maria thought she could wait forever, if she had to.

Was it even waiting, if Maria could spend every moment admiring that smile?

Em climbed to her feet and stepped closer to Maria. With a sheepish shrug, she confessed, "I didn't expect them to have such a strong reaction to me leaving."

Maria chuckled. "The cats or the crew?"

"The cats," Em said, but she frowned as the rest of the question caught up with her. "Oh. Well, the crew, too, I suppose." She let out a self-deprecating laugh. "You know, my head spins after dragon-flight—in a good way," she added, as if the dragons might overhear, "but I thought I might've hallucinated the, umm—" She pulled her shoulders inward. "—squeezing."

Maria squinted at her word choice. "You mean hugging."

"Yes," Em said, holding up a finger. "That."

Maria couldn't help but laugh.

She peered over Em's shoulder, back toward the main deck—to make sure no one had followed them. Then, she asked, "What about me?"

Em blinked at the question. "You?"

Just asking the question made Maria's heart race, but the fear didn't stop her from wanting to know. So, she closed some of the space between them and lowered her voice. "What reaction did you expect me to have?"

Em fixed her gaze somewhere near Maria's throat. "I figured you'd be annoyed that you didn't get your way," she said honestly, "but that you'd get over it."

Maria suppressed a laugh.

No one said things like that to her.

No one but Em.

She was wrong, though. Annoyed didn't even scratch the surface of what Maria would've felt. Remnants of the despair Maria had felt for weeks, while nearing Em's island, still lingered in her chest.

It was no accident that Em underestimated Maria's feelings for her. Maria had woven that lie herself.

Now, it was up to Maria to unravel it.

"I wouldn't have," Maria said.

Em's brows furrowed.

"I wouldn't have gotten over it," Maria confessed. "I would've *never* gotten over it."

Em's lips parted in surprise, and a soft gasp spilled from them. She eyed the wooden boards beneath her feet for a moment, and when she finally spoke, her voice was no more than a whisper. "Why didn't you make me stay?"

"I intended to," Maria admitted, "for a while."

Em nodded, unsurprised. "What changed?"

Gods.

She might as well have asked a hurricane where it began.

"Everything," Maria said with a shrug. "Everything changed."

When Em's posture crumbled inward, Maria barely resisted the urge to lift Em's chin and look at her face.

Was she upset? Nervous? Maria only needed to see Em's bright, expressive eyes, and she'd know.

But she gripped the hilt of her sword, instead, and waited for the impulse to pass.

Em licked her lips, and then, quickly—in that recklessly honest way that only Em would—she said, "I wouldn't have gotten over you, either."

Maria's heart skipped a beat. "Em…"

"The dragons knew—even before I told them," Em admitted, "but I had to see them. I had to know they were all right. Before I could think about me, about what *I* wanted, I needed to know they were okay."

She spoke with urgency, as if she needed Maria to understand, but Maria understood it better than even *Em* did.

Maria understood what Em hid beneath it all.

Beneath the thorns formed by Em's own guilt lay the same kindness Catherine had used against her. Because, contrary to what Em so clearly believed, not even Catherine could kill something that strong.

She could burn it.

She could damage it.

But it would always rise again.

Maria tried to close the remaining space between them, but the damn cat placed *himself* in that sliver of space and meowed up at them.

They both looked down.

"The cat has to go, Em," Maria informed her.

"What?" Em glared up at Maria, while pointing down at Rat-Slayer. "How can you say no to that face?"

Maria looked down at the cat, whose face—if she had to define it—looked more grumpy than cute.

Ugh, fine.

It was cute, too.

It didn't change anything, though.

"Well, let's see," Maria said, returning her attention to her cat-taming surgeon. "I am *the* most feared pirate in all of Aletharia. I kill for sport. My favorite sound is the sound of a naval ship sinking, and my favorite sensation is the warm spray of blood against my skin." She tilted her head and raised both eyebrows. "Does that answer your question?"

Em considered it for a moment, then said, "No."

A surprised laugh burst from Maria's lips, and she threw out her arms in defeat. "All right." She stepped as close to her surgeon as Rat-Slayer would allow and tilted her face toward Em's. "Let's try this, then."

Em's bright green eyes darkened at their proximity.

"There are things I plan to do to you tonight," Maria murmured, "that I can't have an audience for."

Em's mouth fell open, and blood rushed to her face.

Even in the *dark*, she looked red.

Maria crossed her arms and grinned.

"U-umm," Em stammered, "what *kinds* of things?"

Maria's eyebrows arched higher. "You're the color of a fucking apple, Em. You *know* what kinds of things."

Coincidentally, Maria loved apples.

"Just," Em squeaked, "making sure."

Em knelt beside Rat-Slayer, who gave her an extra-grumpy meow. "I know," she sighed. She offered him a conciliatory chin-rub, as she broke the news. "But the captain says you have to go."

Maria stared blankly at both of them. They acted as if the cat didn't have an entire ship to explore.

And an *important* job to do.

"You can stay in my cabin, though!" Em offered. "You'll have the whole bed to yourself until I get there."

"*If* you get there," Maria said.

Em looked up, and her eyes widened.

Maria chuckled at her expression.

Rat-Slayer offered another disgruntled meow.

Em nodded, as if she understood that perfectly. "He says he'll give us privacy in exchange for belly rubs."

Maria rolled her eyes. "Deal."

"She agrees," Em informed the cat. Then, as if the entire conversation hadn't been strange enough, she said, "Goodnight," and the cat immediately slinked off into the night.

Maria shook her head. "I still haven't figured out whether you speak *cat* or the cat speaks *you*."

Emilia giggled—but didn't bother to enlighten her.

CHAPTER 10
Not Wrong

Inside the captain's quarters, the music and laughter faded away, and the steady creaks and groans of the ship rose to reclaim the silence.

As Maria lit each candle on her table, she grew increasingly aware of the silent surgeon standing on the other side of it. "Breathe, love," she muttered. "I can feel your tension from here."

Em frowned, as if she found that hard to believe, but if she could see her *own* face, she'd understand.

Few people were as expressive as Emilia Drakon.

"I just wanted to ask about…" Em trailed off. She winced and then, blurted out, "Judith talked to you?"

"Is that a question or a statement?" Maria asked.

Em lifted her shoulders in a nervous shrug. "Both?"

Maria snorted. "Yes."

Em waited for Maria to elaborate, which Maria had no intention of doing. "She implied that…*Zain* was the reason she and Pelt found out."

"You thought those two figured it out on their own?" Maria said.

"Why shouldn't I?" Em said—in a way that let Maria know

218

exactly how much of an asshole that remark made her. "So…Zain knows."

Maria lit the final candle. "Couldn't you tell?"

"It did sound as if he might've." Em shifted on her feet. "Earlier."

After they'd kissed behind the barrels.

When Em had touched Maria like she was something precious and not something dangerous…

"Did you have any other questions?" Maria spoke with a coldness she didn't feel.

"What are you going to do?" Em asked.

"That's none of your concern, surgeon," Maria said.

Em narrowed her eyes. "None of my concern?"

There it was.

That *bite* in her tone.

Maybe it was wrong for Maria to love it as much as she did, but she simply couldn't help it.

Maria lifted her gaze, peering at the dragon sorceress over the flickering flame of the candle.

Em's green eyes flashed like the fire itself. "Catherine tried to use it against us today and nearly succeeded—because *you* didn't tell me," she reminded Maria. "Pelt and Judith came to me to ask questions. I'm involved, whether my *captain* thinks so or not, and I *am* concerned, whether she likes it or not."

Did Em *know* she flicked her tongue harder against her teeth when she was angry?

Did she know how sexy that one little action was?

"You shouldn't be," Maria said simply.

Em rolled her eyes. "Look, you can be an asshole all you like, but it's not going to change anything," she snapped. "You could stab me, and I'd still care. I'd stab you back! Three times over. But I'd still care."

Maria laughed at that—even as her heart twisted at the confession.

This witch wouldn't stop until she'd shattered every shard of ice within Maria, would she?

"I think you'd go for more than three," Maria teased.

"Mmm," Em said, "maybe."

Maria's smile widened.

Oh, she was lovely.

Lovely, sharp, and destined to ruin Maria in every way.

"Now that we've established it *is* my concern—" Em began.

"I don't think we established that," Maria said.

Em ignored the interruption. "I think we should just…explain it to him."

Maria shook out the wooden splint, extinguishing the small flame. "We call that a confession, darling."

"He'd understand," Em insisted. "He'd have to." She stepped forward. "I can talk to him for you—explain how convincing Catherine can be."

"Zain knew Catherine, too," Maria reminded her, "and unlike you and me, he never liked her." She set out two dented tankards, pewter clanging against the table, and she cocked her head slightly. "Though that likely had more to do with Ingelby than any actual wisdom, but he'll never admit that."

Determined as ever, Em tried again. "If I tell him—"

"You won't," Maria interrupted. With a few long strides, Maria rounded the table. "You knew nothing. You know nothing." When Em tried to look away, Maria took Em's face and turned it back toward her. "You weren't an accomplice, and you're not going to make yourself look like one now." She forced Em to meet her gaze. "Do you understand me?"

A pink flush of anger spread beneath Em's cheeks, and her eyes —wide and bright in the candlelight—darkened. "No."

Maria narrowed her eyes, but Em never cowered. Her breath quickened, but even *that* might've been in desire and not fear.

Maria loved Em's courage. More than anything, she loved it, but gods, why couldn't Em understand?

Maria had done what she'd done out of fear for Em's life. She couldn't watch Em risk her life again—*because* of what Maria had done!

Maria released her. "It was my decision, *my* crime," she said firmly. "I'll handle it."

"You didn't do anything wrong," Em told her.

Maria released an incredulous laugh. "Come on, love. You don't believe that." When she saw only worry and concern in Em's eyes, instead of the judgment that *should've* been there, Maria said, "We're pirates, Em. We don't show mercy. We don't give quarter." She spread out her arms. "I let her *go*."

"So, you're not the unfeeling pirate you pretend to be," Em said. "Is that really such a bad thing?"

With a shake of her head, Maria returned to her table. "To a crew of pirates who signed on to work for the legendary Captain Maria Welles? Yes!"

"I think they'd like who you really are," Em said.

"They wouldn't," Maria assured her, "and stop insinuating that I'm not actually heartless. I am!" She reached for a bottle of rum to fill the tankards—and then decided against it. "When I want to be."

"I think they'd understand," Em said, "if you just—"

Maria braced her hands against the table. "Em," she interrupted. "They won't." She lifted her shoulders in a careless shrug. "They're not *like* you, all right?"

Em tensed.

She averted her gaze—but not before Maria saw the flash of pain in her eyes—and though Maria didn't know the reason for it, the sight opened a deep ache within her chest.

"Oh." The smallness of Em's voice, as she uttered that one word, only intensified the ache.

Had Maria hurt her, somehow?

What had she done?

"They're pirates, love," Maria tried to explain. "They respect me because I make them respect me."

"You can't think that's the only reason," Em said.

"I can, and I do," Maria assured her. "Em, why do you think it was so easy for me to fuck you over?" She threw out her arms. "Because it's all I've done! For ten years! Everyone on this ship has been fucked over by me! That's why they're here! That's why they serve!"

"That's not true." Em's brows furrowed. "Judith—"

"Judith?" Maria said with a bitter laugh. "Oh, Em, you *know* Judith! Do you think she would've joined the navy, if it weren't for me? Do you think she wanted this life?" Her chest grew tight. "Ship captain was my ambition! She took the least dangerous job possible because she wanted to stay close to *me*."

Em watched with a sympathetic frown that Maria neither wanted nor deserved. "She *chose* to help you that day. She told me that."

"Yes," Maria admitted, "but she wouldn't have had the chance, wouldn't have even *known*, if it weren't for me." She shook her head. "She chose the least dangerous job possible, and now, she's a pirate."

"That's not your fault," Em said.

Maria rolled her eyes. "Of course it's my fault." She stepped back. "And Zain? He didn't even want to help! I blackmailed him. Pelt? Want to know about him next?" Maria didn't wait for an answer. "I was prepared to kill him, when he saw us….committing the theft. But he jumped in and started helping. So, he's alive. For now. Until one day, when he hangs for piracy." She sighed, "When we all do."

"The theft?" Em repeated. "Captain, you can't *steal* people."

"Legally, you can," Maria said, her voice as cold and sharp as ice. "I have the scars to prove it."

Sympathetic pain twisted at Em's face.

Maria leaned forward, pressing her hands against the table once more. "And don't *ever* mention the nature of my crime where my crew might hear you."

Em shook her head in disbelief. "You pour so much energy into protecting this reputation—just so they'll respect you," she said, "when the person you *really* are is worthy of more respect than anyone you've ever pretended to be."

Maria blinked.

Em had said those words so quietly, and yet, they blared in Maria's head, as if she'd screamed them.

They pierced through Maria's anger and left her numb with shock—so numb that the muscles in her arms went limp, and she nearly fell forward.

"You can't really think that," Maria said.

Em gave her an incredulous look. "*Of course* I really think that," she scoffed. "You *know* I think that!"

"Well," Maria said breathlessly, "it doesn't matter." Numbness poured through every vein of her body. "You're different."

Em took a step back. "Yeah, I'm wrong. I got it the first time." Her voice shook with that same pain Maria had glimpsed in her eyes a few moments ago. "You don't have to keep saying it."

Maria looked up, her eyes wide. "What?"

"I think wrong. I talk wrong. Everything about me is wrong. I know," Em said. She waved a hand at Maria, but she didn't look at her. "I've heard it my whole life. I don't need to hear it from you, too."

Maria didn't know whether the adrenaline coursing through her was shock or anger. All she knew was that she needed to touch Em. She needed to *see* her.

Maria circled the table as fast as she could, and she grabbed Em by the arms. "Stop saying that. Why are you saying that?" She tilted her head, trying to catch Em's gaze. "I said you're different. Not wrong!"

Em looked up, and the many years of pain Maria saw in those bright, green eyes shattered her. "Everyone says different when they mean wrong."

Oh.

Oh, Em.

Em herself rarely said anything she didn't mean, but just as Maria had learned to *say* the things she didn't mean, Em had learned that other people did.

And after hearing the same lie over and over, Em had learned to interpret it.

Perhaps someone had even told her what it meant.

Someone who *wanted* to see her hurt.

Someone like her mother.

Maria loosened her hold on Em's arms. "It might've been what someone else meant, but it's not what I meant."

Em frowned, as if she couldn't even fathom that—as if she couldn't even fathom that anyone might not hate everything about her. "It's not?"

Maria lifted one hand and slid her fingers through Em's soft, black hair. "No, love," she murmured, "it's not."

"Then, w-what—" Em stammered. She stared absently at Maria's black, leather doublet. "What did you mean, then?"

Maria didn't *want* to answer that question.

She *shouldn't* have answered that question, but Em had sounded so sincere, so desperate.

Before Maria could stop herself, she began to speak.

"I meant—" Maria stepped back, fighting the urge to run. "I meant...how the fuck do you think you did this to me?" Maria pressed her hand over her aching chest to emphasize exactly where this awful, *wonderful* feeling resided. "I'm Captain Maria Welles! Do you think this happens to me often? Ever?" Her voice sounded broken, even to her own ears. "Do you think I fall for everyone?"

Em's eyes widened, and her lips parted.

"When I say you're different, I mean you—"

I mean you're amazing. I mean you're perfect.

I mean...

Gods, what the fuck do I mean?

Maria pressed her palm harder into her chest, as if it would make her heart stop racing. "You do this."

Maria knew that didn't make any sense, but neither did what she felt.

Em had yet to say anything, but she honestly didn't look...*able* to. Her breasts rose and fell beneath her thin, black shirt, and the shock practically radiated from her.

Maria stepped toward her. "I'm a pirate," she said breathlessly. "I don't know what's right anymore."

Em opened her mouth and closed it again, as if she couldn't

remember how to form words. After a sharp inhale, she finally managed to speak, "Yes, you do."

"No, Em," Maria said with a soft laugh, "I don't." Her pulse finally slowed, and she stepped closer to her wonderful surgeon. She pressed her knuckles beneath Em's chin, lifting her face. "All I know is that what's inside you…*isn't* wrong."

Em stared up at Maria with eyes wider than Maria had ever seen before. Quick, erratic breaths fell from her soft, pink lips, and with Maria's fingers so close to Em's neck, she felt the faint tap of Em's rapid pulse.

For just a moment, Maria felt relief—at having said the things she'd held inside for so long, even if they *had* sounded ridiculous once they were out of her mouth.

Then, came the regret.

This wasn't how she'd intended for the night to go.

Maria had intended to celebrate—to find some way to help Em relax.

This day had been tumultuous enough without Maria unleashing more chaos with her ridiculous words. When Em had asked her dangerous, little question, Maria should've refused to answer.

Maria cleared her throat. "I—" She stepped back, suddenly, and dropped her hands. "I need a drink."

Em wobbled on her feet the moment Maria released her.

Maria returned to her table. Then, as if nothing had happened, she resumed her task of fixing a drink for herself and her guest. She considered the rum once more, before retrieving a bottle of wine, instead.

Maria filled both tankards with an old, Aevarian wine Adda had once given her. As far as Maria knew, they didn't make wine in Aevaria anymore, but what else would she do with it, besides drink it?

Sell it back to Adda?

Oh, she could just hear Adda now.

'You ungrateful, little—'

Em stepped toward the table, and Maria looked up at her.

Em opened her mouth and then closed it again.

She stepped back, then forward.

And all the while, Maria watched her with raised eyebrows, nearly overfilling one of the tankards.

Had she...*broken* the witch?

With a jerky shake of her head, Em turned and fled in the direction of the stern windows.

Maria placed the bottle in the center of her table. She followed Em—but...at a more reasonable pace.

When she reached the floor-to-ceiling windows that set the captain's quarters apart from other parts of the ship, Maria took her place beside Em, and they gazed out at the sea together.

The blackish-blue waves rose and fell, carrying the ship toward a near-black horizon.

"Have you eaten anything?" Maria asked.

Em didn't answer.

That might've annoyed Maria—if Em had given any indication that she'd heard the question. As it was, it only worried her.

"Em?"

Em glanced up at Maria and blinked. "Oh," she whispered. Curiosity flashed in her green eyes, but—perhaps out of embarrassment—she chose *not* to ask how long Maria had been there.

Maria crossed her arms and waited.

With another nervous glance toward the windows, Em asked, "How far can we see at night?"

"From *here*? Not far," Maria said with a scoff. "But that's why we have this thing called a crow's nest."

Her taunting tone earned a peeved look from Em, and Maria smiled at the familiar sight.

When Em tried to return her attention to the sea, Maria said, "She isn't out there."

"I wasn't looking for her," Em lied.

"Yes, you were."

Em didn't deny it again. Perhaps she'd remembered how bad of a liar she was. "You don't *know* she's not out there," Em said. "Catherine lies. Everything she does is about misdirection and manipulation. If she compliments you, it's so she can hurt you later. If she let us go, it can only mean—"

Maria couldn't help the bitterness that seeped into her voice. "You don't need to tell *me* what Catherine does."

Em didn't flinch at Maria's tone the way the rest of her crew would have, but she *did* mumble, "Sorry."

Like an annoying, little dagger, guilt pricked at the place between Maria's ribs.

"You know I trust you. It's just—" Em rubbed two fingers against her chest, as if she were struggling to breathe. "I can't help but worry—about you, about Judith, about the crew… I—" Her breath grew shallow, and she gasped. "I can't lose you, too."

Too.

Maria's stomach sank.

Once, she would've misunderstood Em's questioning—the way Zain still did—but she hadn't known the terrible fate of Em's people back then.

Now, she dropped her arms to her side and turned. "I know." Afraid Em wouldn't hear her, Maria took her by the shoulders and turned her. Em *still* didn't meet her gaze, but Maria spoke, anyway —enunciating each word. "I understand."

Em's brows furrowed, and her gaze darted upward. "Captain—"

There it was—a flicker of doubt in her eyes.

"Em," Maria interrupted. She lifted her hands and curled them around Em's soft face before she could look down again. "You don't need to apologize or explain," she said, "because I understand you."

Maria wouldn't have said those words if she didn't mean them. She barely said them when she *did* mean them—and she needed Em to realize that.

Em's jaw shifted against Maria's finger. The movement of Em's mouth had an instant effect on Maria, even when she wished it didn't.

But it didn't feel like the right time to kiss Em's lips—pink and appealing as they were. So, Maria settled for pressing a kiss against Em's forehead, instead.

With the way Em gasped afterward, the way her lips trembled—you'd have thought Maria had kissed her somewhere *far* more sensitive than the forehead.

Maria leaned back on the heels of her boots.

The soft adoration that filled Em's wide, green eyes, in that moment, could've melted the iciest of hearts.

Maria's chest tightened, and she stroked her thumb along Em's warm, reddened cheek. "Come to the table," she urged. "I've fixed us something to drink."

And then, Maria did something that was becoming frighteningly easy to do. She took Em by the hand.

Em watched Maria the entire way—only diverting her wide-eyed gaze when she nearly ran into a chair.

Maria resisted the urge to laugh. All this over a kiss to her forehead?

Or had their intertwined fingers affected her, too?

Maria released Em's hand when they reached the table. "Sit," she instructed, "and blink, goddamn it."

Em's face turned an adorable shade of pink, and she instantly shifted her gaze toward the floorboards.

As Em took her seat, Maria strolled around to the other side of the table. "Have you eaten anything?"

Em picked up the tankard, examining the red liquid inside. "You're wasting more of your wine on me?"

Maria stiffened. "I hate it when you say it like that."

Em blinked. "Oh." Her brows furrowed. "Umm," she tested, "you're…*giving* me more of your wine?"

"Better," Maria said.

Em lifted her eyebrows, as if she didn't understand the difference, and continued, "It didn't work out too well last time, did it?"

"I think it worked out fine," Maria said. When Em opened her mouth to argue, Maria pointed at her. "The wine was not to blame for Jonas's foolishness."

Em nodded, acknowledging that. "And our fight?"

Maria looked away. "It was…small."

But not small enough to be forgettable, apparently.

Em set her tankard on the table.

Maria sighed. She didn't particularly like thinking of that night —when she'd let her anger and jealousy overtake her, when she'd prodded at Em's weakest points.

Striking at someone's most vulnerable points was part of being a good swordsman—part of being a good pirate, even.

But was it part of being a good captain?

A good lover?

"I pushed when you needed me to wait," Maria admitted. "I realize that now."

Em looked up, her eyes wide.

Maria pressed her hands against the wooden table and leaned forward. "In my defense," she said in a sort of conspiratorial whisper, "do you know how hard it is to consider all the ways Catherine might've known you and *not* be able to ask?"

Just the memory made the jealousy thicken in her throat.

"Oh, you asked," Em assured her.

Maria laughed.

Fair enough.

With the same long, wooden table between them and the same red wine, it was impossible for Maria to ignore the similarities between that night and this one—and the vast expanse of how far they'd come.

"Despite how cold—and perhaps even cruel—I was," Maria reminded her, "you still cared enough to lie to my crew, to protect my reputation." She flashed a wicked grin. "Learning *that* was worth our fight."

Em glared at her. "For *you*."

Maria chuckled. "Yes, for me." She straightened and repeated her earlier question. "Have you eaten?"

"Of course," Em said. "We both ate."

Maria frowned. They'd barely seen each other since the battle, and before that...

"You mean this *morning*?"

That didn't count! After everything that had happened, it didn't even feel like the same *day*.

"Yeah, the coconuts," Em said, "near the cliff-side." She picked up her tankard, and a teasing smile curved at the corners of her lips. "The ones I had to show you how to open—after you nearly cut your hand."

Maria scowled at that…*somewhat* accurate accusation. "I knew how to open it. I was just distracted by those giant monsters cuddling with you."

Em's smile vanished. She set down the tankard and narrowed her eyes. "Never," she snarled, pointing her forefinger in warning, "—and I mean *never*—call my dragons *'monsters.'*"

Maria raised her hands in surrender.

Em shot another murderous glare her way, before picking up the tankard.

Maria uncovered the plate of meat and bread Judith had left her —and made a mental note to remind Judith to feed their forgetful surgeon next time, too.

She tore the bread in half and sliced the meat into two slices. "I hardly think our *one* coconut counted," Maria scoffed, "especially after spending the entire day in battle."

Well-accustomed, by now, to Maria's habit of under-exaggerating how much fruit she'd eaten, Em smiled behind her tankard. "*I* ate one. You ate more."

Maria laughed. "Yes, well, I always eat more than you," she reminded her. She passed one plate to Em and took the other for herself. "With one exception."

Em took a bite of her bread and chewed slowly.

Maria sat down across from Em, but she ignored her food—and rested her face against her hand, instead.

Maria only had to wait a minute or two before a puzzled frown began to pull at her precious surgeon's brows.

Em looked up. "What's the exception?"

Maria lifted her eyebrows meaningfully. She leaned back in her chair, and then, with deliberate slowness, she looked down—toward the center of her own thighs.

Em's eyes widened, and she immediately choked.

She dropped the bread and reached for her tankard, and Maria helpfully pushed the bottle toward her, as well.

Throughout the next few moments of choking, Maria caught only a few of Em's complaints.

"Captain—"

More coughing.

"—asshole—"

More coughing.

"—stab you!"

Maria relaxed against the back of the wooden chair and waited for Em to regain her composure. Only when Em slammed her tankard down with finality, did Maria say, "I didn't catch all of that."

Em pinned her with eyes as sharp as daggers. "If I weren't drained of magic right now," she said, careful to enunciate every word, "I would stab you."

Maria laughed. She leaned forward and murmured, "Stabbing doesn't involve magic, darling."

Em leaned forward, too. "No, but healing you does."

Maria had always liked her table—the long, wooden one that separated them now—but in that moment, she would've wished it out of existence, if she could.

If it meant she could grab Em's chair and pull it closer.

If it meant she could grasp Em's thighs and pull *her* closer.

Maria tilted her head, and the cool, stone beads in her left braid brushed the overheated skin of her neck. "What's the matter, surgeon?" Maria taunted. "Are you too sweet to let me suffer?"

Em's lips parted, and a small breath escaped. Then, her brain seemed to restart, and she shook her head.

"No! No, I am not," the flustered surgeon insisted—though the distinct lack of stabbing said otherwise.

Maria let her head fall back against the chair, and she laughed freely. The laughter shook something loose in Maria's chest, and the tension of the day began to unravel.

The panic of seeing her ship under attack faded.

The indescribable feeling of seeing Em struck in the head with a steel sword…weakened.

Even her hatred of Catherine slipped to the back of her mind.

When her laughter tapered, too, Maria looked at Em.

Em must've been staring at her for quite some time—because without meaning to, she'd made eye-contact.

With a lazy smile, Maria asked, "What is it?"

"Hmm?" Em blinked twice, and then, as she likely realized she'd been staring, she averted her gaze. Her cheeks reddened, and she grabbed her tankard. She drank deeply. "I was just…thinking."

"About?" Maria prompted.

"You," Em said irritably. "You're beautiful, okay?"

Maria blinked.

She couldn't remember the last time a woman had used that adjective to describe her, but she knew—without a doubt—that it was before the scars.

Maria didn't doubt women's attraction to her—scars or no scars—but that didn't mean the change in descriptors had escaped her notice.

She was attractive now.

Sexy, now.

But never beautiful.

Yet, Em had called her *beautiful*.

And she'd said it as though it were a fact.

A simple, annoying fact.

A surprised smile pulled at Maria's lips.

Em pushed back her chair, its legs scraping the floorboards. "I'm going to check the windows again."

Maria's smile faded. "Em! You've barely eaten anything." She tapped the table twice. "Eat. The lookouts will send word, if anything changes."

Em shifted in her chair. "What if they don't see it? What if they're too drunk?"

"The ones on lookout aren't drinking with the rest of the crew," Maria assured her. "Regular rum rations—no more than that."

Em's shoulders relaxed slightly. "You're sure?"

"Yes," Maria said.

It wasn't *totally* a lie.

Maria had told them not to drink too much, and she sincerely doubted they'd disobey a direct order from their captain.

Only the woman in front of her did that.

Well, Em *and* Judith—if you counted the Helen law.

Also, Pelt—since he often covered for them.

Hmm. She was growing less certain by the moment.

"We're alive," Maria said. She could feign certainty, whether she felt it or not. "We survived the day."

"The day isn't over yet," Em pointed out.

"Yes, it is," Maria said. She picked up the thin slice of meat and bit into it.

Maria hated the late stages of a voyage, when their supplies began to spoil, but her respect for Judith always grew the strongest during those days—because Judith could make even the plainest food taste interesting.

Examining the meat, Maria asked, "Some kind of pepper?"

Em's anxious gaze darted toward Maria. "I think so," she said. "We ground some up a few weeks ago."

Maria pointed at the food left on Em's plate. "Eat."

Em obeyed without complaint—which might've been the most alarming thing yet. She chewed a bite of her bread, her green eyes glassy and distant.

"For you, this is all new, still," Maria sighed. "For the rest of us, it's just life as a pirate. All victories are temporary. The enemy is *always* still out there."

"I know that," Em said.

"Yet, you don't want to celebrate." Maria set her tankard on the table and gestured in the direction of the main deck. "You don't want to see *them* celebrate."

"That's not true," Em said, but her voice sounded strained. "Is it so bad that I'm concerned?"

"No," Maria said, "but Em…" She took another sip of wine and exhaled slowly. "It's important for the crew to celebrate every win—no matter how small or temporary. It's good for morale, and as their captain, morale is something I have to consider."

"Yeah," Em said with a quick nod. "I get that."

"You're part of my crew, too, love," Maria said.

Em's brows drew together in confusion. "You want *me* to celebrate?"

"I want you to relax," Maria told her, "and yes, in your own way, celebrate."

Em shook her head. "I don't think I can—not with her ship still out there."

Maria took another bite of the spicy meat. "Do you understand rank?" she said, after a moment. "Do you realize that even if we'd killed Catherine, someone would've taken her place within the hour?"

Em still tensed at the mention of Catherine—but less so than when they'd first met. "I suppose," she admitted, "but no one could be as bad as *her*."

Maria snorted—mostly because she remembered thinking similar thoughts. "If only that were true."

Em's frown deepened, but she didn't argue.

Maria set a half-eaten piece of bread on her plate and leaned forward. "I know hyper-vigilance is just part of it. It was for me, too," she said. "But you need to celebrate, love. You need to *rest*."

Em froze—with her own food still in hand. "You think I'm hyper-vigilant?"

Maria lifted her eyebrows in disbelief. "You don't?"

"I—" Em shook her head. "I think I'm reacting rationally."

"Well, yes," Maria agreed. "That *is* usually what we think."

Em gave her a peeved look.

Maria chuckled. "All right." She rested her elbows against the table. "Think of it this way," she suggested. "Earlier, you walked past sailors who were celebrating their own survival after a seemingly hopeless battle. Is that what you saw?"

Confusion twisted at Em's brows.

"Or," Maria continued, "did you only see what might happen to them—if we're attacked again?"

Recognition flickered in Em's eyes. "You—" she stammered. She inhaled sharply. "You're saying my perception is wrong?"

There was that word again.

"Not wrong," Maria repeated. "Different."

Em buried her face in her hands, intertwining her fingers with strands of soft, black hair.

Nothing distressed Maria more than watching Em's self-loathing spirals. The guilt had seeped into Em's veins like poison, and it emerged in times like these.

Before Em could pull at her hair, Maria pushed back her chair and stood. She circled the table and knelt in front of Em's chair.

She placed her hands on Em's knees.

At Maria's touch, Em reflexively released her hair and dropped her hands to her lap.

Stop reacting to her pain, Maria told herself. *Catherine's already learned to use it against you.*

Maria couldn't help it, though. "You told me what happened to your people," she said. "How could I know *that* and think any reaction to it is wrong?"

Em's breath came in shallow pants.

"Nothing about you is wrong," Maria told her.

Em eyed her skeptically. "You keep saying that."

"*You* keep not believing it," Maria countered.

One corner of Em's mouth twitched upward. "Well, after the way you reacted," she muttered, "I thought I might've imagined you saying it the first time."

Maria scowled at Em's teasing. "What was wrong with how I reacted?"

Em just laughed. "So, you," she hesitated, "*don't* think everything about me is wrong?"

Gods, if Maria could have five minutes alone with the person who'd told Em that…

Involuntarily, her fingers tightened around Em's knees, and Em's gaze darted toward Maria's hands.

Maria forced herself to let go. "No, love. I don't."

She climbed to her feet and leaned against the table. Maria

hoped the minuscule amount of space she'd put between them might clear her mind a bit.

Em leaned forward in her seat, and the toe of her shoe brushed Maria's boot. "I'm sorry," Em sighed. "I guess I'm not handling this well."

"What?" Maria crossed her arms. "I stabbed people for questioning *me*. You're doing fine!"

Em laughed at that. "Well, thank you for setting such a low standard, then."

"No need to thank me, love," Maria teased. Her lips curved into a deep smile. "I never mind doing what I want."

Em rolled her eyes.

With a curious frown, Maria took hold of Em's face and lifted it. Her stomach twisted at the sight of those greyish-brown rings around Em's lovely, green eyes.

The last time she'd seen Em's eyes look like *that* was the day they'd met.

"Does using too much magic do this to you?" Maria asked. She traced the darkened skin with her thumb, and Em's pupils dilated at her touch. "It reminds me of when you were starved."

"Oh," Em said breathlessly. "Yeah. It depletes me."

Maria's chest tightened. "Is it as miserable?"

"Honestly?" Em said with a slight grimace. "Yes."

Maria dropped her hand, and frustration pulled her muscles tight. She could force Em to eat if she had to, but she couldn't stop her from using magic.

Em must've noticed Maria's discomfort—because she quickly added, "The recovery's quicker, though!"

Maria tapped two fingers against her leather-clad thigh. "Sleep?" she asked. "Is that what you need?"

"It helps," Em admitted. "Magic is an exchange of energy. Healers, especially—we take from ourselves. If we don't replenish our bodies, the magic runs dry."

"So, you need to eat, too," Maria realized.

"Yes," Em said. "That's why I was so much weaker when we

met. I hadn't eaten regularly in months, and I can't use my magic in that state."

"You should be eating more, then," Maria decided.

With a baffled laugh, Em said, "I think regularly is enough." She looked down, eyeing her own ample curves. "I mean, look at me."

"I will," Maria said with a smirk. "Thank you."

Em's cheeks flushed, and only after a few moments of stunned silence did she mumble, "Stop that."

Maria chuckled. She redirected her attention to Em's face—even though she fully intended to spend *much* of the night admiring Em's curves. "So, now that you've eaten, will you feel better?"

"Eventually," Em assured her. "Sometimes, it takes more to fully recover—a night of rest, a few meals…"

Maria's smile faded. "You shouldn't have skipped a meal, then!"

"I know," Em said defensively. "I was busy. It…wasn't intentional."

"Yes, well," Maria sighed, "next time, I'll tell Judith to *make* you stop and eat—at gunpoint, if necessary."

Em squinted at that. "Wouldn't that break one of your laws?"

With an annoyed tilt of her head, Maria said, "Fine. I'll tell her to tell *me*, and I'll hold you at sword-point myself."

Em flashed that adorably impish smile—the one that always seemed to tie Maria's stomach into knots. "And how is that different from any other night?"

Maria snorted. "Careful, surgeon."

Em's smile deepened, and her bright, green eyes sparkled in the flickering candlelight.

Maria could've melted against the table behind her, if she'd let herself. "Whatever it takes," she said in a more serious tone, "you *will* take care of yourself while aboard my ship. Do you understand me?"

Em's brows furrowed. "Not…really?"

Well, she was nothing, if not honest.

With a short laugh, Maria said, "We'll teach you." Even to her own ears, it sounded more like a threat than an offer. She curled her fingers around the edge of the table and leaned forward. "We didn't have to teach you to work hard. You already did that." She flashed a taunting smile. "So, we'll teach you this, instead."

Em lifted her eyebrows warily—but didn't object.

At the very least, Em had stopped worrying about Catherine. So, Maria considered the first stage of her work complete.

"There's no way to heal yourself tonight, though?" Maria asked. "You have to leave yourself this way—until tomorrow?"

"I wouldn't say *no* way," Em said with an alarming amount of eagerness. "I could still summon the sea goddess. She'd probably call it an overreaction, once she saw my injuries, but—"

Maria scowled at the suggestion. "We talked about this on the island, Em," she said. "It's one thing for the crew to accept a witch who's been working alongside them for months. It's another for them to accept a witch who consorts with evil goddesses."

"Aletha isn't evil!" Em insisted.

"Good luck convincing *them* of that," Maria said.

Em breathed out a frustrated sigh. "It was only a joke."

Maria doubted that. "So, just food and rest. There are no other ways to restore magic?"

"No one's ever mentioned anything…" Em trailed off, suddenly, and to Maria's delight, she flushed.

Maria widened her eyes. "Oh? Why are we turning pink *this* time?" She turned, casting a playful glance over her shoulder. "I don't see anyone with their tits out."

"Oh, fuck you," Em grumbled.

Maria laughed loudly. "What *did* cause the blush, then?"

"Nothing!" Em said quickly. "A…silly memory."

An unpleasant thought made Maria's smile slip. "It wasn't a memory of Catherine, was it?"

Maria hated the thought of Catherine making Em blush—especially now that Maria had claimed that privilege for herself.

Em frowned at her reaction. "Uh, no. Nothing to do with Catherine."

"Good." Maria winced. "I mean…" She tried to think of a response that might hide her feelings a little better—but ultimately gave up. "Good."

Em raised both eyebrows.

Maria cleared her throat. "So, you remembered another way, then?"

Em shifted uncomfortably in her chair. "No." She glanced down at her hands. "I mean, someone *did* mention something once—which made me feel like I was lying when I said no one had mentioned another way," she said in a rush. "But it's not a real way."

"What makes you so sure?" Maria asked.

"Well, the fact that it's so ridiculous, for one!" Em said with a scoff. She fidgeted. "Besides, I misunderstood the other children all the time. They were all older, and they'd known each other since birth—while I'd known none of them," she rambled. "There's also the fact that I tend to interpret things more literally than others do."

"Yes," Maria agreed.

"Oh." Em glanced up at her. "You noticed, then."

Maria smiled. Yes, she'd noticed. She also found it strangely charming. Not that she wanted to admit *that*. "Why don't you tell me what they said? Perhaps, together, we can decide if you misunderstood."

Em grimaced. "Do I have to?"

Realizing that she'd never get a straight answer if she didn't calm Em first, Maria reached behind her and grabbed the remaining piece of bread. She held it out. "Eat this, while you explain."

Em took the bread with a sigh. "Yes, Captain." She bit into it. "After training, I'd sometimes hear the older children—adolescents, really—talking about meeting up at night," she said begrudgingly, "to replenish in…*unauthorized* ways."

Maria's brows furrowed.

"It was probably just an excuse, though!" Em's face reddened again. Right on cue. "To have sex."

Maria's mouth fell open.

Was she suggesting…?

"It wasn't true," Em said—in response to whatever she'd seen on Maria's face, "I don't think."

Maria could no longer hold back her laughter. "Are you telling me your people had witch orgies?"

"No!" Em snapped. "Captain!"

Maria held up her hands in a show of innocence. "Honest question."

Em rolled her eyes. "It was *two* adolescent kids, meeting up for *regular* sex," she said, "I assume."

Maria snorted at that last part.

"Okay, just forget I said anything. Please," Em whimpered. "I regret even remembering it."

"No, no," Maria said, still suppressing laughter. "I like this idea. How would it work, exactly?"

Em glared up at her. "It wouldn't."

"Hypothetically," Maria asked.

With a forceful sigh, Em blew a black strand of hair out of her face. "*If* it were possible, which it's not," she said, tearing the bread, "it would work because sex *also* involves an exchange of energy."

Maria's smile widened. "Interesting."

She couldn't help but think of the night she'd fucked Em in the galley—when Em had used her magic freely with Maria for the first time, before falling so eagerly to her knees afterward.

The pang of arousal that pulsed in response to *that* memory pushed a soft exhale from Maria's lips. She crossed one boot over the other.

"You never tried it," Maria said curiously, "with any of the girls you grew up around?"

"No," Em said. "I told you! They were older." Her blush deepened. "Besides, I didn't even know what they meant. You think I could've participated?"

Maria flashed her most lascivious grin. "Well, you certainly know how to participate *now*."

Em's eyes flared wide midway through a bite of bread, and she nearly choked on it. *Again*. "I do?" She reached for her drink. "I mean, yes. Of course I do."

With an amused snort, Maria grabbed the bottle of wine from

behind her and refilled Em's tankard. "So, what's stopping you from testing the theory now?"

"Captain," Em said with a scowl, "it won't work."

Maria quirked an eyebrow. "You're not even curious?"

Em licked her lips nervously, and the slight waver in her expression confirmed it. "Well…"

Maria lowered her voice to a murmur—pressing at the first sign of weakness. "Wouldn't hurt to try."

Em's eyes darkened, and she shifted in her chair. "I…guess," she stammered, "it wouldn't."

Desire pooled in Maria's center like warm honey.

Confident that she'd locked the door and made all the necessary preparations already, Maria relaxed her muscles against the table behind her. "Besides," she said lazily, "it's not like I *need* a reason to fuck you."

Em's back went rigid, as if those words had been a bolt of electricity, and she nearly crushed her last piece of bread.

Maria stepped forward. She knelt, again, on the floorboards and gently extracted the single bite of bread from Em's hand. She lifted her own hand, holding the bread between her first two fingers. "After all," Maria murmured, "I already have one."

Em eyed the bread between Maria's fingers, much like she had the orange wedge on the tip of Maria's sword—on her first morning aboard the *Wicked Fate*.

Em reached for it, but Maria pulled her hand away, raising an eyebrow in challenge.

A shaky breath fell from Em's lips.

She could reach for it again, and Maria would surrender the bread.

Or…she could play along.

Em dropped her hand to her lap, and Maria offered her the bread once more.

Em leaned forward, her shortened, black hair falling around her ears. Her mouth closed around Maria's fingers, her lips nearly touching the small, black anchor inked into Maria's forefinger.

Her tongue swiped gently between Maria's fingers to take the bread.

Holy fuck.

Arousal pulsed inside of Maria—as intense and excruciating as a stab wound.

Em chewed the bread slowly, and Maria let her hand fall to Em's leg. Maria gripped just behind Em's knee, digging her fingers into the thin, black fabric.

Em gasped.

Maria waited for Em to take another sip of wine, before taking the tankard and placing it on the table.

Then, Maria leaned forward, curled a hand behind Em's neck, and pulled her downward. When Em's mouth met her own—wet and sweet with wine—Maria groaned.

If there was anything Maria had learned from her kisses with Em, it was that the one time Em couldn't bear to *not* touch Maria was when they kissed.

Em's hand came up to curl along the side of Maria's neck, her fingers soft and gentle beneath Maria's ear, entangling with the loose curls at the nape of Maria's neck.

Em's mouth opened for her, and Maria slipped her tongue inside, tasting the sweet drops of wine that lingered on her tongue.

Maria tightened her grip behind Em's knee and pulled her closer—until the warmth of Em's body pressed into Maria's breasts.

Em pulled back—just barely—her sweet breath still mingling with Maria's. "What was it?"

Maria opened her eyes. "Hmm?"

Em's lips twitched. "You said you already had a reason," she reminded Maria. "What was it?"

Maria trailed her fingers up the back of Em's thigh, cursing the seat of the chair for blocking her path. "I'm celebrating."

Em leaned back a bit more. "Do you," she said nervously, "always celebrate victories in that way?"

Maria quirked an eyebrow, wondering if her sweet Em was capable of a bit of jealousy, too. "Not always, but," she said, "it's not a victory I'm celebrating."

Em's frown deepened. "What are you celebrating, then?"

Maria leaned forward and slid her fingers along Em's cheek-bone. "You."

"Me?" Em breathed.

"You came back, Em," Maria whispered. She trailed her hand lower, running her thumb along Em's soft bottom lip. "You chose to stay. With me. I—I didn't lose you."

Em curled her fingers around Maria's forearm—her touch far too kind, far too gentle. "Captain," she said with a sad laugh. "You could've told me you felt like—like *that*."

"I told you I wanted you," Maria reminded her. "What more was there to say?"

"Clearly, a lot more," Em said, "silly pirate!"

A smile pulled at one corner of Maria's mouth. She rose slightly on her feet, bracing her hands against the arms of Em's chair, as she leaned over her. "So," she said, "do you want me to fuck you or not?"

Em's breath caught in her throat, and her voice came out a bit choked. "You know I do."

The confirmation sent a rush of heat through every vein in Maria's body. She tilted her face toward Em's, and the surgeon's eyes fluttered closed. "Of course I do," she said. "Doesn't mean I don't like to hear it."

Em opened her eyes—and narrowed them.

Maria just grinned.

She glanced down at Em's arms. She took hold of Em's left wrist and turned it over, examining each reddened burn.

A strange wariness flickered in Em's bright green eyes, and she inched her right arm backward.

"I suppose I'll have to be gentle with you tonight."

"*You're* going to be gentle?" Emilia teased.

Maria's gaze flicked upward. "I can be gentle."

"Of course." Em widened those beautiful, green eyes of hers and gave an exaggerated nod—only for a giggle to escape a moment later. She covered her mouth with her right hand, as if that could hide it.

Maria didn't want her to hide it, though.

After everything that had happened that day, Maria *needed* the balm of Em's laughter. She needed the assurance that Em was indeed all right—that Catherine hadn't won this one.

Maria rocked back on the heels of her boots and crossed her arms. "You don't think I can be gentle?"

Still suppressing laughter, Em raised both hands. "When have I ever doubted you, Captain?"

Maria's smile faded, and her hand shot out, catching Em's wrist.

She straightened Em's right arm and pushed back her sleeve, exposing the deep burn around Em's right elbow—the one she'd tried to hide a moment earlier.

The one she'd somehow hidden all fucking day.

"What the fuck is this?" Maria snarled.

Em eyed her warily. "Nothing."

"Nothing?" Maria repeated. "That's the best you can do?"

Em tried to pull her arm back, but Maria held it firmly. "I meant to redo the bandage after I washed up, and I," Em sighed, "forgot."

If Maria were any less angry, she might've asked why Em thought *that* explanation would help. As it was, she merely ignored it —while she examined the burn.

The deep, blood-red burn started on the inside of Em's forearm and curled around her elbow, ending somewhere beneath the sleeve of her thin, black shirt.

It seemed to form some kind of shape, but with it still so swollen, Maria couldn't tell what it was. She noticed little, symmetrical segments in the burn—almost like…dragon-scale?

Maria tightened her grip. "Fucking hell, Em."

Normal burns didn't create symmetrical shapes, and they probably didn't run this deep either.

Maria pushed Em's sleeve up around her upper arm to reveal the full design—a blood-red dragon, wrapped around Em's right arm. "You said," she growled, "your burns weren't severe. This is a really *fucking* severe burn. You lied to me."

Em lifted her chin, clearly ready for a fight.

Maria had always loved that look of defiance in Em's eyes—the same one she'd had the day they met—but Maria refused to let her attraction overshadow her anger. "Your mother's not even alive! Who did you let brand you this time?"

"It's not a brand," Em corrected. "It's a rune."

Maria lifted Em's arm higher, urging her to look at it, as well. "Do you see a difference? Because I don't."

Em did look at it, and not a shred of regret passed over her face. "The purpose is different. Even the process is different," she informed Maria. "There isn't even any iron involved in taking a rune."

"Oh, no iron!" Maria said with feigned relief. "Well, that changes everything. It must not even hurt!"

Em scowled at her sarcasm. "You want to know why I hid it?" She jerked her arm free, and this time, Maria let her—for fear of accidentally hurting her. "Because I knew you'd react like this. You've never understood my runes, and you don't even try."

"How am I supposed to understand you letting someone *hurt* you?" Maria argued, even as a hint of guilt pricked at her chest. "*Scar* you?"

Em flicked her gaze toward the many tattoos that covered Maria's dark skin. "Because *you* let someone give you those," she snarled, "hypocrite."

Maria leaned toward her. "Oh, there you are," she sneered. "Always so clever."

Em stared up at her—unflinching.

Maria held out her arms, displaying the largest of her tattoos. "None of these hurt as badly as that *rune* does, and you know it."

"Which is why my people only take one rune," Em said, "except…dragon-riders, who sometimes take more."

"Sometimes?" Maria repeated.

"Well, no one's ever taken three before," Em admitted, "but there were unique reasons for mine."

Maria crossed her arms. "And those reasons *were?*"

As much as it pained her to see Em injured, Maria did *want* to understand.

"I'm not meant to be separated from my dragons," Em told her, "but dragons aren't sea creatures. They live near the sea, but they can't live *at* sea."

The ball of guilt in Maria's chest grew a bit heavier.

Em extended her arm, offering Maria another look at the intricate rune. The deep burn still looked angry and swollen, but Maria had to admit: once it healed, it'd look quite…attractive.

"This," Em said, "keeps me from having to choose between you."

Maria relaxed her shoulders. "It does?"

Em loved her dragons. The last thing Maria wanted was to come *between* the sorceress and her dragons.

"Yes," Em said, and then, her shoulders relaxed, too—as if her body was in sync with Maria's. "My first dragon rune allowed me to communicate with my dragons across greater distances, but I still needed to be on the same island, at least." She lifted her arm. "This one increases that distance. I can speak to them across the sea. Maybe further!"

"Wow," Maria said.

"During the imprisonment, the dragons couldn't speak to me. They didn't even know where I was," Em told her. "Nymeth didn't want that to happen again. She didn't do this to hurt me, Captain. She did it to keep me safe."

Maria looked away, sighing.

Em climbed to her feet and stepped toward Maria. "This rune will make us safer. I can protect us."

"That isn't your job, love," Maria said, but she took Em's arm and examined it with a more open mind. "There was no way to do this without hurting you?"

Em shook her head. "It wasn't as bad as you think," she assured Maria. "Nymeth's fire is more controlled than my mother's. It didn't hurt nearly as much."

Maria released Em's arm. "Well, that just makes me angrier about the other two."

"And even better," Em said with a strangely bright smile, "this time, I was allowed to flinch!"

Maria scowled. "What the fuck do you mean *allowed*?"

Em winced at her tone. "Oh, uh," she said, "maybe it's best if we *don't* discuss my mother tonight."

Maria was going to kill a ghost. She didn't know *how*, but she was going to kill a fucking ghost.

"The adrenaline was enough to delay the pain," Em assured her. "I barely felt it until a few hours ago."

Maria leaned closer. "Yet, when the pain *did* set in, you continued to perform surgeries all day long."

With each movement Maria made, each shift closer, Em's pupils grew larger—proving that even injuries couldn't diminish the effect they had on each other.

With a stubborn glare, Em said, "That's my job."

Maria hooked her fingers through the thin, leather strap of Em's scabbard and pulled her forward. She leaned in close and growled, "Only when I say it is."

The sound Em made when Maria's waist collided with her own decimated every thought in Maria's mind.

Really, what did emotions or arguments matter, when compared to *that* sound?

How could anything matter at all, when the woman Maria loved responded so easily to a single touch?

"Still feeling gentle?" Em said breathlessly.

Maria took Em by the arms—careful to grip her above the burns—and turned her, pressing her up against the table. "That's not the word I'd use, no."

Em swallowed.

With a swift glance toward Em's arm, Maria added, "But I'd say this confirms it."

Em followed Maria's gaze toward the new rune—and then looked back up. "Confirms what?"

Maria tilted her face closer, until Em's wine-scented breath mingled with her own. Her lips curved into a devious smile. "That drastic measures are needed."

Em's eyelashes fluttered with every word Maria spoke against her mouth. "What *kind* of drastic measures?"

Maria stepped back, and Em nearly fell forward.

Maria unbuckled her scabbard. "Get on the table."

Em blinked. "What?"

Maria reconsidered. "No," she amended. "Remove your sword first. *Then*, I want you on my table."

Em's eyes followed each movement of Maria's fingers—the way a starving woman's eyes followed the movement of a knife through meat. "You," she stammered, "w-want me o-on the—"

Maria didn't think she'd ever heard Em stutter *quite* that much. "Yes," Maria said, as she removed her swords. "That is *exactly* how I meant it."

Em's cheeks reddened, and Maria chuckled at the sight.

Maria draped her swords over the back of the recently vacated chair and then moved her fingers to the thongs of her doublet. She loosened each one, before removing the leather doublet, as well.

"Goddess," Em breathed.

Amusement pulled at the corners of Maria's lips. She turned to face Em, her doublet still in hand.

Maria was still clothed from head to toe, and yet, Em reacted as if she'd stripped down to nothing.

"Em?"

Em's wide, green eyes flicked upward. "Hmm?"

Maria suppressed a laugh. "Table, love."

"Oh!"

Em tried to turn toward the table, but Maria caught her hand and pulled her back.

"*If*," Maria added, "this is what you want."

With a shy smile, Em said, "It is."

Maria smiled, too. "Good." She released Em's hand, and with a quick flick of her fingers, she opened the buckle of Em's scabbard. "Don't forget the sword."

"Right," Em muttered, as she loosened the thin, leather scabbard. "I guess it might get in the way."

Maria hung her doublet over the back of the chair and held out her hand for Em's sword.

Em draped the scabbard over Maria's fingers, and Maria stored Em's sword next to her own.

"Should I undress?" Em said nervously.

"You can do whatever you like," Maria reminded her, "but if you're asking for my preference, I'd like to undress you myself."

Em swallowed hard. "Great. That's…great."

Maria tried *really* hard not to laugh.

Em kicked off her black shoes, before stepping toward the table. She curled her hands around the wooden edge and lifted herself up onto the table.

Maria tugged off her leather boots, watching as Em swung her bare feet back and forth above the floor.

When Em started to lean back a little, Maria warned, "Careful around my maps."

Em glanced over her shoulder. Noticing the map Maria had left spread out on the other side of the wine, she pulled her hand back toward herself.

Maria pulled the chair away from the table, its wooden legs scraping against the floorboards. Then, Maria placed herself where the chair had once been.

Em eyed Maria's leather trousers and the poet's shirt tucked into them. "You're not undressing?"

"Not right now," Maria said. "I'm too impatient."

Em laughed at that. "You're always too impatient."

Maria stepped closer and placed her hands on Em's thighs. Em released a small, shuddery breath—only to gasp a moment later, when Maria gripped her thighs and tugged her closer to the edge. "I don't think you'll be complaining about that tonight."

Em gripped the edge of the table nervously. "Have you ever considered using a bed?" she asked. "You know, some people use those, and they're…safer."

Maria leaned toward her. "Is '*safer*' really what you want?"

Em's bright gaze darted up to meet Maria's, and her breath quickened. "No."

Keeping one hand firmly on Em's soft thigh, Maria cupped Em's face with the other. "Didn't think so."

She pressed her mouth against Em's, breathing in the soft moan Em released in response. She slid her hand up Em's thigh—up over her shapely ass.

Maria squeezed, and even with the trousers in the way, the supple flesh molded easily to Maria's hand. "Fuck," she breathed against Em's lips.

Hungrily, Maria dropped her opposite hand to grasp the other side of Em's ass. Em opened her thighs, and Maria pressed herself between them.

Maria lifted Em off the table, and with a surprised giggle, Em threw her arms around Maria's shoulders.

"I'm going to fall!" she complained.

Quirking an eyebrow, Maria murmured, "You think I wouldn't catch you?"

Em smiled and kissed her.

Maria slid her hands along Em's thighs, relishing the magnificence of Em's curves—and that hint of strength beneath. "I can't believe you removed your armor without me."

"I had to bathe!" Em said with a laugh. "Do *you* bathe fully clothed?"

As turned on by Em's sharp tongue as she was by her body, Maria pulled Em into her, lifting and pressing, urging Em to grind against her.

Any further retort Em might've had turned to a soft, "Oh," as she settled into a steady rhythm.

"There you are," Maria whispered. When she felt the seat of Em's trousers dampen against her shirt, arousal flooded Maria, as well. "Gods, you're fucking soaked, aren't you?"

Em's fingers curled into the thin fabric of Maria's shirt, and her head fell back, her soft, black hair falling away from her face.

It wasn't enough for Maria to know it, though. She needed to feel it on her fingers, taste it on her tongue.

Maria set her down, and Em folded forward, gripping the edge of the table, as if it were the edge of a cliff. Maria stepped back, her own chest heaving. "Arms up."

Em glanced up at Maria. Reluctantly, she let go of the table and lifted her burned arms above her head.

Maria carefully noted each burn, as she pulled Em's shirt free from her trousers. "Tell me if I hurt you."

Maria gently pulled the thin, black shirt over Em's head, before tossing it aside. The fabric tousled Em's shortened hair, and Maria couldn't resist the urge to run her fingers through the soft, black strands.

Maria's gaze fell to Em's large, rounded breasts, and Em—almost imperceptibly—tensed. Maria looked up at her. "Did I hurt you?"

"What?" A puzzled frown pulled at Em's lips. "No."

She certainly didn't *sound* like she was in pain. Her voice had gone breathy—the way it did in moments of passion. So, why had she tensed?

When Em closed her arms around her own bare skin, Maria realized the answer. "You're nervous?"

"I'm always a bit nervous," Em said dismissively. "It's just how I am."

That might've been true, but Maria remembered the first time she'd seen Em without a shirt—and how self-conscious Em had acted, despite Maria only looking at her injuries.

Em felt a specific kind of anxiety about her body.

Maria reached out and touched Em's face. "I just need you to tell me one thing," she pleaded. "Do you doubt everyone's attraction to you? Or only mine?"

Distress flickered in Em's green eyes. "W-what?"

"Please, love," Maria whispered. "I need to know."

I need to know if it's my fault.

Maria hid her feelings to protect herself. She'd done it so long, she didn't remember how to do anything else.

Usually, she wouldn't care who got hurt because of it, but…she cared now.

Maria *hated* that she cared, but the insistent ache in her chest confirmed she did. "Please, tell me."

Em's gaze softened at the plea. "Everyone. I think."

Maria's guilt receded a little at that, but confusion rose to take its place.

How could the woman Maria had spent months watching, the woman she'd spent countless nights thinking about, countless nights trying *not* to think about—how could *that* woman doubt her own beauty?

"Surely, someone's told you you're beautiful." Maria traced the high curve of Em's cheekbone with her thumb. "Didn't you listen?"

Em's skin warmed beneath Maria's touch, and her gaze shifted downward. "Catherine told me," she admitted. "Catherine lies."

Maria's hand fell. "Oh." Her heart twisted with painful understanding. "She does," Maria agreed, "but she didn't lie about that."

Em's brows furrowed, but with her head down, Maria couldn't tell whether she believed it or not.

Maria slipped her fingers beneath Em's chin and gently lifted her face. Enchanting, green eyes met Maria's gaze. "Catherine didn't lie about that."

Em blinked slowly, as if bewitched, and then whispered, "How do you know?"

Maria threw out her arms. "Because I'm fucking looking at you!"

Her impatience earned an amused snort from Em. "You were doing so well with the gentleness," she teased, "for *just* a moment."

Maria rolled her eyes. "Well, maybe if you'd look at yourself with clear eyes for…*just* a moment," she mimicked. She stepped closer, and Em eased her thighs open, allowing Maria to step between them.

Maria cupped Em's right breast in her hand, delighting in the heaviness of it, in the way it overfilled her palm.

Angling her mouth above Em's, Maria murmured, "You think anyone could lie about these?"

Em's breath caught.

Maria caressed Em's breasts for a moment—before squeezing them roughly.

Em's eyes instantly fluttered closed, and she moaned against Maria's mouth.

"I thought you wanted gentle," Maria sneered.

She took Em's hardened, pink nipple between two fingers and squeezed it, too.

Em jerked against her. "Oh, fuck you." She gave what Maria assumed was meant to be a glare, but it didn't quite look like one.

"That is the idea, darling," Maria teased.

Em pressed more of her breast into Maria's hand, and Maria sought out Em's throat with her mouth.

Maria kissed and sucked at the most sensitive spot on Em's neck, and Em moaned in her ear.

When she closed her teeth around the skin, Em practically fell onto her. Her fingers slid over Maria's headscarf, her lips pressing against the side of Maria's face, then her forehead.

"I want— I need—" Em gasped. Her fingers found the place where Maria had tied the headscarf. "May I?"

The poor girl didn't seem to be able to string more than two words together, but it wasn't hard to guess what she wanted.

Maria wanted it, too. "Please."

Maria continued to kiss Em's neck, as Em untied the blue headscarf and tossed it onto the table.

Em slid her fingers into Maria's curls, and she pulled Maria's face toward her own. She kissed Maria hungrily, fingers buried deep in Maria's hair.

Maria knew her head was damp with sweat by now, but if Em cared, she gave no indication. She took Em's bottom lip between her teeth, gently biting down, and Em moaned, her head falling back.

Maria unfastened Em's trousers. "I'll need you on the edge," she murmured, before digging her fingers into Em's thighs and jerking her forward.

Maria tugged Em's trousers down her thick thighs and reluctantly broke away from her mouth to finish removing them. When Maria had the thin, black trousers down to Em's knees, she sank to the floor and pulled them the rest of the way off. She carelessly flung them aside.

Em gripped the edge of the table, her bare breasts heaving. She tried to close her thighs—probably to create some kind of pressure —but Maria grabbed her knees and held them apart.

Em gasped as the open air hit her in the most sensitive place. She was as pink as she was wet, and Maria could no longer resist the urge to touch her.

The moment Maria brushed her thumb over Em's clit, however, Em's grip on the table slackened, and she nearly slid off of it.

With a soft laugh, Maria climbed to her feet, never removing her fingers from between Em's thighs. She closed her free hand around Em's thigh and pressed it against her own leather-clad hip, as she continued to slide her fingers along Em's wet, silken vulva.

Em stared at her, eyes dark, mouth open, and after several moments of Maria refusing to plunge her fingers inside or even linger long enough on her clit, Em's soft moans began to lengthen into a whine.

The sound made Maria ache with need. "You know what I want, love." She tilted her face closer and whispered, "Beg me."

Em didn't hesitate. "Please," she gasped. "Oh, please, Captain."

Maria stopped. She hadn't meant to, but from the look of disbelief and desperation Em gave her, she figured it was safe to assume Em thought she had.

Maria removed her fingers from between Em's thighs. She cupped Em's face in her hands, and Em's eyes fluttered, as she no doubt felt her own wetness on her cheek. "Oh, my sweet girl," Maria murmured, "you know I love it when you call me captain."

As a matter of fact, Maria loved hearing it from Em more than anyone else on the ship—because when Em called her captain, she did so with a sincerity Maria had never heard from anyone else.

Em nodded, pupils huge.

"But when we're in here—together, like this—I'm not your captain," Maria told her. "It's important to me that you know that— that I *know* you know that."

Maria lowered her hand slightly, sliding her wet forefinger over Em's bottom lip. Em immediately closed her mouth around Maria's finger, sucking eagerly at her own wetness.

The air left Maria's lungs, and arousal throbbed painfully between her thighs.

Em curled her fingers around Maria's forearm. When she pulled her mouth away from Maria's finger, she said, "Who are you, then, if not my captain?" Her fingers traced the lines of Maria's tattoo—though she never looked at it. "Maria?"

Maria exhaled shakily. She loved the way Em said her name—like it was something precious she'd never break.

Em said Maria's name in a way that made her feel safe, and Maria couldn't fathom how that was even possible.

With a helpless shrug, Maria said, "Yours. I'm just…yours."

Em's green eyes widened, and a glow of adoration burned within them.

Maria dipped her head and pressed her lips against Em's. Em's lips parted, and Maria pushed her tongue inside.

Fuck.

As if the taste of Em's mouth wasn't arousing enough on its own, right *now*, it tasted of Em's arousal. Maria sank her fingers into Em's hair and twisted, angling her head downward for a deeper kiss.

Em moaned into her mouth.

Maria slid her other hand between Em's thighs, finding Em just as wet as she'd left her.

She circled her thumb over Em's clit, and Em jerked forward, gasping. Maria rubbed faster, swallowing every perfect moan and gasp Em had to offer.

And when Maria finally slipped her fingers into Em—one, then two—Em nearly collapsed on the table.

Maria let the hand in Em's hair fall—to catch her around the waist—and Em's hand slid backward.

Maria stilled at the sound of parchment rustling.

With an amused smirk, Maria met Em's startled gaze. "If you keep touching my maps, I'll have to tie you up again." She quickened the stroke of her fingers. "And I already *promised* to be gentle."

The flood of arousal that coated Maria's fingers, as she said that, made Maria moan almost as loudly as Em had.

As Maria struggled to regain control of her own emotions, Em straightened in Maria's arms and returned her trembling hands to the edge of the table.

"Good girl," Maria whispered.

Em's eyes fluttered, and she exhaled a shuddery breath.

Maria closed her mouth over Em's once more, and Em surrendered her weight to Maria, her large, bare breasts pressing against Maria's chest.

When Maria felt a slight tremor in Em's thighs, she pulled back. Em's breathing changed, and her head fell back, eyes closing.

"No. Not yet." Maria needed something *this* wouldn't give her.

Em's eyes flew open, but Maria was already pulling away and dropping to her knees. She wrapped her arms around Em's soft thighs and dragged her forward.

Em gasped, hands scrambling to keep hold of the table.

Maria buried her face between Em's luscious thighs, replacing her fingers with her tongue.

Em tasted sweeter than *anyone* had the right to taste, and she cried out at the first swipe of Maria's tongue. Her hands left the table, flying up to cover her face, and she fell flat on her back.

Maria heard the faint clatter of a tankard, but she merely chuckled and continued to lap at Em's clit.

It didn't take long.

Em had already been so close.

That little tremor of hers returned, and her gasps grew quicker and quicker—until, finally, she cried out. Even with Em's hands closed so tightly over her face, Maria was sure she'd heard a muffled version of her name.

Em didn't sit up, but she let her hands fall to her sides. "Well, I think you finally did it," she breathed. "You killed me."

Maria chuckled. She wiped the wetness around her mouth against the soft, bare flesh of Em's thigh, enjoying the way Em's muscles jerked in response.

Maria then rested her head against the pillow of Em's thigh. She waited until Em's breathing slowed, until every muscle relaxed, to murmur six words into her skin.

Six words that Em, hopefully, wouldn't hear.

"Thank you," Maria said, "for not leaving me."

CHAPTER 11

To Belong

"*No!*"

Em's eyes flew open, and she gasped.

Darkness cloaked her eyes, much as it had in the Regolis dungeons, and the air she sucked in was thick and damp, also…like the air in the dungeons.

It didn't smell like the dungeons, though—with their slimy stone walls and puddles of foul-smelling water.

Emilia shifted on the hard cot beneath her, testing her range of motion. She moved her arms first, then her ankles.

No shackles.

A relieved sigh escaped her lips, and slowly but surely, Emilia's eyes adjusted to the darkness.

She eyed the cracks between the planks of wood—*wood*, not stone—and then the blood-stained surgery table near her bed. In the wooden chest behind the table, the faint gleam of a glass bottle caught her eye.

See? Emilia told herself. *Surgeon's cabin.*

You're in the surgeon's cabin.

Not Regolis.

Not the dungeons.

Emilia relaxed in her cot and reached out a hand to stroke the fur of the ship cat who'd slept next to her.

Rat-Slayer opened one frosty-blue eye and peered at her, before purring softly and falling back to sleep.

"I am needed."

Nymeth's sudden, thundering voice startled Emilia so much that she nearly tumbled right off the side of her cot.

If the ancient dragon had phrased that like a question, Emilia might've had *some* hope of falling back to sleep before sunrise, but she hadn't.

Nymeth had phrased it like an observation.

That she was *already* acting upon.

Emilia threw off her blanket and hurriedly gathered her shoes and weapons. *"No! No, no! I'm fine!"*

Something told Emilia the crew wouldn't react so well to seeing her dragons *without* a prior warning.

Nymeth was quiet for a moment, but then, Emilia sensed a rush of relief on the other side of the bond. *"It felt like you needed me."*

Emilia dropped her weapons and fell back onto the cot. *"It was a nightmare."*

"Well, you must stop having those," Nymeth informed her. *"They're alarming."*

To a dragon as powerful as Nymeth, Emilia supposed everything was as simple as just…*deciding* it would no longer be. *"Believe me. If I could, I would."*

Nymeth grunted at that. *"Well, if I'm not needed, I should return to my half-eaten cattle."*

Emilia found it a bit alarming that the dragon had chosen the plural word, rather than the singular one. She knew how much Emryn ate. Did Nymeth eat more?

With her size, probably.

"Yummy," Emilia said sarcastically.

"Oh, and I suppose your tiny coconuts are better?" the dragon countered.

Emilia laughed.

She'd never win this one. The dragons were simply too carnivorous to understand human eating habits.

With her first two scares of the day out of the way, Emilia searched the shadowy corners of her cabin for the third. That was where her mother's ghastly form usually lurked, after all—in the shadows.

Emilia found no ghosts in her cabin on this particular morning, but she knew better than to let her guard down.

Emilia had walked through the ruins of her people yesterday. Her mother would never let pain of that magnitude go unused.

"Did I ever tell you your mother wanted to be a dragon-rider?"

Emilia blinked at Nymeth's question. She'd assumed the dragon would've been too focused on her meal to listen to Emilia's thoughts.

Clearly, she'd assumed wrong.

"Instead of a chieftess?" Emilia said skeptically.

"Oh, no. Nydia loved power and war," Nymeth said. *"She had to be chieftess, but she wanted to be a dragon-rider, too."*

The sound of bones crunching between dragon teeth made Emilia flinch.

But Nymeth continued to speak, as if nothing were happening. *"The day after Caelu bonded with Camila, Nydia climbed the mountain and confronted me—me, of all dragons—to demand I bond with her."*

Emilia frowned. She'd never heard this story.

"Can you imagine?" Nymeth said. *"The nerve of that mortal! To confront me!"*

The dragon huffed, and the faint sensation of steam warmed Emilia's face.

"What did you tell her?"

"I told her that even if there came a day when there were thousands of dragons in Aletharia," Nymeth said, *"not a single one would ever want her."*

Emilia's eyes widened. The dragons had bonded with Emilia at such an early age that she couldn't remember a time when they *hadn't* known her thoughts and feelings.

Yet, Nymeth had not only refused to bond with a skilled warrior sorceress; she'd also told her no dragon ever would?

"Nydia's skill made her a good chieftess. It wouldn't have made her a good

rider," Nymeth told Emilia. *"Besides, do you think any of us wanted to bond with a soul as cold as hers? We're dragons. We don't like the cold."*

Emilia had a few questions about *that* explanation, but Nymeth didn't give her a chance to ask them.

"Which is why I must finish this carcass before it cools," the dragon added. *"I merely wanted to tell you that if you ever want to hurt her the way she hurts you, you have my permission to remind her of what I said."*

Emilia couldn't imagine *that* going well, but the silence that fell on Nymeth's end informed her the dragon had decided to focus fully on her meal.

Far too awake, now, to go back to sleep, Emilia draped her blanket over Rat-Slayer and climbed off the cot. She grabbed a bucket of seawater and a clean cloth.

Emilia then pulled her black shirt over her head. The fabric scraped over her burns, sending lashes of stinging pain through her arms.

Emilia had already started to reach for the cloth, when she stopped and looked down at her burns.

Emilia *did* feel significantly stronger than she had the night before. It only made sense to *try* healing them—before adding a fresh layer of burn salve.

Emilia rested her hand against one of the burns. The damaged skin stung and pulled at her touch, but with barely any effort, she called forth her magic.

Warmth gathered in her fingers, and Emilia pressed outward.

The pain receded, and power surged in its place.

Emilia had only lost her magic for one night, which was nothing compared to the months she'd gone without it after the imprisonment, but its return never failed to sate her in ways she couldn't describe.

Emilia basked in the warmth of her own power for a moment— before healing the remaining burns.

With growing excitement, Emilia washed up and dressed for the day.

With her magic restored, she had work to do, and Emilia knew exactly whom she wanted to heal first.

~

CRISP, SALT-SCENTED AIR GREETED EMILIA ON THE MAIN DECK, AND the coral-pink sun—just barely cresting the horizon, at this point— heated Emilia's fair skin.

Usually, the pirates were singing their first sea shanties by now, but no one sang this morning.

Either sunrise had come early, or everyone else was rising late. Considering many of them had poisoned their livers past the point of caring the night before, Emilia assumed the latter.

The sound of nearby retching only confirmed her suspicions.

Maria tended to wander the ship when she wasn't at the helm, so Emilia hadn't expected to find the captain immediately.

For all she knew, Maria was still asleep.

After last night, they *both* should've been.

But as Emilia crossed the main deck, the sunlight silhouetted a familiar form atop the quarterdeck—a tall, muscular form with a sword on each side of her waist and the jut of a tricorn on her head.

Goddess. Had anyone ever *had* a more attractive silhouette than Captain Maria Welles?

Emilia couldn't see Maria's face from this distance, but the way the silhouette leaned forward, casually bracing an arm against the wheel, suggested Maria might've spotted Emilia, too.

"Morning, Em."

Emilia spun to look at the short, brown-skinned sailor she'd just passed. He held a hammer in one hand and a bucket of who-knows-what in the other.

Had he been a carpenter's mate? A friend of Jonas?

Or had the captain simply assigned him to ship repairs after the battle?

All Emilia knew for sure was that this man had never spoken to her before today. Despite the trial and all, it still caught her off-guard when someone she didn't know called her by name.

"Hi," Emilia said.

Was that the right response? How would someone who'd actually had friends before respond to that?

The sailor offered a quick smile and returned to his work.

Emilia continued toward the helm. Above her, the masts groaned, and the sails flapped in the wind. The waves crashed against the sides of the ship, as Emilia climbed the steps to the quarterdeck.

Maria's features slowly came into focus—dark, tattooed fingers wrapped around the wooden spokes of the wheel, a bruised mouth and face, and big, brown eyes that followed Emilia's every move.

Had Maria watched her the whole way?

Emilia pointed curiously at the sailor who'd spoken to her. "Do you know that guy's name?"

"Tobias," Maria said. One hand strayed toward her sword. "Why? Did he bother you in some way?"

"What?" Emilia eyed the sword warily. "No!"

Did Maria intend to stab him if he had?

"He just…knew my name, somehow."

With a shake of her head, Maria released the sword. "Everyone on this ship knows your name, love."

"Because of the trial?" Emilia assumed.

Maria snorted. "They've known your name since the day you punched Buchan in the fucking face."

Emilia squinted. "That was my first day aboard."

Maria gave a single nod. "As I said."

Emilia chewed on her bottom lip. "Why don't I know all of their names, then?"

"Probably because none of them have punched a giant, drawn a sword against their captain, offered their freedom in exchange for the crew's, or flown in on the back of a dragon," Maria muttered.

"Are you sure?" Emilia said. "I mean, what are the chances that none of them have done *any* of those?"

"Is that a serious question?" Maria asked.

Emilia laughed and glanced at Maria. "Do you think I could memorize them all overnight?"

"No," Maria said.

With a twirl of her fingers, Emilia asked, "What if I drew little pictures beside their names?"

Maria laughed. "You should still be in bed."

Emilia looked away. Did Maria know about her nightmares? Emilia knew she woke up screaming sometimes. Maybe someone had heard her.

"Why?" she said, voice rising with anxiety. "I feel fine."

Maria gave her a skeptical look. "I know I wasn't there when you *fell* asleep, but I was there when you *weren't* asleep."

Emilia's cheeks flamed at the reminder.

Only Captain Maria Welles would reference intimate acts with such casual indifference.

"I know for a fact," Maria continued, "that—if you're already awake—you didn't sleep enough."

Emilia licked her lips nervously. "Well, you see," she mumbled, "a, umm, dragon woke me up."

"Did you just blame me?" Nymeth asked.

Emilia's eyes widened at the dragon's interruption. *"Would you stop eavesdropping?"*

"When I know you're safe," Nymeth said.

"I told you I was safe!" Emilia reminded her.

"And you also told your human I woke you up." The thunderous clap of dragon wings filled Emilia's mind. *"I don't know if I can believe you anymore."*

"Oh, that's not fair," Emilia complained.

"Em?" Maria called out.

Emilia blinked and glanced at her. "What?"

Concern twisted at Maria's brows. "Are you sure you don't need more sleep?"

"See what you've done?" Emilia shot at the dragon.

"You do need more sleep, though," Nymeth rumbled.

Emilia blinked a few more times, trying her best to look normal —and *not* like she was arguing with a dragon who was miles away, at the moment. "Well, if *I* didn't sleep enough, neither did you."

"Oh, I know I didn't," Maria assured her. "I'd still be asleep, if Zain hadn't pounded on my door until I wanted to kill him." She rolled her eyes. "*'Other people need sleep, too,'* he said. He's lucky I didn't put him to sleep permanently."

Emilia's eyebrows rose.

Right.

Goddess forbid he do his job.

"Was he on night watch, then?" Emilia asked.

Zain had captained the ship during the battle the day before. If he'd been on night watch, that was an awfully long time for someone to stay awake.

"He and Henry took shifts," Maria told her.

With a sympathetic frown, Emilia said, "I could've left earlier, if you needed me to. So you could sleep?"

Maria glared at Emilia, as if she'd just suggested feeding the ship to a sea serpent. "I'd sooner give up sleep for the rest of my life," she snarled, "than lose one moment of last night."

Emilia's eyes widened. She'd…misheard that, right?

Maria wouldn't confess to something like that, would she?

And if she did, would she say it so…angrily?

Maybe. Anger *was* Maria's favorite mask.

Emilia forced out a small: "Oh."

Maria looked away, and her fingers tightened around the wheel. "I just meant…" she trailed off, shaking her head. "I don't know what I meant."

Emilia's throat constricted. "Captain—"

"I can't talk about this here," Maria said.

Emilia glanced out at the few sailors who'd actually managed to leave their hammocks this morning. She doubted any of them cared enough to eavesdrop right now, but Emilia dropped the issue, anyway.

She stepped closer to the captain, and Maria's dark gaze returned to her.

They were alone on the quarterdeck—near enough for someone to overhear, perhaps, but alone. "Do you think anyone would *see*, if I were to do something…totally silent?"

Maria raised both eyebrows. "Elaborate."

Emilia took one more step toward Maria—until she was close enough to smell the hibiscus and citrus on Maria's skin. "It's something I usually wouldn't do in front of them."

Maria's eyebrows arched even higher than before. "Em, you're killing me. Whatever it is, just do it."

Emilia brushed her fingers over one of the bruises on Maria's face, and Maria's dark eyelashes fluttered in response.

Maria dropped her left arm, allowing Emilia to slip between her and the ship's wheel, and when Emilia did, Maria stepped forward, pressing Emilia against it.

Emilia would've used her hand—if Maria wasn't so clearly expecting a kiss.

Instead, Emilia summoned her power—the steady burn of empathy and magic—and let it gather in her mouth, rather than her fingers. She then lifted herself onto her toes and kissed Maria's bruised mouth.

Maria released a soft, breathless moan the moment their lips made contact.

Not quite silent, after all.

Maria slid her free hand beneath Emilia's scabbard, her fingers caressing Emilia's hip, and Emilia let the warm and gentle magic flow from her, into Maria.

Maria let out a quiet gasp, as the temperature of the kiss no doubt rose.

Literally.

Emilia tried to pull away afterward—to check her work—but Maria's mouth followed hers, unwilling to break contact.

Desire surged inside of Emilia, and she melted against her captain.

Maria's thumb traced Emilia's hipbone, and she sighed pleasantly against Emilia's lips. Only after a long, lingering kiss, did she lean back and open her eyes.

Maria kept her right arm braced against the wheel and her left hand on Emilia's hip, as she considered Emilia with eyes so dark they were nearly black.

Emilia considered her right back—well, just her face, really. She smiled at the sight of Maria's smooth, brown skin and her fully-healed, rosy-brown lips.

Not a bruise or cut in sight.

With a curious smile, Maria asked, "Why do you always taste like flowers in the morning?"

Emilia laughed at the question. She hadn't realized they'd spent enough mornings together for Maria to notice such a thing. "It's rose-water," she explained. "It's a pleasant mouth-cleanser."

"Interesting," Maria murmured.

Emilia grabbed Maria's face and turned it—so she could check the bruise she'd seen on the opposite side of Maria's jaw, as well.

Maria frowned—but didn't stop her.

Emilia found only an old, pale scar that crossed Maria's jawline perpendicularly—but no bruises.

"Em," Maria said slowly, "darling." When Emilia looked up at her, she said, "What are you doing?"

"You don't feel the difference?" Emilia asked.

She knew Maria had endured far worse pain than a few bruises in the Regolis dungeons.

They both had.

But surely, she'd noticed when it no longer hurt to kiss.

When Maria's frown only deepened, Emilia said, "Your lips?"

Maria released her hold on Emilia's waist and lifted her fingers to her mouth. With the side of her tattooed thumb, she traced her plump bottom lip—then the top lip, as well. Her eyebrows lifted.

"Better?" Emilia asked.

An excited smile broke across Maria's face. "Sex *does* empower you!"

Emilia blushed and cast a quick glance over her shoulder—to see if anyone was staring. "No. It was probably the food or rest—as I said before."

"You can't prove it *wasn't* the sex," Maria argued.

Emilia couldn't help but laugh at her stubbornness. "Why do you want it to be sex so badly?"

Maria tapped two fingers against the spoke of the wheel and lifted her strong shoulders in an easy shrug. "I find it fascinating," she admitted. "Is that a crime?" Before Emilia could answer, Maria grinned and leaned closer. "Please, say yes. I do love crime."

Emilia laughed again. "And don't we all know it?"

Maria's smile deepened. Her dark gaze drifted downward, and the tip of her tongue slipped out to wet her lips.

Emilia's face grew warm, and with Maria looking at her as if she wanted to test the theory *again*, Emilia doubted the sun was responsible, this time.

The sound of one sailor yelling to another brought Emilia's attention back to the crew. She carefully stepped out from between Maria and the wheel.

"Sorry," Emilia said. "I was actually just going to *touch* your lips, but you seemed so intent on a kiss."

Maria's grin turned wicked. "Well, now that I know it's an *option*, I think I'll need you to kiss all of my wounds," she teased. "Be sure to stab me somewhere interesting the next time we fight."

"I will not!" Emilia said.

Maria folded forward, cackling loudly enough to attract the attention of some severely hungover sailors.

"Captain?" Emilia tilted her head toward them.

Maria glanced down at the main deck, narrowing her eyes at the pirates who'd stopped to watch. "It's not like they don't know," she scoffed. Her attention returned to Emilia. "Do you have any idea how often they talk about who I fuck? It's exhausting."

Emilia remembered Helen fishing for information after some sort of bet they'd all made—and nodded.

"There are things they don't get to know," Maria told Emilia. "What I said on your island, for instance. But I won't live in fear of them overhearing a *joke*."

That didn't surprise Emilia, really. She sometimes wondered if Maria would have any restraint at all if Zain didn't annoy her so much.

"You did kiss me up here once," Emilia said, remembering their first sword fight, "without consideration for who might be watching."

"I wouldn't say *without* consideration." Maria's lips curved. "I did lead you out of their sight first."

Emilia's brows furrowed. "You did?"

"Oh, don't think too much of it," Maria warned. "It was for *my* sake, not yours. I hadn't decided if I wanted to kill you."

The self-destructive spiral Emilia's mother had sent her into that day had left her memories hazy. She remembered the feeling of helplessness, the inability to stop herself from doing something that might've gotten her killed, but the details blurred in her mind.

Until the kiss.

That, Emilia remembered clearly.

She'd never forget that kiss. How could she—when it had shattered her so deeply and irrevocably?

The penetrating stare Maria had fixed on Emilia made her wonder if Maria knew what she was thinking. "Would've kissed you regardless, though."

Emilia's chest fluttered. "What?"

Maria returned her attention to the sea, her tricorn shifting with the movement. "You heard me."

Emilia could barely breathe.

"Whether they'd seen us or not," Maria said, "I had to kiss you then. I couldn't wait any longer."

Any longer?

Emilia remembered the words Maria had whispered to her later that night.

'Was it madness, do you think,' she'd said, *'or desperation?'*

Maria's voice cut through the millions of questions whirling in Emilia's brain. "Here." She didn't look at Emilia. She just held out her compass. "Hold this."

Emilia took the old, wooden compass with a frown. "You need me to hold your compass?"

Maria gave a quick shrug. "I'd send you to Judith, but she's asleep—on the galley floor with Helen, the last time I looked."

Emilia arched her eyebrows at that.

"But I know, the moment I let you run off on your own," Maria said, "you'll try to heal all the injured."

"Well, yeah," Emilia said. "That's my job."

Maria narrowed her eyes. "You need to pace yourself, Em," she said. "I might not know much about magic, but I know *you*. You'll overdo it."

Emilia wanted to argue, but she couldn't honestly deny it.

Emilia had always had a tendency to fixate on her passions—to the point that she forgot to rest or eat, often overused her magic, and overexerted herself.

"What happens after you leave is up to you," Maria told her, "but for the next hour, you'll hold my compass—and *not* use any magic."

Emilia didn't know what to say—because on the surface, this sounded like another of Maria's rude, sneering commands, but underneath all of that, it was…thoughtful.

"You'd really let the injured suffer for an extra hour," Emilia said, "just because you think healing a few bruises might've exhausted me?"

"No," Maria argued, "I'll let them suffer for an hour—because I need someone to hold my compass."

Emilia lifted the wooden compass in her hand. "It's probably the lightest thing you carry."

"Just do as your captain says, for once," Maria said, but her mouth twitched up at the corners as she said it. "Besides, Judith said you'd stabilized them all."

"Stable and pain-free are not the same thing," Emilia informed her.

"They'll survive," Maria insisted. "I would've made you wait to heal me, if you hadn't tricked me with that strangely warm kiss of yours."

Emilia didn't know whether to protest or laugh. "Captain, you are the *last* person who should accuse someone of trickery."

"Well, you did learn from the best," Maria said with a taunting smirk, "didn't you? *Pirate?*"

Emilia rolled her eyes.

"Show me your burns," Maria said.

"Yes, Captain," Emilia said in a playful grumble. She closed her fingers around the compass and held out her arms.

Upon seeing the healed skin, Maria gave a nod of approval. "I want to see the other one, too."

"I can't heal my rune," Emilia said, but she tugged up her sleeve, anyway.

She'd reduced the swelling with her magic, but the design itself still shone red, like a fresh wound.

Maria pursed her lips—but nodded. "Thank you."

Emilia lowered her sleeve and opened her hand.

The wooden compass rested in the center of her palm—old and worn, its darkened stain faded in the places Maria touched most.

Emilia ran her thumb over the top of the box. It felt so smooth and worn beneath her touch. How long had Maria used this compass?

Emilia pressed her own fingers against the faded spots—holding the compass in the way Maria had.

She couldn't help but imagine a younger version of Maria holding it—the cocky, idealistic naval captain, who hadn't yet learned the cruelties of the world.

If they'd met back then, when Emilia, too, had been naïve, would they have fallen for each other?

They wouldn't have fought as much back then. Emilia knew that.

But without those fights, without being forced to accept each other's flaws first and strengths last, would they have fallen quite as hard?

"The compass is still closed, love," Maria said, snatching Emilia out of her reverie. "You do know that, right?"

Emilia looked up, blinking to clear her mind. "Yes."

Maria's brows furrowed. "And…you're aware of how a compass works?"

Emilia might've taken offense at Maria's tone—if she'd had *any* idea where the clasp was. "Not really."

Maria's eyes widened. "You've never used one?"

Emilia shrugged sheepishly. "I've never needed it."

"Not even while dragon-riding?" Maria asked.

Emilia shook her head. "The dragons have—well, I suppose you could call it an internal sense of direction?"

Maria rested her weight against the wooden wheel, studying Emilia with warm, brown eyes. "Oh?"

The captain's show of interest encouraged Emilia, and she soon found herself rambling excitedly.

"Well, yeah. They have this sort of…magical connection to every land and sea in Aletharia," Emilia explained. "As far as I know, the dragons are the only creatures who have that kind of magic—besides the gods, of course." Emilia tapped the side of her forehead. "It's all here for them! No matter where you want to go, they know how to get there—without using maps or compasses or *anything!*"

An affectionate smile curved at Maria's lips.

"You could ask them to take you to see a sea serpent in the Whispering Abyss," Emilia continued, "and they could!" She quirked her head to the side and added, "They *wouldn't*. Nymeth would call you a crazy mortal for asking and threaten to burn your favorite reading tree, if you didn't *stop* asking. But she'd never really burn it—not even if you asked seven more times within the next month."

Maria lifted a scarred eyebrow. "That is a *very* specific example, love."

Emilia winced at the observation. "I might've read a book about sea serpents when I was a kid," she said, "and developed a brief fascination with them."

Maria snorted. "You might have," she repeated. "Did this book of yours, by any chance, mention that no one's ever left the Whispering Abyss alive?"

"Yes," Emilia assured her.

"And you still asked a dragon to take you there?" Maria asked.

"Yes," Emilia repeated.

Maria threw her head back and laughed. "Oh, Em," she sighed. "I like you more and more every day."

Emilia cast a surprised look her way. "You do?"

Maria beckoned her closer. "Come here. I'll show you how to open it."

Emilia stepped toward the captain and offered the compass, but Maria didn't take it. Instead, she closed her left hand around Emilia's. Maria moved Emilia's thumb with her own, placing it against a painted clasp.

Maria pressed against Emilia's thumb, her touch warm and firm, and together, they pressed the clasp inward. The wooden box popped open.

Maria released Emilia's hand. "Hold it still."

The compass needle spun for a moment—before settling into a horizontal position.

"It points north?" Emilia asked.

"Always," Maria told her.

Emilia turned the box in her hand, watching the way the needle shifted with her movement. "We're going west, then," she realized.

Maria grinned. "Not so hard, after all, is it?"

Emilia remembered Zain's words the day before.

'She went east. We went west.'

So, they'd never turned back.

"Where are we headed?"

Maria had already returned her attention to the sea. "Nefala," she said. "Not only do we need to restock supplies, but we need more extensive repairs than we can do at sea." She drummed her fingers against the wheel. "Even if I *hadn't* killed our carpenter—for good reason—we'd still have to return to Nefala."

Maria recited that last part as if she'd said it too many times already—to Zain, Emilia assumed.

"But Nefala is north of Drakon Isle," Emilia said.

"I'm aware, surgeon," Maria said, but she sounded more amused than irritated. "When are you going to learn to trust your captain's navigational skills?"

"When they make sense to me?" Emilia offered.

Maria snorted at that. "Once I'm sure that isn't a storm forming behind us, I'll give the order to turn back. We have enough supplies in the meantime."

Emilia turned and squinted at the eastern horizon. The red-orange sunlight seared her eyes, and she pressed her hand to her forehead.

A few puffs of orange and pink scattered the eastern sky—but nothing more significant than that.

Emilia didn't think it looked like a storm, but she understood the captain's caution. Even the most beautiful clouds had the potential to become tropical storms.

Maria watched Emilia out of the corner of her eye. "Trust me yet, love?"

Emilia turned to face her. With a playful smile, she held her thumb and forefinger an inch apart.

Maria chuckled.

Emilia moved closer to her captain, lured in by the warmth of her laughter. "Since you let me touch your compass," she said, "can I touch the wheel, too?"

Maria didn't even consider it. "No."

Emilia scowled at her quick answer. "Not even once?"

"Never, my sweet surgeon," Maria said with a ruthless smile. "Never."

It'd barely been a day since Emilia had walked amongst the ashes of the Drakon people. Perhaps that was why she'd spent all morning expecting to see her mother in every corner.

Perhaps that was why she didn't even flinch when Nydia Drakon *did* appear—late in the afternoon, directly behind an injured sailor.

Antoine was a young, black-haired sailor—old enough to have served a few years in the Royal Navy, but still younger than anyone Maria liked to employ.

Maria typically didn't employ deserters either. She considered them cowards, and Maria despised cowards.

She'd made an exception for Antoine, though—after learning of his abuse at the hands of a naval officer.

Pelt usually assigned the boy to the more menial tasks aboard the ship, like swabbing the deck or running errands, but with few combat skills, he'd been an easy target, when the Royal Navy had boarded the *Wicked Fate*.

He'd suffered multiple stab wounds and had only survived because Fulke had thrown the injured boy over his shoulder and carried him down to the hold.

Fulke and Judith had explained all of this, while Emilia sutured the sailor's wounds the day before.

Antoine sighed with relief, as Emilia healed the last of his wounds.

Nydia circled the injured sailor. She wore red today—the traditional color of a Drakon warrior. "Why waste your magic on these humans? This child is of no use to you—*or* your human lover, for that matter."

Emilia tried her best to ignore her mother.

She didn't *want* to. She wanted to argue with her—to tell her that, unlike Nydia, Emilia could care about someone regardless of their usefulness.

Emilia wanted to tell Nydia that even in her limited encounters with this young human, he'd treated her better than her mother ever had.

But Illopian sailors were a superstitious sort, and she doubted they'd react well if word got out that Emilia was speaking to people no one else could see.

So, Emilia focused her attention on the lanky, dark-haired sailor, instead. "Better?"

Antoine laughed, "I know it sounds strange, but I think I feel better than I did *before* the attack."

"Why would that sound strange?" Nydia said, her tone thick with disgust. "It's magic, not a cup of tea."

A wave of exhaustion washed over Emilia, and she braced a hand against the surgery table.

Alarm flickered in Antoine's brown eyes, and he reached for her shoulder. "Surgeon?" he said warily. "Are you all right?"

Forcing a smile, Emilia said, "Just a bit tired."

Antoine dropped his hand. "There were a lot of injured sailors in the hold last night," he pointed out. "Maybe you're overworking yourself."

The poor kid didn't even know how much Emilia had done *before* returning to the ship. He'd been in too much pain to listen to Helen's tales.

Between the stress of seeing what was left of her people and the battle that followed, Emilia had exhausted herself before even mounting the dragon.

Still, Emilia couldn't stop. The injured needed her, and really, what was she, if she ceased to be useful?

Nydia's ghastly form drifted to Emilia's side. "Even the human sees your weakness," she sneered. "Didn't I teach you better than this?"

Emilia straightened her posture. Her mother was right. She knew better than to show weakness.

"I'm fine," Emilia assured the sailor.

Antoine frowned—but nodded. "Am I cleared for duty, then?" he asked. "Pelt will want to know."

"Of course," Emilia said, "but light duty."

A boyish grin broke across his face. "Oh, I like the sound of that."

Emilia laughed weakly, and the sailor, who'd nearly bled out a day prior, hopped down from her table.

Now, it was Emilia who felt as if she'd bled out.

Fleeing from the cramped space of the surgeon's cabin, Antoine called back, "Thank you, Em!"

"You're welcome," she mumbled.

Emilia waited until the sailor closed the door, before she allowed herself to collapse.

"Pathetic," Nydia snarled.

Emilia glared at the flickering form of her mother. "You're welcome to do my job *for* me, Mother."

Once upon a time, Emilia would've cringed away from her mother's rage, but Emilia wasn't that person anymore.

"*I* don't work with the enemy," Nydia said. "Nor would I ever devote my life to something as useless as healing."

Maria didn't consider Emilia's work useless.

None of the sailors Emilia had healed today had considered her work useless.

Only her mother saw it that way.

It wasn't the kindest thought, but Emilia vaguely wondered if anyone had ever tried stabbing Nydia. Perhaps a few hours left bleeding would change her mind about healers.

Emilia had never been that type of person, though, before Catherine's betrayal—and even if she had, it wouldn't have changed anything.

Nydia Drakon was a lot of things, but weak wasn't one of them. She would've endured the injury with the unwavering strength of a warrior, just as she'd taught Emilia to do.

"The crew of the *Wicked Fate* isn't my enemy," Emilia told her mother. "They're my—my crew."

The word 'friends' emerged in Emilia's mind, but calling them *that* would've felt…presumptuous.

"Your crew," Nydia repeated. Her red gown swept over the floorboards but never quite touched them. "They fear you. Can't you tell? Humans will *always* fear us." Hatred burned in Nydia's bright, green eyes. "And we've seen what happens when humans fear us, haven't we?"

Emilia's stomach turned at the reminder. "Some of them might still fear me," she admitted, "but the captain doesn't. Judith doesn't. They can unlearn their prejudice, if they want to—if we let them."

Nydia rolled her eyes. "Oh, of course. Your *captain*. Your *lover*," she sneered. "What happened to not trusting her? Now, you think she can do no wrong."

Emilia let out an incredulous laugh. "I can list her flaws better than anyone," she argued. "Believe me."

"Yet, you trust her," Nydia said. "You *love* her."

Emilia frowned. Had her mother listened to her confession on Drakon Isle, or was she only guessing?

Was there even any point in denying it?

"If I *did* love her," Emilia said, "I'd do so with far more caution than I ever had with Catherine."

Nydia scoffed at that. "You know, I hated your first human lover, but at least *she* knew how to wage war," she muttered. "What is this one even doing?"

Emilia blinked.

Had her mother just complimented Catherine?

The person who'd slaughtered their people?

Was Nydia's hatred for Emilia so intense that she'd rather compliment the person who'd murdered their people than let Emilia think, for even a moment, that she might've made a good decision?

Emilia's resolve hardened. "Captain Maria Welles is brilliant in battle," she said—and she meant it, too. "I believe in her more than I *ever* believed in you."

Her mother recoiled, as if she'd been struck.

Her form flickered and faded, like the dying embers of a fire.

"You—"

A knock at the door interrupted whatever Nydia had been about to say, and rather than continue or wait, the ghost flickered once— and vanished.

When Emilia didn't answer the door, it creaked open, and Judith stepped into the surgeon's cabin. She glanced around the dark space —and frowned, when her blue eyes found Emilia.

"Em?"

Emilia climbed to her feet. "Sorry. I, umm—" *Was busy arguing with my dead mother?* "—was distracted."

Judith merely smiled. "Well, sorry to interrupt, but," she sighed, "I was told to drag you down to the galley for the afternoon meal and make you eat with the rest of us, at—"

"At gunpoint, if necessary," Emilia interjected.

Judith crossed her arms, her once-white shirt stretching over her muscles. "How did you know?"

Emilia laughed. "She gave me the same speech."

Judith rolled her eyes. "Of course she did."

❧

SINCE EMILIA OFTEN ASSISTED JUDITH BEFORE AND DURING mealtimes, she usually ate alone—or with Judith, after everyone else had finished eating.

Emilia assumed they'd do the same today, but Judith apparently had other plans.

Judith pressed a bowl and tankard into Emilia's hands, before taking her by the arm and leading her to one of the galley tables, where three familiar faces waited.

Pelt and Helen sat across from each other, and Fulke occupied the corner closest to the bulkhead.

Fulke tried to rest his elbows between bites, but the wooden table teetered beneath the weight of his arms and nearly spilled all three bowls of stew. Fulke then winced and removed his elbows, causing the table to swing back down and nearly spill them all again.

Helen kept eating throughout it all, unconcerned.

Pelt, on the other hand, dropped his spoon and sighed, "We *have* to bolt down this table."

"I told you that last week," Judith reminded him.

She set her bowl next to Helen's and gestured for Emilia to take the seat between Fulke and Pelt.

Emilia walked around to their side—only to freeze, when Pelt shoved back his chair, blocking her path.

Emilia's stomach lurched. Why had Judith assumed her friends would want Emilia to sit with them?

Maybe if she'd asked them first, she could've spared Emilia the embarrassment of being rejected.

Fulke gave Pelt a look of warning, but Pelt merely grinned, flashing a mouthful of shining, gold teeth.

"Hands where I can see them, surgeon," he said. "Need to see if you're hiding any more of those tiny blades."

Judith rolled her eyes. "Oh, just let her eat, Pelt."

But Emilia laughed—with a mix of amusement and relief. She raised her hand and wiggled her fingers. "I'm clean," she said, "unless you count my sword."

Pelt's gaze fell to the lightweight sword that rested against Emilia's hip. "At least I can see that one."

"A lot of good that'll do you," Judith muttered.

Helen snorted mid-bite and spat out an entire mouthful of stew.

Judith grimaced at her—the way she often did the day after they'd slept together.

Pelt glanced between the two of them, before scoffing, "I'm better with a sword than either of *you*."

"Swords are boring," Helen complained. She drank her ale. "They don't do anything—except burn you."

Pelt and Judith exchanged a puzzled look.

"Helen," Judith said slowly, "did you try to blow up a sword?"

"No," Helen said—through a mouthful of stew.

Judith didn't look convinced.

As Emilia pulled out the empty chair to sit down, Fulke leaned forward and signed something to Pelt.

Pelt raised his eyebrows. "Yeah, I think I'll leave that to the captain."

Emilia glanced from Pelt to Fulke. "Leave what to the captain?"

Pelt lifted his tankard to his mouth. "Fighting you."

With a grin, Judith explained to Emilia, "Fulke was just reminding Pelt of how impressed he was, after you fought the captain that day."

Emilia shifted uncomfortably in her chair.

Discussing her self-destructive spiral with Maria—who'd understood it in a way no one else could—was one thing. Discussing it with the people who'd only witnessed her humiliation was another.

Fulke scowled at Judith and made several annoyed hand gestures.

"Sorry," Judith said easily. She turned to Emilia. "I paraphrased—badly, apparently. The phrase he actually used to describe Pelt was '*scared shitless.*'"

Pelt rolled his eyes at them. "I'd never seen anyone hold their own against the captain for that long."

"Except Catherine," Judith said.

"Except Catherine," Pelt agreed.

Emilia drank her ale much faster than usual. Was it possible for Emilia to change the subject without them all *realizing* she was changing the subject?

Helen pointed a gunpowder-covered finger at Pelt. "Hey, I told you the day she punched Buchan," she said. "She might not be able to throw a punch worth a shit, but there was *something* impressive there."

"What do you want?" Pelt grumbled. "A reward?"

An excited grin burst across Helen's face. "There's a reward?"

Judith gave Helen a sympathetic pat on the arm.

Emilia set down her tankard. "Most of you were in the navy. Weren't you trained in sword-fighting?"

"Trained at a basic level? Yeah," Pelt said. His hazel eyes shifted toward her. "Trained like *you*? No."

Emilia swallowed. He couldn't know Catherine was the one who'd trained her, could he?

Only Maria had guessed that.

"The captain *tried* to train me," Judith said. "I hated it! Even a wooden sword hurts when it hits you."

"Bet it hit *you* a lot," Pelt taunted.

In an ever-so-mature defense of her forbidden lover, Helen pulled back on the end of her spoon and flung a piece of potato at Pelt.

Judith pointedly ignored them. "The captain was too competitive for me. I eventually gave up and found an easier teacher, and the captain found…Catherine."

Emilia tensed. When she'd wished for the subject to shift away from her, she hadn't meant for it to shift *toward* Catherine.

"On that note," Pelt said, wiggling the tankard in his hand, "I'm going to need more ale."

He started to stand, but Judith waved for him to sit back down.

"I need more, too," Judith said. She pushed back her chair and stood. "I'll bring back the flagon."

Pelt turned to Emilia. "I might not be the best swordsman on the ship," he said with a flash of his gold teeth, "but I think I make up for it with my dazzling smile."

Emilia laughed at that. "What did you have going for you before the teeth?"

"Good question," Pelt said. He looked up at Judith, as she returned. "Should we ask Sarah?"

Judith rolled her eyes. "Sarah only fucks you because she knows you'll tell me." She refilled Pelt's tankard. "Same reason she fucks Helen."

Helen scowled. "Sarah loves me!" she argued. "She says I have pretty freckles!"

Judith gave her a skeptical look.

"What? You don't agree with her?" Helen said.

Fulke gestured frantically to Judith, but Judith either didn't notice or chose not to heed his warning.

"I think *'pretty'* isn't a word I'd use to describe you," Judith told her.

Fulke covered his face with his massive hand and shook his head, while Pelt just rolled his eyes. "Here we go again," he muttered to Emilia.

As Emilia listened to her friend put her foot further and further into her mouth, Pelt grabbed the flagon of ale and finished refilling everyone's tankards.

"It wasn't an insult!" Judith tried to explain.

"You know," Pelt said, drawing Emilia's attention away from the wreckage, "if we'd had a surgeon like you when *this* happened—" He tapped the butchered-suture scar on his face. "—I wouldn't have almost died."

Sympathy tugged at Emilia's chest. Even if Pelt was comfortable joking about it now, Emilia knew it would've been a terrifying experience.

For all of them, really.

Even Maria—though she'd never admit it.

"No," Emilia agreed, "you wouldn't have."

Pelt smiled, and the smile he offered her now looked so different from his usual ones that Emilia almost didn't recognize him. "Luck seems to be improving now, though. Don't you think, Fulke?"

Fulke—who'd been staring at Judith, as if he wanted to cut *her* tongue out, too—turned his attention toward Pelt. His dark eyebrows lifted.

"Have you seen Antoine?" Pelt said. "He walked up to me earlier, as if nothing had happened. *Walked!*"

Fulke nodded and peered down at Emilia.

Emilia fought the urge to slide beneath the table and hide—until they stopped looking at her like that.

"I thought he was dead when I saw him yesterday." Pelt braced his tanned elbows on the table. "Luckily, Fulke stopped to check his pulse." His gaze returned to Emilia. "Luckier, *too*, that we had you."

Emilia offered a nervous shrug. "It was a few damaged organs. That's all," she told them. "I repaired what I could and removed what I couldn't."

"Damaged organs!" Pelt said with a snort. "That's all!"

Fulke laughed, too, and Emilia shifted in her chair.

Had she said something wrong?

Helen's loud voice cut through their laughter. "You weren't complaining about my freckles last night!"

"I'm not complaining now!" Judith threw out her slender, tanned arms. "And would you lower your voice before the captain hears?"

Emilia cast a wide-eyed glance around the galley. She didn't find the captain anywhere, but she saw plenty of *other* sailors turning to watch.

Fulke must've noticed the same thing Emilia had—because he pushed back his chair and circled around to the other side of the table.

He grabbed Judith by the arm and dragged her to the corner, pushing her into his own chair. Then, he returned and took Judith's chair for himself.

The chair creaked beneath the giant's weight.

Judith leaned toward Emilia and whispered in her ear, "You knew what I was saying, right?"

Emilia offered her a sympathetic smile.

After all, Emilia's brain went a bit fuzzy around women, too.

Maybe not *that* fuzzy, but…

"'*Freckles*' is a new gambling game I came up with!" Pelt told the listening sailors. "See me later, if you're interested."

A few pirates returned their attention to their food, while the rest of them huddled together to whisper.

"You," Pelt said, pointing at Helen and then Judith, "owe me. Again."

"I already owed him the price of a small ship," Judith grumbled to Emilia.

Fulke leaned over the table and swapped his bowl with Judith's —then swapped their tankards, as well.

"Anyway, what I was trying to say before all of that," Pelt said, swirling his hand between Helen and Judith, "was that we're glad you decided to stay."

It took Emilia a moment to realize he was talking to her, and when she did, she dropped her spoon.

Pelt and Fulke exchanged a puzzled look, while Helen seemed oblivious to everything but her stew.

Only Judith seemed to recognize Emilia's shock. "Ah, come on, mate," she whispered in Emilia's ear. She nudged Emilia's shoulder with her own. "You're not *that* surprised, are you?"

Emilia was, though.

It'd been hard enough to accept that Maria and Judith wanted her here, but Pelt and Fulke, too?

Maybe even Helen?

While Emilia failed to think of a single response to Pelt's kind remark, the other four pirates moved on to idle ship gossip.

Emilia wanted to have *normal* responses to these kinds of things —like happiness or gratitude—but the shock cooling in her blood made it impossible for her to even process the words, much less believe them.

No one had ever *wanted* Emilia anywhere.

Her mother hadn't even wanted her *alive*, for Aletha's sake.

Emilia had learned to accept that—to want nothing more than to be tolerated.

How did someone who'd only ever longed to exist without resentment adjust to the possibility of being wanted?

Of belonging?

The mention of storm clouds jerked Emilia's attention back to the conversation.

"We can't sail *into* the storm. If one develops, we'll be stuck out here until it's over," Pelt was telling Judith. "Can you make the supplies last that long?"

"I can stretch what we have, if I have to," Judith said. She pushed back her short, brown hair, before taking another bite of stew. "Won't be fun, but I can."

"Not fun for us, or not fun for you?" Pelt asked.

"Neither," Judith said. She pointed her finger at Pelt. "And the first person to blame the lack of variety on *my* skills is getting punched in the face."

Helen looked up, her eyes alight with excitement.

Pelt scoffed, "*You're* going to punch someone?"

"No." Judith gestured toward Emilia with a tilt of her head. "Em is."

Emilia spun toward her. "What?"

Helen leaned forward. "I love that idea!"

"I don't," Emilia muttered. She'd sworn off punching people in the face after the fight with Buchan.

"I'll help you!" Helen offered. "We'll make your little arms less little!"

Apparently, 'larger' and 'more muscular' were not words Helen knew—not in reference to Emilia, anyway.

"My arms are not little," Emilia grumbled.

Helen made a sudden, alarming attempt at leaping across the table to squeeze Emilia's arms, but Fulke—*thank the goddess*—grabbed Helen's shoulder and shoved her back into her chair.

"Umm, right," Emilia said warily. She turned to Pelt, who'd clearly spoken with the captain recently. "Do you know if we spotted any naval ships today?"

"Not since yesterday," Pelt said—with enough casual indifference that Emilia wondered if she'd imagined the entire battle. "You know who we *did* see, though?" Pelt grinned at Fulke. "The *Ukevort.*"

To Emilia's surprise, the giant cringed.

"What's the *Ukevort?*" Emilia asked them.

Pelt's grin widened. "Ask Fulke."

Emilia turned to the giant. He signed something to her, but Emilia didn't understand those gestures yet.

"He says *'ukevort'* is the Aevarian word for *fortitude,*" Judith said.

Emilia blinked in surprise. "It's an Aevarian ship?"

The human governments of Aevaria collapsed during the Great Drought—thirty years ago, *five* years before Emilia was even born. Trade and currency collapsed along with them, and many of the humans who *didn't* flee to the prosperous Kingdom of Illopia died.

Maria's mother had been one of them.

In the unrest that followed, the Aevarian giants had taken control of the coast and desert lands. Any ship coming out of Aevaria now was likely manned by a crew of Aevarian giants.

"*Yes,*" Fulke signed. He pressed his palm to his chest. "*My people.*"

Emilia nodded.

She'd never actually met an Aevarian giant before Fulke. She'd met other giants—giants from the islands and a few Illopian giants —but no Aevarian ones.

Throughout the history of Aletharia, most races of giants had intermingled with humans so much that these days, they weren't much larger or stronger than the average human.

Aevarian giants, however, had maintained their own culture in the southern lands of Aevaria—marrying and procreating with other giants.

According to legend, the Aevarian giants, even to this day, possessed the strength of a troll and the intelligence of a human.

A dangerous combination—if they chose to make it so.

"Captain thinks they're trading with one of the islands," Pelt said. "King Eldric won't like that."

Of course he wouldn't.

It would be harder to conquer the world if the independent cultures started forming alliances.

Fulke signed his reply, and Judith translated, "He says, 'The *Ukevort* doesn't have enough firepower to defend herself against the

Royal Navy. Her captain will turn back, if he thinks he's been spotted.'"

"Wait," Emilia said. She turned and squinted suspiciously at Fulke. "How do you know how many cannons this specific ship has?"

Pelt's grin returned. "*There* it is."

Rather than give an actual answer, Fulke simply stuck out his tongue—or lack thereof.

Even though she'd suspected as much, Emilia still gasped, "The captain who did *that* to you is nearby?"

"Not just the captain," Pelt interjected. "The boatswain, too."

Emilia didn't want to imply that Pelt's job was any less important than the captain's, but… "Wait, the boatswain cut out your tongue?"

Fulke shook his head and offered a hand gesture that Emilia had seen many times by now.

"Captain."

"No, the boatswain is—" Pelt hesitated, checking with Fulke first. "Can I tell her? I want to tell her."

With an amused roll of his eyes, Fulke nodded.

"The boatswain was Fulke's lover!" Pelt blurted.

Emilia had yet to meet anyone on this ship who enjoyed ship drama as much as Pelt seemed to.

"Your lover saw what the captain did to you and didn't…leave?" Emilia asked.

Fulke made a small correction, and Judith supplied, between bites of stew, "Ex."

"Sorry," Emilia said. "Your *ex*-lover didn't leave?"

"His ex-lover chose the captain over him." Pelt sipped his ale. "Professionally *and* romantically."

"Oh," Emilia said. Her eyes widened. "Oh!"

What kind of person would do that to Fulke?

"Well, if he's nearby," Emilia pointed out, "we can attack him!"

Judith choked on her stew, and Pelt turned to Emilia, his eyes wide. "Easy there, surgeon."

"They hurt Fulke," Emilia said defensively.

Fulke laughed and signed something to her, and since Judith was still choking on her food, Pelt translated, "He says only two of them did that."

"Well, then, we'll only attack those two," Emilia said easily. "How hard could it be? You already said they don't have many cannons."

Fulke shook his head, his grin as wide as ever.

"How hard could it be?" Pelt repeated, enunciating each word. "It's a ship full of giants, Em!"

"We're only worried about two," Emilia reminded him. "We'll just focus on the captain and the lover. Or even just the lover! He sounds awful."

Fulke snorted.

"Or…she?" Emilia said timidly. "They?"

Emilia didn't know Fulke's exact orientation, but she'd gathered he liked men, at least, from the jokes he made, when he wanted to offend Zain.

Not that offending Zain was hard to do.

"*He*," Fulke signed.

Emilia nodded. "Well, how large is he, exactly?"

"Large enough to help cut out Fulke's tongue," Pelt muttered.

Which was exactly why Emilia had asked. "Would you be considered large or small, compared to your old crew?"

Fulke signed his answer, and Judith, having recovered from her choking fit, translated, "'Depends on what you mean.'"

Emilia tried to think of a clearer way to word it. "Well…how big is the ex-lover?"

Whatever Fulke said next caused Pelt to squeeze his eyes shut and cover his face with his hand.

Judith was midway through a bite of stew and took a bit longer to read. "'He says, 'He's bigger where it counts.'" She wrinkled her nose. "Gods, Fulke! Can't you see I'm trying to eat?"

Fulke guffawed, nearly falling out of his chair.

Emilia watched them with a frown. "Height?"

Pelt slowly uncovered his face, and Judith took a suspiciously large drink of ale.

Okay…

Apparently not.

Emilia tried to think of what might be the most important part of a boatswain's body. "Muscle mass?"

Pelt and Judith snorted, while Fulke's smile merely widened.

Helen swallowed her food. "He's talking about the c—"

Fulke slammed his palm over Helen's mouth before she could give it away.

Emilia looked from one person to the next, piecing together their amused expressions with Helen's one-letter hint. *"Oh,"* she mouthed—before sinking as low in her chair as she could.

The table erupted into laughter, and Emilia's face burned hotter.

"Oh, Em," Judith cackled. She tossed her arm around Emilia's shoulder and pulled her close. Throwing an insincere glare at her friends, she said, "It's not *her* fault her mind didn't go there! She loves women! It's possible she's never seen one."

Emilia scowled at that. "I'm a surgeon."

"Oh," Judith snorted. "Maybe it *is* her fault, then."

Emilia rolled her eyes. "What I *didn't* know," she said defensively, "was that Fulke likes to make dirty jokes over dinner."

"You could've warned her, Judith," Pelt scolded.

"About his ex!" Emilia added. "Over dinner!"

Fulke threw back his head, and an even bigger, heartier laugh erupted from his chest. Only when he'd finished, did he sign one last remark.

"Oh, you are just the mushiest, aren't you?" Judith scoffed.

Emilia glanced back and forth between them. "What did he say?" she asked Judith.

Judith turned to Emilia. "He said that's because he saves them for his friends."

Emilia frowned. She'd known Judith, Pelt, and Helen were Fulke's closest friends—besides Maria, of course—but had he forgotten Emilia was there, too?

That she was the target of the entire joke?

If he saved them for his friends, why would he…

Oh.

Her heart raced.

A band of shock tightened around her lungs, and Emilia placed her hand over her aching chest, as she forced herself to speak. "M-me, too? I'm a—"

Fulke nodded.

A friend.

For the first time in her life, Emilia had...*friends*.

CHAPTER 12

The Serpent and the Sword

"*You seem happy,*" Nymeth told her, later that night.

Emilia leaned against the rail, gazing up at the night sky. She couldn't *see* her dragons, but she could imagine them, flying amongst the stars. "*I think I am.*"

Emilia sensed a rush of warmth on the other side of the bond.

"*Good,*" the dragon replied.

The approaching *thud* of someone's leather boots brought a faint smile to Emilia's lips. Many of the sailors aboard the *Wicked Fate* wore boots. Yet, Emilia recognized the sound of Maria's every time.

Perhaps it was Maria's heavy, self-assured gait that set her steps apart from everyone else's, or perhaps it was something simpler—like weight distribution.

All Emilia knew was that her senses were far too attuned to Maria's presence.

Once, she'd told herself it was a survival instinct—because Maria had so often threatened her life.

But now?

Now, Emilia knew it was more.

A warm arm pressed into Emilia's, as a certain pirate captain claimed the spot next to her.

Emilia studied the forearm next to her own. Beneath a thin layer of sweat, tattooed into Maria's smooth, brown skin, was one of the largest of Maria's tattoos—the one that drew Emilia's gaze the most often. A snake coiled around a sword.

The Serpent and the Sword.

Emilia had once read a children's story with that title. She didn't remember much of it—just a detail here and there.

The people of the story had believed the serpent to be a monster, but the true villain had been someone else—though Emilia couldn't remember who.

Apart, the serpent and sword had failed. Together, they'd prevailed.

Someone had died, Emilia thought.

In the end, the story had been about the importance of strength and…deception?

No.

Cunning?

"What's it like?"

Maria's smooth, lilting voice interrupted Emilia's deliberation and drew her gaze upward.

Maria had tilted her head back, exposing the lovely curve of her throat, and she gazed up at the stars—just as Emilia had done before she'd arrived.

"What do you mean?" Emilia said breathlessly.

Maria's warm gaze slid downward, meeting Emilia's with the gentleness of a caress. "Flying."

A little, spiral curl had gotten itself caught in one of Maria's gold earrings, and Emilia curled her fingers inward, aching to free it.

"There's nothing else like it," Emilia said. She returned her attention to the dark blue sky—and the shining stars dusted across it. "The higher we fly, the more the world falls away, and then, I just feel…free."

Even without looking at her, Emilia felt the warmth of Maria's gaze—on her eyes, her cheeks, her lips…

"That's how the sea feels to me," Maria said.

Emilia turned, her eyes wide. "Really?"

Maria pressed more of her weight onto the wooden rail. With an affectionate smile, she drew her arm back—until her tattooed fingers brushed the back of Emilia's hand. "The further I sail from land, the more the world falls away," she sighed, "just as you said."

Emilia's heart fluttered in her chest, and a surprised smile pulled at the corners of her lips.

A crate moved somewhere behind them—a rough scrape of wood against wood—and the warmth of Maria's fingers instantly left Emilia's hand.

Emilia tried *not* to miss the sensation.

Her gaze drifted back toward the unobscured night sky, and the sight drew a soft sigh from Emilia's lips.

"What are you thinking?" Maria murmured.

The truth spilled out far too easily. "When I was a child," Emilia told her, "before I rejoined my people, I used to sleep beneath the stars with the dragons."

Maria's eyebrows rose. "Outside?"

"Well, not always," Emilia assured her. "Most of the time, they preferred to sleep in their caves—with their piles of shiny things." She turned and hooked a finger through the gold chain that hung from Maria's neck.

Maria's eyes darkened. "Sounds comfortable."

"To them, maybe," Emilia said with a scoff. "The night I'm thinking of, though—it was cloudless and cool, and the stars were… breathtaking." She spread her hand in front of her. "I was lying in this bed of soft grass, between Astral and Caelu."

"Darling," Maria halted her, "I don't remember which ones those are."

Emilia's lips twitched. "Violet and blue."

"Ah," Maria said with a nod, "got it."

Emilia suppressed a laugh. "I looked up at the stars and wondered what they must feel like—to touch," she said. "A burning ember? A ball of dragon-fire?"

Maria stopped interrupting, and her gaze softened.

"I wondered if a dragon had ever flown high enough to touch

one," Emilia said. "Would the oxygen deprivation kill them, too? Could a star be hot enough to burn dragon-scale? Nothing else is."

"So curious," Maria murmured.

Emilia's only defense was a small shrug. "Most of the dragons were sleeping. I didn't want to wake them up—especially not for any of *my* silly ideas," she muttered. "But Nymeth doesn't sleep at night."

Maria frowned. "Does she sleep during the day?"

"That is none of her business," Nymeth said.

Emilia ignored the dragon's commentary. "No one knows," she told Maria. "I know she likes to spread her wings beneath the stars, but she's never told me why." She shrugged. "Anyway, she'd heard my thoughts, and she spoke in my mind. She said—"

Nymeth spoke again tonight—though only Emilia heard her—and she repeated the same quote that Emilia now recited to Maria.

"Even dragons have limits, little one."

Maria leaned heavily against the wooden rail, watching Emilia with warm, brown eyes and a small, awestruck smile—as if Emilia had just presented her with a chest of gold.

Emilia blushed beneath her gaze. "Why are you smiling at me like that?"

Maria lifted her strong shoulders in a lazy shrug. "I just liked the story. That's all."

Emilia didn't know *why* Maria would like that story. There was nothing particularly interesting about it. It had only popped into Emilia's head because the stars looked lovely tonight, too.

But the fact that Maria *did* like it made Emilia's body melt like candle-wax.

Maria removed one arm from the rail and turned to Emilia. "Did you come out here expecting to fight?"

Emilia's brows furrowed. "What?"

Maria gestured at where Emilia stood—on the deck, beside the rail. "This is where we meet up to spar."

Emilia pretended not to remember that as well as she did. "I'm not that presumptuous."

Maria lifted a scarred eyebrow. "Then, I suppose you were searching for Catherine again."

Emilia scowled at that assumption. "I'm sorry to be the one to tell you this, Captain, but not everything is about you and Catherine."

Try telling that to anyone else on this ship…

Maria chuckled. "Then, why are you out here?"

Emilia sighed in defeat. "Look, do you want to fight or not?"

Maria threw back her head and laughed. "I knew it!"

Emilia rolled her eyes. Her entire body ached from the battles of the day before—not to mention the constant use of her magic—but she loved sparring with Maria too much to refuse the opportunity.

"We fought every night for a while there," Emilia reminded her, "before we made it back to the island." She shrugged. "You don't want to keep doing that?"

Maria's laughter faded, and her large, brown eyes softened, like warm honey. "Of course I do. I love fighting you." Her hand grazed her sword, as if she were still thinking about it, but she didn't draw it. "You have no idea how *much* I love fighting you."

"But?" Emilia assumed.

"But," Maria said, "I think you need a day off."

"I think *you* need a day off," Emilia countered.

Maria snorted. "We fought enough yesterday to make up for any lost time tonight, don't you think?"

"That was different," Emilia complained. "I didn't get to stab you yesterday."

"And as appealing as that sounds," Maria said, "I think we both need a bit of rest."

Emilia spread out her hands in defeat. "Fine."

"We'll resume our training tomorrow," Maria said, "if you can resist drawing a sword until then."

"Hmm," Emilia said noncommittally, "I can try."

With an amused chuckle, Maria turned and pressed her back against the rail. "Tell me more about how much you love the stars."

Emilia blinked at the request. "Oh," she said with a frown, "I don't know if I'd call it *love*."

"I promise I won't tell anyone," Maria teased.

"*Is* curiosity love?" Emilia asked.

"It seems to lead to it, doesn't it?" Maria seemed to realize a little late that she'd said that out loud—and quickly glanced around them. When she'd ensured no one was eavesdropping, she returned her attention to Emilia and whispered, "It did for us."

The mention—no matter how vague or quiet—of what they felt for each other caused warmth to unfurl inside Emilia's chest. "You were curious about me?"

Maria scoffed at the question. "How could I not be?" She trailed her gaze down Emilia's body. "You were quite the mysterious finding, Emilia Drakon."

How did she *do* that?

How did she say Emilia's name in a way that made Emilia feel as if no one else had ever said it right?

With such slow sensuality.

And deliberate attention to every syllable.

Emilia glanced at Maria, thinking, suddenly, of her little collection of illegal books—of the way she'd sought out anything denied to her—and Emilia realized just how similar the two of them had *always* been.

They'd had different childhoods, different religious beliefs, different careers, different personalities, even, but from the start, they'd both had such…curious souls.

That was why Maria had liked her story.

After all, why did *anyone* like stories?

Because they saw themselves in them.

"They're magnificent," Emilia found herself admitting. "The stars. Especially here—with no land or mountains to obscure the view." She glanced out at the rolling, midnight-blue waves. "The sea, too—with its steady rhythm. It soothes me and amazes me, all at once."

Maria's lips curved at the corners.

Emilia knew if she met Maria's gaze, she'd lose her nerve, but if she just kept talking… "When I'm looking at all of this, I…kind of get it." She bit her lip nervously. "I understand how a younger version of you fell in love with this life."

Oh, no. Why had Emilia said that?

Surely, she could've answered Maria's question without making herself sound like a love-struck fool.

Maria settled more of her weight against her elbow, angling her body closer to Emilia's. The cool leather of her doublet brushed against Emilia's arm. "So, this is what you think about at night? Me? Falling in love with the sea?"

Emilia's face burned with embarrassment.

She'd caught herself thinking of younger versions of Maria a few times today, actually—younger versions of both of them—but Emilia had no intention of admitting *that*.

"What's wrong?" Emilia countered. "Not dirty enough for you?"

Maria chuckled. "Not as dirty as what *I* think about at night."

A traitorous heat coursed through Emilia's body, and she forced herself to keep her gaze on the sea, lest Maria see the curiosity in her face.

Don't think about it.

Whatever you do, don't think about what she *thinks about when she…*

Oh, for Aletha's sake.

Out of the corner of her eye, Emilia could see Maria watching her—and worse, Emilia saw the knowing smile stretching ever wider on Maria's face.

Maria leaned forward, trying and failing to catch Emilia's gaze. "Why are you turning so red, love?"

Emilia's blush deepened. "Go away."

Maria just laughed. Her scarred throat curved, and her strong shoulders trembled.

Asshole.

Beautiful, infuriating asshole.

When she'd finished laughing at Emilia's expense, Maria lowered her gaze. She tilted her head, her curls gathering on her leather-clad shoulder, and her large, brown eyes warmed and softened, like melted butter.

"It's only a small part."

Emilia frowned at the pirate captain. "Hmm?"

A soft, adoring smile curved at the corners of Maria's dusky-pink lips. A smile like that might've made sense, if it were directed at the beautiful, star-speckled sky, but Maria wasn't looking at the sky.

She was looking at Emilia.

"The view of the sea and sky," Maria reminded her. "You imagined it was the part of this life I fell in love with, but it's really only a small part." She held Emilia's gaze. "It's like…a pair of lovely, green eyes."

Emilia still wasn't following.

Maria lifted a hand and traced her tattooed thumb beneath Emilia's cheek, where it curved beneath her eye. "Dazzling. Memorable. Intriguing enough to hold my attention—even as the girl scurries into that little alley she thinks will hide her from me…"

What?

Hide?

Emilia Drakon did not *hide*.

She'd simply stored the stolen bread in a less visible place, before placing *herself* in a less visible place—to watch the events unfold.

She hadn't even known Maria was there yet!

Arrogant pirate.

"The view was lovely and might've drawn me in," Maria continued, oblivious to Emilia's silent objections, "but it wasn't the, er—" Her intense gaze slid down Emilia's body, lingering a bit too long on Emilia's hips. "—main asset."

Emilia held out her hands. "I don't know what you—"

"Asset, Em," Maria repeated. "Ass?"

Emilia's frown deepened.

"The sea and stars are lovely, like your *eyes*," Maria said slowly, as if translating a foreign language, "but not the main draw, like your…" She arched her eyebrows meaningfully.

Emilia shook her head in disbelief. "Captain!"

Maria dissolved into a fit of laughter. "Oh, Fulke can tell you dirty jokes, but I can't?"

Emilia's eyes widened. "Oh my goddess!" she complained. "Can't anyone on this ship keep their mouth shut for five seconds?"

"No, they can't," Maria assured her, "and it's Fulke. Keeping *his* mouth shut doesn't change anything."

Emilia rolled her eyes. "I can't believe he told you," she muttered, "and just so you know, your joke doesn't even make sense. No one falls in love with someone's backside!"

"Have you seen yours?" Maria said.

Emilia ignored that. "It's the most horrid analogy I've ever heard in my life."

"Seriously?" Maria placed a hand against her own chest. "Because I grew up in a tavern. I've heard *far* worse."

Emilia didn't doubt that.

She, however, had heard her first dirty joke from Aletha when she was eleven—and had only realized it was suggestive afterward, when she'd overheard the goddess arguing with the dragons about what kind of humor was age-appropriate and what kind wasn't.

"Fine," Emilia said begrudgingly, "in this awful analogy of yours, what *would* be the buttocks?"

"The buttocks?" Maria repeated in disbelief. "You're just *trying* to ruin my joke, aren't you?"

"As if my effort was needed," Emilia scoffed.

Maria stepped away from the bulwark and then toward Emilia. Her sweet, tropical scent enticed Emilia's senses, and she flashed a wicked grin. "Isn't it obvious?"

Emilia didn't pull away. "Would I ask, if it were?"

Maria chuckled. She tilted her face toward Emilia's, and her breath caressed Emilia's lips, as she whispered, "Power."

"Of course," Emilia said.

With a shrug, Maria said, "As I said."

"It's ridiculous," Emilia insisted. "People don't fall in love with power or…asses."

"Em, I can assure you," Maria said, "many of us fall in love with power."

Emilia pointed a finger in victory. "But not asses!"

That earned a surprised snort from Maria. "Clever," she sneered. "Fine. Power is…tits and ass." She waved her hands in a circle. "The whole package."

"That is not an improvement!" Emilia informed her.

Maria only laughed harder. "I don't know what you want from me."

"All right," Emilia said, stepping closer. "I know part of what you love about your job is this crew. So, if the sea and stars are eyes and the power is…other parts of the body, what's the crew?"

"Oh, my sweet Em," Maria said with a surprisingly fond smile, "it wasn't meant to be this literal."

"Well, I made it literal," Emilia stated. "So, answer the question."

Maria chuckled. "I serve my crew, Em. I don't love them." When Emilia remained unconvinced, Maria pursed her lips. "Fine."

Maria brushed one hand against Emilia's waist.

Emilia tried not to react to Maria's touch—even as the warmth of Maria's fingers seeped through the thin, black fabric of Emilia's shirt.

Maria turned Emilia to face her fully—and examined her, as if the answer were written somewhere on Emilia's body. Maria's gaze drifted down to Emilia's shoes and then back up to her hair.

Okay, since when did Maria take *anything* this seriously?

Much less a joke of her own making…

Maria's dark gaze returned to Emilia's face—to a place she'd touched only a few moments earlier—and her smile returned, too. "Cheekbones."

Unfortunately, that part of Emilia's body chose *that* moment to grow intensely warm.

Maria's smile deepened at the sight of her blush.

Like the predatory villain people believed her to be, Maria closed in at the first sight of weakness. She lifted her hand and traced Emilia's flushed cheek with the backs of her warm, tattooed fingers.

Emilia's pulse quickened at her touch.

"I have a slight—*slight*," Maria emphasized, "fondness for my crew." She lowered her voice to a whisper. "Just as I have a slight fondness for these strong, perfect cheekbones I sometimes get to… kiss."

Get to?

As if it were a privilege?

Emilia's chest grew so heavy it ached.

Maria tucked a lock of short, black hair behind Emilia's ear and leaned forward. Her breath washed over Emilia's cheek first, and then, her lips—soft, warm, and a bit wet—touched Emilia's skin.

Emilia doubted anyone had ever died from a kiss on the cheek, but she was fairly certain *she* was about to. In a desperate attempt at self-preservation, Emilia blurted out, "What about the cats?"

Maria jerked back, as if someone had splashed a tankard full of water in her face. "Fucking hell, Em."

Well, what else could she have said?

'Please stop before I spontaneously combust?'

"The cats are part of shipboard life, too," Emilia said. "You can't leave them out!"

Maria leaned her head back and groaned at the sky—which was responsible for all of this, really. "I am trying to seduce you, and you want to talk about cats?"

"You were trying to seduce me?" Emilia said.

A spark of amusement flickered in Maria's eyes. "I don't love the ship cats. They're not part of this."

Emilia crossed her arms. "Well, just wait until Rat-Slayer hears *that*."

"Ah, for fuck's sake," Maria grumbled. She leaned forward. "If you repeat this to anyone *other* than Rat-Slayer…"

Emilia mimed sealing her own lips.

One side of Maria's mouth quirked upward. She took a small step back and swept her gaze downward again.

Emilia was starting to think Maria was just using this analogy as an excuse to stare—though Emilia didn't understand why Maria wanted to stare at *her*.

With no warning whatsoever, Maria reached out and poked the lower curve of Emilia's stomach.

"Belly," Maria said, as Emilia fought back a sudden burst of giggles. "Soft and cute." When a few of those giggles spilled out,

Maria looked up and grinned, like a child who'd just found a basket of sweet rolls. "Em?" she murmured. "Are you ticklish?"

"No," Emilia lied. She pressed a protective hand over her stomach before Maria could test the theory.

Maria raised a scarred eyebrow.

If Emilia didn't suddenly have to worry about being *tickled*, she might've teased the pirate captain about implying the ship cats were *'soft and cute.'*

As it was, she simply had to plow on to her next question. "I want to know what the soul is."

Maria's smile faded. "No."

"We're talking about love, Captain," Emilia said. "You can't talk about love and not include the soul."

"*You're* talking about love," Maria muttered.

"The sea and stars were what drew you in," Emilia said. "The crew was a part of the job you became fond of. You think the ship cats are soft and cute—"

"Careful, surgeon," Maria grumbled.

"And the power of your position," Emilia continued, "was something you found attractive."

"That's an understatement," Maria said.

"Which means," Emilia said, undeterred by Maria's interruptions, "there's something else—something that meant more to you than all of that."

"I thought you said you *weren't* presumptuous," Maria sneered.

"I want to know what it is," Emilia pleaded.

Maria shook her head. "No." She pointed a tattooed finger directly at Emilia's face. "No."

With a playful smile, Emilia said, "Too difficult of a question for you, Captain?"

Maria narrowed her eyes. "You ruined my joke. You can't mention the soul during a dirty joke!"

Emilia giggled, which only frustrated Maria more.

Maria stepped toward her. "Gods, you're such a—"

She reached for Emilia's waist, but Emilia swiveled out of her hold before Maria could grab her.

Maria simply followed.

"If the question is too difficult for you, Captain," Emilia said, while walking backward, "it's all right to admit defeat."

"Me? Defeat?" Maria said. "Fuck you."

This was almost as much fun as sword-fighting!

Pure, effervescent joy filled Emilia and bubbled out of her in a fit of hysterical laughter. She struggled to keep walking in the midst of it, and Maria caught her.

Emilia tried to squirm out of her captain's hold, but she only managed to turn away.

Maria closed her arm tighter around Emilia's waist, every inch of her pressing against Emilia's back, and she buried her face in the curve of Emilia's neck.

Emilia had to bite her lip, just to hold back a moan.

Maria moved her mouth up Emilia's neck, until it reached the shell of Emilia's ear. "You're mine, now."

Desire shot downward, like a bolt of electricity—straight to Emilia's core.

Maria's hand traced the hilt of Emilia's sword, then her scabbard, then the waistband of her trousers...

"Captain," Emilia gasped.

Maria chuckled. "You ruined my joke, Em."

Between the playfulness of Maria's tone and the caress of her lips against the sensitive skin of Emilia's ear, Emilia didn't know whether to laugh or moan.

"Your joke was awful," Emilia said breathlessly. She tilted her head back, resting it against the gentle slope of Maria's shoulder. "If anything, I redeemed it."

Maria smiled. "Maybe."

She tightened her hold around Emilia's waist, and though their swords and scabbards tangled, forming an unwanted barrier between them, the brief press of Maria's small, soft breasts against Emilia's back was enough to draw a soft moan from her lips.

Maria's eyes dilated, growing wide and dark with lust, and she dipped her head and pressed her mouth against Emilia's.

When Emilia released a pleasant sigh, Maria used that moment to press her tongue into Emilia's mouth. Maria's tongue was hot and gentle against Emilia's, and she explored Emilia's mouth deeply, despite the awkward angle.

Her hand slid downward, tracing the outside of Emilia's thigh, and she moaned into Emilia's mouth.

The strange angle left Emilia with no choice but to surrender most of her weight to Maria, and yet, Maria held her easily.

The creaks and groans of the ship fell away, until all Emilia heard was Maria's quick and heavy breathing.

Maria removed her hand from Emilia's thigh and lifted it to touch Emilia's face. The movement caused a slight shift of their hips, and the clang of steel hitting steel cut through the haze of desire.

"Fucking swords," Maria grumbled.

She unfurled her arm from Emilia's waist and carefully adjusted her own double-belted scabbard.

When she'd freed Emilia's sword, Emilia turned to face her.

"Now, maybe it'll…" Maria began, but she stopped when she noticed Emilia's curious smile. "You are *not* still waiting for me to answer that fucking question."

Still breathless after that kiss, Emilia said, "Well, of course, you don't *have* to answer, but…"

Maria lifted her eyebrows. "But?"

Emilia stepped closer, and Maria's eyes darkened.

"But," Emilia whispered, "I'd love to know."

Maria tilted her head, small, brown curls gathering against one shoulder, and her lips curved upward.

Maria *wanted* to tell her.

From that look alone, Emilia knew Maria wanted to tell her.

Emilia leaned a bit closer, and Maria watched her.

"What is the part that takes hold of you?"

To illustrate her point, Emilia took hold of Maria's black, leather doublet with one hand, and with the other, she took the gold chain around Maria's neck—and she jerked both toward herself.

Their bodies collided, and Maria's thick eyelashes fluttered closed. The wanton moan that spilled from Maria's mouth surprised Emilia as much as it aroused her.

It took all of Emilia's self-control just to finish the question. "The part that owns you?"

Maria opened her eyes, revealing fully blown pupils. "*Nothing,*" she growled, "owns me."

Heat pulsed through every cell of Emilia's body, and she raised herself onto her toes, aching for another taste of Maria's lips.

Maria's dark gaze darted toward Emilia's mouth, but she didn't lean forward—not yet. "You already said it."

Emilia fell back on her heels. "Hmm?"

In the aftermath of that *sound* Maria had made, their little game had faded into a distant memory, and she struggled to even remember the question.

Maria's smile widened. "The answer to your question, love. You said it earlier."

Emilia's brows furrowed, as she tried—and failed—to remember the events that had preceded Maria's moan.

What *had* Emilia said before all of this?

"The…stars?" Emilia guessed.

Maria shook her head slowly. "Before that." She stepped forward and cupped Emilia's face with her hand. "It all falls away," Maria recited, "and I just feel…free."

Emilia's eyes widened.

Maria traced Emilia's cheekbone with her thumb—just as she'd done earlier. "The part of this life that took hold of me—the way you have, my love," she murmured with a kind of reverence Emilia had never heard in her voice before, "was *that* feeling. Sweet, utter freedom."

Emilia's chest tightened, and emotions wracked her so powerfully they took her breath.

Maria slanted her mouth *just* above Emilia's. "Now, please," she whispered. "Kiss me."

Emilia didn't hesitate. With her fingers still wrapped up in Maria's doublet and necklace, Emilia tugged Maria closer and poured every ounce of love coursing through her into the collision of their lips.

Pressing her free hand against Emilia's back, Maria held Emilia just as tightly, and her breath grew quick and ragged against Emilia's mouth.

Every muscle in Emilia's body slackened, and just when Emilia thought she might drown in this moment, someone above them coughed.

Maria released her, instantly. She stepped back, her hand darting toward her sword. Maria gripped the curved hilt of her sword, as she glared up at the sailor who hung in the rigging above them.

By the time Emilia looked up, the sailor had already retreated to a safe place to hide, leaving nothing above them but a trembling line and rustling sails.

"I'll kill him, if he says a word to anyone about this," Maria told Emilia. She raised her voice, before adding, "For his sake, let's hope he heard that."

Emilia suppressed a smile. "I'm sure he just saw us kissing," she assured Maria, "and like you said, they already know, anyway."

"That better be all he saw," Maria said. Then, with a small smile, she whispered, "Come to my quarters?"

Emilia's reply was quiet and sincere. "I'd love to."

CHAPTER 13
A Warning from a Goddess

In the days that followed, the crew settled back into a routine, and even Emilia found herself worrying less and less about Catherine with each passing day.

Emilia still believed Catherine had turned away for a reason, of course—one that wouldn't work out in their favor—but what could she do about it?

With a storm developing in the east, the *Wicked Fate* couldn't return to Nefala for repairs, much less prepare for another battle.

Emilia had only stopped to slip on her shoes, when the large cat behind her let out an impatient meow.

"Yes, yes, sorry," Emilia sighed.

She ambled to the door—barefoot—and opened it so the ship cat could attend to his needs elsewhere.

Emilia returned to the surgery table, where her shoes and scabbard waited, but she froze when she noticed a faint glow beneath the sleeve of her shirt.

Emilia tugged the thin, black sleeve up to her elbow and studied the shining dragon that wrapped itself around her arm.

The glow was dim enough that Emilia doubted anyone would

notice, if they didn't know to look for it. After all, *she* hadn't even noticed it until today.

Still, it gave Emilia more warning than usual of Nymeth's imminent intrusion of her mind.

"Aletha asked about you," came the dragon's voice.

"Aletha?" Emilia frowned. *"What's her interest in me?"*

Nymeth's rumbling laughter filled Emilia's mind. *"Same as always,"* she said, *"or were you unaware that gods don't usually visit mortals throughout their lives?"*

"No, I know that," Emilia assured her.

The truth was Emilia had never known why the goddess visited her. She'd just assumed Aletha liked to check up on her charity case every now and then—to see if Emilia was proving worthy of her second chance at life.

The answer to that question, of course, was no—as Emilia's mother so often pointed out.

"I know her visits seem rare to you," Nymeth added, *"but you must remember that to the gods, mortals live and die in the blink of an eye. Aletha believes she's visiting often, whether she actually is or not."*

Emilia nodded. *"But isn't it like a blink of an eye to you, too?"*

Nymeth was quiet for a moment. *"Dragons live long lives, but they're also typically younger than the gods,"* she said carefully. *"After all, dragons were a creation of the gods."*

Nymeth always answered questions regarding her age with that sort of vagueness. For reasons Emilia had never understood, the dragon refused to give any helpful clues.

"Because you're too clever for your own good," Nymeth informed her, *"and no matter how fond I am of this particular mischievous child, I won't be the reason she learns things before she's ready."*

A delighted smile burst across Emilia's face. *"You're fond of me?"*

"Not for long," Nymeth teased, *"if you continue to stick your nose where it doesn't belong."*

Emilia's smile deepened. She was fond of the dragons, too—even the ones who denied her bits of information for seemingly no reason.

The dragon huffed, and Emilia felt the steam wash over her

face, as if they were standing in front of each other—rather than miles apart.

"Don't start being rude, like your human," Nymeth scolded.

Emilia laughed at the mention of Maria. *"She may be rude,"* Emilia admitted, *"but she grows on you."*

"She grows on you,*"* Nymeth corrected. *"You also have a fondness for Emryn, so I'm not sure I trust your taste."*

Emilia's mouth fell open. *"Emryn is your child!"*

Dragons rarely discussed their parentage or birth—even with Drakon sorcerers. After all, the gods created and hatched some of the dragon eggs themselves.

But Emryn had never kept a secret in his life.

"I never said I don't love him. I simply said you have strange taste," Nymeth assured her. *"Besides, I have many children—not all of them biological."*

Emilia didn't know what Nymeth meant by that, but she supposed Nymeth hadn't meant for her to. *"So, the goddess came to see me?"*

"Oh, no. She knows where you are," Nymeth told her. *"There's nothing on the sea Aletha doesn't know. She just doesn't know* how *you are."*

The dragon rune on Emilia's arm burned just a bit brighter, and the dragon magic in her veins surged.

As Nymeth no doubt soared into the air, Emilia felt a rush of wind around her—on her face, against her neck, beneath her arms.

"Why do I feel stronger?" Emilia wondered.

"Because I do," the dragon told her.

Apparently, that was the only answer Emilia was going to get.

No one could accuse *Nymeth* of being long-winded.

"As I was saying," Nymeth said, as if Emilia had intentionally interrupted her, *"Aletha asked me about you because she knows how acquainted I am with your feelings."*

Emilia's brows furrowed. *"The sea goddess knows about my new rune?"*

"As I said before," Nymeth reminded her, *"there's nothing on the sea Aletha doesn't know."*

Even in a limited form, omniscience was difficult to comprehend —for Emilia, anyway.

Less so for ancient, black dragons, apparently.

"Once I assured the sea goddess you were all right," Nymeth said, *"she asked me to give you a warning."*

Emilia's shoulders tensed.

A warning?

From a goddess?

"Be prepared to summon her," Nymeth said, *"soon."*

Emilia didn't like the sound of that.

"The captain doesn't want me to summon the goddess," Emilia tried to explain. *"I offered on the island, but—"*

"I know," Nymeth assured her. *"I was listening."*

She was?

Emilia hadn't thought Nymeth was nearby during that conversation. Emryn had been, though. Nymeth might've listened through Emryn.

Or even Emilia.

The dragon sighed. *"Your human is afraid—for you and for herself."*

Emilia didn't think Maria would like that observation.

"Whether she likes it or not, it's clear in the way she resists," Nymeth said. *"Humans don't understand this, my child, but fear is the weakest of all motivators. A person who makes a decision out of fear will change their mind the moment something* else *scares them more."*

Emilia's heart raced.

Unfortunately, she'd understood *that* message loud and clear.

Something would happen soon, and whatever it was—it would terrify them all.

Even Maria.

"Great," Emilia muttered, no longer taking care to not speak aloud. "More anxiety! Just what I needed."

And, of course, someone chose that moment to knock on her door.

"Em?"

Emilia smiled warily at the familiar voice and finished buckling her scabbard. "Coming, Judith!"

"Take care, Dragon Child," Nymeth said.

The wind on Emilia's face vanished, and silence fell on the dragon's side of the bond.

Emilia hurried to the door and opened it.

Judith stood outside, already dressed in beige breeches and an off-white, linen shirt—despite the early hour.

If Judith was up this early, Emilia figured it was safe to assume Judith and Helen hadn't stayed up *gambling* the night before. She didn't have time to ask, though, because Judith had other concerns.

The ship cook leaned forward, on her toes, casting a puzzled look over Emilia's shoulder. "Who the fuck were you talking to this time?"

"The cat," Emilia lied.

She didn't really feel like explaining to Judith how a dragon bond worked—or how her rune intensified it.

It'd been hard enough to explain it to Maria.

Judith continued to peer over Emilia's shoulder, her frown only deepening. "What cat?"

"Oh, right," Emilia said with a wince. "I let him out earlier, didn't I?"

Judith returned her attention to Emilia. She arched her eyebrows and waited for further explanation, but Emilia offered none. "Em, you know I adore you, but," she sighed, "you are one *strange* girl."

"Aww," Emilia said, smiling, "I adore you, too."

Judith chuckled and gave Emilia an affectionate pat on the arm. "So, are you still caring for injured sailors, or," she paused to clasp both hands together, as if in prayer, "can I have you back?"

"I healed the last one yesterday, actually," Emilia told her. "Whatever you need today, I'm there."

Judith's entire body sagged with relief. "Thank the gods! The rest of them annoy the hell out of me!"

Emilia frowned. "The rest of whom?"

"Everybody," Judith said with a broad swipe of her arm. "Everybody except you."

Emilia just laughed.

For someone who seemed so laid back, Judith tolerated surprisingly few people in her galley.

"Well, come on, mate," Judith said, as she turned to leave. "And before you ask: no, I haven't broken the Helen law lately; yes, that's why I'm fucking awake!"

With an amused smile, Emilia closed the door and followed the sexually frustrated ship cook.

MULTIPLE TIMES THAT DAY, EMILIA CONSIDERED HUNTING DOWN Maria and telling her about the warning she'd received from Aletha, but despite Maria's fascination with the sea goddess, she didn't always react well to Emilia talking about her.

With her luck, the pirate captain would assume Emilia had summoned the goddess and received the warning that way—and would be so angry about it that she wouldn't even listen to the damn warning.

Besides, if there were any way to prevent this *thing* that might happen, the goddess would've told her.

Emilia did wish she'd been a bit less vague, though.

So, while Emilia chopped potatoes in the sweltering galley of the ship, she tried to focus on less alarming matters—like the storm that might kill them all.

Though it had begun as nothing more than a few puffs of white on the horizon, those clouds had gathered and darkened throughout the last week, and with each passing day, it had become increasingly clear that Maria's instincts were right.

"If we're lucky, we'll avoid it completely," Judith was saying. "Pelt says the captain means to outrun it."

Which explained why they were still sailing west.

"What if we can't, though?" Emilia asked. She dumped a platter of chopped potatoes into a wooden bowl. "I doubt any of the islands are going to welcome a pirate ship, and I *know* the sirens won't."

Judith waved a hand. "Oh, don't you worry about that. The

captain's sailed through hurricanes before." She came to collect the sliced potatoes and gave Emilia's shoulder a nudge when she did. "She's so skilled at navigating storms that people say she has a *magical* gift."

Judith was obviously mocking the idea, but Emilia found it quite plausible.

Not a magical gift, really—but magical *favor*.

The sea goddess had always had a habit of favoring people—a habit that Aria, the wind goddess who both loved and hated her, often criticized.

Aletha had favored Emilia, after all.

And perhaps Emilia was biased, but she fully believed the sea goddess would admire Captain Maria Welles, too, just as Emilia had grown to do.

How could she not?

Judith set down the bowl and turned to remove a pot of boiling water from the fire. "The real question," she told Emilia, "is whether the captain will survive *Adda's* wrath when we return to Nefala—because when we don't return in a timely manner, Adda worries, and she doesn't like it when the captain makes her worry."

Emilia's brows furrowed. She understood that, whether Maria liked to admit it or not, she and Adda had a kind of…mother-daughter relationship. What Emilia didn't understand was what a mother-daughter relationship even looked like. Emilia's relationship with her own mother had been…

Not quite *that*.

Judith glanced back at her, likely misinterpreting Emilia's silence. With a suspicious squint, Judith said, "Ah, you're not still worried about our return, are you?"

"No," Emilia said. It'd been a mistake, she realized, to even mention that to Judith. "It was never a worry," Emilia insisted. "It was just a…thought."

Several days ago, before the sky had made it clear that returning to Nefala wasn't an immediate option, Emilia had expressed mild curiosity—*not* worry—about how Adda might react to seeing her again.

After all, the last time Emilia had come into contact with Adda was after she'd stolen the bread.

Maria insisted Adda would believe the lie she'd fed her, but as Judith liked to point out, Maria was often overconfident.

What if Adda hadn't believed it?

Would she hate Emilia?

Would she then hate her more, when she found out that Maria and Emilia were together?

Would Maria even tell her?

Judith had been far too amused by Emilia's *thought* and hadn't let her forget it since. "Have you shared your concerns with the captain?"

"I told you," Emilia said. "It's a thought, not a concern." She gathered another armful of potatoes to chop. "And no, of course I haven't told the captain!"

Just the thought of doing such a thing made Emilia's face burn with humiliation.

Judith laughed. "Em, you have nothing to worry—ah, I mean," she stopped to hold up a finger, "*think* about."

Emilia scowled at her teasing.

"Adda won't hate you," Judith assured her.

"Well, she didn't seem to *like* me," Emilia pointed out, "the first time I met her."

Judith snorted. "Adda doesn't *seem* to like anyone."

Emilia looked up from her potatoes.

"Look, Adda wasn't young when *I* met her, and that was thirty years ago," Judith said. "She's a cranky, old woman who hasn't *always* had the captain to kill her enemies for her." Judith added several spoonfuls of pepper to the pot. "You have to remember, when the captain was a child, it was Adda who protected *her*—not the other way around."

"I know that," Emilia said.

"You don't do business with pirates, murderers, and thieves without a good deal of ruthlessness—and the ability to hide any humanity you may have." Judith offered Emilia another grin. "Who do you think the captain learned it from?"

Emilia considered that.

Maria had implied once or twice that she'd learned to hide her emotions in the navy, where she'd faced disrespect because of her gender—not that Emilia understood *why* Illopians fixated on such things.

But perhaps that was simply where Maria had first learned its usefulness.

After all, Adda had built her career in Illopia, too, and in the criminal world, Emilia supposed it was even *more* necessary to project a sense of invulnerability.

"If you'd been a stranger in Nefala, walking into the *Shrieking Siren* for the first time, you would've thought Adda hated that little orphan girl," Judith scoffed, "who was always breaking things and getting into fights with grown men." She rolled her eyes at the memories. "But I promise…the captain never doubted Adda's love for her."

Emilia's chest tightened. She couldn't even imagine a childhood like that—knowing that no matter what you did, someone would still love you?

"Adda adores the captain, but she doesn't show it in front of anyone who would use it against her." Judith gave Emilia a meaningful look. "Remind you of someone?"

Maria.

Except Maria *had* shown it—by declaring war on an entire naval fleet, just to protect Emilia.

And Catherine had promptly used it against her.

Emilia's arm ached at the memory.

"The captain wasn't an easy child," Judith said. "Trust me. As the girl who always got in trouble *with* her—even though I've done nothing wrong in my entire life—"

Emilia lifted her eyebrows at that.

"I can assure you she wasn't easy to raise," Judith continued, "but Adda loved her. And if she can love the captain, she'll *like* the woman who makes the captain happy."

Emilia froze. "You think I make the captain happy?"

"And even if she doesn't," Judith said, apparently choosing to ignore that question, "the worst that'll happen is she'll ask the captain to kill you."

"Oh," Emilia said, "well, as long as that's all…"

With no warning whatsoever, Judith burst into laughter. She set the wooden ladle on the table so that she could brace a hand against her flat stomach.

Judith had always enjoyed Emilia's sarcasm, but this was an extreme reaction, even for her.

"What?"

Judith rubbed a fist against her eye. "Ah, it's just—"

Emilia stopped to gape at Judith, when she dissolved into yet *another* fit of laughter. "What could possibly be that funny?"

"Ah, you know, it's just…" Judith snorted. "We learned that magic was dangerous and that witches were these horrible, evil crea-tures." She waved her hand at Emilia. "And yet, here's our horrible, evil creature, worrying her lover's mother might not like her."

Emilia narrowed her eyes. "I already told you I'm not worried!"

"Mm-hmm," Judith said with an infuriating wink.

Emilia rolled her eyes. "Okay, fine!" she relented. "I want her to like me. Is that so ridiculous?"

"No," Judith said, "but it *is* adorable."

Warmth rushed to Emilia's cheeks. "Oh, hush."

Judith's grin widened. She leaned her hip against the table. "The only reason Adda doesn't *typically* approve of the captain's lovers—aside from the fact that the captain moves from one to the next in the time it takes the girl to orgasm—"

Emilia ignored that.

"—is that Adda knows the captain needs someone who won't take her shit," Judith said. "Women let the captain get away with murder. Literally. You don't."

"Uhh, no, she still gets away with murder," Emilia said. "All the time. It's…her career."

"Adda will like you," Judith insisted, "just like the rest of us do!"

The rest of whom? Emilia had spent her entire lifetime learning that it was impossible to like her, actually.

Unless you were a dragon.

Or an animal.

Or a navy admiral, who only *pretended* to like her.

Right. Back to dragons and animals.

"And if she *doesn't* like you," Judith said with a wave of her wooden ladle, "just take solace in the fact that the captain has never followed a rule in her life. Not even Adda's."

"Also, we might die in the storm and never return to Nefala," Emilia added helpfully. "Or the captain might get tired of me and throw me overboard!"

Judith snorted. "That's the spirit!"

The two of them fell silent, when the wooden planks above them creaked. As it was a bit early for the afternoon meal, Judith and Emilia exchanged puzzled looks.

The heavy, clumsy steps suggested that it was either multiple people or one very *loud* one.

Worn, brown boots descended the wooden steps. The pirate's beige, canvas trousers followed, and when the end of a long, bright orange braid came into view, Judith mumbled, "Shit."

Emilia cast a curious smile Judith's way.

Helen stumbled down the last couple of steps, as if she wasn't quite sure where she was. Her hazel eyes scanned the dark galley, before focusing on Emilia.

Emilia had never seen the master gunner so…*clean.*

No gunpowder on her freckled face?

No wood chips in her red hair?

No still-smoking holes in her clothes?

What was *this*?

Helen looked a bit paler than usual, too—though maybe that was just the lack of gunpowder.

Judith stared deliberately into her pot of boiling water. "Food's not ready yet, mate."

Helen glanced at Judith. "Oh, I'm not here to eat." But then, she turned to Emilia. "Am I?"

Emilia stared blankly at her. "I—I can't read your mind, Helen."

"But you're a witch," Helen said.

"Well, yes, but," Emilia said, "telepathic spells are rare and complicated. They require consent of both parties—also, a sacrifice from both parties."

Helen's eyes widened. "A human sacrifice?!"

Emilia frowned. "No? Just a regular one." She didn't know how the gunner had jumped to *that* conclusion. "It's more about what it means to the person than the sacrifice itself. For some people, it can be pain or blood. For others, it's—"

Midway through the explanation, Helen turned to Judith. "Will you translate what she's saying into Illopian for me?"

Emilia scowled at her. "I'm *speaking* Illopian."

Judith reluctantly looked up at Helen. "Do you really not know why you're here?"

"No, I know," Helen said. She gestured toward Emilia. "I was just wondering if she knew more than I did."

Oh, for Aletha's sake.

Judith returned her attention to the simmering water. "Mate, just tell me what you need."

Emilia lifted her eyebrows at Judith's curt tone. No wonder she and Helen had stopped 'gambling,' if these were the types of conversations they were having.

"Nothing from you," Helen said. She waved toward Emilia. "I was looking for the surgeon."

That got Emilia's attention.

She set her knife aside and grabbed a clean rag to wipe her hands. "Are you hurt?"

"I'm hurt*ing*," Helen said.

Emilia quickly circled the table—so she could tend to her possibly injured shipmate. "Another burn?"

"No," Helen said with a bit of a whine. "Just pain."

"Okay." Emilia stepped closer to the large, muscular woman. "Show me where it hurts."

Helen rested her hand against her stomach. "Here."

Judith scoffed in disbelief. "You came to see the ship's surgeon for a stomachache?"

"It's fine if she did," Emilia told her. She returned her attention to Helen. "I need to feel for distention. Do you mind?"

Helen shrugged her large shoulders. "I don't know what that means."

"She's going to touch you," Judith said.

"Oh, good," Helen sighed. "No one else does anymore."

Emilia blinked—and then shot a wide-eyed look in Judith's direction. Coincidentally, Judith chose that moment to concentrate *very* hard on her work.

Emilia glared at her coward of a friend, before returning her attention to Helen. "Stomach," she told Helen. "I need to feel your stomach."

Helen dropped her hand, and Emilia replaced it with her own. She pressed harder, but she didn't feel any distention—just firm, unyielding muscles.

Granted, Emilia would've felt more confident in her examination, if Helen were lying down, but she doubted Judith—or anyone else, for that matter—wanted Helen stretching out on top of the food.

"It's lower, actually," Helen said. She took Emilia's hand and shoved it downward, ignoring the squeak of surprise Emilia gave her, when she did. "There."

Emilia stared up at her, her eyes wide. She carefully removed her hand. "Lower stomach, then?"

"There are two stomachs?" Helen said. "No wonder I'm so hungry."

Judith threw down her ladle, as if Helen had insulted her. "Fine! I'll get you some bread."

Helen smiled at the...quite angry offer. "Thank you!"

Judith made a rude gesture—on her way to do something... considerate.

Emilia really couldn't make sense of these two.

"Umm, no. One stomach," Emilia said slowly. With a wave toward Helen's lower abdomen, she said, "That's more likely... intestinal?"

She considered asking Helen to point it out again—with her own hand, this time—but Helen wasn't even looking at her. She was, instead, watching a certain cook stride toward her with a piece of bread Helen had never actually asked her for.

Judith shoved the bread into Helen's hand. "If you tell the captain I gave you extra food, I will beat you with my ladle."

Helen closed her hand around the bread. "Promise?"

Emilia spread out her arms. "Should I just leave?"

"No!" both of them said, at once.

Helen clasped her hand over her abdomen. "You can't leave *me*! I'm dying!"

"Okay," Emilia said patiently. "Can you give me a few details as to *how*? Do you have other symptoms? Does anything happen before or after the pain?"

Judith slipped past them, returning to the hearth.

Helen's thin, red eyebrows drew closer together. "What kind of symptoms?"

Emilia gestured toward the bread Helen was already shoving into her mouth. "Well, you clearly haven't lost your appetite." She glanced at Helen's other hand. "Based on the location of the pain, I'd say bodily functions would be a good place to start."

Judith grimaced. "Do I need to be here for this?"

Emilia didn't have time to answer that—because Helen suddenly blurted out, with a mouthful of food, "Oh, you mean the bleeding."

Emilia's eyes widened. "You're bleeding?" They'd been sitting there talking and doing...*whatever* Judith and Helen had been doing, while Helen was bleeding? "Helen, you should've led with that!"

Helen lifted her shoulders in a careless shrug. "You're a witch. I assumed you knew."

"Oh, and we're like sharks?" Emilia muttered. "We can smell blood from a mile away?"

"Why are you asking me?" Helen asked. "Don't you know?"

Emilia heaved out a defeated sigh. She looked Helen over, searching for any injuries she might've missed. "Just show me where you're bleeding."

Helen's eyebrows shot upward. "Here?"

Emilia searched the galley for something she could use as a tourniquet, if needed.

Helen shrugged those strong shoulders of hers and unfastened her trousers. "All right. Who am I to tell a surgeon where to do her job?"

By the time Emilia had returned to Helen, the master gunner had already dropped her trousers—right in the middle of the damn galley.

Judith arched both eyebrows, apparently no *longer* uncomfortable watching.

"Helen," Emilia said, her eyes wide, "what in the name of the goddess are you doing?"

Judith leaned against the table in front of her and tilted her head, short, brown hair falling to the side.

Naked from her waist down to her ankles, Helen said, "What you told me to do."

Emilia nodded slowly. "Helen? Have we been discussing your monthly bleeding this entire time?"

"No," Helen said, "we were talking about the pain."

"Yes," Emilia said, "but it might've helped to have known a bit earlier—so I wouldn't have thought it was a wound that needed sutures."

"Sutures?" Helen shrieked. She threw her hands over that mass of orange curls she was displaying to anyone who might come down. "Judith! Help!"

Judith didn't tear her gaze away for a moment. "Totally here for you, mate."

"Oh, for Aletha's sake, I wasn't actually going to—" Emilia squeezed her eyes shut. "Can you just pull up your trousers, please?"

Helen knelt to grab them, but Judith stopped her.

"Wait." Judith smiled and twirled a finger. "Can you do a little circle first?"

Emilia opened her eyes long enough to glare at the shameless cook. "Judith!"

Judith offered an innocent shrug. "Just trying to help."

"No, you're not!" Emilia said.

Helen froze mid-turn—with her bare, freckled backside in Judith's direct line of sight. "*No* circle?"

Judith grinned.

"No circle!" Emilia said.

She grabbed the closest thing to her—a thin slice of pepper, as it turned out—and tossed it at Judith.

Judith dodged it and nearly fell over, laughing.

Helen fastened her beige trousers. "So, can your people fix this kind of thing or not?"

With a bemused frown, Emilia said, "Are 'my people' witches or surgeons?"

Helen leaned forward, clutching her stomach. "I don't care what you are today," she said with a miserable groan, "as long as you make it stop."

Emilia offered her a sympathetic smile. "I'll make you a tea, for now, to ease the cramps, and you can come by the surgeon's cabin later for a tincture."

Helen grabbed Emilia by the shoulders, leaving breadcrumbs on her thin, black shirt. "Thank you!"

"It's no problem at all," Emilia laughed. She turned to Judith. "Do you mind if I boil some water?"

Judith waved encouragingly at the fire-hearth.

Emilia gently removed Helen's hands from her shoulders so she could head to the back to retrieve supplies. "Have you felt weak?" she called back.

Helen shouted her answer, "I never feel weak."

Emilia didn't doubt that.

It took Emilia several moments to gather the ingredients she'd need, and when she returned, she found Helen attempting to sprawl across the closest table, while Judith swatted at her and scolded her for crushing the food.

Emilia set the supplies on the table. "Are you tired, then?"

"Why would you think that?" Helen asked.

Emilia and Judith exchanged a look. "I was just wondering if you might be a bit anemic."

"Well, I don't know what that is, but I'm not tired," Helen said. She glared at Judith. "Just *uncomfortable!*"

Judith rolled her eyes and walked away. She returned with a tankard, and Emilia thanked her.

"She didn't mind me resting on the table the other night," Helen grumbled to Emilia, "but apparently, she just changes the rules whenever she wants."

"There wasn't food on the table the other night!" Judith argued. "We wouldn't have done half the shit we did on that table, if there'd been food on it!"

Emilia's eyes widened, and she cast a horrified look at the table beneath her. "Oh." She carefully removed the loose tea leaves. "Oh, no."

Helen crossed her arms, muscles bulging.

"I'll get the pot." Judith strode toward the fire.

"You didn't use *that* the other night, too, did you?" Emilia muttered.

"Hmm?" Judith called back.

"Nothing," Emilia said. As she prepared the tea, she asked Helen, "Have you had any headaches?"

"Only when I hit my head very hard," Helen said.

"Yes, well," Emilia said with a tilt of her own head, "perhaps we should try not to do that?"

"For five whole days?" Helen said incredulously.

Emilia looked up at the explosion-loving gunner. "I was thinking more like forever," she corrected, "but we can start with five days and go from there."

Helen pouted—like a huge, muscular child. "Fine."

Judith returned with a flagon of boiling water. She poured the water over Emilia's tea leaves, and white steam rushed up from the tankard.

Emilia added a few spoonfuls of honey.

When she finished, Helen stepped forward to sniff the steaming tea. "That'll save my life?"

"You're not actually dying." Emilia wrapped a cloth around the tankard and picked it up. She carried it around the table. "This happens every month, does it not?"

When Emilia reached her, Helen grabbed Emilia's arms so hard that she nearly spilled the boiling tea.

"Yes," Helen said fiercely, "and I die every time."

Emilia started to disagree, but then, she tilted her head in acquiescence. "Yeah, okay. Me, too."

Helen took the tankard from Emilia's hands and immediately lifted it to her mouth.

"Not yet!" Emilia sprang forward, grabbing Helen's wrists to stop her. "It has to steep—and *cool*! Not everything is supposed to burn, you know?"

Helen lowered the tankard. "Are you sure?"

"Very," Emilia said. "Now, please. Take it with you. Drink it when you need it, and if you can manage not to blow anything up for a few hours, I'll see you in the surgeon's cabin later—to give you that tincture."

Helen braced a hand against Emilia's shoulder. "I don't know how we ever survived without you."

Emilia might've called that an overreaction, if it were anyone else, but with Helen and her constant explosions, it truly was a mystery.

Helen was halfway up the steps when Emilia heard her say, "Ow."

"Let it cool!" Emilia yelled.

"Yeth, thurgeon!" Helen called down—with what sounded like a swollen tongue.

Emilia rolled her eyes and turned to face Judith.

Judith sighed, "Ah, that poor chunk of muscle. Sometimes, I wonder if living through that many explosions is good for the brain."

Emilia narrowed her eyes at the ship cook. "Sometimes, I wonder if *you* have any shame at all!"

Judith shrugged her slender shoulders. "I learned my manners from the captain. What do you expect?"

"I suppose you have a point," Emilia muttered.

Amusement sparkled in Judith's bright blue eyes.

"Honestly," Emilia said, "why do you even bother with the tavern girls, when you're *this* into Helen?"

Judith's smile faded. "Appreciating the view when it presents itself doesn't mean I have feelings for her."

Emilia lifted her eyebrows in disbelief. "And what about breaking the Code to sleep with her?"

"It's not a real law!" Judith said defensively. "It was just a little temper tantrum the captain threw because she had to pay for some minor ship repairs."

"A hole in the side of a ship is minor?" Emilia said.

Judith shrugged dismissively. "Besides, the tavern girls are prettier than Helen!" She waved a finger at Emilia. "You can't deny that."

Emilia wasn't sure her definition of pretty was the same as Judith's definition. Like many Illopians, Judith seemed to attribute certain societal expectations to the word—societal expectations that Emilia didn't know or understand.

Rather than discuss all of that, however, Emilia simply said, "And yet…"

Judith leaned against the table behind her and bit her thumbnail thoughtfully. "And yet."

~

"Em?"

Emilia instantly recognized that voice—warm and lilting in the darkness. She released the iron handle of her door and turned to face the pirate captain, who'd called her name.

Maria stood in the dark companionway outside the surgeon's cabin. For how long, Emilia didn't know.

Dressed in her black, leather doublet and her black, leather trousers, Emilia might not have seen her, if it weren't for the light of a nearby porthole.

"Trying to sneak up on me, Captain?"

Maria smiled, and though it was too dark to know for sure, Emilia thought she saw Maria's eyes dilate.

"You walked past me," Maria said. "If I'd meant to sneak up on you, I wouldn't have called your name."

Emilia nodded at that. "Were you waiting for me?"

"Well, what other explanation is there?" Maria said.

"Fair point," Emilia said with a laugh. "What did you need?"

"You," Maria murmured.

Emilia's eyes flared wide. "What?"

Maria stepped closer. "Do you know how hard you are to find? You've been all over the ship today."

Find?

Maria had been looking for her?

"Not really," Emilia argued. "I was in the surgeon's cabin, then the galley, then the surgeon's cabin again to make a tincture, then the galley again. Now, I'm meeting Helen in the surgeon's cabin. Again. Oh, and someone asked me to look at a tooth earlier!" She frowned. "Was that when you were looking for me?"

Maria didn't seem to hear the question. She stepped forward, wood creaking beneath her. "Helen? She's blown something up again, hasn't she?" Maria glared at the narrow, wooden door, as if Helen could see through it. "I'm going to kill her, if she has!"

Emilia held up her hands in a placating gesture. "She didn't blow anything up—that I know of."

Maria reluctantly tore her gaze from the door. "Good," she muttered, "because this ship is damaged enough, as it is."

"I know," Emilia assured her.

"We can't even repair the damage we've already taken," Maria continued, as if Emilia hadn't said anything. "If we take any more, and that storm hits—"

Sympathy pulled at Emilia's chest. "I know."

Maria nodded, and the slight heave of her chest beneath the doublet slowed. "Just…tell her I said—"

"I will," Emilia said.

Maria exhaled slowly, and every muscle in her long, lean body seemed to loosen.

Judith wasn't worried about the storm. No one was worried about the storm—because they all trusted their captain's skill.

But that left only one person to shoulder the worry.

Emilia stepped toward her. "Are you all right?"

"I'm fine," Maria said. She didn't even try to meet Emilia's gaze. "I only wanted to make sure you weren't wasting all of your energy and leaving *me* with no one to fight tonight."

Emilia laughed softly. "Captain, have I ever missed before?"

A small smile tugged at one corner of Maria's lips. "Just don't start tonight. I—I need it."

Emilia's eyes widened at that confession. "Captain—" She reached for Maria's hand.

Maria pulled back. "Tonight," she repeated. Then, as if to soften her rejection, she added, "I hope you're ready to lose."

Emilia forced a smile and countered, "I hope *you're* ready to be stabbed."

Maria turned to leave—but not before flashing one last smirk. "I'm always ready for you, love."

INSIDE THE SURGEON'S CABIN, EMILIA FOUND A CERTAIN LARGE, muscular woman sprawled across her surgery table.

Helen covered her eyes with two unwashed hands. "I'm ready," she said with a dramatic sigh. "Cut me open."

Emilia had no idea why Helen was covering her eyes, but she'd stopped asking questions by this point. "I don't cut people open for cramps, Helen."

Helen dropped her hands and sat up, her long, red braid swinging over her shoulder. "But you said there was a cure!"

Emilia knelt to retrieve a small, glass bottle from one of her wooden chests. "I *said* I'd make you a tincture."

She straightened and held out the bottle, but Helen leaned away, as if it were some kind of explosive.

Not that she would've *ever* backed away from one of those.

With a grimace, Helen said, "Does it taste bad?"

"No worse than Judith's rum," Emilia muttered.

The master gunner gave a miserable groan. "You wouldn't compare it to that if it didn't taste bad!"

Emilia laughed, "Do you want relief or not?"

Helen snatched the bottle from Emilia's hand. She hopped off the surgery table and headed toward the door. "Thank you, Em!"

"I hope you feel better," Emilia told her.

Helen turned to point a dirty finger at Emilia. "You," she said, "are *never* leaving us. Never!"

Emilia's smile deepened.

Once, she might've interpreted that as a threat.

Now, Emilia only hoped it was true.

CHAPTER 14

Sharp Swords and Dirty Moves

Maria slashed her sword downward—and nearly sliced Em's stomach open. Confusion twisted at her brows, and she took a cautious step backward.

That was the third mistake Maria had made that night.

"Are you all right?" Maria said breathlessly.

She would've gladly accepted Em's anger or ridicule after a mistake as dangerous as that one. She would've *deserved* it.

Yet, the only emotion Maria found in Em's expressive, green eyes, in that moment, was concern.

Em adjusted her grip on her sword and then shifted her feet, as well. "Yes."

Maria hesitated for only a moment, before swinging her sword again. Em blocked the blow, and the crash of Em's sword against her own sent a cathartic rush of adrenaline through Maria's bloodstream.

With each swing of her blade, a little more of the tension within Maria's chest unraveled. All day long, the pressure had built up inside of Maria, until she felt as if she might explode, and the stress had devoured her from the inside out.

Her only relief had been thoughts of Em—thoughts of seeing

Em, fighting Em, touching Em. Waiting until nightfall, just to see her, had nearly killed Maria.

She'd even broken down and sought her out once—and that one moment had sustained Maria for hours.

It was ridiculous—the way Maria felt about Em.

It was too strong, too unrelenting.

Em offered Maria the kind of release she hadn't had since Catherine betrayed her, but that comparison wasn't fair—because Em didn't just sate *one* need.

She sated needs Maria didn't even know she had.

Maria didn't want to rely on someone like this—not after the way it had turned out last time—but she comforted herself with the knowledge that it wasn't one-sided.

Em enjoyed their sword fights, too, and Maria had taught her things Catherine hadn't dared to teach her.

Catherine hadn't been *wrong* to fear Em's potential.

Cowardly, yes, but not wrong.

Em didn't have anywhere close to the level of experience Catherine had, but Maria had no doubt that she'd be ready to kill Catherine soon.

And perhaps Maria would have the strength to let her do it.

No.

Don't think about that.

It was Zain's fault, really.

Preparing for a storm was stressful enough without him constantly giving her those accusatory looks.

It'd been over a week.

Maria wished he'd just fucking say it already.

No, I wasn't strong enough to kill her. Is that what you want to hear?

The blade of Maria's sword grazed Em's arm, and Maria froze, as a band of bright red blood blossomed on Em's skin.

"You need to focus," Maria snarled.

Em's eyebrows lifted. "*I* need to focus?"

The bite of accusation in Em's tone made Maria's heart race. Did Em know what was on her mind?

With the tip of her sword, Maria pointed at the cut on Em's arm. "If this were real life, you'd be dead."

"From a cut on the arm?" Em said skeptically. "These are actual swords, in case you've forgotten. I always come away with cuts. So do you."

With her own sword, she gestured toward Maria's arms, and Maria looked down. Sure enough, there were thin slices all along her own arms, as well.

Em was right. You couldn't spar with sharpened swords and not get cut, but usually, Maria had more control than this.

Usually, neither of them were bleeding *this* early.

"And if this were real life," Emilia countered, "my dragons would eat you—for making me bleed and then blaming *me* for it."

Maria's cheeks warmed. "I wasn't blaming you. I just wanted you to focus."

Okay, so maybe I wanted me to focus.

Maria looked up, opening her mouth to apologize, but the words died on her lips, as she caught sight of the shining dragon, curling around Em's elbow.

Literally *shining*.

Like a star.

On Em's…skin.

Strange as it might've been, there was something absolutely beautiful about the way Em's skin glowed.

Maria forced herself to look away from the intricate design—long enough to check their surroundings. Maria wasn't sure how the crew would react to Em's new habit of shining like gold.

When she returned her attention to Em, she found a familiar sort of distance in Em's green eyes. It reminded Maria of that moment on Drakon Isle—after the navy had shot down one of Em's dragons.

"Are you talking to your dragons right now?"

Em blinked, and her eyes refocused on Maria. "Umm, sort of." She winced. "I had to explain that I wasn't actually giving her permission to eat you."

Maria wasn't sure whether to feel grateful or concerned. "Which one wants to eat me?"

Em offered an apologetic smile. "Nymeth."

Oh, the big, scary one!

Wonderful.

With a curious frown, Em asked, "How did you know?"

Maria shot a pointed look at Em's arm.

Em looked down. "Oh, shit!" She shoved her sleeve down over the dragon rune, and the thin, black fabric of her shirt dimmed its golden glow. "I usually keep the sleeve down."

Naturally, though, it had drifted up, while fighting.

Maria wasn't complaining. "It's kind of hot."

Em's brows furrowed. "Not really. A bit warm, perhaps, but no warmer than any other magic."

Oh, sweet surgeon.

Honestly, Maria should've expected Em to misunderstand that one. "Sexy, Em. It's sexy."

Em's eyes widened. "It is?"

Maria waited until Em glanced down at the shining rune, now covered by her sleeve, to make her move.

In one swift movement, Maria stepped forward and lifted her sword. She slashed downward, and though Em raised her sword, she did so a moment too late.

Maria stilled the blade a moment before it would've slid into Em's shoulder. "You are so easily distracted."

Em narrowed her eyes. "Only when you say things like *that!*"

Maria chuckled. "Perhaps you should tell those dragons of yours to stay out of your head so you can focus."

"The dragons weren't the ones using the word 'sexy!'" Em wrinkled her nose at the thought. "Thank the goddess."

Maria stepped back and lowered her sword. "Your concentration is shit tonight, and it'll get you killed."

Em tightened her grip on her own sword. "And am I supposed to keep pretending yours isn't worse?"

Maria scowled and thrust her sword at Em again.

This time, Em caught her blade and flung it away.

Maria cast another glance at the covered rune, before saying, "She really wants to eat me?"

"Don't take it personally. Nymeth dislikes most humans and has a tendency toward violence." Em flashed a cute smile. "Much like a certain pirate captain I know."

Maria tried not to laugh.

Em's smile faded, and she sighed, "She's aware that your self-control is a bit looser than usual, and she's not impressed by your fear of discussing it."

Maria's smile faded, too. "I am *not* afraid."

Em tilted her head, strands of silky, obsidian hair sliding to the side. She quirked her eyebrows in challenge. "Go ahead, then. Discuss it."

How did this woman manage to turn Maria on and infuriate her at the same goddamned time?

Maria swung her sword, but Em easily blocked it.

Wait.

When had Maria lost the upper hand in this fight?

Well, if Maria couldn't get rid of her own distractions, she needed to keep Em in a similar state. With a flick of her blade, she gestured toward Em's arm. "Do all of your runes glow like that?"

Em didn't even look down. "You're not distracting me again, Captain. It's time to learn new tricks."

Maria raised an eyebrow at that challenge, and a tendril of excitement licked up into Maria's chest.

Maria lifted her blade once more, but she hesitated, when Em's eyes grew distant again.

"Nymeth says this rune is unlike any rune a Drakon sorcerer has ever taken," Em said, "because it was crafted of pure dragon magic, rather than the weaker form that runs through our veins." With a quick eye roll, she scoffed, "No offense, she says."

Maria smiled. Em had answered her question, after all. "Is that a no, then?"

"The others might glow, at times," Em assumed, "but not like this one."

Fainter, then.

Easier to hide.

Maria slashed her sword at Em, and Em parried.

With an enticing smile, Em said, "You'd have a much better chance of winning, if you'd just tell me what has you so aggressive tonight."

Maria leaned toward her. "I'm always aggressive, and I always win," she snarled in her surgeon's face, "and I've never needed to *talk* in order to do so."

"Oh," Em said, "I forgot! You usually deal with things by killing people." She cast her gaze about the moonlit deck. "Who did you have in mind tonight?"

It took every ounce of Maria's faltering self-control not to laugh. "You, if you don't shut your fucking mouth."

The moonlight sparkled in Em's emerald eyes.

Maria thrust her sword upward, but Em twisted out of the way and struck back. The dragon sorceress stopped her sword just inches from Maria's ribs.

Fuck. She was incredible tonight.

"When I kill someone," Maria informed her, "I always have multiple reasons to do so." She lowered her sword. "Buchan, for instance. What he did to you was the final straw, not the first."

"What he did to *me?*" Em repeated. "I thought you killed him because he lied to you."

"As I said." Maria gave her a careless shrug. "Multiple reasons."

A mixture of surprise and curiosity flickered across Em's face for a moment, before she smiled. "Yet, you don't deny that *this*…is one of them."

Maria rolled her eyes.

Persistent, little witch.

With a growl of frustration, Maria swung her blade, but Em blocked it as if it were nothing.

"Look, I want to give you what you need," Em said—with more sincerity than either of them had offered all night, "but at least tell me *why* you need it."

A flash of orange and a flicker of movement in her peripheral drew Maria's attention toward their left. Her eyes widened, as she found several people, who hadn't been standing there moments before.

Helen, Pelt, and a few younger deckhands.

Behind them, more pirates strolled toward them with extra bottles of rum in their hands.

Maria huffed out an annoyed sigh. "Don't say that here." With a jerk of her head, she directed Em's attention toward the quickly gathering crowd.

Em's face paled. "Captain, why do we have an audience?" she asked. "Did you triple the number of sailors on night watch?"

"None of *them* are on night watch," Maria said. "They're here because their captain and surgeon are fighting, and someone opened his big mouth about it."

Maria shot a murderous glare at Pelt, and the boatswain flashed a gold-toothed grin in response.

"No more talk of what I told you in private," Maria murmured.

Em kept her wide-eyed gaze on the crowd. "Obviously."

"And try to keep that sleeve down," Maria added.

Em once again pressed the sleeve of her black shirt down over the dragon rune. "Yes, Captain."

Over the next two hours, the crowd expanded to include half the crew.

Maria stopped to catch her breath, and Em glanced out at the surrounding crowd of pirates.

With a baffled shake of her head, Em said, "I guess we've become more interesting than whatever gambling game they were playing?"

Maria wiped the back of her hand beneath her drenched head-scarf. "It's cute," she teased, "that you think we haven't *become* the gambling game."

Em turned to Maria. "What?"

With an arch of her eyebrows, Maria straightened. She called over her shoulder to her boatswain. "Pelt?"

"Yes, Captain?" he called back.

Flashing a smug smirk at Em, Maria said, "How many people bet that *I'd* win the most bouts?"

"All but two, Captain," Pelt said.

Instantly forgetting her desire to see Em's reaction, Maria spun to face the boatswain. "Two people bet *against* me?"

"Oh, of course," Em grumbled. "I just found out most of the ship thinks I don't stand a chance, and you're upset because two people think I do."

Maria ignored her. "Who the fuck bet against *me?*"

The entire crowd seemed to take a collective step back, but one gunpowder-covered hand shot into the air.

Maria narrowed her eyes at her master gunner.

"Oh, really?" Em said. "Thank you, Helen!"

Helen blew a kiss to Em, and Maria's glare turned murderous.

"Don't get your hopes up, love," Maria told Em. "Helen's never won a bet in her life."

Helen gave a small nod. "That's true."

Em's shoulders fell. "Oh."

Maria returned her attention to Pelt. "Who else?"

Pelt cast a much-too-quick glance over his shoulder, before saying, "He's not here."

Maria knew of only one person who'd be so easily picked out of a crowd. "I'm going to kill Fulke."

Em's eyes brightened. "Fulke bet on me?"

"He loses bets, too," Maria assured her.

Em merely smiled, and a defiant gleam flashed in her stunning, green eyes. "I don't care."

Maria tried to keep scowling—for the sake of the pirates who'd dared bet against her—but damn, it was hard not to smile when Em gave her that look.

"Actually," Pelt interjected, "Fulke has won a few bets, regarding the two of you, recently."

Em's brows furrowed. "A few?" Now, she turned to face the boatswain, too, her sword swinging at her side. "Just how many times *have* you gambled on us?"

"I lost count," Pelt said simply.

Em stared blankly at him. "I can't believe you people."

"If it makes you feel better, this is the first time it's been about fighting," Pelt offered. "Usually, it's over whether you two will fuck or kill each other."

"That does the *opposite* of making me feel better," Em informed him.

Maria pointed her sword at the boatswain. "I'm going to outlaw gambling on this ship, if you don't find a new subject."

"What?" Pelt whined. "That's not fair!"

"Now, you know how I feel," Helen told him.

Pelt scowled at her. "No one knows how you feel, Helen."

Maria turned away from them. "You can forfeit now, if you want," she told Em. She spread out her arms, her blade gleaming in the moonlight. "Helen and Fulke are going to lose their bets, either way. Might as well save your energy."

Em spun toward her, eyes wide and incredulous. "Your arrogance knows no bounds! I've beaten you tonight as many times as you've beaten me! It could go either way."

That was, unfortunately, true.

A sliver of pale skin caught Maria's eye, and her gaze drifted downward. Her sword must've caught Em's trousers, at some point, and left a tear in the upper thigh. Maria forced her gaze upward.

"Yes, but you're tired," she pointed out.

The pirates cheered in agreement—because, of course, with her dear Em being so prone to pinkness, she was visibly flushed with exhaustion tonight.

"You're tired, too!" Em said.

That was also true.

The muscles in Maria's arms and legs had begun to ache nearly an hour ago, and her abdomen muscles burned fiercely. Not to mention, the warm flush spreading from her head to her toes, and the sweat dripping from her hair.

*But…*Maria hid it better. "Absolutely not, love," she lied. "I'm not even close to being done with you."

Em squinted, not buying it for a moment.

Fortunately, the rest of the crew was more gullible.

"I never yield," Em told her.

You do when I kiss you.

But Maria couldn't say that—not with their captivated audience.

"Punch her in the face," Helen yelled out, hands curled around her mouth, "like you did Buchan!"

Both Em and Maria turned to frown at the gunner.

"I'm not…punching anyone," Em said. "This is a sword fight, Helen! That's not how they work."

"See?" Maria stepped closer to Em. "The person who bet on *you* doesn't even know what's going on."

Em cast a sidelong glance at her.

"Yield now," Maria urged, "and save yourself some embarrassment later."

Em turned to face her. She lifted her sword and pressed its sharp tip against Maria's doublet. The sensation sent a jolt of excitement into Maria's throat.

"If you want me to yield, Captain," Em said, "you'll have to make me."

Maria raised an eyebrow, and the little sparks of excitement inside her ignited into one, burning-hot flame.

Well, now, she *had* to win.

Maria flicked the blade of her sword against Em's, and the two of them began to fight once more.

They fought twice after that—with Maria winning the first fight and Em somehow winning the second.

With as exhausted as they both were, by that point, Maria usually would've ended the night there.

After all, pushing yourself to your limits in sword-fighting was beneficial. Pushing yourself *past* them was not.

But for the sake of their audience, Maria suggested one last bout to break the tie, and Em, out of pure stubbornness, agreed.

The fight didn't start out well.

With a few clever moves, Em managed to disarm Maria of her first sword, and Maria had no choice but to draw her second.

Maria struck harder and faster this time, and with a final twist of her blade, she knocked Em's sword from her hand.

The steel blade slid across the deck, clanging and scraping, and Em followed its movement with her gaze.

Maria used that brief moment of distraction to step toward her, and at a close and almost…*sensual* angle, Maria pressed her sword against Em's throat.

Em's wide, green eyes shifted to meet Maria's.

"You lose," Maria whispered.

One side of Em's soft, pink mouth quirked upward. "Do I?"

Maria froze, as a sharp point pressed into her inner thigh.

That fucking dagger.

"Femoral artery," Em whispered, "in case you need a reminder."

She'd *wanted* Maria to step closer.

Damn it. How did Em always find a way to use Maria's arrogance against her?

She knew her too well; that's how!

"We didn't have much gambling in my culture." Em licked her lips, and Maria couldn't help but follow the gentle slide of Em's pink tongue. "Can you tell me, Captain, who wins in a draw?"

"Pelt," Maria said.

"Really?" Em said. "He wins all of it?"

"Pelt arranges the bets," Maria explained. "He takes a bit regardless, but he only wins when no one else does." Her gaze flicked toward Pelt—just long enough to see the eager smile on his face and decide he would *not* win today.

Maria carefully removed her sword from Em's throat, holding it up in a show of surrender. When Em only frowned, Maria tossed the sword aside.

The crowd released a collective gasp.

"Did you just…*yield?*" Em said incredulously.

Maria said nothing.

With confusion twisting at every muscle in her face, Em removed her dagger from Maria's thigh.

Maria waited until the enchanted blade reached Em's side, before reaching forward and sliding her fingers around Em's wrist.

Before Em registered what she was doing, Maria hooked her ankle behind Em's legs and jerked them forward, knocking Em flat on her back.

Maria wrenched the dagger from Em's hand on the way down, and a harsh *whoosh* of air left Em's lungs the moment she hit the deck.

Maria tossed the dagger aside and sank down on top of the witch, before she could catch her breath. She straddled Em's soft, wide hips and shoved Em's hands above her head.

"That was," Em gasped, clearly trying to force air back into her lungs, "a dirty move."

Maria forced Em's arms closer together—pressing them to the deck, above her head—so she could hold Em's wrists with one arm, instead of two.

"It also," Em said, inhaling sharply, "hurt."

Maria shifted her gaze downward—to meet Em's. "Lesson one, my sweet surgeon," she murmured, "never trust a pirate to yield, if they don't *say* they yield." She tilted her chin thoughtfully. "Actually, even if we do say it, you still shouldn't trust us."

Em narrowed her eyes at that.

"Lesson two," Maria whispered, closing her free hand around Em's throat, "blades aren't your only weapons." Em's abdomen muscles tensed beneath Maria's thighs, and Maria grinned at her reaction. "You, of all people, should know that. *Witch.*"

Em glared up at her. "I hate you."

Maria leaned in close—until she could feel Em's breath on her lips. "Oh, I know you do, love," she cooed, "but you also lo—" She stopped and glanced up at the surrounding pirates. "Probably shouldn't say that here."

Em squirmed beneath her, and the movement of her waist between Maria's thighs put pressure in all the right places, sending jolts of arousal into Maria's body.

Maria pressed her leather boots into the sides of Em's legs to hold her still.

It didn't work.

"Just yield," she said breathlessly.

Em continued to fight. "Fuck you."

Maria chuckled and tightened her hold around Em's throat.

That...*did* make her stop.

Satisfied for the moment, Maria loosened her grip, and Em immediately started fighting again.

When Em nearly threw off Maria's balance with all of that squirming, Maria grumbled, "Oh, no, you don't," and adjusted her position over Em.

Maria slid her body lower and wedged one thigh between Em's —smiling when Em's eyes went wide.

The rough wood of the deck pressed into Maria's knee, but something much warmer and softer pressed against Maria's thigh.

Em tried—almost experimentally—to push Maria off, but her eyes fluttered when the movement only placed more pressure against a *very* sensitive spot.

"What's the matter, darling?" Maria taunted.

"I'm," Em said breathlessly, "going to stab you."

Maria laughed. "Yield, and I might let you."

"Oh, no," Em said, her brows high. "You don't get to know when it's coming. Not after this."

Maria only laughed harder. She tilted her head, a few loose curls sliding over her leather doublet. "You've already lost, love."

Em pressed the back of her head against the deck, as if that could free her throat from Maria's grasp. Despite the shortened state of her hair, the silky, black strands still fanned out around her head.

"That doesn't mean I have to yield."

"That's exactly what it means," Maria argued.

No longer able to hear the conversation, the crowd pressed closer.

Maria merely lowered her voice more. "Yield."

Em's dazzling, green eyes hardened with resolve. "No."

Stubborn witch.

Em jerked so suddenly and so forcefully at her wrists that she nearly knocked Maria's arm off of them.

Maria responded by putting enough pressure on Em's throat to make her light-headed. When Em's eyelashes fluttered, Maria arched her eyebrows.

Em swallowed, causing her throat to rise beneath Maria's fingers, and then, she licked her lips.

Maria let her gaze slide down to those lips—those pink, parted lips.

Maria could end this with a single kiss.

If it weren't for their audience.

As it was, it seemed Maria would have to resort to some…*dirtier* moves, as Em had so aptly put it.

Maria pressed her forearm harder against Em's wrists and adjusted her hips. Careful to keep the movement subtle enough that no one but Em would notice, Maria pressed upward with her thigh.

Em gasped, and her eyes dilated, growing wide and dark with arousal.

Maria's own clit pulsed at the sight. She ground her thigh against Em once more, and Em's head fell back, her eyelids sliding closed.

"Nnnnnh, Captain," Em said, not-so-subtly holding back a moan.

Maria lowered her lips to Em's ear and whispered, "I bet you are so wet right now."

Em's eyes popped open. "Captain!"

Maria pulled back. "Shhh," she said with a laugh, "they'll just think I'm asking you to yield—which you should, by the way."

"You're evil," Em hissed. "Pure evil!"

Maria snorted, "I'm Captain Maria Welles, darling. Where have *you* been?"

Em pursed her lips.

"Yield," Maria whispered, "and we can finish this in my quarters."

To drive home her point, Maria pressed her thigh forward again, and this time, Em's hips arched *into* Maria's touch, clearly seeking more.

The ache between Maria's own thighs sharpened.

A sudden rush of desperation rose within her, and Maria dipped her head toward Em's. Their breath mingled—warm and wet—and their lips almost touched.

Until a murmur from a nearby pirate reminded Maria of where she was.

Maria groaned in frustration. The plan had been to torment Em, not herself. "Please," she whispered against Em's lips, "yield, so I can fucking kiss you."

Em's eyes softened at her plea. "Fine," she sighed, "but I'm still going to stab you later."

Maria pulled back to grin at her. "I'd expect no less."

With a roll of her eyes, Em called out, "I yield!"

A collective cheer rose from the crowd of pirates.

"I promise you won't regret it," Maria whispered.

"I already regret it, you asshole," Em said. "Now, get off of me." She flashed a caustic smile, before adding, "Captain."

Maria chuckled and climbed off of her. She rose to her full height and offered her scarred hand to Em.

To her amusement, Em pushed Maria's hand away and insisted on climbing to her feet with no help.

Em and Maria separated to gather their discarded weapons, and by the time they returned to each other, the crowd of sailors had collapsed into chaos.

Confident that no one cared to watch *them* anymore, Maria rested her palm against the curve of Em's back. She leaned in close, brushing her lips against Em's ear, and whispered, "Come, love."

Em sneered, "Yes, Captain," but out of the corner of her eye, Maria saw Em smile as she said it.

Maria's body ached all over, but she hadn't felt an ounce of stress in hours. Em had soothed Maria in the way only she could.

CHAPTER 15

A Message from the Dead

One of the most disconcerting aspects of dreaming was how Emilia never remembered the person standing in front of her was dead until *after* she awoke.

Silas Drakon, the chief agrarian sorcerer, knelt in front of a young Emilia Drakon. His green tunic and trousers had probably collected more dirt- and grass-stains than any other clothing on the island, and a stray, green leaf stuck up out of his light brown hair.

Emilia's mother often said that agrarian sorcerers were adults who spent their days playing in the dirt.

Emilia doubted anyone '*played*' as much as Silas did.

"What's the matter?"

"Nothing," Emilia lied.

Most adults attempted to make eye-contact with Emilia, though she'd never understood why.

Silas didn't.

She wondered if he shared her anxiety about it.

Instead, he eyed Emilia's clasped hands with raised eyebrows. "You won't show me what's under there?"

Emilia cast a quick glance at the older children, and Silas followed her gaze. He nodded.

"It's hard for you, isn't it?" he said—too quietly for the other kids to hear. "Making friends?"

Emilia blushed.

It wasn't just hard. It was impossible.

It was a language Emilia could never understand.

But Emilia didn't have the words to explain that. So, she just nodded.

Silas straightened and addressed the other children. "We're finished with today's lesson. You may go."

As the other children gathered their things and left the field of small plants, Emilia remained on the ground with her hands clasped tightly together.

When a few older children hesitated at the edge of the field—likely just to discuss their evening plans or something—Silas repeated, irritably, "You may *go*."

The children took their discussions elsewhere.

Silas knelt, and his pale face entered Emilia's vision once more. With a nod toward Emilia's clasped hands, he said, "Now, let me see what you've done."

Emilia braced herself for insults and anger—for the reactions her mother would've had. "I messed up."

To Emilia's surprise, Silas only said, "Good."

Emilia looked up, her eyes wide.

"Mistakes are how we learn."

Emilia had never heard *that* before.

Silas didn't even seem to notice her shock. He nodded toward her closed hands. "Let me see."

Emilia reluctantly opened her hands to reveal the plant that had sprouted from the center of her palm.

Silas winced—possibly because of the redness of her skin or the blood that tried to ooze out between the roots—but he didn't ridicule her. "It's because you're a healer," he told her. "I know you haven't taken your runes yet, but this only makes it more obvious."

Most sorcerers didn't take their runes until they were far older than Emilia was now, but the leaders had noticed Emilia's proclivity for healing years ago.

Camila had even begun training her privately.

Advanced studies, she'd called it, with a smile.

"Your style of magic involves stealing something from yourself and giving it to someone else," Silas explained, "but plant magic isn't like that."

Emilia didn't fully understand that. She only knew the other children didn't have plants sprouting from *their* skin.

"Plants aren't parasites. They're friends," Silas said, and Emilia realized he really meant that. "The flower doesn't want to take from you. It wants to involve you." He raked a calloused forefinger through the dark soil, drawing a circle. "We grow faster together."

Emilia thought of the way her dragons used to tell her to eat so she'd grow—and had an amusing thought of plants telling each other the same thing.

To eat their dead people and grow.

Indeed, her plant *did* grow, and the pink bud of a flower formed at the end of a long, green stem.

Emilia eyed the bud warily. "Can you fix it?"

"Of course. Simple transfer," Silas mumbled. He hesitated—and then looked up from the soil. "The roots are in your veins. It *will* hurt to remove them."

"Pain doesn't scare me anymore."

It wasn't a boast. Emilia felt no emotion whatsoever in saying it.

It was a fact—nothing more, nothing less.

Emilia's mother had killed the part of her that feared pain.

The agrarian sorcerer's thick, brown eyebrows creased, but he nodded. "Shouldn't be a problem, then."

His large, calloused hands, gritty with soil, curled around her wrists. "Bring your hand into the circle."

Silas pulled Emilia's small hands forward, and she was stunned to find that this stout, broad-shouldered man had a far gentler touch than her mother.

The longer she thought about it, though, the more it made sense.

Silas's experience with the fragility of plants had taught him gentleness, whereas Nydia's experience with battle had taught her brutality.

Size meant nothing, when compared to experience.

Silas released her hands, and his green eyes shifted upward—again, not to Emilia's eyes, exactly, more to her nose. "In order to not kill the flower, we'll need to remove one root at a time."

Emilia nodded.

She imagined that'd be safest for her hand, as well—not that Silas seemed too concerned about *that*.

He had warned her of the pain, though, which was more concern than her mother had ever shown her.

Silas curled his dirty fingers around the flower, and a faint glow radiated from his pale-skinned hand. He drew his hand upward, and though he never touched the plant, it followed his movement.

A root tugged harshly at Emilia's vein, like a person trying to free their ankle from a gap in the rocks, and when the root came free, a spurt of Emilia's blood came with it.

Silas grimaced at the sight. "I, uhh, don't see a lot of blood in my line of work," he admitted. He went to work on the next root, and after a few moments of silence, he began to speak again. "It was always hard for me, too." His jaw tightened. "Making friends."

Distracted, for a moment, from the pain, Emilia looked up at the man who might've been her father.

He let out a nervous laugh. "I was always saying the wrong things."

"That's—that's what I do," Emilia stammered.

Silas nodded. "It might've been worse for me, if it hadn't been for Nydia." He let out another shaky laugh. "She tends to scare people away."

That was…true, of course.

Even adults were terrified of Nydia Drakon, but…in context, that statement made no sense to Emilia.

Emilia's mother was far more likely to *be* the bully than to protect anyone from them.

"You grew up with her?" Emilia asked.

Silas nodded. "I was a few years older."

Emilia remembered some of the things Camila had said about Emilia's mother, while they were training, and said, "So, you grew up with Camila, too."

"Yes. She was kind, of course," Silas said easily. He lifted his hand again, and another blood-soaked root ripped itself from Emilia's skin. "All healers are."

Emilia had heard this before.

Healers were kind. Warriors were cruel. Agrarian sorcerers were content, and oracles were enigmatic.

It was what most of her people believed.

Emilia didn't know if it was true or not. If she were being honest, she didn't think she'd had enough experience with kindness to even recognize it.

"Nydia and Camila were closer, then," Silas said.

Emilia's frown deepened. She couldn't imagine her mother and Camila *ever* being close.

They hated each other.

Silas continued to mutter to himself, almost as if he'd forgotten Emilia was listening. "Sometimes, I wondered if Nydia was only befriending me to make Camila jealous."

"Jealous?"

Emilia knew the meaning of the word, of course, but she didn't understand how it could apply to her mother or Camila.

Silas winced. "Ah. See?" His cheeks reddened, and Emilia couldn't tell if he were embarrassed or in pain. "There I go, saying the wrong thing again."

Why was that the wrong thing, though?

Was it because Emilia hadn't understood him?

Or because he was worried she *had?*

Silas leaned forward. "Don't…mention this to your mother," he pleaded. "It was only a suspicion. I never…" He cringed. "You won't tell her, will you?"

Emilia lifted her eyebrows. "My mother barely even talks to me."

"Oh." Silas furrowed his brows—and then, he returned to removing the roots from Emilia's hand.

Emilia studied Silas's pale hands, his round face.

It wasn't much, but…their similarities had to mean something.

Nydia Drakon wielded her words with the deadly precision of a blade.

She didn't stumble over them like Emilia did.

Like Silas did.

Nydia wanted to hurt Emilia. Silas didn't.

Surely, Emilia had *one* parent who didn't want to hurt her.

"You and my mother are friends, then," Emilia said.

Silas froze—but said nothing.

Emilia's heart raced, and anxiety swirled in her stomach. "I've seen you visit her," she admitted, "at night?"

The only indication that Silas had even heard her was the gradual blush that spread beneath his skin.

Emilia winced as another root ripped itself from her palm. "It's just that," she stammered, "some of the other children have two parents, who are friends."

Silas finally looked up at her, and the mix of horror and frustration that flashed in his big, green eyes silenced Emilia. "Now, you're doing it."

Emilia held her breath. "What?"

"Saying the thing you shouldn't say," Silas said.

Emilia's stomach plummeted. "Oh."

Without an answer, without another *word*, Silas returned his attention to the plant, and this time, Emilia accepted the silence for what it was.

Rejection.

Silas had never told her he was her father, and he hadn't wanted to talk about it, either—because he didn't *want* Emilia.

And why would he?

Why would *anyone* want Emilia?

Silas removed the rest of the plant as quickly as possible, but even though the pain increased with each removal, it paled in comparison to the humiliation that churned inside of Emilia.

When he finished, Silas lifted the plant from Emilia's hand and lowered it toward the soil.

Like blood-soaked fingers, the roots reached for the ground, easily slipping beneath the blanket of soil.

Emilia climbed to her feet—and staggered, as a wave of exhaustion and light-headedness swept over her.

"You'll need to see a healer," Silas told her.

"I'm fine," Emilia muttered.

Her hand ached and bled, as if it'd been stabbed by a hundred tiny daggers or a hundred giant mosquitoes—she couldn't decide which—but all that mattered to her now was finding a place where she could be alone.

Her rising emotions would spill out soon, and Emilia knew better than to cry in front of anyone.

Emilia's mother didn't tolerate weakness, and tears, her mother told her, were weakness.

"You'll need to eat certain nutrients," Silas said, his gaze still fixed on the dirt beneath his hands, "to replenish what the plant took from you."

Emilia's eyes burned, and her throat constricted. She couldn't hold out much longer. "Can I go now?"

Silas still didn't look up, but he nodded.

Emilia fled from the field as fast as her feet would take her. Blood dripped from her hand with each step. Her head swam, and her muscles ached with exhaustion—but she could only focus on *not* crying.

She'd been such a fool.

She could just hear her mother's voice now.

'Pathetic, useless child.'

'You dared to hope for more?'

The agrarian fields came to an end, and the paths diverged—up the mountain or down to the village.

Emilia hesitated, as she so often did on her hardest days.

She wanted nothing more, in that moment, than to take the mountain path, find whatever cave the dragons had chosen for the night, curl up with them, and never, *ever* come back.

Perhaps her mother would come to drag her back, or perhaps

she wouldn't. But Emilia missed the simplicity of living amongst dragons.

People were so complicated.

And Emilia was so tired of *begging* to be tolerated.

This was what the sea goddess had asked Emilia to do, though. Aletha had told Emilia, several years earlier, that it would be hard— but that Emilia needed to train with her own people.

There were things the dragons couldn't teach her.

So, Emilia's feet fell upon the village path.

The green of trees gave way to the brown of tents, and the cacophony of birdsong gave way to a cacophony of voices.

And Emilia kept walking.

Don't cry.

Don't. Cry.

"Hey, Dragon Child."

Emilia froze.

Mateo sat on a large stone, near one of the warrior tents, and Ayanna—a pretty, agrarian sorcerer, whose green tunic looked lovely against her tawny skin—sat next to him.

Mateo was nineteen now, and he no longer trained with Emilia *or* Ayanna. Yet, here they were, together.

"Emilia," she corrected. "I'm Emilia."

"Whatever you say, Dragon Child," Mateo sneered, and Ayanna giggled—as if he'd told a funny joke.

But he hadn't…told a joke, had he?

Emilia eyed Ayanna curiously.

Had she always been that pretty?

If so, why was Emilia suddenly so aware of it?

Mateo looped a muscular arm around Ayanna's slender shoulders, and she didn't pull away.

His attention never left Emilia, though. Mateo tilted his head, and a predatory delight flashed in his green eyes. "What happened to your hand, Dragon Child?"

Emilia didn't understand his insistence on calling her that. Was it simply because she'd asked him not to?

Ayanna offered her small, lovely smile to Mateo. "She was the last to leave Silas's lesson today."

Mateo's teeth flashed. "Really?"

Emilia wiped her bleeding palm against her black trousers and tried not to wince at the pressure.

"I wonder what that was about."

Emilia had *no* intention of telling him.

Luckily—or *unluckily*, as it turned out—someone had overheard them. Leather shifted, and grass rustled, as the warrior stepped out of her tent.

"Emilia."

That icy voice chilled every drop of Emilia's blood.

Nydia's shadow fell over Emilia—dark and ominous—and Emilia turned to face her mother.

The confusion and frustration of interacting with Mateo and Ayanna had displaced Emilia's sadness enough that she didn't think she was at risk of crying anymore, but that didn't mean she was ready for the barrage of insults her mother would throw at her.

Emilia eyed the path behind her mother longingly.

Healers and warriors lived on opposite sides of the village. If she ran toward her own tent now, how far would she get before her mother caught her?

Would Nydia Drakon even deign to chase a child?

Perhaps she'd just hurl a fireball in Emilia's direction. It wouldn't be the first time.

Almost as if she knew what Emilia was thinking, Nydia crossed her arms, the sleeves of her red dress clinging to her muscles. "In the tent. Now."

Her tent?

She wanted Emilia to come into *her* tent?

Emilia hadn't thought she was allowed to do that.

Nydia's black eyebrows lifted. "I said *now*, girl."

Behind Emilia, Mateo taunted, "Run to mommy, Dragon Child." He laughed lowly. "Maybe she'll do you a favor and kill you permanently this time."

Ayanna giggled at that remark, and Emilia decided perhaps Ayanna wasn't so pretty, after all.

Nydia narrowed her eyes—not at Mateo, of course, but at Emilia.

She stepped back and shoved the leather flap of her tent open. With a jerk of her head that swung her long, black braids, Nydia directed Emilia inside.

Emilia slipped beneath her mother's arm.

Nydia stepped in behind her and let the flap fall closed. With audible disgust, she said, "I don't know why you let that boy talk to you like that."

Emilia frowned at her mother. "He's an adult now."

Nydia scoffed at that. "Hardly."

She cast a puzzled look over Emilia's head, as if she'd expected to see someone much taller behind her, and Emilia resisted the urge to turn and look.

Had she expected Mateo to follow them?

"Where's Camila?" Nydia asked her.

"I haven't seen her since this morning," Emilia said.

Nydia's dark brows furrowed. "Then, why are you here?"

Umm. Okay.

Emilia turned to leave.

Nydia sighed and snatched up the back of Emilia's shirt. "I wasn't telling you to leave, foolish child!"

The fabric tugged against Emilia's throat, and she stopped.

Nydia spun Emilia around, her sharp fingernails digging into Emilia's shoulder. "I sent Camila to retrieve you from your tent," she said, voice thick with impatience. "I was asking how you ended up here without seeing her first."

She'd sprouted a plant from her hand. That's how.

"I hadn't made it back to my tent yet," Emilia said.

Nydia tilted her chin, and her sharp gaze bore into Emilia with such intensity that Emilia wondered if her mother were reading her mind.

But no, telepathic spells required consent, and on the list of things Emilia would never do, giving her mother access to her mind was near the top.

"The girl wasn't lying, then," Nydia said.

So, she'd heard Ayanna's remark, too.

"What did Silas want with you?"

Emilia couldn't talk about Silas right now. Not when her mother would probably kill her—*again*—at the first sight of tears. "Nothing."

Nydia narrowed her eyes suspiciously, but she didn't press the issue. "Well, no matter. You're here now."

Emilia figured her mother would just ask Silas later, during his visit.

What *did* they talk about at night?

Nydia stepped past Emilia and strolled toward the heavy, wooden table in the center of her tent.

Most people filled their tents with a few treasured items and comfortable places to sit, sleep, and eat.

Emilia had filled hers with the books her dragons had helped her...*obtain* from Illopian shipwrecks.

But her mother's tent held none of those things.

There was a bed, at least.

One bed—in the corner, covered in red blankets that matched her mother's warrior-red clothing.

Besides that, her mother had only the round, wooden table in the center of her tent—which didn't even have chairs.

Did she stand while she ate?

It honestly wouldn't surprise Emilia if she did.

Nydia Drakon was nothing, if not utilitarian.

After all, this was the woman who'd sentenced her newborn baby to death because of a possible future mistake—the woman who'd never shared a warm word with anyone, not even her daughter.

Especially not her daughter.

Nydia braced her hands against the heavy, wooden table. Her long, black braids swung forward, as she studied something on the surface of the table.

Emilia tip-toed forward, trying to peer at the tall table—without attracting her mother's attention.

Oh.

Someone had burned a map of Aletharia into the surface of the wooden table. Considering the precision with which her mother wielded magical fire, Emilia had no doubt Nydia had done it herself.

Nydia moved wooden figurines from one part of the map to the other, as if she were playing a game, but of course, Nydia Drakon did not play games.

Her long, claw-like fingernails closed around a figurine with thick tentacles—not unlike those of an octopus.

Emilia recognized that symbol from her books.

It was the symbol of Aletha's children.

Sea creatures.

Nydia's cold, unfeeling gaze found Emilia. "How much do you know of the sirens?"

Emilia's eyes widened. The fear and sadness of the day faded away at the prospect of discussing something from her books.

"Everything!" she blurted out. "What do you want to know?" She bounced on the balls of her feet. "Oh, they're amazing! Did you know they wield magic with their voices? And they live hundreds of years?"

Nydia gave an unimpressed arch of her eyebrows.

"At least four times the lifespan of a human!" Emilia continued. "The only sea creatures that live longer than sirens are sea serpents, kraken, and this one type of shark that's native to the Whispering Abyss."

Nydia leaned back on her heels and crossed her arms. "Did I *ask* for your eccentric ramblings?"

Emilia's brows furrowed. "Yes?"

Nydia rolled her eyes. "No, I did not."

Emilia was pretty sure she had, though.

"I asked how much you knew," Nydia reminded her. "You could've just said 'a disturbing amount.'"

Were there limits to how much a person was supposed to know?

Nydia moved the octopus figurine toward the part of the map that represented the Illopian Mountains.

"The Kingdom of Illopia will not always wage war within the bounds it adheres to now," Nydia said—as if Emilia had *any* idea what she was talking about. "One day, you'll—*we'll* need alliances."

Emilia tried to remember something from her books about *alliances*.

Nydia sighed, "You and Camila are our only dragon-riders, at the moment." Resentment flashed within her green eyes. "Their preference for healers will never make sense to me. A warrior sorceress is *far* more useful on dragon-back than a healer."

Emilia frowned at her mother's words.

Flying wasn't about usefulness. It was about the bond between person and dragon.

How did Emilia's mother not understand that?

"It limits my choices." Nydia eyed Emilia as if she were nothing more than a speck of dirt. "Out of the two of you—you, a useless child, and her, our chief healer—I would, of course, prefer to send Camila, but apparently, she's become too weak to overcome her own limitations."

Oh! Emilia's mother must've misunderstood the situation.

Camila had only stopped flying because of her illness, and it had been Caelu who suggested she stop.

"Chronic pain isn't weakness," Emilia informed her mother. "Quite the opposite, actually."

Nydia rolled her eyes. "You sound just like her."

Well, yes.

Because she was right.

"Regardless," Nydia said, "it leaves us with *you.*"

Emilia ignored the way her mother sneered the word 'you,' because at least Nydia seemed to be insulting Emilia for a *reason* this time. "Leaves me for what?"

Nydia tapped the top of the octopus figurine, her fingernail clicking against the wood. "We need a dragon-rider," she said, "to forge an alliance with the sirens."

The only part of that Emilia actually understood was the dragon-riding part. "How would I do that?"

Frustration burned in Nydia's green eyes. "Well, first, you'll have to learn to carry on a conversation."

Emilia didn't like the sound of that. "With whom?"

"The siren queen," Nydia said, "and her daughter."

"Both of them?" Emilia asked.

"The princess is around your age," Nydia said. "Interacting with her should be simple for you."

Unless what had happened outside counted as a conversation, it would *not* be simple for Emilia.

"Queen Amathea, on the other hand, is vicious," Nydia said. "For her, you'll need training—if you want to survive the encounter." She leaned forward and tilted her chin. "*I* wouldn't mind if she tore you apart with her teeth, but I'd prefer the treaty was signed first." Her green eyes darkened with hatred. "Just in case the sea goddess decides to put you back together again, and the future Aster saw comes true."

"Aster saw me get ripped apart?" Emilia asked.

"No," Nydia assured her. Her lips curled up at the corners. "What he saw in *your* future was…worse."

Emilia didn't know what was worse than being eaten alive—only that her mother seemed quite pleased with the prospect of…*worse.*

Nydia straightened and stepped back. "It will take years before you're ready. Training, practice flights, more training… You'll start all of that next week."

Nydia circled the round table, and Emilia fought the urge to step back, as her mother approached.

Dirt shifted beneath Nydia's shoes, and the red dress hugged her form, like a fresh coat of blood.

Her smile widened. "Before we start, however," she said, "you, Emilia Drakon, will take your runes."

Emilia's mouth fell open.

The youngest Drakon sorcerer to ever take their runes had been Nydia, and even *she* had been fifteen.

Even the older children, who trained with Emilia each day, hadn't taken their runes yet.

Mateo had taken his recently—on his nineteenth birthday. Emilia distinctly remembered her mother sneering in disgust when he'd cried out in pain.

And Ayanna—she'd only just begun to *talk* to Silas about taking hers. They hadn't even set a date yet!

Emilia forced herself to speak. "The leaders—"

"Have all agreed," Nydia assured her. "A few of them voiced some concerns about the dangers—and the pain. I've chosen to ignore their concerns."

Naturally.

"But they're in agreement that you've mastered your restorative magic at an unprecedented age," Nydia said, "and that you've demonstrated enough with other magicks that there can be no doubt what you are."

Hadn't Silas said something similar?

'This only makes it more obvious,' he'd said.

"I think you'll survive it," Nydia said—in a tone that made Emilia think that was a lament and not a reassurance. Her gaze swept up and down Emilia's preadolescent form. "You're not much younger than I was, are you? I was fifteen. You're what? Fourteen?"

"Twelve," Emilia corrected.

Had her mother *really* forgotten which year she'd given birth, or was this just another way of demonstrating how insignificant Emilia was to her?

Nydia waved a hand, as if those two years were *not* important and formative. "You'll survive."

Some people didn't, though.

It was rare. The healers usually took care of the infections and blood loss, but people *had* died before.

Emilia distinctly remembered the story of a man whose heart had given out—from the pain or shock. The healers had tried to save him, but by the time they'd reached him, he'd already died.

"You'll take two runes, instead of one," Nydia informed her, "like Camila did." She braced her hand against the table and tapped Emilia's ankle with her shoe. "One to strengthen your magic and another to strengthen your connection to the dragons."

Emilia had known of Camila's dragon rune, of course, but she'd never actually seen it. "When?"

"A week from today," Nydia told her.

Emilia didn't fear the pain. She only feared her reaction to it—and her mother's reaction to *that*.

A wise fear, as it turned out.

"It's an honor, and you'll accept it." Nydia pushed away from the table and stepped toward Emilia.

Emilia looked up, as her mother loomed over her.

Outside, the tropical heat was stifling, but beneath her mother's sinister shadow, Emilia's blood cooled.

"And you will *not*," Nydia snarled, "embarrass me by crying."

People far older and larger than Emilia had cried while taking their runes, but Emilia's mother hadn't.

And that was all that mattered.

Nydia's hand shot out like a claw, and Emilia stumbled into the table. Nydia grabbed Emilia's chin and dragged her forward. "Do you understand me?"

Emilia forced air through her lungs. "I won't cry."

"You better not," Nydia said. She leaned closer, and her sharp fingernails cut into Emilia's skin. "If I see you so much as wince, you will not *live* to regret it."

Emilia's heart pounded against her chest.

"Let the sea goddess bring you back again," Nydia hissed. "I'll kill you every single time."

Emilia tried to shake her head, but Nydia held her still. "I—I don't know," she stammered. "I don't know if that's even something I can control."

Nydia released her so suddenly that Emilia fell against the table. "You'll learn to."

Emilia ignored the pain in her face as well as she could. Even if she was bleeding, she couldn't heal it right now, anyway. "How am I supposed to do that?"

Emilia could barely control her facial expressions when she *wasn't* in pain.

Nydia twisted her wrist, eyeing her own slender fingers, as if she were trying on a leather glove. "Did you think I'd stake my dignity on a worthless child's promise?" A gleam of delight flashed in Nydia's eyes, and malice radiated from her in waves. "Your training for the sirens begins next week, but your training for the runes, my dear, begins tonight."

Goddess, help me.

Emilia eyed the opening of the tent, as her body urged her to run. She didn't even want to ask, but…

"How does someone train for their runes?"

With another twist of her wrist, Nydia conjured a swirling ball of fire. "Like this."

Emilia tried to run, but Nydia jerked her forward.

She slammed her hand against Emilia's chest, and flames erupted over Emilia's clothes and skin.

Emilia screamed.

THE SCREAM RIPPED EMILIA FROM HER SLEEP, AND SHE JERKED AWAKE in the darkness of the surgeon's cabin.

She panted for air she couldn't seem to find, and her entire body throbbed in time with her pulse.

The scream had left Emilia's throat raw, and her chest ached— but that was because of her rapid pulse, *not* because of her mother's fire.

Right?

There was no fire.

Not anymore.

Emilia tested the mobility of her wrists and ankles.

Up.

Down.

Out.

She rubbed her scarred wrists against her trousers, letting the soft, black fabric soothe her.

Free.

Safe.

I'm free.

I'm safe.

Emilia told herself these things, even if she didn't really feel them—and hoped her body would listen.

She breathed in and out, in and out—until her pulse slowed, and her head stopped spinning.

Emilia had nearly convinced herself the danger was over, when a familiar, cool voice proved her wrong.

"You sleep like a scared, little girl."

Emilia squeezed her eyes shut and curled her fingers into the wool blanket.

Not now.

Please, not now.

She couldn't do this now.

But when Emilia reopened her eyes, she, indeed, found her dead mother seated at the end of the cot.

In the total darkness of the surgeon's cabin, Nydia's ethereal form emitted a faint, silver glow. She'd aged since that day in her tent—strands of white woven into her long, black braids—but Emilia had aged, too.

Emilia reminded herself, as she stared at the mother she still instinctually feared, that she was no longer a defenseless child, no longer at her mother's mercy.

Emilia sat up in her cot and drew her legs up toward herself. She narrowed her eyes. "Leave."

Nydia tilted her head, her long, dark braids sliding along the front of her red dress. "You dare demand things of me," she sneered, "you ungrateful child?"

"I'm no more a child than you are," Emilia said—just as much for her own sake as her mother's.

The memories still whirled—too fresh in her mind.

Nydia delighted in triggering Emilia's panic attacks. *This* time, Emilia didn't intend to give her the satisfaction.

Her mother had won the day she'd pushed Emilia into a self-destructive spiral—the one that had nearly gotten Emilia killed by the captain she now loved.

Emilia wouldn't let her win again.

"If you really wanted me to leave," Nydia said, "you would've banished me by now."

"I've been busy," Emilia informed her. She could do this. She *had* to do this. "You're not a priority to me, Mother."

The furniture rattled against the walls.

If Emilia hadn't known her mother's anger as well as she did, she might've thought the storm had caught up with them.

But Emilia *did* know her mother's anger.

She'd learned to avoid it the way a sailor learned to avoid storms, the way prey animals learned to avoid their predators.

Nydia glared murderously at Emilia, and though the silver glow had washed out her tawny skin a bit, her green eyes burned as fiercely as ever. "I should leave you to your fate," she growled. "I shouldn't lift a finger to help you or your pathetic humans."

Emilia's humans?

Her crew.

Emilia knew she shouldn't ask—that she shouldn't even humor her mother long enough to find out.

But the goddess of the sea had sent her a warning.

What if Maria *was* in danger?

What if they all were?

"What are you talking about?" Emilia said warily. "You'd *never* help my crew—or me, for that matter."

Nydia bared her teeth, her sharp cheekbones lifting. "I have done nothing *but* help you," she snarled, "and the dragons, who only ever adored *you*."

Jealousy.

As a child, Emilia couldn't think of her mother as someone capable of such a petty emotion, but now? She *heard* it. "You didn't help me. You hurt me."

"I did both," Nydia argued. "Do you think you could've withstood weeks of torture without me?"

Honestly?

Emilia had often wondered if she could have.

Nydia had always called Emilia weak, and Emilia had believed it. Even as she'd endured unimaginable pain, even as she'd refused to give even a shred of information in exchange for a moment of relief, she'd wondered if her mother were the only reason she did.

It was so dehumanizing—to feel beholden to someone who'd hurt her the way her mother had.

Nydia clearly knew that, too.

She flashed toward Emilia, suddenly—in a way only a spectre could. One moment, she sat at the end of Emilia's cot. The next, she stood in front of Emilia.

Her feet never touched the floorboards.

Emilia's heart stopped.

Behind her mother's faintly glowing form, shadows stretched outward, like the wings of a dragon, and when she reached *out*, the shadows formed claws.

Emilia couldn't banish a spirit—not without preparation—but if she could reach her sword…

The claws closed around Emilia's face, and pain tore through her skin.

Illusion.

It's just an illusion.

But Emilia didn't know if it was.

She hoped, but she didn't know. What Emilia *knew* was that the pain felt real.

And the fingernails that sliced into Emilia's jaw—those felt real, too.

"You think you're safe, now that I'm dead, don't you?" her mother growled. "You'll never be safe."

Her voice stretched and echoed in the small cabin, as if wooden walls couldn't contain her—as if *death* itself couldn't contain her.

Emilia's fingers closed around the hilt of the sword she'd kept strapped next to her pillow, and with a shrill *shing*, she drew her blade. She pointed its sharp tip at her mother's flickering, near-transparent form.

Nydia froze.

"I've killed enough people with this that it should work, shouldn't it?" Emilia asked. "Teach me one last lesson, Mother. What does lifeblood do to the dead?"

The flicker of fear that flashed in her mother's eyes told Emilia she'd guessed correctly.

It would *hurt*.

"I'd come back," Nydia warned.

"Oh, I hope so," Emilia said with a vicious smile, "because next time, I'll banish you for good."

The shadowy claws receded, and Nydia jerked back her hand, as if Emilia had burned her.

Ironic, really—considering it had always been the other way around.

Emilia didn't lower her sword. Instead, she stood and stepped toward Nydia, backing her toward the surgeon's table—the *bloodstained* surgeon's table.

Nydia must've realized that—because she froze. "You foolish child," she hissed. "You need me."

"No." Emilia forced herself to say the words, whether she believed them or not. "I've never needed you."

Nydia scoffed in disbelief. "How dare you…"

"Your days of hurting me, Mother," Emilia said, her chin high, "and causing me to hurt *myself* are over."

Rage simmered in Nydia's luminous, green eyes. "I'm dead because of you! We are *all* dead because of you!"

Guilt twisted at Emilia's stomach, but she couldn't give in to it. "I've spent every minute of every day, since the day it happened, hating myself for trusting her," she admitted, "but I can't change the past."

Nydia's eyes darkened. "Believe me. I'm aware."

The resentment in that remark stung a little, but Emilia had never known anything *but* her mother's resentment. She'd grown used to that sting long ago.

"What do you want from me?" Emilia asked.

"I told you," Nydia said. "I'm here to help you."

Emilia's face still burned, where Nydia's fingernails had sunk into her skin. "You're here to *hurt* me."

Nydia let out a cruel laugh. "Oh, you poor baby," she sneered. "Holding your pathetic, human weapon, and *whining* that your mother likes to hurt you."

Emilia tightened her hold on the sword.

"Your little weapons won't help you, Emilia," Nydia warned. "Human weapons won't stop him."

Emilia blinked. "Him?"

Not Catherine, then.

King Eldric, perhaps?

Why wouldn't a weapon stop King Eldric?

Nydia's lips curled up at the corners. "Oh, *now*, you want to know?" She shook her head in disgust. "You haven't even realized why you had that dream, have you?" Her ethereal form drifted closer. "Think about it. What did we discuss that day? Why would you need to remember that *now*?"

Emilia's blood ran cold.

Her mother knew what she'd dreamt? How was that possible?

Nydia's smile turned smug. "When you're ready to stop wallowing in your feelings, like a child, and beg me for help," she sneered, "let me know."

With that, her mother vanished into thin air.

Emilia lowered her sword and blinked in the total darkness of her cabin.

What the hell?

CHAPTER 16

The Nature of Fire

Emilia couldn't spend another moment in her cabin—not after a nightmare *and* a visit from her mother.

Her anxiety forced her to move, to find open air, where her lungs *might* remember their function.

It wasn't a new habit.

Fleeing to the main deck of a ship might've been, but even on Drakon Isle, Emilia had always needed open air, when her anxiety whirled out of control.

She'd once left her own rune ceremony to stand on the beach and catch her breath—not because of the pain, but because there'd been so many people.

Emilia's mind and body weren't always rational in their reactions to things, but after what Nydia told her, Emilia thought a bit of panic was warranted.

She leaned against the deck rail, grateful, at least, that the adrenaline hadn't left her queasy.

This time.

The vibrant, azure-blue waves were reckless today, splashing and spraying the sides of the ship. Toward the east, the storm clouds had

366

only grown taller and darker, but here, the tropical sun still shone brightly.

It was as if only the sea knew what was coming.

Emilia couldn't think about that—not if she wanted to slow her heart-rate. So, she fixed her gaze on the blue water below, following the steady rise and fall of the sea, counting each rhythmic crash of the waves.

Emilia's chest loosened, and she inhaled the salt air.

Her mother's words made no sense to her.

Emilia's enemies, Maria's enemies—they were all human.

Humans died by the sword.

Even the untouchable King Eldric would bleed out, if someone dared to stab him.

So, who had Nydia meant?

As usual, Nymeth gave no warning, before her low, rumbling voice interrupted Emilia's deliberation. *"I've tried to explain to Emryn that this rune is for emergencies, only,"* the dragon began, *"but does he listen? No."*

A weak smile pulled at the corners of Emilia's lips. She was fairly certain Nymeth had used it for a few non-emergencies herself.

The dragon stopped in the middle of her own rant, just to rebuke Emilia, *"And who gave you the right to decide what's an emergency and what isn't?"*

Emilia's smile deepened. *"Sorry, Nymeth."*

It wasn't Emilia's fault the dragon read every thought that crossed her mind.

"I heard that, too," Nymeth growled. *"Anyway, Emryn wanted me to tell you he saw a rainbow near your favorite creek today."*

Warm and gentle affection filled Emilia at the thought. *"A rainbow? Does that mean it's raining there?"*

"Sometimes. The weather's quite erratic here," Nymeth said. *"It keeps ruining my dinner. Do you know how hard it is to roast cattle when it's raining?"*

Emilia tried not to laugh at that. *"I can imagine."*

"What's the point of breathing fire, if I have to eat the beast raw?" Nymeth rumbled. *"Ah, but while we're on the topic of weather, if your*

human gives you any say in the matter, keep sailing west. I distinctly heard Aletha call this storm 'fun,' which, as you well know, means deadly."

Emilia's smile faded. *"Will you be all right?"*

"We'll take shelter in the caves, if it comes to that," Nymeth assured her. *"Don't concern yourself with us."*

Easier said than done.

"Tell Emryn I said thank you." A hint of a smile returned to Emilia's face. *"I needed a rainbow today."*

"No," Nymeth said. *"I will not encourage this."*

She totally would, though.

"Wait, what did you mean by…" Nymeth trailed off.

After discussing the younger, green dragon, who Nymeth pretended to not adore—though Emilia knew she did—she'd expected to sense amusement or false outrage, perhaps, on the other side of the bond, but what she sensed, instead, was *real* outrage.

A blaze of *real,* dangerous outrage.

"Someone hurt you," Nymeth said. *"I'm on my way."*

Emilia's eyes widened. *"No! Nymeth, I'm fine!"*

"You're not," the dragon told her.

Sure, Emilia's jaw still burned, where her mother had dug those claws into her skin, but…they'd been shadows. Shadows didn't inflict injuries.

Did they?

"It's not a real injury," Emilia tried to tell her. *"It's in my head."*

Emilia assumed the pain was like her flashbacks. It felt real now, but in an hour or so, when she'd managed to calm herself, the pain would fade.

"On your head, you mean," Nymeth corrected. The thunderous beat of dragon wings echoed behind her voice, warning Emilia that the ancient dragon was, indeed, on her way. *"And it is most certainly real."*

Emilia gripped the wooden rail in front of her and glanced first toward the bow of the ship, then toward the stern. Sailors moved along the deck, many of them just beginning their work for the day.

Emilia could only hope the captain and crew of the *Wicked Fate* were ready to see a massive, black dragon in the sky—if Emilia failed to talk the dragon down.

"Nymeth, you can't just fly out here every time I have a minor injury," Emilia said.

The ancient dragon growled in Emilia's mind, and Emilia nearly shuddered at the sound. *"Watch me."*

Emilia decided to try a different approach. *"You can't do anything about it, anyway—not to this person."*

Nymeth was quiet for a moment. *"Do you mean…"*

The dragon didn't finish the question, but a painful heat began to spread through Emilia. It expanded in Emilia's chest—until it had nowhere to go but up.

Flames shot upward, burning the inside of Emilia's throat, until she felt the urge to open her jaws and…

Oh.

Was this how it felt to breathe fire?

Only when the burning stopped, did Nymeth's dangerous growl fill Emilia's mind. *"Nydia Drakon."*

Emilia felt thin tendrils of flame curling between her teeth.

Nymeth's teeth.

This dragon bond was…disorienting, sometimes.

"Banish her," Nymeth demanded. When Emilia didn't instantly agree, the dragon continued, *"Nydia will use every opportunity to hurt you, and clearly, death has not changed her. She must go. If you don't know how to banish a spirit, I'll teach you."*

Emilia had obviously never done it before, but she had a vague understanding of the spell. *"I—I can't."* She shifted her weight from one foot to the other. *"I think she knows something—about Aletha's warning."*

"Of course she knows something," Nymeth scoffed. *"She knows everything there was to know. Nydia nearly drove her brother mad, forcing him to look into your future over and over, to tell her every detail."*

Emilia frowned. *"My mother hurt Aster?"*

When had that happened? Before Emilia was born, perhaps?

"Don't you understand?" Nymeth said. *"Nydia wants power over you.*

It's what she's always wanted—what she's always had. No amount of information is worth that."

"*It might be, if it saves lives,*" Emilia argued. "*The people on this ship are important to me. I need to know if they're in danger.*"

"*They are.*" The dragon's voice was cold and rough in Emilia's mind. "*Do you feel better now?*"

Actually, Emilia *felt* as if she might vomit. "*You knew and didn't tell me?*"

Nymeth didn't make a habit of showing sympathy toward anyone, which was why it surprised Emilia, when she sensed a bit of regret on the other side of the bond.

"*I tell you what I can. I tell you what you're ready to know,*" Nymeth tried to explain. "*Your mother tells you what she's ready for you to know.*"

Interesting, how no one was giving Emilia a choice in the matter.

"*Who do you trust?*" Nymeth asked. "*Me or her?*"

Emilia sighed, "*Well, you, of course, but—*"

"*Then, banish her,*" Nymeth interrupted. "*Banish Nydia Drakon to the realms of hell, where she belongs.*"

Emilia's eyebrows rose at that. "*I never realized you felt so strongly.*"

"*Oh, I tried not to,*" the dragon assured her. "*I tried to remember the Drakon people needed her. I am ageless. I'm not meant to care more for one child than an entire people. Yet, it tormented me to even see her breathe—day after day.*"

Another burst of fire burned the inside of Emilia's throat.

Emilia remembered a conversation she'd overheard as a child— between Aletha and Nymeth. She'd been playing with Emryn and had only caught bits and pieces of what Aletha had said to the dragon.

"*It is done. The child lives again—and does well enough here with you,*" she'd said. "*It's been five years. You must let this go.*" There'd been a pause, as Nymeth had no doubt responded. "*We'll keep the child away from her for as long as we can. You know that's all we can do.*" There'd been a laugh—the quiet, mischievous laugh of the sea goddess. "*And Aria says I favor people…*"

Had Nymeth wanted to kill Emilia's mother?

Had the sea goddess dissuaded her?

Emilia had been too young, back then, to make sense of it, and she hadn't thought of it much since.

"Why?" she asked the dragon.

"Why do you think?" Nymeth said. *"Because of you, Dragon Child. We took care of you, bonded with you. Then, I was expected to let you return to that mortal—and sense every time she hurt you? Over and over?"*

Over the years, Emilia had seen the dragons challenge Nydia whenever she'd hurt Emilia, but she hadn't realized it had bothered them *this* much—that it'd bothered Nymeth this much.

Nymeth's growl filled every space of Emilia's mind, resonating with ancient, transcendent power. *"It is not in the nature of Fire to not burn when someone hurts her child."*

Child?

"My mother hurt a dragon?"

The one thing Emilia and her mother had always had in common was their loyalty to the dragons.

The heat that had burned in Emilia's throat cooled, and the fury on Nymeth's side of the bond faded.

"Not…a dragon," Nymeth sighed. *"You, little one. It was you that she hurt."*

Emilia didn't understand.

"We raised you, did we not?" Nymeth said. *"We did as well as we could, anyway."*

"Yes." Somehow, even in Emilia's mind, her voice sounded breathless.

The dragon's wings rustled, as if she were closing them around herself.

She'd landed somewhere, then.

"You are a dragon-rider," Nymeth said, *"but you're more than that, too. How could you not be?"*

More?

Emilia had always been less than.

Never…*more.*

A strange sensation pricked at Emilia's senses. The bond

between them pulled tight, like a bowstring, and Nymeth warned, *"Someone's seen your rune."*

"Did your tattoo just…glow?"

The sudden intrusion of a human voice—audible to her ears and not just her mind—startled Emilia. She spun around, coming face-to-face with Zain.

Emilia didn't think she'd ever seen the quartermaster gape before, but he was most certainly gaping now.

At Emilia's exposed forearm.

Emilia forced herself to stammer out a response, "Oh, no, it, umm—"

Wait.

Tattoo?

Zain thought Emilia's rune was a tattoo?

With no…ink?

"It's actually—"

"Never mind," Zain interrupted. His near-black gaze shifted upward. "I just realized I don't care."

Emilia's brows furrowed.

"Well?" Zain arched a thick, black eyebrow. "Are you coming or not?"

Emilia peered behind the quartermaster, searching for some clue of what he meant. "Where?"

Zain scowled. "Do you even have to ask?"

Emilia glanced up toward the helm and noticed Maria's dark, gorgeous form, outlined in sunlight. She nodded. "The captain sent you to get me?"

"Of course," Zain said. "Because what else was I elected quartermaster to do—besides fetch the captain's," he paused, his gaze flicking downward, *"you?"*

Had he forgotten the word for *surgeon?*

"Every time she sees you wandering around," Zain continued, "awake at some ungodly hour."

"You're awake, too," Emilia pointed out, "and it's well after sunrise."

"Yes, well, I actually sleep at night," Zain told her, "instead of fighting for the crew's entertainment."

Oh.

So, he'd heard about the sword-fights, then.

"The captain and I actually fight for—"

Zain interrupted her with another grimace. "I don't want to hear about your foreplay."

Oh, for Aletha's sake.

"That's not it, either!"

Zain held up a hand to silence her. "I don't want to hear about this. I don't want to hear about your weird tattoo. I don't even want to talk to you at all."

Emilia sighed, "And here I thought you were warming up to me."

"Ew," Zain said. "What gave you that idea?"

"You voted in my favor," Emilia told him, "during the trial?"

"Don't remind me," Zain muttered.

But…he'd literally just asked her to.

"Move your feet, surgeon," Zain snapped. "I have other things to do today."

Emilia rolled her eyes and followed the surly quartermaster. "You know, I could just go to her by myself," she offered. "I know the way."

Zain didn't even look at her. "No."

Emilia spread her arms in defeat.

Zain didn't speak for the rest of the walk—not even when a spray of seawater hit them both, and Zain stopped to wipe his hands over his red waistcoat.

He glared at the sea, as if it had personally offended him, and resumed walking.

The saltwater had left Emilia's jaw stinging, but that pain wasn't real either, was it?

Zain would've said something, if Emilia had claw marks all over her face, right?

After all, when had Zain Amari ever kept an opinion to himself?

At the bottom of the steps, Emilia looked up and found Maria's dark brown eyes fixed on her—and her alone. She climbed the steps to the quarterdeck with Maria's gaze warming her skin, like a second sun.

Maria's leather tricorn and blue headscarf kept her curls secured, but the brisk winds wreaked havoc on the loose sleeves of her shirt. She alternated her hands on the wheel, as she pushed the sleeves higher around her arms.

Zain strode past the pirate captain, heading for the taffrail, and Emilia stopped beside her.

"You wanted to see me, Captain?"

Maria's intense stare *still* didn't waver. It was impressive, really—especially to Emilia, who could barely stare at her own shoes for this long. "I already see you," she murmured. "I want more than that."

Emilia's face warmed. "What do you want, then?"

One side of Maria's mouth pulled upward, but she kept whatever she was thinking to herself. For once.

Her gaze finally returned to the sea, releasing Emilia from its hold.

Her dark, tattooed fingers tightened around the wooden spokes of the wheel. She pulled the wheel a little to the right, the muscles in her forearms shifting with the movement. "Are you all right?"

"Oh, uhh," Emilia stammered.

Why would Maria ask *that?*

Emilia peered down at the main deck—toward the place she'd stood only minutes earlier. She wondered how Maria had even recognized her from here. Emilia didn't recognize anyone.

With such limited visibility, perhaps Maria had assumed Emilia had gone to the rail to vomit—as she often did after panic attacks.

From this distance, she couldn't have known.

"I'm fine," Emilia said. "No…sea sickness today."

Maria's jaw shifted. "It was never sea sickness. You don't need to lie to *me* about it."

Emilia's stomach fluttered with nervousness and shame. If Maria knew that, did she know about Emilia's nightmares, too?

Had she always known?

"So, you," Emilia said, "*didn't* need anything from me?"

Maria peered up at the roughly flapping sails. "I told you what I needed. I needed to know if you were all right."

From the taffrail, Zain called back, "Can we move any faster?"

"We're moving faster than the storm," Maria told her quartermaster. "That's all we need to do."

"It's a bad one," Emilia warned. "This storm."

Because Nymeth was right. When Aletha called a storm 'fun,' she meant a specific *kind* of fun—with Aria—which was the opposite of fun for everyone *but* the two goddesses.

According to Drakon teachings, Aria was the more considerate and rational of the two, but when it came to this, both of them could be quite…single-minded.

Zain returned to the helm, wood creaking beneath his polished boots. "And how would you know that, surgeon?"

Emilia glanced at him, and upon seeing his shrewd scowl, swiftly shifted her attention back toward the captain. Emilia absently smoothed the thin, black sleeve of her shirt over her rune, and Maria's dark gaze followed the path of Emilia's fingers.

"Dragons?" she guessed.

Emilia tried to ignore Zain's stare, as she nodded.

Zain rolled his eyes. "Why can't anything ever be normal with you?" he grumbled at Emilia, before returning to the stern.

Maria held Emilia's gaze for a moment longer, quirking a scarred eyebrow.

Emilia offered a helpless shrug. "I don't know what I did to make him hate me so much."

Maria snorted. "You don't have to *do* anything to make Zain hate you. He just wakes up that way."

"I heard that," he called back.

"I meant for you to," Maria assured him. With that wicked smirk that never failed to make Emilia's stomach flip, Maria said, "Don't worry, love. Zain will always hate *me* more than he hates you."

"You won't hear me deny it," Zain muttered.

Emilia sometimes wondered if these two enjoyed tormenting each other. She *knew* Maria enjoyed it.

"Tell me what you need," Maria said.

Emilia's brows furrowed. "You called me here," she reminded Maria, "not the other way around."

"And you gave me what I needed," Maria told her. "Now, I want to know what you need."

Emilia let out a baffled laugh. "I don't need anything."

Maria pulled the wheel to the left. "Yes, you do." She shot a pointed look at Emilia's shifting feet.

Apparently, the excess adrenaline affected Emilia's body, even when she'd practically forgotten about it.

"Decide what it is, and tell me," Maria said, as she watched the rolling waves. "The worst I can say is no."

Emilia gave her a skeptical look.

This was, after all, the vicious Captain Maria Welles they were talking about. Emilia had no doubt Maria could think of far worse things to say than no.

"Em," Maria said impatiently.

See?

A few more minutes, and she'd be threatening to kill someone.

"Fine." Emilia considered the way Maria had dealt with her own excess adrenaline the day before, and she realized, "I need to fight."

Maria glanced at Emilia, her eyes wide. "Now?"

Before Emilia could answer, Zain said, "The captain can't fight. She has work to do!"

Maria rolled her eyes at his interruption.

"I realize that," Emilia told him, "which is why I wouldn't have mentioned it, if she hadn't insisted."

Zain continued, as if Emilia hadn't said anything, "It would also disrupt everyone *else's* work, and you did enough of that last night."

"Oh, would you shut the fuck up?" Maria said. "No one asked you." She never tore her gaze from the sea, even as she argued with Zain. "Besides, if you weren't making assumptions about things you weren't awake to see, you'd know: we didn't disrupt anyone's work."

"I was awake to see it *before*," Zain said, "when it was you and Catherine Rochester doing this same…*dance*."

Tension rippled through Maria, starting with the muscle in her jaw and moving toward the muscles in her arms.

Emilia scowled at the quartermaster. "I can't see how that's relevant, at the moment."

"Ignore him," Maria told Emilia. "I do."

Maybe that's what Maria wanted Zain to think, but Emilia knew better. Even if her voice sounded calm, the anger that pulled at her muscles said otherwise.

Apparently deciding against provoking Maria further, Zain turned away from them.

Emilia wondered how many of these remarks Maria had 'ignored' lately—and if that had anything to do with how stressed Maria had been the day before.

Perhaps it was time for Emilia to tell the quartermaster what *she* thought of his little jabs.

Before Emilia could say something she might regret, however, Maria said, "You really want to fight right now?"

Maria kept one hand on the wheel, while the other curled and uncurled around the hilt of her sword.

Was she actually thinking about it?

"Yes," Emilia admitted, "but I know we can't."

"I wish you were wrong." Maria motioned toward Zain with a tilt of her head. "I wish *he* was wrong." She let go of her sword and sighed, "But he's not."

"I know," Emilia assured her. "I understand."

"You'll tell me why, though, won't you?" Maria's smooth voice dripped with sensuality—even when it had no right to. "Most people need to be dragged out of their hammocks in the mornings. Yet, you woke up ready to fight. Why?"

Nope.

No amount of sensuality could convince Emilia to answer *that* question.

Maria took a quick step to the side—quick enough that Emilia barely noticed it, until Maria hooked her fingers through Emilia's scabbard and tugged.

A squeak of surprise escaped Emilia's lips, as the front of her body collided with Maria's left hip.

The curved handle of a steel sword pressed into Emilia's stomach, but honestly, how could she care for any minor discomfort when she'd just entered the orbit of Maria's beautiful, brown eyes?

Maria's warm fingers slid around Emilia's leather scabbard, lightly caressing the curve of Emilia's hip.

Maria leaned in and whispered, with her mouth slanted just above Emilia's, "Please."

A nervous laugh left Emilia's lips—and fell against Maria's. "Can't a girl just wake up in the mood for violence?"

Maria grinned. "*My* girl can."

Emilia's stomach did another delightful, little flip, even as she shook her head in disbelief.

Between Maria's *ridiculous* flirting and the nearness of her body —the warmth of her seeping into Emilia, her alluring, tropical scent enticing Emilia's senses, ensuring she'd never want to breathe anything else—Emilia had nearly forgotten about her mother's visit.

Until Maria's smile faded.

The warmth drained from Maria as rapidly as rum from a breached barrel. She grasped Emilia's chin between her thumb and her forefinger and turned it to the side. "What the fuck is this?"

As it turned out, Zain *would*, in fact, see claw marks on someone's face and say nothing about it.

In Maria's haste, she'd released her hold on the helm, and the wooden wheel spun wildly, now.

The ship shifted beneath their feet, and Zain turned to see what had happened. "Captain?"

Without looking, without even loosening her grip on Emilia's face, Maria reached out with her free hand and caught the wheel, curling three fingers around it. The ship steadied beneath them, even as Maria refused to tear her gaze from Emilia's face.

"Who," Maria growled, "did this?" She spoke each word as if it were a struggle to get out—as if the quiet rage in her eyes had clogged her throat, as well.

Maria turned Emilia's head in the other direction, examining the scratches on the left side, as well.

Emilia tried to remove her face from Maria's grasp, but Maria didn't yield an inch. "It's not that bad."

"Don't tell *me* it's not bad," Maria said with an incredulous scoff. "I'm fucking looking at it."

You wouldn't be, if I'd realized I needed to heal it.

Emilia tried to free her face by turning it back toward the left—and nearly caused Maria's thumb to slide over one of the bleeding wounds.

"Don't hurt yourself. If you want me to let go, I'll let go," Maria said. She pulled Emilia's face back toward her own, forcing Emilia to meet her gaze. "But at least tell me who to fucking kill first."

"Kill?" Emilia repeated. "Captain, it's a scratch!"

Maria turned Emilia's face again, and Emilia lifted her eyebrows in disbelief.

Had she shape-shifted into a wooden puppet?

"I can't believe I didn't see the blood before," Maria muttered, "but you weren't turning your head or—" Her eyes widened, and she jerked Emilia's face back toward her own. "Were you hiding this from me?"

"I would've done a better job of it, if I were," Emilia assured her.

Maria gave a small nod at that.

Emilia flashed a sharp, sardonic smile. "Can you stop jerking my head around now?"

"Oh." Maria let go of Emilia's chin. "Sorry."

Emilia tried to step back, but Maria caught her arm, fingers curling gently, even in the midst of her rage.

"Em," Maria said. "Tell me who I'm killing."

She wasn't leaving much room for debate, was she?

"No one," Emilia told her. "It's a few scratches. I've dealt with far worse wounds than this."

"Scratches?" Maria repeated. Was this the first time she'd actually heard Emilia? Her frown deepened, and she reached for Emilia's face again—before deciding against it. "Fingernails? Fingernails did…*that?*"

Emilia remembered those eerie claws her mother had sprouted and muttered, "Something like that."

"Em," Maria said, her tone low and dangerous. "Give me a name, or I swear to the gods I'll slit every fucking throat on this ship until you do."

Emilia's eyes widened. "Goddess!"

"Not yours," Maria said—as if one less throat made a difference.

"Well, that's a relief," Emilia said. "For a moment there, I thought you were going to overreact."

Maria ignored her sarcasm.

Nymeth and Maria were more similar than either of them realized.

Kill first. Ask questions later.

"Those are too deep to be scratches," Maria told her. "You're either lying to me, which I'd hope you wouldn't do, or someone really fucking hurt you."

Emilia sighed, "If I told you their fingernails grew as long as bread knives, would you believe me?"

Maria jerked Emilia closer. "Give me the name."

Emilia stared up at the pirate captain, unsure of what to say. The last thing she wanted to do was talk about her mother—especially here, where people might hear. "Shouldn't you be watching the sea?"

Maria still had a firm grip on the wheel, but she hadn't looked away from Emilia's face in quite some time. "Yes, because islands pop up out of nowhere every day," she scoffed. "Don't change the subject."

Emilia couldn't help but smile a little at the sarcasm.

"Name, Em," Maria growled.

Emilia closed her eyes and sighed. "Nydia."

Confusion pulled at Maria's scarred brows. "I don't have any sailors by that name."

"No, you don't," Emilia said, "because she isn't a sailor. She's a warrior and a chieftess." Emilia lowered her voice. "A *dead* warrior and chieftess."

Maria's eyes flashed. "Your mother did this?"

Emilia cast an alarmed glance around them, hoping no one had heard that.

At least Zain was still turned away.

"How the fuck is that possible?" Maria asked.

The better question was: how did Maria manage to sound angrier now than when she'd threatened to murder an entire crew?

"I don't know," Emilia said. "When it happened, I thought it… hadn't, really." A sudden wave of shame turned her stomach. "I thought it wasn't real."

Maria's dark brown eyes softened, and she gave a subtle nod. "You don't trust your own mind."

Emilia looked down, unable to meet her gaze.

Maria turned to Zain. "Quartermaster? I'm taking a break," she called out. "Man the helm until I return."

Zain strode toward them. "Yes, Captain."

Emilia wondered how much of their conversation he'd over-heard, how much he'd purposely ignored.

He took the helm, and Maria took Emilia by the arm. "Come with me," she murmured in Emilia's ear.

From a distance, it might've looked as if Maria were dragging Emilia down the steps, but in reality, her touch was achingly gentle every step of the way.

She led Emilia around the steps, toward the door that separated the main deck from the captain's quarters. They stopped outside it —cloaked from the crew by the shadows of the quarterdeck.

Maria released her arm. "Tell me what happened."

Emilia shrugged. "My mother visits from time to time. It was nothing out of the ordinary, really."

Maria narrowed her eyes. "Your mother leaving you injured and bleeding is 'nothing out of the ordinary?'"

Emilia thought of the memory from her nightmare—of the *training* her mother had given her. "Well…"

Maria's fingers curled tightly around the hilt of her right sword. She looked away, turning her head with enough force to swing those small, beaded braids she wore at the front of her hair.

Emilia licked her lips nervously. "How could I have known it was real?" She held out her hands, curling her fingers inward. "I mean, she had these…*claws.*"

Maria lifted her eyebrows. "Lots of women have claws, love. Especially the ones who don't need to concern themselves with fucking other women." She cocked her head. "Even some of the ones who do."

The absurd timing of that remark caught Emilia completely off guard. "Captain!" She shook her head to rid herself of the thought, but no, Maria had *burned* that one into her mind. "Why would you even—" she sputtered. "We were talking about my mother! No one wants to think of their mother doing…*that!*"

Maria's lips twitched with each new wave of horror that shuddered over Emilia's face.

Emilia pressed her fingers into her eyes, rubbing them miserably. She couldn't help but remember Silas's words. "Even if it *was* implied that their mother might've engaged in such an activity."

"Wait, what?" Maria's look of mild amusement turned to one of confusion. "Your mother liked women?"

"I don't know!" Emilia said. She dropped her hands. "Would it really surprise you, if she did?"

"Me? No," Maria scoffed. "I'm only surprised when someone *doesn't* like women."

Despite everything, Emilia actually laughed at that.

Attraction might've been a force outside of one's control, but… well, women *were* quite phenomenal, weren't they?

Though anger remained coiled in Maria's muscles, like a viper waiting to strike, she still smiled at the sound of Emilia's laugh. "You have to tell me more, love," she said with a wiggle of her fingers. "You can't just drop a theory like that on me and not tell me where it came from."

"Oh, uhh…" Emilia blushed and let the words spill out in a rush, "Well, my possible-father once implied my mother might've had some kind of relationship with a woman who, honestly, deserved *way* better, but I didn't understand him, at the time." Emilia took a breath so quick it barely counted. "And it's not like I ever asked her about it—because come on, does my mother *seem* like the kind of person you ask about that?"

Maria's eyebrows rose higher with each word that came out of Emilia's mouth. "Why would your father mention your mother's sexual relationships to you?"

"Possible-father," Emilia corrected.

Maria rephrased the question. "Why would anyone?"

"We don't *know* it was a sexual relationship," Emilia said. "It might've been a…toxic friendship."

Maria's brows furrowed.

"But," Emilia said reluctantly, "probably…because he knew I was too young to know what he meant."

"Darling," Maria said, "how young is too young?"

Emilia lifted her chin. "Twelve."

Maria snorted.

Emilia's mouth fell open. "Oh, and I'm to believe you knew what sex was when you were twelve?"

"I grew up in a tavern, love," Maria reminded her.

Emilia scowled at the smug pirate. "Well, the rest of us learned these things at a normal age."

The corners of Maria's full, rosy-brown lips curved upward. "And what, my love, *is* a normal age?"

"I'm not going to keep answering your questions, just so you can laugh at me!" Emilia said—but after a few moments of Maria watching her with that expectant smile, Emilia sighed. "Eighteen?" When Maria's eyes widened, Emilia tried again. "Sixteen?"

"Em," Maria said. "Why are you guessing?"

"I'm not," Emilia lied. "Fifteen?" She leaned forward. "Which age would you *not* laugh at?"

To her dismay, Maria laughed even without an answer. "Em! You had to have known before then!"

"Who was going to tell me?" Emilia said. "The dragons?" She wrinkled her nose. "They probably don't even know *how* our species has sex. They'd have me all confused, describing wings and such."

"Dear gods," Maria muttered under her breath.

How did Maria always manage to make Emilia feel like the strangest person in all of Aletharia?

They couldn't *all* grow up around pirates and thieves! Some people were raised by dragons!

Or…

Well…

"It didn't hurt me to not know," Emilia said, growing more defensive by the moment. "I figured it out before it was time to try it, didn't I?"

"Try?"

Emilia knew she'd chosen the wrong word the moment the smirk vanished from Maria's face.

"No. You—you must've…" Maria trailed off. "At least a few times before…"

Emilia wasn't used to *Maria* being the one who couldn't finish a sentence. "I must've what?"

Pure horror twisted at the captain's scars. "Tell me I'm wrong." She took a quick, almost desperate step toward Emilia. "Tell me Catherine wasn't your first."

Seriously?

Wasn't talking about Emilia's mother bad enough? Now, Maria wanted to talk about Catherine?

Couldn't they discuss the weather, instead?

Apples, perhaps?

Maria loved to talk about fruit.

"Em?"

"No! Of course she wasn't my first—" Emilia winced a little, before finishing the sentence, "kiss."

Maria had *almost* relaxed—until she'd heard the last word. "You're fucking kidding me."

"Sure," Emilia said, "if it'll end this conversation."

Maria ignored that remark. "Every time I think I know just how low she'll sink, I discover a new low!"

Emilia rolled her eyes. "Oh, for Aletha's sake! I wasn't a child! I knew what I was doing."

Maria didn't even look at her.

"Catherine massacred my people." Emilia stepped forward. "She imprisoned both of us! Had us tortured! She ruined the lives of everyone who sided with you—all those years ago. And you think seducing a grown woman was somehow worse?"

"Not worse. Just," Maria hesitated, "cruel."

"You're Captain Maria Welles," Emilia said with a shrug. "You're supposed to be okay with cruel."

Maria pinned her with a dangerous glare. "Not when it comes to you."

Emilia blinked.

These little confessions became less and less rare every day, and yet, they never ceased to make Emilia's heart skip a beat.

"Everyone *thinks* they love their first, Em," Maria said. "I had to talk Judith out of proposing to the first girl she fucked. Couldn't even tell me her name!"

That…didn't surprise Emilia, actually.

After all, this was the same Judith who'd tried to have sex during a battle and ended up blowing a hole in the side of the ship, thereby creating the Helen law.

"You say you knew what you were doing," Maria said, "but Catherine knew what she was doing, too."

"I told you when we met," Emilia reminded her. "I was easy to manipulate once."

Maria gave a single nod. "Yes. You did."

The tightness in Emilia's chest increased to an unbearable level, and she looked away. "Must we talk about Catherine right now? This isn't even *about* her."

"No," Maria said, ice in her tone. "It's about someone *else* who enjoys hurting you."

Aiming for a bit of levity, Emilia said, "It's become quite the popular sport. Perhaps you should join in!"

Maria didn't laugh. "Em."

"Sorry," Emilia muttered.

Maria stepped toward her, and the quiet creak of wood beneath her worn, leather boot was louder, even, than her voice. "Tell me how to stop this."

Emilia stared up at the pirate captain, stunned by the sudden change in her demeanor, by the quiet plea in her tone. "There's nothing you can do."

Maria grasped Emilia's elbows, her fingers warm against Emilia's skin. "Don't tell me that."

"Captain." Emilia didn't understand the anguish she saw in Maria's eyes, nor did she know how to soothe it. "It's the truth."

Maria released Emilia's arms. She spun on the heels of her boots, flexing her fingers in frustration. "Fuck!" For a moment, she just stared at the heavy, wooden door. Then, she spun back toward Emilia, renewed determination in her gaze. Her sword left its sheath with a soft *shing*. "Summon her, and I'll stab her."

Emilia merely lifted her eyebrows at the sword.

She knew the law against drawing weapons outside of battle didn't apply to Maria, but you'd think the pirate would show a *little* restraint every now and then.

Ha.

Maria?

Restraint?

Who was she kidding?

"You can't stab a ghost, Captain," Emilia said. "Not really. They're not corporeal."

"I can fucking try," Maria assured her.

Emilia pressed her lips together, trying—and failing—not to smile at the thought of Maria attempting to stab someone she couldn't even see.

Maria was less amused.

"I don't know what the living can do to the dead," Emilia admitted. "It's possible we can displace them. I have a theory about a way we might hurt them—a theory that holds a bit more weight after my mother's reaction today…"

Emilia's gaze strayed back toward Maria's sword, as she realized…Maria's sword had taken *far* more lives than her own had.

It might actually intimidate Nydia—for a moment.

Until she remembered Maria couldn't see her.

Emilia shrugged. "But it's my first haunting. I'm still learning."

"Your first—" Maria shook her head. She looked away, and a beam of sunlight caught her blade, gleaming. "If we can't injure her because she's non-corporeal, how did she injure you?"

"I wish I knew," Emilia said, "but this is my first—"

"Haunting, yes," Maria interrupted. She looked at Emilia, eyes dancing. "You could've warned me, you know?" she teased. "That my life was about to get so much stranger when I hired you."

"Well, that's what you get, Captain," Emilia said with a playful smile, "when you trick people."

Maria's lips curved. "Ah. I still think it worked out in my favor."

Emilia rolled her eyes. "I can't summon her either—just so you know. She's a ghost, not a goddess. She doesn't exist in the living world until she chooses to."

All traces of humor drained from Maria's face. "So, she has all the power, then."

"She's my mother," Emilia said with a bitter laugh. "She's always had the power."

If there was anything about Nydia that Maria—with her own shameless love of power—might've understood, Emilia would've thought it was that.

Yet, that only seemed to distress Maria more. She sheathed her sword, finally, but her fingers remained curled around it. "Do you think she planned this?"

Emilia stared blankly at her. "Do I think my mother died a terrible death, just so she could haunt me?"

Maria winced at that. "Fair point."

"At most, she's grasping for what little power is still available to her," Emilia said. "She can't kill me anymore, and she knows that. I'm the last of our kind. That makes me her only anchor to this world."

Maria's dark brown eyes cut toward Emilia—as sharp as a blade. "Does it *look* like your survival is my only concern?"

Well...no.

In addition to the fury burning in Maria's eyes, Emilia didn't think she'd seen the pirate captain's muscles unclench *once* since she'd seen the wounds.

Not even the leather doublet and trousers could hide the tension that radiated from every part of her.

Emilia didn't know *why* it bothered Maria so much. Emilia was clearly all right, and it wasn't as if she didn't have a high enough pain tolerance to handle it.

Maria, of all people, knew she did.

Emilia only knew she wanted to soothe Maria in any way she could. "I can banish her."

"What does that mean?" Maria asked.

Emilia's throat tightened, and she rubbed her wrist against her own scabbard, letting the leather scratch against her skin. "It's…a spell," she admitted. "They say it's a fate worse than death, that the dead risk it anytime they make themselves known in this world."

"When they haunt someone," Maria realized.

Emilia nodded. "I wondered, when I was a child, if it were just another scary story—a cautionary tale to discourage us from hanging around after we die."

Maria stepped closer. "But?"

"But my mother reacts with fear when I mention it," Emilia said, "and Nymeth wants me to do it."

"The dragon," Maria said with a nod.

"The dragons know magic better than any of us," Emilia said. "If Nymeth says it can be done, it can."

"Then, do it," Maria said. "Why let her continue to hurt you, if you can end it now?"

Because I think you might be in danger, and I'll do whatever it takes to protect you?

Emilia couldn't bring herself to say something as ridiculous as that, though. So, instead, she said, "It's complicated."

Maria's brows creased. "It's not—" She took a slow, careful step toward Emilia. She lifted her hand to touch Emilia's jaw again—but stopped midway, clenching her fingers into a fist. Her hand dropped. "It's not because you think you deserve this, is it?"

"No," Emilia said.

"Good." Maria nodded. "I just know you've endangered your-self before because of—"

"I know I deserve it, of course," Emilia assured her, "but that's not the reason."

Maria stepped back, distress twisting at her scars. "Em…"

"The reason," Emilia said, "is that I need supplies."

It wasn't a lie.

Emilia did need certain things for the spell, and while she knew she deserved far worse than anything her mother had ever done to her, that wasn't why Emilia had hesitated to banish her.

At least, she didn't *think* it was.

Maria exhaled, suddenly, and Emilia wondered if she'd been holding her breath. "Tell me what you need," she said. "I'll find it for you. If I have to raid every ship in the sea, I'll find what you need."

Emilia glanced toward the main deck, wondering which ships Maria meant. She hadn't seen any in over a week.

"No, you're right," Maria sighed, though Emilia hadn't said a word. "There aren't any out there."

Emilia cast a bemused look at Maria. That uncanny perceptive-ness of hers was downright unnerving, sometimes.

"It's illegal for Illopian merchants to trade with the islands," Maria explained. "I prefer the Azure Sea for that very reason." She tilted her head, a thin, brown braid sliding along her jaw, and the corners of her mouth tilted upward. "The ships we do encounter out here tend to be the ones I like to *sink*."

Maria said the word 'sink' the way some people said far more… illicit words—with her teeth gleaming in her mouth and delight burning in her eyes.

"Naval ships," Emilia said.

Maria nodded. The delight fled her eyes as quickly as it had come. "But right now, even those are gone."

Perhaps that was what was bothering Maria.

Murder withdrawals.

With a soft laugh, Emilia told her, "That's probably because we've already sunk most of them."

Maria's brows furrowed. "Darling, the Kingdom of Illopia is the largest naval power in all of Aletharia."

Considering Drakon Isle hadn't even had ships, much less a navy, Emilia didn't quite understand Maria's point. "I know. I saw the fleet."

Maria shook her head. "That was one fleet, Em," she said. "The Royal Navy has hundreds of ships."

Emilia paled. "Hundreds?"

No one had ever told her *that*.

"Sorry, love," Maria sighed, "but when Catherine returns—provided she isn't demoted after failing so spectacularly—she'll come back with just as many ships, if not more, than we've already sunk."

Emilia's heart raced.

Goddess, what if they came back with more dragon-killing weapons, too? What if Emilia wasn't there to help?

"A demotion is possible," Maria told her. "She lost a lot of ships in that battle. King Eldric won't forgive that as easily as he's forgiven her other failures."

Her other failures being Em and Maria, of course.

"You said yourself that someone else would take her place," Emilia muttered.

Maria nodded. "I'm sorry, love," she said gently. "I thought you knew. You didn't see them in Regolis?"

Emilia pressed her back against the door, letting the coolness of the wood seep into her skin. "I was unconscious when they moved me from the ship to the dungeons. All I saw for weeks was darkness."

Pain twisted at Maria's brows. She stepped toward Emilia, and this time, when she lifted her hands to touch Emilia's face, she didn't hesitate.

Emilia's breath caught, as Maria leaned into her, as her warm fingers curled around Emilia's cheeks.

Maria captured Emilia's senses, one by one, drew them all

toward her—until all Emilia heard was the sound of Maria's breath, until all she smelled was the leather Maria wore and the hibiscus and oranges on her skin, until all Emilia felt was the gentle touch of Maria's hands, as they cradled Emilia's bleeding face as if it were a precious gemstone.

"I promise you, Emilia Drakon," Maria murmured. "We will destroy them."

Emilia blinked up at her remarkable captain.

Here, a pit of despair had opened wide, prepared to swallow Emilia whole, and Maria held her above it with just a few words.

"How can you think that," Emilia said, words soft and timid, "when we've been ineffective so far?"

"Ineffective?" Maria scoffed. Her lips quirked up at the edges. "How dare you say such a thing?" Before Emilia could remind Maria of the *hundreds* of ships she'd just mentioned, Maria said, "Make no mistake, my sweet surgeon, what you did will cripple them."

Emilia ached to touch Maria, too.

After all, why should Maria be the only one allowed such indulgences—in the middle of the day?

Emilia brushed her fingers along the cool leather of Maria's doublet, and Maria's eyelashes fluttered, as if Emilia had touched bare skin.

"Careful, surgeon," Maria teased.

Emilia's lips twitched at the warning. "Do you truly think we made a difference?"

"You think I'd do what I do, if I didn't?" Maria leaned in, letting her tricorn tip back, as she pressed her head to Emilia's. "They fear us for a reason, Em."

Emilia relished the sensation of Maria's skin against her own, of Maria's breath against her face. Someone could walk past at any moment, and this would end.

Until then, Emilia adored what she had.

"And why is that," Emilia asked, "Captain?"

Maria let out a short laugh. "Because I'm Captain Maria Welles, and you're the Dragon Child." Her lips brushed Emilia's. "We're fucking legends, Em. We could rule the seas together, and they know it."

Emilia had never heard anyone use the term *Dragon Child* and mean anything remotely positive by it.

No one besides Nymeth and Aletha, anyway.

Yet, just as Maria saw her own infamy as fuel for her power, she clearly thought the same of Emilia's.

Maria's thumbs traced Emilia's cheeks. "We'll destroy every last one of them," she growled against Emilia's lips. "I swear to you. Somehow, we'll do it."

Emilia leaned forward, desperate for Maria to kiss her already.

Instead, Maria pulled back and let her hand slide down to Emilia's jaw. She tilted Emilia's face, her eyes narrowing on the bleeding wounds. "We'll destroy your bitch of a mother, too, if she keeps—" She stopped mid-sentence, and her gaze flicked up to meet Emilia's. "Witch. Witch of a mother."

Right.

As if Emilia hadn't heard Maria insult her mother a billion times already.

With a lift of her eyebrows, Emilia said, "I do hope you haven't been using those words interchangeably."

Maria grinned wickedly at that. "Gods, I wish we could fight right now." She dropped her hands and stepped back. "But I have to get back to the helm."

"I know," Emilia assured her.

Maria held up a tattooed finger. She closed the space between them once more and began to tug at Emilia's scabbard. "Left you a bit crooked here."

Each touch and pull sent another rush of desire through Emilia's body, and Emilia wondered how Maria managed to make her feel these things without even kissing her.

"There," Maria murmured. Her hands fell away from the weapon belt. "Henry's taking the helm after the first meal. I have some work to do after that, but *then...*" Her deep, brown eyes shifted up toward Emilia's face. "You're mine for the rest of the day."

As in...*before* nightfall?

"Yours to—" Emilia sputtered, "to fight, right?"

Maria stepped back. "Enjoy your day, love."

Emilia spread out her arms in confusion. "That's not an answer." When Maria turned to leave, Emilia called after her, "Hey, are we fighting or not?"

She heard Maria's chuckle even from there.

"Get to work, surgeon."

Emilia glared at the back of her head. "Captain!"

CHAPTER 17
Learning the Ropes

Aside from popping above deck to remove the occasional splinter or, once, to nurse a smashed thumbnail—poor guy—Emilia spent most of the day working in the galley with Judith.

A shaft of red-orange light streamed in through the portholes, illuminating the tables and floorboards in front of Emilia. As she sliced potatoes for the evening meal, the fiery light occasionally caught the blade of her knife, as well, gleaming in the dark space.

Potatoes, Emilia had learned, were not only one of the most versatile vegetables on the ship—but also one of the longer-lasting ones.

While Emilia scooped them into a bowl, she continued to question Nymeth—as she'd been doing for an hour straight, *"You have to tell me more than just that."*

"I am one of the most powerful creatures in all of Aletharia. I don't have to do anything. Except nap. Now."

"And I will let you take your nap," Emilia promised, *"as soon as you tell me what kind of danger we're facing."*

The dragon growled. *"You're lucky I can't burn you right now."*

Emilia suppressed a smile. She suspected one of the reasons

she'd failed so thoroughly in holding onto her hatred for Maria was that the pirate shared a few too many qualities with the dragons Emilia adored—including their habit of showing affection through threats.

"Just give me one clue. One sentence!"

"One?" Nymeth sounded skeptical. *"All right, Dragon Child. One sentence."* When Emilia didn't object, the dragon said, *"Evil spreads among you."*

Emilia frowned.

What kind of clue was that?

The dragon was supposed to tell Emilia what kind of threat awaited the captain and crew of the *Wicked Fate*—not describe the general state of a pirate ship!

"But—"

"No," Nymeth interrupted. *"You said one sentence. Your deal, girl, not mine."*

Emilia pressed with a bit too much indignation, and her knife hit not only the potato but the wooden table beneath it. A small jolt of pain shot from her wrist to her elbow. *"I assumed you'd pick a better sentence!"*

An infuriating rumble of laughter resounded in Emilia's mind. *"When dealing with a mind as clever as yours, one cannot be too specific."*

"Sure, you can!" Emilia thought the dragon was overestimating her, anyway. *"Who's going to stop you?"*

"No more questions!" Nymeth said. *"If I don't get my nap, I'll get cranky, and who knows what will happen, then? I might just breathe in the direction of someone's favorite tree."*

Emilia's mouth fell open. *"You would never."*

"Do you intend to test me?"

Emilia sliced the next potato with even more vigor than the last. *"Good dragons don't threaten trees!"*

The dragon's low chuckle filled Emilia's mind. *"If you knew anything of my countless years in the lands of Aletharia, you'd know: I am not a good dragon."*

Emilia's brows furrowed.

What was that supposed to mean?

"Em?"

If the sudden closeness of Judith's voice hadn't already startled Emilia, the *clang* of the pot she dropped onto the table next to Emilia would have.

Emilia looked up at the ship cook, blinking.

Judith stood beside Emilia, sleeves of her thin, beige shirt rolled up around her tanned arms and sweat dripping from her short, brown hair.

Emilia discreetly touched her own black sleeve, ensuring it still covered her rune. "Sorry," she said with a wince. "Did you…say something?"

"Just your name." Judith rested her slender hip against the table and folded her arms over her chest. "You've been quiet today."

"Not from my perspective," Nymeth grumbled.

Emilia forced herself not to roll her eyes at the dragon—since Judith would likely assume the eye-roll was for her. "You call everyone quiet, Judith. You once told the captain she was being quiet, and I happen to know she's not even capable of it."

Judith arched an eyebrow. "I bet you do."

Heat rushed to Emilia's face. "Not at *all* what I meant by that."

Judith snorted. "You've been quieter than usual."

Emilia's chest fluttered. She cast another glance at the sleeve that covered her rune. Judith would freak out if she saw it, but once she got over the *burned-into-Emilia's-skin* part, would she understand?

"You may tell who you need to tell about the rune," Nymeth said begrudgingly, *"but Aletha's warning was for you and you alone."*

"I know."

But how did Emilia explain her preoccupation without mentioning the warning from the goddess?

"I'm sorry," was all Emilia could think to say. "I've had a lot on my mind lately."

Something about Emilia's tone or facial expression must've alarmed Judith—because her smile faded, and her brows creased with concern. "You should've said something, mate." She dropped her arms and stepped toward Emilia. "I'm always here to talk."

Emilia's heart raced.

As busy as they were, and Judith wanted Emilia to just…pass the burden on to her? Even if Emilia *could* do such a thing, she wouldn't.

"Thank you," Emilia said, her throat too tight, "but I can't." She offered a sad, apologetic smile. "Yet."

To her surprise, Judith just nodded.

She placed a hand—damp with either water or sweat, Emilia didn't know which—on Emilia's shoulder. "Let me know when you're ready."

The kindness of that remark crashed over Emilia, crushing her chest and leaving her unable to respond.

And though Emilia had healed it hours ago, her jaw ached, too, as if to remind her that she, of all people, deserved cruelty, not kindness.

Judith picked up the pot and carried it to a table near the fire-hearth.

"Do you see now?" Emilia thought, hoping Nymeth still listened. *"Do you see why I must protect them?"*

The dragon didn't answer.

Evil spreads among you.

Emilia reconsidered those words.

Illopians used the word 'evil' for things that were illegal or misunderstood, like piracy or witchcraft.

Dragons, on the other hand, thought of evil not as a specific thing or person, but as the *intention* of bringing harm.

"Is someone on the ship planning to hurt someone?"

Nymeth didn't answer that question, either—not that Emilia had expected her to.

What else could it be, though?

Unless…

What if she'd used the word 'spread' for a reason?

What if that was the clue?

"It's not a disease, is it?"

Still, the ancient dragon offered only silence.

It couldn't be a disease, though, could it? Emilia knew how to treat diseases! She wouldn't need to summon a goddess for that.

"Have you noticed we're missing a crate of apples?"

Emilia looked up at Judith. "What?"

Judith dumped a bowl of chopped carrots into the pot, before nodding toward the empty spot on the table next to her. "I left a crate of apples there during the afternoon meal, and now, it's gone."

Emilia stared blankly at the empty spot.

Not the empty crate, no. The entirely empty *spot*.

What kind of imbecile would steal not one apple, but an entire crate of them?

Silly question.

Emilia knew *exactly* which imbecile would do that.

"I'll catch her red-handed, eventually," Judith said, "and I'll hit her in the head with a pot. A big one!"

"The tricorn might provide some cushioning there," Emilia warned.

"Shall I hit her on the ass, then?" Judith asked.

Wood creaked somewhere above them, and the two of them looked up. The soft creaking continued toward the steps.

"Maybe she's coming back to return them," Emilia suggested.

Judith gave her an incredulous look. "Ah, come on, Em. You know her better than that."

Emilia nodded.

It was true. Remorse was a foreign concept to Captain Maria Welles.

Most of the time.

Tattered, brown boots descended the wooden steps, and Emilia tried again. "Were you expecting Helen today?"

Judith made a disgusted sound in the back of her throat. "Why would I expect *her*?"

Emilia lifted her eyebrows.

Had Emilia sounded this silly when *she'd* been in denial?

Probably.

The boatswain soon came into view, and before he could even greet them, Judith said, "If you're coming to ask for more ale, the answer's no. I've had enough of you gluttons today!"

Pelt reached the bottom of the steps and stopped. The bemused look he gave Judith made the skin around his scar twitch. "I don't know who stole from you *this* time, but I'm actually here for the surgeon."

"Same person who always does," Judith grumbled.

Emilia set aside her knife. "Is someone injured?"

"No." Pelt tilted his head and squinted thoughtfully. "Possibly. I'm not sure."

Emilia's brows furrowed. "You're not sure?"

Pelt turned to Judith. "Do you need her right now?"

"Not if she has her own work to do." Judith examined a bulb of garlic with a frown. "Surgeon's work comes first."

"It can wait," Pelt assured them, "if you're busy."

Emilia also turned to Judith, concerned about leaving her before the evening meal was done.

Judith looked up—and blinked, as she found both of them watching her. "Go! We finished most of the preparation already. I'll come find you if I need you."

Emilia nodded. She carried her bowl of sliced potatoes to Judith, and while Judith added them to the pot, Emilia grabbed a rag to clean her hands.

"So, who's possibly hurt," Emilia said, as she dipped the cloth into the bucket of sea water, "and why do we not know if they are or not?"

"He's an older deckhand." Pelt crossed his arms. "Most stubborn bastard you'll ever meet."

Judith looked up. "Cornelius?"

Pelt nodded, and the look of disgust the two of them shared unleashed a flutter of anxiety in Emilia's stomach.

"Who's Cornelius," Emilia asked, "and why do I get the feeling there's something I should know about him?"

"Because there is," Judith said.

Pelt shot a warning glare her way. "No, there isn't."

But one didn't spend her entire life around Captain Maria Welles—without developing an immunity to glares. Judith pointed her wooden ladle, like a sword. "You tell her, or I'll knock out the gold teeth, as well."

Emilia glanced back and forth between them, not sure whether to intervene or wait for them to sort it out.

They *usually* sorted it out.

With…minimal violence.

Pelt rolled his eyes. He reluctantly shifted his attention toward Emilia. "You might recognize him."

Emilia didn't see how. She worked on an entirely different part of the ship from the deckhands—*two* entirely different parts of the ship.

Emilia doubted she would've even seen Pelt as often as she did, if he weren't the boatswain—and a close friend of Judith's.

The closest Emilia might've come to this deckhand was during mealtimes. Perhaps she'd served him once or twice, or he could've been part of Pelt's gambling crowd.

But Emilia wouldn't recognize him after such a brief encounter. With a defeated shrug, she said, "How?"

Judith opened her mouth to answer, but Pelt interrupted, "Can't we find out if he even *needs* her help, before we tell her why she shouldn't help him?"

Judith scowled at him. "Whose side are you on, anyway?"

"You know I have no love for the man," Pelt assured her. "I just don't want to be short a deckhand."

Judith scoffed in disgust, "Don't be such a selfish prick."

Pelt's mouth fell open. "Me?"

Emilia's gaze bounced between the two pirates, as they once again began to bicker. Judith had once told Emilia that Pelt was like a brother—that she wanted to strangle.

Often.

Considering Judith's white-knuckled grip on the ladle, Emilia figured it was safe to assume Judith was mere moments away from strangling him now.

"Can someone just tell me why I'd recognize him?"

Judith silenced the boatswain by pointing her ladle at his head— like she might've done with her pistol, if it weren't against the Code. Her bright blue eyes shifted toward Emilia. "After the trial, the captain asked me to keep an eye on the people who voted against you."

Emilia blinked. "She did what?"

"Oh, don't act like *that's* extreme," Judith said. "She wanted to kill them all, but I talked her down from that, didn't I?"

Emilia's eyes widened.

Maria wanted to murder her own sailors?

Oh. Actually, that wasn't surprising, after all.

"So, this Cornelius," Emilia said hesitantly. "He thinks I endangered the crew."

With a disgusted roll of her eyes, Judith said, "Oh, I wouldn't even give him that. The trial could've been about anything, and he still would've voted against you—because you're a witch, and you know what he is?" Judith slapped the wooden ladle against the table. "He's a fucking bigot!"

Pelt lifted his eyebrows—but didn't argue.

Emilia couldn't help but smile at Judith's outburst.

Judith had once believed the same of witches as any other Illopian, but when she'd realized Emilia was one, when she'd realized she'd been taught wrong, she hadn't just changed her own mindset.

She'd come out ready to fight anyone who didn't.

And Emilia adored her for that.

"Let him die," Judith declared. "If you'd been executed, like he wanted, you wouldn't be here to help him, anyway."

"Gods, Judith. I don't even know if he's injured yet," Pelt sighed, "much less *dying*."

"How do you not know?" Emilia asked.

"Isn't it obvious?" Judith grumbled. "The little imbecile doesn't want to be touched by a witch, so he's hiding his injury."

Emilia froze. Her stomach dropped, and her head spun.

She didn't know this deckhand. He certainly didn't know *her*. Yet, he hated her so much he'd rather suffer than let her touch him?

Touch?

Somehow, that was harder to accept than the fact that he'd wanted her dead.

Probably because Emilia had been accepting people wanting her dead her entire life.

"Is that true?" she asked Pelt.

Something in Pelt's expression faltered, before he said, "I think so."

Emilia sank into the nearest chair, gripping her knees.

Of course, people still hated her. She'd known that.

Oh, they thought they could hide it, but it was always there. The venom lurked in their tone, their gaze, in the very air around them…

Emilia always knew, but…*goddess*, it was exhausting sometimes.

"Let him die." Judith dumped a bowl of chopped cabbage into the pot. "The captain will support you. She wanted to slit his throat, anyway."

"I can't do that," Emilia sighed. "I've never refused to treat anyone, and I'm not going to start now."

Judith turned to stare at her. "Em, you're a pirate now! You don't have to take the high road!"

"It's not the high road," Emilia said. "It's my job."

Pelt strode forward. He pressed a hand against the table behind her and looked down at her. He smelled of sweat—even from there. "Just help me figure out if he's actually injured or not. If he is—and you *don't* want to treat him—I'll pretend I knew nothing."

"You better," Judith muttered under her breath.

Emilia looked up at the boatswain. She already knew she'd find a way to treat the guy, regardless, but Pelt's offer made her smile. "You'd do that?"

Pelt shrugged his lean shoulders. "As I said, I have no love for the man." He shot an amused look at Judith. "Besides, it's easier to hide *that* than the captain slitting his throat or Judith bludgeoning him to death with cooking equipment."

Judith pointed her wooden ladle at him. "And don't think you wouldn't be helping me dispose of the body, if I did."

With a shrug, Pelt said, "I helped you with Jonas, didn't I?"

Emilia's eyes widened. "Jonas? You—you knew?"

But Jonas and Pelt had been friends, hadn't they?

Pelt flashed a mouthful of gold teeth at her. "You thought Judith carried him to the bilge by *herself*?"

"Oh, like you were much help!" Judith complained. "You dropped him every time you saw a rat!"

Pelt shuddered at the memory. "Who wouldn't?"

Emilia glanced back and forth between them, her jaw slack. She knew they'd only been following their captain's orders, but still, the person Jonas had committed the crime against—the crime Maria covered to protect Emilia's secret—*was* Emilia.

Maria had killed him *because* of Emilia.

She looked up at Pelt. "When you told everyone I got drunk with the captain that night—"

"The captain carried you to her quarters," Pelt explained, "and left a trail of blood behind her."

So, he'd known Emilia was injured.

Pelt hadn't just spread Maria's lie because he liked to gossip— though he *did* like to gossip. He'd spread the lie because his captain needed him to. Pelt was loyal to Maria, whether Maria realized it or not.

"Tell me why you think he's injured," Emilia said.

Pelt pushed away from the table. "It'll take a while, and I have some work to do." He looked back at her. "Do you mind continuing this above deck?"

"Not at all." Emilia climbed to her feet and glanced at Judith. "Are you sure you won't need me?"

"Go, go, go." Judith waved her hand at Emilia. "Go be a terrible pirate."

Emilia suppressed a smile. When Judith was in *this* mood, it was easy to see how she and Maria had grown so close.

Emilia followed the boatswain toward the steps. "Where are we going, anyway?"

"Well, I was thinking…" He turned toward her. "How do you feel about learning the ropes?"

"The ropes?" Emilia repeated.

"Knots, surgeon," Pelt said. "I'll teach you to tie a few knots, if you want to learn."

"I *always* want to learn," Emilia assured him.

His brows twisted at that. "Surgeons are a *strange* breed."

After listening to all of the unusual things Pelt had noticed about Cornelius throughout the last week or so, Emilia agreed the deckhand might've been hiding an ankle injury, but she couldn't say for sure without looking at him—especially considering his age.

Since Pelt refused to let her see the deckhand before he was sure, Emilia offered the boatswain a few more tips on what to look for.

"And if you notice a sort of…stench—"

"It's infection," Pelt assumed. He traced that horrid scar on his cheek with his forefinger. "I remember."

Emilia offered him a sympathetic smile.

Pelt pointed at the rope. "Try the knot again."

Emilia took the rope in both hands and formed her loop. She was just about to start the second step, when a familiar shadow fell over them.

"Why is my surgeon playing with rope?"

Pelt jumped at the sound of Maria's voice. He cast a wide-eyed look over his shoulder, where the pirate captain loomed. "Captain," he said with an exaggerated smile. "How long have you been there?"

Maria lifted a scarred eyebrow.

Emilia thought the boatswain's reaction was a bit strange, but she assumed it had more to do with Cornelius than anything they were doing now. He probably feared Maria would hear about Cornelius and decide to slit his throat, after all.

"I'm tying knots," Emilia told her.

Maria kept her gaze on Pelt. "Is that so?"

Pelt cringed away from his captain's glare—clearly less immune to these things than Judith.

Emilia formed a second loop, before trying to fold them. "I did well enough on the first three, but I can't seem to get the hang of this one."

"I wonder why," Maria growled at the boatswain.

Pelt scratched the back of his head, his thin, brown ponytail wiggling with the movement.

"Probably because I haven't had ten years to learn these things," Emilia muttered, "like the rest of you."

Maria shoved Pelt forward. "Tell her."

At *that*, Emilia turned to look at them, rope still in hand. Her eyebrows rose at the sight of Pelt's guilty smile. "Tell me what?"

Though Maria wasn't actually any taller than Pelt, she seemed to tower over him, when he shrank away from her like that. She'd removed her tricorn, too—as she often did during the hottest hours of the day—so she didn't even have *it* to blame.

"You're, erm," Pelt said with a wince, "not going to be able to tie that…particular knot."

Emilia frowned. "But you said I almost had it."

"Did he, now?" Maria said.

He carefully avoided Maria's gaze. "It was kind of a…prank?"

Was that an Illopian word?

Emilia didn't think she'd heard it before. "A what?"

Pelt looked to Maria for assistance. "A joke?"

Well, Emilia definitely knew that one. "The knot is a joke?"

"He's messing with you, Em," Maria told her. "He's always doing it to our new sailors, and he wastes *hours* of everyone's day in order to do it."

"Two hours, at most," Pelt said defensively.

Maria scowled at him. "I don't *have* two hours, and neither do you."

"Sure, I do!" Pelt said, but when Maria's glare turned murderous, he quickly took it back. "I mean, no, I don't."

"Messing with me?" Emilia repeated. She glanced down at her partially tied rope. "This…*isn't* the fourth knot, then?"

Maria wrinkled her nose at the sight of the thing. "Darling, that isn't a knot at all."

Emilia scowled at her—and then at Pelt, when *he* burst into laughter.

He pointed a calloused finger at her. "You held a tiny knife to my throat. You deserved it."

"Tool," Maria corrected, lips twitching. "Not a knife."

Well, technically, it was a tool, *called* a surgical knife, but Emilia wasn't about to point that out.

Emilia held out the rope. "The first three knots were real, though, right?"

"Yes, love," Maria assured her. "They were real."

Pelt leaned toward Maria. "It wouldn't have been half as hilarious, if she hadn't been so eager to learn!"

To Emilia's dismay, the impatience that had driven Maria to intervene was apparently not enough to stop her from laughing. "I know."

Emilia glared at them. "Oh, you are *both* assholes!"

Pursing her lips to stifle her laughter, Maria held out a scarred hand. "Would you like to learn a *real* fourth knot?"

"No," Emilia lied. When Maria gave her a skeptical look, Emilia said, "How many times do I have to tell you, Captain? I won't fall for the same trick twice."

Maria's smile widened. "If it were a trick, I couldn't demonstrate. Did Pelt demonstrate the last one?"

Emilia blinked, as she realized, "No." She glanced at Pelt, who merely grinned. "He *described* the steps."

"Always ask for a demonstration," Maria said. She flicked her gaze toward her outstretched hand.

Really?

That was it?

Maria thought she could demand something from Emilia with a single look?

Emilia glanced down at the rope in her hand, and then, with a roll of her eyes, she placed it in Maria's scarred hand. The infuriating smirk Maria flashed in response made Emilia want to snatch the rope back.

Maria stepped toward Emilia, and her alluring scent tickled Emilia's senses. She turned so Emilia could watch, her warm upper arm brushing Emilia's. "Watch and learn, surgeon."

Emilia tried to glare at her—but failed to do much more than ogle.

Goddess, how did she manage to look even better now than she had that morning?

Must've been the apples.

Where was she hiding them, anyway?

Maria looped the rope around her tattooed fingers, before leaning toward Emilia. Her warm lips brushed Emilia's ear. "If you wanted to play with rope this badly, you could've told me."

Emilia's eyes widened.

She hadn't meant…

Had she?

Emilia looked up—just in time to see Maria's full lips curve into a shamelessly wicked grin.

Oh, for Aletha's sake.

"You know *I'm* always ready to play."

Emilia scowled at her incorrigible captain. "Would you stop?"

Maria blinked innocently. "Stop what?"

Emilia rolled her eyes. She leaned forward to glance at Pelt, but the boatswain was squinting up at the sails, oblivious to his captain's antics.

"Eyes on me, surgeon," Maria said.

Emilia shot a peeved look at the pirate captain, before fixing her gaze on the rope in her hands.

Or…trying to, anyway.

Maria pulled swiftly at the tail of the rope, and with her thin sleeves pushed up around her arms, it was all too easy for Emilia to watch the flex of muscle in Maria's tattooed forearms. "Got it?"

Emilia looked up, eyes wide. "Mmm-hmm."

Maria returned her attention to the knot. The heat had left a glossy sheen of sweat on her brown skin, and a single drop traced a path down her bicep.

"And that?"

Emilia blinked.

Oh, no. What had she missed now?

"Mmm-hmm," Emilia lied.

Pelt might've played a trick on her, but at least Emilia could concentrate when *he* was teaching her.

Maria held out the rope. "Would you like to try it?"

"Oh, I don't think that'd be a good idea," Emilia muttered.

Maria chuckled, as if she knew exactly why Emilia had refused, but…she didn't, did she?

Maria tossed the rope aside, before turning toward Pelt. "Get back to work, boatswain."

"Aye, aye, Captain." Before Pelt walked away, however, he said, "Thanks for the free entertainment, Em!"

Emilia glared at the back of his head.

Maria stepped past Emilia and leaned against the rail. She opened a small, cloth pouch that hung next to her sword and removed a shiny, red apple.

She wiped it against her leather doublet before lifting the fruit to her lips. The *crunch* that followed brought Emilia's attention back to the captain.

With an incredulous shake of her head, Emilia said, "You better not let Judith catch you with that."

Eyes widening slightly, Maria glanced from one side of the deck to the other. "Is she up here?"

Emilia considered lying, just to see if Maria would throw the apple into the sea to save herself, but she couldn't bring herself to spoil Maria's snack. Even if she *had* probably eaten ten of them already. "No."

Maria relaxed her leather-clad shoulders and took another bite of the fruit.

"Where's the rest of the crate?" Emilia asked.

"Like I'd tell you," Maria said with a mouthful of apple. "You can't even lie about Judith. I saw you thinking about it."

She did *not*.

"I lied to you about being a witch, didn't I?" Emilia reminded her.

A quick laugh escaped Maria's lips, and a tiny drop of juice came with it, sliding along the corner of Maria's plump, bottom lip. She ran a tattooed thumb beneath her mouth, wiping it away.

"You didn't lie," Maria argued. "You did everything you could to *avoid* lying."

"I lied by omission," Emilia told her. "Successfully."

Until Jonas had ruined it.

When Emilia caught herself watching every subtle curve and twitch of Maria's lips, as she chewed the apple, she realized she needed to get herself *away* from Maria.

At least, until she regained some semblance of concentration.

"Well, if you don't need me for anything," Emilia said, "I should get back to the galley."

Just as Emilia turned away, however, Maria said, "I *do* need you for something."

Emilia spun toward her. "Oh?"

Maria hadn't moved, but her gaze had, roaming Emilia's curves with a kind of feral hunger that made Emilia wonder if Maria had mistaken *her* for the apple. "Mmm-hmm."

Mmm-hmm? Was she mocking Emilia, now? She *had* noticed Emilia getting distracted during her demonstration, hadn't she?

The smirk that pulled at one side of Maria's mouth confirmed it.

"Captain," Emilia said irritably, "do you actually need me or not?"

Maria bit into her apple. "I just said I did, didn't I?"

Emilia narrowed her eyes suspiciously. "All right." She crossed her arms. "What do you need, then?"

Warmth simmered in Maria's large, brown eyes, and as she chewed her fruit, those eyes trailed down Emilia's body and back up again, as if Maria were trying to choose a specific *part* of Emilia's body.

To chop off or stare at, Emilia wasn't sure.

Maria's gaze returned to Emilia's face, and she swallowed. "Do you really want to know?"

Emilia was about ready to throw something at her.

Too bad *Emilia* didn't have pockets full of apples.

"I wouldn't have asked, if I didn't."

Maria pushed away from the wooden rail and stepped toward Emilia. With the apple still in hand, Maria pressed her tattooed knuckles beneath Emilia's chin.

Maria tilted her head, brown curls brushing her shoulder, as she examined one side of Emilia's face and then the other. "You healed it?"

Emilia tried to nod, before remembering that Maria's hand was beneath her chin. "Yes, Captain."

Maria's gaze flicked upward, and her lips curved.

What in the name of the goddess was this devious pirate up to?

"Was *that* what you needed?" Emilia asked.

"No." Maria removed her hand from Emilia's jaw and bit into the apple.

Emilia threw out her arms in frustration. "Do I have to solve a riddle to get a damn answer?"

Maria snorted at that.

She circled Emilia, the deck creaking beneath her worn, leather boots. The creaking stopped, and Emilia straightened, as the warmth of Maria's body pressed against her back.

Maria's breath fell against the back of Emilia's neck first, then the shell of her ear. "What I *need*, my love," she murmured, "is to sit on your face."

Emilia jerked forward, as heat shot straight to her clit, like a lightning bolt.

There was no slow spread to the desire today.

Nope. It was quick and hot and catastrophic.

Emilia didn't even realize her knees *had* buckled, until Maria's arm slid around her waist to catch her.

Maria buried her face in Emilia's short, black hair and chuckled. "You did *say* you wanted to know, didn't you?"

Emilia was going to stab her!

After she drowned beneath Maria's strong thighs, preferably.

No. No, no, no.

Don't think that!

Stop thinking that!

Cloth rustled behind Emilia, as Maria pocketed the apple to free her hands.

"That isn't a need, Captain," Emilia told her. "It's a want!"

Maria flattened her palm against Emilia's stomach, pressing Emilia's ass harder against her. "I disagree."

With Maria pressed so close to her, heat consumed Emilia, melting every muscle and nerve beneath her waist. A small part of her wanted nothing more than to close her eyes and let her head fall back against Maria's shoulder—to surrender *everything* to her.

The other part of her had a vague recollection of where she was. "Also," Emilia gasped, "you can't say things like that. Here!"

Maria's smug chuckle filled Emilia's ear, annoying her as much as it turned her on.

Maria's fingers drifted toward Emilia's scabbard, before curling beneath it. She jerked the belt toward herself, pulling Emilia against her leather-clad waist.

With another soft gasp, Emilia glanced around to ensure no one had seen them. Maria knew her ship better than anyone, of course, and would've known where they were visible and where they weren't.

But again, Maria was *also* exceedingly arrogant.

With a teasing smile that Emilia felt against her ear, Maria whispered, "I'm the captain of this ship. I can do whatever the fuck I want."

Well, that wasn't even true.

Someone could call a vote or start a mutiny.

Not that Emilia would call a vote over…this.

"Em?" Maria's breath grew ragged in Emilia's ear. "Do you want to come to my quarters or not?"

So, Maria's playful mood wasn't *totally* without seriousness, then.

Emilia glanced toward the setting sun—now a deep red on the horizon. "Now?"

"Well, you can't leave me like this for long." Maria's voice sounded almost like a whine. "Oh, you can, of course, but please, don't."

Emilia's eyebrows rose. She'd thought *she* was the one losing her battle with self-control, but apparently, it went both ways. "There's so much of the day left."

They'd never spent an entire night together before.

"Didn't I say you'd be mine as soon as I was done with my work?" Maria bit the lobe of Emilia's ear, and Emilia barely held back a moan. "Say no, if you want, but it seems to *me* like you want to say yes."

Emilia blushed at how easily Maria read every reaction of her body. "What about Judith? Dinner?"

"Oh, don't worry, love," Maria teased. "I'll make sure you have plenty to eat."

Emilia didn't even *want* to know if Maria meant that to be an innuendo.

With a soft laugh, Maria admitted, "I sent someone else to help her. If you want to spend the evening with me, you're free to do so."

Then…Maria hadn't just cleared her own schedule for the rest of the night. She'd cleared Emilia's, too.

"Okay," Emilia mumbled.

Maria snorted. "Don't just say 'okay.' This is your choice. Tell me you want this, or tell me you don't."

"I want this," Emilia said.

She'd never wanted anything more.

Maria released her. "Let's go, then."

Emilia exhaled shakily and *prayed* she remembered how to walk.

CHAPTER 18

Stay with Me

Maria didn't even bother to close the door to the captain's quarters, before shoving Emilia against it.

The heavy, wooden door slammed closed beneath their combined weight, and the collision pushed the air from Emilia's lungs.

Maria's warmth surrounded Emilia, as she closed her hands around Emilia's face and pressed her mouth against Emilia's.

Maria kissed Emilia as if she were starved for the taste of her, her tongue pressing and sliding, her mouth open and hungry. She kissed as if she'd counted every moment since that morning, every moment until she could do *this*.

She tasted of ferocity and of…well, apple—her tongue still sticky and sweet from all the fruit she'd eaten.

Emilia traced her fingers along Maria's arms, over her scarred wrists—which felt so similar to Emilia's—down her tattooed forearms, along the bends of her elbows, up to the bunched up fabric around her biceps.

Maria pressed closer, her muscles flattening against Emilia, their weapons clanging softly between them.

Maria tilted Emilia's head back against the door and trailed her mouth lower, lips hot and wet against Emilia's skin.

She lingered for a moment at the soft curve of Emilia's jaw, and the unexpected gentleness of the kiss Maria placed there—exactly where those strange claws had pierced Emilia's skin—contrasted so sharply with her usual aggression that it took Emilia's breath.

That kiss had been deliberate.

Thoughtful.

Maria's thumb slid over Emilia's cheek, and her gorgeous, brown eyes shifted to meet Emilia's. "How many scars would you have, if it weren't for magic?"

Emilia swallowed uneasily. The truth was…she probably wouldn't have much skin *left*, if it weren't for magic. She'd been burned alive more times than she could count. But all Emilia said was, "A lot."

Maria's lips didn't part. Her eyes didn't widen. She'd likely come to that conclusion long ago.

But her hands softened around Emilia's face, and she moved to lean her head against Emilia's. A few stray curls had escaped from the top of Maria's headscarf, and they tickled Emilia's skin in a way that had become *so* pleasantly familiar.

"You know I'll be whatever you need, love," Maria whispered. She ran her thumbs beneath Emilia's cheekbones. "Do you need me gentle?"

The emotion expanded inside Emilia's throat, leaving her barely able to breathe, much less voice all of the thoughts pouring through her head.

You've always been perfect.

Every way you've ever touched me has been perfect.

I want what you want, and you already said what you want.

A heady warmth unfurled inside of Emilia at the mere memory of what Maria had said she wanted.

Needed.

Emilia shook her head slowly, and the corners of Maria's full lips curved into a deep smile.

Maria slid one hand into Emilia's hair, her fingers entangling with the silky, black strands. "So," she said, breath washing over Emilia's lips, "if I said I wanted to tie you up and fuck your face while you're helpless beneath me—" Maria lifted her eyebrows, when Emilia gasped. "—you *wouldn't* be against that?"

Nope.

Definitely *not* against it.

Heat poured through Emilia's body, like lava, melting every muscle and nerve ending in its path. Without meaning to, Emilia had arched against Maria, and Maria had clearly felt it, her gaze drifting downward.

How did she just…*say* things like that?

Was it possible to *talk* someone to an orgasm?

Because if it was, Maria would find a way to do it.

Maria dropped one hand with a curious sort of amusement and curled her fingers around Emilia's hip, just above the scabbard.

Her gaze slid back to Emilia's face, and her smile cracked open, teeth shining in the fading light.

Considering the fire that burned beneath Emilia's skin, at the moment, Emilia had no doubt Maria had seen the flush of her cheeks and neck, too.

Emilia hadn't managed to say a word, since Maria's question— if you could *call* it that. But Maria must've read the answer easily enough in the reaction of her body—because she murmured, "Good to know."

Maria tugged Emilia's hair back, exposing her throat and ripping another soft gasp from Emilia's lips. Then, Maria dropped her head to Emilia's neck.

She kissed the place between Emilia's ear and her throat, and Emilia's gasp turned to a moan.

Maria trailed her lips lower. She pressed one kiss after another against Emilia's throat, each one less gentle than the last.

When she reached the deep curve of Emilia's neck, where even the warmth of her breath danced along Emilia's nerves like electricity, Maria twisted Emilia's hair and closed her teeth around the skin.

The bite sent a pang of pleasure ricocheting through Emilia's body, until it found its destination between her legs. Emilia's muscles clenched, and her head hit the door behind her.

She gasped out, "Maria. *Oh.*"

Maria's lips curved against Emilia's skin—forming a smile that *felt* as alluring as it must've looked. "Yes," she whispered, breath caressing Emilia's skin. "Say my name. Please, just—"

She bit down again, and Emilia gave her what she wanted.

Maria soothed the bite with her tongue, lapping gently at the skin. Only when Emilia relaxed against her, did she close her mouth again and suck.

Emilia reached back for something to hold on to and found only the cool, iron handle of Maria's door.

The hand around Emilia's hip slid forward. Maria fumbled with the buckle of Emilia's scabbard, while keeping up her relentless assault on Emilia's neck.

Maria was definitely leaving marks tonight. Emilia just hoped she remembered to heal them in the morning.

Maria leaned back on the heels of her boots and removed Emilia's scabbard. She gently dropped the weapon belt to the floor, and the sheathed blade landed with a soft *thud.*

She pressed a kiss just beneath Emilia's jaw, as she tugged the thin, black shirt from Emilia's trousers.

Maria was less careful with the shirt than she'd been with the weapon, tugging it over Emilia's head and tossing it aside, as if it hadn't had a right to exist in the first place.

Maria's dark gaze fell to Emilia's exposed breasts, and her lips parted. "Fuck," she said in an exhale.

You'd think she'd never seen them before.

After seeing women in corsets—with breasts like Jane's—how did Maria react like *this* to Emilia's?

Maria curled her hand beneath Emilia's right breast, letting its heavy weight overfill her palm.

She took the other breast into her hand, as well, squeezing, as Emilia tried not to moan at her touch.

"Do you have any idea how perfect..." Maria trailed off. Her gaze never strayed from Emilia's breasts, as she muttered, "No, of course you don't."

Was she talking to Emilia or herself?

Maria's head fell to Emilia's breasts, as if it were inevitable, as if she simply couldn't help herself.

Emilia sucked in a sharp breath, as Maria lavished wet, opened-mouthed kisses along the deep curves of her breasts.

Even as she panted for breath, even as she squeezed the tarnished door handle, Emilia couldn't help but admire the beautiful, brown curls peeking out from beneath Maria's blue headscarf.

She reached carefully toward the little blue knot at the nape of Maria's neck, and Maria tilted her head, offering her easier access.

Emilia worked her thumb into the knot and pulled the damp, blue headscarf free. Maria's curls spilled around her face.

The loose, brown curls softened Maria's scarred face, revealing a side of her she usually kept hidden from the world. Maria was always gorgeous, always beautiful, of course, but there was something particularly lovely about what lay beneath her façade.

Maria shook her head slowly, her smile deepening. "You can't keep doing this to me."

Emilia blinked out of her thoughts. "Me? I haven't done anything," she complained. "Yet."

"Yet," Maria said with a snort. She leaned toward Emilia, her fingers sliding along Emilia's hips. "If you even knew the way you looked at me sometimes…" Maria exhaled shakily.

Emilia blushed. She hadn't meant to look at Maria in any certain way, but really, how could she not?

"Right." Maria unfastened Emilia's trousers with far too much nonchalance. "Get those off, and get on my bed. I need to undress."

Emilia gave her a peeved look, but when Maria stepped away and the open air hit Emilia's bare breasts, she instinctually crossed her arms over them.

Maria stopped and glanced back at Emilia, giving her a look that, if Emilia hadn't known better, she would've called a…*pout.*

Hiding any amusement she might've felt at the thought of Captain Maria Welles *pouting,* Emilia stepped away from the door.

She watched as Maria methodically loosened each thong of her doublet, and she teased, "We're actually using a bed for once?"

Maria's lips curved. "It serves the purpose well enough." She removed the double-belted scabbard first, then the doublet, draping both over the back of her chair. "I know it's small, but only one of us needs to lie down, right?"

Okay, *that* image had done nothing to cool Emilia's skin.

At this rate, she'd pass out before she made it to the bed.

Maria quirked a brow in amusement. "Unless you'd prefer the floor? It'll be less comfortable for you, but…well, my seat's the same."

Every inch of Emilia's skin burned. She pointed a trembling finger at Maria. "Stop talking. No more talking."

Maria tilted her head back and laughed, and Emilia vacillated between annoyance for the laughter and adoration for the sensual curve of Maria's throat.

Emilia kicked off her black shoes, and Maria turned to face the stern windows. She unfastened her leather trousers and pulled the thin, billowing shirt free.

Emilia was just about to remove her own trousers, when Maria tugged the white shirt over her head.

Emilia stilled at the sight of Maria's bare back—with its toned muscles and slight curves.

She'd always thought a woman's back was a particularly attractive part of the body—not that there were many parts of a woman Emilia *didn't* find attractive.

But the slopes of her shoulders, the arch of her back—there was something so enticing about it.

Perhaps because it was so nice to touch?

To trace with her fingers?

With her tongue.

Even when she was young and still coming to terms with her sexuality, she'd noticed it. The sirens hadn't worn clothes, after all, since they only hindered their ability to swim.

What a shock *that* had been for Emilia.

Nerissa's back, of course, had looked nothing like Maria's—with her scattering of blue, iridescent scale and her more-than-ample curves.

Catherine, however, had shared many qualities with Maria. Both of them tall, both of them muscular.

Aside from the deep contrast in their skin tones, the only major difference between Catherine's back and Maria's was that Catherine hadn't had a single scar.

She'd likely never broken a rule in her life—certainly not since she'd joined the Royal Navy.

Maria, on the other hand, had more scars than Emilia could count. No matter how many times Emilia saw that asymmetrical web of raised lines along Maria's back, it never ceased to take her breath.

Many of the scars varied in shade. Some were dark; others were pale. A few were closer to amaranth, similar in shade to the deep scar that cut across Maria's eye.

Regardless of shade, though, they all contrasted enough with the brown tone of Maria's skin that Emilia could see them across the captain's quarters—even in the fading sunlight that shone through her windows.

Emilia realized, in that moment, that when Maria asked how many scars Emilia would've had, what she'd really been asking was, *As many as me?"*

Maria finished removing her boots, which she'd apparently unlaced while Emilia was lost in thought, and she tossed them aside.

Maria cast an amused glance over her shoulder, when she noticed Emilia hadn't moved. "Surgeon?"

"Hmm?" Emilia blinked to clear her mind. "Oh."

Maria snorted. "Simple task, Em. On the bed."

Emilia glared at the pirate captain for that remark. "It's not my fault you're undressing in front of me!"

"I'm not in front of you," Maria said. "I turned around."

Maria dropped her trousers.

Emilia's eyes widened. "That's still— You're still—" she stammered. "Oh, for Aletha's sake!"

Maria folded forward as she laughed, further exposing the curves of her toned ass to Emilia's gaze.

Emilia tried not to stare. Definitely didn't succeed, though. "I'd probably be better off with you facing me. It's not like your butt's any less distracting than your—*oh, goddess.*"

Maria had, in fact, turned to face Emilia, and Emilia was *not* better off. Maria grinned. "You were saying?"

Maria hadn't removed the strip of linen around her breasts yet —a small mercy, considering Emilia's habit of staring at them—but every *other* inch of Maria's golden-brown skin was bare to Emilia's gaze.

Well, except for the place that was hidden by the small triangle of brown curls between her thighs.

Emilia forced herself to look away—before she forgot the plan and sank to her knees here and now.

"Bed, love," Maria said with an amused smile. "Unless you've changed your mind?"

"No," Emilia said—a bit too quickly. "I have not."

Before Maria could find another reason to laugh at her, Emilia strolled toward the bed. She sat down on the edge of the mattress, which promptly sank beneath her.

Emilia forgot, sometimes, that Maria slept on a cloud every night—while Emilia slept on a rock.

She slid her trousers down to her ankles and bent to remove them, and Maria strode toward her table.

The pirate captain dipped her hand into the center of a small spool of rope on her table, and Emilia instantly flushed.

Maria glanced back at Emilia, before wrapping the rope around her fingers. "Do you still want…" Rather than finish the question, she simply lifted the rope.

Mouth dry, Emilia only nodded.

Maria's eyes darkened. "Then, lie down."

With a few, long strides, Maria closed the space between herself and Emilia, and she climbed onto the bed, sitting upright on her knees.

Emilia shuffled backward on the bed, until her hands brushed the pillow, and she stared up at Maria, her breath shallow.

Maria glanced from Emilia to the pillow and back again. Lifting a scarred eyebrow, she teased, "You love to test my patience, don't you?"

Emilia rolled her eyes. "Everything tests your patience when you have none."

Maria laughed at that. She crawled forward and swung her thigh over Emilia's hips, straddling her.

Emilia's breath caught in her throat, and Maria leaned forward to kiss her.

Slowly.

Indulgently.

When Maria pulled back, Emilia let her gaze fall to Maria's still-wrapped chest.

Holding herself up with one arm, Emilia pointed at the strip of linen. "May I?"

An affectionate smile pulled at the corners of Maria's lips. "Whatever you want, love." With a tattooed finger, she lifted Emilia's chin. "Always."

Emilia's chest fluttered. She untied the strip of linen and let it fall to the bed, and with Maria raised up on her knees, Emilia found her face mere inches away from Maria's small, beautiful breasts.

Desperate yearning spilled from her in a sigh, and Emilia practically fell against them. She kissed the place between Maria's breasts, and Maria gasped.

Emilia kissed her way along the slight curve of Maria's breast, until she reached Maria's dark brown nipple. Emilia closed her mouth around it, feeling it harden against her tongue.

Maria swayed forward, folding her free arm around Emilia's head before she could fall. She buried her face in Emilia's thick, black hair, groaning as Emilia licked and sucked at her nipple.

A drop of Maria's arousal fell against Emilia's bare stomach, and Emilia moaned against her breast.

Emilia shifted her attention to the other breast, and Maria released another gasp, as Emilia took that nipple into her mouth.

Maria let her left hand fall to Emilia's shoulder, as well, and the rope dangling from her fingers tickled Emilia's shoulder-blade.

Maria's head fell back, and she panted for breath.

As Emilia lavished her attention on Maria's perfect breasts, Maria pressed herself against Emilia's stomach, soaking Emilia's skin with a single slide of her hips.

The sticky wetness served as a much-needed reminder of the even better place Emilia wanted to put her tongue.

Maria must've had a similar thought—because with a single shove against Emilia's shoulder, she pushed Emilia onto her back. "I need you now, Em. *Please.*"

Emilia nodded eagerly.

Maria unspooled the rope. "I'm going to tie your wrists now. If you get uncomfortable, at any point, you need only to tell me."

Throat tight with desire, Emilia forced out a breathless, "I will."

"Good." Maria braced her knees on either side of Emilia's chest. She draped the rope over the pillow, next to Emilia's head, and took each of Emilia's wrists into her hands. "We'll need these," Maria said, lifting Emilia's arms above her head, "here."

When Maria's wet core slid over Emilia's breasts, Emilia squeezed her eyes shut and moaned.

Maria's voice came out strained, as she said, "It'll be where you want it soon enough."

Emilia couldn't help but moan again at that.

Perhaps Emilia *shouldn't* have agreed to the rope. Even an extra moment's wait was torture.

Maria took the rope into her hands. She looped one side around Emilia's left wrist and the other around Emilia's right wrist. Then, she took each end and slid them between the wooden slats of her headboard.

As Maria tied the rope, the backs of Emilia's fingers brushed against the wood.

Emilia opened her eyes and peered up at her wrists. "You're not just…tying them together?"

"Not this time." Maria's dark brown eyes shifted to meet Emilia's. "Is that all right?"

"Yeah," Emilia said. "Whatever you want."

Maria grinned, her eyes dancing with mischief. "Don't tell me *that*. I'll have every part of you tied up."

Emilia clenched her thighs at the thought.

Maria kept her gaze on Emilia, as she skillfully tied the knot. "I swear…I wasn't even thinking about tying you up—until I saw you with that rope."

She *had* been thinking about the rest, though?

Maria tugged gently at the knot, before leaning back and pressing herself against Emilia's breasts. Aside from the slight flutter of her eyelashes, Maria gave no indication the pressure had affected her.

Meanwhile, Emilia was about to combust.

With a nod toward Emilia's wrists, Maria said, "Not too tight, is it?"

"No," Emilia said breathlessly. "It's fine."

Maria's dark gaze bore into Emilia. "And if you change your mind," she said slowly, "you *can* free yourself? Without using too much of your magic?"

"I can," Emilia assured her.

She'd only used her healing magic once today. She had plenty left for minor magicks.

"Good," Maria murmured. She traced her tattooed thumb over Emilia's lips, before pressing into them.

Emilia opened her mouth, allowing Maria to slide her thumb inside. Maria pressed down on Emilia's tongue, urging Emilia to open her mouth wider.

Maria's eyes dilated, pools of black swallowing rings of brown, and she arched her slender hips, coating Emilia's skin in her arousal.

When Maria began to grind herself harder against the softness of Emilia's breasts, Emilia worried she'd changed her mind about where she wanted to come.

"Please," Emilia gasped. "Maria, *please*."

Maria gave a sharp inhale at the sound of her own name, and without another moment of hesitation, she crawled forward and lowered herself onto Emilia's face.

Whatever illusion of self-control Maria had maintained until then dissolved the moment her wetness soaked Emilia's skin. "Fuck," she breathed.

Emilia moaned at the way Maria's soft heat surrounded her, at the way her bittersweet arousal flooded Emilia's mouth. She licked lightly, and Maria arched forward, curling her fingers into the pillow.

"Fuck. Oh, *f-fuck*," Maria whispered.

A few more drops of arousal slid down Emilia's face, and her own clit throbbed at the sensation.

She didn't think she'd ever *felt* Maria this wet.

Could this be—was *this* what Maria pictured when she touched herself at night?

Oh, goddess. It was, wasn't it?

Maria rocked forward once. Her head fell back, and a surprisingly loud moan spilled from her lips.

Emilia slipped her tongue between Maria's wet folds, seeking out her clit but finding it just out of reach. Emilia considered taking Maria's thighs and moving her into a better position, but after a quick tug at her tied wrists, she remembered why she couldn't.

Maria let her lick for a few moments—apparently enjoying the feel of Emilia's tongue regardless—before finally leaning back.

She twisted her fingers into Emilia's thick, black hair and pushed firmly, burying Emilia's face deep between her thighs. Maria rubbed herself against Emilia's tongue, her arousal flooding Emilia's mouth.

"Do you see what you've done to me?" Maria growled out. "*Taste* what you've done to me?"

Emilia moaned against her.

Oh, goddess, it was heavenly.

How did anyone live their entire life without feeling *this*?

Maria quickened her pace. She braced one hand against the wooden headboard of her small bed, and she kept the other twisted in Emilia's hair, as she rocked hard and fast against Emilia's mouth.

Desire flooded Emilia with every small thrust, and Emilia squeezed her thighs together to ease the ache.

"Just think," Maria said, a tight strain in her voice, "if you hadn't let me tie you up, you could touch yourself, but now, you'll have to wait for me."

Emilia let out a soft whimper—though Maria's weight muffled the sound.

Maria bucked harder and faster, coating Emilia's tongue with more arousal. "Gods, Em. *Fuck.*"

Well, Maria was saying her favorite word a lot.

That was a good sign, right?

Emilia's lungs ached.

Maria had been careful to let her breathe often, but she seemed to be nearing the edge now.

Her movements grew quick and erratic, and there was a slight tremor in her muscles. Maria's fingers twisted tighter into Emilia's hair, suddenly, and the muscles in her thighs clenched around Emilia's face.

The sweet, breathless cry Maria released, at that moment, was so beautiful it made Emilia's head spin with pleasure—though that *could've* been the lack of oxygen, actually.

Emilia licked gently, relishing the sweet flood of pleasure that slid around her tongue and into her mouth.

Maria's fingers and legs trembled, as she climbed off of Emilia and collapsed on the bed next to her. There wasn't really room on the bed for two people, but Maria fit her long body between Emilia and the wall, anyway.

Maria stretched out on her back and threw her arm over her face, before adding one more breathless, *"Fuck,"* just for good measure.

An exhausted giggle bubbled up from Emilia's chest, and Maria lifted her arm, peering curiously at her. "Wow," Emilia breathed, feeling half-drunk from it all. "That was…*oh, wow.*"

The corners of Maria's lips curved upward. "Yes."

By now, Emilia had grown familiar with Maria's habit of turning cold after sex—of antagonizing and pushing Emilia away by whatever means necessary.

So, when Maria rolled onto her side to face Emilia, Emilia braced herself for anything she might say.

But all Maria said was, "You were amazing."

A compliment?

That was…unusual.

Maria brushed her tattooed knuckles along Emilia's soaked jaw —which she'd had no way to wipe clean—and Maria's smile sharpened. "And look at what I've done to you."

As if Emilia hadn't already blushed enough for one lifetime, her cheeks heated even *more*. Emilia clenched her thighs against another rush of desire. "Well, you know, I," she stammered, "I loved it."

Maria chuckled. "Of course you did." Casually—*leisurely*, really —Maria reached above Emilia's head and untied the rope. Without ever even *looking* at it, she freed Emilia's wrists. "I've never met a woman who loved eating pussy as much as you do."

Emilia rubbed the scars around her wrists, barely paying attention—until Maria said *that*. Emilia's eyes flared wide, and she looked at Maria.

With a soft laugh, Maria said, "Not an insult, love."

Well, that was a relief, but it did little to ease the flames burning beneath Emilia's skin.

Maria couldn't *know* how much Emilia enjoyed it. She was just guessing. She had to have been!

Maria scooted closer—until one of her breasts brushed Emilia's arm. "Why are you so…" she trailed off. Her smile faded, and her mouth rounded, as if she were whispering, *'Oh.'*

Emilia's brows furrowed.

Oh, what?

"Was that," Maria hesitated, "your first time?" Her eyebrows rose. "Doing that?"

Oh, no.

How had Maria guessed?

Had Emilia been bad at it?

Maria's…reaction had implied the opposite, hadn't it?

Avoiding her gaze, Emilia mumbled, "Depends on which part you mean."

That only made Maria's eyes widen more. "Surely, you did it with Catherine? At least once?"

Oh, for Aletha's sake!

Emilia didn't want to talk about Catherine!

At a time like this!

But Maria answered her own question. "No," she said under her breath. "I suppose she would've needed to portray herself as gentle and…timid—to keep you comfortable and maintain the façade…"

Emilia sat up, reaching for the coarse blanket, folded at the end of Maria's bed.

Maria didn't seem to notice. "Still, you could've done it to her. That wouldn't have messed with her façade."

"Captain!" Emilia said.

Maria looked up at her, blinking. "What?"

The nerve of her.

To feign innocence after all of that.

Flustered by the line of questioning, Emilia blurted out her first thought, "I'd…be too heavy." When she realized she'd said that out loud, she quickly devolved into stammering, "W-wouldn't I?"

"Ah, don't be silly," Maria said with a dismissive scoff. "Not for me. But if you're worried about it, there are ways…" Mischief flashed in her dark, brown eyes, and she held up a finger. "Give me a moment to recover, and I'll show you."

Oh, for the love of…

If Emilia blushed any harder, she'd melt right into the damn mattress.

"Captain," Emilia said, finally. "Why would you mention Catherine? After we— When we're still— Right now?"

Maria's brows creased, and she slid her gaze up and down Emilia's undressed form.

Feeling even more self-conscious than usual, Emilia held the blanket closer to her chest.

"Oh," Maria said, as if she'd only just noticed Emilia's discomfort. "Shit, Em. I didn't mean to—"

Emilia frowned, stunned by the apology.

Maria raised herself into a sitting position. She tilted her head, curls sliding along her bare shoulder. "Mentioning Catherine was thoughtless." She rested a hand against her—also bare—chest. "I'm thoughtless. You know that."

"Wait, so you—" Emilia's frown deepened. "You *weren't* trying to make me leave?"

Maria's eyes widened. "That's what you thought?"

"It's what you do," Emilia said with a shrug. "Not that I'm complaining! I understand that you like to be alone afterward. I *do* wish you'd just say that, instead of—"

Maria smiled, as Emilia proceeded to do just what she said she *wasn't* doing. "Em," she interrupted, "it's all right to complain. The way I was before—I knew what I said would hurt you. I was an asshole."

Emilia couldn't disagree with that. "I don't mind leaving when you need me to, though. If you need something, I'll do it. You just have to tell me."

Maria's smile softened. "I know that now." She shifted closer to Emilia and gently removed the blanket from Emilia's hand. "Do *you* want to leave?"

"Only if you want me to," Emilia said honestly.

"I don't," Maria told her. "Not yet." She offered her scarred hand to Emilia. "Come back to me. Please?"

Emilia didn't even need to think about it. She placed her hand in Maria's and let the pirate captain pull her close.

Something burst inside Emilia's chest, as Maria pulled Emilia into her lap and wrapped her muscular arms around Emilia's back.

Maria buried her face in Emilia's hair. "I'm shit at this, but I *am* trying." She kissed the top of Emilia's head. "You know that, right?"

Emilia nodded, her cheek pressed against the base of Maria's throat. "Hey, don't worry. As long as you don't murder everyone I care about, you're ahead in *my* eyes."

A surprised snort burst from Maria's lips. "Em!"

Emilia laughed. She reached out—cautiously—and wrapped her arms around Maria's lower back. The sigh Maria released into Emilia's hair sent flutters of warmth all throughout her body.

Emilia realized, in that moment, there had been a part of her that had assumed she'd never hold anyone like this again—that had assumed no one would hold *her* like this again.

Almost as if she knew what Emilia was thinking, Maria murmured, "Catherine's a part of us, whether we like it or not—whether my *crew* likes it or not." Her warm mouth touched Emilia's forehead. "But I *swear* to you: I didn't mean to make you feel vulnerable like that."

Emilia's chest ached, and her eyes burned. Her fingers trembled against Maria's back, as she fought against the urge to do something ridiculous, like cry.

"I've never wanted you to feel like that." Maria hummed thoughtfully. "Well, maybe for one, enraged moment, when I thought Catherine might've sent you…"

Emilia rolled her eyes. "I can't believe you ever thought that."

"Me either." Maria ran her fingers through Emilia's hair. "I was giving Catherine *way* too much credit."

Emilia released a soft laugh.

They were talking about Catherine, still, but it wasn't sending Emilia into a panic anymore. Emilia felt less vulnerable here, in Maria's arms, than she had in months—regardless of whom they were discussing. It seemed impossible, and yet, it was true.

"What do you say?" Maria murmured into Emilia's hair. "Was…what we just did a sufficient alternative to fighting, or do you still need me on the deck?"

Emilia blushed at the reminder. "More than sufficient." She ran her fingertips along the curve of Maria's back, hesitating as she came to the first scar.

"It's all right," Maria said. "You can touch them."

Emilia gently traced her forefinger along the scar, waiting for Maria to tense, but she never did.

Both fury and empathy poured through Emilia in waves, as she traced the path of a whip that should've *never* been allowed to touch Maria.

"You have the gentlest touch of anyone I've ever known," Maria said. "It blows my mind that you can swing a fucking sword with that hand."

Emilia let out a weak laugh. "Well, I do cut people open with it, as well. Lots of slicing involved there."

Maria pressed her mouth against Emilia's bare shoulder, scattering chills over her skin. "My dangerous, little surgeon."

Emilia rolled her eyes at Maria's teasing. "Do you really intend for us to spend the entire night in here?"

Maria moved her lips to Emilia's ear and whispered, "Why do you think I stole a whole crate of apples?"

Emilia burst into a fit of laughter, and Maria merely held her tighter throughout it all. "You would've done that, regardless!"

"That may be true," Maria said. She ran her fingers down Emilia's spine, smiling when Emilia shuddered at her touch. "I did eat half of them already."

"That's not even possible," Emilia giggled.

Maria trailed her hands lower, cupping them around the soft curves of Emilia's ass.

Clearly, she'd *recovered* from earlier.

"Judith will leave some stew at the door, after everyone's finished eating." Maria kissed Emilia's neck. "It'll have cooled by then, but...it's a small price to pay—to have you all to myself for a night."

Emilia suppressed another shudder.

It was such a small thing, really, but Emilia couldn't believe Maria had actually made this happen. She'd arranged for them to have an entire night together.

Emilia couldn't help but think of the morning after Jonas attacked her. Maria had arranged her time to spend with Emilia that night, as well, hadn't she?

More for vengeful reasons than romantic ones, but still...

Emilia pulled back to peer up at her wonderful captain. "I love you."

Maria's large, brown eyes widened at those words. She smiled and lifted a hand to touch Emilia's face. "You have to stop saying that. You'll spoil me." But then, she leaned forward and pressed her mouth to Emilia's ear. "And I adore *you*, my sweet surgeon."

Emilia couldn't remember a moment better than this one.

Later that night, after far too many hours of lovemaking and more apples than any one person should eat in a night, Maria curled up behind Emilia and slipped her arm around Emilia's waist.

Emilia's heart gave a surprised flutter at the embrace, and that flutter only quickened, when Maria buried her face in the curve of Emilia's neck.

Her quick, uneven breaths caressed the sensitive skin of Emilia's neck, and with the same caution she might use with a dragon, Emilia lifted her hand and rested it against the tattooed skin of Maria's forearm.

Maria released a pleasant sigh against Emilia's skin.

Emilia assumed Maria was simply fitting herself onto the cramped bed in the only way she could—until Maria's breathing slowed against her neck.

When Maria began to snore softly, Emilia's eyes widened.

Maria had fallen asleep.

She'd *actually* fallen asleep.

With Emilia next to her!

Emilia couldn't bear the thought of accidentally crossing one of Maria's boundaries, so she quickly tried to extract Maria's arm from around her waist.

A task that was *much* harder than it looked.

Did Maria even need to be this strong, really?

Was it actually necessary for the captain of a pirate ship to have *this* kind of grip?

When Emilia failed to actually remove Maria's arm, she tried squeezing out from underneath it, instead.

Emilia squealed, as this resulted in the lower half of her body sliding off the bed.

The only consolation to Emilia's predicament was that it had awoken the sleeping pirate behind her.

Maria stilled for a moment, before tightening her hold around Emilia's ribs and hauling her back onto the narrow bed. "What the fuck were you doing?"

Emilia hated how much she loved the sleepy lilt in Maria's voice. She hated how much it made her want to stay. "I was going back to the surgeon's cabin," she said, breathless from her struggle, "so you can sleep."

Maria nuzzled her face against Emilia's neck and grumbled drowsily, "You'd rather sleep on that rock than in my bed?"

Forget the bed. Maria's *arms* were more comfortable than Emilia's cot.

Maria's arms were more comfortable than a lot of things, actually.

"Well, no." Emilia trailed her fingers along Maria's forearm, and Maria pressed herself closer to Emilia's back. "But don't you *need* me to leave? So you can sleep?"

"I was sleeping fine," Maria complained, "until you started flopping about, like a fucking fish."

Emilia pursed her lips at that description. "But you usually need me to leave, do you not?"

Maria tugged Emilia backward, and Emilia tried not to moan, as Maria's breasts pressed against her back.

"You're softer than my blanket," Maria murmured into Emilia's neck. "You're not going anywhere."

Emilia cast a bemused look at the coarse blanket. "Well, it isn't the softest blanket in the world, is it?"

Maria groaned miserably. "Shut the fuck up, and go to sleep. No more flopping."

Emilia tried to shoot a glare over her shoulder, but she doubted Maria saw it. "I was carefully maneuvering, not flopping!"

Maria snorted at that. "Carefully, she says."

"I was so graceful!" Emilia said. "Until the end."

Maria just chuckled. "Sure, you were, surgeon."

Emilia rolled her eyes and reached for the blanket—until she remembered why she'd thrown it off in the first place. She turned in Maria's arms, ignoring Maria's growl of frustration. "You want me to stay?"

Maria opened her eyes, blinking drowsily. "Haven't I already said that?"

When she was *this* sleepy, Captain Maria Welles looked less like a dangerous pirate and more like a grumpy cat.

No wonder Rat-Slayer liked her.

With an affectionate smile, Emilia said, "Not in so many words."

Maria gave another weary blink. "You're staying with me and replacing my blanket." Her hand traced the curve of Emilia's hip, and her tired, brown eyes shifted downward. "My old one didn't have *these*."

Emilia scowled at the half-asleep pirate. "Stop comparing me to inanimate objects."

Maria probably thought she could lessen the impact of such a request with a joke, but *nothing* could lessen the impact of this.

And the last thing Emilia wanted was for Maria to regret her decision. "Are you sure you want this?"

Maria's gaze softened. "I'm sure." She lifted her hand and touched Emilia's face. "I want this. I want…you. Stay with me, love. Sleep. Next to me."

Her words were disjointed and jerky, as if they didn't quite fit together in Maria's mind, and yet, her dark gaze was steady and sure, as it held Emilia's.

Emilia forced an exhale of breath through the flood of emotion surrounding her lungs. She understood the magnitude of this gesture in the way others wouldn't have—just as Maria had understood the magnitude of the trust Emilia had offered her.

Emilia gave the only response anyone could, when faced with a gesture like that one: "I'd love to."

An adoring smile curved at the corners of Maria's lips. "Good." She dropped her arm, curling it tightly around Emilia's lower back. She gathered Emilia close and pressed her face into Emilia's hair. "Good."

Emilia slipped her fingers into Maria's brown curls and kissed the scar on Maria's throat. When Maria gave a strangely delicate moan in response, Emilia thought her heart might burst.

CHAPTER 19

Strays

A few hours later, Emilia learned one of the reasons Maria didn't like for people to sleep in her quarters.

For one, half-asleep moment, Emilia assumed the ship was just rocking over some particularly rough waves, but when Maria's twisting and turning nearly threw Emilia from the bed, her eyes snapped open.

For the second time in one night, Emilia found herself hanging halfway off the bed. She grasped the wooden bed-frame and pulled herself back onto the bed, before casting a worried look at Maria.

Her chest tightened.

Maria had kicked the blanket off of them, at some point, and she lay, naked, in the middle of the bed.

In the pale blue moonlight that streamed in through the stern windows, a layer of cold sweat glistened on Maria's brown skin, and her damp, brown curls stuck to her neck and face.

Her full, rosy-brown lips trembled, and every so often, they'd form a silent word that looked like, '*No.*'

Emilia had never seen Maria like this, and with a twist of sympathy, she realized why.

This wasn't the fear of Captain Maria Welles.

Always cloaked in anger or rage.

This was Maria.

Just...Maria.

Afraid.

Emilia leaned over her. She curled her hands around Maria's strong, sweat-slick shoulders and shook them.

"Captain?" she called out. "Captain, wake up."

Maria didn't open her eyes, but she twisted and nearly knocked Emilia off the bed a second time.

Emilia crawled closer to Maria and shook her again.

"It's a nightmare!" Emilia said. "Captain, wake up."

Of *course* Maria hadn't wanted people to see her like this. Emilia hadn't wanted anyone to see *her* nightmares, either.

A small cry spilled from Maria's lips, and something inside Emilia shattered at the sound.

Emilia cradled Maria's face in her hands, and the pirate captain relaxed beneath her touch. "Maria?"

Emilia spoke the name quietly—too quietly for anyone outside the captain's quarters to hear—and Maria stirred. She might not have reacted to Emilia calling her captain, but she'd reacted to her name.

Maria tried to turn again, but Emilia grabbed her shoulders before she could. Maria whined pitifully.

Oh, it felt so wrong.

Emilia shouldn't have seen this. Maria wouldn't have wanted her to see this!

Except...she'd asked her to stay.

Emilia rubbed Maria's shoulders, and the muscles relaxed beneath her fingers. "Don't feel like this. It's a dream. *Please.* Let me help you *not* feel this."

Maria stilled beneath Emilia's hands, but she didn't open her eyes. So, Emilia shook her one more time.

"Maria?"

Maria folded forward so suddenly that it might've thrown Emilia off the bed *again*, if Maria hadn't also grasped Emilia's wrists and snatched them forward.

Throwing her leg around Emilia, she slammed Emilia against the bed. Maria straddled her hips and pressed down on her wrists, effectively pinning Emilia beneath her.

With Maria's nude form blocking the moonlight, Emilia realized Maria probably couldn't see her face.

With as much enthusiasm as she could muster, while out of breath, Emilia said, "You're awake!"

Mission accomplished.

Sort of.

Maria froze. "Em?"

Before Emilia even confirmed her guess, Maria's muscles had already begun to relax against her.

Emilia tried not to notice Maria's warm center pressing against the lower curve of her stomach.

They really should've dressed before falling asleep.

"Yep," Emilia said with a nervous laugh. "I'm softer than your blanket. Apparently. Remember?"

"Of course I remember," Maria muttered.

She released Emilia's wrists and leaned back, her weight pressing Emilia's hips into the mattress. Maria rested one sweaty palm against her bare thigh and ran the other over her face.

The change in position caused the moonlight to cascade over Maria's face, and when Maria dropped her other hand to her thigh, Emilia saw the shame and regret that betrayed itself in Maria's expression.

The sight made Emilia's stomach whirl with concern. "If you've changed your mind, I can leave."

Maria held out her hands, gesturing toward Emilia's position beneath her. "Don't you *want* to leave?"

The exhaustion and resignation in Maria's voice tore at Emilia's heart. "Captain, you didn't hurt me."

Maria lifted a scarred eyebrow. "What if I had?"

"You didn't," Emilia insisted.

Maria tilted her head, and her dense, brown curls brushed a scar on her shoulder—a raised, amaranth line, where the whip had perhaps missed its mark.

Emilia could burn them all for what they'd done to her captain. "I have them, too, you know? Nightmares."

Maria's gaze softened. "I thought you might," she said. "It's why you prefer the discomfort of that cot over sleeping below deck with the others."

Emilia nodded.

"And," Maria added, "it's why you never sleep."

Maria *had* suspected, then.

She always had.

"I sleep…enough," Emilia lied.

Maria didn't look convinced, but she didn't argue either. With a sigh, she climbed off of Emilia, and she moved to sit at the edge of the bed. "I suppose it's just part of it. The trauma?" she said. "I always thought it might be, but…it's nice to know, I guess."

Emilia raised herself into a sitting position, gazing sadly at the slope of Maria's scarred back. She'd never heard Maria's words so stilted, so unsure. "I was afraid it was just me," she admitted, "honestly."

Maria glanced over her shoulder. "I take it they didn't discuss nightmares in any of your books?"

"My surgical books?" Emilia said with a sad laugh. "They taught me about illnesses I could cut out." Her throat constricted, and her next words came out strained. "What they did to us—I— well, I think those things make their home in a place you *can't* cut out."

Maria's expression softened, and she patted the spot next to her.

Emilia didn't hesitate. She crawled to the edge of the bed and swung her legs over the side. "Not without taking more than we meant to, anyway."

Maria watched her with a mournful smile. "Can't have the good without the bad, can we?"

"I don't think so," Emilia whispered.

Maria exhaled heavily. She braced her elbows on her thighs and buried her scarred face in her hands.

Emilia reached out—but hesitated. "Do you mind if I touch you?"

Maria's hands muffled her laughter. "Never, darling. I *never* mind when you touch me."

Every word rang with sincerity, and they opened a deep ache inside Emilia's chest.

Emilia rested her fingers against Maria's deeply-scarred shoulder-blade and leaned her head against Maria's unyielding bicep.

Maria released a pleasant sigh into her hands, and when Emilia pressed her lips against Maria's skin, every muscle in Maria's body seemed to relax.

If Emilia couldn't heal the wound in front of her, the only thing she could think to do was cut herself open, too. "In mine," Emilia said, "usually, I just relive the events as they happened, but sometimes, the dream changes a detail or two. It gets worse."

Maria lifted her face from her hands. She turned to look at Emilia, her lips parted.

Emilia kept her gaze on the bedding beneath them. "Sometimes, they win." Her voice cracked. "I'm too weak to withstand the drugs and the torture, and I tell them what they want to know." Her lungs constricted, and she gasped for breath. "I endanger my dragons."

Maria's eyes widened.

No, no, no.

Why had Emilia thought she could lay herself bare like this? She'd only been trying to help, but she couldn't handle this.

She should've known she couldn't handle this.

Tears spilled down her cheeks.

Maria moved so quickly that Emilia barely noticed she had, until she found herself enclosed in Maria's arms.

Maria pressed her face into Emilia's hair. "You didn't have to do that, Em. You didn't have to—"

But you felt vulnerable.

And you shouldn't feel that alone.

Emilia couldn't bring herself to say those words, though. It felt wrong to say them out loud.

Maria ran her fingers through the soft strands of Emilia's hair. "It was Judith in this one," she whispered. "She died during the mutiny. I was too weak to send her away. My choices—*my*…choices got her killed."

Emilia's heart shattered at the captain's confession, and she couldn't help but sob. She gripped Maria's narrow waist. "She didn't die," she said soothingly. "You're not weak, Captain. You've *never* been weak."

Maria kissed Emilia's hair. "Neither are you."

Emilia shook her head against Maria's shoulder, and a laugh of disbelief escaped her lips. "*I* am."

Maria pulled back, and she lifted her hands to grasp Emilia's face. She forced Emilia to look up—to look into Maria's lovely, brown eyes. "You're not," she argued. "*We're* strong. Say those words. If you said them about me, you can say them about yourself."

Emilia tried to shake her head, but Maria held her face still, not letting her refuse. "I can't say that."

"Yes, you can," Maria said. "You're not going to comfort me and then refuse to accept it in return."

Emilia laughed at the absurdity of that. She'd only stated the truth about Maria.

Once she included herself, it was no longer true.

"We're strong," Maria said slowly. She pressed her forehead against Emilia's and stroked her thumbs over Emilia's cheeks. "We're strong. Repeat it."

Emilia could still hear her mother's sneering voice.

Every time she'd told Emilia what she was.

'Healers are weak.'

'You're weak.'

When Emilia didn't speak, Maria hardened her voice. "That's an order, surgeon. Repeat the fucking words."

Emilia had to force every ridiculous word past her lips. "W-we…are…strong."

Oddly enough, Emilia's mother did *not* pop out of the shadows to sneer at her.

Nothing terrible happened, actually, and Maria, instead, rewarded Emilia with a kiss on the forehead and another embrace.

Goddess, Emilia had never been hugged like this.

She hadn't even known Maria *could* hug like this.

Desperate and intense—with unyielding strength.

"Now," Maria said, and Emilia could practically *hear* the smirk in her voice, "say, *'My mother's a lying bitch, and nothing she ever said about me was true.'*"

A surprised burst of laughter spilled out of Emilia's mouth, and her entire body shook in Maria's arms. "I'm not saying that."

Maria shrugged her shoulders. "Worth a try."

They laughed together for a few moments—until Emilia barely remembered the tears on her face.

Maria wound Emilia's smooth, black hair around her fingers, and she rested her chin against the top of Emilia's head. Their breasts pressed together, and their hips touched, too—only their legs angled apart.

When Maria finally spoke again, she whispered something Emilia had never expected to hear from her.

"Please, don't—don't ever leave me."

Certain she must've misheard that, Emilia pulled back to look up at Maria.

Maria loosened her grip on Emilia's shoulders and waited, her eyes wide and vulnerable, her lips open. Her small breasts rose and fell with every quick and shallow breath.

Emilia didn't even know if they were at a point where she *should* make that promise, and yet, the words spilled out easily, as if they were a simple truth. "I won't." Emilia wrapped her fingers around Maria's wrist and squeezed. "I won't leave you."

The scars on Maria's face twisted, as if she were in pain. She let her hands fall, but not before intertwining her tattooed fingers with Emilia's. "Don't make that promise, if you mean to break it."

"I don't."

Emilia looked down as the tattooed fingers within her grasp trembled.

Captain Maria Welles was trembling?

No. *Maria* was trembling.

Emilia lifted those trembling fingers to her lips and kissed them. "I'll only leave, when you ask me to."

Maria shook her head. "That won't happen."

Emilia rested her chin on their joined hands and smiled up at Maria. "You say that now, but…"

Maria didn't wait for her to finish.

She pressed upward with her fingers, lifting Emilia's face toward her own. Then, Maria dipped her head and pressed her mouth against Emilia's. A shaky breath spilled out against Emilia's lips.

'You're mine until death.'

Maria had once said that playfully.

Menacingly.

Emilia wondered, if she were to say it again, would it sound more like a plea?

Maria pushed Emilia back, and she climbed on top of her, as she deepened the kiss. Maria's skin slid against Emilia's, and her nipples—near-black in the darkness—hardened against Emilia. Yet, her hands never left Emilia's face.

When Maria pulled back, Emilia said, "You should get some more sleep."

"I am tired," Maria admitted, "but I don't know if I can."

Emilia had never been taken care of by anyone. She didn't even know what it *looked* like.

But she reached up and squeezed the warm hand against her face. "Let me get the blanket, and we'll see if we can get you back to sleep."

Maria offered her the softest smile Emilia had ever seen. "*I'll* get the blanket," she corrected. "You stay."

Maria climbed off the bed, and as Emilia adjusted the pillow, Maria knelt to grab the blanket from the floorboards. She returned to the bed, every inch of her skin bare and utterly gorgeous in the moonlight.

With her muscles and grace, Maria looked as strong and powerful as ever. Yet, tonight, Emilia had glimpsed the fragile soul beneath it all.

Maria spread out the blanket. She draped the thick fabric over Emilia's bare skin—and smiled, when Emilia blushed. She then slipped underneath the blanket and curled into Emilia's side, like a cat.

Maria slung a tattooed forearm over Emilia's stomach and hooked her legs between Emilia's. Then, she rested her head against Emilia's bare breasts.

Emilia raised her hands, as she wondered what to do with them. She remembered the way Maria had occasionally soothed her—by stroking her fingers through Emilia's hair—and she lowered her hand, until it hovered above Maria's thick, brown curls.

"Do you want me to touch your hair," Emilia asked, "the way you do mine?"

"Yes," Maria said against Emilia's breast, "please." The rush of breath caused Emilia's nipple to harden, and Maria lifted her eyebrows in amusement.

"Stop," Emilia said. "We're sleeping, remember?"

"It was an accident," Maria mumbled—right before blowing another stream of air against Emilia's breast and proving herself to be the biggest liar in Aletharia.

Emilia rolled her eyes.

She entangled her fingers in Maria's soft, brown curls and then gently slid her fingers downward.

Maria practically purred against her.

A comfortable silence settled between them, filled only by the steady creaks and groans of the ship, and it was all too easy for Emilia to lose track of time like that—with Maria's long body curled around her own, with her fingers in Maria's beautiful curls, with the scent of hibiscus and oranges surrounding her.

Just when Emilia began to wonder if Maria had fallen asleep, Maria nuzzled her face into Emilia's left breast and said, "Have I mentioned that you have the softest fucking tits?"

"Once or twice." Emilia suppressed a shudder at her touch. "What happened to going back to sleep?"

"Careful what you wish for, love," Maria warned. "If I *do* sleep like this, I might lose my ability to sleep without you."

Emilia wished the prospect of that didn't appeal to her so much. "You say that like it's a bad thing."

Maria's lips curved into a smile that Emilia felt against her skin. That smile faltered a moment later, however, as Maria traced a thin, white scar on Emilia's stomach. "Where did you get this one?"

The only scars Emilia had ever retained—besides her runes, of course—were the ones she'd received when she didn't have the magic to heal herself.

The ones from the Regolis dungeons.

"Ah, that," Emilia sighed. "An Illopian guard thought he could intimidate me with a stab wound. The fool didn't even know where my essential organs were."

Maria snorted at that. "Well, you're not the easiest person to intimidate, Emilia Drakon."

"You'd know, wouldn't you?" Emilia said.

Maria chuckled. "I would." She looked up at Emilia. "I take it no one's ever told you not to feed strays?"

"No!" Emilia tried to sit up, but Maria laughed and pushed her back down. "Why would they say that?"

"I haven't the faintest idea, my sweet surgeon." Maria turned her head to hide a smile.

Emilia eyed Maria suspiciously. "It doesn't make sense. Why would anyone want me to let an animal starve?"

"Because, as the saying goes," Maria explained, "if you give them what they want, they'll come back for more."

Emilia blinked in the moonlit darkness. "Well, yes. Animals need to eat more than once in their lifetime! I just don't understand these Illopian teachings."

Maria lifted herself onto her arms, holding herself above Emilia. "And that, my love," she teased, "is why you'll never be free of me. Me *or* Rat-Slayer."

Emilia spread out her hands tiredly. "That doesn't make sense either. Rat-Slayer isn't a stray. He lives on the ship. And I don't *feed* you."

Maria merely laughed.

That night, Emilia slept better than she had in months, and

when she *did* have a nightmare—just one—she awoke in Maria's arms, with Maria's warm, lilting voice in her ear.

"It's over, love. I have you. It's over."

Sometimes, the thing someone feared most turned out to be the best thing that could happen to them.

EMILIA AWOKE THE NEXT MORNING IN A BRIGHT, OPEN SPACE—SO entirely different from the surgeon's cabin that she didn't even need to think about where she was.

The floor-to-ceiling windows of the captain's quarters bathed the bed in warm, yellow sunlight, and Emilia resisted the urge to toss off the blanket.

She sat up, blinking wearily at her surroundings.

No ghosts, for once.

Emilia glanced at the sliver of empty space beside her—and then looked around the captain's quarters, as well. She found the usual spools of rope on the floor and the mess of maps spread over the table.

Emilia even found her own clothes—her scabbard draped over the table and a discarded pool of black that just so happened to be her shirt in the middle of the floor.

What Emilia *didn't* find were the captain's weapons.

Or her clothes.

Or her.

Emilia sighed. She'd had a whole night with Maria.

She couldn't expect a goodbye, too.

The incessant scratching at the captain's door informed Emilia that she needed to get some actual clothes on.

Quickly.

She pulled on her trousers and then hurried to retrieve the shirt Maria had thrown across the cabin.

Emilia ambled to the door, still fastening her trousers. She twisted the iron handle, and the door creaked open to reveal a large, silver-and-white cat.

Emilia knelt in front of the tabby cat. "I'm sorry." She reached out and rubbed his silver ear. "If I'd known I wasn't coming back to the surgeon's cabin last night, I would've told you. You know that."

Rat-Slayer gave a less-than-impressed meow.

Emilia rose to her feet and stepped aside, allowing the cat to slink past her.

As she pulled the heavy, wooden door closed, the silver-and-white tabby rounded the table and leapt into the wooden crate behind the captain's chair.

Emilia planted her hands on her hips. "Well, she didn't hide it very well, did she?"

Rat-Slayer turned two full rotations, before plopping his over-sized body in the large crate.

Emilia slipped on her shoes and returned to the table to retrieve her sword and enchanted dagger.

She slid the leather scabbard over her shoulder and around her waist, adjusting the buckle on her way to the door. Emilia had just reached for the door handle—*again*—when the door swung open on its own.

Emilia jumped back, startled.

"Leaving so soon?"

Captain Maria Welles filled the doorway in a way that made her seem far larger than she actually was.

The leather tricorn might've added an inch to her height, though it was more likely just her posture.

Her pride.

Her.

Once she'd regained her composure, Emilia gestured toward the sunlit windows behind her. "The sun's up, and I need to bathe before work."

Maria stepped into the captain's quarters without waiting for Emilia to move. Her leather-clad hip slid against Emilia's, as she stepped past. "You know, there are some sailors who rise *after* the sun."

Emilia shot a baffled look toward the windows. "I *did* rise after the sun."

Maria shut the door, eliminating Emilia's only means of escape. Emilia turned to give her an incredulous look.

Maria grinned and stepped closer. "You don't need to bathe," she teased. "You just need a bit of this." She uncorked a familiar glass bottle and dipped a finger into it.

Emilia smelled the hibiscus and oranges, even *before* Maria pressed a wet fingertip against Emilia's neck.

"Stop!" Emilia laughed, pushing her away. "That's not a substitute for bathing, you filthy pirate! Please, tell me you know that."

Maria's smile widened. "You'd be the first to notice, if I didn't."

"I guess I would," Emilia muttered.

Maria tried to apply another drop of oil, and Emilia pushed her away again. Unfortunately, Maria interpreted all playful fighting as encouragement.

"Stop!" Emilia couldn't help but giggle, as she swatted Maria's hand away for the third time. "You already left marks on me. I don't need to smell like you, too!"

"Wouldn't be the first time." Maria reached for her again. "At least this time doesn't require you dislocating a shoulder first."

Emilia dodged her. "Speaking of marks, I'll need you to point those out to me? So I can heal them?"

Maria's eyebrows lifted. "So, if I don't point them out, you'll stay in here all day?"

Where did Maria even *find* this kind of energy in the mornings?

Especially after they used so much last night.

"That isn't what I said," Emilia informed her. "Now, show me where they are, or you'll never leave them again."

That got Maria's attention.

"What?" Maria whined. "But you enjoyed that!"

Emilia blushed at the reminder—but didn't let it soften her resolve. "Captain! Where are they?"

Maria tilted her head, a thin braid brushing the dark leather of her doublet. Her warm, brown gaze lingered for a suspiciously long time on a specific part of Emilia's neck. "Oh, I think you're good."

Emilia gave her a skeptical look. "I know better than to believe you."

Maria just laughed. "Then, why did you ask?"

Emilia cast a quick glance around Maria's quarters. "Do you have something reflective I could use?"

"My sword," Maria said, "or the water." Her gaze flicked toward the bucket of water beside the table, and she smiled. "Oh! You could wash up in here!"

Emilia scowled at the ridiculous suggestion. "With the water you've already used?"

"I'd get you more, obviously," Maria assured her. She rested a hand against the center of her black, leather doublet. "I promise not to watch."

No one had *ever* sounded less sincere.

Emilia shook her head in disbelief. "How many lies can one pirate captain tell before noon?"

Maria leaned toward her. "So many."

Emilia couldn't even suppress her smile at *that* one. "Why are you trying to keep me in here, anyway? Don't you have work to do?"

"Eventually," Maria said dismissively. "Oh! I know what you need." She strode toward the table, her long, leather-clad legs easily swallowing the space. She froze mid-step. "Em?"

Emilia lifted her eyebrows. "Yes, Captain?"

Maria spun toward her. "Why is there a cat in my crate?"

Emilia peered around the pirate captain—to where Rat-Slayer slept comfortably in his newly-acquired crate. "I refuse to believe this is the first time you've lost a crate to a cat."

Maria narrowed her eyes at that. "Why is there a cat in my quarters at all?"

"He was scratching at the door," Emilia scoffed. "What was I supposed to do? Leave him outside?"

Maria rolled her eyes. "He has a whole ship!"

"Yes," Emilia agreed, "including the captain's quarters—and his new crate."

"*His* new—" Maria threw out her arms. She circled the crate and chair and knelt in front of her sackful of apples. She thrust her hand into the sack, grumbling as she did, "Last time I hire a cat-taming witch!"

Maria really thought she was fooling someone with her complaints, but Emilia knew better.

Rat-Slayer did, too.

Maria returned to Emilia with two shiny, red apples in hand. She offered one to Emilia. "The surgeon's cabin doesn't have these, does it?"

Emilia accepted the apple with a wry smile. "No, but the galley would—if you didn't steal them all."

Maria lifted her own apple to her lips. "It was for a good cause."

"Mm-hmm," Emilia said. "I'm not sure Judith would agree with that description."

The corners of Maria's lips pulled upward, even as she chewed her apple. "If she'd seen you last night, she would have."

Emilia's face warmed at that remark. "You're ridiculous," she muttered. "I'm supposed to be meeting Pelt on the main deck soon."

Maria's brows furrowed. "Why?"

"Long story." Emilia shrugged. "A possible injury."

"Fine. I'll let you go," Maria said, as if there'd been any other option. She stepped closer and pressed the tip of her finger to Emilia's neck, scattering chills over Emilia's skin with a single touch. "This is the only one you need to worry about. The collar of your shirt hides the other."

Emilia replaced Maria's finger with her own. The warmth of her magic enveloped her hand, before seeping into the skin of her neck.

Maria watched with such rapt fascination that you'd think Emilia was resurrecting the dead, instead of healing a slight discoloration on her skin. When Emilia finished, Maria lifted the apple to her mouth and bit into it. "You're magnificent."

Emilia's eyes widened at the much-too-strong word—that she must've misheard. "It's just healing magic."

"Your magic is beautiful and intriguing," Maria said, "like every other part of you." She swallowed a bite of fruit. "And if you ever learn to look at yourself through eyes that don't belong to your mother, you might realize that."

Emilia's chest tightened, and her throat constricted.

Maria thought Emilia was beautiful and intriguing?

She thought Emilia's *magic* was beautiful and intriguing?

Even more absurd—she thought Emilia looked at herself through her mother's eyes.

She didn't.

Did she?

Maria's warm, brown eyes never left Emilia's face. "Thank you for last night."

Emilia's pulse quickened. "You did the same for me," she said breathlessly, "after my nightmare."

Maria shook her head slowly. "Not the same."

Emilia didn't know what to say.

She didn't even know if she *could* say anything.

After a long pause, though, Emilia managed to force out a single word, "Anytime."

Maria returned to her table. "Goodbye, surgeon."

Emilia suppressed a smile. She'd gotten her goodbye, after all. "Goodbye, Captain."

Emilia had already stepped out of the captain's quarters and closed the door behind her, before she heard Maria yell through the door.

"Em! You left the cat!"

CHAPTER 20
Her Place

About four years into her naval training, Maria and Anne—a small, red-haired seamstress Maria had met a few hours earlier—shared one last kiss outside the large, stone tavern, before going their separate ways.

Maria waited until the thin woman disappeared down a dark, cobblestone street, and then, she turned to head back toward the Regolis training yard.

"You skipped our fight for *her*?"

Maria ran into Catherine Rochester so suddenly and unexpectedly that she nearly fell backward.

Maria glanced up at the stone tavern and then at the torch-lit street behind it, wondering where exactly the tall, blonde sailor had been hiding.

"Did you follow me?" Recovering her balance, Maria brushed past her sparring partner with a look of disbelief. "What the fuck, Cat?"

"Oh, don't flatter yourself," Catherine scoffed. The echoing thud of her boots informed Maria that Catherine was *still* doing the thing she claimed she hadn't. "I don't need to follow you to know where *you've* gotten off to."

Maria couldn't, for the life of her, figure out what Catherine wanted from her. Maria loved having her as a sparring partner, of course, but the rest of their relationship confused her.

She'd yet to figure out whether Cat actually wanted to fuck her or just wanted to make sure no one else did.

Maria understood jealousy. It was the jealous and competitive nature of Catherine Rochester that had intrigued Maria in the first place.

She'd finally come across a woman with ambition equal to her own—a level of ambition that, in the Kingdom of Illopia, only men were allowed to have.

But the muddled nature of Catherine's attitude toward Maria often left her fumbling.

With a lift of her not-yet-scarred eyebrows, Maria said, "I'm sorry I crave the touch of a woman every now and then." She stopped and spun toward Catherine. "You should try it sometime."

Catherine came to a perfect halt, as if she'd learned the size and speed of Maria's every step.

Maria took hold of the fine, white linen of Cat's cravat— perfectly folded and free of even the smallest speck of dust—and tugged it forward. "Might make you less of a bitch."

Catherine narrowed her light blue eyes, but the pull of the thin fabric against her pale throat drew a quick breath from her lips, all the same. "Yes, well," she sneered, "I'm sure you have a whole *list* of whores to recommend." She glanced over her shoulder, toward the tavern they'd just left. "What about that one? Was she as dirty as her clothes?"

Maria followed her gaze with a frown. She'd never even considered the state of the girl's dress, but of course, Catherine Rochester, in all her Regolis-bred bitchiness, had. "Anne wasn't a whore. Not that I would've liked her any less, if she had been."

That seemed to agitate Catherine *more*, if it were even possible. "Street-rat, then."

Maria released the cravat, before she gave in and choked Catherine with it. Cat knew enough of Maria's background to *know* what she was saying—to know exactly which buttons she was pushing.

Maria led the way onto an unlit street, and the steady thud of Cat's boots followed.

"Can't say I'm surprised," the blonde sailor mused. "What is it they say? Like calls to like?"

Maria had never possessed much patience, as it was, and Catherine knew exactly how to use up what little she had. Maria turned and shoved her closest friend against the alley wall. Catherine's long, blonde braid shone like polished gold in the moonlight.

"What did you just call me?"

Catherine's thin, pink lips curved into a deep smile. "Am I wrong?"

Maria's hand strayed toward her sword, and like a shark drawn to the scent of blood, Cat leaned closer.

"Not too busy for a sword-fight *now*, are you?"

Maria quirked an eyebrow, and her anger easily gave way to excitement. She released Catherine and stepped back. With a grin, she said, "Race you there."

Then, she took off—with Catherine's laughter and footsteps not far behind.

Maria's quill stilled against the current page of the captain's log. She shouldn't have been thinking about Cat today.

Admiral Catherine Rochester of the fucking Royal Navy, perhaps.

But not Cat.

Not her supposed friend of years ago.

She shouldn't have mentioned her to Em the night before, either.

Em hadn't hesitated to forgive her, of course. She never had.

But Maria knew she'd made Em uncomfortable. She knew Zain's remarks were starting to affect her.

Maria dipped her quill in a well of ink, as she reminded herself of all the things that had happened *since* those days.

The huge, fucking scar over her eye was one of them. Did Zain think she'd forgotten about that?

Hadn't Maria proven by now that she'd decimate the entire Royal Navy, given the chance?

Of course Maria would kill Catherine, if she could!

If Catherine hadn't held a pistol to Em's head.

If Catherine hadn't ordered her men to torture Em.

Yes, Maria thought about the past sometimes.

Yes, she occasionally wished Catherine had been the person Maria thought she was, instead of a useless coward, who'd rather cover up King Eldric's atrocities than rebel against them.

But that didn't mean she'd *wanted* to help Catherine escape. It didn't mean she was secretly relieved that Catherine was still alive.

Perhaps Zain thought it did, but he was wrong.

A sudden knock at the door startled Maria, and she had to catch the well of ink before it spilled. She looked toward the door.

Had Em returned?

The weight on Maria's chest lifted at the mere prospect of seeing Em again. "Forget something?"

When no response came, Maria's smile faded.

Not Em, then.

With a sigh, she said, "Door's unlocked."

The heavy, wooden door creaked open, and the last person Maria wanted to see, in that moment, stepped inside.

"Captain," Zain said curtly.

Maria returned her attention to her neglected captain's log. "Does Henry need a break?"

Zain closed the door behind him. "No."

The floorboards creaked beneath the quartermaster's polished, leather boots, as he intruded further into Maria's space. The chair across from Maria scraped against the floor, and Zain took a seat at her table—without waiting for an invitation.

It took a conscious effort for Maria to keep writing—to resist the urge to squeeze the quill in her hand until it broke. "What is it, then? Have you run out of snide remarks?"

Zain ignored that. "I think it's time we talked."

Maria set the quill aside and closed her worn, leather-bound captain's log. She leaned back in her chair, projecting complete and utter confidence, whether she felt it or not. "About fucking time."

Zain's eyes narrowed. "I'd be careful what you wish for, Captain."

"The only one who need be careful, quartermaster," Maria said, "is you."

Zain raked his hand down his green waistcoat, his fingers lingering on a brass button—one Maria vaguely remembered popping off. "I don't know if you noticed, but I asked Phillip to mend my coat."

Maria had never understood Zain's need for small talk at times like this. It didn't soften her mood. It just made her more restless.

She'd actually found it a relief that Em hadn't seemed eager to learn that particular social custom.

"You know I would've had someone fix it in Nefala," Maria muttered. "It's not like you didn't have plenty of waistcoats to wear in the meantime."

Zain's obsidian gaze flicked toward Maria's black, leather doublet and her black, leather trousers. "Some of us prefer a little variety in our wardrobe."

Maria followed his gaze—and shrugged.

Zain liked his coats. She liked her swords.

It was his gold to spend as he wished.

Same as hers.

"Yes, well," Maria said, "I'm happy for you and your mended coat. Now, say what you came to say."

Maria was actually quite impressed by her own restraint. Considering the glare he shot her way, Maria figured it was safe to assume Zain was not.

"I *tried* to give you the benefit of the doubt," Zain said. "Truly, I did."

Maria looked away, feigning indifference, even as her pulse spiked.

"I knew there was something in the way Catherine looked at you that day—with that sort of…recognition." Zain's jaw shifted. "Something in the way she gave Em over to you, as if she'd just struck a deal."

Maria didn't even know whether to deny it—because all she remembered was the relief she'd felt at having Em in her arms again.

She'd watched Catherine's *hand*, not her eyes.

She'd watched *Em's* eyes, not Catherine's.

"And when you showed no concern for the results of the search, I told myself you simply believed she'd drowned, as many of our other sailors did," Zain continued, "but that wasn't the case, was it?"

Maria let her gaze drift toward him, and she curled her fingers around the curved handle of her sword. "That sounds like an accusation, quartermaster."

Zain neither confirmed nor denied it. "I questioned Pelt and Judith first. Judith was useless, as expected." He rolled his eyes. "But Pelt informed me he'd already questioned *Em*—that there'd be no need for me to do it, as well, since he'd tell me everything she said."

Maria tensed at the mention of her surgeon.

No.

Don't bring Em into this.

She's not to blame.

"Apparently, she told him nothing," Zain said, and Maria breathed a sigh of relief. "I assumed that meant she didn't know. After all, if she *knew* you'd done something so…questionable, in regards to the woman who destroyed her people, surely she'd never forgive you. Yet, every time I made any sort of remark about it in front of her, she looked at me as if she wanted to gut me."

Had she, really?

Maria couldn't help the surge of pride she felt at that bit of information—even if she *did* wish Em would be more careful about not implicating herself.

Zain watched her reaction closely. "After what Catherine did to her, Em should be the least forgiving of your…mistake."

The ounce of self-preservation that stopped Zain from making the accusation aloud was the *only* thing keeping Maria's sword in its scabbard.

"Instead, she's out there, viciously guarding your secrets like some kind of—" A look of genuine misery crossed the quartermaster's face the moment his own analogy caught up with him. "Oh, you know, like a—"

It was too late, though.

Maria was already laughing. "Dragon?"

Zain was less amused. "Joke all you want, but you need to realize: you can only fail to kill someone so many times before the crew starts asking questions."

The smile vanished from Maria's face. She leaned forward, tightening her grip around her right sword. "And what do you intend to tell them, when they do?" she sneered. "That *you'd* make a better captain?"

If Zain were even aware of the dangerous undertone in her voice, he gave no indication. "Depending on how our talk goes, perhaps I'll tell them that our captain shouldn't be someone who once loved the enemy."

Maria was on her feet before she even realized it. She pressed her hands against the table, leaning over it. "I never loved Catherine Rochester!"

Zain arched an eyebrow at the show of emotion.

Fuck.

Just what she needed.

Maria pushed away from the long, wooden table. She paced to calm herself. "I might've thought I needed her. I might've cared for her. I might've never known what I actually felt toward her," she admitted, "but I never loved her."

Zain made no move to stand. "Interesting."

Maria clenched her jaw. She spun toward him. "What is *interesting*?"

"I was prepared to discount anything that came out of your

mouth," Zain said with a lift of his slender shoulders, "but that actually sounded like the truth—perhaps the first truth you've ever spoken about her."

Maria's lips parted. She turned away, lest he learn even more from her reaction than he already had. She strolled toward the stern windows, the sunlight warming her skin.

"Do you remember what I said the day you told me about Edward?" Zain asked.

Maria forced herself not to tense at the mention of Lieutenant Ingelby. This conversation was uncomfortable enough without Maria cluing Zain in to the fact that she'd sort of decapitated his ex-lover.

"You said, 'You mean she sleeps with men, too?'" Maria recalled. "To which, I replied, 'How the fuck should I know?'"

A lot of memories faded after a decade or so, but the memories of *that* day were forever branded into her mind—into *all* of their minds.

"Which I thought was an odd question," Zain muttered, "since she was your lover at the time."

"Not lover," Maria corrected. "I admit we blurred the lines between platonic and sexual sometimes, but can you blame us? Ship life gets lonely. And the choices in the navy were limited for those of us who loved women." She turned to grin at him. "I wouldn't expect you to understand."

"My choices were limited, too," Zain assured her, "because unlike you, I have standards. I don't just sleep with anyone of a particular gender."

Maria's grin tilted tauntingly. "Sounds exhausting."

"Anyway," Zain said with a roll of his eyes, "I was actually referring to something I said *after* that?"

Maria's smile vanished. "You said you'd never trust me where Catherine was concerned."

Zain gave a small nod. "That hasn't changed."

Maria narrowed her eyes. "You want Catherine dead because she made you a pirate."

Zain shot to his feet. "You say that like it's small. That day changed the entire trajectory of my life. I can't even visit my family in Regolis anymore, and you know none of *them* are setting foot in Nefala."

Maria wouldn't let him guilt-trip her—not here, not now. "It's not my fault your mother thinks her feet are too precious for the streets I grew up walking."

Zain stepped closer to her. "Do *not* speak of my mother."

"I have nothing against your mother," Maria scoffed. "Do you think I'd help you provide for her, if I did?"

She just occasionally got tired of people acting as if they were better, simply because of where and how they were born.

"You don't like Judith's brother, and you provide for him," Zain pointed out.

He…might've had a point there.

"I wasn't saying it like it was small," Maria informed him. "I was saying it like it was one reason. One!" She stepped toward him. "Meanwhile, I have a whole *list* of reasons. Count my scars, and then add more. *That's* how many reasons I have to want Catherine dead."

Zain gripped his own sword. "Yet, you seem incapable of accomplishing it."

Red-hot rage pulsed within Maria. "Fuck you."

Zain must not have recognized how close she was to killing him—because he continued, "It's ironic, really—considering how skilled you seem to be at killing everyone *else*."

Maria leaned toward him, gripping her sword so tightly that it shifted within its sheath. "Keep pushing me, and I might just prove you right."

"Oh, but Captain," Zain sneered, "what a mess that would make."

EMILIA NEEDED TO TALK TO THE CAPTAIN. AFTER SPEAKING WITH Pelt, she was more sure of that than ever.

She was so fixated on the problem at hand that she didn't even see the captain's door swinging open until it nearly smacked her in the face.

Emilia stumbled back. "Oh! Captain! I'd hoped to—" She froze, as she saw *who* had stepped out of the captain's quarters. "Sorry. You're not…the captain."

Zain closed the door behind him. "Not yet."

The embarrassed smile that had briefly overtaken Emilia's face vanished. "What is *that* supposed to mean?"

Zain stepped toward her, not past her. Rather than answering her question, he said, "I'd give her a moment to cool off, if I were you."

Anger and protectiveness surged inside of Emilia, and her body surged *with* it, her shoulders straightening, her chin lifting. "And why would she need to cool off?"

Zain's eyes—like obsidian pebbles in the shadows—skimmed up and down Emilia's form.

Not like Maria's eyes did.

His eyes never lingered, never carried any heat.

They conveyed only cold, condescending appraisal.

"What would that matter to *you*, surgeon?"

"What would it matter to me," Emilia repeated, "if you hurt my captain? Is that a serious question?"

"Your captain," Zain said, his eyes dark.

Nymeth's low voice filled Emilia's mind. *"Do you need me?"*

For once, Emilia didn't tell the dragon no. *"I'll let you know."*

Nymeth said nothing more, but Emilia sensed the rising excitement on the dragon's side of the bond.

Zain's eyes narrowed on Emilia's arm. "Your tattoo's glowing again." When Emilia made no move to hide the rune, he looked up. "Tell me, surgeon. How do you remain loyal to her after what she did?"

Emilia held herself completely still. Even if Zain already knew, she wouldn't confirm it. "The captain's done a lot of things. You'll have to be more specific."

Zain did no such thing. "Perhaps you feel obligated to forgive her—because you think she did what she did for you—but you should know: the captain's judgement has always been questionable, where Catherine Rochester is concerned."

Don't react.

Don't show weakness.

"Questionable to you, perhaps," Emilia said.

Zain scoffed in disbelief. "Do you think she's even noticed how devoted to her you've become? Do you think she even has the humility to appreciate it?"

Oh, Emilia knew *exactly* what was happening now. "Appreciation? You think I care about that? I'm a witch working on a ship with people who think my mere existence is evil." With a bitter laugh, she gestured toward the deck. "Even now, I'm trying to help someone who doesn't even want me to touch him!"

Zain lifted a thick eyebrow. "You are?"

Zain was probably the last person Emilia wanted to discuss Cornelius with. So, she just sighed, "I don't care if the captain appreciates me, and if I did, I'd *tell* her. I wouldn't conspire against her."

A muscle shifted in Zain's jaw. "Is that what you think I'm doing?"

Emilia offered a bitter smile. "I've learned to recognize manipulation when I see it."

A faint smile curled at Zain's lips, as well. "From the captain, no doubt."

"No," she said, "from Catherine." Emilia was the one who stepped forward, this time, and she could tell the quartermaster didn't like that change. "You, however, could use a bit more practice, I think."

Zain's smile faded. "Excuse me?"

"You're worried about the captain's judgement," Emilia said, "but you're the one being manipulated."

"Me?" Zain balked. "I wasn't the one who gave Catherine what she wanted that day!"

"What she wanted?" Emilia repeated. "You think Catherine's ambitions have ever been that simple? Oh, you think the captain's ambitious. You think she's obsessive. You think she's manipulative, but she's none of those things, compared to Catherine. Why do you think Catherine keeps winning?"

Zain lifted his chin. "I knew Catherine."

"You think you did," Emilia said, "but trust me. No one knows Catherine. Not until you've been part of her game—and *lost*. There were a thousand ways Catherine might've survived, but do you know what none of those would've done—that this one did?" She pointed her finger at Zain. "This. You're the one giving Catherine what she wants, quartermaster."

His eyes narrowed. "Your place—"

"My place," Emilia interrupted, "is between anyone who dares hurt her and her." She stepped closer. "Now, tell me…how far you intend to take this."

For the first time, she saw a flicker of hesitation in Zain's dark eyes. "And if I intend to mutiny? What would you do, then?" His gaze drifted toward Emilia's waist, where she carried her sword.

But Emilia didn't need her sword.

Not for this.

A familiar warmth spread over her skin.

She knew the moment her dragon rune began to glow—because Zain's eyes darted toward it.

The distant roar of a dragon made those eyes flare wider, and he looked up, briefly meeting Emilia's gaze.

Until Emilia glanced a bit higher and accidentally met a *different* pair of dark brown eyes.

Oops.

In the heat of the moment, Emilia must've missed the telltale creak of the door opening behind Zain—because it *was* no longer closed.

Maria leaned in the doorway with her arms folded over her chest and her eyes dangerously narrowed.

Maybe she hadn't heard anything.

Maria lifted a scarred eyebrow.

*Or…*maybe she had.

Zain followed Emilia's gaze and turned, hesitantly, toward the door. When he found the captain behind him, he simply said, "Do you see what I mean?"

The pirate captain gave Emilia a brief break from her deadly glare, as she directed it at Zain, instead.

Zain's lip curled, as he sneered, "How does it feel to have your own personal dragon?"

Her personal dragon?

Nymeth didn't listen to Maria.

She barely listened to Emilia.

Maria didn't even blink. "Good."

With a scoff of disgust, Zain turned to leave.

"Ensure the crew doesn't panic," Maria told him.

"Yes, Captain," he grumbled.

As soon as the quartermaster was out of sight, Maria's glare cut right back to Emilia, slicing her to the core.

Emilia crossed her arms, as if that might protect her.

Several moments of tense silence followed, before Maria finally said, "Well?" Her long, tattooed fingers drummed an impatient rhythm against her upper arm. "Are your dragons attacking us or not?"

"What? No!" Emilia said with a laugh. She lifted her shoulders. "They're just…stretching their wings."

Maria arched her eyebrows. "This far west of Drakon Isle?"

Emilia winced at that. "Dragons can be pretty loud, Captain. They're not as close as they sound."

"Mm-hmm," Maria said skeptically. She dropped her arms and stepped aside. "In my quarters. Now."

Emilia sighed at her tone. "Fine," she muttered, "but only because I needed to talk to you, anyway."

Emilia stepped into the spacious, sunlit cabin, and the heat of Maria's glare followed her. "Look, I get it." She turned to face Maria. "You told me not to get involved, and you think that's what I did."

Maria slammed the heavy, wooden door behind her. "That's exactly what you did!"

Emilia didn't even flinch. "You didn't hear what he said."

"I don't care what he said!" Maria stepped toward Emilia, heat pouring off of her in waves. "I don't need you to defend me, surgeon."

Emilia leaned forward. "I never said you did!"

Maria closed the last bit of space between them. "Why can't you understand that I *need* you to stay out of it?" Her breath fell against Emilia's face, sweet with apple and rum. "That this could go badly, and I need you to survive, if it does!"

"Why can't *you* understand," Emilia countered, "that I can't just listen to him talk about you like that?" She tapped the back of her fingers against Maria's muscular arm. "Why can't you understand that I think you deserve better?"

Maria froze. The anger fled her face in an instant, leaving a brief vacancy in its place. She fell back on the heels of her boots and whispered, "Em."

Emilia licked her lips nervously, wondering if she'd been too honest, but before she could even think about taking it back, Maria's fingers closed around Emilia's arm and pulled her forward.

Maria's lips crashed against Emilia's, and Emilia's eyes slid closed. Overwhelming warmth poured through Emilia, taking her breath and all of the tension in her muscles with it.

Emilia would've thought she'd developed some immunity to these kisses by now—especially after sharing so many the night before—but this kiss destroyed her as thoroughly as their very first had.

With a soft giggle, Emilia said, "This isn't how you discipline *all* the sailors who don't follow orders, is it?"

"No," Maria assured her. "It only works on you."

Emilia opened her eyes, smile instantly fading. "Works? Works?" She stepped back. "Captain!"

Maria wrapped an arm around Emilia's waist, before she could retreat any further. Her laughter spilled out against Emilia's mouth. "I'm kidding!"

Emilia resisted Maria's attempt at another kiss. "I'm never trusting a kiss from you again."

"No," Maria whined. "It was a joke. I swear!"

Emilia narrowed her eyes. "Mm-hmm."

"Ah, come on, love. You have to believe me," Maria said—though her continued laughter sounded less than remorseful. She pressed a warm hand against Emilia's face. "Besides, you know my secret already."

Squinting curiously, Emilia said, "What secret?"

Maria brushed her soft, warm mouth against Emilia's, as she said, "I prefer the taste of rebellion."

Emilia probably shouldn't have given in so easily, but *goddess*, it was hard to resist those perfect, full lips of Maria's. She closed her eyes and surrendered herself over to the pure elation of kissing Maria.

So quietly that Emilia might not have heard her, if she hadn't *felt* the vibration of the words against her lips, Maria said, "I do appreciate you."

Emilia pulled back in shock. "You *did* hear him."

Maria didn't confirm or deny it, but she added, "Even if you do scare the hell out of me sometimes."

Emilia's chest tightened.

Had Captain Maria Welles just admitted fear?

Without lies or façades?

She'd just…said it?

Maria slid the backs of her fingers along the curve of Emilia's cheek and released a soft laugh. "Darling, you can't hide a single emotion on this face."

As opposed to Maria, who could hide them all.

"I can hide…things," Emilia lied.

Maria's eyebrows rose.

Emilia cleared her throat. "Anyway," she said, drawing out the word, "I actually had a reason to come here, believe it or not."

"Did you?" Maria murmured.

Emilia didn't like how skeptical she sounded. She stepped back, and Maria reluctantly dropped her arm. "Yes."

Maria leaned forward conspiratorially. "And it *wasn't* to breathe fire at my quartermaster?"

"Well…no," Emilia said. "Dragon sorcerers can't breathe fire.

Some of them can *wield* fire, but we can't breathe it." She waved her hands. "Our bodies are too soft and fleshy. They can't withstand the heat."

Maria snorted. "No, I suppose you couldn't *literally* breathe fire."

Emilia frowned.

Oh.

Maria didn't mock her, though. She only smiled. "And your other reason was?"

Emilia wanted to reiterate that 'breathing fire' wasn't amongst her reasons at *all*, but Maria probably wouldn't believe her, anyway. "I need you to…"

When she didn't finish, Maria fell serious. "Em, I'm your captain. You can ask me for what you need."

Emilia shifted from one foot to the other. She kept her gaze on the floorboards, as she blurted out, "I need you to order someone to let me look at their leg."

Maria blinked, as if she'd expected something a bit more…difficult. "Leg?" Her brows furrowed. "I take it this concerns that 'possible injury' you were helping Pelt with? Is it a certain injury, then?"

"Well, I can't say if it's certain until I've seen it, but…" Emilia stopped when she noticed Maria's amused smile. "Oh. I did it again, didn't I?"

Maria shook her head. "No. That one was on me."

Emilia wasn't so sure, but she'd never known of Maria to lie for the sake of her feelings *before*. "His mobility has deteriorated steadily since the battle," she told Maria. "If I had to guess, I'd say infection."

"Since the battle?" Maria repeated. She glanced toward the stern windows and squinted, as if she'd lost track of the days that had passed since then.

Easy to do on a ship.

"Do you mean," she asked, "one of the sailors you healed after the battle never got better?"

"Wow," Emilia said dryly. "I see how much faith *you* have in me."

Maria's lips twitched. "You didn't heal him, then."

"No," Emilia confirmed, "I did not."

Maria's gaze darted toward the large, wooden table in the center of the cabin. "I don't understand," she said, but before Emilia could explain, she turned and strolled toward her table. "Apple and rum?"

The sudden change in subject nearly gave Emilia whiplash. "What?"

Maria turned to look at her. "I'm famished," she said—though Emilia was fairly certain the pirate had eaten less than an hour ago. "I'm getting myself an apple." She extended a tattooed finger toward Emilia. "Would you like one?"

"I'm fine," Emilia assured her.

Maria nodded. "Just rum, then. Got it."

That wasn't exactly what Emilia said, but…close enough, she supposed. "After the battle, I checked on all of our wounded daily— the ones I *knew* about, anyway. This sailor never came to me."

Maria set two tankards on the table, pewter clanging against wood. "I don't understand why he wouldn't. Didn't he know he was wounded?"

"It's…*hypothetically* possible to not feel a wound," Emilia admitted, "but in these circumstances, I'd say it's unlikely that was the case."

Maria went to her cabinet to retrieve a bottle of rum. "Then, why wouldn't he have come to you?"

Emilia ran her hand through her short, black hair, finding it even wavier than usual.

Had the humidity risen that much in one day?

Was that a bad sign?

"I suppose he thought it'd heal on its own."

Maria spun around, saffron-gold liquid splashing over the sides of the bottle in her hand. "But why risk it?" she snapped. "Ten fucking years without a surgeon! I finally give them one, and they don't even use you? What sense does that make?"

Startled by the sudden flare of Maria's rage, Emilia shrank back. "Well…because—because it's me."

Maria's grip loosened around the rum bottle, and confusion flickered in her large, brown eyes. "What?"

Guilt twisted in Emilia's stomach. "It's because the surgeon you gave them was…a witch."

The spark of rage in Maria's eyes cooled into something far more dangerous—the kind of rage that simmered, rather than burning bright. "Name."

Emilia frowned. "What?"

"Name," Maria growled. "Give me the name."

It'd been so long since the trial. Would Maria even remember that Cornelius had voted against Emilia?

"Pelt didn't mention his surname, but he's called Cornelius," Emilia offered. "Do you know him?"

Maria slammed the bottle against the table so hard it nearly shattered. "I knew I should've killed him!"

Apparently, she did.

"Captain," Emilia said with a nervous smile, "you realize a vote ceases to be democratic, if you kill everyone who votes the way you don't like?"

Maria scowled at her. "Does it look like I care?"

"Not at the moment, no," Emilia muttered.

Maria gripped the hilt of her sword. "This is my ship, and I don't tolerate this behavior on *my* ship."

Emilia lifted her eyebrows. "This behavior being…concealing a wound?"

Emilia had done *that* before.

"This behavior being prejudice," Maria corrected. "You are my surgeon, Em! I won't have someone making you feel less-than because of your bloodline."

Warmth unfurled in Emilia's chest, and she offered her tempestuous captain a grateful smile. "If it's any consolation, he's probably in pain right now."

"Not enough pain," Maria said, "clearly."

Emilia wondered what *would* be enough pain, in Maria's opinion. She had no doubt the pirate captain had something in mind. "How much do you know about him?"

"Plenty," Maria scoffed. "He was on my first ship."

Emilia blinked in surprise. "He sided with you during the mutiny, then."

"Reluctantly," Maria muttered.

Emilia supposed everyone had lines they wouldn't cross.

Well, maybe not Catherine.

Or King Eldric.

Or a good portion of the Royal Navy.

But for those who *did* draw the line somewhere, how did bigotry so often end up on the wrong side of it?

Maria removed the cork from the bottle. "The ship where my First Mate mutinied against me was the first ship I *captained*, by the way," she said, "not my first altogether." A smile spread across her face, softening the anger that had been there moments before. "My first altogether was this massive beauty called...the *Glorious Destiny*."

Emilia's eyes widened. "The one you stole!"

The one she'd renamed the *Wicked Fate*.

Maria grinned. "Never got over my first love."

Oh, Emilia adored that.

She couldn't even explain why. She just did.

Emilia supposed it was simply the possibility that something had remained unstained by betrayal.

Unlike herself.

"Yeah, I've known Cornelius for a while—not always as his captain either." Maria filled each tankard with rum. "Believe it or not, I know *every* sailor in my service—at least in part. I may not have chosen them all personally, like I did you, but I'm always here when they sign my Code."

Emilia's gaze darted toward the swords that hung from Maria's waist. She wondered if Maria handled everyone's signing the way she'd handled Emilia's.

"Unlike *naval* captains," Maria bragged, "I do take the time to notice everyone who serves me."

A small smile pulled at the corners of Emilia's lips. Maria had the arrogance to turn literally *anything* into a boast, but this partic-ular one, Emilia thought, was a good one.

"What's he like?"

Maria considered that for a moment. "Ornery, but experienced," she answered. "He's good on the lines. Not good in combat, but he can do most jobs on the main deck." She frowned. "He doesn't climb—not since I've known him, anyway. That's a job best left to younger sailors, but he'll do most anything else."

Emilia nodded. "And you haven't noticed him favoring one leg recently?"

Maria rolled her eyes. "I said I knew him, not that I spend *time* with him. He's an asshole, remember?"

Emilia held up her hands. "Just asking."

Maria leaned over her table. "I don't pester every sailor as often as I pester you, you know?"

Emilia widened her eyes playfully. "How would you ever find the time?"

Maria chuckled. She picked up both tankards of rum and brought them around the table. She held one out to Emilia.

Emilia accepted it with a murmur of thanks.

"Apparently, someone saw blood on his trousers the day of the battle, but when Pelt asked about it, Cornelius said it was someone else's blood." Emilia lifted the tankard to her mouth. "Pelt didn't think much about it—until he noticed Cornelius limping."

Maria nodded. "Then, he came to you."

"Not immediately," Emilia said. "He watched for a few days. He came to me when he noticed it getting *worse*."

Maria tipped back the rum, as if it were nothing more than water.

Of course, with as little fresh water as they had access to these days, it might as well have been.

"And you're sure it isn't just…unexplained pain?" Maria asked. "The older sailors, especially, experience that."

"Chronic pain does increase with age for some people," Emilia admitted, "but it doesn't explain the blood." The burn of the rum left her throat and tongue tingling. "The limp presented after the battle, and there was blood on his trousers that day."

Maria's brows furrowed. "How many people can hide a sword wound, though?"

"Depends on how shallow it was," Emilia told her. "Perhaps the blade only grazed his shin."

"And progressed to a limp?" Maria said skeptically.

Emilia nodded. "Any wound left untreated, especially in the unsanitary conditions of a ship, can—"

"Unsanitary?" Maria interrupted. "I'll have you know the *Wicked Fate* is as clean as a cat!"

Emilia squinted at that. "I doubt it, but also…you're aware that a cat's claws can cause infection, right?"

Maria didn't answer, but she *did* purse her lips.

"Infections worsen over time," Emilia continued. "It might explain why he's now struggling to walk."

Maria lowered her tankard, letting it rest against her black, leather doublet. "Wouldn't an infection also cause fever and hallucinations?" Her brows creased. "I mean, it did—when it happened to me."

Emilia couldn't help but notice the nervous twitch of Maria's finger against the tankard, and her chest tightened with sympathy.

"Your eye or," she hesitated, "your back?"

"Eye." A bitter smile curled at Maria's lips. "Catherine was inexperienced. She learned her lesson when her *trophy* nearly perished before she even got it back to Regolis." She eyed the remaining rum in her tankard. "They were more careful with my…lacerations."

Emilia's stomach turned. Even if she knew Maria's choice of words matched Catherine's attitude, it still nauseated her to think anyone could see Maria in that way—that anyone would hurt her like that.

The Illopian guards had tortured both of them, but somehow, Emilia found it far easier to bear the thought of her own pain than the thought of Maria's.

"Many infections cause fever," Emilia said, "but not everyone's body responds the same." She shrugged. "Even if he does have a mild fever, he might hide it."

Maria downed the rest of her rum. "Let him die, then."

"Captain!" Emilia had thought they were past this!

Maria returned to her table. "He's gone to *so* much trouble to ensure he suffers, rather than receive help from the ship's surgeon." She set down her empty tankard with a *clang*. "So, let him."

Emilia nearly shivered at Maria's tone. "I can't do that, Captain."

Maria picked up the bottle of rum and examined it. "Perhaps we should try a bit of Judith's rum. Maybe, *then*, you'd have a change of heart."

Emilia stared blankly at her. "You want me to get drunk and be okay with murder?"

Maria spread out her arms. "Isn't that what piracy is?"

Emilia rolled her eyes. "I'd still try to help him, even if I were drunk. I just might not be able to hold my hand steady during the surgery!"

Maria shrugged those strong shoulders of hers. "Better than nothing, I suppose."

"I'm not touching Judith's rum!" Emilia insisted.

Maria exhaled heavily. "At least you've learned *some* things from me…"

"I'm also not letting him die," Emilia added.

"Just not the right things," Maria muttered.

"This is what you hired me to do, Captain," Emilia reminded her.

Maria refilled her tankard. "I don't know if I'd say *that*." When she finished, she held out her hand. "You need more, too." Before Emilia could object, she added, "It's the non-toxic kind, I promise."

Emilia stepped forward and offered her tankard. "Just so you know, I only believe you because I've *had* Judith's rum, and I remember how it tasted."

Maria's mouth quirked up at the corners. "Tastes like a rotting corpse, doesn't it?"

Emilia grimaced at the thought. "I wouldn't know. I don't make a habit of tasting rotting corpses."

Maria poured the rum into Emilia's tankard. "Em, this guy hates you because of something you can't help." She extended her arm over the table, offering Emilia the tankard. "He doesn't deserve to live."

Emilia took it. "That isn't my decision to make."

"Why not?" Maria scoffed. "I make that decision all the time." She lifted the tankard to her lips. "Do you want me to make it for you? *Please,* let me."

Emilia sighed at that. "I have to heal him."

"Not according to your captain," Maria sang behind her tankard.

Emilia shook her head in disbelief. "Sometimes, I wonder how there's *anyone* left alive on this ship."

Maria hummed irritably. "It's Zain's fault."

"Captain," Emilia said, "I heal the sick, and this sailor might be sick." She set down her tankard and circled the table, closing the space between them. "And even if we *were* going to let him die, I'd still need to see the leg. What if it's a disease?"

Her heart raced, as Nymeth's warning echoed in her mind. She didn't think she'd need to summon a goddess to treat a disease, but that didn't stop her from worrying.

Maria turned toward her. "A disease?"

Emilia wanted to tell Maria everything, then—about Aletha's warning and Nymeth's clue—but she'd promised not to share it with anyone.

Maria set down the tankard. "Fine," she groaned, "but if you want *me* to spare someone's life, you'll have to wait until I eat my apple. I don't let anyone live, unless I've had something sweet first."

Emilia couldn't help but laugh at that. "Had you had something sweet the day you spared *my* life?"

"Oh, yes." Maria leaned in close and murmured, "I had you."

Warmth rushed to Emilia's face. "You…kissed me. You didn't *have* me," she stammered. "There's a difference. Isn't there?"

Maria just laughed. She knelt behind her wooden chair and rifled through the sack for an apple. "Are you sure you don't want one?"

Emilia heard the *crunch* of the apple, before Maria was even visible. "I don't usually eat until noon."

Maria rose to her full height. "Madness."

How was that madness? It was literally the meal schedule of the entire ship.

"So," Emilia said, once Maria was safely chewing her fruit, "will you order him to let me look at him?"

"No," Maria said with her mouth full. "You will."

Emilia assumed the absurdly large bite Maria had just taken was responsible for her mishearing that. "What?"

With another *crunch* of the apple, Maria ensured Emilia wouldn't get an answer anytime soon. "Oh, Em." She turned the apple in her hand, examining it. "This is a good one." Before Emilia even realized what she was doing, Maria's legs had swallowed the space between them. She presented the shiny, red fruit to Emilia. "Here."

Emilia blinked at the fruit that was suddenly inches from her mouth. At least Maria was offering her the untouched side, this time. "Captain, this is important!"

"So is this," Maria said. "Go on. One bite."

With a roll of her eyes, Emilia dipped her head. Maria held the apple between three fingers, as Emilia bit into it. The sweet juice flooded Emilia's mouth, and she chewed the apple slowly.

Maria's gaze followed every movement of Emilia's mouth. "Well?"

Emilia swallowed. "It's good."

Maria grinned wickedly. "Told you so."

"*Now*, will you order him to report for an examination?" Emilia asked.

"No," Maria said again. She lifted the apple to her mouth. "I told you. You're going to do it."

Emilia frowned at that. "I…can't. I'm not the captain."

Maria chewed the apple slowly. "What does that have to do with anything?"

Emilia stared blankly at her. "I can't give orders."

One side of Maria's mouth twitched upward. "Who told you that?"

Emilia briefly considered taking the apple hostage. Perhaps, *then*, she'd get a real answer.

If Maria didn't stab her first.

Maria leaned against the table behind her and took another bite of her apple. "A ship's surgeon, my love, has the authority to order *anyone* on the ship to report for examination," she said with a mischievous smile, "and to decide whether or not they're fit for duty."

Emilia's eyes widened. "Oh."

Maria lowered her voice to a whisper. "Anyone includes your captain, by the way."

"What?" Emilia sputtered.

Maria swallowed her fruit. "You're actually the only person aboard this ship who can remove me *without* a vote. Simply deem me unfit for duty because of madness or whatever, and I'm gone."

"If this is part of my job," Emilia asked, "why has no one mentioned it until now?"

"Ah, well," Maria said, and her smile widened, "it wasn't an accident that I neglected to tell you."

Emilia narrowed her eyes at that. "Captain!"

Maria held out the half-eaten apple. "More?"

Emilia didn't even look at the fruit. "Captain."

Maria just laughed. "You're focusing on the wrong part again, love." She lifted the apple to her mouth. "I've told you now, haven't I?"

"You're ridiculous," Emilia grumbled.

The corners of Maria's lips curved as she chewed. "There are some who say a ship's surgeon is the most powerful person aboard the ship. I couldn't have that, now could I? *I* like to be the most powerful."

"I'm aware," Emilia assured her.

Maria's smile was positively shameless. "If you insist on helping this imbecile, simply order him to report for examination, and he'll have to adhere."

Emilia couldn't believe it was that easy. "What's to stop him from saying no?"

"Himself," Maria told her. "Cornelius served in the Royal Navy for thirty years before I even *joined*. If there's anything he respects, it's naval structure. You'd have the authority in the navy. He'll submit to it here."

Emilia didn't even know what to *do* with authority. She couldn't think of a single time in her life when she'd had power over anyone.

"Hell, it took him eight years to stop saluting me," Maria said with a scoff. "*After* we left the navy!"

Emilia had never seen a pirate salute Maria—not seriously, anyway. She'd seen naval sailors salute Catherine, though. "What's the significance of a salute?"

Maria had just taken another bite of her apple, but at Emilia's question, she stopped chewing. "Hmm."

Many Illopians would've responded to Emilia's curiosity with condescension, but as she so often did, Maria met Emilia's curiosity with her own. "You didn't have anything similar on Drakon Isle?"

"I don't think so," Emilia said. "The first time I'd ever seen a salute was—"

"Catherine, yes," Maria finished. With a wave of her apple, she gestured toward the floor. "Bowing?"

"No," Emilia said with a laugh. "We don't do that."

Maria lifted a scarred eyebrow. "Never? Not even to your mother?"

"My mother was a chieftess, chosen by my people," Emilia told her, "not a queen. My people didn't have royalty. We actually found the idea quite repulsive." Her eyes widened, and she extended her hand in apology. "No offense to you or the sirens, of course."

Maria froze, the apple inches from her mouth. "Sirens have royalty?"

"Yes," Emilia said easily. "You're very similar."

Maria stared blankly at her. "They have fins!"

"Well, everyone has peculiarities, Captain." Emilia waved her hand between them. "We have two legs, but you don't see anyone complaining about that."

"Because having two legs is normal!" Maria said.

Emilia quirked her head to the side and lifted her eyebrows. "Not according to four-legged creatures."

A small smile broke through Maria's confusion. "Right," she

said with a shake of her head, "so your mother was elected, like captain and quartermaster of a ship?"

"Yes," Emilia confirmed. "She also led us during battle—because she was our chief warrior. So, she had that in common with you, as well."

Maria grimaced. "Don't compare me to her."

"Umm," Emilia said, "with Catherine, then?"

"That works." Maria took another bite. "So, when your mother led your people, did she ever require any sort of greeting?" she tried again. "Some sort of acknowledgement of her power over them?"

Emilia shook her head. "Why would she? She knew she was in charge. She didn't need anyone to tell her that."

Maria gave a surprised snort of laughter.

Emilia frowned. "Did I say something wrong?"

"Not wrong." Maria placed the apple on the table and leaned forward, curling her tattooed fingers around its wooden edge. "I just find your perspective," she paused to lick the juice from her lips, "fascinating."

Emilia didn't understand *why*.

"In the Royal Navy, a salute is a show of respect," Maria explained, "but as you've just…*unintentionally* pointed out, it's just that—a show." She pushed away from the table and stepped toward Emilia. "Sailors will salute you to your face and whisper behind your back—that you're too soft, too emotional, too mad…"

More bitterness seeped into Maria's voice with each recitation, and her teeth flashed in the candlelight.

How many times had Maria overheard someone insult her?

How long had she held on to this vicious rage?

'That's just the nature of leadership, love,' Maria had once said. *'They'll be questioning my judgement for a totally different reason by next week.'*

"Why would they do it, then?" Emilia said. "If they don't respect you, why pretend to?"

Maria shrugged. "Well, depending on the captain or circumstance, you can be whipped for not saluting a superior officer."

How brutal.

And pointless.

"Then, it's a gesture of fear," Emilia pointed out, "not respect."

Maria leaned back on the heels of her boots. She crossed her arms, the loose fabric of her white shirt flattening against her brown skin. "They're essentially the same," she said, "don't you think?"

"No, I don't," Emilia said with a frown. "Not at all, actually. They're entirely different emotions."

"Well, there's certainly an overlap," Maria said.

"No," Emilia argued. "I feared my mother, but I never respected her. I don't fear you, but I *do* respect you. There is no overlap. They're different emotions."

An amused smile twitched at the edges of Maria's mouth. "You don't fear me at all?"

"No," Emilia said, "and quite frankly, when you *tried* to make me fear you, I respected you less."

Laughter burst from Maria's lips, and she dropped her arms and folded forward as even more spilled out.

Emilia's confusion only grew. "What?"

Maria straightened and leaned toward Emilia. "You, my sweet surgeon," she teased, "have a unique gift for demonstrating to me *just* how much I prefer sincerity over show."

Emilia didn't fully understand that, but she agreed with the part she did. "I prefer sincerity, too."

"Yes," Maria said with a smile. "I *have* noticed."

And even though Maria had used that taunting tone of hers, a smile tugged at Emilia's lips, as well.

Maria stepped closer. "One thing, love. You're not confronting Cornelius alone. If you must do this, you'll take Fulke and Pelt with you."

"I thought you said he'd adhere to the authority," Emilia said.

"Knowing how to handle him and trusting him are two different things," Maria said. "I don't trust him with you. I *won't* trust him with you."

Emilia sighed, "Captain…"

"Pelt will be there because he knows how to talk to the guy. He deals with him every day," Maria told her. "Fulke will be there because he knows how to crush the guy."

Emilia rolled her eyes. "I'll be fine."

"Em," Maria said slowly. "Your authority extends to this. Mine extends to your safety. You'll take backup, or you won't do it. Do you understand me?"

Emilia crossed her arms. "Yes, Captain."

Maria smiled. "Good." She glanced toward her windows. "Go on, now. I'd hate for you to miss our sword-fight because of this."

"I would never," Emilia assured her.

As Emilia turned to leave, Maria called after her, "Don't forget, love. You might not be allowed to draw a sword, but I am. If you come to your senses and decide he deserves to be stabbed, rather than healed, let me know."

"Not happening, Captain," Emilia called back.

CHAPTER 21

It Spreads Among You

Rat-Slayer paced the small surgeon's cabin, while Emilia waited for the injured deckhand to arrive.

His incessant meows—*wails*, really—worried Emilia, and she knelt beside the large tabby.

Emilia soothingly stroked his silver ears. "What is it? You're sensing something, aren't you?"

Rat-Slayer blinked his frosty-blue eyes at her, and Emilia *felt* his agitation—the sense of wrongness that had set him on edge.

"Magic," Emilia guessed, "but not like mine."

To test the theory, she summoned a bit of healing magic into her palm and offered it to the cat. Rat-Slayer immediately nuzzled into her warmed hand.

"Magic meant to harm, not help." Emilia repeated the dragon's words, "Evil spreads among you."

Rat-Slayer looked up, recognition flashing in his reflective eyes, and he let out another chilling wail.

"Don't worry," Emilia whispered, stroking his fur. "I'm here. No one will hurt you, while I'm around."

The narrow, cabin door creaked open, and Emilia heard a gruff voice complain, "She's not even here!"

479

Emilia jumped to her feet, much to Rat-Slayer's dismay. "I'm here!" She pointed toward the silver tabby at her feet. "I was just talking to the cat."

The three pirates frowned at her.

It was amazing that Fulke—with his tremendous height and bulk—managed to squeeze himself into the surgeon's cabin at all, but the poor guy knocked several wooden chests over in the process.

When one of the glass bottles inside shattered, his large, brown eyes flared wide.

Emilia held up her hands. "It's all right. Not your fault."

Still, Fulke winced and looked down.

Pelt—with his lanky form—had a much easier time of it, sliding in on the other side of the surgery table.

Cornelius, however, didn't even *try* to enter.

Even if Emilia hadn't known the other two men, she still would've recognized Cornelius on sight.

Not because of the stringy, grey hair, tied back at the nape of his neck. Not because of the rigidness of his muscles or the deep wrinkles between his brows.

No, it was the pure, unadulterated disgust seething in his grey-blue eyes that gave him away.

"Do you see what I mean?" he hissed at Pelt.

Since Emilia had stayed here, with Rat-Slayer, while Pelt and Fulke had gone to collect Cornelius, she could only guess at the things he might've said about her, but considering the way Pelt cocked his head and arched his eyebrows in warning, Emilia figured it was safe to assume that whatever the deckhand had said was...*less* than nice.

Cornelius shrank back and looked to Fulke for support, but Fulke simply crossed his enormous arms across his chest.

Was Cornelius so accustomed to finding allies in his awful ideology that he thought he'd find one here, too?

Emilia hoped not.

Rat-Slayer chose that moment to emerge from behind the surgery table, and though Emilia had pointed at him already, his appearance startled Cornelius and caused him to stumble onto his injured leg.

The deckhand yelped and fell against the door.

Pelt's eyebrows rose. "You certainly *sound* injured."

"I'm not!" Cornelius said, though the gravelly pain in his voice said otherwise. "I don't need a surgeon!"

Pelt ignored his objection. He turned to Emilia, gesturing toward the cat at her feet. "Smart cat."

"Of course," Emilia said with a smile. "Why do you think he's our master ship cat?"

"We have a master ship cat?" Pelt snorted. "Does the captain know we have a master ship cat?"

"She pays him in chin rubs," Emilia informed him.

"The captain?" Pelt said with a scoff. "Like anyone would ever believe *that*."

Emilia and Rat-Slayer exchanged a knowing look.

Cornelius watched them with a grimace. "You're all mad."

Well, Emilia supposed the tension wasn't easing anytime soon. She stepped forward and extended her hand—the way Illopians often did.

If there was anything she'd learned from her time on the run, it was that mimicking Illopian behavior made people like *this* a bit less hostile. "Hi. I'm Em."

His eyes narrowed. "I know who you are, witch!" he spat. "The nerve of you! To think I'd touch those witch hands of yours!"

Couldn't work *every* time, she supposed.

Emilia examined her outstretched hand. The only difference in her hand and most other sailors' hands was that she'd recently washed *hers*. "Well, I don't have any other hands, so…" She dropped her arm.

Fulke snorted.

While Fulke's attention was on Emilia, Pelt's never left Cornelius. He stepped toward him, and when the deckhand looked up at him, Pelt snarled, "She's your surgeon. You'll address her as such."

The change in Pelt's tone stunned Emilia. She'd never heard Pelt speak like that. She supposed he was boatswain for a reason, of course, but this intimidating version of him was so at odds with the easy-going version she saw during mealtimes.

"It's fine with me, if he calls me a witch," Emilia told the boatswain. "It's just a word. I'm not bothered by it."

Pelt's hazel eyes shifted toward her. He pursed his lips and then stepped past her. He motioned for Emilia to follow. So, she did.

The two of them huddled in the opposite corner of the surgeon's cabin, while Rat-Slayer sniffed at the deckhand's injured leg.

"You need to understand something, Em," Pelt said. "People like Cornelius can only be handled in one way."

Murder?

No, no. They wouldn't be here, if it was murder.

Emilia had *clearly* been spending too much time around the captain.

"I'm guessing my way is wrong?" Emilia said.

Pelt tilted his head and winced, as if he didn't want to say yes, but…*yes*. "Have you ever noticed that the captain handles different people in different ways?"

"Yes," Emilia admitted. "I find it a bit confusing, to be honest."

"Yes, well," Pelt said with a nod, "she does it because it works. Some pirates respond well to a gentle nudge, while others only respect a shove."

Emilia squinted at that. "I don't know if I'd call anything the captain does '*gentle*.'"

"Perhaps not," Pelt chuckled. "Trust me, Em. I deal with Cornelius every day. I know how to handle him."

"Okay," Emilia said easily.

"If you give an inch, he'll take a mile," Pelt told her. "Now, the good news is…he respects naval structure, and in the navy, the three of us would hold rank—surgeon, boatswain, master-at-arms." He pointed at Fulke, who quirked a dark eyebrow at them. His calloused finger swung toward Cornelius. "*He* wouldn't. That makes this all too easy—*if* we can be a bit more…rigid."

Emilia was fairly certain that by *'we,'* Pelt meant *her*. "I didn't even know surgeons *were* naval officers."

Pelt slapped her on the shoulder so hard Emilia thought it might bruise. "Well, that's why you have me!"

For that *and* minor shoulder injuries, apparently.

"Oh, I—" Emilia shifted uneasily. "I don't know if I can do that. I'm not like the captain."

Pelt's brows furrowed. "Don't worry! I just told you I'd explain all the naval shit to you."

Emilia found his word-choice amusing, considering he'd advised her to follow it *rigidly*. "It's not the information. It's—" she sighed. "I can't change personalities like that. I'm the way I am all the time."

"I see," Pelt said with a nod. "Don't think of it as changing your personality. Think of it as…changing your communication style."

Emilia offered an apologetic smile. "I don't think I'm any good at that either."

Pelt chuckled at her honesty. "All right. How about this? You handle the healing, and I'll handle the rest." Before Emilia could agree, he held up a calloused finger. "But…you have to *let* me handle it."

"Okay," Emilia said.

"Are you sure?" Pelt asked. "Because that means when I tell him not to call you a witch, you don't get to correct me."

"I'll…try my best," Emilia amended.

Pelt snorted at that.

A sudden hiss drew their attention toward the deckhand, who'd pressed himself up against the door in an effort to avoid the cat.

Pelt leaned toward her. "You can tell me the truth," he whispered. "Are you controlling that thing right now?"

Emilia heaved out an exasperated sigh. "I don't control the cats."

"Oh," Pelt said with a wink, "of course not."

Emilia scowled. "Why are you winking?"

"Because I know *nothing*," Pelt whispered. He gave an exaggerated nod and another wink, too.

"Clearly," Emilia muttered.

"Can someone get this cat?" Cornelius shrieked.

Fulke bent forward and gathered the large tabby into his thickly muscled arms. Rat-Slayer relaxed against the giant's chest and purred, as Fulke ran his huge, black-skinned hand over the cat's silver-and-white fur.

Emilia smiled. "Still think I'm controlling him?"

Pelt gave her a puzzled look. "Yes."

Emilia returned to Cornelius. "Can you tell me *where* you've felt pain recently?" She ignored the glare he shot her way. "Foot? Ankle? Knee? All of the above?"

"I told him already." Cornelius jabbed a pale, wrinkled finger at Pelt. "There's nothing wrong with me!"

Pelt joined them near the door, easily avoiding the deckhand's outstretched finger. "Yes, but the cat proved otherwise."

"The cat proved nothing!" Cornelius snarled. "The witch cast some kind of spell on it. That's all it was!"

Pelt grasped the stout sailor's shoulder in a way that seemed *not-so-gentle*—if the whitening of Pelt's tanned knuckles was any indication. "*Surgeon.*"

Between gritted teeth, Cornelius said, "The *surgeon* cast some kind of spell on it."

Maria had said Pelt knew how to talk to the guy, while Fulke knew how to crush him. Considering Fulke was currently petting a cat, while Pelt crushed someone's shoulder, Emilia thought the captain had it a bit backward.

"You know, this would be easier, if you'd cooperate," Emilia told Cornelius, "but if you don't want to talk to me, that's fine." She spread out her arms. "You'll just have to let me look at it."

A muscle ticked in the deckhand's jaw.

"Remove your trousers," Emilia said, gesturing toward the surgery table, "and climb up there."

Cornelius balked at the demand. "Absolutely not."

Fulke placed Rat-Slayer on the floor and stepped toward the deckhand, as if he intended to pick him up and *put* him on the surgery table.

But Pelt slapped Cornelius's shoulder, before Fulke could.

Emilia's shoulder ached in sympathy. Pelt might've been scrawnier than a lot of sailors, but he was *definitely* stronger than he looked.

"Come on, sailor," Pelt goaded the deckhand. "You've probably waited your entire life to hear a woman tell you to remove your trousers."

Emilia grimaced at the implication.

As if the trigger had been pulled, a deranged sort of rage burst in Cornelius's blue-grey eyes. He shoved Pelt backward. "That's not a woman!" He shouted so loudly that his skin reddened from the exertion, and he jabbed that pale finger of his in Emilia's direction. "To be a woman, you have to be human, and *that's* not human!"

Pelt raised his eyebrows at Fulke.

That was it.

No words. Just a look.

Fulke snatched Cornelius backward, crushing the deckhand against his chest, and Pelt swung his fist.

The sequence of events took place so quickly that Emilia didn't even realize what was happening until she heard the quiet *thump* of a fist against a jaw.

Emilia scrambled forward as quickly as she could, arms raised, as she squealed, "What are you doing?"

Pelt stepped back, wincing. "Nothing." He rubbed his reddened knuckles against his thick trousers.

Emilia gave him an incredulous look. "I saw you."

Cornelius's head rolled against Fulke's chest, and he let out a long, pained groan.

At least he wasn't bleeding.

Yet.

"Yes, well, you saw me do nothing, then," Pelt continued to lie. "Right, Fulke?"

Emilia turned toward the giant, who was still holding the recipient of the punch that supposedly didn't happen.

Fulke signed with his free hand.

"He says he saw nothing," Pelt said. He examined his reddened knuckles with a grimace. "Doesn't have a tongue, you know?"

Emilia scowled at the supposedly gentle giant. "You can't use that, Fulke! No one *sees* with their tongue."

Fulke shrugged his huge shoulders, jostling their...probably-concussed deckhand.

"This is the surgeon's cabin!" Emilia scolded the two pirates. "People come here to be healed, not punched!"

Pelt held up a finger. "If I punched him—not saying I did, but *if* it happened—it'd be totally legal. The Code only prohibits drawing weapons. It says nothing about fighting." He gestured toward Emilia. "As I'm sure you remember."

Emilia narrowed her eyes at that. "I punched Buchan on the deck, not in the surgeon's cabin!"

"Oh." Pelt turned to Fulke. "Well, we can do that! You can carry him to the deck next time, can't you?"

Fulke nodded—until Emilia glared at him, at which point, he began to shake his head vigorously, instead.

"There will be no more punching!" Emilia said.

Pelt pouted. "The *captain* would let me punch him."

Cornelius's head must've stopped spinning, by this point, because he suddenly cried out, "This is a hostile work environment!"

Fulke looked down at the angry deckhand, while Pelt muttered, "This is piracy."

Emilia shook her head at all of them. "Table. Now."

Cornelius didn't have time to object—because Fulke closed both hands around the sailor's arms and lifted him off the ground.

Fulke carried the much smaller man to the surgery table and set him on top of it. He reached for the deckhand's trousers, as well, but Cornelius slapped his hands away.

"I can do it!"

Fulke held up both hands and stepped back.

Pelt followed Emilia to the surgery table. "Are you sure you don't need one more punch?" he whispered. "If we let Fulke do it, we can call it sedation."

Emilia had to clamp her hand over her mouth to stifle a sudden giggle.

Pelt grinned, gold teeth flashing in the candlelight. "*There's* the woman who punched Buchan."

"Stop it!" Emilia hissed at him.

Pelt's smile only widened. "Helen will be delighted to know you're still in there."

These damn pirates were *determined* to bring out the worst in Emilia!

Though he still wore underclothes, Emilia offered the deckhand a wool blanket for privacy, but Cornelius swatted it away with the petulance of a child. Emilia sighed and set it on the table, next to him.

She then knelt to retrieve a surgical blade from one of the wooden chests on the floor.

"This is ridiculous," Cornelius griped. "I've served on this ship with no surgeon for ten years. I don't need one now. Not for a little cut!"

Pelt raised an eyebrow. "Oh, so there *is* a wound, then."

Cornelius grunted and refused to say anything more.

Emilia climbed to her feet. "Even little 'cuts' can be dangerous, if bacteria gets into the open wound."

Cornelius wrinkled his nose at her. "And what is that? Witch-speak?"

"It's surgeon-speak, dumbass," Pelt muttered.

Cornelius scoffed at that.

Behind the deckhand's back, Fulke met Emilia's gaze, before rolling his eyes.

Emilia suppressed a smile. Dealing with Cornelius was no easy feat, but having friends in the cabin with her eased the strain of it.

She froze.

Friends.

She'd thought it on her own—and not just about Judith and Maria, or even Helen, but about Fulke and Pelt, too.

Emilia had dared to think it.

She circled around to examine the deckhand's injured leg. "All right. Let me just—"

Emilia nearly dropped the blade.

She'd thought she was prepared for whatever she might find, but nothing could've prepared her for this.

Pelt watched her worriedly. "Is something wrong?"

Well, yes.

Very wrong.

Emilia didn't want to alarm them, though.

Not yet.

So, Emilia said nothing, as she knelt in front of the sailor and stared in horror at the blue, bloodless skin that stretched from his knee to his foot.

It didn't take long for Emilia to find the site of the original wound. The tissue had long since died, and a blackened web stretched outward from the wound.

But the *blue*...

The blue made no sense.

Unless...

Emilia fought to keep her voice steady, as she asked the deckhand, "How long has it been like this?"

"There's nothing wrong with it," Cornelius insisted.

Emilia wondered if the infection had rotted his brain as well as his skin. There was no way he thought this was normal.

Cornelius was either willing to die for his hatred, or he was in deep, *deep* denial.

Pelt stepped behind her—and gasped, "What the fuck?" He glanced down at Emilia. "That's not...normal, is it?"

Emilia needed to understand what had happened. So, she braced a hand against Cornelius's knee to hold him still, and she lifted the surgical blade. She pressed the sharpened steel into the blackened skin.

Clink.

What the...

Emilia pressed harder, but the blade didn't move.

She looked up at Cornelius, searching for signs of pain, but he was watching Rat-Slayer, not Emilia.

When he'd fallen on his leg and yelped, perhaps he hadn't felt the pain in his leg at all. Perhaps he'd felt it higher.

Perhaps he felt nothing in his leg.

Emilia tried again, pressing the blade downward. The grating sound of steel against stone caused her to jerk her hand back.

Hard.

Dry.

Stone.

"Can we get this over with already?" Cornelius said. "I do have other things to do today."

His reaction—or lack thereof—was enough to alarm Pelt. "Em?"

Emilia sliced harder, putting as much force behind the small blade as she might've put behind a sword.

Scrape.

"Em," Pelt said again. "Shouldn't it be…bleeding?"

A blue, bloodless leg?

No.

But it shouldn't have been *this* dry.

Emilia licked her lips and pleaded with her heart to stop racing. She glanced up at the Aevarian giant, who stood behind Cornelius. "I'll need your help."

Fulke nodded.

Pelt stepped closer. "What about me?"

"I need you," Emilia said breathlessly, "to get the captain."

Pelt cringed. "Eh. I don't know if I can do that," he mumbled. "The captain ordered me not to leave your side."

"Pelt." Emilia rose to her feet, clinging to any calm left inside of her. "I *need* the captain. Now."

Pelt must've seen something in her expression—because his eyes widened. "Aye, surgeon," he said, and without another moment of hesitation, he ran.

Maria rushed into the surgeon's cabin, strides ahead of her boatswain. Somewhere along the way, she'd overtaken him, and he'd never fully caught up.

For just a moment, when Maria saw the deckhand stretched out on the surgery table with his eyes closed, she thought her surgeon had killed him, after all, but then, Maria noticed the steady rise and fall of his chest and Fulke's massive hands, clasped around the sailor's shoulders.

Pelt stepped into the surgeon's cabin, still panting from his sprint across the ship. "Well, look at that. Must've punched him, after all."

Maria lifted an eyebrow, but her curiosity turned to concern when Em didn't even react to the joke.

Pelt's smile faded, too.

Something was wrong.

Em tied the tourniquet around the sailor's thigh. "It's a sedation spell," she said distractedly. "It'll give me time to prepare him for the amputation. I hope."

Maria stepped toward the table. "Sorry, love. Did you say amputation?"

Em looked up, and the fear in her bright, green eyes paralyzed Maria. "No higher than the thigh. I hope."

She was saying those two words a lot today.

"But Em…" Maria curled her fingers around Em's arm, noticing how Em relaxed slightly at her touch. "You don't like to amputate."

Maria hadn't observed as many of Em's surgeries as Judith had, but she'd observed enough to know that Em always tried everything else first.

And she'd yet to fail.

"No, I don't," Em said in a rush. "Too many risks. No point in amputating, if I can just heal. But I *can't*…just heal." She gasped for breath. "I can't heal this."

Maria had never seen Em look so…*lost*, but she imagined it was how she would've looked, too, had someone taken her ability to fight or sail. "Breathe, love. Amputation isn't the worst thing in the world."

"It is, if it doesn't work," Em whispered.

Maria's brows furrowed. "Why wouldn't it?"

Em shook her head, as if to clear her mind. "I have to get the bone saw, but…here." She placed a small, dry blade into Maria's hand. "Try to cut his leg."

Maria examined the tiny blade with a frown.

Aside from a thin layer of grey dust along the side of the blade, it didn't look as if it'd been used at all.

Maria stepped closer to the surgery table. She looked over the old deckhand, who actually had his mouth shut, for once—though not for the best reason—before letting her gaze settle on his outstretched legs.

She bit back a gasp.

One leg was a typical, sun-tanned beige, while the other was a chilling shade of blue—starting at the knee and continuing to the foot.

Like the skin of a corpse.

Maria looked up at Em. "This is some kind of infection?"

Em withdrew a large bone saw from one of the wooden chests. "*Some* kind of infection, yes. Have I ever seen one like it? No."

Maria didn't understand what Em meant—nor had she ever seen Em look so unsure, while caring for a wounded sailor. This was the one place where Emilia Drakon had always held some kind of confidence. "Em," she said warily. "What's wrong?"

Em carried the bone saw as comfortably as she carried a sword. If Maria hadn't recognized the panic flashing in Em's bright, green eyes, she might not have known the surgeon was worried at all. "Try to cut the leg. Then, you'll understand."

Maria leaned forward. "The part that's discolored?"

"Yes," Em told her. "Below the knee."

Maria had never used this sort of blade in her life, but she curled her fist around it and raised it into the air. She thrust the knife downward into the shin.

Or she tried to.

The tiny, steel blade clanged against something so hard it sent a jolt of pain all the way to Maria's elbow.

"What the hell?" Pelt said.

Em rolled her eyes. "I told you to cut, not stab."

If she hadn't been so shocked, Maria might've laughed at Em's admonishment. What did it matter how roughly she'd stabbed the deckhand, if his leg was as hard as a fucking rock?

But *why* was it as hard as a fucking rock?

Could she have hit bone, perhaps?

Maria stepped closer and tried to stab Cornelius again—only to growl in frustration as the blade refused to penetrate his leg. She pulled back the surgical knife and examined it.

There wasn't a drop of blood on it.

"Your knife isn't sharp enough," Maria grumbled.

Em lifted her eyebrows. "Yes, it is." When Maria turned toward Pelt with a contemplative frown, Em sighed, "There's no need to test it on anyone, Captain."

Eyes widening, Pelt took a step back.

Fulke released the sailor's shoulder and moved closer to Maria. He balled up his enormous fist in front of Maria to ensure she was watching and then thumped it against the blue-skinned leg.

The dense *thud* that followed did *not* sound human.

Cornelius didn't move a muscle.

Either the sleeping spell was more powerful than Em had implied, or he hadn't felt it.

Maria turned to Em, her eyes wide.

"Bone," Pelt guessed. "That sound—it was…bone, right?"

"Just beneath the skin?" Em said.

Pulling herself out of her brief moment of shock, Maria held out the dry knife. "Where's the blood?"

Em nodded, as if Maria had asked the right question. "It's stone," she said with a solemn frown. "The blood, the vessels—it's all turned to stone."

Pelt shook his head in denial. "That's…not possible." He glanced at Maria. "Is it?"

"How should I know?" Maria said breathlessly. "I've never *heard* of it happening before."

"That's because it hasn't happened before, or at least I don't think it has," Em told them. "This is an infection unlike any I've seen before. If I could study it, I would, but I don't have time. The human body needs blood flow. If it keeps spreading, he'll die."

Maria's stomach dropped. "It's spreading?"

Em moved to stand beside Maria. She pointed to the blackened wound. "It's taken about two weeks for the infection to spread from here to the knee." She lifted her finger to point at a quick swipe of black ink, just above the knee. "When I sent Pelt to get you, that was still flesh and blood. Try to cut it now."

Maria eyed her warily for a moment, before turning to do as the surgeon asked. The small, steel blade clinked against something as solid as a mountain.

Her grip tightened around the knife.

"Is it contagious?" Pelt asked.

"I don't know," Emilia said honestly.

Maria spun to face the boatswain. "No," she said firmly. "Until we know more, it's *not* contagious."

Pelt gave a solemn nod. "Aye, Captain."

Maria turned toward Fulke, as well. "The exact nature of this infection does not leave this cabin."

Fulke nodded easily.

Maria glanced at her surgeon. "Do you know how it happened?"

Em bit her lip. "I have a theory."

Cornelius stirred in his sleep, and all three of them glanced at him.

"The magic's wearing off. I can try it again, but," Em sighed, "we'll need the bite strap, just in case."

"I'll get it," Fulke signed.

Maria nodded.

Fulke would know where it was, since he'd helped with the ship's last amputation—the one that had ended in a sailor's death.

Maria turned to Em. "What do you need?"

"Fulke's agreed to hold the upper half of Cornelius's body," Em told her. "If someone could hold the lower half—" She glanced at Pelt, who'd gone surprisingly pale. "If you think you can handle it, I mean."

Captain Maria Welles, of course, was no stranger to blood. "You guard the door, Pelt. I'll hold him."

Pelt breathed a sigh of relief. "Aye, Captain."

"I'll cut here, where I still can," Em said, resting the saw against his thigh, "but we need to move quickly—before the infection spreads further."

Maria nodded and moved into position. "I suppose you'll tell me your *theory* after we've finished here?"

"Yes, but I have to warn you, Captain," Em said with a solemn frown, "you're not going to like it."

Maria was sure she wouldn't.

CHAPTER 22

Gods and Seashell Stew

"Em, wait!"

Maria chased after Em, climbing the wooden steps outside the surgeon's cabin. When Em opened the hatch, orange, evening light rushed into the dark space, along with a burst of noise—pirates yelling, waves crashing.

Even in a perfect situation, Em wouldn't have heard her over *that*. Still, Maria yelled, "Em!"

Em was out onto the main deck, before Maria could catch her.

Maria emerged soon afterward, squinting at the barrage of light. She held her hand against her headscarf to shield her eyes—and wished she'd had time to grab her tricorn before the surgery.

It wasn't hard to spot Em amongst the sea of sailors—with her shortened, black hair and her lovely, wide curves, all clad in black.

Maria rushed toward her. She took Em by the arm and turned her.

Em looked up at Maria, eyes wide and unfocused. "Captain? What do you need?"

Maria couldn't tell whether Em was panicking or just in shock. "You're covered in blood, Em—in the middle of the day, on the main deck."

"Oh." Em looked down at the splatter of blood on her fair-skinned arms and the thick, wet patches on her black shirt and trousers. She then looked up, watching as three sailors strode past.

None of them turned to look at Em or Maria, but that didn't mean no one *else* on the ship had noticed.

"Sorry, Captain."

Maria stepped closer, her chest twisting with worry. "Don't apologize. Just come with me."

The flash of panic reignited in Em's eyes, and when Maria tugged at her arm, Em resisted. "I—I can't," she stammered. "I—I need to do something."

"You *need* to come with me," Maria corrected. "You need to clean yourself up, and you can't use your own cabin for that because, well, it's in use, isn't it?"

Was that the most *delicate* way to say there was an angry, amputated bigot who'd be bleeding and cursing in the surgeon's cabin for the foreseeable future?

Probably not.

But how else would she say it?

Em shook her head, but the motion was quick and jerky.

Panic.

This was panic.

"You don't understand," Em was mumbling.

"Then, you can *explain* in my quarters," Maria said firmly.

The concern of Em drawing unwanted attention offered Maria a convenient excuse, but really, it was concern for Em that drove her to act.

Whether Em realized it yet or not, she *needed* a quiet space.

Maria had seen Em like this enough to know that—to know that the chaotic, main deck of a ship would only overload Em's senses at a time like this.

"I need supplies," Em muttered.

Well, *that* wasn't the response Maria had expected. "Supplies?"

Em looked up, her bright, green eyes wide, as if she'd only just remembered Maria could hear her.

When it became clear Em couldn't—or wouldn't—elaborate, Maria whispered, "Em, please."

The plea cracked through the haze of Em's anxiety, and she nodded. "Yes, Captain."

Taking Em's arm, Maria led her toward the captain's quarters. She positioned herself in front of Em in case anyone stopped them to ask questions.

News would spread of the amputation, of course.

Screaming tended to draw a bit of attention, after all. It was... inconvenient in that way.

But that didn't mean anyone had to know the exact nature of Cornelius's infection.

Not until Maria knew more, anyway.

Not until Em *told* her more.

The odd thing was that Em had barely shown any unease at all during the amputation itself. She'd only panicked afterward, and the only clue she'd given Maria as to why was this mention of supplies.

Supplies for *what*?

Em had already finished the surgery. She'd already dressed the wound. She'd already given instructions to the sailors Pelt had sent to stay with Cornelius.

What did she have left to do?

As awful as any amputation was, it'd been amazing to watch Em work. Maria had seen larger, stronger ship carpenters tremble throughout the process, but Em had handled it all with ease.

Maria supposed that was just the wonder of having a real surgeon, for once.

She hated when Adda was right.

When they reached the captain's quarters, Maria unlocked her door and ushered Em inside.

Yellowish light flickered along the walls, and Maria glanced at the candles on her table. She'd rushed out in such a hurry when Pelt had come to get her that she hadn't had time to blow out the candles.

"He already hated me," Em mumbled, "and now, I've taken his leg."

Maria turned to her. "It's his own fault. If he'd come to you sooner, you might not have had to."

"Might not," Em repeated.

Maria frowned worriedly. She needed to know what was wrong with Em. She stepped closer and pressed her hand against the curve of Em's lower back, urging her toward her bed. "Sit."

Em moved—almost mindlessly—toward the bed.

When she sank down on the edge of the mattress, Maria went to retrieve two empty buckets. "I'll get some seawater."

"Seawater," Em repeated. She looked up at Maria. "I need seawater."

Maria stopped and nodded. "I'm aware." She shot a bemused look at Em's bloodied clothing and skin.

Em glanced down at herself. "Should I sit in a chair, instead?"

"It'll be fine," Maria said with a laugh. "There's not much on your trousers, anyway."

And it wasn't as if Maria hadn't waltzed around her quarters, covered in blood, a few times herself.

"I need seawater—but not just for cleaning," Em tried to explain. "Can I come with you?"

"No," Maria said irritably. "I know it's hard for you, but you need to sit the fuck still for a moment."

It might've been the pot calling the kettle black, but at least Maria's habit of wandering was a little less…frantic.

What Em did was less like wandering and more like running from one task to the next without ever stopping to breathe or… *explain* things to her captain.

"What could you need seawater for, anyway?" Maria asked. "If not for cleaning yourself up?"

Em looked away. "It's better if you don't know."

"Like hell it is," Maria snarled.

Em pressed her lips together.

Maria sighed. She hated seeing Em in such a tormented state and not knowing how to help, and as hypocritical as it might've been for Maria, of all people, to think it, she also hated that Em wouldn't let her *in*.

Especially after last night.

"Make peace with it however you need to," Maria said, "but when I get back, you're telling me what's going on."

Em stared at the floorboards beneath her shoes and clasped her hands between her knees, squeezing her fingers.

Maria spun on the heels of her boots. The empty, wooden buckets swung in her hands, flopping against her thighs. She'd nearly reached the door when a hint of light caught the corner of her eye.

Maria glanced over her shoulder to find that beautiful tracery of a dragon shining along the bend of Em's arm.

Dragons?

What could dragons have to do with *this*?

WHEN MARIA RETURNED TO HER QUARTERS, SHE FOUND EM *standing* by the table. "Hmm," Maria muttered, "I thought I said to sit the fuck still." She dropped the buckets next to Em's feet, water sloshing over the sides. "Must've imagined it."

Em turned to Maria and held out an old, pewter bowl that she'd likely found in Maria's cabinets—when she'd been *not* sitting still. "Can I use this?"

"Probably," Maria said. "Can you tell me why you need it?"

Em pulled the bowl back toward herself. "I'd rather not."

"Em," Maria said irritably. "You said you'd tell me your theory as soon as you finished the amputation."

"My theory, yes," Em agreed, "but I never said I'd tell you this."

"Em…" Maria tried to step toward her, but the toe of her boot hit one of the wooden buckets and sent seawater splashing over the side. She looked down, relieved to find it hadn't fallen over, at least.

She narrowed her eyes at the threads of green algae floating near the surface of the water. "What imbecile drew up this water and didn't remove the seaweed?"

Maria tried to remember who'd handed it to her.

"Seaweed?" Em repeated. Her eyes brightened, and she knelt

beside the bucket. "I need that!" She lifted a string of seaweed from the water.

Maria stared blankly at her. "You need…seaweed?"

"Small life," Em said distractedly. She climbed to her feet, water still dripping from the seaweed, and she draped the stringy, green plant over her palm.

Maria shook her head.

Em picked the *worst* times to start speaking that witchy gibberish of hers.

"Bowl, seaweed…" Maria listed. "What are you doing? Making stew?"

"Don't forget seawater," Em mumbled.

Maria grimaced. "Really *bad* stew?"

Em looked up, suddenly. "Do you have a seashell?"

Maria's eyes widened. "Perhaps you should leave the *recipe* part of the cooking to Judith, love."

A small laugh escaped Em's lips, and Maria's chest lifted at the sound. She hadn't realized how much she'd needed to hear Em's laughter until that moment.

Her surgeon was still in there.

Beneath…whatever this was.

"Do you have a seashell or not?" Em tried again.

With a sigh, Maria turned and strode toward her wooden chests. She knelt in front of one and pushed back the lid. It creaked on its hinges, and she rifled inside the chest, pushing aside old books and clothes, until she found a few large seashells at the bottom.

"Does it matter which sea it's from?" Maria asked.

"No." The soft *pat* of Em's flat, leather shoes informed Maria of her approach. "Any sea will do."

Maria removed a remarkably large, mostly white seashell from the chest and climbed to her feet. She turned to Em, offering the shell. "Here. This one's large enough that I'm not worried you'll try to eat it."

With a giggle, Em said, "I'm not making stew."

When Em tried to take the seashell, Maria closed her hands around it. "Then, tell me what you *are* doing."

Em dropped her hands. "Please, Captain," she said. "It'd be better for you, if you didn't know."

"How would it be better for me," Maria asked, "to not know what my surgeon's doing?"

Em lifted her shoulders in a slow, uneasy shrug. "I believe they call it plausible deniability?"

Maria *really* didn't like the sound of that.

"You're trying to protect me," Maria realized. She gave a quick nod—because of course Em was trying to protect her. Just as she'd done earlier. "I'm Captain Maria Welles. I don't need anyone to protect me."

Em rolled her eyes. "Oh, drop the arrogance. You're not untouchable, and you know it!"

Maria *did* know it. With Zain possibly on the verge of mutiny, she was more aware of it than ever.

That didn't mean she'd ever admit it.

"I'm your captain, and I *will* know what my surgeon is doing," Maria told her. She stepped closer. "If I have to watch your every move, I will know. So, save us both some time, and just fucking tell me."

Em narrowed her eyes. "I hope you're not trying to intimidate me, Captain."

Maria flashed a vicious smile. "Why would I waste my time?"

"You're more than just my captain, and I don't want you affected by my actions," Em explained. "But I have to do this."

Maria set the large, white shell with its spirals of pink and gold on the table, but when Em reached for it, Maria caught her wrist.

A quick gasp escaped Em's lips, and Maria tugged her forward. Em's soft curves melded to Maria, unleashing an unexpected wave of desire.

Gods, it was hard to focus around this woman.

Em's eyelashes fluttered, and her breath caught in her throat.

At least Maria knew the feeling was mutual.

Maria rubbed Em's wrist with her thumb, tracing the scars left by shackles—the scars they shared. "Em." She tilted her face toward Em's. "Tell me. Please."

Em's lips parted, and her soft exhale of breath fell against Maria's lips. "I'm summoning Aletha."

Maria dropped her wrist. "What?!"

Em fell back on her heels. "I'm summoning the goddess of the sea," she reiterated, "and now, you know why I didn't want to tell you."

Maria couldn't believe this. Not only had Em planned to disobey a direct order, but she'd thought she could do it without her captain knowing?

Where did she think she was going to hide a whole fucking goddess?

Under the bed?

Em's gaze roamed Maria's face with patient curiosity, as she waited for a response.

"I told you no," Maria snarled. "On Drakon Isle, I told you *no*."

"Yes," Em said easily, "because you were afraid of what people might think." She leaned forward, determination flashing in her bright green eyes. "I'm sorry, but that's not a good enough reason for me."

Anger coursed through Maria, burning her from the inside out.

The nerve of this witch!

To suggest *she* was afraid!

Sometimes, Maria admired Em's bravery. Other times, she adored it.

But every now and then, it infuriated her.

"I am afraid," Maria growled, "of *nothing*."

Em didn't even flinch. "Prove it."

Maria let her hand curl around the cool hilt of her sword. "Careful, surgeon."

"We need Aletha, and you don't want me to summon her because you think the crew won't approve," Em said. "What do you call that, if not fear?"

"A desire to hold my position here," Maria told her, "to remain captain of *my* ship!" She pressed her hand to her chest, her pulse racing against her palm. "I told you on Drakon Isle! I told you how it'd look if you aligned yourself with a goddess they believed to be evil. Things have only gotten worse since then! Zain's threatening mutiny, and you want to do this now? How do you think he'll react, if I let you do this?"

A sympathetic frown pulled at Em's brows. "I'm not asking you to *let* me do anything," she informed Maria. "I'm telling you what I'm going to do."

Maria scoffed in disbelief.

Em stepped closer. "I don't *want* you to lose your ship. I love that you're my captain," she confessed. "I love how much you love *being* captain. I love how much you love this ship."

A strange warmth settled in Maria's chest.

"But as much as I don't want to see you lose your ship," Em continued, "I want to see you die *less*."

So, that's what this was about.

The panic she'd seen in Em earlier—that's what had caused it. She thought Maria's life was in danger.

"It's one infection, Em! You're a brilliant surgeon. You'll figure it out." Maria let out an incredulous laugh. "You don't need a goddess to explain human disease to you."

She'd genuinely thought that would calm Em—which was why she was so taken aback when it didn't.

"Human disease?" Em repeated. "You think this is human? Captain—" She shook her head in disbelief. "The inside of his leg turned to stone, like the innards of a mountain."

Well, yes, but…

What other kind of disease was there?

"What are you saying, Em?" Maria scoffed. "That it was magic?" Just suggesting it made unease crawl beneath Maria's skin.

A magical disease would only reinforce Illopia's fear of magic, and since Em was the only magic-wielder aboard the *Wicked Fate*, it certainly wouldn't paint *her* in the best light.

People like Cornelius would suddenly find more…allies.

"It's not magic, is it?" Maria asked warily.

Em shrugged, but the flash of pain in her bright green eyes confirmed it.

"Shit." Maria ran her hand over her headscarf, accidentally

jostling a few curls loose. "It's gone, isn't it? You cut it off. Literally. It must be gone! Right?"

"I hope," Em said simply.

Oh, why couldn't she just lie?

Just this once.

"I assume there wasn't a way to heal it with magic?" Maria asked. "That would've been easier to hide."

It was a foolish question, really.

Maria understood Em's magic had limits, and she'd known the moment Em mentioned amputation that she'd already tried everything else.

'Healing spells are good for mending,' Em had once told her, *'not as good for reconstruction.'*

Which category did stone-limbs fall under?

"I tried," Em assured her. She extended her hand, staring at it, as if she could see her magic. "It was so *wrong*, so powerful. My magic couldn't touch it."

Maria didn't understand what she meant. As an Illopian, she'd been taught all magic was wrong, but Em talked as if *this* magic had been different.

As if *this* magic were the only one that was wrong.

"We shouldn't jump to conclusions," Maria said—a bit too quickly. "There's no reason to assume it's magic." She shrugged. "Don't humans sometimes develop growths that are like…stone?"

"This was different," Em said. "Come on, Captain. Surely, you felt something? The cat and I did."

Maria frowned. "The cat?"

"I let him out before the amputation," Em told her. "I didn't want to traumatize him."

Maria nearly laughed. She'd seen that cat disembowel rats before—and he'd probably seen *Maria* disembowel some people, too.

"If this disease *is* magical, which I still find hard to believe," Maria said, "how did Cornelius catch it?"

Em's brows furrowed. "It's not a virus, Captain. It's an infection from a wound. You *saw* the sword wound, didn't you?"

"The black crevice with the, er," Maria paused to wave her hand in a circle, "spider-web around it?"

Em tilted her head at that, her soft, black hair sliding toward her chin. "That's…one way to describe it."

"Then, it can't be magic!" Maria insisted. "If it came from a sword wound, it must be a normal infection."

Swords were specifically non-magical items! That was what made them great.

A memory came unbidden to Maria's mind—of a certain surgeon wielding a sword inflamed with dragon-fire—but Maria dismissed it.

That wasn't magic, really.

Was it?

Em sighed. She withdrew a long, slender dagger—the beautiful one with a dragon carved into the handle, the one Maria had seen many times before. "This is an enchanted blade."

"So you've said," Maria acknowledged, though she still didn't know what it meant.

Em turned the blade over, tracing the dragon with her opposite finger. "My mother gave it to me before she died."

"Your mother?" Maria repeated.

There was no way the woman who'd drowned and tortured Em had also given her gifts.

What sense did that make?

Em offered her an amused smile. "Believe me. I was just as confused as you." Her gaze dropped to the shining, steel blade. "I didn't understand until one, lucid moment in the Regolis dungeons—when I finally realized *how* she'd intended for me to use it."

Maria waited for Em to elaborate.

"She told me when she gave it to me that there are two types of enchanted daggers, but that our people had only ever had use of one." Em held the long dagger between them, balancing it in each hand. "There are blades that absorb magic and blades that deliver it."

Maria eyed the dagger warily. Em had stabbed her with it

before, so she knew *it*, at least, didn't hold any magical infections. Pointing at it, she guessed, "This one absorbs?"

"Yes," Em confirmed. "It takes in the essence of things. Its purpose is to store the magic—for me to withdraw later." She drew the blade back toward herself. "You see, my people have no use for a blade that delivers magic, since we can wield magic on our own. But a blade that holds the destructive magic of a dead warrior sorceress, so a *healer* might withdraw it later—to set fire to the crowd that had gathered around the gallows, for instance—*might* have its use."

Maria's eyebrows rose. Zain had told her of the incident months ago, but this was the first time she'd heard *Em* speak of it.

"Do you know who'd have use of the other kind of enchanted blade, though?" Em asked. "Do you know who *can't* wield the magic on their own?"

"Humans," Maria realized.

Em nodded. "The Illopian Royal Navy."

Maria shook her head at that. "The Royal Navy doesn't use magic. They hate magic. It's outlawed."

"Captain," Em said with a sigh, "you're walking proof that they don't care about laws or morals."

The mention of Maria's crime—her *first* crime—still sent a bit of anxiety skittering underneath her skin. No one spoke of it as brazenly as Em did.

But that was because others saw her moment of emotion as weakness, while Em saw it as strength.

"Morals, no. But laws?" Maria said with a grimace. "As fucked up as it is, there are no explicit laws in the Kingdom of Illopia regarding human trafficking."

Em's eyes widened. Clearly, she'd assumed otherwise.

"The laws regarding magic, on the other hand," Maria told her, "are explicit and, for the most part, universally agreed upon."

Em shook her head. "That's—"

"Fucked up, yes," Maria said. "As I said."

Em merely shook her head again, as if she couldn't wrap her mind around it. "Still," she said, "after the things you've seen them do—the things *I've* seen them do—you can't think they're above hypocrisy!"

"There's a difference in other forms of hypocrisy and breaking the *law*," Maria insisted. "Their sense of self-righteousness comes from their ability to follow and enforce the law. They believe it makes them the good guys—even as they commit atrocities like the ones you and I have seen."

Em's soft, pink lips twisted with a hint of cynicism. "I think you're overestimating them. Some people, I think…don't have limits."

Maria might not have known Em before the imprisonment, but she knew—Maria *knew*—where that kind of cynicism came from.

"You have mountain priests in your kingdom," Em reminded her, "who receive prophecies." She stepped toward Maria. "What do you think prophecies *are*, Captain?"

"Petra tells them things, and they write it down. That's what they tell people, at least." Maria shrugged a shoulder. "I've always suspected they were making it all up. Or…eating the wrong mushrooms."

Em's brows furrowed. "Well, I can't speak for their diets, but I *can* tell you that divination is magic." She closed the last shred of space between them. "Summoning a god? Also, magic."

Maria shook her head, ready to deny it again—when Em stunned her by touching Maria's face. Maria's breath caught in her throat, and she fought back the urge to lean into Em's wondrously gentle touch.

"Captain, you say you don't see yourself as an Illopian anymore," Em said, "but you still think like one."

Pairing harsh words with a gentle touch was an intriguing talent that Em *probably* didn't realize she had.

"How?" Maria breathed.

Em's hand warmed against Maria's face, and a strange glow enveloped her fingers. Then, that warmth flowed *into* Maria, filling her with something…*pleasant*—something that felt like…life.

And kindness.

And the very essence of…Em.

Maria closed her eyes and exhaled shakily.

"You can't kill magic. Not with hate. Not with fear," Em said softly. "You can outlaw it, sure, but all you're actually doing is sending it into hiding. Try as they might, Illopians will never truly eradicate magic."

Maria opened her eyes. "Why not?" she whispered.

She didn't know *why* she'd whispered. Maria supposed she'd just felt as if she were in the presence of something too magnificent, too wondrous, to scare away.

"Because magic is in everything." Em blinked emerald-green eyes that were just as beautiful and dazzling as her magic. "It's the first thing we're taught as Drakon sorcerers—the first things the dragons ever told *me*. Magic exists in everything."

Maria held on to her every word. "How can that be?"

"It's in the earth you walk on. It's in the air you breathe." Em slid her hand downward, tracing the path of Maria's carotid artery. Maria shuddered, as Em's soft fingers scattered chills along her skin. "It's the very life inside of you. Everything in Aletharia is magic."

Gods. Was it any wonder that Maria was ready to do almost anything for this woman?

With her lovely touch and her lovely words?

With the way every part of her fed something in Maria that had starved for too long?

"Everything?" Maria repeated. "Even humans?"

"Some creatures wield magic, and some don't," Em told her, "but the magic doesn't cease to exist, simply because you can't wield it."

Maria watched Em's hand fall to her side and tried to talk sense into the part of herself that wanted to grab Em's hand and put it back on her face.

"That's why humans fear it," Em said. "Humans—Illopian humans, especially—have a habit of hating what they can't control."

Maria couldn't argue with that. She'd learned long ago that the Kingdom of Illopia destroyed what they couldn't control—and the people who got caught in that destruction often faced an even worse fate.

"What they don't understand is that my people don't control magic either," Em said. "We exist *with* things. We don't force them to do what they're not meant to do."

"Like infect someone," Maria assumed.

Em offered a small shrug. "If I had to guess, I'd say Petra has somehow convinced King Eldric that this awful magick is a kind he can control—through the use of enchanted blades. The irony, though, is that not only is this a magick that can't be controlled, it's also one that can't be *wielded*—because it's divine magic."

A chill slid down Maria's spine. "Petra? Divine magic? What are you trying to say, Em?"

Surely, Maria had heard her incorrectly.

"Think about it, Captain," Em said. "The infection turned Cornelius's leg to stone. Petra is the god of mountains. What are mountains formed from?"

"That's a huge leap," Maria said.

"Not that huge," Em argued. "My magic wouldn't touch it. Dragon magic is one of the most powerful magicks in all of Aletharia, and I wield dragon magic." She held out her hand, and that familiar light unfurled from it, once more. "I can affect siren magic and wind magic, but I couldn't touch *this*. Because even a dragon can't fight a god."

Maria shook her head firmly. "No. No. Our enemy is Catherine, not Petra. Not a fucking god!"

"What makes you so sure?" Em challenged.

Maria threw out her arms. "Because it's ridiculous!" she said with a near-hysterical laugh. "Look, I get that *your* life might've been all magic and gods, but sometimes, Em, things are just flesh and blood!"

"It's funny you would say that," Em snarled right back, "because what was missing in that surgeon's cabin just now was exactly that! *Flesh and blood!*"

Maria refused to accept it. "You're paranoid. Our enemy is Catherine Rochester. A human. Not a god."

"You don't even believe that!" Em accused. "You were the one who told *me* it didn't matter who was admiral—that it'd be the same, regardless. Catherine is a tool for a larger power." Em quirked her head, before adding, "A horrendous tool, who I'd like to see reduced to ash and bone by my dragons—but a tool, nonetheless."

Despite the confusion and frustration whirling through her, Maria smiled at that. "No blood?"

Em offered a playful roll of her eyes. "We can stab her first," she offered, "if you insist."

Maria leaned toward her. "I absolutely insist."

Em laughed, but her smile faded soon afterward. "Captain, I know when I'm out of my depth. Do you?"

Maria's jaw tightened. Historically, no. Maria did *not* usually know. "We don't need a goddess."

Em leaned closer. "Captain, your arrogance might've made sense, when your enemies were all clad in blue and easy to kill, but that's not the case anymore. We're up against a god, and the only creature who can tell us how to fight a god is another god—or… goddess, in this case."

"We're not fighting a god, Em," Maria stated. "That isn't the war I signed up to fight."

Em spread out her arms. "Well, damn. I suppose someone forgot to check with you before infecting one of your sailors," she said. "Don't worry. We'll write a letter and get it all straightened out."

Maria suppressed a smile. Ah, that sharp tongue of Em's would be her undoing every time. "Couldn't we give it a bit more time?" she asked. "If he gets better, we won't need your goddess."

"And if he doesn't?" Em said. "We might not have more time, Captain. It might already be spreading."

"You'll figure it out," Maria assured her.

Em didn't see herself as clearly as Maria did. She didn't see how quickly and easily she rose to every challenge.

She'd handle this one, too. Maria knew it.

"What if I don't?" Em's voice rose in panic. "People will die, Captain! You could die! Judith could die! Helen, Fulke, Pelt…" She staggered backward, hands trembling at her sides. "Goddamn it, I care about too many people on this ship! I tried not to, but I do! And I can't—I can't—" Em gasped, breasts heaving beneath her thin, black shirt. "I can't lose you, too."

Em lifted her hands to cover her face, but Maria stepped forward and grasped her arms to stop her.

"Em," Maria breathed.

Her heart broke at the sight of Em like this, but what shattered her more was the knowledge that *this* had been there all along, just beneath the surface.

Em had been thinking like this, *suffering* like this, the entire time, and she'd bottled it up. She'd let the panic rage inside, while feigning calm on the outside.

Maria pressed her fingers beneath Em's chin and lifted—until Em's wide, green eyes met hers. "Even if we do lose someone, it won't be your fault."

"I can't." Em's chest continued to rise and fall, her breath escaping in quick, erratic gasps. "Please. *Please*, Captain." Her eyes glistened. "I can't lose you."

Maria's chest pulled so tight it hurt, and she curled her hands around Em's soft face. Resting her forehead against Em's, she murmured, "Oh, my sweet surgeon. You were supposed to hate me."

"I know," Em said with a sound that was as much a sob as it was a laugh. "Goddess, what is *wrong* with me?"

"Nothing." Maria traced her thumbs along the gentle curves of Em's face. "You're strong, smart, and…still kind, somehow—whether you're ready to admit it or not. Nothing's wrong with you, love. *Nothing.*"

Em tried to shake her head, but Maria still held her face. "I'm not strong. I'm literally terrified right now."

"That's not weakness, love," Maria murmured. "It's just…a scar."

At that, Em relaxed.

Maria felt it. In every part of her that touched Em, she felt it— as each muscle in Em's body stopped trembling.

Em rested her hands against Maria's hips, just beneath the scabbard, and when she spoke again, her voice no longer shook. "You were supposed to hate me, too, you know?"

"Do you want to know a secret?" Maria whispered. She let her mouth brush against Em's, savoring the way Em arched against her, when she did. "I never really did. Not for long."

With a soft laugh, Em admitted, "You fooled me."

"I'm a pirate, darling," Maria murmured against her lips. "Fooling you is my job." Maria tightened her hold on Em's face and closed her lips over Em's. She let herself enjoy the silky warmth of Em's mouth—for just a moment—before pulling back. "Do you trust her?"

Em blinked up at her. "Aletha? Yes."

Maria let her hands slide downward, resting them against Em's shoulders, instead. She still couldn't bring herself to break contact completely. "Because this is a *goddess* we're discussing," she said. "You say Petra enslaves people. What's to stop the sea goddess from doing the same?"

Em shook her head. "Petra shackles people with greed. Aletha fills them with curiosity and wanderlust. What's more freeing than that?"

Maria glanced around her quarters, considering the life those particular feelings had driven *her* toward. "Suppose you have a point."

The warmth of Em's hands remained steady on Maria's hips. "Bargaining with a goddess is always a bit dangerous, but it's better than the alternative." Em flashed her little impish smile that never failed to make Maria's stomach flip. "Besides, when has danger ever stopped Captain Maria Welles?"

When, indeed?

A slow grin spread across Maria's face. "All right. Tell me what we need to do."

~

MARIA COULD HONESTLY SAY SHE'D NEVER FOUND ANOTHER SAILOR sitting cross-legged on the floorboards as often as she found Emilia Drakon sitting cross-legged on the floorboards.

You'd think chairs didn't exist.

Em looked up at her. "Are you sure you want to be here for this? You can still leave and pretend you knew nothing."

Maria folded her arms over her chest. "Show me how it works, and then, I'll decide."

Em nodded. "First, we'll need our bowl of seawater." She adjusted the bowl in front of her—that she'd already filled with water. "Actually, it doesn't have to be a bowl. This is just me improvising. Usually, I'd walk out *into* the sea, but I figured that might raise some eyebrows."

"At our current depth?" Maria said. "I'd say so."

Em laughed. She placed a single thread of seaweed in the bowl. "Next, we need our small life."

With an exaggerated sigh, Maria said, "Please, translate for those of us who don't speak *witch*."

Em offered a baffled shrug. "It's…small life," she said. "Literally just a…small life-form."

Maria blinked at that. "Oh."

"It represents life and kindness," Em explained, "and the Sea's care for all creatures—no matter how small or vulnerable."

Maria pointed skeptically toward the green algae. "The sea goddess cares about seaweed?"

"Yes," Em said slowly.

"But *no* one cares about seaweed," Maria argued. "It's annoying."

Em's lips quirked upward. "Aletha does."

Maria shook her head in confusion. "It simply isn't possible."

With another quiet laugh, Em picked up the large, mostly white seashell. "This represents death—since the creature inside has died. And strength." She placed the shell in the center of the bowl, displacing enough water that it flowed over the sides. "We must respect all: life and death, kindness and strength."

Maria tilted her head curiously at that. If those were, indeed, the Sea's values, it was easy to see why the sea goddess had favored Em.

"Is that all?" Maria waved her hand toward the bowl of seawater and…*stuff*. "Is your seashell and algae stew going to summon the goddess now?"

"Not quite," Em said. She drew that beautiful, enchanted dagger once more.

Maria straightened. "What do you mean to do with that?"

"The most important part of a summon is sacrifice." Em positioned the shining blade over her palm.

Maria stepped toward her. "You're not cutting *yourself*!"

Em offered her a baffled smile. "You want me to cut someone *else*?"

"Well…maybe," Maria muttered, "if you have to." She glanced around. "I'm sure I could find someone."

Em laughed loudly at that. "Contrary to popular belief, Captain, most sorcerers don't sacrifice other people—or any creature, for that matter—for our magic, and if we did, it wouldn't summon a *god*."

Maria took another step toward Em. "Why not?"

"Because summoning a god requires *self*-sacrifice," Em said. "Now, that could mean all sorts of things, but the simplest form is blood and pain." She held up the dagger and her open palm for emphasis.

A jolt of shock traveled through Maria, and she glanced down at the thick scar in the center of her *own* palm. "Pain."

With a knowing look, Em murmured, "A lot of nerve endings in the hand."

Maria looked up, her chest fluttering, as she met Em's gaze.

On her first full day aboard, when Em had seemingly guessed how painful Maria's wound would've been, she hadn't been guessing at all. She'd *known*. She'd known because she'd done it to herself.

Maria narrowed her eyes. "What kind of *not*-evil goddess refuses to see you unless you hurt yourself?"

Em's brows drew inward. "Aletha didn't create this magic. It's dragon magic, and it needs sacrifice. That isn't Aletha's fault. I'm the one who chose blood and pain."

Maria didn't think she could just *watch* Em do that to herself. "What are your other choices?"

"I'm not sure, but I don't want to risk it," Em admitted. "I know from experience this sacrifice is enough, and I'm not afraid of the pain."

So she'd proven.

Many times over.

Maria gave a reluctant nod. "All right."

Em offered her a gentle smile. "Well, we've reached the point where you should probably leave." She glanced toward the door. "I promise, if I'm caught, I'll tell them I did it without your knowledge."

Maria's lips curved. Humility or not, Zain had been wrong about Maria not appreciating Em's loyalty.

Em didn't give her loyalty freely. She'd made Maria earn it.

But when she did give it, there was no loyalty quite like Em's.

Maria had realized it when Em had called her captain and meant it, and Em had never proven her wrong. She adored Em's loyalty and had no idea how to live up to it—or *why* Em thought she already had.

"You're not going to get caught," Maria decided, "because I'm not leaving."

Em's brows furrowed. "But if you're here when—"

"If I'm here," Maria interrupted, "I'll kill whoever finds us."

"Kill?" Em sputtered. "I'd rather you not."

Maria turned and strode toward the door. She pulled out her large, brass skeleton key and slid it into the lock. She turned the key, and the lock slid into place with a quiet *thunk*. "Unless they're Fulke, it's unlikely they'll break down the door, anyway." She returned to Em's side. "But if they do, I'll handle it."

Em's brows twisted with worry. "I don't want you to lose your ship."

"I won't," Maria insisted, "but I also won't see you executed in some attempt to protect me. It's simply not happening." She crossed her arms. "If this must be done, it'll be done with my protection."

Em's soft jawline shifted, as if she were grinding her teeth. "I don't know…"

"You didn't ask my permission to summon a goddess," Maria pointed out, "and I'm not asking yours to stay." Her gaze drifted back toward Em's strange, little bowl. "Besides, how often does a pirate captain get the chance to watch someone summon a goddess with seashell stew? How could I pass *that* up?"

"Stop calling it stew!" Em laughed.

Maria flashed a wicked grin. "Make me."

Em rolled her eyes. "There's something else, though." She gently placed the dagger in her lap. "You can't see her without participating in the spell."

"Oh," Maria said. The slight dip of disappointment in her stomach surprised her. She hadn't realized how much Em had piqued her curiosity already. "So, you have to have magic to meet a goddess?"

Em shook her head quickly. "No. You have to participate." She tapped her finger against the long, enchanted blade. "It requires self-sacrifice—from anyone who wants to see her. *Anyone.*"

Maria nodded in understanding. "I have to cut my hand."

"I could do it for you, but," Em hesitated, "Captain, I don't know if I can hurt you like that. Deliberately."

Maria scoffed, "Em, you've stabbed me before."

"Yes, but that was to prove a point," Em said—with an adorably mischievous smile, "*and* it was fun."

"It was," Maria agreed, "and this will be, too. I've never seen a goddess before." She stepped forward and offered her hand—purposefully choosing the one that didn't yet bear a scar. "I want you to do it."

Em glanced at Maria's outstretched hand, and she must've realized which one Maria had offered her—because she quickly said, "I'll heal it afterward, if Aletha doesn't heal it first. She usually does."

"The sea goddess has healing magic, too?" Maria asked.

A bright smile burst across Em's face. "Oh, she's incredible! You'll see!" she paused. "If you're sure, that is."

"I am," Maria told her.

Em nodded toward the floorboards. "Sit down."

Maria dropped her hand. "I have to sit on the floorboards for this?" She pointed toward her table. "I have chairs! And a bed!"

"Trust me," Em told her. "When she makes her entrance, you don't want to have far to fall."

Maria froze. "What is *that* supposed to mean?" When Em didn't immediately answer, Maria said, "Em! You better not let her damage my ship."

"She'll fix anything she breaks, I'm sure," Em said with a shrug.

"No," Maria said, drawing out the word. "There will be no breaking. *None!* Do you understand me?"

Em suppressed another laugh. "Just sit down."

Maria grunted irritably. "Fine." She sat down across from Em, on the other side of the small bowl. Though she'd tried to adjust her swords, as she did, they still shifted and pressed into the floor. She glared at the raven-haired sorceress in front of her. "This is hard to do when you're wearing swords."

Em patted the long, slender sword against her hip. "What do you think I'm wearing? A quill?"

Maria pinned her with a petulant glare. "You only have one," she grumbled, "and yours is…smaller."

"Mmm-hmm," Em said with a teasing smile. "I also complain less."

Maria unfastened her scabbard and loosened the belts so that her swords could move more freely. "Next time, we're doing it on the bed."

"Fine," Em said with a shrug. "Just don't complain to me when your bed's soaked through with water and seaweed."

Maria grimaced at the thought.

Em lifted the enchanted dagger, its blade flashing in the candle-light. "I can start with myself, or—"

Maria cut her off, "I'm Captain. I'm first." She rolled her sleeve up to her elbow, exposing her tattooed forearm. Then, Maria extended her arm, offering Em the unscarred hand once more. "Do it."

Em reached across the bowl and curled her fingers beneath Maria's hand. She lowered Maria's hand toward the bowl and rested the blade of her dagger against Maria's palm. "I can take your pain."

Maria narrowed her eyes. Yes, she remembered that particular magic of Em's—the way Em had stolen Maria's pain after she stabbed her and taken it into herself, instead. "Only for you to feel your own, as well? I don't think so. If you even try, I'll have you whipped."

A surprised laugh burst from Em's lips. "You will not."

Maria shrugged. "I'll have you drowned, then."

Em rolled her eyes. "You definitely won't do that!"

Maria lifted an eyebrow. "Test me."

Maria hoped she *didn't*.

Em shook her head in amusement. Then, with no further warning, Em's fingers closed around Maria's hand, and she sliced into Maria's palm.

There was an empty moment between the slicing of her flesh, and the moment Maria's brain processed it.

Then, the pain ignited—sharp, quick, and intense.

Between clenched teeth, Maria said, "No warning?"

Em offered an apologetic smile. "Something I've learned as a healer," she explained. "It hurts worse, if you give them time to tense."

"In that case," Maria forced out, "thank you."

Em's hand remained steady and gentle beneath Maria's, even as Maria's palm filled with blood. "Are you sure you don't want me to take the pain?"

"Don't," Maria growled, "you dare."

Em's brows creased, but she acquiesced. "Are you ready for me to let go?"

Maria gave a single nod.

When Maria had cut open her other hand, long ago, in her escape from the Regolis dungeons, her fingers had twitched for what felt like forever afterward, and she'd struggled to hold her hand in certain positions.

Whether it was because of the precision of Em's cut or the way Em had held her hand throughout, Maria didn't know, but that hadn't happened this time.

Em gently released Maria's hand.

Maria kept her hand over the bowl, experimentally curling her fingers. Each movement increased the pain, but her muscles and tendons didn't resist.

Whatever she'd damaged when she'd cut the other hand, Em had apparently left it intact with this one.

"What now?"

Em opened her own hand, flexing her fingers. "I need to do mine now—unless," she paused, looking up at Maria, "you wanted to do it?"

Maria nodded. "I can." She tilted her head to the side, watching as a stream of crimson slid over her thumb. "As long as you're not afraid of getting a bit of my blood on you."

"I'm not afraid of blood, no," Em assured her.

Maria snorted, "Of course not." She held out her scarred hand. "I'll cut with this one. Put your hand in the other one."

Em handed Maria the enchanted dagger, and then, she rested her hand in Maria's bleeding palm. "It'd be more sanitary to clean the blade, at least, but—"

"Em," Maria teased, "I fucked your face last night. I think we're past that level of sanitary."

Em's eyes widened, and her hand nearly slipped from Maria's blood-soaked palm. "Captain!" she hissed, as if someone were actually in the cabin with them. "You can't just...say those things!"

Maria closed her fingers around Em's hand to hold it still. The pressure unleashed another wave of pain, but it was nothing Maria couldn't handle. "Really?" She lifted the perfectly-weighted dagger and grinned shamelessly at Em. "Who's going to stop me?"

Em glanced around the captain's quarters again.

"Oh, I get it!" Maria realized. "You're afraid your *god*-mother is going to hear about your…nightly activities." Her grin widened. "Pun intended."

Em scowled at her. "Very funny," she grumbled, "and Aletha isn't my mother! She's just the woman who gave me life." Maria arched an eyebrow, and Em wrinkled her nose. "I didn't think that through before I said it."

Maria chuckled. "So it would seem." She rested the shining blade of the dagger against Em's fair-skinned palm. "Are you ready?"

Em nodded. "Don't be afraid to cut deep."

Maria met her gaze. "I never am."

Maria pressed the dagger into Em's hand. The flesh parted beneath the sharp blade, and deep red blood blossomed in its wake.

Em closed her eyes and exhaled through her nose, but she made no sound. She barely even tensed.

Maria kept a steady hold on Em's hand, as she removed the dagger. A thick layer of blood gleamed on the blade, though Maria couldn't have said how much of it was her own and how much was Em's.

"Is that good?" Maria asked.

Em nodded—even before she opened her eyes. "Rest the blade over the top of the bowl."

Maria did as she asked. The blade balanced easily, and the water in the bowl seemed to shift.

"Usually," Em said, her voice shockingly steady, "I squeeze my hand to quicken the blood flow, but since there are two of us…" She turned her hand over and clasped it with Maria's. "*This* makes more sense."

Maria winced a little at the increased pressure, but she intertwined her fingers with Em's, anyway. They squeezed each other's hand, and a steady flow of blood splashed into the water below.

Maria's eyes widened, as the water in the bowl began to rise and fall, like the waves of the ocean. "Em?"

"She's responding," Em said.

As if that made *any* sense.

Maria might've voiced her annoyance, if Em hadn't begun to murmur something in Drakoní.

Maria fell silent, listening to the beautiful cadence of Em's voice. She'd so rarely heard Em speak in her own language.

It was unlike anything Maria had ever heard.

Drakoní syllables were heavier than Illopian—but far more lyrical.

So smooth and honeyed.

The familiar glow of Em's magic enveloped their joined hands, and a wondrous sensation filled Maria. For just a moment, it was as if their very *emotions* had touched.

"What was that?" Maria said breathlessly.

Em's green eyes remained unfocused. "*Magyck*."

Maria's brows furrowed. She wondered if Em even realized she'd pronounced that word in her own tongue, rather than Illopian.

At least the words were similar enough that Maria didn't need to ask for a translation.

The sea roared outside the ship, and Maria's eyes flared wide. "Em?!"

Em's bright gaze refocused on Maria, and she cringed. "You can explain away a rogue wave, can't you?"

"What?" Maria snapped—only a moment before her ship tilted, and everything went dark.

CHAPTER 23

Goddess of the Sea

"Hand?"

The unfamiliar voice with its otherworldly accent roused Maria from her brief moment of unconsciousness—if *that* was what it had been.

Maria pushed herself up onto her arms, stunned to find herself on the floor of the captain's quarters. Her hand ached from the pressure, still slick with blood.

The wound in Maria's hand jogged her memory, and with a sudden surge of panic, she called out into the darkness, "Em? Em!"

"I'm here, Captain," Em said, from several steps away. "I'm just trying to relight these candles."

Maria glanced in the direction of Em's voice, and with the blue moonlight streaming through the stern windows, she found Em easily—standing next to the long, wooden table.

Maria's shoulders sagged with relief.

But then…if Em was by the table, who'd spoken to Maria a moment before?

Whose large shadow fell over her now?

The unfamiliar voice spoke once more. "I'd help, but fire doesn't exactly fall within my realm of expertise."

522

Em laughed at that. "I know, Aletha."

Aletha?

Oh.

Maria scrambled into a sitting position. Her sheathed swords scraped the floorboards, as she turned to face the woman behind her.

Maria looked up.

And up.

And up.

She met a pair of cerulean eyes that were as deep and unsettling as the sea itself, and as Maria stared into them, they seemed to roll and whirl, like the waves.

Maria's arms buckled beneath her, and she nearly fell.

Again.

Maria had once paid a good deal of gold to have a *very* illegal figurehead created for the *Wicked Fate*—in the shape of the sea goddess. So, she'd become quite familiar with many of Aletha's unusual features.

Which was why Maria wasn't surprised by Aletha's smooth, blue skin or the wavelike curves of her body—or even the cerulean fins that stuck out from her head, where her ears should've been.

Maria could've even gotten used to those unnerving eyes, given a moment or two.

But Em really should've warned Maria about the goddess's *size.*

Aletha wasn't large in the way giants were large. No, it was more like the goddess had tried to match a typical human's size and missed—by a *lot.*

Her strange, blue skin also seemed to pour forth a steady stream of seawater. If Aletha were to venture too close to Maria's maps, at any point, she'd ruin them!

Maria intended to let Em know exactly how she felt about these unforgivable omissions—as soon as the goddess stopped staring at her.

Aletha tilted her too-large head to the side, flowing waves of midnight-blue hair sliding over her shoulder. Without ever looking at Em, she told her, "I think your fearless pirate over here is scared of me."

Flickering, yellow light danced across the walls of the captain's quarters, as Em lit a second candle.

Em turned to glare at the goddess.

To glare!

At the *goddess*!

"Be nice to her," Em warned, "or I'll tell the dragons."

Aletha looked up at Em, and her strange, blue lips curved into an amused smile. "Oh, as if the dragons didn't offer to eat her the moment they saw her!"

Em pursed her lips. "You're all ridiculous."

"We're playful," Aletha corrected. "It's a good sign!" She raised her dark blue eyebrows. "The dragons weren't so playful with your last lover, were they?"

Em looked away. "No."

Aletha spread out her dripping arms. "See?"

Maria eyed the item of clothing that hung from the goddess's curves. She supposed it was a pale-blue gown of some sort, but it looked nothing like the heavier, longer gowns worn in Illopia.

There was no corset—barely any shape to it at all, actually— and the goddess's legs, from her knees to her feet, were completely and totally visible.

Maria had always dressed in what was considered masculine clothing in Illopian fashion. So, of course, she wasn't one to judge someone *else's* bold clothing choices.

It was just…an interesting garment.

With each passing moment, Aletha's smile grew ever wider. "You haven't heard anything I've said. Have you, human?"

Maria blinked up at her.

"Hand," Aletha said slowly, as if she'd said it four times already. She held out her own hand. It looked mostly human—if you didn't count the blue skin or the thin, translucent webbing between her fingers.

"Captain, let her heal you," Em said with a gentle smile. "She won't hurt you. I won't let her."

Maria sought out her surgeon's familiar, green eyes. Part of her wanted to jump to her feet and run to Em's side.

The other part of her worried that'd look like fear.

It *wasn't* fear, by the way.

Maria was absolutely comfortable around this goddess—with her strange clothing and strange eyes.

She simply thought there was too much distance between her and Em, at the moment. That was all.

"It's true. She'd never forgive me if I harmed you," Aletha assured Maria. "She already blames me for your little fall."

Maria carefully removed her blood-slick hand from the floorboards and held it out to the goddess.

Aletha stepped toward Maria. Water splashed, like raindrops, onto the wood beneath them, and the goddess held her blue, webbed fingers over Maria's.

A sudden rush of water poured out of them.

The cool seawater flowed over Maria's palm, washing away the blood and pain and leaving no trace of the wound.

Maria lifted her hand, turning it this way and that.

Puddles of water splashed beneath Em's shoes, as she returned to Maria's side. "Yes, well," Em scolded Aletha, "you don't always have to ride in on the biggest wave."

"I am the Sea!" Aletha said, her voice suddenly booming, like the crash of a wave. "How dare you object to the size of my waves?"

Maria imagined anyone else would've fallen to their knees and begged for forgiveness in that moment, but Em just rolled her eyes.

"I just want my captain kept safe. That's all."

The goddess seemed to melt, her large shoulders sliding downward. "Your *captain*," she cooed. "As if I don't know what else she is to you."

Em's cheeks reddened, and she fell abruptly silent.

Maria glanced back and forth between the two of them, both brows raised. Somehow, in all of her imaginings, she'd never expected her dragon-riding surgeon and the sea goddess to carry on like…*this*.

After all, who talked to a goddess like that?

Dragon-riding surgeons, apparently.

Aletha laughed, "Aww, look at you." She pressed her webbed hand against Em's reddened face, and Em didn't cringe away—not from the strangeness of her hand *or* the cool water that streamed out of it. "You mortals change so much in the blink of an eye."

"I was sixteen years old the last time you visited," Em said. "That's a bit more than the blink of an eye."

"To *you*," Aletha scoffed. She trailed her hand up and smoothed it over Em's black hair, thoroughly drenching it. "This has changed, hasn't it?"

Em shot a quick glance at Maria, before saying, "Yes. Someone chopped it off recently."

Maria suppressed a smile.

"You look less like your mother now," Aletha murmured, "more like you." Before Em could react to that, the goddess took hold of Em's shoulders and spun her around. Aletha's dark blue eyebrows drew together, and she jabbed her fingers into Em's back.

Em spread out her hands. "Umm? Ow?"

"What happened to your spikes?" Aletha asked.

Em rolled her eyes, as if this bizarre series of events had happened before. "Drakon sorcerers don't have spikes, Aletha. You're thinking of the dragons."

"Am I?" Aletha waved that strange, blue hand of hers. "Oh, you know you all look alike to me."

Maria squinted at that.

Em turned around—but stopped to frown at Maria. "Captain? Why are you still on the floor?"

Oh, Maria didn't know!

Shock?

The literal deity standing in front of her, perhaps?

Em offered her hand to Maria.

Maria should've refused Em's offer of help—retain what little pride she had left—but goddamn it, if she wasn't *already* missing Em's touch.

Maria shifted both legs beneath her and curled her fingers around Em's, pulling herself to her feet.

Em's gaze darted downward, as Maria rose to her full height, and Maria quickly released Em's hand so she could catch her swords against her hips.

With an annoyed sigh, Maria adjusted the scabbard, re-tightening its leather belts.

Em stepped closer. "You know," she said, lowering her voice to a whisper, "you're kind of adorable when you're freaked out."

Maria narrowed her eyes at the surgeon.

She'd changed her mind. She hadn't missed Em's touch, after all.

Much.

Maria leaned toward her. "I'm *not* freaked out," she growled, "and no one calls Captain Maria Welles adorable."

Em tried to suppress her smile—but didn't succeed. "Sorry, Captain."

Maria hadn't heard a *hint* of sincerity in that. "Careful, surgeon."

Em's eyes sparkled—before darting toward Aletha. She took a quick step back, and Maria turned to look at the sea goddess, as well.

Aletha eyed them both with an intrigued smile. "You two remind me so much of…" she trailed off. "Well, no matter."

"So much of whom, Aletha?" Em prodded.

Aletha shrugged her blue shoulders. "No one of consequence."

Maria turned to Em. "Perhaps you should get on with it," she whispered, "before someone comes knocking on my door about that wave."

Aletha overheard, apparently. "Oh, that won't happen."

Em and Maria both turned to look at the goddess.

When it became clear she didn't intend to elaborate, Maria said, "Why not?"

"You seemed so concerned about interruptions," Aletha said with a shrug. "So, I ensured we'd have none."

Maria would've said her concern was more about arrests or mutinies than interruptions, but…

Wait, what was that last part?

"Er," Maria sputtered, "how?"

"You can't stop time or anything," Em said with a look that was more curious than concerned, "can you?"

Aletha pursed her lips thoughtfully. "I don't know! I've never tried." A mischievous smile spread across her face. "What I certainly *can* do, however, is ensure the sailors aboard this ship are having too much fun to worry about a little wave."

Maria held up a hand. "That isn't possible," she informed the goddess. "Zain doesn't have fun."

Aletha laughed. "He does tonight."

Maria looked to Em for support. "It's not possible."

Em rested her hand against Maria's upper arm, as if to comfort her—even as she spoke to the goddess, "This *fun* doesn't involve dangerous activities, like jumping overboard, does it?"

Was that likely?

"Of course not!" Aletha said. "Why does everyone think I drive people to do such dangerous things?"

Em gave Maria a long, meaningful look. "I have no idea."

Maria scowled. "Don't look at me! You court danger as much as I do!" She tapped a finger against her own chest. "You court me, and I *am* danger."

Em's brows furrowed. "I don't think you're making the point you think you're making."

A hint of concern flashed in Aletha's strange, cerulean eyes, only to vanish a moment later. "Ah, you've both made it this far," she muttered. "I couldn't have done *too* much harm."

"What does she mean by that?" Maria whispered to Em.

Em didn't answer. "Aletha," she said. "I assume you're aware of our problem?"

Aletha lifted an eyebrow. "You think you have only one?"

They better have only one.

"I think we have an immediate problem we're aware of," Em

corrected, "and any other problems we might have *hopefully* won't kill us off as quickly."

"Hopefully," Aletha agreed.

Em sighed and tried again, "You're aware of the infection?"

Aletha shuddered at the mere thought of it. "Of course I'm aware of it. I could *feel* it, crawling across my seas like a disease." She backtracked, "Well, I suppose it was a disease, but you understand, don't you? It made me *roll*." The goddess pressed a hand to her stomach and frowned at Em. "What's the mortal word for it?"

"Nauseous," Em provided.

"Nauseous." Aletha recited the word slowly, as if she were trying it out—experimenting to see if her mouth would form the word. "Yes. Nauseous."

Maria couldn't make sense of the way the sea goddess spoke. She spoke Illopian well enough, but she spoke it as if it had changed recently, and no one had told her.

Her accent was unusual, as well.

A bit lilting like an Illopian accent, a bit smooth like Em's, when she spoke her native tongue, a bit staccato like an Aevarian's, and a bit tonal like a Caluxian's.

It was, at once, unlike anything Maria had ever heard, and *like* everything she'd ever heard.

It was a paradox.

An ever-intriguing mystery.

Like Em.

"And do you still feel the…disease?" Em asked.

"No," Aletha said, "but that doesn't mean it ceased to exist. When you tossed the diseased limb into the sea, I destroyed the magic inside—because within my own realm, my magic is more powerful than his." She sighed, "But Petra's magic isn't easy to destroy."

"Petra?" Maria stammered. "Then—" She extended her arm toward Em. "You agree with her? You think the god of mountains did this?"

With a curious quirk of her head, the sea goddess said, "Think?

It's one thing to not believe your mortal lover, but…you're even prepared to not believe *me*."

That wasn't true.

Not totally.

"Petra abhors magic," Maria reminded the goddess.

"Petra *is* magic," Aletha corrected, "just as I am."

Maria shook her head in confusion. "You have sirens and sea monsters. Petra has mountains and gold. What's magical about those?"

Aletha glanced at Em, who shrugged helplessly.

The goddess stepped toward Maria, and unlike Em, she didn't approach Maria's misconceptions with gentleness. Only the cruel, unforgiving nature of the sea whirled in *her* tumultuous, blue eyes.

"Petra created the trolls that used to eat people like you alive," Aletha sneered, "the ones who laughed at the sounds of your screams." She flicked her fingers, splashing water at the gold chain Maria wore around her neck. "But he flashes a bit of shiny metal in front of you, and you forget all about them."

Maria didn't yield an inch, even as her heart raced.

Aletha leaned in close and whispered, "They didn't forget about *you*, though. I can assure you of that."

"Aletha!" Em snapped.

Aletha's whirling, blue eyes shifted toward Em, and though she didn't look afraid, though she had no *reason* to be afraid, the goddess held up both hands and stepped back.

Maria gripped the cool, steel hilt of her sword and forced her breathing back into a steady rhythm.

Could this goddess end all of their lives here and now?

Of course.

Was Captain Maria Welles intimidated by that?

No.

Maybe.

She hadn't decided.

"Mountain trolls haven't been seen in decades," Maria pointed out. "According to the stories, Petra killed them so Illopians could safely mine gold."

Did Maria believe that? Not really—though it was more that she doubted trolls ever existed in the first place.

Maria had grown skeptical of the things she hadn't seen with her own eyes—especially after all of the things she *had* seen with her own eyes.

People lied.

Her gaze drifted toward Em.

Most people lied.

With a grimace, Maria added, "Supposedly, it was to repay the Illopian kings for eradicating magic."

Aletha held up a finger. "Remind me, pirate," she said, teeth sharp around the words. "Did the stories say Petra killed the trolls, or did they say the mountains swallowed them whole?"

Maria shrugged. It'd been years since she'd even heard them. "Does it matter?"

"Oh, yes," Aletha said. "It absolutely matters."

"Swallowed, Captain," Em reminded her. "Not killed." Her brows creased. "They're still alive."

"Starving in the bellies of the mountains," Aletha agreed, "where your people will eventually find them."

Maria narrowed her eyes. "Illopians are not my people. My people are on this ship." She pointed at the wood beneath her feet. "I claim no one else. Not anymore."

Aletha gave a slow nod. "Yes. That's what I liked about you," she said, "but you'll have to work harder than that, if you hope to shake off his influence. Born of his land or not, he still sank his teeth into you in one way or another."

Maria frowned at that choice of words. "You know where I was born? Or…where I *wasn't* born?"

"I am the Sea," Aletha said simply. "I know everything on the Sea." A mischievous smile pulled at her lips. "Especially *you*, Captain Maria Welles."

Maria didn't know what to think of that.

She knew nothing of gods and magic, but if Em's magic had such strongly defined limits, surely gods had limits, as well?

One would hope, anyway.

Maria turned to Em and lowered her voice. "Did you tell her?"

With an amused smile, Em said, "No, Captain."

Maria eyed Aletha skeptically. "I wasn't born on the sea. I was born on land."

"But you moved from one land to another by sea," Aletha reminded her, "did you not?"

And she'd spent most of her life at sea since.

Aletha giggled at Maria's expression. "I've known all there was to know about you for quite some time, Captain Maria Welles. Are you truly surprised?"

Well…yes.

"Surely, you didn't think a pirate could see the success you have *without* the Sea's favor?" Aletha's whirling, blue eyes widened, as she, apparently, found the answer in Maria's expression. "Oh, you *are* an arrogant one, aren't you? How amusing!"

Maria didn't like the goddess's patronizing tone—nor did she like the fact that this goddess thought she could take credit for Maria's success.

Before Maria could voice her frustration, however, Aletha continued, "It goes without saying, of course, that I wasn't surprised when my favorite dragon sorceress ended up on your ship."

Em blinked at that. "You weren't?"

Aletha offered Em a smile that Maria suspected was reserved for her—and her alone.

That, Maria could relate to.

"Of course." Aletha stepped closer and placed her hand on Em's arm, further drenching the thin, black shirt. "You were forged from the magic of dragons, Dragon Child. It's in your *blood* to love the fire."

"You know, then," Em whispered to the goddess, "that I—that I love her?"

So, Maria was fire in this analogy?

Lethal.

Unstoppable.

Hot?

Maria supposed she could live with that.

"Everything on the sea," Aletha reminded her.

Em's head tilted, and a sudden coolness shuddered over her. "Then, you knew about Catherine, as well."

A slight wariness entered the goddess's eyes. "I did, and my heart ached for you. It did, but—" She dropped her hand and stepped back, already anticipating Em's reaction. "But there was nothing I could do."

"Nothing?" Em took one step forward, for every step the goddess retreated. "You could've left me dead! My mother was right. You should have left me dead!"

Maria's eyes widened. "Em!"

Aletha held up a hand to silence Maria. "Let her say what she needs to say. She's been waiting to say it for a while."

Let Em say awful things about herself?

Maria didn't know if she could do that.

"I thought—" Em's voice broke. "I thought *you* thought I could stop it. I assumed you would've only brought me back if you knew my mother was wrong. But you didn't know that." Her hands trembled at her sides. "You knew all along I'd be the end of my people, didn't you? You knew all along that everyone would've been better off, if I'd stayed dead!"

Maria's chest twisted in agony, and she no longer cared whether the goddess struck her dead for it. She rushed to Em's side, taking her by the arm. "Don't," she breathed. "Em, *please*, don't say that."

Em didn't meet her gaze. "Why not? It's the truth."

"No, it's not," Maria tried to tell her.

But Em wasn't listening. Not really. "Yes, it is! She knew all along that I didn't deserve to live, and she let me think I did!"

Maria supposed she'd known Em believed these things, but knowing it and hearing it said aloud were two different kinds of agony. "Em, please." Relying on instinct, Maria pressed her fingers beneath Em's chin, urging Em to meet her gaze. "You're wrong. You're wrong, all right?"

Every muscle in Em's body stilled the moment she met Maria's gaze. Her eyes widened, and her brows creased with sympathy.

Because of *course* she'd react to Maria's pain with more kindness than she'd ever offered her own. "Captain?"

"These wounds will take time to heal," the goddess said. *"I hope you can learn patience, Captain Maria Welles."*

Maria glanced at Aletha, her eyes wide.

Had the goddess just spoken in her mind?

Aletha held her gaze—but said nothing more.

Em had to have heard that, right?

But as Em glanced back and forth between Maria and Aletha, Maria realized she hadn't. The goddess of the sea had spoken those words for Maria alone.

"You deserved a chance at life, regardless of what might've come of it," Aletha told Em—aloud, now.

Em tried to shake her head, and Maria dropped her hand so she could. "I destroyed them. I destroyed my people."

"No, Dragon Child," Aletha said, "you didn't."

"My mother tried to kill Catherine, and I stopped her," Em informed the goddess. "If you'd left me dead, Catherine would've died, and the Drakon people would've survived. My life doomed them."

"No, Dragon Child," Aletha said again, her brows creased, "the Drakon people were doomed, regardless."

Em froze. "What?"

Aletha sighed, "Your death would've delayed their end. It wouldn't have saved them."

Em shook her head. "My mother—"

"Was willing to go to great lengths to extend her own life," Aletha interrupted, "and the lives of those who followed her. Mortals are terribly short-sighted, though. They never consider the centuries to come."

"Centuries?" Em repeated. She threw out her arms, as if Aletha had only confirmed her point. "That still leaves me at fault for *my* people dying!"

"As I said," Aletha sighed, "short-sighted mortals."

Maria couldn't help but think that for someone who'd lived for so long, this goddess was quite inept at comforting the person she clearly cared for.

And that was saying a lot, coming from Maria.

"It doesn't matter who would've died or when," Aletha told the person to whom it did, in fact, matter. "What matters is that you needed to live—for the sake of more than just *your* people."

Em's brows furrowed. "What does that mean?"

Aletha didn't elaborate, but she did step forward.

Maria stepped out of her way.

"I need you to understand something." The goddess lifted her hand and touched Em's face again, just as she had before. "You never hurt your people. Greedy, cowardly mortals did, one of which *you* are not."

Maria and the goddess agreed on that, at least.

Sadness glistened in Em's bright, green eyes. "I did, though."

"No," Aletha said.

Em didn't look like she believed it, but she stopped arguing. "The infection," she said in a quiet, pained tone. "Tell me how to save *these* people, at least."

Aletha dropped her hand. "Tell me what you think of the infection." She gave Em an appraising look. "You've made yourself quite the expert in these matters, after all."

Em rolled her eyes at that. "Choosing to study all methods, rather than just one, doesn't make me an expert. It makes me versatile."

Leave it to Em to reject a compliment on the basis of perceived accuracy.

When Aletha's expectant expression didn't waver, Em sighed, "I suppose…it reminded me of some infectious diseases I've seen. One of them involved skin death—spreading from one limb to the next. Surgeons slow the progression of that disease with amputation, which is why I tried that with this one."

"A good start," Aletha praised. "What other things have you considered?"

"Its progression might share certain similarities with wasting diseases," Em said. "If so, it would lead to a slow and painful death, rather than a quick one."

When had Em found the time to consider these things? Before the amputation?

After?

During?

"And how do you suppose it spreads?" Aletha prompted.

Maria *thought* that was why they'd summoned the goddess—to ask precisely that.

"If it spreads like similar infectious diseases," Em guessed, "then, it might do so through bodily fluids."

"Well, then, we have nothing to worry about with Cornelius," Maria interjected. "No one would fuck him." When Em turned to scowl at her, Maria said, "Could *you* spend five minutes with the guy?"

Aletha flashed a wicked grin at Maria. "What if it doesn't *take* five minutes?"

Maria grimaced at that unwelcome thought. "I'm ever so grateful it was always women for me."

Aletha laughed loudly at that. "Oh, I do like her," she told Em.

"I knew you would," Em muttered. She turned to Maria. "I just need to know… You are aware that's not the *only* bodily fluid, right?"

The question reminded Maria of another question Em had asked the night they met, and Maria couldn't resist the temptation to respond in the same way she had then. "Vaguely."

The subtle twitch of Em's lips told Maria *she* remembered it, too.

"So, what you're saying is," Maria said, "when I do decide to kill this guy, I should do so with minimal blood spill?" She shrugged. "Disappointing, but doable."

"That wasn't at all what I was saying," Em said, "but close enough, I suppose."

"While your knowledge of human disease has served you well thus far," Aletha told Em, "*this*, my dear Dragon Child, is the part where you must think like a sorcerer, rather than a surgeon."

Maria didn't have the faintest idea of what *that* meant, but Em must've understood—because her brows furrowed in thought.

"Magic relies on intent, inner strength, and emotion," Em mumbled, "but the victim of the magical infection wasn't the one who cast the spell. So, how could that relate?"

Aletha reached out and touched Em's shoulder with her dripping hand. "You're one of the cleverest sorcerers I've ever known. Tell me what you think."

"Emotion," Em offered. "Perhaps it uses emotion—seeks it out, like a parasite infecting specific cells."

Em likely couldn't see it—with her gaze averted, as it so often was—but Maria saw the flash of pride in Aletha's eyes the moment Em guessed correctly.

"And what emotion do you think," Aletha asked, "Petra's magic, specifically, might crave?"

Em stepped back—not quite pacing, but not standing still either. "He used greed to trap the Illopians." She gestured with her hands. "But with trolls, he—he uses a sort of hunger."

"Judith ensures no one on this ship goes hungry," Maria reminded her.

"It's not that sort of hunger," Em told her. "Trolls, they're—" She wiggled her fingers, as if calling the words to her. "The reason the legends depict them as mindless creatures is that they literally *are*. It's cruel, really—to create a creature with no mind of its own, driven only by an insatiable hunger that urges them to eat without concern for who they might hurt—" Her eyes widened, and she spun toward Aletha. "It's selfishness. That cruel narrow-mindedness you get from greed and insatiable hunger—it's…*selfish*."

"People concerned only with their own needs are awfully easy to manipulate, aren't they?" Aletha said.

Em glanced at Maria. "Cornelius can't empathize with my kind because he thinks only of himself."

"Cornelius doesn't empathize with *anyone*," Maria agreed, "because he thinks only of himself."

The color drained from Em's face, and panic flashed within her green eyes. "I can't control emotion, Captain," she said, voice shaking. "I can clean a wound, but I can't *make* someone care about people!"

Maria didn't have any reassuring words for her—because, well, she had a point. She turned to the goddess. "This is a pirate ship. Greed and selfishness are sort of expected here."

"Well, you better find some way to keep it in check," Aletha said, as unforgiving as the sea—or…well, *herself*, "Captain Maria Welles."

Maria touched the gold she wore around her neck, wondering how this insane goddess expected her to weed out the same emotions she felt from time to time herself.

"The person who attacked Cornelius—how did he know he'd be such a…" Maria trailed off in thought.

"Fertile breeding ground?" Em offered.

Maria pointed at Em. It was as good a description as any. "—for this magical disease?"

Em shrugged. "Did Catherine know Cornelius?"

Maria grimaced at the realization. "Ah."

"If she knew him as well as you do," Em said with a sigh, "she likely knew that Cornelius would not only provide the right emotion, but that he'd hide the infection, rather than letting a *witch* touch him."

"Providing enough time," Aletha added, "for it to threaten the rest of the crew."

"I don't know if she knew him as well as I did," Maria admitted, "but Catherine served on the same ship."

Perhaps Zain was right, and Maria's connection to Catherine *would* continue to endanger the crew.

Em turned to Aletha. "Is it still a threat," she asked worriedly, "to the rest of the crew?"

"I don't know," Aletha told her. "I don't sense the magic anymore—nor do I sense its wrongness. Perhaps the Illopian admiral underestimated how quickly you'd find the infection."

Maria's eyes widened. "Fuck!" she snapped, attracting the attention of both women. She threw out her arm, gesturing toward the east. "That was why she turned away, wasn't it? To give it time to spread."

Aletha offered a reluctant nod.

Maria shook her head in frustration. She'd known Catherine would have an ulterior motive, of course.

It was fucking Catherine!

But goddamn it, just once, Maria wanted to not be a pawn in Catherine's fucking games.

Was it madness that she kept hoping she'd one day win?

This time, it was Em who stepped toward *Maria*. "You heard Aletha. Catherine underestimated us." She leaned closer, until the gentle scents of rosewater and honey caressed Maria's senses. "And that's why she'll lose."

Maria's lips curved at the corners. "Catherine underestimated *you*. She always underestimates you."

Em mirrored her smile. "A problem you don't have."

How had she done that? How had Em known exactly what Maria needed to hear?

"I might have once," Maria said, "but unlike our dear Catherine Rochester, I learn from my mistakes."

Em's smile deepened. "And that's why you'll win."

Maria leaned toward her. "*We'll* win," she corrected. She bit her bottom lip, before remembering their spectator. "Also, we summoned a goddess for help—a goddess who's been fairly useless so far."

Em's eyes widened slightly, but if the goddess were offended by Maria's blunt remark, she didn't show it.

Aletha chuckled. "I can tell you what you need to know, pirate, but you won't like it when I do."

Could gods see the future, or was she merely assuming?

"We need to know how to fight this," Em insisted. "My mother offered to tell me what I needed to know—before I even knew what the problem was. But Nymeth made me promise to trust *you*, instead."

She had?

Maria glanced at the intricate dragon rune on Em's arm and wondered how much of Em's day-to-day life she missed, simply by not knowing what lay on the other side of that dragon bond.

"I know," Aletha said, "and you were wise to listen. Your mother would've used the information to control you."

"And we're to believe you won't?" Maria said.

Aletha bared her teeth in a dangerous smile, and Maria wondered if she'd just *imagined* seeing sharp points on the ends of those teeth. "When bargaining with the gods, one should expect to uphold their end of the deal, but don't worry. We are usually more honest in our deals than pirates."

"I don't like this," Maria informed Em. "She's only helping in order to use you."

Em glanced up at Maria, eyebrows lifting. "And you were different, how?"

Maria shrugged shamelessly. "I'm a pirate."

"She's a goddess," Em countered.

Maria sighed. Couldn't Em see the danger this deal might pose?

Then again, Em had seen the danger with Maria—and had made the deal, anyway.

"The dream your mother pressed upon you," Aletha told Em, "do you remember it?"

"She—" Em's eyes widened. "She can do that?"

"Do you," Aletha repeated, "remember it?"

Em nodded. "It was a memory of—of when she trained me." Her hand drifted toward her chest, as if she could still feel whatever had happened in the dream.

The way Em's face twisted with pain at the mere memory of it sent a surge of fury through Maria. What kind of fucked-up training had Em's mother subjected her to?

"You're focusing on the wrong part of the memory," Aletha told Em, "though I understand why." Her jaw tightened, as if she, too, found the memory unbearable. "Something else happened."

Em shook her head in bewilderment, until she realized, "The treaty! That was the day she told me—that she'd send me to forge an alliance with the sirens."

Maria spun toward Em. "The what?"

Aletha nodded. "Only a dragon-rider could safely enter siren territory."

Maria couldn't believe this. "Your mother sent you to forge an alliance with a species that might eat you?"

Em barely even blinked. "That surprises you?"

Surprises? No.

Infuriates? Yes.

"If it helps," Em offered, "sirens rarely eat my kind. According to Nerissa, we taste like charred magic."

Maria's brows furrowed. "Who's Nerissa?"

"Oh, umm…" Em's gaze darted toward Aletha.

Had Maria imagined it, or had Aletha just flashed some sort of…smirk at Em?

"It's not that they *can't* eat sorcerers—or even that they won't," Em continued. "They just prefer not to. Nerissa says it feels a bit like cannibalism."

There was that name again.

"Wait." Maria's frown deepened. "Eating a witch feels like cannibalism, but eating a human doesn't?"

Em shrugged. "You're not magical creatures."

Maria waved her hand between Em and herself. "But our bodies look the same."

"We're not discussing appearance, Captain," Em reminded her. "We're discussing taste."

Oh, for fuck's sake.

"And how does eating a fish feel?" Maria said. "Just trying to establish where the lines are."

It hadn't even been a serious question, but of course, Em had a serious answer. "Fish are friends, and sirens don't eat their friends."

Maria stared blankly at her. "Just humans, then."

Em wrinkled her nose. "Now that you mention it, they *are* quite picky, aren't they? Compared to dragons, anyway."

"Compared to anything," Maria muttered. Her gaze darted between Em and the goddess. "What did this treaty entail, then? If it didn't need to include not eating you?"

"Well," Em said, "it was an acknowledgment of the threat Petra —and by extension, the Kingdom of Illopia—posed to all magical creatures."

Maria found it strange to hear Em refer to herself as a magical creature, even if the description was *technically* accurate.

"In the event of a clear threat to magical creatures," Em explained, "the Drakon people would invoke the treaty, and the sirens would send aid." She turned to Aletha. "What still doesn't make sense to me is that my people didn't have *time* to call for aid, and my mother would've known that—as often as she used the oracles. So, what was the point of it all?"

"That *is* the question, isn't it?" Aletha tilted her head, long, dark-blue waves flowing over her shoulder. "Wouldn't you say, Dragon Child, that the genocide of an entire race of magical creatures constitutes as a clear threat to all?"

"Yes, but my people are gone," Em reminded her. "There's no one left to invoke the treaty."

"Isn't there?" Aletha said with a smile. "I happen to see a Drakon sorcerer standing in front of me now."

Em blinked. "You mean," she sputtered, "my mother meant for *me* to invoke the treaty? All along?"

Aletha lifted her bare, blue-skinned shoulders, and her strange garment slid lower around her arms. "You could call Nydia Drakon a lot of things, but unprepared wasn't one of them."

"I'll call her whatever I want," Maria muttered under her breath.

"No," Em said with a nervous laugh. She shook her head. "I can't invoke a treaty by myself! They'd never honor it."

"The sirens are *my* creatures," Aletha assured her. "They'll honor the treaty—as long as *you're* brave enough to confront them."

"I am. Of course," Em said, "but—"

"What?" Maria interrupted. She looked from Em to the goddess who *supposedly* cared for her. "You're telling her to confront ferocious sirens? By herself?"

"Careful, pirate," the goddess said, using Maria's own choice of phrase. "I wouldn't want you to insult my beloved creatures in front of me."

Em gave Maria a baffled look. "I forged the alliance by myself, didn't I?"

"You shouldn't have," Maria said, and if she'd had a mother with any sort of warmth in her heart, she wouldn't have!

"If you're so concerned for her," Aletha said with a taunting smile, "you could always accompany her."

Ah, this goddess truly annoyed Maria sometimes.

"Even if I were concerned," she said begrudgingly, "I couldn't sail the *Wicked Fate* into siren-infested waters. They'd wreck her! She'd be in pieces!" Just the thought of such a thing turned Maria's stomach.

Em lifted her eyebrows in amusement. "No concern for the sailors they'd eat alive, though."

Maria waved a hand dismissively. "Yes, that, too."

"My creatures are intelligent, pirate," Aletha snarled. "Contrary to what people like *you* seem to think, they can communicate."

Maria looked to Em for confirmation.

Em nodded easily. "They might even speak Illopian for you."

"If you ask nicely," Aletha added.

Maria narrowed her eyes suspiciously. "Will I have time to ask *before* they rip my ship apart?"

Em winced. "That part could…present a problem."

"That's what I thought," Maria said.

"Well, it's not as if you *have* to accompany me," Em reminded her. "The dragons will take me into siren territory. I'll invoke the treaty and return to you with whatever aid they offer."

Dread settled deep in Maria's gut, cooling her from the inside out. "You're already talking as if you intend to do it. They're sirens, Em!"

"With powerful magic," Em said, an excited smile curving at her lips. "They could be of real help to us!"

"We don't need help! Especially not at that price," Maria snapped. "You're talking about leaving me, Em!"

The last part had slipped out before Maria could stop it, and the surprise Maria felt at her own words mirrored itself in Em's wide, green eyes.

"Not for long," Em said—in barely a whisper.

Maria swallowed, forcing back her emotions, forcing a coolness into her tone that she didn't feel. "And if they kill you? How long would it be, then?"

"They will *not* kill the Dragon Child," Aletha said.

Em glanced at Aletha, confusion flickering across her face, before she returned her attention to Maria. "I can die here, too, Captain. We all can—if we don't find a way to fight this."

"According to her," Maria said, pointing at the sea goddess. "What if this is all just a way to get you to do her bidding?"

"You saw Cornelius's leg," Em reminded her. "It turned to stone. *Mountain.* It has to be Petra's magic."

"You said you wouldn't leave," Maria heard herself say.

Shit.

Why did these things keep coming out of her mouth?

Em's brows creased. "I don't want to leave you, but what choice do I have? We can't fight this alone."

"Why not?" Maria scoffed. "We've gotten this far, haven't we? I've fought the Royal Navy for ten years!" She spread out her arms. "I've never needed gods or sirens—just my swords, my ship, and my crew."

Em's gaze dropped to Maria's waist—to the swords she wore at her hips.

"Oh, the arrogance to even think such a thing!" came a familiar laugh from her left. "It's incredible!"

Maria turned to glare at the goddess.

"Humans are such amusing creatures!" Aletha said.

This goddess had been far more intimidating before she'd started laughing so much.

At Maria.

Aletha stepped closer, water dripping from her skin. "You have no idea how many times you've survived, simply because I enjoy you."

"Aletha," Em said warily.

"Oh, relax," the sea goddess cooed at Em. "As long as I'm amused, I'm not decimating her for her insolence. You'd prefer I didn't, I assume?"

"Very much so," Em said.

Aletha returned her attention to Maria, her strange, cerulean eyes whirling faster than ever. The air seemed to press against Maria's skin, the way the sea might've at its deepest and darkest depths, and Aletha's voice grew muffled, as if she were speaking underwater. "This is one of those times, by the way."

"What do you mean?" Em asked.

Aletha's dreadful gaze left Maria, and the pressure went with it.

Maria swayed on her feet, barely able to find her bearings after such an awful sensation.

What even *was* that?

"Oh, darling. Didn't the dragons tell you what Aria and I have been up to for the last," Aletha paused to count on her fingers, "*many* days? I lost count."

Even through her haze of confusion, Maria saw the deep blush that spread beneath Em's skin, reddening her ears as well as her face.

Maria watched her surgeon curiously, as she tried to make sense of Em's reaction. "Aria? The wind goddess?"

Aletha grinned, and yes, her teeth *were* pointed! "The one and only," she murmured, "infuriating, sanctimonious, *gorgeous* goddess of wind."

Maria thought, suddenly, of the forbidden book that lay in one of the wooden chests behind her—with its graphic descriptions of Aletha and Aria. Together. "The storm?!"

Aletha chuckled, "Well, we had to hold back the Illopian naval fleet somehow, didn't we? Who says you can't mix business with pleasure?"

"Fleet?" Em said. "She has another one? Already?"

Maria cared about the naval fleet, too, of course, but there were more important questions to ask. "You mean it's true? Storms actually form when you—"

"Sometimes," Aletha said, each syllable slow and playful. "I suppose that little book of yours did get a few things right."

Em threw up her hands and groaned in misery, "Oh, goddess. Of *course* she knows about the book!"

Aletha and Maria both burst into laughter.

Relieved the goddess wasn't laughing at her, for once, Maria quirked a curious brow. "What did it get wrong?"

Em shot an incredulous look at Maria. "Must you ask these things?"

"Yes," Maria said.

Aletha just smiled. "Well, it vastly underestimates the role her wings play in our lovemaking, for one."

Maria's eyes widened. "She has wings?"

"Oh, yes. Great, tremendous ones!" Aletha frowned. "Haven't you ever seen a statue of her?"

It'd been hard enough to find images of Aletha, and the Azure Islands had entire *temples* dedicated to her.

"The wind goddess isn't as forbidden as you are, of course, but," Maria told the goddess, "her worship is *also* outlawed in the Kingdom of Illopia."

The difference was that Illopians had mostly forgotten the wind goddess, while the sea goddess lived on as a symbol of evil.

"A pity," Aletha sighed. "She used to create some of the most *beautiful* temples—before your ridiculous laws." A wistful smile curved at her dark blue lips. "She still does—in parts of the Caluxian Empire. You should visit sometime, if you can survive the cold."

Maria shuddered at the thought.

Aletha giggled, "Our dragon sorceress had the same reaction when I suggested it to her."

Out of the corner of her eye, Maria saw Em nod.

"I'd suggest you visit the one off the shores of Aevaria," Aletha said, "but I accidentally flooded it a few centuries ago. Aria still hasn't forgiven me for that."

Maria blinked. "A few centuries?"

Aletha flashed a mischievous smile. "Oh, did I forget to mention she's a sanctimonious shrew?"

"Aletha!" Em said. "Stop insulting Aria before you bring the storm here!" When Maria shot a wide-eyed look her way, Em quickly added, "I didn't mean it like *that*! I meant she'd get angry and *come* here!"

Maria's eyebrows arched ever higher.

Em glared at her. "That wasn't a dirty pun, so stop looking at me like it was!"

Maria couldn't help but laugh.

"Aria won't leave her position until I've returned," Aletha assured them. "She knows how important it is that we give you time to seek help—if you dare to do so."

Maria instantly stopped laughing. She turned to the goddess. "And if we don't?"

Aletha shrugged. "I imagine that wouldn't fare well for any of us —least of all, *you*."

Maria had made enough threats in her lifetime to recognize one when she heard it. "You say Petra's cruel. You say he's the threat. Yet, you force people to do your bidding all the same."

"Captain," Em whispered.

All traces of humor had left the sea goddess's face. "Oh, no, I don't force. I'm simply vengeful, when wronged. Can you not relate, Captain Maria Welles?"

Maria clenched her jaw at that. "No one has wronged you. We're simply refusing to do your bidding—if it means risking our lives to do it."

"*I'm* not refusing to do anything," Em interjected.

Aletha let out a cruel laugh. "You'll risk your life at sea, either way. You really prefer that to spending a few days around my creatures?"

"Your creatures are vicious!" Maria snarled.

"Captain!" Em breathed.

Silent rage whirled in Aletha's eyes. "As are you, and yet, our dear Em has found something appealing in you."

"The sirens are *her* creatures," Em whispered. When Maria glanced at her, she said, "How do you react when someone insults the people you love?"

She…had a point, actually.

Not that Maria *did* love many people.

"Of course, our darling dragon sorceress also found something appealing in *my* creatures," Aletha said, turning to Em, "didn't you? Seeing as one was your…sexual awakening?"

Em's skin turned an incriminating shade of pink. "What? Don't call her that. She wasn't *that*."

Aletha shrugged. "According to Emryn——"

"Emryn needs to keep his jaws shut," Em snapped, "and I will *tell* him that in just a moment." She held up the arm with the dragon rune for emphasis.

"He *is* the most talkative dragon of the bunch, isn't he?" Aletha said with a laugh. "I can find out anything I want from him."

Maria didn't even question the 'talkative dragon' part because she was too caught up on the part about Em. "You fucked a fish-per——" She cast a wary glance at the goddess, before correcting herself, "——a siren?"

Em spread out her hands in frustration. "No! We've been over this. My *sexual* experiences were limited," she reminded Maria. "Which is why I was complaining about Aletha's choice of words. Nerissa wasn't a sexual awakening. She was just a regular *I'm-attracted-to-women* awakening."

Maria cocked her head slightly. "Em, that usually *is*…called a sexual awakening."

"See?" Aletha said.

Em blinked—and then shook her head in defeat. "This language is so strange sometimes."

Maria snorted at that. "Nerissa, was it? I've heard that name a few times today."

"And you would've heard it again," Em said, "once the sea goddess, who likes to cause *trouble*, had left."

Aletha flicked her fingers, sending a splash of water directly into Em's face.

Em simply blinked a few times and wiped it away.

"So, you were going to tell me?" Maria said.

Em rolled her eyes. "Have I ever omitted anything important?"

Maria raised an eyebrow. "You mean, besides the fact that you're a witch?"

"It wasn't important," Em muttered, "at the time."

Maria scowled at that.

"Is it Princess Nerissa or just Nerissa?" Aletha asked Em. "I forget."

Em shrugged. "She didn't introduce herself with the title."

"Princess?" Maria's eyes widened. "She's a princess?"

"Well, she's the daughter of the siren queen, so…" Em winced. "Yes."

Maria shook her head in disbelief.

"Oh, even if the girl wasn't a special kind of siren with a special title," Aletha said—unhelpfully, "you really couldn't blame our dragon sorceress for falling for her. Sirens are so beautiful and alluring that no one can resist them."

"Why are you implying that I loved her?" Em said with a frown. "I didn't love her!"

"And their breasts!" Aletha continued, as if Em hadn't said anything. "Have you ever seen their breasts, pirate?"

Too baffled to speak, Maria simply shook her head.

"They're phenomenal. You'll see," Aletha told her. She pushed her wavy, blue hair over her shoulder. "But of *course* they're phenomenal. I created them. Do you think *I'd* cut corners on the important parts?"

"Oh, for the love of the goddess!" Em complained—to that same goddess. "What are you even trying to do?"

But Maria *knew* what the sea goddess was doing, if she dared to believe it. It'd been there—in the phrase: 'You'll see.'

Even if Aletha trusted her creatures enough to send Em into their territory, she also cared enough about Em to not want her to go alone.

She wanted to ensure Maria went with her—by any means necessary.

"Then, you and the wind goddess intend to hold back Catherine's fleet," Maria assumed, "until we've entered siren territory?"

"We?" Em repeated.

That cruel smile curled again at Aletha's dark blue lips. "Perhaps," she murmured, "as long as *you* intend to do it." She stepped closer. "You must understand, pirate: Aria and I are doing what we're doing because we care for the future of humanity."

Aletha leaned in—close enough that the scent of the sea swirled around Maria's head, close enough that drops of seawater splashed against Maria's leather boots.

"If you can't find it within yourself to care for the future of Aletharia, pirate," Aletha snarled, "if you can't find it within yourself to see past yourself, past your ship, past your little vendetta… then Aria and I will have no reason to hold them back any longer."

"Aletha!" Em complained.

Aletha held up a webbed hand. "Quiet, Dragon Child," she said—without a hint of kindness. "I appreciate that you want to protect her, but it's time your pirate captain understood her predicament."

Maria narrowed her eyes. "And my predicament is: do your bidding, or face certain death?"

"If that's how you interpret it," Aletha said.

Maria didn't break eye-contact with Aletha, even as she spoke to Em, "I thought you said Illopians were wrong to call her cruel."

Em didn't respond.

She probably couldn't—after whatever Aletha had done to silence her.

Aletha tilted her face toward Maria's. "You, of all people, should know, *Captain Maria Welles*," she hissed, "our reputations always come from somewhere."

Maria's heart raced, and she gripped the cool, steel hilt of her sword. A lot of good her swords would do her now—but it was just a habit, a place to funnel the emotions she couldn't let show.

Like fear.

"And if you really want to know how cruel the Sea can be," Aletha whispered, "let something happen to my favorite dragon sorceress." The goddess bared her sharp teeth, like a beast. "Be careless with her life, and my favor will turn from you in the blink of an eye. And then, you'll find, *pirate*, that the wrath of the Sea is something no ship captain wants to behold."

Maria had no doubt about that.

Aletha stepped back. "I'll know when you've made your decision, and the storm will follow." Her blue eyes shifted toward Em, and she dropped her hand.

Em clutched her throat and gasped, as if whatever had stolen her voice had finally released her.

"Be safe, Dragon Child," Aletha said—before dissolving into a burst of water that splashed the floorboards with enough force to soak them both.

"I think that went well," Em said, still clutching her throat. "Don't you?"

Maria glared at her.

CHAPTER 24

Uncharted Waters

After checking with Zain and a few other members of the crew, Maria returned to the captain's quarters to find Em on the floorboards again.

On her hands and knees, this time.

Maria closed the door behind her, cocking her head at the sight.

Em scrubbed the floorboards with a rag. "Did you find out what kind of fun she used to distract them?"

"Fuck if I know," Maria grumbled. "I could barely carry on a conversation with them. It's as if they're all drunk. Yet, there isn't a drop of rum in sight."

"Probably dehydrated, if there's no rum," Em muttered.

Maria strode toward her. "Em?" She stood over her strange surgeon and crossed her arms. "Why the fuck are you in my floor *this* time?"

"Not summoning a goddess!" Em assured her. She wiped at another puddle. "Sirens can do that, you know? Make humans behave as if they're drunk?"

"Can they?" Maria said cooly.

"Yeah," Em told her. "The magic is in their kiss. It makes the human's head spin with a sort of euphoria—intoxicates you and makes you easier to, well…"

"Know this from experience, do you?" Maria said.

Em stopped what she was doing and looked up at Maria. "No, actually. It doesn't work on my kind."

Maria lifted an eyebrow. "Get off the fucking floor."

Em's brows furrowed. "I was just cleaning up the puddles."

"It's water, Em," Maria said, enunciating each word. She gestured toward the stern windows. "We're on a fucking ship."

Em pointed up at her, still making no move to get off of her knees. "You're not in the best mood."

"No," Maria agreed, "I'm not."

Em sank her teeth into her bottom lip, and Maria's entire body ached at the sight.

"Em," Maria said slowly. "Get *up*."

Her frown deepened. "Why?"

Why did she even need to know? That was the real question!

"Because my mind tends to go places when you're on your knees," Maria snarled, "and I don't want it to go there right now."

Em's eyes widened.

She'd asked.

Em looked down at the floorboards beneath her and then up at Maria—a deep flush spreading beneath her skin, all the while. "Really?"

"Em! Up!" Maria took hold of her arm and hauled her to her feet. She leaned toward Em. "Also, because cleaning fucking water is the most ridiculous excuse I've ever seen anyone use to avoid a problem."

Em pursed her lips. "What's a good one, then?"

Maria felt her own lips twitch in amusement—and just had to *hope* rolling her eyes would draw Em's attention away from them.

How dare Em be so charming and adorable, when Maria was angry with her?

Em sighed, "Look, I'm sorry Aletha got all scary there at the end. She's the Sea! It's what she does."

Maria narrowed her eyes at that. "She didn't *scare* me."

Em held up both hands. "You're right. I'm so sorry. I should've used a word that *means* 'scary' but doesn't hurt your legendary-pirate-captain pride."

Maria shook her head, no longer able to suppress her laughter. "You're delightful. You know that?"

A surprised smile broke across Em's face. "Aletha's like that sometimes, but she hasn't killed *me* yet, has she?"

"Well, you are remarkably hard to kill," Maria said. "Even when someone did kill you, you came back."

Em gave a small nod at that. "You have nothing to worry about, Captain. I'd never let her hurt you."

Maria stared blankly at her. "She's a goddess, Em."

"Yes, which means she gets away with being a bit scary some-times, but it doesn't mean I'm going to let her hurt you," Em said—as if stopping a sea goddess were some simple task. "Come on. You know the Sea! You can't tame her. You can only hold on and…ride the wave."

Maria gave Em a suspicious look. "Are you trying to soften me with nautical metaphors?"

Em's eyebrows rose at the idea. "I hadn't thought of it, actually. Do you think it'd work?"

Maria snorted, "Coming from your mouth? Probably."

A sheepish smile pulled at the corners of Em's soft, pink lips.

Maria lifted her hand and brushed her dark, tattooed fingers along Em's pale throat. "Did she hurt you?"

"No," Em said, her voice suddenly breathless. "It was annoying—because I really wanted to talk—"

Maria chuckled. "I bet you did."

Em rolled her eyes at Maria's interruption. "But not painful."

Maria trailed her fingers downward, watching as Em's dark eyelashes fluttered in response. "Little did she know, all she had to do to shut *you* up was kiss you."

Em's eyes narrowed. "You're not funny."

Maria flashed a wicked smirk. "Sure, I am."

She tilted her face toward Em's, and Em swallowed, causing her soft throat to move beneath Maria's fingertips.

A rush of need poured through Maria, and she closed her fingers around Em's throat and kissed her.

Em gasped against Maria's mouth, before melting against her, fingers closing around Maria's arms.

Maria forced herself to pull back. "Try as you might," she murmured, "you will *not* distract me."

Em opened her eyes, outrage flashing within them. "You kissed *me*, you asshole!"

Maria laughed loudly, and Em pushed her away.

Em crossed her arms and averted her gaze—but not before Maria saw the flush of desire in her cheeks and the dilation of her emerald-green eyes.

In hopes that a little distance would improve her focus, Maria strode toward her table. Only two of the candles flickered in front of her, so she picked up the wooden splint to light the rest. "We can't sail into siren territory, Em. The crew would turn against me."

A soft rustle of fabric told Maria that Em had probably dropped her arms, had perhaps even turned to look at her.

"I know," Em said, "which is why I'm not asking you to. I'll fly in on dragon-back. My dragons are nearby, anyway. After earlier, Nymeth wanted to remain close in case I needed any…assistance."

Earlier, being when Em had scared the shit out of Zain with her dragons, Maria assumed.

"I thought you said they sounded closer than they were," Maria pointed out.

She could practically *hear* Em cringing at her own slip. "Well, that wasn't false," Em said defensively. "They did sound closer than they were."

Maria turned to give Em a peeved look.

Em shrugged. "You've seen the size of Nymeth's wings! It's not her fault she moves so quickly!"

Maria exhaled heavily and shook the wooden splint in her hand, extinguishing the small flame.

The floor-to-ceiling windows bathed Em's form in pale blue moonlight, allowing Em's fair skin and raven hair to take on varying shades of blue.

So beautiful.

And after such a *long* day.

The dragon rune along Em's arm radiated its lovely, golden light, and after a moment or so of silence, Em spoke aloud, "Nymeth says we can leave tomorrow."

Panic seized Maria's chest at the suggestion. "No!"

The light of Em's dragon rune faded. "No?"

So much for not getting distracted.

"No," Maria repeated. "You're not leaving us."

It was almost as if they were back where they were months ago —only this time, Maria wasn't tricking Em into signing her life away for her own amusement.

She was pleading with Em.

Shamefully pleading.

"We're talking about man-eating sirens, Em," Maria said. "They could kill you."

"They won't," Em assured her. "My dragons would never allow it, and the treaty doesn't either."

"How do sirens even sign a treaty?" Maria said with a frustrated wave of her hand. "Can they even write?"

"Some of them can," Em said with a laugh, "but it was forged with magic, anyway, so…"

Maria eyed her curiously. "You really forged an alliance with such a dangerous species at…what? Eighteen? Younger?"

If it was an awakening of sorts, probably younger.

"Fifteen," Em said.

Maria shook her head in disbelief. "Fuck."

"It had to be a dragon-rider," Em said with a shrug. "My mother trained me for three years before she sent me—if that helps."

"It doesn't," Maria informed her.

All that meant was that her mother had looked at a twelve-year-old and chose to send *her* into danger.

Em offered another shrug, helpless to explain her mother's lack of concern any better.

"Were you scared?" Maria asked.

"At fifteen? Yeah," Em said with a short laugh. "Excited, too, though." She glanced at Maria, eyes sparkling in the moonlight. "It's funny how easily those two emotions mix."

And there it was—the reason Maria had always known Em would make a good pirate.

The two of them were alike in that way—too exhilarated by the danger to turn away.

From each other *or* from what lay ahead.

"If you must go," Maria said, "you'll take me."

Em froze. "But," she stammered, brows furrowing, "you can't. You—you just said you couldn't."

"I shouldn't," Maria said.

"Then, don't," Em told her. "Captain, I don't *want* you to lose your ship. I understand how much you love being captain, and I'd never ask you to risk that—"

"Do you understand how much I love you?" Maria interrupted. She pushed away from her table and strode toward Em. "You're asking me to risk you."

Em's lips parted.

The floorboards creaked beneath Maria's boots, as she closed the space between them. "I'd risk everything before you. Do you understand that?"

Em stared up at Maria, her breath quick and shallow. Either she hadn't heard the question, or she'd lost all ability to answer it.

Maria wouldn't risk the former. She pressed her knuckles beneath Em's chin, urging Em to meet her gaze. When Em's gaze finally *did* collide with hers, Maria's chest fluttered. "Everything."

Wonder and astonishment glistened in Em's bright green eyes. "That's...not possible," she whispered.

Maria leaned in close. "Why the fuck isn't it?"

A small, surprised laugh spilled from Em's lips. She shook her head, a smile curving at her lips. "How will you convince the crew?"

"I'm captain. I don't need to convince them," Maria said. "I'll set us on course for siren territory, and with as close as we already are, Zain'll have a hard fucking time staging a mutiny before we get there."

Em's smile faded. "What about while we're gone?"

Maria shrugged. "We'll just have to hope their faith in me will be enough to stay their hand."

"Hope?" Em said warily.

"They know Zain can't handle storms or battles," Maria told her, "not like I can. Perhaps they'll doubt his ability to escape siren-infested waters, as well."

Em nodded. "And dragon-inhabited skies."

Maria lifted her eyebrows. "You're still bringing the dragons?"

Em laughed at the question. "If I tried going without them, I'd have a mutiny on *my* hands."

Maria didn't relish the idea of justifying the presence of multiple dragons to a frightened crew—along with everything else she'd need to justify in the coming days—but since Maria was *also* prepared to do whatever it took to remain at Em's side, she couldn't exactly blame the dragons.

"Dragon mutinies?" Maria said with a tilt of her head. "Can't say I have any experience with those."

Unlike human ones.

"The dragons will keep us safe," Em assured her. "Even if sirens *could* stand against a dragon, they wouldn't."

Maria frowned curiously at that. "Why not?"

Em blinked, as if she hadn't expected that question. "Well, the dragons were the gods' first creation. You'd have to be awfully arrogant to risk the wrath of the gods."

As the Illopian Royal Navy was doing now?

"It's also a long-held belief that the very threads of Aletharia would unravel, if dragons ceased to exist." Em's brows furrowed. "You've never heard that?"

"Not in the Kingdom of Illopia," Maria muttered.

That seemed to surprise Em. "That's why the Drakon people were created—to protect the dragons and, therefore, protect Aletharia." She sighed, "And it's all fallen to me now."

No wonder the sea goddess hadn't doubted Em would risk *her* life.

"I don't understand," Maria said. "Why would Aletharia unravel without dragons?"

Em licked her lips thoughtfully. "Do you remember when I told you about dragon magic and how it differed from divine magic?"

How absurd that she even needed to ask—that she thought there was even a chance Maria could forget a single detail of that night.

In the galley.

In the chair.

With Em on her knees.

Goddamn it.

There went her focus again.

Em's frown deepened. "Captain?"

Maria ran her hand along her thin headscarf, squeezing her eyes shut in frustration. "Yeah, I remember."

Would the sea goddess forgive them, if they took a brief break from planning?

A few hours, at most.

From what Maria had seen earlier, she figured Aletha was the one goddess who might actually *understand* this sort of distraction.

"Well," Em said with a concerned frown, "it was, of course, divine magic that created Aletharia—and the dragons, too. But the magic that's woven throughout Aletharia, the magic our world thrives on—that's dragon magic." She shrugged. "Or so the tales say."

Tales not told in the Kingdom of Illopia, apparently.

Would anything change in the way Illopians viewed dragons, if they'd heard those tales?

Or had the dragons' history of burning entire cities to the ground created a fear that could never be dispelled?

"Do you think King Eldric knows of this belief?" Maria asked. "He wants to kill the dragons. I know he doesn't care for the rest of Aletharia, but surely, he wouldn't risk the downfall of his own kingdom?"

"That *is* the question, isn't it?" Em sighed. "I suppose we'll find out in time."

Perhaps it wasn't even true.

How likely was it, really? That Aletharia would cease to thrive without *one* species?

Maria touched Em's face once more, tracing her soft jawline, then her cheek. A smile pulled at her lips, when Em's eyes fluttered. "I can't believe I've let you convince me to sail into siren territory."

Em opened her eyes. "I did no convincing," she said defensively. "I literally just offered to go on my own."

"It's absolute madness," Maria muttered.

"Aletha did more convincing than I did," Em continued, "when she told you about Nerissa."

Maria ignored her objections. "These are uncharted waters for me, Em," she said. "Do you understand how significant that is? I've been doing this for eleven years, and it's a line I've never crossed—a line *no* ship captain has ever crossed and lived to tell of it."

Em's lips curved into a deep smile. "Sounds like the perfect challenge for Captain Maria Welles."

Maria couldn't deny the rush of excitement that poured through her at the thought. "You better not be wrong about this goddess of yours."

Em shrugged. "She resurrected a baby that no one wanted—and that no one ever would." Her smile faded at the reminder. "How terrible can she be?"

Maria might've reacted differently to those words—if it hadn't been for the private message the goddess had spoken into Maria's mind.

Patience.

With a slow exhale, Maria said, "One day, you'll realize that isn't true."

Em looked up at her. "What?"

"One day, you'll realize the person who told you that was lying," Maria said. "Maybe no one wanted you then, but they do now." She cupped both hands around Em's face and leaned in close. "*I* do now."

Em's eyes widened, shining like gemstones. "Captain," she breathed.

A sad laugh spilled from Maria's lips, as she tried to make sense of Em's inability to accept something that was so clear to everyone else.

But then, wounds re-inflicted—over and over again—were the hardest to heal. That's what the sea goddess had wanted Maria to understand.

Maria forced herself to release Em, to take a step back—before she blurted out any more confessions. "As late as it is already," she sighed, "I suppose we'll have to skip our sparring, after all."

Em glanced toward the stern windows, as if she'd already forgotten the moonlight and the dark blue waves rising and falling beneath it. "I thought we might have to," she admitted, "after I saw the nature of his infection."

After she'd already decided to summon a *goddess*, she meant.

Em winced and added, "Sorry."

Maria stepped forward and brushed her fingers over the hilt of Em's sword—the one she'd carefully chosen *for* Em. When Em's eyes darkened at her proximity, Maria teased, "You can make it up to me later."

Em's cheeks flushed.

With a sigh, Maria said, "I am *not* looking forward to this fight with Zain." She quirked an eyebrow. "Though I might enjoy it a bit more, if he gives me a reason to kill him during it."

Em scoffed at that. "You would not—because you don't actually hate him as much as you pretend to."

How dare she accuse Maria of such a thing?

"I most certainly do!" Maria said.

Em lifted her eyebrows skeptically. "I'll believe it when I see it."

Maria leaned closer. "Then, I'll ensure you do see it."

There was a chance Maria would have to make good on that threat—if Zain chose to mutiny and lost. In such an event, public execution was the only reasonable response on a pirate ship.

After all, pirates didn't take prisoners, did they?

"Perhaps you should discuss it with him now," Em suggested. "If he's truly behaving as if he's drunk, he might be more amendable than usual."

Maria snorted, "Zain does not do *'amendable,'* love. Not even when he's drunk."

"I said *more* amendable," Em said, "not totally amendable."

Maria shook her head. "And what will you do, while I'm gone? Not more water-cleaning, I hope?"

Em rolled her eyes at Maria's teasing. "I was just trying to help," she paused, grimacing, "you forget we summoned a sea goddess."

Maria snorted. "No chance of that, love."

"I need to go down to the surgeon's cabin," Em told her, "and make sure the person Pelt left with Cornelius wasn't *also* affected by Aletha's…*fun*." Her brows furrowed. "Speaking of Pelt," Em said, suddenly, "you should know: your boatswain is violent!"

"I do know that," Maria said.

An amusing spark of anger flashed in Em's green eyes. "What?"

Maria gave a playful arch of her eyebrows. "His ever-annoying hobby," she muttered, "is taking bets from pirates. How do you *think* he collects on those bets?"

Em glared at her. "You said to take him because he knew how to *talk* to Cornelius and to take Fulke because he knew how to *crush* Cornelius."

Maria nodded. "I lied."

With two words, Maria had turned what started as an amusing spark of rage into a wholly entertaining *blaze* of it.

"You *what?*"

Maria tilted her face toward Em's. "I am a pirate, my love," she taunted. "Why are you always so surprised?"

Em pushed her away. "I have no idea!"

Maria chuckled. "Ah, come on. I knew if I told you to take Fulke for the violent reason, you'd think, 'Oh, Fulke only looks scary. He doesn't actually behave that way,'" she said, "but if I'd told you to take Pelt for the violent reason, you'd say you didn't need him—because you're quite capable of punching someone yourself."

"I *am* quite capable of punching someone!" Em said.

"I remember," Maria assured her. She leaned in close and lowered her voice, as if divulging a secret. "But darling, you and I both know you're too selective in your punching—a problem Pelt does not have."

"You are so manipulative!" Em snapped.

Maria spread out her arms shamelessly. "Pirate."

"You got someone punched, Captain!" Em said.

"Good," Maria said with a shrug. "It was for the good of the ship, Em. He needed to be punched."

"He needed to be punched and then lose his leg?" Em challenged.

"Well, I didn't anticipate the amputation," Maria admitted, "but I won't pretend to pity the guy. Anything less than death is better than he deserves."

Em shook her head in disbelief.

"Painful death," Maria added.

"You would make the *worst* healer," Em informed her.

Maria laughed. "Good thing I have you, then."

Em pursed her lips to hide her amusement, but Maria saw it, anyway. The poor girl just didn't know *how* to hide her emotions.

They were always there—in her beautiful, expressive eyes.

Em pointed a fair-skinned finger right at her captain's face. "No more manipulating me."

Maria clasped both hands over her chest in a show of sincerity. "I wouldn't dream of it."

Em rolled her eyes. "I need to check on the sailor *you* had tormented."

Well, that wasn't fair.

It wasn't as if Maria had *ordered* Pelt to punch him.

Perhaps she'd considered it, but then, she'd realized it'd likely happen on its own—leaving Maria absolutely innocent in the matter.

And *not* on the other end of one of Zain's lectures.

Win-win.

"You'll come back to my quarters afterward," Maria said, as Em turned to leave, "won't you?"

Em glanced back at her. "Do you mean," she hesitated, "you want me to sleep here tonight?"

Maria dragged one boot along the floorboards, focusing on the soft *scrape*, rather than the quick tap of her own pulse. "Well, you can't sleep in the surgeon's cabin tonight—not while it's in use."

"No," Em said, "but I could sleep below deck."

"You won't be comfortable there," Maria said.

She didn't need to say why. They both knew about the nightmares now.

"Maybe not, but I'd sleep there before I made *you* uncomfortable." Em studied Maria with a frown. "I need to know you're ready for this."

Maria's chest ached at the question—at the sincerity she heard in it.

When trauma resulted in strange behaviors, people often reacted with ridicule or scorn, but Em didn't.

She never had.

The day of their first sword-fight, when Maria had been prepared to skip meals—just so she could be alone while her emotions surged—Em had offered to fix the bowl and let Maria take it with her.

Em had acted as if Maria deserved to eat, regardless—even if it was Maria's own choice that would've stopped her. She'd understood what Maria needed.

Before she'd known anything, she'd *understood*.

"I'm ready," Maria said, surprising herself with her own certainty. She stepped toward Em, drawn forward by a force she couldn't explain. "After last night," she whispered, "I *know* this is what I want."

Em smiled, and the relief that spilled from her lips was audible. "Oh, Captain." She cupped Maria's face and leaned forward onto her toes.

Em kissed Maria with the kind of adoration Maria could *feel*—in the gentleness of Em's touch, in the sweet exhale of her breath, in the lingering slowness of the kiss itself.

Maria didn't have enough strength inside her to break a kiss like this one—and probably never would have, if someone hadn't chosen that moment to knock on her door.

Reluctantly, Maria called out, "What is it?"

"It's Zain, Captain," his voice came, muffled, through the door. "You're needed at the helm."

Maria groaned in frustration, and Em offered a sympathetic smile.

"At least you don't have to go looking for him now."

Maria pinned her with an annoyed scowl.

That was *not* a positive.

Zain pounded on the door again, as if she hadn't heard him the first fucking time. "Now, Captain!"

Maria gripped the hilt of her sword, and Em's gaze flicked toward it.

"Don't," Em warned. "You'll regret it."

"I assure you," Maria growled, "I won't."

With a wary lift of her eyebrows, Em went to get the door.

Zain sprung through it the moment she opened it. "Finally!" he snarled, before he realized it was Em who stood before him. "What are you doing in here?"

"Leaving." Em stepped past him, only stopping to call back, "I'll see you soon, Captain."

Maria smiled at the promise—until she remembered Zain was watching. She forced all emotion from her face, as she turned toward him. "What's the problem?"

Zain waited until the door closed behind Em to ask, "Soon? She's coming back?"

Maria rolled her eyes. "I refuse to believe you're the only person on this ship who doesn't know we fuck."

Zain wrinkled his nose at the reminder. "I knew before anyone else, actually."

"Then, why are you asking?" Maria said.

"Well, because you have that…*thing*," Zain paused, his thick eyebrows twisting, "you know, where you don't like people around? At night?"

See?

Scorn.

Maria turned away, generously choosing to ignore his question, rather than stab him for it. She strode toward her table. "Care to tell me why you were breaking down my door? Or have you forgotten?"

Zain hooked a thumb over his shoulder. "I'd rather discuss it on the way."

Maria drew her sword.

Zain dropped his hand, his eyes wide. "Or not."

Lifting her eyebrows at his reaction, Maria grabbed a cloth from her table, as she circled it. She sank down in her chair and positioned the sword across her leather-clad thighs.

"If we're in danger of hitting something, I'm sure Henry knows to turn the fucking wheel." She wiped the cloth across the sharp, steel blade. "Tell me *now*."

Even though Maria had made it clear already that she was only cleaning her sword, Zain still eyed the blade warily, as he joined her at the table.

"Something knocked us off course," Zain told her. "There was this rogue wave that I…don't quite remember. It must've been that." At Maria's arched eyebrows, he said, "I think I had some bad rum."

Maria suppressed a smile. "Bad rum?"

If only the 'bad rum' had lasted longer.

"Yeah," Zain said with a grimace, "perhaps a bit of Judith's rum was mixed into the batch somehow."

Maria scoffed, "You'd know, if it was."

Zain gave a reluctant nod to that.

If there was anything they all had in common, it was that they'd never forget the taste of Judith's rum. Only a few of them were mad enough to try it *again*, though—Judith and Helen, namely.

"How could a wave have knocked us off course," Maria asked, "when I never charted a course to begin with? We're running from a storm. As long as the wave didn't knock us back *into* the storm, we're not off course."

Considering the sea and wind goddesses had created the storm to protect them, she doubted Aletha would've knocked them back into it.

"Well, I assume you didn't mean for us to be where we are now!" Zain said.

Maria rolled her hand expectantly. "Which is?"

"If we don't take action now," Zain said quietly, "we'll enter siren territory within the next two days."

Maria's eyes widened.

No.

They should've been weeks away, still.

"How big was that fucking wave?" Maria said.

Zain pressed his hands against the table and leaned forward eagerly. "Did you have the bad rum, too?"

Maria wrinkled her nose. "Something like that."

"Well, I don't entirely know," Zain admitted, "but it didn't damage the ship. So, it couldn't have been *that* big." He leaned back. "Yet, I can see the Illopian mountain range from the helm. Without a spyglass!"

Maria shook her head in disbelief. That presumptuous goddess had pushed them toward siren territory before Maria had even agreed to it!

Before she'd even heard the idea!

No wonder Aletha had been so amused by Maria's arrogance. She was no better.

"So, you see, now, why I wanted to discuss this on the way to the helm." Zain gestured toward the door. "We must take action immediately."

"No," Maria said.

His arm fell to his side. "What?"

"No." Maria returned her attention to her sword. "We're taking no action."

Zain nodded solemnly. "It's the bad rum, still. It'll wear off soon."

Maria rolled her eyes. Perhaps she shouldn't have used that excuse, after all. "It's not the bad rum."

"It must be," Zain said. "It's the only explanation."

Maria flipped her sword—to clean the other side. "Not the only one. It could be that I'd intended to chart a course toward siren territory already."

"Oh, dear," Zain mumbled. "Your rum was *really* bad."

"It isn't the rum!" Maria said.

Zain spread out his hands in frustration. "It's either the rum or a joke."

"Oh, as if you'd even recognize a joke," Maria scoffed.

"I recognize insanity," Zain said. "Captain, sailing toward siren territory is the very definition of endangering the crew! You wouldn't do that."

"I would," Maria told him, "if I thought there was more danger in sailing *away* from it."

Zain flung out his arms. "That makes less sense than anything else you've said!"

Maria couldn't tell him about the goddess—for obvious reasons—so what was she left with? "The storm isn't letting up anytime soon, and we can only guess at what lies on the other side of it. If we can't return to Nefala for repairs, we'll have to seek help *here*."

Zain gestured toward the stern windows. "There are islands out there, full of *humans*, and you want to ask the things that eat us for help? You've lost your mind!"

Maria forced herself to keep cleaning her blade. It would've been easier, if this could've waited until morning, at least. Perhaps then, she would've had time to plan her lies. "The Azure Islands don't welcome sailors who fly a black flag, and you know it. A few too many pirates have found them to be easy prey—without the protection of any kind of navy."

"So, we take down the flag," Zain said. "Simple enough."

Maria scowled. "Then, they'll think we're an Illopian naval ship. Have you forgotten the *Wicked Fate* is a warship?"

Zain gave a begrudging nod.

Islanders distrusted pirates, but they *feared* the Kingdom of Illopia.

After all, King Eldric didn't seek out allies. He conquered them.

The ones who refused to bow either died in the way Em's people had—or the king found other…*uses* for them. The years of bitterness and anger had hardened Maria, and yet, the memory still turned her stomach.

"You can't think sirens are a better option," Zain argued. "How dangerous can islanders be, really? Surely, not as lethal as a siren's teeth or magic?"

Maria still knew so little of what siren magic did. She knew they wrecked ships, somehow, but no one had ever lived to tell the story of how.

"We can take longboats in the middle of the night," Zain said, "raid their villages. We *are* pirates, after all."

Maria glared at him for that suggestion. "We attack naval ships, not innocent islanders."

Zain arched a black eyebrow. "You pick the most inconvenient times to have a conscience."

Maria wrinkled her nose in disgust. "It's not a conscience. It's discernment—of who I want as an enemy and who I don't."

"And the all-powerful Kingdom of Illopia is who you want," Zain said, "instead of some measly island village who worships an evil goddess?"

Maria forced herself not to react to the 'evil goddess' part. "Yes."

Zain threw up his hands. "Goddamn it, Captain!"

Maria sometimes wondered if the reason Zain annoyed her so much was that his 'morals' reminded her a bit of Catherine's—too dependent on how they served him.

It was cruel to compare the two. Maria knew that.

Even at Zain's worst, he didn't deserve a comparison to Catherine, but still, it frustrated her.

It was better, Maria thought, to have no morals at all—than to use them the way Catherine did.

"What makes you think the sirens will even stop to listen to our request?" Zain asked. "They'll kill us the moment we enter their territory. What's to stop them?" He let out a near-hysterical laugh. "How do we even communicate with them? They're fish!"

"Em," Maria answered. "Em is who will stop them, and Em is how we'll communicate with them."

Zain nodded slowly. Bitterness seethed, like venom, in his obsidian eyes. "I should've known."

Maria moved her hand, curling her fingers around the hilt of her sword. "You should've known *what*?"

"It was the witch," Zain accused. "She was with you when I arrived—right before you started spouting all of this nonsense." He held out his hand. "She already convinced you to sail into dragon territory. Of course she'd have you sailing into the territory of some other kind of monster now!"

Maria climbed to her feet, sword clutched at her side. "The witch?"

"Yes!" Zain circled the table to confront Maria. "The witch has poisoned your mind, Captain!" He tapped a finger against his head. "It's what they do!"

Maria stepped toward him. "They?"

"Witches!" Zain said, voice rising. "Come on, Captain! Snap out of it!"

Maria fisted the lapel of Zain's waistcoat and shoved him back. The table scraped backward as he fell against it, but when he tried to get up, Maria pressed her sword over his chest. He froze, bronze skin paling a shade or two.

"I thought, when you voted in her favor," Maria snarled, "that you were one of the people I *didn't* need to consider killing. Clearly, I was wrong."

"Captain," Zain gasped, "you can't—"

"Can't I?" Maria challenged. "After the threats you've made, I think killing you would solve several of my problems."

His eyes narrowed. "It might create more."

"And I might forget to care about that possibility," Maria warned, "if you continue to talk about my surgeon the way you do." Maria leaned forward, letting her dangerously sharp blade press him into the table. "She saved a sailor's life today—one who deserved to live even less than you do. Yet, here you are, talking about her as you always have. I've had enough of it!"

She spat out the last sentence with enough vitriol to make Zain flinch.

"I won't have bigotry on my ship," Maria snarled, "especially not from my fucking quartermaster." She slid her sword upward, until it dug into his throat. "You'll lose this attitude, or you'll lose your head. Do you understand your choices, quartermaster?"

Zain swallowed, causing the blade to press harder against his throat. "Yes, Captain."

Maria released him and stepped back. The table shook with the release of their combined weight. She returned to her chair and rested her sword against her thighs.

Zain straightened, legs trembling as they found the floor. He checked his throat for blood, but he found none, of course.

Maria wielded her swords with precision. He wouldn't bleed until she wanted him to bleed.

Which would happen sooner, rather than later, if he kept pushing her where Em was concerned.

"I don't trust her to keep us alive in siren territory," Zain said carefully. "Am I allowed to say that?"

Maria chose *not* to acknowledge the resentment in his tone. She reached for the cleaning cloth. "I suppose."

Zain retreated to the opposite side of the table, before collapsing into the chair. "How has the…*surgeon* suggested she might keep us alive?"

"Dragons," Maria said.

"Wonderful." Zain looked away, grinding his teeth so hard Maria could practically hear it. "Does the…*Em* have a back-up plan?"

Maria stared at him in disbelief. "The Em does."

Zain's dark gaze darted toward her. With a grimace, he said, "Er…what was it?"

Maria returned her attention to cleaning her sword. "Em is familiar with the sirens. Her people had a treaty with them. It'll protect her—and might protect us, as well," she explained, "though it'd probably be more accurate to call her dragons the back-up plan."

"Of course her people associated with…" Zain trailed off. "I mean…" He shifted uncomfortably on the wooden seat. "How familiar are we talking?"

That was *not* a question Maria wanted to answer. "Familiar enough."

Zain crossed one leg over the other, forcing himself to relax against the back of the chair. "Captain, if you want to change our heading, you'll have to give me more than that."

"It seems Em had a," Maria said, wiping her sword, "prior relationship with the siren princess."

Zain clasped a hand over his chest. "You mean to tell me that the woman who loves *you* has a thing for bloodthirsty murderers?" He glanced at the sword in Maria's lap, just as she finished cleaning it, and said, "Captain, I would've never guessed."

Maria sighed heavily. "Will you just adjust our fucking heading?"

As much as it annoyed her, Maria knew Zain well enough to know his animated reactions were good signs. He'd acknowledged a bit of his own familiarity with Em, rather than distancing her with words like, *'the witch.'*

"Captain," Zain said with a sigh, "I can't adjust our heading on the basis of lovers and treaties. I'm still not convinced we'll survive."

"You can, and you will." Maria set aside the cloth and sheathed her sword. "Also, she's an *ex*-lover, not a lover."

Zain's eyebrows rose at the correction, but for once, he kept his derisive opinions to himself.

The silence was delightful.

"Captain, we can't—"

"It's an order, quartermaster," Maria interrupted.

Zain sighed, "Fine." He dropped his boots to the floor and rose to his feet. "I'll leave things as they are, for now, but in the morning, when the rum has worn off, and you're thinking clearly, we'll talk again."

Maria rolled her eyes. "It isn't the rum."

"Goodnight, Captain."

The exact words Zain had used in his little taunt didn't register in Maria's mind until after he left: *'The woman who loves you?'*

Zain knew Em loved her.

Did he know Maria loved Em, too?

If so, Maria no longer had just one enemy who knew her weakness. She had two.

~

"WHAT THE—"

Emilia froze mid-step, squinting at the vaguely human shapes, sprawled across the wooden steps.

With nothing but a bit of moonlight streaming through the portholes, it was far too dark for Emilia to identify the companionway-defilers, but when she saw the long, red braid draped across the steps and the small breasts of a shorter, dark-haired woman on top, Emilia realized—with dismay—whom she'd stumbled upon.

"Judith?" Emilia threw her hand over her eyes. "Helen?"

Judith looked up. "Em?"

"Well, now that we're all acquainted," Emilia said miserably, "why are you on the steps?"

Judith's brows furrowed. "I don't…remember."

"Seemed like a good idea at the time," Helen said.

Aletha.

Of course it was Aletha's fault!

"I just needed to check on an injured sailor," Emilia whimpered.

"Well, what's stopping you?" Helen asked.

"Us, Helen," Judith told her. "We're in her way."

Emilia waved her hand blindly. "Just naked women blocking the entire companionway. No big deal."

Judith snorted. "You all right, mate?"

"Absolutely," Emilia said—with a bit too much enthusiasm, "if I could just…squeeze through."

Judith peered around at the limited space on the steps and said, "I don't know how safe that'd be."

Helen shot up on her elbows, as if she'd just thought of a brilliant idea. "How high can you jump?"

"I don't know!" Emilia squeaked.

Judith pressed a hand against Helen's muscular shoulder and

shoved her back down. "We have to get up, you oaf!" she scoffed. "Give me my damn shirt."

Helen fumbled around the dark space until she found a white shirt. As Judith climbed to her feet, Helen held the large shirt out to her. The still-white portions of the shirt glowed blue in the moonlight.

The problem was that most of the shirt was *not* still white.

"We're not totally naked, you know?" Helen told Emilia. "Judith hadn't let me remove her breeches yet."

Emilia stared deliberately at the porthole. "That's lovely."

Judith took the shirt from Helen—but only so that she could wave it in front of the master gunner's face. "Does this *look* like my shirt to you?"

Helen cocked her head to the side, her long, red braid sliding over her freckled shoulder. "It's white."

"Your shirt was white, too, Helen!" Judith reminded her. She waved the shirt wildly. "This is twice my size and covered in gunpowder!"

Helen pointed a finger at her bare chest. "It's mine?"

Judith tossed the shirt at Helen. "Where the fuck did you put my shirt, Helen?"

Emilia gestured toward the deck above her. "I think I'll just…go back up for a moment."

Judith held out her hand. "No, no, no. You have a job to do. You stay right there." She resumed her hobby of glaring at Helen. "Besides, if you leave, Helen will forget we're getting out of your way."

"I'm not that forgetful!" Helen objected.

"You can't even remember which shirt is mine," Judith said. "I'll give you a hint. It's the one *not* covered in gunpowder! I'm a cook, love. A cook!"

Helen winced, as she looked over her shoulder. "Well, that might've changed, if I'm lying on it."

"Oh, for fuck's sake," Judith grumbled.

Helen pulled a white, linen shirt out from underneath her—that was, indeed, hosting a few new gunpowder stains. She reluctantly offered it to Judith.

Judith snatched it from her hand. "Why would you have my shirt underneath you?"

"I didn't want to get splinters!" Helen said.

"You blow things up! Constantly!" Judith reminded her. "You get splinters for fun!"

"Yes, and I go to our little surgeon here to remove them," Helen said, gesturing toward Emilia. "Do you think she wants to remove a splinter from my ass?"

"Oh my goddess," Emilia whined at the boards above her. "Please, don't ask me to answer that."

Judith shook her head. "We are never drinking that much of my brother's rum again." Her brows furrowed. "We did drink some, didn't we?"

Helen shrugged. "I don't remember drinking any."

"Well, neither do I," Judith admitted, "but we must've drunk *something*." She waved toward Helen. "*You*, I'd believe, had blacked out on a bit of normal rum. Underneath all that muscle, you have the stomach of a mouse! I, however, can handle my rum."

Helen lifted her chin. "I like to think I have the stomach of a rat, not a mouse."

Judith wrinkled her nose. "What's the difference?"

"A rat will eat anything," Helen told her. "Mice only eat cheese and grain."

"That's not true," Judith said.

"It is so!" Helen leaned forward. "What would you know? Do you cook for rats and mice, too?"

Judith rubbed her forehead tiredly. "Em, help me out here."

"I'll think about it," Emilia offered, "*when* you're fully dressed."

Judith laughed, "Drives a hard bargain, that girl." She tossed the stained shirt over her head and pulled it down. Then, she tucked its long tail into her unfastened breeches. "Have you seen my pistol?"

"Please, tell me Helen isn't on top of that, too," Emilia muttered.

She didn't have the energy for another surgery.

Helen pointed toward her boots at the end of the steps. "Ah! It's in my boot! Mine's in the other! See?"

"How did they get there?" Judith plucked both flintlock pistols from the boots and handed one to Helen—as if she knew, without looking, which one was which. "Trousers and shirt, Helen. Hurry."

Emilia kept herself occupied by adding up her list of grievances to discuss with the sea goddess at their next meeting.

Seeing her friends naked was near the top.

When the two women finished dressing, they stepped aside to allow Emilia to squeeze past.

She hurried down the steps without even stopping to talk. "Rats are slightly less selective in their diets than mice. I'm glad you two made up. Goodnight!"

Judith looked up at Helen. "We made up?"

"I didn't know we were fighting," Helen told her.

Judith squinted suspiciously at that. "You've been avoiding me for nearly two weeks!"

Helen leaned toward her. "That's because you said you didn't like my freckles!"

"I never said that," Judith complained.

"I heard it with my own ears!" Helen argued.

Emilia swiftly escaped into the surgeon's cabin, as the bickering began once more.

CHAPTER 25

The Kraken

"Y ou fucked a fish-person?" Judith exclaimed.

Emilia threw up her hands. "Why does everyone keep asking me that?"

Judith turned to Maria. "Everyone?"

Half-sitting on the table Judith was using to slice her carrots, Maria leaned forward and whispered, "I asked the same question."

As if that weren't obvious.

It'd been nearly two days since the sea goddess had set them on this mission, and though the crew grew more tense with each nautical mile, no one had mutinied.

Yet.

Emilia and Maria had done what they could to put the crew at ease over the last day or so, but they'd finally realized they needed their best on the job.

Judith.

Wonderful, charismatic Judith.

"You cannot call them fish-people!" Em pointed at Judith and then at Maria. "Do you understand me? You'll offend them, and they'll rip you apart!"

Maria leaned toward Judith again. "Also, they didn't fuck."

577

Judith tapped the wooden ladle against Maria's arm. "Well, I'm sure that put *you* at ease."

Maria scowled at her. "I am not a jealous woman."

"Yes, you are," Judith said.

Maria reached for an apple in a nearby crate, only for Judith to slap her hand away. She jerked her hand back, shooting a betrayed look Judith's way. "I'm nowhere near as bad as Catherine."

"Oh, what a boast!" Judith said with feigned awe. She slapped Maria's arm with the ladle, when Maria reached for the apple again. "The woman followed you without your knowledge, and you weren't even together!"

Emilia looked up from her own platter of sliced vegetables, knife still in hand. "She did what?"

Maria scooted further onto the table. She rested her hands against her leather-clad thighs, probably wanting Judith to think she'd given up on the apples. "I knew I shouldn't have told you about that."

Judith scoffed, "And who else would you have told?"

Emilia glanced back and forth between them, curious to hear more of this. She'd heard so little of Maria's relationship with Catherine.

She knew their relationship had been more platonic than romantic—while still occasionally sexual—but Maria didn't speak much of it.

And Emilia had never wanted her to.

Was it, by any chance, a good sign that Emilia had responded with curiosity to the mention of Catherine, rather than panic?

Was her mind finally recovering?

"How *do* they fuck?" Judith asked.

Emilia nearly dropped her knife, as the question jolted her thoughts back to the present. "What?"

Judith waved the ladle uncomfortably. "Oh, you know, they have those fins...*there*. Don't they?"

"She's asking if your ex-lover had a pussy," Maria said.

Emilia narrowed her eyes at her indelicate captain. "I'd imagine sirens have all kinds of genitalia—just as we do."

Maria turned back toward Judith and shrugged. "Sometimes, you just have to come out and say it."

"And sometimes, you don't," Emilia muttered.

Judith squinted curiously at Emilia. "You say you imagine? Do you mean you and the siren never *touched*?"

"We touched," Emilia said defensively, "just not everywhere." When both women stared at her for a little too long, Emilia blurted out, "I was fifteen!"

Judith and Maria exchanged an amused look.

"Oh, not you, too!" Emilia complained at Judith.

Judith offered an apologetic shrug and pointed the wooden ladle at Maria. "I grew up with *her*."

"She wasn't very good at it back then," Maria told Emilia, "if that makes you feel better."

Judith glared at the captain. "You don't know that!"

Maria flashed a taunting smirk. "The questions you asked me afterward were quite telling."

Judith rolled her eyes. "Some confidant you are!"

While they teased each other, Emilia carried the platter of sliced vegetables to the pot. "If you have any *relevant* questions—*not* relating to genitalia—I'd be happy to answer those."

Judith pursed her lips, as if these parameters were somehow difficult for her. "Hands!" she said—with a clap so loud and sudden that Emilia flinched at the sound. "What do they have, instead of hands?"

Emilia's brows furrowed. "They have…hands," she said slowly. "Who told you they didn't have hands?"

"My baby brother," Judith said.

Maria lifted her eyebrows. "The one who's never been sober a day in his life? The one who brews poisonous corpse-juice and calls it rum?"

Emilia wrinkled her nose at that description.

"It is rum!" Judith said. "The whole crew drank it the other day, apparently—though no one remembers why. If it was as bad as you say, they'd remember!"

Maria shot a bemused look Emilia's way.

Neither of them knew why the crew had collectively chosen to blame Judith's rum for Aletha's magic—or how no one had noticed that there wasn't enough rum missing to account for this possibility —but they couldn't exactly correct them all either.

Not without confessing to summoning a goddess.

Emilia finished emptying the platter and turned away—only for Judith to grasp her wrist, pulling her to a stop.

"I thought of another," Judith said with a good deal of serious-ness. "Is it gross to kiss a cannibal?"

Emilia stared blankly at her. "How is this relevant?"

Maria had been slyly reaching toward the crate of apples, until she'd heard the question—at which point, she'd spun toward them. "No, no. Answer the question, surgeon. It's important."

Emilia narrowed her eyes at her curious captain.

No, it absolutely was *not* important.

"First of all, sirens don't consider themselves cannibals. Humans are an entirely different species," Emilia said, "and second, no, it wasn't gross."

Maria seemed disappointed by that answer.

Judith leaned toward her. "But how did it, you know, taste? Do they taste like fish or human flesh?"

Maria pointed a tattooed finger at Judith, as if she'd asked the right question. "Or blood! Was it like that metallic taste when you cough up a mouthful of it?"

Judith grimaced at the description. "Captain, we don't *all* get into fights regularly."

"None of those, if you must know," Emilia told them. "Now, do you have any questions that would actually *help* you reassure the crew?"

Judith waved the ladle dismissively. "You underestimate how many of them find talk of kissing a pretty girl relaxing. Even the fishy kind."

"Don't call them fishy!" Emilia scolded.

Maria finally managed to steal an apple, while Judith's back was turned. She lifted it to her mouth. "Don't kiss them either. Em says that's how they get you."

"It's one use of their magic," Emilia agreed.

Maria might've gotten away with her fruit theft—if it hadn't been for the *crunch* of her apple.

Judith spun around just in time to smack the apple out of Maria's hand.

The fruit skidded across the floorboards with a slow *thuh-thump, thuh-thump, thuh-thump.*

Maria spread out her hands. "What the fuck?"

"You've had enough apples!" Judith snapped.

"There's no such thing." Maria chewed and swallowed the single bite that had made it safely into her mouth. "And what good is it on the floor?"

"Think of it as punishment," Judith sneered, "for stealing a crate of my apples—and then trying to steal *more*!"

"The cat stole your crate," Maria said. She pointed a tattooed finger at Emilia. "Em let him."

Emilia frowned at that. "You still ate the apples."

Maria turned to scowl at her. "Whose side are you on, anyway?"

Emilia just rolled her eyes.

Judith jabbed the wooden ladle at Maria's doublet, as if it were a sword. "No more apples," she snarled, "or so help me, gods, I'll feed you to the sirens myself!"

"And they call *me* the madwoman," Maria scoffed.

Emilia reached out and pushed the ladle down. "We're not feeding anyone to the sirens."

"Speak for yourself," Judith grunted.

"How about this?" Emilia suggested, spreading out her hands in a placating gesture. "We'll tell you the plan we've devised, and you can decide if any of it will be useful in reassuring the crew."

Judith quirked her head, curiosity shining in her bright, blue eyes. "You devised a plan?"

Maria leaned forward, and the muscles in her tattooed forearms flexed, as she gripped the table. "What do you think we were doing all night?"

Judith pressed her tongue to her cheek and lifted her eyebrows. She didn't say a word, but apparently, she didn't need to.

Maria's grin was absolutely shameless. "Well, yes, we did a bit of that, too." She shrugged her strong shoulders. "What can I say? We're multitaskers."

Emilia looked away, her eyes wide. Did those two really need to tell each other *everything*?

Judith turned toward Emilia. With an amused smile, she took Emilia by the arm and guided her to a nearby chair. "Well, if she has you that sleep-deprived, you better have a seat." She pushed Emilia into the chair. "I'll get us some ale, and you can tell me about that plan."

Because of course they needed ale for that.

THROUGHOUT THE DAY, WHEN EMILIA WASN'T HELPING JUDITH IN the galley or caring for Cornelius in the surgeon's quarters, she was stealing moments with Maria—to discuss their departure from the ship.

"We might be away from the *Wicked Fate* for a few days," Emilia warned. "When my mother sent me to forge the alliance, I was there for an entire summer."

Maria rested her arm against the wooden rail, angling herself toward Emilia. "Where will they expect us to sleep, then?" Her gaze flicked to the right, as a group of sailors strolled past them. "Underwater?"

"No," Emilia said with a laugh. "They know we breathe air. When I was there, I slept in a cave."

Maria's attention returned to Emilia. "Cozy."

Emilia smiled at her sarcasm. "It's not that bad. I slept in plenty of caves when I lived amongst dragons. It was either a cave or the grass, depending on the weather."

Maria's dark brown eyes shifted downward, taking in each and every curve of Emilia's body—though Emilia had no idea what relevance *they* held to this conversation. "I'm beginning to see why you get along so well with my cats."

Emilia squinted at that. "The ship cats don't sleep in caves *or* grass, Captain."

"No, but they sleep in strange places," Maria said. "One time, I found Rat-Slayer sleeping beneath a cannon. Can you imagine if there'd been a battle?"

"He sleeps there because of the light that comes in around it," Emilia told her. "He likes the sunbeams."

Maria looked away and shook her head, as if there were something strange about Emilia knowing that.

Perhaps if Maria spoke with the cats every once in a while, she'd know it, too.

"Couldn't we just *tell* them we'd prefer to return to our ship and sleep in our own beds?" Maria tilted her head slightly, before correcting herself, "My own bed?"

"They'll probably want to keep us close," Emilia said.

Maria narrowed her eyes at that. "I won't be held prisoner. I've had enough of that for one lifetime."

As had Emilia.

Nymeth chose that moment to give her opinion. *"If you want to cheer her up, you should remind her of the part of sleeping in a cave she might enjoy. Cuddling."*

Emilia resisted the urge to roll her eyes. *"Are dragons supposed to speculate on whom their riders cuddle with?"*

"Supposed to?" Nymeth said with a low, rumbling laugh. *"As if anyone would dare set rules for dragons!"*

"Well, perhaps they should," Emilia said.

"Perhaps I'd incinerate them for having the audacity," Nymeth countered. *"Besides, dragons don't need to speculate. We know—when we're close enough. Or when we've heightened the bond—the way you and I have."*

Yes, well, when Emilia agreed to take Nymeth's rune, she hadn't realized she was also agreeing to the ancient dragon teasing her about cuddling.

These things should come with warnings.

"All you should really worry about," Nymeth added, *"is whether or not I've… 'speculated' on the location of your clothes during these nightly activities."*

"People fear you because you breathe fire," Emilia complained. *"Wait until they find out you make jokes, too."*

Nymeth chuckled. *"At least mine are more sophisticated than Emryn's."*

"I don't know what a sophisticated joke is," Emilia said, *"but I don't think I've ever heard one from any of you."*

Maria cast a frantic glance over her shoulder, before placing her tall, lean form in front of Emilia. "Can you not ask those fire-breathing beasts of yours to stop talking to you while everyone can see?"

Emilia blinked once, refocusing her attention on Maria. "Nymeth was…giving me advice."

"Emryn agrees with me," Nymeth continued. *"He thinks you should tell your shiny human about cuddling."*

"Oh, will you just go eat a cow or something?" Emilia complained.

"We did that already," Nymeth said.

"Em!" Maria said. She cast another glance around the deck, before returning her attention to Emilia.

Emilia winced. "Sorry. You can't actually silence a dragon. They're quite loud, you know?" Her brows furrowed. "Wait, how did you even know that I—" She looked toward the dragon rune on her arm.

"No, it's covered," Maria assured her. "It was your face."

Emilia looked up. "What's wrong with my face?"

Maria snorted. "Nothing's wrong with your face." Her leather-clad shoulders lifted in a vague sort of shrug. "You just get this…*look* whenever you're talking to your dragons." She glanced over her shoulder. "I can't be the only one who's noticed."

Emilia paled, as she considered every time she'd spoken to her dragons in front of Maria. "There's a look?"

"Yes." An amused smirk tugged at one side of Maria's mouth. "Sort of distant, sort of annoyed." She leaned closer. "Do your dragons annoy you?"

"I adore them!" Emilia said with a scoff. "So, yes."

Maria laughed in that wonderfully loud way she did sometimes —the one that made her large, brown eyes crinkle at the corners. "Are they still coming?"

Emilia offered a sly smile. "Don't you hear them?"

It was easy to understand how Maria missed the distant flap of dragon wings, which held only slight differences to the steady flapping of the ship's sails.

Perhaps, if Emilia hadn't sensed their nearness, hadn't felt the surge of dragon magic—of pure *life*—in her blood, she might've missed it, too.

Then again, Emilia *knew* the sound of her dragons.

Maria's eyes widened, and with an amusing amount of eagerness, she spun toward the sound. Her long, muscular body curved forward, as she grasped the wooden rail and squinted out at the great, winged shadows in the distance.

Maria had spent the last few days acting as if relying on Emilia's dragons to protect her ship was an inconvenience. Yet, the same, lovely spark of wonder that had danced within her eyes on Drakon Isle, as she'd beheld dragons for the first time, danced within them now. "I can barely see them," she gasped. "Yet, we can hear them from here!"

"Like I said," Emilia reminded her, "they're loud."

Maria chuckled. "Is that all of them we're hearing?" She looked at Emilia. "Or just the big one?"

"Likely just Nymeth," Emilia assumed. "She's the loudest by far."

"I should think so," Maria laughed.

As the five dragons drew closer to the *Wicked Fate*, someone in the crow's nest called out a warning, and shouts of alarm rang out from the crew.

Maria's smile faded, but she didn't even turn to look. "I spend all day warning them the dragons are coming so they *won't* panic, and what do they do the moment your dragons arrive?"

"Panic?" Emilia offered.

Maria shot an unamused look her way. "Do you see the hardships you cause me?"

"Oh, no," Emilia said sarcastically. She pointed toward her dragons. "Shall I tell them to go home and leave us at the mercy of the sirens, then?"

Maria's eyes darkened. "Surgeon," she said, as if the title alone were some kind of warning.

A warning Emilia deliberately ignored.

A smile pulled at one corner of Emilia's lips, and she stepped closer. "Was that a yes, Captain?"

Maria quirked a scarred eyebrow at that. She pushed away from the rail and turned to face Emilia. Her dark gaze trailed downward, the subtle warmth within burning hotter with each passing moment. "Perhaps we should discuss this in my quarters."

Now?

With a nervous laugh, Emilia said, "Why would we do that, Captain?"

Maria stepped closer—because that was what she always did when Emilia showed a hint of weakness.

Really, Emilia should've expected it by now.

"Because," Maria said, "even if the entire crew is—*annoyingly*—betting on us, there are still things I can't do to you with them watching."

Emilia's heart raced, tapping painfully against her ribs, and her breath grew shallow. "Like what?"

The sensuality of Maria's low chuckle rippled through Emilia's body. The pirate captain stepped forward, eyes dark and dilated. "Like," Maria said, speaking slowly enough for Emilia to see the languid flick of her tongue, "kiss you."

Her dark gaze lingered on Emilia's lips, and Emilia exhaled shakily. As much as *she* wanted that kiss, as well, she was relieved Maria had said only that.

The tropical sun could only explain so *much* overheating, after all.

But then, Maria leaned closer. "Like," she said again, and this time, she pressed her warm, wet mouth against Emilia's ear and whispered, "push you to your knees and—"

Emilia gasped and grabbed hold of Maria's doublet at the same moment the lookout called down another warning.

"Alert! All hands!"

Maria pulled back mid-sentence, her eyes wide.

Unfortunately, even shock wasn't enough to quell the painful throb of desire between Emilia's thighs.

Maria carefully extracted Emilia's hands from her clothes and pushed them down. "I have to go."

"What?" Emilia breathed.

Perhaps if her pulse would quieten down, Emilia could actually *hear* Maria.

"Get down to the hold," Maria said distractedly.

Emilia frowned at that. "It's only the dragons."

Maria gave a quick shake of her head. "No."

"Well," Emilia sputtered, "what is it, then?"

It was Nymeth, not Maria, who answered Emilia's question. *"You have another guest, Dragon Child."* Before Emilia could ask any more, the dragon added, *"An uninvited one."*

Maria rushed to the helm, where her quartermaster and helmsman awaited. She would've liked to have thought her surgeon had *obeyed* her orders, but the hurried footsteps behind her own said otherwise.

"What is it?" Em asked, as they crossed the main deck. "Do you know?"

"Danger," Maria called over her shoulder. "Unspecified danger."

Another shout came down from the crow's nest, louder this time. "Something in the water!"

"Something," Em repeated. Her voice grew more breathless, as she struggled to keep pace with Maria's long strides. "Isn't it *usually* specified?"

"Usually, yes," Maria said. "If he could see what it was or where it was, he'd tell us. Clearly, he can't."

"And that's bad," Emilia assumed.

Maria glanced at the surgeon, but didn't slow her steps. "Possibly," she said, stressing the word. "When it was dragons, he said dragons. When it was a ship, he said fucking ship." She shook her head in frustration. Not frustration at Em, of course. Em was too new to sailing to know the lookouts' calls already. It was frustration at her own emotions—at her inability to fully cloak them. "If it were a person, he would've said, 'Man overboard.' If it were an object— even one he couldn't identify—he might've said something like, 'Object off the bow.' For him to be that vague, he must not know what or where it is."

Em watched her with a frown. "Which points to?"

"Coral," Maria said—a bit too quickly. "Coral reefs look like shadows sometimes. It's probably coral."

Em squinted, as if she doubted the honesty in Maria's answer. For someone with no talent for lying herself, Em had grown surprisingly quick at recognizing when Maria was doing it.

She missed a few, still, but apparently, she'd had enough experience with Maria's lies to recognize a lot of them. "You're this concerned over a coral reef?"

"Who said I was concerned?" Maria snapped.

Em ignored Maria's anger, clearly already aware of what hid beneath it. "So, it's something large, then."

"I hate it when you do that," Maria complained.

Note to self: Stop falling for clever girls.

"Under the ship?" Em continued. "He's seeing it all around. That's why he doesn't know where it is."

Maria cast a puzzled look at her. "You're guessing all of this?"

"For now," Em told her. "When my dragons arrive, they might be able to confirm our theories."

Our theories?

"I thought I told you to get down to the hold," Maria grumbled.

Em ignored that, as usual. "How much of a threat do whales pose to a ship this size?"

"Depends on the size of the whale," Maria said, "but…not much. Not if we move quickly."

"And if it's bigger than a whale?" Em asked.

Maria scowled at her. "It's not."

Maria took the steps up to the quarterdeck two at a time, and the creak of Em's footsteps followed.

Zain met Maria at the top of the steps. "What do you think?" he said breathlessly. "Whale? Squid?"

"She thinks coral," Em said—with a playfulness that did *not* fit the situation.

Maria couldn't deny the brief lift of amusement it had given her, though.

Zain peered around Maria, as if he hadn't realized Maria had a tagalong. He shook his head solemnly. "It's already moving us, Captain. It can't be coral."

At that, all of Maria's amusement died. "Full sail."

Zain gave a quick nod. He called out the command to the sailors below, as Maria hurried to take the helm. Henry stepped aside the moment he saw her.

Em went to the taffrail to peer down at the sea that frothed and bubbled, like a stew recently stirred.

As the sailors passed along Maria's commands from stern to bow, another call came from the crow's nest. "Creature in the water! Creature in the water!"

Well, at least they had made *some* progress on the details.

The masts and sails of the *Wicked Fate* groaned in protest, as the dragons drew near.

"They know not to get too close, right?" Maria yelled over her shoulder.

"Yeah," Em called back. "They'll stay high."

With a curl of his lip, Zain looked up at the flying beasts. "Can't they let us deal with one creature at a time?"

"Dragons have better sight than humans," Em told him. "They're going to show me what they see."

Zain scowled at Maria. "What does she mean '*show*' her?"

Maria didn't understand it much better than he did. So, she ignored the question and pulled on the wheel with all of her strength. If the creature was, indeed, below them, any direction— taken quickly enough—would do.

Em ran to her side. "It's swimming up!" she warned. "I can't see what it is yet, but it's enormous!"

Maria glanced at her surgeon, stunned. Was it really possible that Em could see better with dragons than a human could with a spyglass? "How enormous?"

Zain just shook his head. "And here I thought the healing magic and glowing tattoos were weird."

"Bigger than us," Em said.

Zain spun toward her. "That's not possible."

"It came from the deep," Em said with a frown. "Deep, *deep* sea. A bottom dweller, perhaps."

"Squid?" Zain assumed.

"Perhaps," Maria said. She spotted Pelt on the main deck and gestured toward him with a jerk of her head. "Tell Pelt to get word to the gunners. I want them on the cannons, just in case."

"Aye, Captain." Zain turned to leave.

Em blinked rapidly, as if the dragons had shown her too many images, at once. "Oh. Oh, goddess."

Maria looked at her. "What?"

"Not squid," was all Em managed to say, before the sea exploded around them.

Maria ducked her head, blinded by the dome of seawater that burst around them, jetting into the air, before splashing over the deck and back into the sea.

The creature slammed into the bottom of their ship with a force like that of a cannon blast. It might've knocked Maria off her feet, if she hadn't been gripping the wheel so tightly.

Still, a scream pierced the air, as a sailor no doubt fell from the rigging.

Maria wiped desperately at her eyes. She couldn't see the falling sailor through the continuous spray of water, but she *heard* him, all right—every moment of the way, his agonized screech spiraling downward, until it ended with a sickening *thwack*.

Maria's senses seemed to reengage after that, and the cries of the crew filled the silence left by the end of that one sailor's scream.

She registered the quick footsteps behind her, just in time, and reached out blindly, catching Em's wrist in her free hand. "No!" she screamed. "Don't move!"

Em tried to pull herself free. "I have to help him!"

This was just one of the many reasons it was better to have her surgeon below deck. Em was far too empathetic to show any restraint at a time like this.

"No!" Maria couldn't let go of the wheel, so her only option was to ensure her grip on Em's wrist was unbreakable. "Not yet! Don't move…*yet*. That's an order!" Desperation closed around her throat, and before she could stop herself, she cried out, "Please!"

Em immediately stopped fighting, and those bright, expressive eyes of hers shifted to meet Maria's.

"I need you," Maria gasped, "here."

Em nodded, though the conflict still warred in her eyes. "You can let go. I won't leave you. I swear."

Maria reluctantly released Em's wrist and finally let herself look *up*.

All around the ship, tentacles as wide as tree trunks—no less than eight of them—reached into the air.

Each greyish-purple tentacle wiggled and unfurled, almost experimentally, as if the thing were stretching its limbs, testing its mobility outside the water.

Em grabbed Maria's arm and whispered, "Brace yourself," just a moment before those tentacles slid back toward the water.

Though the movement was slow, the pale, mauve tentacles slammed against the hull of the ship with a *splat* as loud as some explosions.

The hull groaned and cracked under the pressure, and though Maria pulled the wheel with all of her might, her ship refused to do anything more than writhe within the creature's grasp.

All across the deck, pirates screamed and ran, some slipping on the translucent slime the creature had slathered over the deck.

Maria turned to Em and said, voice dull with shock, "Kraken?"

Em nodded.

With his impeccable timing, Zain ran toward them, screeching like a banshee, "Squid! Squid! Captain, it's a giant squid!"

Both of them turned to frown at him.

He slid to a stop, panting.

"A squid, Zain?" Maria said, brows high. "What kind of fucking squid do you think grows *this* big?"

"The giant kind?" Zain offered.

Em's response was far kinder than Maria's. "They're both cephalopods, but they're not the same species."

Zain's dark brows furrowed. "Cepher-what?"

Em squinted, as if she couldn't figure out whether she'd mistranslated a word or simply used one he didn't know. "They're similar creatures—but not the *same*," she tried again. "Similar behaviors. Similar habitats. *Not*-so-similar diets, unfortunately." She winced a little at that last part.

Zain turned to Maria. "What is she saying?"

"Kraken, Zain," Maria said. "It's a kraken."

"A young one," Em offered, "if that helps."

Maria shot an incredulous look at Em. If *this* was a young one, how fucking big were the grown ones?

"It can't be," Zain said, his near-black eyes wide. "This is the Azure Sea, not the Whispering Abyss!"

"The Whispering Abyss is home to sea monsters, yes," Em told him, "but no one ever said it was home to *all* of them. Some of the smaller monsters stay with the sirens."

Zain waved his hands around himself, gesturing wildly toward the giant tentacles holding their ship. "Smaller?!"

Em shrugged. "Compared to others, yes."

Maria couldn't really criticize Zain's skepticism. Though she'd heard stories of kraken in the Azure Sea, she'd, too, often attributed them to sailors' habits of exaggerating.

If they somehow survived this, Maria would never dismiss them again.

The tentacles pulled once more—sluggish in their movements—and the ship groaned dangerously.

Em cringed at the sound. "He probably hasn't decided how he wants to eat us yet."

"How comforting," Maria muttered.

"Their mouths aren't as large as you might think," Em said.

Well, Maria just so happened to consider *any* mouth capable of devouring a ship too large.

Pelt raced up the steps, casting alarmed glances at the slimy, mauve tentacle on the starboard side of the quarterdeck.

Em didn't even wait for him to speak, before blurting out, "Did he survive? The sailor who fell—is he alive?"

Maria couldn't even bring herself to rebuke Em for it. After all, was having a surgeon who cared too much to restrain herself the worst thing in the world?

Caught off-guard by the question, Pelt just blinked. "Erm, didn't see, actually." His gaze darted back the way he'd come. "But I'm sure, if he's breathing, somebody'll get him to the hold for you."

Em nodded. "Are there more injured? Do you know?"

Zain shot a peeved look at Maria, and she sighed.

"Em," Maria snapped, "there will be time for this later! *If* we survive. We're trying to save the crew right now, not the guy who's probably dead already."

Em flinched at that, before looking away. "Sorry."

Zain gave Maria an approving look, even as Maria longed to take it all back. She couldn't remember the last time she'd made Em flinch like that.

Damn it.

Maria *knew* why Em obsessed over every life like that. She was the last person who should've made Em feel guilty about it—even if it *was* expected of her.

Pelt turned to Maria. "The gunners are awaiting your orders."

Maria nodded and tried to clear her mind of distractions. "Aim at the closest tentacles, and—"

"No!" Em interrupted.

Maria turned toward her, glaring openly now.

"Oh, for fuck's sake," Zain said, stepping forward, "a surgeon shouldn't be on the quarterdeck during a crisis, anyway. If you won't remove her, I will."

At that, Maria grasped Em's arm and pulled her close. Em squeaked in surprise, as the side of her body collided with Maria's.

"She's here on my orders, and you won't fucking touch her!" Maria snarled at him. "She's here because I need her knowledge of magical creatures, and if you have a problem with that, you can fuck off!"

Em watched her curiously—but said nothing.

Zain held up his hands and took a step back. Any approval Maria had earned from him was gone now.

Fuck him, then.

Maria didn't need his approval.

She needed Em.

Here.

With her.

"Captain?" Em said.

Maria glared at her. "Don't."

Unfortunately, Em didn't back down as easily as Zain. "If you want my knowledge of magical creatures, I'm offering it now. Don't fire at him."

Zain scoffed, "She can't be serious."

Maria occasionally admired Em's ability to care for creatures that were so unlike herself. It'd been one of the aspects of Em that had always intrigued her.

But right now, she didn't have time for it. "If we don't fire at it, surgeon," she growled, "it'll eat us."

Em didn't flinch this time. "Not necessarily."

Maria shook her head in frustration. "When we've encountered squid in the past—"

"This isn't a squid," Em interrupted. "It's a kraken. Cannons won't scare him. They'll make him fight harder, and he'll crush the ship on his way down."

Maria's brows furrowed.

Em wanted to protect the ship? Not the kraken?

"So, you propose we let it eat us, instead?" Zain said.

"No," Em sighed. She kept her gaze on Maria, even as she answered Zain. "Think about it, Captain. He's sunk every ship he's ever caught. Do you understand what that means?"

"That he's hungry?" Maria assumed.

"And that we need to kill it!" Zain added.

Em pinned him with an exasperated look. "We can't kill him. It'd take more firepower than we even have."

"Not if we use your dragons," Zain argued.

Honestly, Em had been quite patient with him up until that point, but now, she unleashed the full force of her *'were-you-born-yesterday'* stare. "You want my dragons to burn a creature who has *us* in his grasp?"

Zain's brows furrowed. "Well…"

"We're on a wooden ship," Em continued, "in case you've forgotten." She lifted her eyebrows. "You are aware of what fire does to wood, aren't you?"

"Of course I'm aware!" Zain snapped.

Maria suppressed a laugh. "What do you intend for us to do," she asked Em, "if we can't kill the kraken?"

"I know more about wooden ships than you could ever dream to," Zain muttered under his breath, "you…witch-turned-pirate."

Pelt snorted in amusement, and Zain glared at him.

Em leaned toward Maria. "We can't kill him, but we *can* trick him."

Maria arched an eyebrow at the woman, who just so happened to be the worst liar Maria had ever met. "*You're* proposing trickery?"

Em narrowed her eyes at Maria's teasing. "He's young, which means he's not the most *clever* kraken."

"There are clever kraken?" Maria asked.

Em ignored that. "Nymeth thinks he'll let us go, if we trick him into thinking we're a friend."

"Who's Nymeth?" Zain said.

Maria pointed vaguely toward the sky. "Big one."

Both Zain and Pelt glanced up at the dragons circling overhead, and Maria gestured for Em to continue while they were distracted.

"You're going to think I've lost my mind," Em said.

"Already do," Maria said with a shrug. "Keep going."

Em scowled at that, but she continued, anyway, "The sirens communicate with him through song. Dragons, obviously, can't sing, but we can."

There was no fucking way Em was about to suggest…

"We have to sing to him."

Maria shook her head, outright refusing to believe it. Em had *not* said that. She hadn't fucking said that.

The longer Maria shook her head, the more concerned Em looked. "Captain?"

"You've gone mad," Maria said. "You've gone completely and utterly mad!"

Em tilted her head to the side, her choppy, black hair falling against her ear. "I did warn you."

Maria leaned toward her. "You want us to battle a kraken with a fucking sea shanty?"

"It was Nymeth's idea, actually," Em said.

Zain tore his attention from the dragons to frown at the two of them. "Wait, what was that?"

"I asked you if you understood what it meant," Em reminded her, "that he'd sunk every ship he'd ever caught." She stepped closer. "It means, Captain, that your instincts as a ship captain will get you killed because *their* instincts as ship captains got *them* killed. To get a different outcome, you must try something different."

Well, singing to the monster was fucking different, all right.

The nearest mauve tentacle twitched, and the ship gave a dangerous groan in response.

"Captain," Pelt called out, "we need your orders."

"Tell them to fire the cannons," Zain told her.

Maria knew that was the only rational response, and yet, she couldn't tear her gaze from Em.

'Try something different.'

She had a point.

An absolutely mad, impossible point.

But a point, nonetheless.

No other ship had survived the encounter.

"I know you love your ship," Em said softly. "This is the only way to save it."

With another shake of her head, Maria turned toward her boatswain and sighed, "Tell the gunners not to fire. Yet."

Zain's eyes widened. "Captain!"

Maria forced herself not to cringe, as she continued, "And spread the word to the crew that we're…*singing*."

Pelt didn't look as outraged as Zain had, at least. Just… surprised. "Captain?"

"Pick a song everyone knows," Maria told him. "I want every sailor on this ship singing." She rolled her eyes at her own orders. "The last thing we need is to sing to this thing and it not even hear us."

Pelt nodded slowly. "Are you certain, Captain?"

Fuck, no.

But Maria couldn't say that. "Yes, boatswain."

"Captain, why are you listening to her?" Zain complained. "This is madness, and you know it!"

Maria didn't even look at him. "If we make it through one song, and it doesn't release us," she told Pelt, "the gunners will fire, as originally planned."

With a worried frown, Em said, "Just one song?"

Maria turned toward her. "Yes, one song." She held a finger in front of Em's face. "You have one chance, Em. One fucking chance. Do you understand me?"

Em merely nodded. "Yes, Captain."

Maria returned her gaze to Pelt. "Do it now."

Pelt didn't hesitate. "Aye, Captain."

The word spread with surprising speed, and before Maria knew it, the first line of her own favorite sea shanty began to ring out across the ship.

"My home, I've found, in you…"

Maria forced herself to sing with the crew, even as she grew more and more angry with Em—for convincing her to do this.

Of all the ways to die!

The ship rocked, as the creature's tentacles began to unfurl.

Maria's eyes widened.

Was it working?

As sailors all over the ship took notice, they began to sing louder.

After the first stanza, Em looked up at Maria, her green eyes bright with excitement. "I know this one!"

Maria couldn't help but smile. "Then, sing it, love."

For the first time aboard this ship, Em joined in on one of their songs. She had a pleasant voice, actually. Too timid to be a musician's voice, of course, but smooth and lovely—like when she'd spoken in her own language in Maria's quarters.

Maria held her surgeon's gaze, as they sang the chorus together.

"The shore's a distant memory,
Your open waters set me free,
No walls, no bounds, just endless blue,
My home, oh sea, is you."

Absurd, little chills slid over Maria's skin, and as the song ended, Maria had to resist the urge to pull Em close—right there, in view of her crew, while her ship was in the grasp of a fucking kraken. It couldn't have *been* more ridiculous.

Yet, something about singing with Em, about singing with her crew, had left Maria's chest warm and unsteady.

"Nymeth says we did well," Em whispered to her.

Maria was just about to remind Em that Nymeth wasn't the creature they needed to impress, when the ship jolted beneath her feet. She reached for Em's hand, just in case, but as she looked around, she realized those pale, purple tentacles weren't closing around them.

They were unfurling.

"I don't believe it," Zain muttered.

With eight, enormous splashes, the slimy, mauve tentacles slipped down the hull of the ship and back into the sea.

"He's swimming back down," Em told them. "The dragons are showing me. He let us go!"

Maria let out a soft, disbelieving laugh. "I gave you one chance." She lifted both eyebrows, and her lips curved into a deep smile. "Good work."

Em blushed.

Cheers rang out from the crew, and though most of them seemed reluctant to peer over the slimy rails of the ship, the calls from the lookout confirmed the kraken had, indeed, released them.

Still, Maria needed to see it for herself. She offered the helm to Henry, who was all too eager to take it back—now that the danger had passed.

Then, she turned to Em and gestured toward the taffrail with a tilt of her head. "With me."

Maria strode toward the taffrail—with Em's footfalls not far behind. She opted to keep her hands at her sides, lest she accidentally touch a bit of kraken slime, and she peered over the wooden rail.

The bright blue waters still bubbled and frothed beneath them, disturbed by the brief struggle that had taken place. Yet, the kraken was long gone.

"He swam back down," Em said, "to the deepest, darkest depths of the sea, where he usually lurks."

Maria glanced at her. "The dragons told you that?"

Em nodded. "They've been around for longer than any of us. They're usually right about these things."

And so they had been.

Zain trudged past them, his obsidian eyes wide and dull. "That's it. I'm done. I'm going to bed."

Em turned to frown at him. "But it's the middle of the day."

"Done," he called back. "I said I was done!"

Em turned to Maria, pointing over her shoulder. "I might need to check him for symptoms of shock."

Maria snorted. "One problem at a time, Em." She shook her head. "I can't believe we defeated a kraken with a song. Do you know how they'll react if we tell this story in Nefala? They'll think we've gone mad!" She leaned toward Em. "*Have* we gone mad?"

Em offered her a gentle smile. "I don't think so."

Maria let out a short laugh and decided this day required far more rum. She pulled out her leather pocket-flask and removed its cork. Pressing the leather container to her lips, she tipped her head back and drank.

The rum slid down her throat with a familiar burn.

When Maria finished, she exhaled sharply and offered the flask to Em. The fact that Em accepted it without a second thought warmed Maria's chest even more than the rum had.

Em flashed a playful smile. "Still think I should've gone down to the hold, when you told me to?"

"We'd all be dead, if you had," Maria admitted.

See? Maria wasn't *that* arrogant.

She could admit she was wrong.

On the rare occasion she actually was.

The very, *very* rare occasion.

Em and Maria shared the rest of the rum in her flask, passing it back and forth after each sip. Maria spent much of that time watching the waters below, half-expecting another tentacle to burst from the sea.

It never did.

Perhaps the dragons were right, and the kraken had returned to his deep-sea home. If that were true, though, how long until something brought him back?

"You said the sirens communicate with him." Maria turned to Em. "Did the sirens send him to attack us?"

Em nodded. "We're just outside their territory. I'd assume that little kraken is their first line of defense."

"I wish you'd stop calling it little," Maria said with an incredulous look. "Will they send more after us?"

Almost as if she'd been waiting for that question, Em said, simply, "No."

Maria frowned at the certainty in her tone. "You think the sirens will let us enter their territory, unimpeded, simply because we sang a song?"

"The sirens will find out what the kraken knows, which isn't much—because the kraken has a limited understanding of his surroundings," Em explained. "He knew he held a ship because we were within his grasp, but he can't see above the water. He won't have known about the dragons."

"Which means the sirens won't know about the dragons," Maria assumed.

"Not yet," Em agreed. "They'll know we sang to the creature, but they won't know who told us to *sing*. And they'll *want* to know who told us to sing."

As thunderous dragon wings flapped overhead, Maria looked up at the nearest one—the violet one, from the looks of it. "And when they see it was dragons?"

Em smiled at the question. "They'll know it's me. The sirens know who travels with dragons."

Maria tried her best to ignore the little flip of delight in her stomach. "And they'll hesitate to attack us, then," she assumed, "because of your treaty."

"It'd be a mistake, if they didn't," Em said.

Maria returned her attention to the gorgeous Azure Sea. "This is dangerous, love. Nothing we're doing is certain. Nothing we're doing is rational." She crossed her arms. "I don't like it."

Em looked up at her and smiled. "Yes, you do."

A slow smile spread across Maria's face, as well. She cast a sidelong glance at Em and said, "Yes, I do."

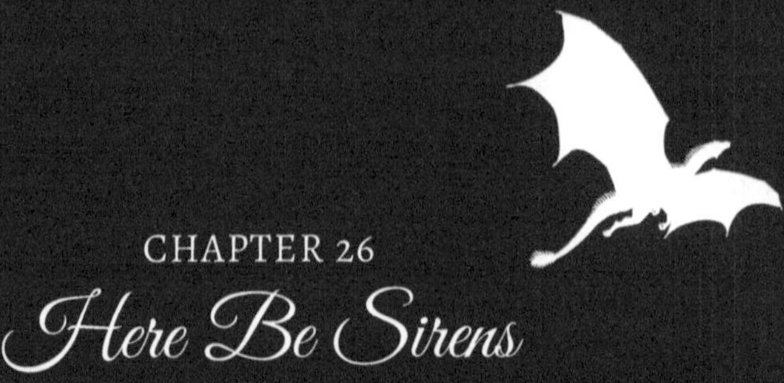

CHAPTER 26

Here Be Sirens

Siren-infested waters didn't come with warning bells or discernible lines.

No trap ever had, after all.

Aside from the kraken, there were no changes in the water, no signs of danger. The water a sailor died in looked no different from the water they lived on.

Maria had taken the helm the moment the jagged outcrops of the Illopian Mountains became visible.

It wasn't that Henry was a bad helmsman. He was excellent, actually.

Maria had grown fond of the older helmsman during her first naval assignment and was grateful to still have him as part of her crew after so many years.

She owed part of that to Em. If she hadn't healed Henry's liver when she did, they'd have lost him months ago. Maria sometimes wondered if Em even realized how many people they would've lost without her.

No, it wasn't that Henry was a bad helmsman. He just didn't have the quick reflexes needed to navigate such a rocky coast.

No one did.

Except Captain Maria Welles, of course.

Maria had taken the helm with all of her usual confidence and hadn't even questioned whether she'd need help—until she spotted the shark fins.

Usually, a ship as large as the *Wicked Fate* wouldn't need to concern herself with something as small as a shark, but *usually*, there weren't hundreds of them.

"What the fuck?"

The alarming number of grey fins circled the ship in a wide arc —distantly enough that Maria didn't think they'd sail through them anytime soon, but still near enough that Maria saw them without her spyglass.

Maria cast curious glances at the two dragons flying on either side of their ship. The one on the left sometimes blended into the blue sky, her scale such a light shade of shimmering blue that Maria often recognized her more by the shadow she cast over the water than her shape itself.

The dragon flying to the right of the ship was about half the size of the blue one and possessed those familiar, shining green scales Maria remembered from Drakon Isle.

Emryn, Em had called him.

The massive, black dragon—who had the impressive talent of making nearly every human in Aletharia piss themselves at the mere sight of her—flew behind the *Wicked Fate,* like the dark, ominous shadow she was.

The other two dragons, whose names Maria had long since forgotten, had flown on ahead of them. Maria hadn't seen them in hours.

She wondered if any of these dragons knew what those damn sharks were up to—and if they'd conveyed the information to Em already.

The steps below the quarterdeck creaked, and Maria looked down to find Pelt ascending them.

The boatswain likely had his hands full, since their quartermaster had ended *his* day prematurely.

When Pelt reached the helm, he said, "What's with the sharks?"

"Fuck, if I know," Maria muttered. "Where's Em?"

"Last I saw her, she was cleaning Cornelius's wounds," Pelt said with a grimace. "I thought about offering to help, but..." His scarred face twisted with increasing amounts of disgust. "That shit was gross."

Maria arched her eyebrows. She remembered the state of *his* wounds, once upon a time. "Really, Pelt?"

"Hey." Pelt held up his hands defensively. "You didn't see it!"

Maria had been there when Em cut the fucking thing off.

Pelt turned toward the strange arc of shark fins and held up a calloused hand to shield his eyes. "It's odd, isn't it? Francis thinks they're a bad omen."

Maria rolled her eyes. "Francis thinks everything's a bad omen. Every time he finds a hollow pocket in his bread, he tells someone they're going to die."

"Hey, my ma believed in the bread, too," Pelt said with a wave of his finger. "Got it right a few times."

"A few?" Maria repeated. "How many times did she get it wrong?"

"Ah, you don't keep count of that," Pelt told her, "not if you know what's good for you."

Maria snorted. "Well, tell Francis and whichever deckhands he's been blathering to *this* time that we're fine. Sharks pose no danger to a ship as big as ours."

Pelt glanced at her. "Even in these numbers?"

"They're still sharks," Maria said. "I wouldn't want to be in the longboat with those around, but as long as we're aboard the *Wicked Fate*, we're fine."

The problem was...Maria still didn't know when she and Em would be *boarding* said longboat.

Pelt nodded. "Aye. I'll spread the word." He turned to leave— and froze. He cocked his head slightly, then changed directions. Pelt approached the taffrail and peered into the waters below. "Er... Captain?"

Maria glanced over her shoulder, though she had no hope of seeing what he'd seen. "What is it, now?"

Pelt turned toward her. "Is it possible we're already in siren-infested waters?"

"Very possible," Maria admitted. "Why?"

Pelt hooked a thumb over his shoulder. "I think I just saw a… head."

Maria frowned. "A what?"

"Two of them, actually," Pelt mumbled. "I thought I saw one back there. So, I came over to look, and there was another, right here, looking up at me."

Maria could barely hear him, much less understand him. "You saw a human head?" she assumed. Did he mean a person overboard? No. He'd asked about siren-infested waters. "Or the head of a siren?"

"Something like that," Pelt said distractedly.

"Oh, for fuck's sake," Maria grumbled. She pulled out her old, brass spyglass and took a closer look at those sharks.

If Pelt had, indeed, seen a siren behind them, there were likely sirens in front of them, as well.

The sharks, as it turned out, were not alone.

Maria's blood cooled, as she saw the numerous human-like heads poking out of the water behind a barrier of sharks.

Human-like, in a broad sense, of course—as Maria had never seen a *human* with fins sticking out of their head.

"Whoever we have in the crow's nest," Maria muttered, "must've gone to bed with Zain."

Pelt's voice was full of confusion now. "Captain?"

Maria lowered the spyglass. "We're here." She inhaled through her nose, careful to keep her voice calm. "Reduce sail, and prepare to drop anchor."

Pelt sprang into action. "Aye, aye, Captain."

"And someone find me my fucking surgeon!" Maria screamed after him.

Maybe not so calm, after all.

"You're holding a cat," Maria muttered. "Again."

It had taken until after they'd already anchored the *Wicked Fate* for someone to find Em and send her to the quarterdeck.

Maria understood that. Mostly.

Em was exceptionally hard to find sometimes—often bouncing from one side of the ship to the other to remove splinters or nurse a smashed hand.

And the kraken had left her *several* injuries to attend to.

What Maria *didn't* understand was why Em had come to her with a large, purring feline in her arms.

Em glanced down at Rat-Slayer, feigning shock. "Well, look at that."

Maria ignored her sarcasm. "We're surrounded by hundreds of sirens, and you stopped to grab a cat?"

Em shrugged. "Pelt was worried you'd flay someone alive, if I didn't come immediately."

"And you stopped to grab a cat?" Maria repeated.

"I already *had* the cat," Em said with a laugh. She stroked her fingers through Rat-Slayer's striped fur. "After I finished redressing Cornelius's wound, I stopped to give Rat-Slayer some treats."

Confusion twisted at Maria's face. "Treats? What treats?" An alarming thought occurred to her, then, and she quickly searched the cat's silver-and-white fur for traces of blood. "Not...human flesh?"

"Why does everyone keep asking me that?" Em said.

Maria looked up, eyebrows rising. "Everyone?"

"No, I'm not feeding Cornelius to the cats," Em said with an exasperated sigh. "When there's flesh that needs to be cut away, I dispose of it properly."

Maria didn't know what *that* meant. "Then, what are you feeding my cats?" she asked. "And why?"

Em quirked her head slightly, her short, black hair rustling in the dragon-induced wind. "Well, the 'why' is simple. They're the best cats in all of Aletharia, and the best cats deserve treats."

Maria thought that might be a slight exaggeration, but the ever-so-proud *meow* Rat-Slayer offered in response suggested he felt otherwise.

This witch was *really* spoiling Maria's cats.

"You forgot to answer the first question," Maria said.

Em licked her soft, pink lips—the way she often did when she was nervous—leaving them visibly wet and even more appealing than usual. "I didn't forget, per se. I just…thought it best I didn't answer it."

"*You* thought it best?" Maria said.

Em stared deliberately at Rat-Slayer's silver-and-white fur, as she slid her fingers through it. "Yes."

Maria crossed her arms, the rolled-up sleeves of her shirt bunching around her muscles. "Em. Tell me you're not stealing food from the galley."

"Not at all," Em assured her. "Unlike you, I ask for it."

Maria narrowed her eyes. "Em!"

She'd said Em's name loudly enough that two of the sailors on the deck beneath them looked up.

Maria lowered her voice. "They'll never keep the ship free of rats, if you're spoiling their dinner!"

"It wasn't that much," Em scoffed. She clutched the huge cat close to her chest. "Besides, they deserve it."

She'd use that argument for anything, wouldn't she?

Maria rolled her eyes. "They're here to do an important job, Em."

"Yes, and they do that job very well," Em said. She bent her head toward Rat-Slayer's fluffy, silver ear and murmured, "Don't you? You're the best slayer of rats Aletharia's ever seen, aren't you?"

Maria didn't *have* a soft spot.

Not a single one.

If Em were any less charming with that massive ball of fluff in her arms, Maria would've put her foot down.

Hard.

No soft spots.

"If I start seeing rats on this ship," Maria warned, "you'll never set foot in that galley again."

Em's brows furrowed. "Well, that's just punishing Judith, isn't it?"

A cruel smile curled at Maria's lips. "Oh, I'm well-aware of how much you enjoy working with her. If you had to sit still for even an hour, you'd go mad."

Em's eyes widened a little, and she bent toward the silver tabby. "She's being rude again, Rat-Slayer."

The cat's frosty-blue eyes shifted toward Maria, and he gave a curt meow.

Blinking in shock, Maria rocked back on the heels of her boots. She might've forgotten her irritation, too, if she hadn't noticed the impish, little smile curving at the corners of Em's lips.

Gods, what was it about that fucking smile?

And how were they supposed to go out and face deadly sea creatures with Em looking like *that*?

Em would simply have to stop smiling.

Yes. Maria would order her to stop smiling.

For the safety of the crew.

With a shake of her head, Maria decided against it. "Put the cat down. We have matters to attend to."

Em glanced toward the unattended wheel. "We don't need anyone at the helm right now?"

"We're anchored," Maria told her.

"Oh!" Em knelt and gently placed Rat-Slayer on the deck. He stepped toward her, but she smiled and shook her head. "It wouldn't be safe for you, but we'll come back as soon as we can. I promise."

Maria lifted her eyebrows. Surely, the cat didn't want to come with them.

In the *water*.

Em gave Rat-Slayer one last chin rub, before climbing to her feet. Her thin, leather scabbard had shifted at some point, leaving her sword hanging against the front of her thigh.

With a frown, she adjusted it.

Maria considered offering to fix it for her. After all, how often would she have the opportunity to touch Em's wonderfully soft hips over the next few days?

If Maria thought too long about that, she'd probably change her mind about the whole thing.

Rat-Slayer circled Em's ankles once more, rubbing his head against her. She offered him another smile.

Finally, Em looked up at Maria. "Are you ready?"

"Haven't decided yet," Maria muttered. At Em's concerned look, Maria grinned and gestured toward the steps. "We're meeting Fulke and Pelt on the main deck. Starboard side. Longboat should be ready."

Em nodded and turned to leave.

Maria started to follow—but hesitated, when Rat-Slayer rubbed his ear against her boot. She looked down, blinking at the cat.

She knelt, one leather-clad knee touching the deck, and she slid her fingers through his fur. The soft purr he offered in response made Maria's lips curve.

"It's nothing personal, love," she murmured. "Your job here just happens to be an important one."

Rat-Slayer lifted his little chin and meowed at that.

When Maria looked up, she found Em, not just watching, but *smiling* at them.

Maria narrowed her eyes at the surgeon. "Stop that."

"YOU DON'T USE THAT SMILE ON NERISSA, DO YOU?"

The question caught Emilia so off-guard that she nearly tripped over her own feet. She spun toward Maria, her eyes wide. "What smile?"

Maria rested her hand against her right sword and shifted from one boot to the other. "What?" Her gaze wandered in every direction *but* Emilia's. "I didn't say anything."

Emilia scowled at the obvious lie. "Yes, you did!"

Maria's warm, brown eyes finally settled on Emilia. "Fine. Maybe I did, but I didn't *mean* to say it. Out loud." She grimaced. "Can we just pretend I didn't?"

Emilia's eyes widened. If there was anything Captain Maria Welles was known for, it was taking control.

She *lived* for control—got off on it, even!

So, how was Emilia supposed to react to Maria admitting to a lack of it?

"Captain," Emilia said with a worried frown, "Aletha didn't make you…insecure, did she?"

Emilia hadn't thought much about Aletha's mischievous, little remarks—because Maria hadn't acted as if they'd bothered her.

Maria had teased Emilia about her history with the siren, but she hadn't shown any signs of jealousy.

Not like she had when she'd realized Emilia's connection to Catherine, anyway—when her voice and words had turned as sharp as her swords.

"Insecure?" Maria repeated. She spread out her long, tattooed arms. "I'm Captain Maria Welles. I don't *get* insecure."

Emilia lifted her eyebrows skeptically.

It was true that Maria was the most infuriatingly arrogant person in all of Aletharia, but…she was also human—reluctant as Maria might've been to admit that.

Emilia stepped closer to her arrogant, *human* captain. "Don't worry. If blackmailing me, tricking me, and threatening to kill me wasn't enough to stop me from loving you, a siren princess won't be either."

Maria's lips twitched with each new item on the list. She let her arms fall to her sides, and the rigidness of her posture melted away. "There are certain words you shouldn't be saying out here, you know?" she murmured. "Insecure. Aletha. *Love*…"

Emilia laughed. "I'll need a quill and parchment for that list."

Maria's smile deepened. "They're waiting for us, love."

Emilia leaned in close and whispered, "I thought we weren't supposed to say 'love.'"

Almost as if she couldn't help it, Maria threw her head back and laughed. "Goddamn it." She pressed a warm hand against Emilia's back and pushed her in the direction of the longboat. "Not another word out of you."

Emilia proved she'd heard that by saying more words. "I still don't understand the question. How do you *use* a smile? And are you saying I have more than one?"

"Yes," was all Maria said.

Emilia sighed. Apparently, a few words of explanation were too much to ask for.

Emilia slowed her steps, as she caught sight of a familiar group of pirates, waiting near the rail. "I thought you said we were meeting Pelt and Fulke."

"I did," Maria said.

Pelt, indeed, waited by the rail, but among the two women who waited with him—neither of whom Maria had mentioned—a certain giant was nowhere to be found.

Maria strode on ahead of Emilia. "Boatswain," she said, when she reached him, "where's our master-at-arms?"

Pelt's eyes—wider than Emilia had ever seen them—swiveled toward Maria. He blinked a few times, as if waking from a trance. "Oh! Aye. He took a nap after the kraken attack. I think he's on his way now."

Maria squinted suspiciously. "Him, too?"

Emilia eyed Helen and Judith, noticing the way the women leaned over the wooden rail, nearly tumbling overboard just to see what waited below.

With a concerned frown, Emilia went to the rail, too, and peered down at the gently lapping water.

A group of older sirens swam beneath them, and as they watched, the smallest of the group—a siren with pale pink hair and translucent pink fins—lifted her hand from the water and waved at Judith.

The one next to her—a large siren with fiery-orange fins and equally fiery hair—waved at Helen.

Emilia rolled her eyes. "They'll convince you to jump into the sea, if you keep staring at them."

Both women jumped and glanced at Emilia with the same wide-eyed expression she'd seen on Pelt.

The interaction must've piqued Maria's curiosity—because she joined Emilia near the rail. When she peered over it, her dark brown eyes grew wide.

"Oh, no, you don't!" Emilia pushed the pirate captain away from the rail. "I'm not jumping in to save you!"

An amused smile quirked at the corners of Maria's rosy-brown lips. "But you'd jump in to save them?"

Emilia waved her hand toward the oblivious cook and master gunner. "*They* weren't properly warned. You were!"

Maria scoffed at that. "They're sailors! They were warned. We all were."

Judith raked her fingers through her short, brown hair. "Yes, but no one said they'd be *this* pretty."

"That's literally what they said," Maria muttered.

"Yes, but *this* pretty?" Judith continued to argue.

Pelt rejoined them. "I don't know if it's possible to prepare for such a thing."

When the four pirates tried to peer over the rail again, Emilia said, "Try to keep in mind *why* they want you to jump overboard— and how painful it'll be when they tear you apart with their teeth."

"I mean, it sounded painful before," Pelt mumbled, "but for some reason, it doesn't sound so bad now."

"Oh my goddess!" Emilia complained. She snapped her fingers in front of their faces. "Blink. Blink. Blink. All of you. Now!"

The four pirates blinked obediently.

"Am I going to have to tie you all up?" Emilia said.

She deliberately ignored Maria's arched eyebrow.

"Eh, I don't think that'd help much," Pelt muttered. "I've seen your knots."

Emilia glared at him. "You taught them to me!"

Pelt grimaced and lifted his shoulders. "Did I teach them *well*, though?"

"You could ask me to do it," Maria offered, her smile positively wicked. "You *know* mine are good."

Emilia's eyes widened, and her face burned.

It was possible—in an ideal world—that Pelt and Helen hadn't caught that. Fully.

But the look Judith shot Maria's way left no question as to whether *she'd* understood it.

Oh, what was the world coming to when Emilia couldn't innocently threaten to tie people up?

Helen stepped forward, holding both hands up, as if she had something quite serious to announce. "Have you all noticed something?"

Judith groaned, "Don't say it, Helen."

Helen leaned forward and whispered, "Their tits are *huge*."

Judith shook her head in defeat.

"What?" Helen said, glaring at Judith and Pelt. "You were both thinking it, too."

"Sure," Pelt agreed, "but we're too polite to say it."

Judith gave him a skeptical look. "You? Polite?"

Pelt tilted his head toward Helen. "More polite than *her*."

Helen held out her hands in a gesture that Emilia hoped was only *coincidentally* cup-shaped. "Just…fucking massive."

Maria glanced at Emilia. "Can they hear her?"

Emilia nodded.

"I've seen big tits before," Helen assured them all. "I've seen Jane's and Em's…"

Emilia's eyes widened even further at the mention of her own… breasts.

Helen stopped mid-sentence, when Maria crossed her arms and pinned Helen with an expectant look. "Clothed!" Helen told her. "I've seen them clothed!"

Maria's glare didn't waver.

"Obviously, I've seen Jane's unclothed," Helen admitted, "but Em's were always covered."

Had Maria blinked yet?

Emilia hadn't seen her blink.

"Doesn't mean they don't jiggle beneath the shirt," Helen continued, as if she had a death wish. "We all know what a jiggle means." She looked to Judith and Pelt for help, but neither of them were touching *that*.

As Helen whined at her friends for betraying her, Maria let her gaze drift toward Emilia. She raised a scarred eyebrow, and her lips twitched.

And Emilia realized…*ah*, Maria was doing this for her own enjoyment.

Emilia might've felt sorry for Helen, if she hadn't so clearly brought it on herself.

"All I was saying was that these are massive, even for someone who's seen the kinds of tits *I've* seen," Helen continued.

"I'm starting to think I need to add some more things to my Code," Maria muttered.

Helen's freckled face paled in horror. "You'd stop people from letting me see their tits?"

"Letting you?" Judith repeated—with a suspicious amount of interest. "Who's *letting* you? Besides Jane."

Pelt held up a placating hand. "Helen could've said it in a more delicate way, perhaps, but she did have a point about the tits."

Did Pelt think *that* was a more delicate way?

All four pirates looked to Emilia.

Emilia shook her head in disbelief. "Are you seriously asking me why their breasts are large?"

Judith shrugged. "I mean, it's fine, if you don't know."

"The extra fat keeps them warm in deep waters," Emilia said irritably. "Can you all behave yourselves now?"

"I think the fact that we're pirates means no," Pelt said.

"Do they store the extra fat everywhere?" Helen asked.

Judith spread out her hand. "Why wouldn't they? It did seem to be around their stomach, as well, didn't it?"

Helen turned toward her. "Yes, but they have that tail fin, remember? Doesn't the fin remove two essential body parts that could hold a bit of curve?"

"Two? I'm counting at least three," Judith said with a frown. "Were you counting both thighs as one?"

Helen counted again on her fingers. *Slowly.*

"Well, they could still have an ass," Pelt told them, "if the tail fin starts below it."

"No wonder sirens eat you," Emilia muttered under her breath.

Pelt turned eagerly to Emilia. "Do you think we could ask them to do a little jump? Like the one dolphins and orcas do? Then, we'd know if they had an ass."

Helen pointed a finger at him. "That's a good idea!"

"No, it's not!" Emilia told them. "It's the worst idea I've ever heard! What is wrong with you people?"

"Don't ask them *that*," Maria said. "We don't have time for the list."

"How am I supposed to keep you all safe," Emilia complained, "when you're clearly trying to die?"

Helen's thin, red eyebrows drew inward. "Oh, I don't think they can blame us for being curious! I think they *want* us curious. Otherwise, what's all the waving and nipples about?"

Emilia knew she shouldn't have asked. She did. But she simply couldn't help herself. "Nipples?"

Pelt stepped forward to assist Helen with this one. He leaned in, as if to share a secret, and whispered, "I don't know if you noticed, but they forgot to cover their nipples."

Emilia cast a pleading look at her captain—who didn't even bother to rescue her.

"He's right," Helen hissed. "They're totally bare!"

Emilia heaved out the longest sigh of her life. "There's nothing covering *any* part of them—because they don't wear clothes." She glanced from one pirate to the next. "Did you notice that, or were you only looking at their nipples?"

Pelt stepped back and looked from Judith to Helen, drawing a finger across his throat. "I don't think we should answer that one."

Emilia looked up at Maria. "They're going to die, and they're going to deserve it."

Maria shrugged. "I tried to tell you. Everyone on this ship deserves to die. That's why I kill them."

"No, you should've seen mine," Helen was telling the other two. "She had orange nipples—like her fins! Did you see that? Orange nipples!"

"Huh, must've missed it," Pelt said. "I'll go look again!" He stepped toward the rail.

Maria grabbed him by his shirt and dragged him back.

Judith eyed Helen with a strange look. "What do you mean, *yours*?"

Helen lifted her chin, orange braid sliding down her back. "Well, she waved at me, didn't she?"

"Of course she waved at you," Judith scoffed. "You were staring at her orange nipples. What else could she do?"

"It wasn't just that," Helen argued. "She wanted to eat me. I could tell!"

"Well, perhaps she skipped a meal, and you looked like a big one," Judith said with a wave of her hand. "Little does she know, the big ones are hard to cook."

Helen frowned. "I don't think they cook us before they eat us. I think they just dive in, like a shark."

"Well, it's amazing they don't get sick, then!" Judith said. Her blue eyes traveled Helen's body. "You'd be tough to eat, either way —all that muscle. What kind of seasoning would they even put on you?"

"Seasoning?" Helen repeated.

"Oh, don't tell me they eat unseasoned meat, too!" Judith said, clearly ready to go down and teach some sea creatures how to cook. "Nah, with standards that low, they'd eat any of us, given the chance."

Helen tapped her hand against her chest, face reddening with rage. "But they'd eat me first!"

Judith threw an arm out toward the rail. "Well, the pink one would eat me first! How do you like that?"

"One of them would eat me, too, right?" Pelt said in a panicked tone. "They don't *only* like women, do they?"

"Oh, for Aletha's sake," Emilia sighed. She turned to Maria. "I really think we're going to have to tie them up."

"We'll have to gag them, too," Maria said.

"Where is your armor?"

Nymeth's voice entered Emilia's mind so suddenly that she nearly jumped out of her skin.

"Goddess!" Emilia thought. *"Can't you ever start with a hi?"*

"Your armor, rider," Nymeth said impatiently. *"Where is it?"*

"In the surgeon's cabin," Emilia told her. *"In a chest."*

"That is not where it's meant to be," Nymeth growled. *"It is meant to be worn by my rider. Why aren't you wearing it?"*

Emilia winced. She hadn't evoked that sort of response from Nymeth in years. Not since she was a much-too-curious child with a certain green dragon willing to entertain all of her curiosities—no matter how dangerous they proved to be.

"Sorry," she said, *"but why would I need it? I'm not flying today."*

"You're not an arrogant human," Nymeth scolded. *"You don't get to make arrogant assumptions."*

"It's not an arrogant assumption. It's a regular assumption," Emilia argued. *"I'm traveling with the captain, and under no circumstances will I abandon her."*

"I never implied you would," Nymeth assured her.

"Then, how could I fly?" Emilia asked. *"Unless there's been some change in the way dragon magic works, and you can bond with humans now?"*

The disgust in Nymeth's voice was so thick it was audible. *"I cannot and would not."*

Emilia suppressed a laugh. *"Then, how would I fly?"*

"Even if you don't fly, you can still wear dragon-scale," Nymeth said. *"It'll protect you against other things."*

"I can't imagine sea creatures fighting with fire," Emilia pointed out.

"Not just fire, but weapons, too," Nymeth reminded her. *"It might protect you from their warriors' tridents."*

"They aim for the throat," Emilia told her. *"No dragon-scale there."*

"If you keep arguing, Dragon Child," Nymeth rumbled, *"I might regret donating my scale to you at all."*

Emilia tried her best not to smile. *"I'm sorry. You know I appreciate the armor, don't you?"*

"Of course I know. Our souls are linked," Nymeth said irritably. *"That doesn't mean I'll accept any less than a yes. Dragon-scale is not meant to collect dust, rider."*

A hint of guilt pricked Emilia's chest. When she'd lived on Drakon Isle, she would've never shown such carelessness, but living amongst pirates had changed her. *"You're right."*

"Don't worry," Caelu said kindly. *"Your human will understand."*

"And if she doesn't," Emryn interjected, *"we'll burn her."*

Emilia lifted her head toward the sky and glared at the small, green dragon, circling their ship. *"Emryn!"*

"We're not burning the human," Caelu told Emryn, *"because our rider loves her."*

"She loved the other human, too," Emryn reminded the blue dragon, *"but we still intend to burn her."*

"Oh, but we always wanted to burn the other one," Caelu said. *"We like this one!"*

"Only because she's shiny," Emryn argued.

"That is not the only reason!" Caelu said.

In her time away from the dragons, Emilia had nearly forgotten how overwhelming it could get, when all of her dragons were talking, at once.

And Astral and Igrunn hadn't even returned yet.

"If you two don't stop arguing," Nymeth warned the younger dragons, *"I'll send you both home, and we'll take care of the Dragon Child without you."*

Emryn and Caelu immediately fell silent.

Thousands of years old, and they still obeyed their mother.

"They better," Nymeth said with a low, rumbling laugh. *"Wear your scale, Dragon Child."*

The dragons had distracted Emilia so much that she hadn't noticed Maria sliding behind her—until Maria's fingers curled around her hip and her mouth brushed the shell of Emilia's ear.

"You have that look again, love," Maria whispered in her ear. "You're talking to your dragons."

With the heat of Maria's body behind her and the warmth of Maria's breath on her ear, it was all Emilia could do to not shudder. "I was, yes," she admitted. "Sorry. Nymeth wants me to wear dragon-scale."

Maria's gentle fingers slid lower, stopping just beneath Emilia's hipbone. "Probably not a bad idea."

Emilia cast a nervous glance at the other pirates. Did Maria realize how close they stood to each other?

Did she realize how intimate it must've looked?

Maria must've noticed the direction of Emilia's gaze—because she whispered, "Relax. They can't even bring themselves to blink, at the moment, much less look at *us*. I could slide my hand down your trousers, and they *still* wouldn't look away from those sirens."

It was true that the three of them had made it back to the rail already and had gone right back to salivating over those sirens. But Emilia hoped Maria didn't intend to *test* that theory.

"Since Fulke isn't here yet, anyway," Emilia asked, "should I go down and get my armor?"

Maria rested her face against Emilia's shoulder, inhaling softly. Chills scattered along the back of Emilia's neck, and every part of her ached to lean into Maria's touch.

"You'll need to dress in my quarters," Maria whispered against her shoulder, "won't you?"

Emilia swallowed. "Ideally, yes. Is that all right?"

Maria lifted her mouth to Emilia's ear, and Emilia *felt* the smirk curving at Maria's lips. "Of course, love. On one condition."

Emilia rolled her eyes at that last part—because she already knew what Maria was going to say.

"Let me help you," Maria whispered in her ear.

A shiver traveled through Emilia at the mere memory of the ways Maria had touched her the last time she'd…*helped*. "I don't think we have time."

"Oh, I know what I'm doing now," Maria said. She tilted her face closer and whispered, "I can be quick."

A rush of desire poured through Emilia, and as her senses narrowed to that one point of contact, where Maria's fingers rested against her, she suddenly wished Maria would dig them into her hip —the way she often did when they kissed.

"Okay," Emilia breathed.

Maria chuckled at the one word answer. "We have a deal, then?"

'One of these days, Em,' Maria had once told her, *'you're going to learn to stop making deals with pirates.'*

Apparently, this…was not that day.

"Yes, Captain."

"You truly have no concerns about the sharks?"

Em looked up at Maria, body rising and falling in time with the longboat. "The sharks listen to the sirens. They're only as dangerous as the sirens are."

Maria slid closer to her surgeon. With the water splashing against the sides of the boat and the waves crashing against nearby rocks, she'd barely heard her.

Fulke occupied the other half of their small, wooden boat, as he rowed them toward the rocky coast. He handled the choppy waves with ease—the way only a giant could.

As the sky blazed around them in shades of orange and rouge and a red sun burned on the horizon, Maria wondered if she should've brought a lantern.

She hadn't thought about it before—since the sun hadn't begun to set when they'd first loaded the longboat—but that had been before she'd had to wait for Fulke and assist Em with her armor.

The armor alone had delayed them by a half hour, at least.

Could they have shaved a good twenty minutes or so off of that time, if Maria had behaved herself?

Perhaps.

But what was the use in being a pirate, if you didn't misbehave whenever you had the chance?

"Only as dangerous as the sirens," Maria called out over the waves, "is pretty fucking dangerous, Em."

Em laughed at that. "They won't let the sharks eat you. I promise." Maria *almost* relaxed—until Em added, "Because if the sharks eat you, they can't."

Maria narrowed her eyes at the unhelpful surgeon. "Remind me why I let you talk me into this."

"It was Aletha who talked you into it, not me," Em corrected, "and I believe she did so by mentioning…phenomenal breasts?"

Maria rolled her eyes. "That was *not* what convinced me."

Though she had to admit…Aletha hadn't lied.

All around them, curious heads poked out of the water to watch them pass.

Portions of the webbed fins that flared from the sirens' heads poked out, as well—the colors of those fins as varied as the colors of their hair and skin.

Behind Em, Fulke caught Maria's gaze and shot a meaningful look at Em's tousled, black hair—as if to indicate that he knew exactly who'd tousled it.

Maria didn't feel any shame about what she'd done, but for Em's sake, she still smoothed a hand over the silky, black strands.

Honestly, it wasn't even Maria's fault.

Not…totally, anyway.

Em's hair was always a bit tousled.

A consequence of living aboard a ship with any sort of curl in your hair. Maria—with her own wild curls—relied on her head-scarves for that very reason.

Em deserved some of the blame, as well—for letting Judith, of all people, cut it.

And for moaning the way she did, when Maria pulled it.

Yes, Maria could think of plenty of people to blame, besides herself, and she'd tell Fulke as much later.

Em blinked up at her. "What are you doing?"

With a start, Maria realized she was still touching Em's hair. She immediately dropped her hand. "Something in your hair," she muttered.

"What?" Em's hand shot toward her head.

Fulke rolled his eyes at Maria.

He was awfully judgmental for someone who'd *coincidentally* gone to bed at the same time as Zain.

Oh, if those two ever…

Maria shuddered to even *think* of such horror.

Zain was the horror, of course.

Not Fulke.

Fulke was lovely—when he wasn't judging Maria.

Pale, bluish-white fingers curled over the hull of the boat, and Maria jolted toward Em, eliminating any and all space between them on the sturdy, wooden thwart.

The siren jerked his hand back and slipped down into the water, as if Maria's reaction had scared *him*.

Em—who'd apparently missed the whole thing—peered around Maria. "What happened?"

"I think one of them tried to touch me," Maria said.

Em leaned back, waving a hand dismissively. "Oh, no, it's their *kiss* that disorients you, not their touch."

As if that were the only thing Maria needed to fear.

Not their appetite for human flesh.

Or their fucking sharks.

Just their kiss.

Out of sheer habit, Maria's hand drifted toward one of her sheathed swords.

Em's bright green eyes followed the movement. "Don't," she whispered. "If you draw a weapon with their children nearby, they'll react aggressively."

"I know. I haven't drawn it yet, have I?" Maria said. Her brows furrowed. "Wait. Did you say *children?*"

Em lifted her eyebrows. "You don't see them?"

Maria swept her gaze around their boat, taking note of the sirens who lurked in the waters around them. Indeed, some of them did look smaller than the others—with smaller faces and smaller eyes. Even their fins were shorter than those of the adult sirens.

Children.

Maria had never even heard anyone *mention* siren children. She'd never even considered the possibility.

Though it was obvious, now.

Why *wouldn't* sirens have children?

"They're curious," Em said with a soft smile. "Some of them have probably never seen a living human!"

Maria turned to Em, raising an eyebrow at the sight of her smile. Only Emilia Drakon would enjoy an experience like this one.

"Must you add the *'living'* part?" Maria complained.

"I must, if I'm to be honest," Em said with a shrug. "I'm sure they've seen plenty of *dead* humans already."

Maria snorted. It was her own fault, if she hadn't learned by now that she shouldn't look to Emilia Drakon for a pretty lie.

Pretty eyes, perhaps.

Pretty breasts, pretty hips.

Pretty smiles.

Pretty, long spiels about her special interests.

But *not* pretty lies.

Never those.

Maria leaned back against the side of the longboat, positioning herself slightly behind Em—where Em's armor-clad shoulder brushed Maria's leather doublet. "You said they can hear us, but how?" Maria whispered in Em's ear. "With the fins on their heads?"

"Those are the opercular fins," Em told her, "and no, they can't hear with fins. They have ears, just like us—only theirs are better protected than ours."

"Really?" Maria breathed. She glanced at a nearby siren, watching as the creature's lilac-colored fins folded against her head, when she sank beneath the water. "Fascinating! Their ears are beneath the fins?"

While Maria watched the siren, Em watched *her*. "I like this side of you." An adoring smile curved at the corners of her lips. "You're so curious."

Maria turned to glare at the mischievous witch. Did she have to make it sound so *sweet?*

"I'm only gathering information," Maria argued, "to ensure the safety of my crew."

"Mm-hmm," Em said, her green eyes sparkling. "Information about opercular fins?"

"Information," Maria corrected, "about whether they can hear us or not."

"Except I already told you they can," Em said.

A fluttering mix of excitement and amusement flared in Maria's belly.

Maria braced her arm on the wooden hull and tilted her face toward Em's. She lowered her voice, breath dancing along Em's mouth. "You're such a pain."

Em's gaze dropped to Maria's lips and darkened. "As are you."

"I'm captain," Maria taunted. "I'm allowed to be."

Em rolled her eyes. She opened her mouth to say something else, but then, she seemed to notice, at the same time Maria did, that the boat had stopped.

Maria turned toward Fulke.

He'd leaned a little to the side, peering into the water beneath them. His dark brown eyes shifted to meet Maria's. He freed his hands and signed, *"I think I might've hit one of them with an oar."* When Maria's eyebrows rose, Fulke continued, *"They've closed in around us. I don't think they want us going any further."*

"It'll be dark soon," Maria reminded him. "We can't stay here."

Maria noticed Em frowning at Fulke's large hand, as if she'd missed a few words. So, Maria repeated what he'd said.

Em nodded midway through the second sentence. "He's right. We should wait here."

"For what?" Maria said. She waved a hand toward a green-finned siren who'd just peered into their boat, eyes dark and hungry. "Them to eat us?"

Em leaned toward the green-finned siren. "Do you know who I am?"

The siren tilted her head at an almost painful angle, and Em spoke again—in her own language, this time.

Recognition flickered in the siren's much-too-large eyes. She looked up at the dragons and then back at Em. *"Drakon,"* the siren said, enunciating the word far more harshly than Em ever had. *"Drakon Apaer."*

Maria turned to Em. "What did she say?"

"Dragon Child," Em told her. "It's Drakoní for Dragon Child."

As absurd as it was, Maria longed to try the words out for herself—to see how they felt on her tongue.

Would they feel as smooth as they sounded, when Em spoke them? Or would Maria butcher the pronunciation, as she suspected the siren had?

The siren said something else, and though Maria recognized none of the words around it, she recognized the name the siren had spoken.

Nerissa.

"She's coming," Em whispered to Maria.

"Who is?" Maria said, though she knew already.

As if in answer, the swarm of sirens parted.

Water rippled in the distance, and somewhere beneath the surface, something swam toward them.

Aside from the rare flash of shimmering turquoise, Maria saw nothing of the creature itself—not at first—but the V-shaped wake of the creature moved toward them at a speed no human could match.

"Em?" Maria said.

Em rested her wondrously gentle hand against Maria's leather-clad thigh, and Maria tried not to lean *too* obviously into her touch. "Don't worry."

"I'm not," Maria lied.

Still, she hoped Em wouldn't move her hand too soon.

The creature swam with incomparable grace, each stroke longer and more precise than a human's, and her tail-fin occasionally emerged from the water—her scales a pale turquoise, translucent and sparkling.

Midway through the crowd of sirens, the creature emerged from the water to look at them.

No, not them.

Em.

She'd looked directly at Em.

Long, greenish-blue hair floated along the surface of the water

—just a shade darker than her tail-fin and the smaller, translucent fins along her forearms.

Her turquoise, opercular fins twitched at the sight of Em, and the corners of her mouth curved upward.

"Nerissa?" Maria assumed.

"Nerissa," Em agreed.

With a graceful dive, the siren princess disappeared once more beneath the deep, azure-blue waters.

"She hasn't seen you since you were fifteen," Maria muttered. "Yet, she recognizes you from a distance?"

"What makes you think she recognized me?" Em asked.

Maria stared blankly at her. Had they been watching the same creature?

The longboat rocked, and when the siren princess reemerged, she was nearly close enough to touch. Her fingers—webbed, like Aletha's—curled over the hull of the boat, and she lifted herself from the water.

Maria hadn't seen it from so far away, but this close, she realized the siren princess wore a crown of sorts—though it was nowhere near the size or weight of the crowns King Eldric wore.

It was a thin crown—more of a tiara, really—made of coral and pearl, interlaced tightly with strands of the siren's turquoise-blue hair.

If the siren had even *seen* Maria and Fulke in the boat with Em, she gave no indication of it. Her large, sea-blue eyes never left Em. "Emilia Drakon."

Her voice was softer than any human's, her words as melodic as a song.

Em removed her hand from Maria's thigh. "Nerissa," she said with a stunned smile. "How have you been?"

Maria wondered why Em was speaking in Illopian, when the first siren had already proven they didn't speak Illopian. She'd even opened her mouth to ask as much—when the siren's gaze shifted toward *her*.

Maria froze at the sight of those much-too-large, turquoise eyes.

Apparently one step ahead of Maria, the siren princess asked, "Are we speaking the mountain-worshiper's tongue for *her* sake?"

"Both of theirs," Em said, motioning toward Fulke, as well, "but yes—if you don't mind."

Nerissa returned her attention to Em. "When have I ever minded accommodating *you*, Emilia Drakon?"

Maria didn't think she liked this princess.

Using her arms, Nerissa gracefully lifted herself, once more, against the side of their boat, before allowing her large, bare breasts to flop over *into* it.

Considering the timing of the *flopping*, Maria doubted it was an accident.

Em's gaze immediately dropped to the siren's large, pale breasts, and she flushed scarlet at the sight.

Maria didn't blame her for this, of course.

She could barely take her eyes off of the siren's breasts herself, and Em had *always* been known to change colors, like an octopus, at the sight of breasts.

Maria did, however, see through the siren's coy act.

"Em," she whispered.

Em blinked—and somehow, impossibly, turned an even darker shade of red. "Umm, right." She stared deliberately at the bottom of the boat. "We were hoping to talk to your breasts—*queen*! Your queen!"

Maria rested her elbow against her thigh, covering her mouth to stifle the laughter.

Fulke took no such precautions.

While the two of them laughed at their ever-so-eloquent surgeon, and that ever-so-eloquent surgeon sank as low in the boat as she could, Nerissa merely tilted her head, feigning cluelessness.

"Who is 'we?'" Nerissa asked.

Em cast a wary glance at Maria. "My captain and I."

Nerissa turned her full attention toward Maria. "Captain, hmm?" She shifted her arms, when she moved, and she somehow managed to reposition her breasts at the perfect viewing angle for Maria.

Maria couldn't bring herself to look away.

It's magic. You can't help it because it's magic, Maria told herself.

She remembered the way Em had forced them all to blink, and she tried to make herself do it.

But her eyes refused to cooperate.

"Yes. My captain," Em told the siren. "What of it?"

Helen had been right about the strange nipples, Maria realized. The siren princess's nipples were nearly the same shade of turquoise as her fins.

"Are you sure that's *all* she is?" Nerissa said with a smile. "Because she looks at me as if I've touched her favorite plaything, even though I haven't touched you yet."

That was enough to snap Maria out of it. "Yet?"

Nerissa lifted a sea-blue eyebrow, clearly impressed that Maria had broken her spell—or that *something* had.

Em, on the other hand, glared at her. "I'm not your plaything," she reminded Maria. "Can we get as upset about that as we do the 'yet?'"

Maria shrugged, her shoulder brushing Em's. "You know you're more than that."

Em's eyes softened, though they still held a *slight* spark of annoyance.

It should've been a crime to look that sexy, while annoyed.

Smiling, annoyed—gods, couldn't Em choose an emotion that wouldn't torment Maria in this way?

Did she even have any?

"*More* than that?" Nerissa repeated—long after Maria had forgotten she was even there. "But doesn't 'captain' imply *less* than that?"

"No," Maria said.

Nerissa giggled at her one-word answer.

Maria knew the sirens probably understood a bit of ship life—considering their diets consisted of sailors, sailors, and more sailors—but that didn't mean they knew anything of what it meant to be captain.

Then again, Nerissa spoke flawless Illopian, despite the other sirens not even recognizing the language. So, it was possible she knew more about this, as well.

How much did a siren princess need to know?

"Captain or not," Nerissa told Em, "I don't think it'd be wise to take a human to the Turquoise Palace."

The what?

"It's decided already," Em said—with little warmth left in her tone. "I won't leave my captain."

Maria hated how much those words soothed her.

A hint of distress flashed across Nerissa's beautiful features. "We're not enemies, Emilia. I don't know why you'd speak as if we are."

Maria and Fulke shared a puzzled look.

Em had only stated her decision. How pliable must she have been once—for Nerissa to think a slightly cooled voice was speaking as if they were enemies?

How pliable had her mother trained her to be?

Em softened her tone. "I know we're not," she sighed, "but I don't trust as easily as I once did—and I'm also not sure I like the way you were treating my friends."

Nerissa lifted her chin, drops of seawater sliding down her pale throat. She glanced at Maria, pursing her lips. "If you don't like the way I treat them, you certainly won't like the way the *queen* does."

She said 'queen' with such an impersonal tone that Maria wondered if the siren princess had the kind of relationship with her mother that Em had with hers.

Perhaps that was the reason they'd grown so close.

"No," Em said, "but *she* won't be bothered if I'm less than happy with her."

The corners of Nerissa's lips twitched at that. "Fair point," she said with a giggle. "I may have taken it a bit too personally. I have missed you, Emilia."

Maria shifted uncomfortably on the thwart—only realizing her mistake when the boat rocked with her movement, and all eyes shifted toward her.

"Splinter," Maria lied.

That only seemed to worry Em more. "Where?" she asked. "We need to remove it before it gets infected."

Damn it. Why had Maria chosen *that* lie to give to a fucking surgeon?

Fulke shook his big head at her.

Judgemental bastard.

"I'm fine."

Em didn't accept that, of course. She lifted Maria's hand, examining each tattooed finger. "Was it here?"

While Em continued her examination of Maria's perfectly unharmed hand, Nerissa offered her a quiet warning, "I was so relieved when I heard they'd seen dragons—because I knew it meant you'd survived."

Em looked up, her brows furrowed.

"But you need to know," Nerissa whispered, "there were sirens in the palace who had other…reactions."

Maria wasn't sure Em had processed the warning—since she'd never stopped frowning at the first part.

"Survived?" Em repeated. "Then, you knew."

Nerissa squirmed at the accusation, water sloshing around her. "Word spreads. It's a small sea, after all."

Maria wouldn't have called the Azure Sea small.

Broken up by islands, yes, but not small.

The color drained from Em's face, and her fingers loosened—until Maria's hand fell from her grasp. "They know what happened to my people. Yet, they aren't happy to see me alive."

"*Some* of them aren't," Nerissa said, "only because they know why you've come." She shrugged her bare shoulders. "Every species has selfishness, even ours." Her gaze drifted toward Maria, lingering on the gold chain Maria wore around her neck. "Though I'd say we have far less than the mountain-worshippers."

Maria briefly wondered if she should've tucked the gold beneath her doublet before leaving the ship.

You couldn't have *paid* her to do it now, though—not when it would've told the little siren princess she had some kind of power over Maria.

"I just didn't want you to go in unprepared," Nerissa said. "My mother listens to a lot of voices, besides my own, but you know mine will always be for you."

Em's eyes narrowed, mirroring the same suspicion Maria felt.

The siren's words were too sweet to believe, and it *was* in a siren's nature, after all, to kill you *sweetly*.

"You were young when you sided with me," Em said. "Your feelings might've changed since then."

Nerissa pulled back, water splashing as she slipped further into it. "My feelings *have* changed," she said, forcing sharp words through even sharper teeth. "When I was young, I hoped we'd align ourselves with your people simply because you had dragons. Now, I hope for it because I'm sick of watching the mountain god have his way with Aletharia, while Aletha's own children do *nothing* to stop him!"

A surprised smile pulled at Em's lips. "I see."

Nerissa shoved her drenched, turquoise hair over her shoulder. "Do we have an understanding now?"

Em nodded. "We do."

Nerissa exhaled, and the brief flash of anger in her strange eyes faded. She kicked her tail-fin, pushing herself closer to the boat. "I suppose," she said softly, "you were serious about not trusting as easily."

"Very," Em said.

Sympathy pulled at the siren's blue eyebrows. "What did those mountain-worshippers *do* to you?"

Em looked down at her gloved hands, entangled in her lap.

Maria followed her gaze, her chest tightening—because unlike the siren princess, Maria knew why Em had looked *there*, of all places. She knew the scars those leather gloves hid—the same reddened scars that marred Maria's own wrists.

"You don't want to know," Em mumbled.

Maria wanted nothing more than to slip her hand into Em's and intertwine their fingers—to squeeze Em's hand and remind her she wasn't alone, to remind her Maria understood.

Fulke would see, of course, which wasn't ideal, but Maria trusted him to not perceive it as something other than what it was.

Unfortunately, they were surrounded by sirens, and if there was anything Maria had learned in her many years as captain, it was to never show emotion in front of a possible enemy.

Maria had no choice but to settle for something more discreet. She rested her arm along the wooden hull—where no one would see—and she brushed her thumb along the center of Em's spine.

The dragon scale was thick and cool against Maria's skin, but not so thick that Em didn't feel it, clearly—because she straightened at Maria's touch.

Insignificant as it might've been, Maria believed Em would understand the meaning behind that touch.

Shared scars, shared pain.

You're not alone.

Em looked up at Maria, and the gratitude that flashed so vividly within her dazzling, green eyes tore at Maria's heart.

They touched only in one, small spot. Yet, Maria felt it every-where—even in the place nothing *could* touch.

A splash on Fulke's side of the boat shattered that feeling, and both of them turned to look at the giant.

Apparently, it wasn't Fulke who'd splashed—but a small, siren child. Mostly submerged in water, the little boy stared up at Fulke with curious, coral-pink eyes, and his pink, opercular fins twitched with excitement.

Amusement pulled at the edges of Fulke's mouth, and he raised a large, dark-skinned hand to wave.

The boy's eyes widened, and he swam closer to the boat. He lifted his own webbed hand from the water and mirrored Fulke's slow wave.

Fulke let out that same loud, rumbling laugh he'd always given in moments of joy, and the boy swam backward, startled by the sound.

Nerissa giggled. She said something to the boy—*sang* it, really—in what must've been her own language. Maria had thought her voice was lovely, when she spoke, but now, as the siren sang, Maria realized it was so much *more* than lovely.

It was magic.

It soothed every muscle in Maria's body.

She'd never heard anything like it.

The boy sang, too—a response of some kind. Even at his age, his voice sounded more pleasant than any human voice ever had, though it clearly wasn't as developed as Nerissa's.

The boy stuck to the same few notes, while Nerissa's soft, soprano voice soared and dipped with ease.

Maria wondered if sirens learned their first musical notes the way humans learned their first words.

Nerissa splashed the boy playfully, and he slipped back in the water. "He's curious about your size," she told Fulke. "He hasn't learned about giants yet."

Fulke gave an understanding nod. Then, he twisted so far in the boat that he knocked Em into Maria's lap—not that Maria was *complaining*—just so he could smile at the boy.

Maria caught Em around the waist and lifted an eyebrow at her, while Fulke did nothing but flash his widest, brightest grin.

The boy beamed back, flashing a mouthful of razor-sharp teeth.

Maria jolted back in shock, accidentally throwing Em out of her lap and into the bottom of the boat.

While Em struggled to find her way back onto the thwart—*without* rocking the boat too much in the process—Maria struggled to regain her composure.

Fortunately, Em was too busy planting her face in the bottom of the boat to see what had startled Maria.

Unfortunately, Nerissa had apparently seen it all—because *she* immediately turned and smiled at Maria.

Baring every one of her deadly, shark-like teeth.

Maria's heart raced.

She suddenly understood why the sirens at the ship had used *closed*-mouth smiles to flirt with Helen and Judith.

This…probably wasn't the reaction they'd desired.

Nerissa, on the other hand, clearly *had* desired it.

When Em finally made it back onto the wooden thwart, she grasped Maria's arm worriedly. "What happened?"

Maria forced herself to look away from Nerissa's teeth—long enough to meet Em's worried gaze. Her words came out in a breathless whisper, "I wish you'd been a little more clear in your descriptions."

Em's brows furrowed. She cast a puzzled look at Nerissa, but the mischievous, fucking siren princess had already stopped smiling. Em's gaze dropped to Nerissa's perfect breasts, as she clearly came to the wrong conclusion. She turned back toward Maria.

"You mean the breasts?" Em whispered. "I didn't think that would bother you. You grew up in a tavern, for Aletha's sake."

"Not the breasts." Maria threw out her hands in frustration. "The teeth, Em! The fucking teeth!"

Several curious heads poked out of the water.

At least the child was gone.

Em glanced again at Nerissa, who was now barely suppressing laughter. With a sigh, she returned her attention to Maria. She tightened her grip around Maria's arm and pulled her close—until Maria's leather tricorn nearly brushed Em's forehead.

"I told you they had smiles like sharks."

"I thought you meant not to trust them," Maria said.

With a puzzled frown, Em said, "If I'd meant that, I would've said it." She lowered her voice. "Also, that's not a nice generalization to make, Captain!"

Maria stared blankly at her. "They literally eat us," she hissed. "I think it's a *safe* generalization to make."

"Yes, and what do you think they eat you *with*?" Em asked. "Teeth. Shark-like teeth." She spun toward Nerissa, eyes flashing. "And I don't know what *you* think is so funny."

Nerissa fluttered her perfect eyelashes. "Oh, Emilia, darling, it was an accident! I had no idea your fearless ship captain was afraid of a *smile*."

Maria glared at her, hand flying to her sword.

Em grabbed Maria's wrist to stop her. She returned her attention to Nerissa. "It's Em, now, if you don't mind," she said, voice as sharp as the siren's teeth, "and don't insult my captain."

Nerissa floated on her back, breasts emerging from the water like gently sloping mountains. "I'm sorry! No one ever taught me not to play with my food!"

Em narrowed her eyes. "Nerissa."

"It isn't my fault," Nerissa whined.

Maria glanced at Fulke—who had, somehow, managed *not* to laugh at her. "Not a word about this to anyone."

The smile Fulke offered her was surprisingly sympathetic. *"I'll take it to my grave,"* he signed, *"Captain."*

With that, Maria finally let herself relax.

"Are you *sure* you want to take her with you?" Nerissa asked. "I can't promise no one will smile at her."

"I'm sure." Em pointedly ignored the other remark. "Now, can you tell me who I'll be seeing tonight?"

Nerissa sobered at that. With a flick of her turquoise tail-fin, she flipped and swam closer to the boat. "You'll confront the queen and her warriors first, just as you did last time. If you survive that, you'll meet with the full court."

Maria's momentary calm shattered. "*If* she survives?"

Nerissa shrugged her wet shoulders. "Most don't."

With a wince, Em shifted toward Maria. "The siren warriors are…indiscriminate. They'll kill you for any and all missteps."

"And you didn't think I needed to know this?" Maria snarled.

"I mean, I kind of told you," Em said, "vaguely."

Maria narrowed her eyes at that last part.

"She survived last time," Nerissa pointed out. "I'd say *you're* in more danger than she is."

Fulke signed a question, and Em and Maria, almost in unison, shook their heads.

Nerissa glanced back and forth, eyes wide and curious.

Maria translated for her, "He wants to come along—because he's worried about us."

Nerissa nodded her thanks. "I wouldn't recommend it. A giant would be more welcome than a human, of course." She shot a disdainful look in Maria's direction. "But larger numbers wouldn't be."

"Two is already more than they like," Em assumed.

"And three would look like a threat," Nerissa said.

Maria shrugged. "Perhaps we want it to look like a threat."

Nerissa lifted a sea-blue eyebrow. "Perhaps you want to get yourselves killed, then."

Em leaned closer to Maria. "I only survived the first time because I listened to Nerissa's advice," she said softly. "My mother's training was…*lacking* in areas."

"Not surprising," Maria said with a slight growl, "considering how lacking *she* was in areas."

Nerissa perked up at that. "I think the human and I might agree on something, after all!" She nodded toward Em's dragon rune—barely visible beneath the pushed-up, disheveled sleeve of her shirt. "I see she gave you another one."

Em glanced down at the rune, before straightening her sleeve. "No. Nymeth gave me that one, actually."

Nerissa looked up at her, eyes wide. "The dragon?" she gasped. "You've been marked by the dragons themselves?"

"What does that matter?" Em's brows furrowed. "It's a rune, like any other."

Nerissa shook her head slowly. "Not according to *our* legends."

"So, what advice did she give you," Maria asked Em, "that saved your life?"

"Oh, umm. There was a lot." Em shifted uneasily—so much so that her soft thigh brushed against Maria's. "We spent about two months, discussing it."

Maria stared blankly at her. "Two months?"

A pink flush rose in Em's cheeks. "There may have been some… *kissing* happening. Around that time."

Ah.

Nerissa leaned heavily against the boat, waves of drenched, turquoise hair sliding over her breasts. "I can replicate the experience for you," she murmured to Maria, "if you have the time."

Maria scowled at the *clearly* hungry siren. "I don't."

Nerissa shrugged, drops of water sliding down her shoulders. "Then, I see only one option," she said. "Em was the first of her kind to survive the Turquoise Palace. If you want to be the first of *yours*, you'll have to follow her lead."

Maria narrowed her eyes. "I'm Captain Maria Welles. I follow no one."

Nerissa let out a deceptively sweet laugh. "Your name means nothing here. You'd taste the same as any other ship captain." Her gaze slid downward, pupils visibly dilating. "Which is good, I've heard."

"Nerissa," Em scolded.

"The last several to sink in these waters were men, which I just don't have a taste for. But you?" The siren licked her lips hungrily. "*You*, I could do."

"Nerissa!" Em said again.

Maria suddenly understood how so many sailors had plunged to their deaths for these creatures.

Nerissa turned her attention toward Em. "I just want her to understand how little *I* care whether she gets herself killed or not."

"I care," Em informed her.

"Then, tell her to get over herself," Nerissa said, words slow and enunciated, "and follow your lead."

Em cast a reluctant glance in Maria's direction.

The siren's gaze was merciless, when it returned to Maria. "Can you do it, or shall I expect an early dinner?"

Maria glared at the siren princess, but then, she looked down at Em—the brilliant and daring surgeon, who'd fascinated her from the start.

The dragon sorceress, who'd endured the absolute worst of humanity and still found it within herself to care for humans.

The woman who'd withstood an unimaginable amount of torture for her dragons—and had even withstood several moments of it for Maria.

Surgeon, swordsman, dragon-rider.

She was everything.

Utterly everything.

To Maria.

Maria wouldn't have admitted it to another soul, but the truth was…

She'd follow Emilia Drakon anywhere.

She'd followed her *here*, hadn't she?

But these were truths that the siren princess hadn't earned the right to hear. So, when Maria's attention returned to her, all she said was, "I suppose we'll see, won't we?"

Nerissa merely shrugged. "Very well." She let go of the boat and slipped back into the water. "Follow me, then." As she spun with a flick of her tail-fin, she called back, "Oh, and Em? I like what you've done to your hair." Her turquoise fins twitched. "It's cute!"

With a pointed look at Maria's sword, Em said, "I had help."

CHAPTER 27

The Turquoise Palace

For the second time since she'd brought Em aboard her ship, Maria found herself following Em to a place she'd never been.

Only this time was decidedly…*wetter*.

Maria splashed through the shallow water, loose rocks shifting and crackling beneath her boots. "This is a fucking cave, Em, not a palace. Why did your *ex-lover* call it a palace? Was she mocking us?"

"It was one summer," Em called back to her. "It really wasn't that serious." She cast a quick glance over her shoulder. "And no, she wasn't mocking us."

A drop of shockingly cold water splattered against the sleeve of Maria's shirt, and she glared up at the wet rocks above them. "Then, why is it a cave?"

Em stopped to wait for her. "If you had even an ounce of patience," she teased, "you'd find out."

Maria climbed a small slope of rock to join Em. "The usefulness of patience is widely overstated."

With an amused laugh, Em said, "And what would you say the usefulness of complaining is?"

Maria shrugged. "Makes me feel better."

"I'm sure," Em said sarcastically.

They'd parted ways with Fulke and Nerissa at the mouth of the cave—with Maria ordering Fulke back to the *Wicked Fate* and Nerissa promising to see them inside the palace.

The palace that didn't seem to *exist*.

Em climbed a set of dark grey stones, stacked like stairs, and stepped up onto some kind of flat surface.

Maria followed her blindly. It was a dark cave, after all. What other way was there?

Maria didn't notice the cave smoothing around them. She'd *barely* noticed the firelight that flickered up ahead.

The slick slide of boot against rock turned to a low thud, as Maria stepped onto flat, sea-blue stone. She froze and looked up, as a hall of blue opened before her.

Her breath caught at the sheer beauty of the stone—pale, sea-blue with webs of gold woven throughout.

Em must've noticed the absence of Maria's steps because she stopped, too. She turned toward Maria—her form a lovely shadow in this shining hall.

"Welcome to the Turquoise Palace, Captain."

Maria blinked. "We were in a cave." She glanced back the way they'd come. "What happened to the cave?"

Em let out a soft laugh. "It's still here, Captain."

Maria spun a full circle, until she faced Em once more—and that glimmering, blue hall behind her. With a slow nod, she said, "A hidden palace."

Em's smile deepened. "A hidden palace."

First, dragons. Now, hidden palaces.

What kind of excitement would Em bring into her life next?

Maria stepped forward, gazing up at the shining, pale blue walls with their asymmetrical veins of gold and brown. "Sirens can paint *and* sing?"

"Paint?" Em repeated. "Captain, it's turquoise."

"The gemstone?" Maria dragged the toe of her boot over the smooth stone. "Impossible."

"I'd imagine, with thousands of years' worth of siren magic," Em said, "most things are possible."

Maria shook her head in denial. "They sing." She held up a hand. "I'll accept controlling kraken and luring sailors to their deaths, but… shaping stone to perfection? Accumulating it all in one place? No."

Em shrugged. "I don't know how they did it—because I can't wield siren magic myself—but I can tell you that siren magic is seduction. Every aspect of it is meant to lure you and hold you. When you set foot in here, they don't *want* you to want to leave."

Maria shivered. Not at what she'd said, but at the cool air of the cave, of course. "So, our attraction isn't just to the siren's body, but to everything they do?"

"Exactly," Em said. "Their magic *is* allure."

Whereas the Drakon sorcerers wielded practical forms of magic, sirens wielded something…*prettier*.

And darker.

Maria let her gaze drift back toward the dazzling, stone walls. "This much turquoise would sell for a good bit of gold."

"The cavern won't fit on your ship, Captain," Em said dryly.

Maria shrugged one shoulder. "I don't even know how Adda would sell it. In pieces, perhaps?"

Em grimaced. "Please, don't say that too loudly."

Maria cast an alarmed glance at Em.

Could the sirens hear them?

Maria hadn't seen any.

Em looked up at the turquoise ceiling, and a smile pulled at the corners of her lips. "I was awestruck, too—the first time I came here," she told Maria. "Nerissa said it wasn't even the most beautiful one they'd made. There's an Opal Palace near the coast of Aevaria. She said it's like existing within a rainbow."

"I'm not awestruck," Maria had already begun to say—before the rest of that statement caught up with her. "Wait. Aevaria?"

The desert lands where Maria was born?

Maria hadn't lived there long enough to call it home, but Adda had. Her mother had, too.

Before it had become her grave.

"Sirens do swim, you know?" Em said, witty as ever. "There is a *reason* for their fins."

Maria suppressed a smile. "But the maps—"

"Your maps only tell you where their territory is," Em explained, "where they feed and raise their children. The maps warn you to stay away from *here*—because the people who didn't never came back."

Their children.

The sirens weren't vicious about protecting their territory out of malicious intent—but because there were children here.

Maria had never even considered the possibility.

No Illopian had.

"They eat us here, too, though," Maria pointed out.

"Yes," Em said with a nod, "they eat you."

The memory of the sirens' shark-like teeth sent another chill down Maria's spine. "With the teeth."

Em laughed. "With the teeth." With a tilt of her head, she motioned toward the end of the blue hall, where its walls curved like a snake. "We should go."

Maria followed, the low thud of her leather boots echoing through the stone hall. She searched for signs of water but found none. "How can they move in here?"

Em tapped the floor with her shoe. "The water flows beneath us," she explained. "They swim."

Maria frowned at that. "To where?"

"You'll see," Em said. The walls curved, and they found themselves at the end of another sea-blue hall. "Try to remember: sirens don't create these palaces for themselves. They're traps—for their food."

Maria preferred *not* to remember that, thank you very much. "It's awfully…extravagant for a trap."

"Well, humans do have a tendency toward greed, don't they?" Em pointed out. They continued toward the next serpentine curve. "Sirens use their palaces in the same way humans use theirs—for the most part. Except these are also designed to trap us inside."

Only Em would say something like that so casually.

Maria came to an abrupt stop, grasping Em's arm to stop her, too. "And we just walked inside?"

"Why do you think I brought dragons?" Pure viciousness flashed in Em's beautiful, green eyes. "They'll boil them all, if they even try."

A rush of heat poured through Maria's veins, and she let her gaze drift downward, admiring just how fierce Em looked—with her gorgeous curves all cloaked in dragon-scale.

Gods, Maria couldn't control herself around this side of Em.

She forced herself to release Em's arm, rather than pull her closer. "Siren soup," Maria said breathlessly.

"I think they'll want to avoid that," Em whispered, "don't you?"

"Have I mentioned," Maria murmured, "that you are an incredible asset to me?"

Em tilted her head at that. "I thought I was a pain."

Maria chuckled. "Well, lucky for us," she said, waving a hand toward the scars that marred her face, "I've learned to tolerate pain."

Em crossed her arms. "Am I an asset, or are you tolerating me?"

Somewhere deep within the halls of the Turquoise Palace, a woman began to sing. Her voice—a warm, rich alto—pulled Maria's attention, and then, it pulled her feet, too.

Maria began to walk.

"Captain?" Em rushed to catch up with her—which did make sense, considering she was the only one of them who actually knew where they were going.

So, why were Maria's feet still moving?

"It's the queen," Em said breathlessly. She eyed Maria with a concerned frown. "That voice you're hearing—it's hers. She's waiting in the throne room."

"Throne room?" Maria repeated.

What kind of throne did a siren sit on?

"Ah, ah.
La, ah, ah, ah.

La-ahh.
La-ah-ahh."

For the first few refrains of her song, the siren sang no discernible words. She only vocalized. Yet, her voice soared and plummeted with passion and depth unlike anything Maria had ever heard.

It was…physical—what the music did to Maria.

Each note drew her forward, pulling the blood in her veins, like currents of the sea. Her very bones moved like puppets on a string.

Em watched her, worry pulling at the soft curves of her face. "I'd heard humans were more susceptible to it, but I didn't realize it was *this* powerful. I suppose my magic protects me from it."

Maria tried to slow her steps, but she couldn't.

The queen's alluring timbres resonated through the halls of the palace—and in Maria's bones, too—and her repetitive sounds evolved into unfamiliar words.

With a soft gasp, Em staggered to a halt.

"What is it?" Maria called over her shoulder, though she still couldn't find the will to stop.

When Em saw the space opening up between them again, she rushed to close it. "It's Drakoní," she said breathlessly. "She's singing in Drakoní."

It really was such a harmonious language—with each smooth syllable flowing gently toward the next.

Maria understood why they'd use it for a song. She wondered, though, if there were a darker reason.

If their magic couldn't seduce Em as easily, perhaps they hoped *this* would.

Maria glanced at her. "You must miss hearing it."

A hint of pain flashed in Em's eyes. "Sometimes," she sighed. "I try not to think about it—that I might never hear it spoken again? It's…overwhelming."

Maria's chest ached for her. "You could speak it to me," she offered. "I won't understand a fucking word, but…you could. If you wanted."

Em's gaze softened. "Was that a selfless offer, Captain?" she teased. "What kind of pirate are you?"

"I mean, if you told anyone, I'd kill you, so…" Maria shrugged.

Em laughed at the familiar threat. She glanced down at Maria's boots. "You slowed down," she realized. "It must be because you were talking!"

Maria suspected it had more to do with the person she was talking *to* than the act of talking itself.

"Keep talking! Tell me…" Em paused to think. "Ah! Tell me what you think of the Turquoise Palace! Is it as nice as the one in Regolis?"

"How should I know?" Maria said with a scoff. "I'm a street urchin from Nefala. You think they let people like me set foot in the Illopian palace?"

Em's brows furrowed. "You were a naval captain."

"A new pair of boots doesn't make my feet worthy of their floors," Maria muttered.

Em's frown only deepened. "You didn't even *live* on the streets, though. You lived in a tavern."

Maria smiled at Em's ever-so-literal interpretation of things. "Which are so notoriously *clean*."

Em nodded. "Well, now, you're the most infamous pirate in all of Aletharia *and* a giant asshole," she reminded Maria. "You're no street urchin anymore."

Maria grinned at that. "I have risen through the ranks of villainy a bit, haven't I?"

"Assholery, as well." Em drifted closer to Maria with each step— her body language almost…*protective*. "Would they have let Catherine set foot in one?"

Maria shot a stunned look at Em, impressed that she hadn't tensed when she said the name. Perhaps Em had made some progress over the last month or so. "Yes."

"Because she's from Regolis?" Em assumed.

Maria tilted her head thoughtfully. "Yes, and no. Many of the families from Regolis are of noble birth."

"What is that?" Em said.

"Ah," Maria said with a frown, "it's hard to explain to someone whose people had no concept of royalty."

"I understand enough to know that royalty has to do with your people's obsession with bloodlines," Em offered.

"Not my people," Maria corrected, "but yes. Most of the people who live in Regolis aren't like the rest of us. They're of noble bloodlines." She waved her hand, as she tried to think of a better way to explain it. "Families born into wealth and power."

Recognition flickered in Em's eyes. "Catherine was *born* into power? No wonder she's such a…" she trailed off, as if she couldn't think of an insult strong enough.

Maria loved her for that. "High-class bitch?"

"No, no, that insult means nothing to me," Em said with a sigh. "I need one that translates better."

Maria laughed at that. "I eagerly await your decision," she teased. "Anyway, Catherine's father was Commodore Rochester—well, the *first* Commodore Rochester, before *her*—and her mother was the Honorable daughter of Viscount Lanivet."

Em's emerald-green eyes registered no recognition.

So, Maria added, "Someone with power."

"Ah," Em said with a nod, "and that's how she ended up in the navy, too? She was born into it?"

Maria's steps slowed again. "No." The memories pricked at her chest. "If Catherine had been born a boy, yes, but as a girl, she had to fight for it."

Em frowned. "But she was born into a powerful family—"

"A powerful family who didn't support her ambitions," Maria said. "They wanted her to marry a nobleman and reproduce—to be a pretty face in a pretty home. Catherine didn't want that. She had to fight off her mother's constant marital arrangements and her father's constant condescension." Maria released a pained sigh. "She had it easier than me, I'd say, but she had to fight for it, too. We both did."

"That's why you were close to her," Em realized.

"It's why I *needed* her," Maria corrected. A wave of shame rose in her throat—especially since Em, of all people, knew how wonderful

Judith was. "I had Judes. That should've been enough for me, but it wasn't. She had no ambition, no interest in rising through the ranks," Maria pleaded with Em to understand. "She didn't *understand* me."

Em's expression held no judgement.

That, more than anything, shattered Maria's walls. "I needed someone as selfish as I was—someone who wanted what people said they couldn't have. I needed someone willing to do anything for their own ambition, someone as vicious and insatiable as me."

Em's brows creased with sympathy.

"Judith was so good, so…*content*, and I wasn't," Maria snarled. "I never have been."

Em opened her mouth, as if she wanted to argue with some part of that, but Maria didn't give her the chance.

"Cat, though? Oh, she was ambitious and greedy—so fucking greedy! She was ready to do whatever it took to advance in a career dominated by men," Maria said. "She was everything she wasn't supposed to be, just like me. And a hell of a good sparring partner, at that! We were the same." She shook her head sadly. "I *thought* we were the same."

"Catherine offered what you needed," Em mumbled, "at the time."

The accuracy of that statement startled Maria—until she realized *why* Em understood it so well.

Cat had become what Em needed, at the time, too.

She was what everyone needed—until she wasn't.

That was her unfailing method.

"I suppose I let her down as much as she did me," Maria said with a bitter laugh, "because, as it turned out, I only *thought* I'd do anything for what I wanted. Catherine Rochester actually would."

Em pursed her lips at that. "You say that like it's a weakness, but it isn't. You showed more strength in that one day than she's shown her entire life."

Maria froze.

She turned to face Em, her heart pounding.

Em's words pierced her so deeply that she didn't know whether she was bleeding out or healing.

Em respected her, *admired* her—not because of who she pretended to be, in order to make everyone *else* respect her, but because of who Maria actually was.

The things Maria *hadn't* been ruthless enough to do.

Em stopped, too, and an excited smile burst across her face. "You stopped walking! You did it!"

No.

Em had done it.

Em—with her wonderful, sincere words.

With empathy strong enough to break any spell.

The gorgeous, alto voice soared higher and louder, and the magical tug at Maria's feet grew stronger.

Em winced at the rise in volume. "We should hurry, though—before she resorts to something more powerful."

Maria's eyes widened. "More powerful?"

What could be more powerful than *this*?

Em led the way through the sinuous, blue halls—coiled at the bottom of a mountain, like a sea-snake—and Maria stopped resisting the pull in her bones.

Emotion resonated in each line of the siren's song, and Maria recognized only a few words along the way.

Aletha.
Drakon.
Magyck.
More…*magyck.*
More *Aletha?*

"What is the song about?" Maria asked, finally.

"Oh, it's one of their sacred songs," Em said with an awed smile, "about Aletha." She laughed, "I didn't even realize they *could* sing it in Drakoní!"

It clearly meant a lot to Em—to hear her own tongue so long after watching her people perish—and Maria loved that for her. She just…hoped these creatures weren't cruel enough to use it against Em.

According to the stories, they were, but Maria knew better than anyone…the stories were often wrong.

"They must really love Aletha," Maria said.

Em nodded. "Humans tend to think of islanders as the ones who worship Aletha, and we do, of course," she admitted, "but the sirens are her children. They'd do anything for the goddess who gave them life."

"Including what we're asking them to do?" Maria asked.

"I think so," Em said.

Maria hoped she was right.

The sound of gushing water, which had begun as a faint ghost of a noise, grew louder, now, and Maria realized it wasn't just the sea she was hearing.

That steady rush of water was coming from somewhere *inside* the palace—forming a constant, ambient background beneath the siren's melody.

Maria might've asked Em about it, if the next curve hadn't brought not only the answer to her question, but also the most dazzling sight she'd ever seen.

A long pool of impossibly blue water stretched before them, its rippling surface reflecting the walls of turquoise around it.

Maria couldn't even see the bottom of the pool. It ran so deep, likely bubbling up from some underground lake beneath the mountain.

What loomed before them must've been the sirens' idea of a throne room. Maria had never set foot in one herself, but she figured it was safe to assume no human throne room had ever looked like *this*.

Beyond the pool, moonlight poured through a small opening in the cave, casting shimmering light over the water's surface.

That opening also provided an entrance for a thin waterfall, which cascaded over the turquoise stone and supplied a steady rush of water to the pool.

Near the end of the hall, algae and large stones emerged from the pool, and an imposing throne of coral rose from the water, as well.

It didn't look too comfortable, but it was stunning.

How had they even created it?

Several large sirens lurked around the coral throne, and Maria assumed these were what Nerissa referred to as the siren *warriors*—since unlike other sirens, these actually wore some sort of clothing.

No, clothing was the wrong word.

Armor.

The siren warriors wore armor, crafted from leather and what looked alarmingly like…bone.

Oh, shit. It wasn't human, was it?

If they didn't eat the bone, perhaps they repurposed it. Ah, but what about the skin? They did eat the skin, didn't they? The leather —it wasn't…

It wasn't, right?

Maria's stomach rolled at the thought.

"Captain?"

Maria looked up to find Em several steps ahead of her. With a miserable shake of her head, she followed.

The siren warriors were just as round-bodied as any other siren. Yet, even without *seeing* the muscle definition, Maria knew it was there—in the imposing width of their shoulders and the thickness of their biceps.

Not to mention, the ease with which they carried those massive, white tridents—which *also* reminded Maria a bit of bone.

She considered asking Em about it, but ultimately decided she'd rather not know.

Em must've been counting their steps—because she stopped and reached out, grasping Maria's hand to stop her, too. "Now, we wait," she whispered.

Maria gave in to the temptation to squeeze Em's hand once, before letting go—relishing the brief warmth of her hand, the brief comfort of her touch.

In the center of the siren warriors, curled upon her coral throne the way a seal might curl upon a rock, a beautiful woman hummed the end of her song.

Iridescent, rose-pink scales shimmered with each flick of the woman's tail-fin, and long, locks of rose-pink hair lay over her heavy, rounded breasts.

Queen Amathea.

That was what Em had called her.

The woman's beauty made Maria's head spin, as if she'd had too much rum. It made her want to fall to the stone floor and offer herself—even as all rational thought told her to do otherwise.

Even Em, who seemed to have a slight immunity to their magic, grew breathless at the sight of the queen.

Queen Amathea ended her beautiful song and spoke in clear Illopian, as her daughter had likely advised her to do. "Approach."

Em's green eyes shifted toward Maria, and at her side, she carefully folded two fingers, leaving only three.

Three steps.

Maria begrudgingly obeyed.

A flicker of pale-blue caught her attention, and she realized Nerissa lurked behind her mother's throne.

Maria hoped the siren princess wasn't *gloating* about this. She didn't think she'd forgive anyone present, if she was. .

Em included.

Immediately, upon the third step of Maria's boots, the siren warriors surged forward in the pool, thrusting their tridents into the air, stopping mere inches from their throats.

Em didn't flinch, but Maria certainly did.

Maria's hand reflexively went to her sword, but with Em's warnings in mind, she resisted the urge to draw it.

"Dragon Child," Queen Amathea said, her voice as slow and sensual as a caress, "you've grown up."

"As one does," Em muttered.

Maria glanced at her, brows high.

The air in the room thickened with unease.

Queen Amathea's alluring smile, however, never wavered. "We

were so horrified to hear of what the humans had done to your people."

Em nodded. "I would hope so."

Well, it was a good thing Em's mother had never thought to involve her in *human* politics.

If Maria didn't think it'd get her killed by the sharp, three-bladed weapons, currently aimed at them, she might've advised the queen to skip the small talk, before Em accidentally insulted everyone present.

Then again, what was Em expected to say to something like that? Bringing up a recent genocide *was* an uncomfortable way to begin a conversation.

The siren queen must've realized that—because while her warriors tensed, she didn't. "In a show of gratitude for you not hurting our kraken during the encounter, we've allowed you to enter our territory."

Okay, now, *Maria* wanted to insult her.

"Well, fortunately for all of us," Em said, "the dragons were there to offer a nonviolent alternative."

At the mention of Em's dragons, Amathea shifted uneasily on her coral throne. "My daughter tells me that the ship full of *food* you've brought with you is not for our consumption."

Maria didn't miss the way the queen's hungry, pink eyes had shifted toward *her*, when she'd said that.

"It is not," Em assured her.

The queen's nostrils flared, and her gaze traveled up and down Maria's form. "And that this appetizing…*morsel* is not, either?"

Appetizing?

Maria was appetizing?

Em narrowed her eyes at the siren. "I'd advise you not to even think about it."

The queen's gaze flicked toward Em, and the razor-sharp points of the warriors' tridents inched closer. "Was that a threat," she said, "Dragon Child?"

"Take it how you must," Em said, "as long as you don't touch her."

Damn.

Em was making the threats now?

Maria couldn't think of many times she'd wanted Em more than she did now—which was ironic, considering they'd probably die before she could act on it.

Amathea straightened on her throne, rage flashing like fire within her rose-pink eyes. "Our little treaty might protect you, Dragon Child, but it doesn't protect the humans you brought with you," she said—through shark-like teeth. "Now, you have a total of three hundred of your breaths to explain why we shouldn't devour every human in our territory."

Shit.

Em didn't tremble. She barely even blinked. She simply held out her hand and began to count on her fingers. "I have dragons," she said, "and the goddess of the sea sent us. Was that quick enough for you?"

And people had actually wondered why Maria had brought Em onto her ship. Hadn't they ever seen her go?

Several sirens gasped, and even the queen herself grew several shades paler.

Em forced a smile and, only as an afterthought, did she add, "Queen."

As Maria struggled to hide her own smile, someone behind the queen showed even less restraint. A familiar giggle drew Maria's attention to the siren behind the throne.

Nerissa.

Slowly, Amathea turned toward her giggling daughter. "Is something funny, Nerissa?"

Nerissa pressed her soft lips together to stifle her own laughter. "Of course not, my queen," she said pleasantly. "A fish tickled my tail-fin. That's all."

She swam backward in the deep, blue water, until she was nearly horizontal. Her aforementioned, sea-blue tail-fin emerged to offer a playful little flick.

Somehow, Amathea managed to look even *more* disgusted by her daughter's behavior. Only when she turned away with a huff, did Nerissa's sea-blue gaze return to Em. With a sly smile, she winked.

Amathea waved her webbed fingers, the movement quick and uneasy. "Warriors."

The siren warriors immediately withdrew their tridents and retreated deeper into the pool of water.

Maria's lungs fully deflated for the first time in what must've been quite a while, and she finally let go of her sword.

The siren queen shifted uncomfortably on her coral throne. "The goddess herself? Sent you? To see *me*?"

Em nodded.

Amathea released a quivering breath, as if this were the greatest honor she'd ever received. "Had I have known, your greeting would've been warmer."

"One would assume," Em said.

No matter how magically seductive the sirens were, Maria could've ignored all of them, just to watch Em.

Amathea turned to her nearest warrior—a large man with flowing, green hair. "Titus, spread the word that the human ship is not to be touched." She shot a warning glare at Em, before adding, "For *now*."

Titus lowered his head, long, green hair falling into the water. "Yes, my Queen." The warrior dove deep into the pool of water, vanishing from sight.

Without thinking, Maria stepped forward to peer into the deep pool, curious about where the siren warrior had gone. She didn't realize her mistake until someone sang a sudden, shrill note.

She looked up to find a siren warrior, propelled into the air by his own magic, his trident raised. Her heart sputtered to a stop.

Maria reached for her sword, even though she knew it was too late, but at the last moment, Em stepped in front of her.

Maria screamed out in panic, sword already drawn, but the siren was plummeting rapidly toward them.

Time slowed, stretching the worst moment of Maria's life into what felt like hours—*hours* of those deadly spikes plunging toward Em's throat.

Somewhere behind the siren warrior, Maria noticed the queen jerk forward on her throne, just before a siren with turquoise-blue fins jetted toward them.

Amathea screamed something.

No.

No, she *sang* something.

She sang something loud and clear and powerful, and everything suddenly…stopped.

The center spike of the trident touched Em's soft throat, just as the siren warrior froze mid-air, several feet above the turquoise floor.

Maria stumbled back, gasping for breath.

Em, however, stood totally still—merely glaring at the deadly creature, as he hung in the air, like some kind of suspended sculpture.

Maria stared at the spike that touched Em's throat, her heart racing.

Fuck.

Aside from the slight lift of her chin the moment the spike touched her throat, Em hadn't moved.

She'd barely even *tensed.*

Had Em known the queen would stop him?

How had the queen even done it?

Em had stood in front of Maria, unflinching—even in the face of certain death. She'd been spectacular.

Spectacular and…fucking *insane*!

Maria grasped Em's arm and jerked her backward. "What have I told you about risking your life for mine?"

Even to her own ears, her voice sounded broken and desperate.

"Something I ignored, I'm sure," Em muttered.

Maria's head spun violently, and she didn't know whether she was about to pass out or vomit.

"Just like *you* ignored the three steps rule," Em said.

"I fucked up! I know!" Maria snapped. She pressed her free hand to her chest. "But I die for that! Not you!"

Em stepped closer, eyes flashing. "*You* don't die at all."

"Yes, Dragon Child," Queen Amathea said, once she'd finished humming her warrior back into the water—however *that* worked. She curled her shimmering tail-fin along the bottom of her coral throne. "You've made your stance on that clear."

With her head buzzing as loud as it was, Maria had nearly forgotten the sirens were still there.

Em turned to face Amathea. "Good."

The distant roar of dragons punctuated her remark, and every siren in the room shifted nervously at the sound.

"It seems we have much to discuss," the siren queen said, "Dragon Child."

TO BE CONTINUED...

Book 3

The story of Emilia Drakon and Captain Maria Welles will continue in *The Dragon Child* (*Lesbians, Pirates, & Dragons: Book 3*).

The Aletharian Appendices

Appendix A

GODS OF ALETHARIA

A**letha** - the goddess of the sea, worshipped by islanders, sirens, and sailors, abhorred by the Kingdom of Illopia. Though she rules all seas, she guards the Whispering Abyss most viciously, since it is home to her sea monsters. Even when she tries to appear human, she often retains many of the features of her sea creatures, including fins, webbed fingers, and pointed teeth. Her personality remains a mystery because while some describe her as tempestuous, mischievous, and cruel, others describe her as kind.

ARIA - THE GODDESS OF WIND, WORSHIPPED BY THE WINDIEST climates of Aletharia, including the Caluxian Empire and parts of Aevaria. She often appears with giant, white wings and radiant skin. She rules the skies and avoids contact with humans as much as possible. Those who have met her describe her as cautious, just, benevolent, and perhaps a bit self-righteous.

. . .

PETRA - THE GOD OF MOUNTAINS, WORSHIPPED BY THE KINGDOM OF Illopia, feared by all. He rules the mountains and all who rely on them. Unlike other gods, he appears with no inhuman characteristics, likely due to the fear of magic he's fostered in his own worshippers. He, instead, appears as a frail, light-skinned man with a long, white beard. Due to the infrequency of his appearances, little is known of his personality, though both gods and dragons describe him as greedy, self-centered, and ambitious.

FIRE - A LONG-FORGOTTEN GODDESS, WHOSE NAME WAS FORGOTTEN with her. It was once said that she burned the night stars into existence. The few who remember her say she perished long ago, when Petra captured her within a volcano. No one has seen her since.

NATURE - ANOTHER FORGOTTEN GOD WITH NO REMAINING TEMPLES. It's said he was once worshipped within the Kingdom of Illopia before perishing at the hands of Petra. Nothing more is remembered of him.

Appendix B

MAGICKS OF ALETHARIA

Divine Magic - magic that runs only in the veins of the gods. It's the only form of magic that includes creation. Further capabilities of divine magic can vary from god to god and are often specific to that particular god's realm of power. Gods are able to give or return life, as it is a form of creation.

Dragon Magic - magic that exists within dragons and within the Drakon sorcerers who were forged from it. Dragons brought their own form of magic into the world, and it's believed that Aletharia thrives because of it. Dragon magic is powerful but limited. It involves wielding the magic in all things—but not creating it.

Destructive Magic - a form of dragon magic, wielded by dragons and Drakon sorcerers. This form of magic is useful in combat. Only some Drakon sorcerers can wield this kind of magic easily, and the ones who do are called *warriors*. Traditionally, they identify themselves by wearing red clothing.

RESTORATIVE MAGIC - ANOTHER FORM OF DRAGON MAGIC, WIELDED by dragons and Drakon sorcerers. This form of magic is useful in caring for others, but not useful in defending oneself. Only some Drakon sorcerers can wield this kind of magic easily, and the ones who do are called *healers*. Traditionally, they identify themselves by wearing blue clothing.

PLANT MAGIC - ANOTHER FORM OF DRAGON MAGIC, WIELDED BY dragons and Drakon sorcerers. This form of magic is useful in producing food and supplies. Only some Drakon sorcerers can wield this kind of magic easily, and the ones who do are called *agrarian sorcerers*. Traditionally, they identify themselves by wearing green clothing.

DIVINATION - ANOTHER FORM OF DRAGON MAGIC, WIELDED BY dragons and Drakon sorcerers. This form of magic is useful in determining future events and is often utilized before a major event, such as the birth of a child. Only some Drakon sorcerers can wield this kind of magic, and the ones who do are called *oracles*. Traditionally, they identify themselves by wearing violet clothing.

DRAGON BONDING - A RARE FORM OF DRAGON MAGIC THAT CAN only exist between a dragon and a Drakon sorcerer. This form of magic allows the sorcerer to link telepathically and empathically with dragons—and therefore, ride them. Since this magic exists within dragons alone, only a dragon can choose the rider. Though any Drakon sorcerer can be chosen, few ever are. There's often only one dragon-rider per generation. Traditionally, dragon-riders identify themselves by wearing some form of black clothing.

. . .

GIANT MAGIC - A LIMITED FORM OF MAGIC THAT EXISTS WITHIN giants. Like humans, giants are *not* magic-wielders. Because of this, many assume they have no magic at all—especially within the Kingdom of Illopia. However, their tremendous strength doesn't come from increased size alone. There is a limited form of magic within them.

SEA MAGIC - MAGIC CREATED AND WIELDED BY THE GODDESS OF THE sea. The sea goddess often bestows it on her sea monsters. Examples of this include kraken, sea serpents, and leviathans.

SIREN MAGIC - A FORM OF SEA MAGIC, UNIQUE TO SIRENS. THIS form of magic is attractive and alluring. It's a powerful kind of influence, wielded through music. Through song, a siren can influence humans and sea creatures to do as the siren wishes. It's said that it's pleasant to fall under their spell—until they eat you.

WIND MAGIC - MAGIC CREATED AND WIELDED BY THE GODDESS OF wind. The wind goddess often bestows it on her wind creatures. Examples of this include the Pegasi, phoenixes, and other magical birds.

MOUNTAIN MAGIC - MAGIC CREATED AND WIELDED BY THE GOD OF mountains. The mountain god bestowed it on his mountain creatures. An example of this includes trolls.

<h1 style="text-align:center">Appendix C</h1>

MAGICAL CREATURES OF ALETHARIA

Gods - beings of tremendous power and age, with no known birth, who created Aletharia and many of the creatures within it. Only three of these gods are currently worshipped within Aletharia, but the oldest creatures of Aletharia remember there being more.

DRAGONS - THE FIRST CREATION OF ALETHARIA. BECAUSE OF THEIR power and relation to the gods, dragons are often considered demigods. With the exception of the gods themselves, dragons are the most powerful creatures in all of Aletharia. They can live for thousands of years, and there is one dragon who's believed to be even older.

DRAKON SORCERERS - A POWERFUL KIND OF MAGIC-WIELDER, created through dragon magic for the purpose of protecting the dragons of Aletharia. Drakon sorcerers usually develop affinities for specific forms of dragon magic and are, therefore, dependent upon each other for support. Along with wielding dragon magic, some Drakon sorcerers may also bond with dragons and become *dragon-riders*. While Drakon sorcerers can vary in appearance as much as humans can, their dragon-green eyes often mark them as different.

Village Witches - A weaker form of magic-wielder, believed to be descended from a Drakon sorcerer. They often use their limited abilities to perform magic tricks for gold. Since magic is feared and outlawed in the Kingdom of Illopia, these people are often hanged with enraptured audiences.

Sirens - Beautiful sea creatures, able to wield sea magic through song. As natural predators, they use their beauty and magic to lure, deceive, and devour humans. They share some physical characteristics with their prey. However, they also have teeth capable of rending flesh from bone and various fins that aid in swimming, such as the *tail-fin*, the *opercular fins*, and the *glider-fins*. Not much is known of their culture, since no one has ever lived to tell of it. Though death at their hands is quite painful, sailors have been known to jump to their deaths, anyway—with one captain's log detailing his sailor's final words as, "She's just too beautiful."

Giants - Non-magic-wielding humanoids with size and strength beyond that of humans. Giants exist within every land and culture and have intermingled with humans enough so that their unexplained size and strength is seen as no more magical than a different hair color or skin tone. However, the answer to their size and strength does, in fact, lie in magic. Aevarian giants are unique in that they've maintained a separate culture and have rarely inter-married. Because of this, Aevarian giants are said to be as strong as trolls and as intelligent as humans. *Disclaimer: This theory has not been tested against a real troll.*

. . .

Sea Monsters - creatures endowed with sea magic, created by the goddess of the sea. The largest sea monsters dwell in the Whispering Abyss, while the smaller ones often dwell in other seas. Since no human has ever survived a voyage into the Whispering Abyss, one can only speculate on what might dwell within it. A few of the better-known sea monsters include kraken, sea serpents, and leviathans.

Wind Creatures - creatures endowed with wind magic, created by the goddess of wind. Like the wind goddess herself, wind creatures are often reserved and wary of human contact. Among those identified from afar were Pegasi, phoenixes, and thunderbirds.

Trolls - creatures endowed with mountain magic, created by the god of mountains. These creatures are significantly larger and stronger than humans and are driven by insatiable hunger. With no ability to think, they act on hunger alone, devouring any living thing in their path. It's easy to outsmart them, but impossible to overpower them. They lived within the Illopian Mountains, hindering the mining of gold, until one day, when the mountains opened up and swallowed them whole—supposedly, in reward for the eradication of magic in the Kingdom of Illopia.

Appendix D

LANDS OF ALETHARIA

The Kingdom of Illopia - the most powerful and prosperous dominion in all of Aletharia, ruled by the same royal family for hundreds of years. Its unrivaled navy has allowed it to conquer many lands and peoples. Because of this, the kingdom encompasses a variety of lands and climates. Magic is outlawed in the Kingdom of Illopia, and it is believed that the kingdom prospers because of this. Gold is the currency of the realm, and worship of Petra, the god of mountains, is the only worship allowed.

THE CALUXIAN EMPIRE - AN EXTENSIVE EMPIRE IN THE ICY northern lands of Aletharia. They have no known navy, and they refuse to trade with other lands. Due to their isolation and the towering walls around their lands, most believe them to be xenophobic—though little is actually known of them. Because of their windy climate, they worship Aria, goddess of wind.

. . .

Aevaria - THE SPARSELY POPULATED DESERT LANDS OF SOUTHERN Aletharia. Before the Great Drought, a human monarchy ruled over Aevaria, and the kingdom prospered through trade with the Azure Islands and the Kingdom of Illopia. During the drought, trade and government collapsed, forcing many people to either flee or starve. The Aevarian giants eventually rebuilt the kingdom and assumed control of it, but much of the human population had either died or immigrated by then. People of Aevaria have been known to worship both Aletha and Aria, goddesses of sea and wind.

The Azure Islands - AN ARCHIPELAGO IN THE AZURE SEA, MADE UP of independent island villages. Despite their history of peaceful coexistence with other lands, they're vilified by the Kingdom of Illopia for their worship of Aletha, goddess of the sea.

Drakon Isle - A LARGE TROPICAL ISLAND THAT IS HOME TO dragons and Drakon sorcerers. The Drakon people wield dragon magic and use it to sustain their culture. They live amongst dragons and are believed to have tamed the godlike beasts. Long vilified for their use of magic, their influence with dragons, and their worship of Aletha, Drakon sorcerers are considered enemies of the Kingdom of Illopia.

FOR FURTHER DETAILS, CONSULT ALETHARIAN MAP.

Author's Note

Oh, gosh, where do I start?

Thank you for reading this—for joining me in this second installment of *Lesbians, Pirates, & Dragons*.

Thank you for following me throughout my journey of writing and rewriting (and rewriting and rewriting and…thinking it was finished, then rewriting again, thinking it was finished *again*, then rewriting *again*, etcetera).

Every book I've written has involved a lot of rewrites, but this one terrified me in ways that I *still* can't put into words. I lost count of how many times I rewrote it. Were all of those times necessary? Well, it depends on who you ask, probably. I think it was.

I love my characters and my world. I couldn't write them, if I didn't, and for them, I *needed* to get it right. For you, too, I needed to get it right.

I really hope I have.

It never ceases to amaze me how each book I write feels like climbing an even higher mountain than the last, and somehow, I never remember how I climbed it the last time.

Nor do I retain any self-assurance from it. I'm always sure that *this* is the mountain that will send me tumbling down to a painful, embarrassing death—with limbs all broken and akimbo.

This mountain came with so many obstacles—external and internal. I wrote in the midst of ups and downs in my physical and mental health. Mostly downs, honestly. *Lots* of downs.

I had to learn what autistic burnout does to me. That was new.

It's always terrifying to release a book.

Writing is cutting out pieces of your soul and sewing them into the work, and publishing is then offering up those pieces to be trampled on or cherished.

My own trauma is on the page, and that's terrifying.

I always think it'll get easier, but it doesn't. It's always scary. It's always asking courage of me that I'm not sure I have.

But it's worth it, and I know that.

It always feels a little dramatic to say books saved my life, but they did. Reading and writing have been there at the lowest points of my life, pulling me out of holes I didn't think I could escape.

If *my* books can do that for anyone, it's worth every ounce of fear.

One thing I've always liked about the second book of a series is that it tends to be where the characters start to heal, and this is very much a book about trauma and healing. It's also about the self-loathing and helplessness you feel when you think you're not healing "fast enough."

If you take one thing from Em and Maria in this book, I hope it's that there's no such thing as "fast enough." Whether you still feel broken because of something that happened many years ago, like Maria—like *me*, honestly—or you're still reeling from something that happened recently, like Em, it's natural.

Trauma changes us. On physical and emotional levels, it changes the way our brains work, and one of the hardest *parts* of healing is realizing that it can't bring back the person we were.

Please, know…the person you were deserved better, but the person you are, now, does, too. You're worthy of love, just as you are.

You're doing your best, and that's enough. That's *more* than enough.

I hope you know that, and I hope this book was something good for you—whether it was entertainment or something that made you feel less alone.

Em and Maria will be back for at least one more book—that I am *so* excited to write. I hope you'll join me again for that. For updates, check my website, sign up for my newsletter, or follow me on social media.

Thank you again for reading, and thank you for all of the messages and comments you've sent my way. I couldn't do this without you.

As always, please, remember that you deserve love, happy endings, and all the lesbian pirates your heart desires.

Lots of love,
Britney

Also by Britney Jackson

LESBIANS, PIRATES, AND DRAGONS:

Pirates of Aletharia

Goddess of the Sea

The Dragon Child
(Coming Soon)

CREATURES OF DARKNESS SERIES:

The Stone of the Eklektos

The Tomb of Blood

The Assassins of Light

The Reign of Darkness

About the Author

Britney Jackson is a multi-award-winning author of LGBTQ speculative fiction. She's adored books for as long as she can remember and has loved writing for almost as long.

She has a passion for creating the kind of heroes she needed when she was younger: heroines with mental illness, flaws, and traumatic pasts. She centers her books around strong, lesbian and bisexual women who find courage, love, and happy endings.

She resides in Alabama with her two kids and the snuggliest cat you'll ever meet. She has a Bachelor of Science in Fine Arts and Religion and did her graduate work in English.

Learn more at britneyjackson.com.